PHILLI

The Burning Man

The Undertaker's
Widow

Also by Phillip Margolin

PHILLIP MARGOLIN OMNIBUS

The Burning Man
The Undertaker's Widow

PHILLIP MARGOLIN

timewarner
paperbacks

A *Time Warner* Paperback

This omnibus edition first published in Great Britain by
Time Warner Paperbacks in 2003
Phillip Margolin Omnibus Copyright © Phillip Margolin 2003

Previously published separately:
The Burning Man first published in Great Britain in 1996 by
Little, Brown and Company
Published by Warner Books in 1997
Reprinted by Time Warner Paperbacks in 2002
Copyright © Phillip M. Margolin 1996

The Undertaker's Widow first published in Great Britain in 1998 by
Little, Brown and Company
Published by Warner Books in 1998
Reprinted 1999, 2000
Reprinted by Time Warner Paperbacks in 2002
Copyright © Phillip M. Margolin 1999

A CIP catalogue record for this book
is available from the British Library.

ISBN 0 7515 3507 9

Printed and bound in Great Britain by
Clays Ltd, St Ives plc

Time Warner Paperbacks
An imprint of
Time Warner Books UK
Brettenham House
Lancaster Place
London WC2E 7EN

www.TimeWarnerBooks.co.uk

The Burning Man

For Bart C. and his parents,
Phillip and Kaye,
who never gave up hope.

ACKNOWLEDGEMENTS

Some of the events in *The Burning Man* are similar to incidents that actually occurred in a murder case that I handled many years ago, so I want to make it crystal clear that no character in this book is intended to represent a real, live human being. This book is peopled by fictional characters whose personalities and motivations I invented for the purpose of entertaining my readers with a make-believe tale.

Some very real people helped me in the writing of *The Burning Man*. I want to thank Judy Margolin, Bart Reid, Dr. Donald Trunkey, Dr. Stanley Abrams, Robert Palladino, Detective Patric Montgomery of the Oregon State Police, Dr. Benson Schaeffer and my friend and fellow writer Dr. Michael Palmer for sharing their technical knowledge with me.

The comments of Jay Margulies, Pam Webb, Vince Kohler, Susan Svetkey, Larry Matasar, Jerry, Joseph, Eleonore and Doreen Margolin and Norman and Helen Stamm, who were kind enough to read my first draft, were greatly appreciated.

I also want to thank the dynamic duo of Lori Lipsky and Elisa Petrini, the world champions of tag-team editing, for riding to my rescue, Estelle Laurence for her careful copy editing, and everyone (and I mean everyone) at Doubleday and Bantam Books.

Finally, I never get tired of thanking Jean Naggar and everyone at her agency for taking such good care of me, and Doreen, Daniel and Ami Margolin for putting up with me.

PART ONE

CRASH AND BURN

CHAPTER ONE

1

On the day the gods chose for his destruction, Peter Hale ate his breakfast on the terrace of his condominium. The sun was just beginning its ascent above the city of Portland and a blood-red aura surrounded the flat, black silhouette of Mount Hood. The dark metropolis looked like an ink-black carpet crisscrossed by Christmas lights. A poet would have savored the sunrise for its beauty, but Peter enjoyed the advent of day for another reason. He believed that Galileo was wrong when he imagined an Earth that revolved around the sun. In his heart of hearts, Peter knew that the sun that was slowly rising over his city revolved around him.

A crumb from his bran muffin fell onto the leg of Peter's gray Armani trousers. He flicked it off, then took a sip of the café latte he had brewed in the espresso machine that graced the marble counter of his designer kitchen. Peter lived in the condo, drove a fire-engine-red Porsche and pulled in a high five-figure salary as a fourth-year associate at Hale, Greaves,

Strobridge, Marquand and Bartlett. The salary did not cover all his expenses and Peter was a bit overextended right now, but he never had any trouble obtaining mortgages, car loans or things of that sort since everyone knew he was the son of Richard Hale, one of the firm's founding partners and a past president of the Oregon State Bar. With all this, Peter was not a happy camper.

The living room drapes moved. Peter looked over his shoulder. Priscilla padded across the terrace wearing only an oversized Trailblazer tee shirt. She was a flight attendant with United. Peter had dated her on and off for a few months. Most men would have killed for such a lover, but Priscilla was talking about 'commitment' with increasing frequency and Peter was finding it more and more difficult to avoid discussions of the dreaded 'C' word.

Priscilla bent down and kissed Peter on the cheek. Peter's head moved slightly and she sensed the rebuff.

'Boy, are you a grouch this morning,' Priscilla said, straining to keep the hurt out of her voice.

'Yeah, well, I've got to get to court,' he answered brusquely.

'How is the case going?'

'Great for Sir Richard. Not so good for me.'

Priscilla sat across from Peter. 'What's wrong?' she asked.

'The same damn thing that's been wrong since I made the mistake of going to work for my father.'

Peter did not try to disguise his bitterness. It felt good to vent his anger.

'Last night, right after court, Sir Richard informed me that he would be cross-examining all of the defendant's important witnesses and giving the closing argument.'

'Your father has let you try some part of the case, hasn't he?'

'He's let me examine a few insignificant witnesses. That's about it.'

'Oh, Peter. I'm so sorry. I know how much you've been counting on being lead counsel.'

'Yeah, well,' Peter shrugged, 'I should have known better. My father just has to hog the glory.'

Peter looked out toward the sunrise, but his thoughts were turned inward. When his father asked him if he wanted to work at Hale, Greaves, Peter had imagined serving a brief apprenticeship followed quickly by a succession of major cases in which he would act as lead counsel, winning multimillion-dollar verdicts and establishing his credentials in the legal community. It had taken four years serving as Richard Hale's vassal to bring him to his senses. He had worked on *Elliot v. Northwest Maritime* from day one and he knew more about the case than his father ever would. If his father would not let him be lead counsel in *Elliot*, he had little hope of being lead counsel in a major case in the near future. He had to get out from under his father's influence. If necessary, even leave Hale, Greaves. A new start with a new firm might be the answer. He would seriously consider a move when the Elliot case was over.

The senior partners in Hale, Greaves, Strobridge, Marquand and Bartlett looked out from corner offices on the fortieth floor of the Continental Trust Building at the rivers, towering mountains and lush green hills that made Portland, Oregon, so unique. Though the skyscraper was new, the firm's quarters were decorated with heavy, dark woods, polished brass fittings and fine old antiques, giving the place an air of timeless quality.

At precisely 7:30 A.M., Peter entered a small, windowless conference room where he and his father met before court every morning to review the witnesses who would testify that day and to discuss any legal issues that might arise. Peter's father still had the same massive build that helped him win second team All-American honors in football and an NCAA wrestling championship at Oregon State in 1956. He owned a full head of white hair and his craggy face was outfitted with a broken nose and a cauliflower ear. Richard Hale practiced law the way he played sports, full steam ahead and take no prisoners. This morning, Peter's father was striding back and forth in front of a low credenza in his shirtsleeves, a phone receiver plastered to his ear, muttering 'Jesus Christ!' at increasing decibel levels each time he made a turn.

Peter took off his suit jacket and hung it behind the door on a hanger. He noted with distaste that his father had flung his jacket onto a corner of the long conference table where it lay crumpled in a heap. Richard loved playing the humble, hulking man of the people in front of juries and he thought that the disheveled clothes helped his image. Peter could not imagine wearing a suit that had not been freshly pressed.

'When will you know?' his father barked, as Peter took several files from his attaché case and arranged them in a neat pile.

'No, goddamn it, that won't do. We're in the middle of the goddamn trial. We've been in court for two weeks.'

Richard paused. His features softened. 'I know it couldn't be helped, but you don't know Judge Pruitt.'

He paused again, listening intently. Then, his face turned scarlet with anger.

'Look, Bill, this isn't that difficult. I told you I needed the goddamn things two weeks ago. This is what happens when you wait until the last minute.

'Well, you better,' Richard threatened, ending the conversation by slamming down the phone.

'What's up?' Peter asked.

'Ned Schuster was in a car wreck,' Richard answered distractedly, running his fingers through his hair. 'He's in the hospital.'

'Who?'

'Schuster. He's supposed to testify today. Now, Bill Ebling says they can't get the papers to court because Schuster had the only copy.'

Peter had no idea what his father was talking about. He glanced down at his files. There was one for each witness and none was for a Ned Schuster. When he looked up, his father was leaning against the wall. His face was as pale as chalk and he was rubbing both sides of his jaw vigorously.

'Dad?' Peter asked, frightened by his father's ashen pallor and the beads of sweat that suddenly bathed his face. Instead of answering, Richard grimaced in pain and began rubbing his breast with a clenched fist. Peter froze.

'Heart attack,' Richard gasped.

Peter snapped out of his trance and raced around the conference table.

'I need to lie down,' Richard managed, as his knees sagged. Peter caught him before he hit the floor.

'Help!' Peter screamed. A young woman stuck her head in the door. Her eyes widened.

'Call 911, fast! My father is having a heart attack.'

When Peter looked down, Richard's teeth were

clenched and his eyes were squeezed tight. He continued to rub his chest vigorously as if trying to erase his pain.

'Hold on, Dad,' Peter begged. 'The medics are coming.'

Richard's body jerked. His eyes glazed over. The two men were sprawled on the floor. Peter held his father's head in his lap. He was concentrating so hard on his father that he didn't notice the room filling with people.

Suddenly, Richard's eyes opened and he gasped, 'Mistrial.'

'What?'

'Get . . . mistrial . . . Must . . .'

'Don't talk. Please, Dad. Save your strength.'

Richard grabbed Peter's wrist and squeezed so hard his fingers left raw, red impressions.

'Must . . . Mistrial,' he managed again.

'Yes, I will,' Peter promised, just as someone called, 'Let me through.' Peter looked toward the doorway. He recognized the older woman who was pushing through the crowd as a nurse the firm had hired to assist in working up personal injury cases. A moment later, Peter was standing on the far side of the conference table as the nurse tried to save his father's life.

The idea of Richard Hale dying sucked the air right out of Peter. He slumped onto a chair just as two medics rushed into the room with oxygen, a stretcher and a portable IV. Peter's mother had died several years ago after a long illness and her death had been expected, but Peter saw his father as a mountain that would last forever. When he looked up he could not see his father through the crush of medical personnel who surrounded him. What if Richard didn't pull through? he asked himself. Peter's heart beat so rapidly he had to will himself to calm down. The anxiety attack passed. He opened his eyes and saw his briefcase and his files. The trial! Peter looked at his watch. It was almost time to go to court. Suddenly, the people in front of the door were backing away and the medics were rushing out of the room with a stretcher that supported his father. Peter wanted to follow them to the hospital, but someone had to tell Mrs. Elliot what had happened and ask Judge Pruitt for a mistrial. There was no way he could see his father now anyway. Peter knew he would probably have to stay in the hospital waiting room for hours before the doctors could tell him anything.

Peter stepped out of the conference room into the hall. It was empty. Everyone had followed the medics to the elevator. Peter walked away from the crowd and left the offices by a back door that opened near the men's room. He was trembling and flushed. He went to the rest room sink and splashed cold water on his face. Then, he leaned forward and looked at himself in the mirror. His brown, blow-dried hair was a mess, his shirt was rumpled and his tie had been wrenched to one side. Peter took out a pocket comb and wet it. When his hair looked presentable, he tucked in his shirt and straightened his tie.

Peter examined himself again. He saw a man whose genetic inheritance from his mother had softened the sharp features his father had contributed. Peter had his father's intense blue eyes, but he also had his mother's smooth, high cheekbones. His nose was straight instead of craggy and his lips were thinner than Richard Hale's. At five feet ten, one hundred and sixty pounds, he was slender and wiry with none of the bulk or height of his father.

Peter straightened up. He felt back in control of

himself and the situation. There was nothing he could do for his father now. Richard would be unconscious or drugged for hours. Peter decided that he would quickly explain what happened to the judge before going to the hospital. Certainly, Pruitt would grant a mistrial under the circumstances. No judge would require the trial to go on when the lead counsel had been stricken with a heart attack.

Peter took the elevator to the lobby. The courthouse was only a few blocks away. As he rushed toward it, an unsettling thought suddenly occurred to him. Mrs. Elliot was suffering terribly. He could see how hard it was for her to sit through her trial, both physically and emotionally. If a mistrial was declared, Mrs. Elliot would have to suffer through a second trial. In a second trial, the defense would have transcripts of Mrs. Elliot's witnesses and would know all of their strategy. Delay always helped the defendant when the plaintiff had a strong case. And the plaintiff's case was almost finished. Only two short witnesses remained.

Peter paused inside the courthouse doors. Lawyers, litigants, policemen and clerks swirled around him, the noise from dozens of conversations formed a constant din, but he was oblivious to the crowd. Was his father thinking clearly when he told Peter to ask for a mistrial? He had been in unbearable pain. Did his father really want to abort the case when it was going so well? Would Richard even remember his order when he recovered from the trauma of his coronary? Peter was certain that following his father's wishes was not in Mrs. Elliot's best interest, but the thought of disobeying Richard Hale's command terrified him.

Peter realized that he was trembling. He took a deep breath and willed himself to calm down. A lawyer's first duty was to his client. Why, then, had his father told him to ask for a mistrial? It took a moment for the answer to dawn on Peter. Richard Hale had no confidence in Peter's ability to take over the case.

Peter's fear gave way to a sense of outrage. He squared his shoulders and strode across the lobby toward the elevators. By the time the elevator doors opened, Peter was ready to go to court. He would show his father just how good he was. He would win *Elliot*. Then, he would place the multimillion-dollar judgment in front of Richard Hale, irrefutable proof that he was ready, willing and able to step up to the big time.

Alvin Pruitt was a cadaverous jurist with a military crew cut, beady, bloodshot eyes and sunken cheeks that always seemed to be covered by gray stubble. He was foul-tempered and ran his courtroom like a Marine barracks. By the time Peter walked into court, he was ten minutes late and the judge was furious.

'I hope you have a good explanation for your tardiness, Mr. Hale.'

'I do, sir. There's been an emergency. May I approach the bench?'

Pruitt frowned and searched the room beyond Peter. 'Where is your father?'

'That's what I want to tell you,' Peter answered, as he pushed through the low gate that separated the spectators from the area before the bench.

Pruitt beckoned Peter forward, then addressed the attorney representing Northwest Maritime and their driver.

'Mr. Compton, you'd better get up here.'

Peter paused at the plaintiff's table to say hello to his client. Nellie Elliot was a washed-out woman who had been worn down by poverty, the untimely death of her husband and the grueling task of raising five young children when life added a final insult by putting her in the path of a Northwest Maritime truck. Now, Mrs. Elliot was a wheelchair-bound quadriplegic and her lawsuit was worth millions.

'What's wrong?' Mrs. Elliot asked. Since the accident, she could move only her head, which bobbed toward her left shoulder as she spoke in the halting, slurred speech that was another product of the defendant's negligence.

'I'll fill you in after I confer with the judge,' Peter answered with a reassuring smile.

'Well?' Judge Pruitt asked impatiently.

Peter spoke quietly, so his voice would not reach his client.

'Your Honor, my father had a heart attack just as we were leaving for court.'

Lyle Compton looked stricken and the judge's hard-bitten demeanor disappeared. Both men had known Richard Hale for more than twenty years. Though Judge Pruitt was brusque with all who appeared before him, he had the highest regard for Richard. Richard and Lyle Compton had been friendly adversaries in countless courtroom battles.

'Is he going to be all right?' Pruitt asked with genuine concern.

'I don't know.'

'Well, I'll adjourn court and we'll reconvene tomorrow so you can bring us up to date,' the judge said.

Peter had been afraid the judge might try to stop the trial on his own. 'There's no reason to adjourn,' he said, hoping he did not sound as anxious as he felt. 'I won't be able to see my father for hours.'

Judge Pruitt's brow furrowed. He looked at Peter as

if he was certain he had misunderstood him.

'You don't plan on continuing the trial, do you?' the judge asked.

'Oh, certainly. After all, our case is almost over and there's Mrs. Elliot to consider. It would be awfully hard for her to go through a second trial.'

'Yes, well that may be, but your father is lead counsel,' the judge said.

Lyle Compton was short, bald and rotund. He usually had a disarming smile on his face. He represented insurance companies for a living, but he was sympathetic to plaintiffs and was fair and charmingly nonadversarial until he was forced into the courtroom.

'Peter, it wouldn't be right to make you continue this case,' Compton said with sincerity. 'Mrs. Elliot has a right to be represented by the best. If you move for a continuance or a mistrial, I'm not going to object.'

Peter kept control of his facial expression, but he was seething. He believed Compton was trying to sucker him into moving for a mistrial so he could save his case. And that crack about Mrs. Elliot deserving the best . . . Peter's heart hardened. He would show Compton what it was like to really go up against the best.

'I appreciate your concern, Mr. Compton, but I'm prepared to continue.'

'Do you feel that you're ready to do that, Mr. Hale?' the judge asked. 'You've never been lead counsel in a case this complex, have you?'

'No, Your Honor, but I worked on this case from the beginning. I prepared the witnesses, wrote the pleadings and the legal memos. In all modesty, I believe I know the ins and outs of Mrs. Elliot's lawsuit as well, if not better, than my father.'

'Is this what your client wants?' the judge asked.

'I haven't had an opportunity to confer with her. She doesn't know what happened.'

Judge Pruitt looked troubled. 'Well, why don't you take a few minutes to confer with Mrs. Elliot. But before you do, I have to tell you that I think you're making a big mistake if you go ahead. You should be with your father in the hospital. I know you're thinking of your client's interests, which is commendable, but I can't imagine how you're going to be able to focus on this case without knowing that your father has pulled through.'

Peter felt a brief flash of elation. The trial was going to continue and he was going to try it by himself. Then, as Peter walked over to his client, a moment of self-doubt assailed him. Aside from his mistrust of Peter's abilities, was there some other reason why his father had ordered Peter to ask for a mistrial? Peter remembered how upset his father had been just before his heart attack. What had that been about? Some witness and some papers. As Peter sat down next to Mrs. Elliot, he tried to review everything he knew about the case. He could think of no witness who needed to testify other than the two who were scheduled for this morning and no papers that had to be introduced.

Before he could consider the matter further, Mrs. Elliot swung her wheelchair so she could face Peter.

'Where's Mr. Hale?' she asked fearfully.

Peter promptly forgot about the mystery witness and said, 'Mrs. Elliot, I want you to stay calm. I have some news for you that may be a bit disturbing.'

'Plaintiff rests,' Peter declared in a voice that conveyed to the jury the confidence he felt in his case. His last two witnesses had been terrific and Peter could not conceive of a juror who was not convinced that Nellie Elliot should be awarded millions to compensate her for the negligence of Northwest Maritime's driver.

'May I confer with Mr. Hale for a moment?' Lyle Compton asked Judge Pruitt.

'Why don't I send the jury out for lunch, Mr. Compton. As soon as you're finished talking to Mr. Hale, you can make any motions you may have. We'll start the defense case after lunch.'

'That would be fine, Your Honor.'

When the jurors were gone, Compton motioned Peter to join him out of earshot of Mrs. Elliot. Peter felt he was on top of the world as he crossed the courtroom. During a phone call to the hospital, he had been assured that his father would make a full recovery, and he was on the brink of winning his first million-dollar verdict.

'Peter,' Compton said in a low voice, 'I'm prepared to recommend a settlement of 1.5 million. I think that's a fair offer.'

Peter's chest swelled. Compton was on the ropes and he knew it. The offer was a last-ditch attempt to save his client the several million dollars more Peter was confident the jury would award.

'Sorry, Lyle, but I don't think that's enough.'

Compton seemed uneasy. 'Look, Peter, I feel very uncomfortable about the way this case is proceeding. You shouldn't have continued to try this matter. You're too inexperienced.'

'Oh,' Peter replied, fighting hard not to smirk. 'Why don't we let the jury decide that.'

Compton looked down. He took a deep breath and exhaled.

'I probably shouldn't do this, but I don't want to take

advantage of you. I respect your father tremendously and, because of that, I feel compelled to tell you that you have problems with your case. Under the circumstances, this is a very good offer.'

Peter wanted to laugh in Compton's face. Problems with his case, indeed. Did Compton think he would fall for this transparent attempt to prey on the insecurities of a young lawyer trying his first big case. He felt great seeing one of the best insurance defense attorneys in the state squirming like a worm on a hook.

'Lyle, I appreciate your concern, but it's no go.'

Compton looked distraught. 'All right. I tried, Peter, but I have a client, too.'

As soon as the lawyers were back at their respective tables, Mrs. Elliot asked, 'What happens now?'

'Mr. Compton will probably move for a directed verdict. It's nothing to worry about. It's routine. The defense always does that after the plaintiff rests. He's going to argue that we haven't produced enough evidence to let the case go to the jury. He has to make his record.'

'He won't win?' she asked anxiously.

'Of course not,' Peter answered with a confident smile. 'To rule against us, the judge would have to find that there is no reasonable interpretation of the evidence that could support our position. It's an almost impossible burden to meet.'

'I have a motion for the court,' Compton said, sounding almost apologetic.

'What is the basis for your motion, Mr. Compton?' Judge Pruitt asked.

'Your Honor, plaintiff's complaint alleges that Northwest Maritime is a corporation registered in the state of Oregon. It is in paragraph one of the complaint.'

Peter looked down at the pleading that had been filed a year and a half before to formally put the case before the court. Mrs. Elliot's complaint alleged that Northwest Maritime was a corporation doing business in Oregon, that a truck driven by one of its agents had caused her injury and that the driver was negligent in the way he drove. It was a simple, straightforward court document.

'Our answer denied each and every allegation in the complaint,' Compton went on. 'When a defendant does that, it becomes plaintiff's duty to prove each and every allegation in the complaint. I kept track of the evidence and I submit that Mrs. Elliot has failed to prove the existence of the corporation.'

Peter did not hear anything else Compton said. It was as if the engines on a plane in which he was flying stopped suddenly and the plane began plummeting downward at a dizzying speed. Peter had assumed that his father had entered the corporate documents on one of the occasions he had been in the law library researching legal issues. Now, it looked as if the evidence had never been produced.

Suddenly, Peter remembered Ned Schuster, the mystery witness who had been in the accident. The man who was bringing the documents his father was so upset about, right before he'd had his coronary. They must have been the documents that would prove that Northwest Maritime was a corporation. That's why Richard had implored Peter to move for a mistrial.

'. . . to dismiss the case against Northwest Maritime and grant a directed verdict for my client,' Compton concluded.

Judge Pruitt looked very upset. He turned toward Peter, who was rereading the complaint as if, somehow, he could will the words to change. This point that

Compton had raised was such a little thing. A technicality. Everyone knew Northwest Maritime was a corporation. It owned huge buildings and declared its existence from immense signs with fat red letters. The missing document was so small. A notarized paper that took up no space at all.

'Mr. Hale,' the judge stated quietly, 'I've been expecting this. The answer does deny the existence of the corporation. That does put the burden on you to prove your allegation regarding the corporation. This morning, I looked up the case law in anticipation of this motion.'

'The . . . the driver. Mr. Hardesty. I believe he said . . .'

Judge Pruitt shook his head. 'No, sir. The question was never put to him.'

'But Mrs. Elliot? What about her?' Peter asked pathetically. 'If you dismiss the case against Northwest Maritime, only the driver will be left and he doesn't have the money to pay for Mrs. Elliot's bills. She's paralyzed. You know Northwest Maritime is liable.'

Peter stopped. The judge could not look him in the eye and Lyle Compton looked sick, like a child who has played a successful practical joke and now feels guilty about it.

'Mr. Hale,' Judge Pruitt said, 'there is nothing I can do in this case. You did not prove that Northwest Maritime is a corporation. No reasonable jury could conclude it was from the facts in evidence and the jurors may not go outside the evidence produced in court. If I deny Mr. Compton's motion, he will appeal and the court of appeals will reverse me. They have upheld motions of this sort in seven reported cases I have found. My hands are tied.'

Judge Pruitt turned toward Lyle Compton and Peter sank onto his seat. His head was spinning. He had no idea what he should do. He thought he might be sick.

'I'm granting your motion, Mr. Compton. A verdict will be directed for Northwest Maritime. The case against Mr. Hardesty will proceed.'

Peter felt the wheels of Mrs. Elliot's wheelchair bumping against his chair.

'What is it? What is it?' she asked, her slurred voice trembling with panic and fear. With each repetition, Mrs. Elliot grew louder and more strident and everyone in the courtroom looked at Peter to hear the answer he would give to this poor, crippled woman who would not receive one cent for the anguish and horror she had been through. Peter wanted to answer her, but he could not speak. He could only sit, eyes staring straight ahead, as his world went up in flames.

2

After court, Peter staggered back to Hale, Greaves in a daze. Martin Strobridge was one of the most eloquent attorneys in the state of Oregon, but he was struck dumb by Peter's account of his attempt to try *Elliot v. Northwest Maritime.* When Strobridge recovered his senses, he issued an order that no one was to tell Richard what had happened for fear of sending him into another cardiac arrest. Then, he suspended Peter from all his duties at the firm until a committee reviewed his conduct. Strobridge had no idea how grateful Peter was for the opportunity to stay away from the firm where he would be the object of derision as soon as the office grapevine spread the news of his disgrace.

Peter drove directly from his office to the hospital. He was allowed into the intensive care unit for only a few minutes. Richard's doctor assured Peter that his father's condition was not serious and that Richard would be out of the hospital within the week, but the shock of seeing his father hooked up to IV drips and blinking machinery was as great as the trauma of losing *Elliot*. Though he had never seen him play, Peter's image of his father always involved football. He thought of Richard Hale as a man of boundless energy who crashed through lines and smashed into opponents. The Richard Hale who stared at him with heavy-lidded eyes was old and frail and his speech was barely coherent. Peter tried to smile. He made a few feeble attempts at conversation. Then, he stumbled out of his father's room before his allotted time was up, grateful that the drugs his father had been given prevented him from thinking clearly enough to ask about the outcome of the Elliot case.

In the intervening days between his debacle and the inevitable summons to the offices of Hale, Greaves, Peter hid in his apartment trying to imagine a scenario in which his life would go on as before. Thankfully, Priscilla had flown off to some unknown destination leaving him alone with his despair. Peter knew that there would have to be some consequences for his actions, but by the time the phone call came requesting his appearance at the firm Peter had created a fantasy in which he apologized and promised to never do anything so foolish ever again, and all was forgiven.

On one of Peter's visits to the hospital, his father had asked about *Elliot* and Peter had answered that everything was taken care of. As soon as he entered his father's massive, corner office on the day he was summoned, Peter knew that someone had finally broken the news of Peter's disgrace to his father. The man who slumped down across from Peter behind the vast oak desk was tired. He studied Peter with weary eyes. He had lost weight in the hospital and his ruddy complexion was now pasty. After a moment, Richard shook his head slowly and sadly.

'Sit down, Peter,' Richard said, indicating a high-backed leather chair. Peter sat.

'I never imagined that it would come to this.'

Peter wanted to protest, to defend himself, but there was a lump in his throat the size of an apple and he could only look down at the polished desktop.

'You wanted to be lead counsel in a big case. That's why you did this, isn't it?'

Peter nodded.

'I know how much you resented me for denying you your chance.' Peter looked up, surprised. He had no idea he was so transparent. 'But I could not permit it.'

Richard sighed. He looked defeated.

'I've tried to fool myself about you, Peter, but what you've done has forced me to face the truth. You are a highly intelligent young man. I have your scores on IQ tests to prove it. But you have never lived up to your potential. You didn't apply yourself in high school, so I had to use my pull to get you into a good university, where you partied for four years, achieving grades that were so low that I had to call in every chip I could find to get you into law school. Then I did the same thing to get you a job with this firm, hoping against hope that you would finally change into a responsible adult.

'In part, I blame myself for your failures. I know I wasn't around as much as I should have been when you were growing up, because I was working so damned hard to build this firm. And when I was around, I tried to make up for my absences by spoiling you rotten. With the wisdom of hindsight, I see now that you would have been better off getting through life without so much of my help. Maybe, if you had been forced to deal with failure, you would have developed the toughness, the moral fiber . . .'

Richard's voice trailed off. He closed his eyes and rubbed the lids. When he opened them he looked sad and resigned.

'Well, it doesn't matter now. Regardless of who's to blame, you are who you are and that is why I could not let you try *Elliot*. I know you possess the intelligence to be a good lawyer, but you are lazy and self-centered. You have always taken the easy way out. You have never given one hundred percent of yourself to anything. For you, trying *Elliot* was an opportunity to show off your trial skills and gain advancement in the firm, but this case was Mrs. Elliot's life. Your arrogance and your thoughtlessness have deprived that poor woman of the money she needs for medical care and her children. You have destroyed her future and her children's future and, the saddest thing for me, as your father, is that I don't believe you care.'

'Dad, I . . .' Peter started, but Richard shook his head.

'There is nothing left to say, Peter. Mrs. Elliot will sue this firm for malpractice and I will have to tell her lawyers that you disobeyed my direct order to ask for a mistrial, that you misled Judge Pruitt so you could have your day in the sun and that your conduct was a blatant example of malpractice. Naturally, under the circumstances, you can no longer remain here. As a favor to me, the firm will give you the option of resigning. That, however, is the last favor you will ever get from me.'

Richard leaned forward. He rested his elbows on the desk and clasped his hands.

'It pains me to say this, but I must be blunt with you, for your own good. This may be your last chance to be saved. I've thought about what I am going to say long and hard and I hope and pray that I'm doing the right thing. First, I've changed my will to disinherit you. Second, I will never give you another penny. You have not earned the way you live. From now on, you must live according to what you earn.'

The words hit Peter like a hammer and he could only stare, openmouthed. His father was turning his back on him, his law firm was taking away his job. Not one more penny, Richard had said. How would he meet his payments on the Porsche and the condo? How would he pay his debts? And the will. Disinherited, Richard had said.

'Dad,' Peter managed, 'I know I was wrong. I'm sorry. I . . . It's just . . .'

Richard shook his head. 'Save your breath, Peter. I love you, but I can't stand the sight of you anymore. You have no idea how hard it is for me to admit to myself that my only child is a failure. I had such high hopes for you. But you let everyone down. Me, the firm, Mrs. Elliot.'

'You can't do this. You can't cut me out of your life.'

'No, I can't. I'm going to give you one, last chance to make something of yourself.'

Peter collapsed with relief, feeling like a hiker lost for days in the forest, near death and bereft of hope, who suddenly hears the voice of his rescuer.

'Anything, Dad. I know I was wrong. I'll do what you want.'

'You're not going to like what I'm about to propose, but I see it as the only way out for you. If you can prove to me that you are a responsible adult, I will reconsider my decision to disinherit you. To that end, I've spoken to an old friend, Amos Geary. Amos and I go way back. We played football together at Oregon State and we were once partners. He has a practice in Whitaker, a small town of about thirteen thousand in eastern Oregon, and the contract to provide indigent defense for Whitaker County and several other small counties around there. His associate just quit. He's willing to give you the job. It pays seventeen thousand to start.'

Peter could not believe his ears. He'd been to Whitaker to take depositions, two years ago. There were four streets in Whitaker. When the wind blew, you couldn't see the buildings for the dust. If it wasn't for the college, which was packed with Future Farmers of America, there wouldn't be any life at all.

'I won't do it,' he said, shaking his head from side to side.

'Then, we have nothing more to say to each other.'

Peter stood up. He'd had enough.

'That's where you're wrong.' Peter's voice shook and tears welled up in his eyes. 'You may have nothing to say to me, but I have plenty to say to you. You call me self-centered. You are the most arrogant son of a bitch I've ever met. You call yourself a father. You were never a father to me. Mom raised me. You put in appearances and made rules. And it sure is no surprise to me that you think I'm a failure. You let me know how little you thought of me every chance you had when I was growing up. My grades were never good enough. I never put out enough at sports. Well, I'll tell you this, no one could live up to your standards. All-American, high school valedictorian, first in your law school class. How was I supposed to compete with a god?

'But I tried and you never gave me credit for trying. And now, when I was ready to show you what I could do in court, you stepped on me, every chance you could. You're afraid to admit how good a lawyer I am. Well, I'll show you. I'll get a job with another firm. I'll make partner and Hale, Greaves can kiss my ass.'

Richard listened to Peter's tirade calmly. When Peter was through, Richard asked, 'What firm will give you a job after the stunt you pulled? They all know what you did. You're the talk of the Portland legal community. How are you going to get a job once your potential employer talks to us? I will tell you flat out that no one here will give you a recommendation.'

Peter's bravado disappeared. He knew that what his father said was true.

'You may not believe me,' Richard said, 'but I do love you. You have no idea how it hurts me to cast you out. But I have to do it for your sake. Go to Whitaker. There won't be any temptations for you there. Learn to stand on your own two feet and live within your means. Learn how to be a good lawyer. Learn to be a man.'

CHAPTER TWO

The sun was a blistering disk that mercilessly baked the brown dirt covering the vast expanse of wasteland east of Whitaker. There were no clouds to compete with it in the pale blue and unforgiving sky. The young Oregon state trooper was grateful for his Stetson and fervently wished for a breeze that would cool him down and create a cloud of swirling dust thick enough to obscure the thing that lay among the sagebrush halfway down the gully. When Dr. Guisti's vehicle appeared, shimmering in the heat like a toy trapped in a bubble of molten glass, the trooper was intentionally standing with his back to the thing. One long look before radioing for assistance had been enough.

The trooper knew it was disrespectful to think of the young woman as a thing, but she no longer resembled any woman he had ever known. The creatures of the desert had feasted on her flesh, the elements had had their way with her, and something else had been at her.

Some person whom the trooper also had trouble thinking of in human terms.

A group of students from a geology class at Whitaker
State College on a field trip with their professor had
found the body. They huddled together while members
of the Major Crime Team took their statements. The
young trooper noticed that they too averted their eyes
from the gully, even though there was no way they
could see the body from where they were standing.

The City of Whitaker had a sixteen-person police
force. The county sheriff's office was even smaller, with
one under-sheriff and five deputies. On those rare
occasions when a major crime occurred, it was investigated by a Major Crime Team, which consisted of a
detective from the small Oregon State Police office
headquartered in Whitaker, the Whitaker County sheriff, or his designee, a member of the Whitaker Police
Department and police from neighboring Blaine and
Cayuse counties. Since the body was found outside the
city limits of Whitaker, and because the Oregon State
Police had taken the initial call, the team had
designated Detective Jason Dagget of the Oregon State
Police as the officer in charge.

Dagget had summoned a forensic team from the
Oregon State Crime Lab to the scene and they were
working the area around the body. Then he called
Dr. Harold Guisti, a tall, anorexic man with a florid
complexion who had practiced family medicine in
Whitaker for thirty years and contracted with the state
medical examiner to perform autopsies in Whitaker,
Blaine and Cayuse counties. The doctor's battered
Range Rover bounced to a stop in front of Detective
Dagget. The detective went around to the driver's
door. Dr. Guisti stepped out. A sudden wind blew
dust in the doctor's eyes and spread his thinning

gray hair across his partially exposed scalp.

'Where's she at?' Guisti asked, as soon as the wind died down.

'In the gully. We think she was killed somewhere else and dumped down there. We haven't found much blood. She's also naked, but there are no clothes.'

Guisti grunted, then stepped over the lip of the gully, cautiously edging sideways down the wall far enough away from the body so that anything he dislodged in his descent would not foul the crime scene.

'How was she killed?' he asked Dagget, who was following behind.

'She was butchered, Harold. Plain and simple.'

Guisti had been hoping that the woman had been shot or poisoned, because there had been another body discovered in an outcropping of rock two months ago, naked and butchered. Guisti believed the weapon used was a hatchet of some kind. He was hoping he would not come to the same conclusion when he examined this young female, because he did not want to think about what that would mean for the people of Whitaker, Cayuse and Blaine.

PART TWO

A FINGER EXERCISE
FOR HELL

CHAPTER THREE

1

Surrounding the City of Whitaker was farmland made green by irrigation systems that tapped into the Camas River, but beyond the farms, hot, dusty winds blew tumbleweeds across vast flatlands that were broken only occasionally by high, brown hills. As Peter drove through the desert, he felt his spirit burning up and crumbling slowly to gray ash and he entered the City of Whitaker as empty as the arid land that encircled it.

Peter spent his first night in Whitaker at the Riverview Motel, which was clean, quiet and actually had a view of the Camas River. After breakfast, Peter walked from the motel to the offices of Amos Geary. He was exhausted from tossing and turning all night in strange surroundings as his emotions shifted from boiling rage at the injustices that life had heaped upon him to feelings of fear and utter despair as he struggled with the very real possibility that he might have lost forever the love of his father.

The walk from the motel took Peter through

Wishing Well Park, which ran the length of the town between High Street and the Camas River. There was a wistful beauty in the slow-moving Camas, but Peter found the town as dry and uninteresting as the wastelands that surrounded it. The biggest bookstore was the Christian Bookshop; you could easily find a store that fixed saddles but none that made café lattes and the town's only movie theater featured wholesome family entertainment. Peter thought of Whitaker as a finger exercise for the architect who designed hell.

City center started at High and First where the courthouse stood. Peter turned up First Street to Main. Running parallel to Main Street was Broad Street. Elm, the street farthest from the river, started commercial, then curved through a pleasant, tree-shaded, residential section of town until it arrived at the campus of Whitaker State College. On the other side of the college was the hospital.

As Peter walked, he saw battered Ford pickups in the parking spaces and noticed more cowboy hats than he had seen all of last year in Portland. When he reached Main and Fourth, he checked the slip of paper with Geary's address. On both sides of Main were old, two- and three-story brick buildings. Peter saw Dot's coffee shop, B.J.'s beauty salon and an orange-and-black Rexall sign, but no law office. Then, he glanced up a story and saw AMOS J. GEARY, ATTORNEY-AT-LAW painted in flaking gold letters on a second-floor window. Peter backtracked and found a narrow doorway between the beauty salon and the coffee shop. The door opened directly into a cramped stairwell. Dingy, green linoleum was secured to the stairs by dented brass runners. It creaked underfoot as Peter climbed to the second floor.

The hall at the top of the stairs was dark and musty. Geary's name and profession were painted in black on a door to the left of the stairwell. The door stuck and Peter had to push hard to get it open. A middle-aged woman with hennaed hair was sitting behind a desk working at a word processor, the only item in the reception area that did not look as if it had been purchased in a secondhand store.

Two issues of *Field and Stream* and a dog-eared copy of *Sports Illustrated* lay on a low Formica-topped end table next to a couch made of cracked, red imitation leather. A ceiling fixture lit by a dim bulb and a little sunlight that managed to work its way through the dirt-covered front window conspired to cast a dull yellow glow over the room. Peter could not help comparing this antiquated dump to the elegant offices from which he had so recently been evicted. The memory of the plush carpets, brass fixtures and polished woods made his stomach seize up in rage and frustration. It just was not fair.

The woman looked up when the door opened and stared at Peter through glasses with thick, black plastic rims.

'I'm Peter Hale. I have an appointment with Mr. Geary for nine.'

The woman eyed him suspiciously.

'You're the young man who's going to work here, aren't you?'

'Yes, ma'am.'

'Well, take a seat. Mr. Geary's not in, just yet. But I expect he'll be along any minute. He has court at ten.'

The secretary-receptionist went back to her work without another word. Peter was shocked by her abrupt dismissal, but decided against reprimanding the woman. She'd probably be typing his work and it did not pay to alienate what appeared to be the only support staff in the office.

Peter sat on the couch. After a while, he looked around the reception room. Except for some cracks in the ceiling plaster, he did not see anything he had not seen the first time he looked. Peter glanced at his watch. It was nine-fifteen. He decided to check out the *Sports Illustrated.* It was nine months old but Peter thumbed through it anyway. He was finished skimming it by nine-thirty and was deciding whether to read an article on a Peruvian boxer or start on *Field and Stream* when the door to the law office opened.

Amos Geary's face was a beet-red matrix of busted blood vessels. What was left of his unkempt hair was a dingy gray and he had compensated for its loss by growing a shaggy, walrus mustache. His bloodshot eyes were lost in folds of puffy flesh. Geary was as tall as Peter's father and looked twice as heavy. His stomach sagged over his belt and the buttons on his shirt looked as if they were about to pop. Peter was wearing a tailored gray pinstripe suit and a tasteful maroon tie. Geary was wearing an awful aquamarine tie spotted with stains that matched those on his rumpled brown suit. Peter's facial muscles twitched with the effort it took to hide his distaste.

Geary studied the young man from the open doorway, mentally reconstructing his face with his mother's features deleted and his father's expanded.

'Peter Hale, I presume?'

'Mr. Geary?' Peter asked hesitantly while he studied Geary's sagging jowls and bulbous, red-veined nose. Geary shifted his battered briefcase and extended his right hand. It was sweaty and Peter withdrew his own after a light touch as if he feared he could contract alcoholism from the brief contact.

'How was the drive?' Geary asked, ignoring the slight and Peter's discomfort.

'Fine,' Peter responded, flinching slightly as Geary's alcohol- and mouthwash-drenched breath hit him full in the face.

'Glad to hear it.'

'Don't forget you have court at ten,' the secretary reminded Geary.

'What case, Clara?'

'*Judd.*'

'Oh, lord. Not *Judd*,' Geary answered, turning his back on Peter and trudging down a dark and dingy hall.

'Follow me,' Geary called over his shoulder. Peter trailed his new boss to a poorly lit office that stank of stale smoke. Geary tossed his briefcase on top of a mess of files and papers stacked atop a battle-scarred, wooden desk. Peter sat on a straight-backed chair in front of the desk. While Geary rummaged through a dilapidated gray metal filing cabinet for the *Judd* file, Peter looked around the office. On one wall, among diplomas and certificates attesting to Geary's admission to various state and federal bars, was a black-and-white team photo of the 1956 Oregon State football team. Geary caught Peter looking at it.

'I'm in the front, kneeling down. Your father's behind me on the right. I opened holes for him for four years and I've got cleat marks on my back to prove it,' Geary said with a brusque laugh.

Peter forced a smile. He was not in the mood to listen to an old drunk wax nostalgic about the man who had exiled him to this big zero. Then, he noticed a framed law degree to the right of Geary's OSU diploma.

'You went to Harvard?' Peter asked, trying not to sound incredulous.

'Class of '59. Does that surprise you?'

'Well . . . Uh, no,' Peter said, flushing because Geary had read him so easily.

'It should. A Harvard man stuck out here in the boonies. But, then, you're stuck here with me, aren't you?'

This time, Peter flushed from anger. Geary found the *Judd* file and slumped onto a slat-back chair behind the desk.

'Your father told me everything when he asked me to hire you. To be honest, I was against it. Not because I was unsympathetic to Dick's attempts to save your soul. I just didn't want to put my practice at risk while your father was fighting for your salvation.'

'If you didn't want me here,' Peter asked resentfully, 'why did you agree to hire me?'

Geary folded his hands behind his head, leaned back and studied Peter without rancor.

'I owe your father a great debt. Supervising your stay in purgatory will take a little off the top. But I made it clear to Dick that I'll drop you like a hot coal if you fuck up. I have a sense of honor, but not a shred of sentimentality. Do we understand each other?'

Peter nodded.

'Good,' Geary said. 'Now, let me tell you the facts of life in Whitaker. There are fifteen lawyers in private practice in this county. Five of them work at Sissler, MacAfee and Petersen. They handle every insurance defense case in Whitaker and the five surrounding counties. Those boys make the big bucks. The other ten attorneys, including yours truly, do not. We fight over the scraps. There's the occasional personal injury case. One good old boy runs his four-by-four into some other good old boy's four-by-four. I write wills, I handle divorces. If it walks through the door and it doesn't take a lot of expertise, I'm your man.

'Then, there's crime. Crime does pay, only not for the criminals. You're probably wondering how I can afford these palatial digs. Well, I'll let you in on the secret. About fifteen years ago, the state decided to contract out indigent defense and I was firstest with the mostest. I've had the contract for Whitaker, Blaine and Cayuse counties, ever since. It pays my overhead and makes me a small profit. It's easy money and I aim to keep it. That's where you come in. You're gonna become the Perry Mason of Whitaker County.'

Peter was gripped by deep depression. He had not gone to law school to muck around in the swamp called criminal law. Real lawyers sued for millions or handled massive business deals. On a scale of one to ten, with ten being the most prestigious type of legal practice, criminal law was a minus seventy-two.

'I hope my father didn't misrepresent my qualifications, Mr. Geary,' Peter said hesitantly. 'I've never handled a criminal case.'

'Peter, we're not talking crime-of-the-century. We're talking shoplifts at J. C. Penney, driving while stupid. Most of these cases will plead out and the rest could be handled by Forrest Gump. Your dad told me about some of the cases you've tried on your own and some of the ones you've second-chaired. I'd say that you're probably one of the most experienced attorneys in town, right now. So, don't sweat the small stuff.

'Now, here's my plan,' Geary said, fishing through his desk until he found a cigarette. 'Your office is next door.' A plume of smoke blew across the desk and Peter held his breath to avoid breathing in the foul, cancerous discharge. 'The walls are paper-thin, so we don't need an intercom. Settle in. Read through the twenty case files on your desk. Keep a copy of the Criminal Code at your right hand, a copy of the Constitutions of the

United States and the state of Oregon at your left, and a copy of the Oregon State Bar Criminal Law Handbook within easy reach. If you have any questions, try not to bother me with them. I'm very busy.'

Peter looked stunned. Geary grinned maliciously.

'Welcome to the real world, son. And have a nice day. Now, scat. I have to go to the ninth circle of hell to fight the devil for Elmo Judd's soul.'

2

Whitaker State College was founded as an agricultural school to service eastern Oregon in 1942, but had since developed a decent liberal arts program. The older, brick buildings surrounded a quadrangle at the center of the campus and were covered with ivy. The legislature had funded an expansion program in the late fifties and, again, in the early eighties, and a school of business, the football stadium, a new athletic facility and a block of two-story, brick dormitories were among the newer-looking buildings that spread out from the hub.

In the shadow of the business school was a large blacktop parking area. Shortly before 10 P.M., evening classes ended and the faculty and off-campus students emptied into the lot. Christopher Mammon drove a dull green Chevy when he did not want to attract attention. Tonight, the Chevy was parked as inconspicuously as possible in the shadows of a large oak tree on the edge of the lot because there were two kilos of cocaine in separate Ziploc bags under the driver's seat.

The Chevy was a normal-size car, but Mammon was so massive that there was barely room for Kevin Booth in the front seat. Mammon's body was so large it approached the grotesque. At a flabby two hundred pounds, Booth had been big enough to play high school football, but alongside Mammon's enormous lats, awesome thighs and mile-wide chest, he appeared to be one dimensional.

Booth looked over his shoulder through the rear window as he had several times each minute since Mammon parked. After a few seconds, Booth twisted forward and drummed his fingers nervously on the dashboard.

'Where is that bitch? She said nine forty-five and it's after ten.'

'Relax, man.' Mammon's eyes were closed and he sounded bored. Booth could not believe how calm Mammon was with this much dope in the car. Of course, Mammon was always calm. When you were that big only King Kong could raise your blood pressure. If they were arrested and went to jail, Mammon would be the king of the beasts in a jungle filled with wild animals. Booth would die in prison, prey for the lowliest of meat-eaters.

'There's something about that cunt I don't trust,' Booth told Mammon, as he looked anxiously over his shoulder again.

'You don't trust anyone. That's your problem,' Mammon said, opening his eyes and lifting his huge head from the headrest.

'If this deal gets fucked up, Rafael is gonna be really pissed,' Booth said, more to himself than Mammon. Booth could not decide who scared him more, Mammon or the slender man with the lifeless eyes who supplied Booth with cocaine.

'That's why you should be glad I'm dealing with your buddy, this time.'

'But what if the bitch doesn't show?'

'She'll be here,' Mammon assured Booth, a hint of menace creeping into his voice. 'She knows what would happen to her if she let me down.'

Booth imagined the things Mammon would do to punish the blonde if she crossed them. Then he imagined what Rafael might do to him if the sale did not go through. One of Rafael's mules had dropped off the two kilos at Booth's house early this evening. Booth's part in the transaction was turning over the cocaine to Mammon and giving the thirty thousand the girl was bringing to another of Rafael's mules. Objectively, Booth was only a go-between, but Booth had vouched for Mammon.

'What if she goes to the cops?' Booth asked anxiously. 'She's been acting squirrelly lately.'

Mammon sighed. He switched on the dome light. Then, he took a mirror and a razor blade from the map holder on the driver's door and handed them to Booth. Mammon opened one of the Ziploc bags and dipped a slender coke spoon into the bag. Mammon held the spoon over the mirror. Booth fixed on the white powder, hypnotized by it.

'I need some peace and quiet, Kevin. If you promise to shut up, I'll let you have a little nose candy.'

Booth's brain told him it was dangerous to use in public. It was also a form of suicide to use any of Rafael's cocaine before the deal went through, because Rafael would weigh the dope if it was returned. Booth thought about turning down Mammon's offer, but his need overcame all objections and he leaned forward greedily as the white powder cascaded onto the mirror to form a small mound. Booth separated the white powder into several thin lines, then rolled a ten-dollar bill tight and inserted it into his nostril. Using the bill like a straw, he sucked up the coke, then leaned back to enjoy the rush. Mammon returned the razor blade and the mirror to the map holder and turned off the dome light. He started to close his eyes when a voice next to his ear said, 'Freeze,' and he turned slightly to his left to find himself staring into the barrel of a gun.

CHAPTER FOUR

1

Peter spent his second morning in Whitaker looking for a place to live. After lunch, he went to the office. As soon as he opened the door, Clara Schoen thrust a case file at him.

'Mr. Geary called from Blaine County. He'll be there all day. He wants you to interview this man at the jail.'

'The jail? Where is that?' Peter asked nervously, as pictures of drooling psychopaths and perverts danced in his head. He had never been to any jail.

'It's a block from the courthouse,' the secretary told him, shaking her head.

Peter opened the file. On the right side was an order appointing Amos Geary to represent Christopher Eugene Mammon. Beneath the order was a complaint filed by the district attorney charging Mammon with possession of a controlled substance: cocaine. Peter cleared his throat.

'Uh, Mrs. Schoen, what exactly am I supposed to do with Mr. Mammon?'

'How am I supposed to know what you're supposed to do? Am I a lawyer? I just do the typing here, Mr. Hale. Didn't they teach you what to do in law school?'

The narrow, concrete room in the Whitaker jail where attorneys met their clients was about the length of a dog run and doubled as the jail law library. It was poorly lit, cold in winter and stifling hot in summer. The so-called library consisted of two handmade wooden bookshelves containing a one-volume edition of the Oregon Criminal Code, a one-volume edition of the evidence code and a worn set of Oregon Supreme Court and Court of Appeals cases. A high window with thick, escape-proof glass let some light into the room. The rest of the light was provided by two bulbs that hung from the ceiling in wire cages.

Peter sat on a metal folding chair in front of a rickety wooden table with his back to the far wall, nervously waiting to meet his first criminal client. His fingers were drumming a solo on Mammon's case file when the door to the interview room opened. Peter stood. A guard stepped aside and all the light from the hall was obliterated by the man who filled the doorway.

'Knock when you want me,' the guard said. Then, Peter heard the lock on the thick metal door snap shut, trapping him inside the overheated coffin of a room. Christopher Mammon moved under one of the caged lightbulbs and Peter sucked in a breath. He was used to large men. His father was large, Amos Geary was large. But Christopher Mammon was bizarre. Curly black hair hung down over his high, flat forehead and cascaded over his massive shoulders. Tufts of hair stuck out of the collar of an orange jail-issue jumpsuit that was stretched taut across his gargantuan chest. The jumpsuit had short sleeves and Peter could see snake and panther tattoos rippling along Mammon's forearms and biceps whenever he moved. About the only parts of Mammon that were not grotesquely big were his cold blue eyes, which were narrow and focused like a predator's, and his ears, which were tiny and delicate.

'Good afternoon, Mr. Mammon. I'm Peter Hale, the attorney the court appointed to represent you,' Peter said nervously, holding out one of Amos Geary's business cards. The card disappeared in Mammon's hand. He examined it, then examined Peter.

'If you're my lawyer, why isn't your name on this card?' Mammon asked in a voice that was velvety smooth and very scary. It was the sort of purr that might issue from a hungry leopard while it was deciding what part of a staked goat to eat first.

'Well, actually, the court appointed Amos Geary. He'll represent you, if we go to trial. I work with him. In fact, I've just started. My cards are on order,' Peter babbled, managing a tiny smile he hoped would convey his perfect harmlessness and the fact that he should be considered a friend and not dinner.

'I see,' Mammon said, returning Peter's smile with an ominous glare.

'Mr. Geary is in Blaine County this afternoon. He wanted me to conduct the first interview. Why don't you sit down and we can get started.'

Peter sat on his folding chair and took a pen and pad out of his attaché case. Mammon remained standing. Clara had placed an interview form on the left side of the file. Peter scanned some of the questions on the form, then, without looking up, he said, 'There's some background information I'll need. Can you give me your date of birth?'

Mammon tilted his head to one side and read the interview form upside down.

'Can I see that?' he asked, pointing at the form.

Peter hesitated, then took the form out of the file and handed it to Mammon. Mammon studied the form for a moment, then slowly ripped it into tiny pieces.

'If Geary's my lawyer I'll talk to Geary and not some flunky.'

As Mammon let the pieces of the form flutter from his fingers like a mini-snowstorm it suddenly occurred to Peter that he was locked in the interview room and there was only a flimsy wooden table separating him from a very dangerous wild animal.

'Yes, well, I'm an experienced attorney and anything you tell me is confidential. I'll only talk about our conversation to Mr. Geary,' Peter told Mammon in an attempt to steer his client out of the world of ultra-violent kung fu flicks and graphic slasher movies.

'Just how experienced are you, Peter?' Mammon asked.

'I've been a lawyer for four years.'

'And how many criminal cases have you handled?'

'Well, none, but, uhm, I have tried many complex legal matters and I . . .'

Mammon held up his hand and Peter stopped talking. Mammon rested his hands on the table and it buckled. Then, he leaned across the table until his face was inches from Peter's.

'You just lied to me, didn't you, Peter?'

Peter turned pale. His voice caught in his throat and all he could manage was, 'I . . . I . . .'

Mammon held him with his eyes for a moment. Then he went to the door and pounded on it. The locks snapped open and Mammon walked out of the room. It took a moment for Peter to realize that he was still alive.

2

Peter's only other visit to Whitaker had been spent humiliating and browbeating a local attorney and his client. After the deposition, Peter had celebrated at the Stallion, a bar popular with the students at Whitaker State, where he met a nurse named Rhonda something whom he fascinated with his description of the devastation visited on his adversary. The next morning, Rhonda had written her name and phone number on a piece of motel stationery before she left for the hospital. Since the Stallion provided the only good memory Peter had of Whitaker, it was here that he ran as soon as he escaped the jail.

'What am I going to do?' Peter asked himself, as he started on his second Jack Daniel's. He could not endure another encounter with a Mammon-like individual. It was out of the question. But what was his alternative? Being a lawyer was all Peter knew and no one except Amos Geary would offer him a job after the Elliot fiasco.

Peter longed for his condo, now owned by a Merrill, Lynch exec who had gotten it at a fire-sale price because of Peter's sudden descent into poverty, and his Porsche, which he had been forced to trade in for a used Subaru. He wanted a job of which he could be proud. Most of all, he needed to reclaim his dignity. But his material possessions, his job and his dignity had been stripped from him. He was, he thought bitterly, as big a failure as one could become.

'Peter Hale?'

Peter looked up and found a tall, solidly built man in a business suit staring down at him.

'Steve Mancini,' the man said. 'We went to law school together.'

'Right!' Peter said, breaking into a smile.

'Mind if I sit down?' Mancini asked as he slid into the booth across from Peter.

'Hell, no. What are you drinking?'

'No, no. It's on me. I'm half owner of this joint.'

Mancini signaled for a waitress.

'You live in Whitaker?' Peter asked incredulously, unable to fathom why any sane person would choose to live in a town without one decent clothing store.

'Live here and practice law here. But what are you doing in Whitaker? I thought you went to work for your father's firm. Are you out on a case?'

'Uh, yes and no,' Peter said, stalling for time. There was no way he was going to tell Mancini the truth, but what could he say?

'There you are,' a woman said, and Peter looked over his shoulder into a pair of hazel eyes that had no room for him and were filled with Steve Mancini. Standing next to the beautiful brunette was a rugged-looking man with the broad shoulders and thick forearms of someone who labors for a living. He had curly black hair, a bushy mustache and blue eyes and he was grinning widely at Steve.

Mancini stood and kissed the woman on her cheek. Then, he took her hand.

'Pete, this is my fiancée, Donna Harmon, and her brother, Gary.'

A law school memory of Steve Mancini and a pretty

blond wife made Peter frown for a moment, but he caught himself and said, 'Hey, congratulations.'

'Thank you,' Donna answered with a satisfied grin.

'When is the wedding?'

'We're tying the knot in a few weeks,' Mancini answered, as he ushered Donna into the booth and sat beside her. Gary slid in next to Peter.

'Do you have the tickets?' Gary asked.

'What tickets?' Mancini asked deadpan.

Gary looked panicky. 'My football tickets. The season tickets. You . . . you didn't forget my tickets, did you, Steve?'

'Don't tease him, Steve,' Donna said sternly. 'Of course, he has them, Gary.'

'Here they are, buddy,' Mancini said, pulling an envelope out of his suit jacket.

Gary Harmon's face lit up and he started to grab for the tickets.

'What do you say first, Gary?' Donna asked gently.

Gary looked confused for a second and Peter examined him more closely. The guy looked normal, but he was acting like a kid.

Gary's face suddenly broke into a grin and he said, 'Thanks, Steve.'

'Hey, guy, you're welcome.'

Gary took the tickets and examined them as if they were a priceless work of art.

'So, Pete,' Mancini asked, 'what brings you to Whitaker?'

Peter had hoped that Mancini had forgotten the question, but the arrival of Donna and Gary Harmon had given him time to invent an answer.

'I'm working for Amos Geary.'

'Geary?' The expression on Mancini's face registered disapproval. 'I never pictured you as the type to practice small-town law. I thought you were aiming for a partnership in a megafirm.'

'Yeah, that's what I thought. I was working in my father's firm in Portland. Hale, Greaves. But I got tired of the rat race and Dad's an old friend of Amos. They played ball together at Oregon State.'

Mancini forced a smile and he and Donna congratulated Peter on his new job.

'How did you get to Whitaker?' Peter asked to divert Mancini's attention.

'Didn't you see the trophy case when you walked in?'

'Well, no, I . . .'

'Then, check it out when you leave. In my senior year, I quarterbacked the Stallions to the NCAA Division II title, Whitaker State's only national championship in any sport.'

'Tell about the run, Steve,' Gary begged, leaning forward eagerly.

'You've heard this story a million times,' Donna chided her brother.

'But I haven't,' Peter said, hoping that Mancini would not press him further on his reason for being in Whitaker if he could keep him talking football.

'Looks like you're overruled,' Mancini laughed. He put his arm around Donna and leaned back in the booth.

'It was the fourth quarter. Texas A&I had a three-point lead and we were backed up on our own six with less than a minute on the clock. I was supposed to hand off to Rick Sandusky, but the son of a bitch slipped. I turned back toward the line, only to be confronted by three of the biggest human beings I have ever seen. Their eyes were red-rimmed, steam was coming out of their nostrils and I could see that they were dying to commit an act of extreme violence on yours truly. That's when I was inspired to make one of the greatest runs in football history. You can find a wall-size photo of me in the Whitaker gym galloping the last ten yards before the end zone. In this town, Pete, I'm an immortal.

'After graduation, most of the class gravitated to the big city, but people remember me here. I've got a great practice, I'm big in the Chamber of Commerce and,' Mancini added, puffing up his chest, 'my ship may soon be sailing into the dock.'

'Oh?'

'Yeah. Bend has the inside track on the next Winter Olympics and I'm involved with some guys who are building condos just fifteen minutes away from Mount Bachelor.'

'How long have you been in town?' Donna asked.

Peter decided that Steve's fiancée was every bit as good-looking as the wife he remembered.

'This is my second day,' he said.

'Have you found a place to live?'

Peter shook his head. 'I'm still at the Riverview Motel.'

'We can't have that,' Donna said, turning to her fiancé. 'Can't you help him, Steve?'

'I think so. I own a few rental properties near the college, if you're interested.'

'I've got my own house,' Gary said proudly.

'You shouldn't interrupt, Gary,' Donna reprimanded her brother gently. 'Peter and Steve are talking.'

Gary stopped smiling. 'I'm sorry,' he apologized, looking down at the table.

It suddenly dawned on Peter that Gary Harmon was retarded. Peter shifted a little toward the wall. Gary looked harmless enough, but Peter had still not recovered fully from his encounter with Christopher

Mammon and he felt uncomfortable sitting so close to a person whose behavior he could not predict.

'Gary just moved into his own home and he's working as a janitor at the college,' Donna explained. 'He's very excited. It's his first job.'

'Oh, yeah,' Peter said, trying to be sociable. 'Do you like your job?'

Gary frowned and considered his answer. 'It's hard, but Mr. Ness says I'm doing good. He says I work real hard.'

'Well, that's great,' Peter answered lamely, at a loss for anything else to say.

'I think I might have a place for you,' Mancini said. 'It's furnished and only three quarters of a mile from town, not too far from my house.'

Mancini took out a business card and wrote an address on the back. Donna looked at her watch.

'We'd better go. Mom's expecting us.'

'It was good seeing you,' Mancini told Peter. 'Give me a call after you look at the house. I'll take you out to lunch and give you the lowdown on Whitaker. And, since you'll be living here, I'll send you an invite to the wedding.'

Mancini followed Donna and her brother out of the bar and Peter ordered a pitcher of beer and a burger with everything. He felt a little better. At least he knew someone in town. Peter remembered Steve Mancini as a real party animal. If there was anything going on in this hopeless burg, he would know about it.

When Peter finished eating, he suddenly remembered the last name of the nurse he had spent the evening with the last time he had been in Whitaker. It was Kates. Rhonda Kates. He decided to go back to the motel and give her a call.

On the way out of the Stallion, Peter looked in the

trophy case. There was Mancini's helmet and cleats, a program from the championship game and a photo of Mancini's famous run. Fame and fortune, Peter thought wistfully. Steve Mancini certainly seemed to have it all.

CHAPTER FIVE

At six-thirty on Friday morning of his second week in town, Peter awoke in the house he was renting from Steve Mancini, then ran four miles through the quiet streets of Whitaker. The houses Peter passed were not split levels or indistinguishable tract homes. They were old, wood frame houses with gables and front porches that stood in yards rimmed by white picket fences where swings hung from the thick, gnarled limbs of ancient oaks. In the half light of early morning it was easy to imagine the glow behind the curtained windows was cast by an oil lamp and that the rickety garage doors would open wide, barn style, to reveal a horse and buggy.

After his run, Peter showered, dressed for court and brewed a café latte in the espresso machine he had brought with him from Portland. He drank the latte with his breakfast at a rickety wooden table in his postage-stamp-size kitchen. Amos Geary had been dragging Peter around Blaine, Whitaker and Cayuse counties so he could meet the D.A.'s, judges and court personnel. Geary had not let Peter handle anything by himself but Peter was starting to realize that criminal law was not that difficult. After breakfast, Peter walked to the courthouse to watch Geary handle the preliminary hearing in Christopher Mammon's case.

Criminal complaints in felony cases were lodged in the district court, but only a circuit court had jurisdiction to try a felony. There were two ways to change the jurisdiction of a felony case to the circuit court: a grand jury could meet in secret and hand down an indictment or a district court judge could hold a preliminary hearing in open court and order the case bound over to circuit court. District attorneys loathed preliminary hearings because they gave defense attorneys the opportunity to hear the state's case and cross-examine the state's witnesses. It was very rare to hold a prelim in cases as serious as Mammon's. Amos Geary had been shaking his head about the development all week, but he was not going to look a gift horse in the mouth.

The four-story courthouse was the tallest building in Whitaker. It was a square, no-nonsense edifice of gray stone and it stood at the end of High Street across from Wishing Well Park. The office of the district attorney was on the top floor above the two circuit courts. The administrative offices and the traffic court were on street level. Misdemeanor cases and certain preliminary matters in felony cases were handled in the district court, where the preliminary hearing for Christopher Mammon and Kevin Booth was to be held.

Peter walked up the central staircase to the second-floor courtroom and found Steve Mancini standing in the hall talking to the cutest thing Peter had seen since moving to Whitaker. Peter figured her for five two at the most. She had curly red hair, freckles that made her look like a high schooler and a body that was definitely not adolescent. Just looking at her made Peter feel all mushy and downright lascivious at the same time.

Mancini waved Peter over. 'You're here to help Amos with the prelim, aren't you?'

'Yeah. He wanted me to sit in,' Peter said, fighting to keep from staring at the redhead.

'Then, you should meet Becky O'Shay, Whitaker's most vicious prosecutor. Becky, this is Peter Hale. Watch out for him. He's a big-city lawyer who's moved to the sticks to prey on innocent young things like you.'

O'Shay looked up at Peter and he swore she was gazing into his eyes with something more than polite curiosity.

'Pleased to meet you, Peter,' she said. Her voice sounded like the trill of clear water rushing over smooth stones in a mountain stream. O'Shay extended a tiny, delicate hand. Peter took it and felt a jolt of electricity.

'Time to go, boys and girls,' Mancini said.

'Are you involved in this case?' Peter asked him.

'I'm representing Kevin Booth, the co-defendant.'

O'Shay entered the courtroom and Peter watched her walk to the prosecution's counsel table. When he tore his eyes from her, he saw Christopher Mammon sitting with Amos Geary at the defense table. The two were chatting as if they were old friends and Geary did not seem the least bit intimidated.

To Mammon's right was Kevin Booth. Mancini's client was a mess. His jumpsuit sagged on him, his dirty black hair was uncombed and pimples dotted his pale skin. The contrast between Booth and Christopher

Mammon was amazing. Although they were facing sentences that would keep them in prison for eons, Mammon looked as if he was going to fall asleep, while Booth's prominent Adam's apple bobbed up and down from fright and he could not keep his hands still. When Mancini sat beside him, he jumped.

Peter edged behind Mammon and Geary and sat at the end of the table. His boss looked up at him with bloodshot eyes.

'Good morning, Mr. Geary,' Peter said.

Before Geary could reply, the bailiff rapped his gavel and District Court Judge Brett Staley, a short, balding man with thick glasses, ascended to the bench. Becky O'Shay told Judge Staley that Earl Ridgely, the district attorney, was on vacation and she was handling the preliminary hearing. Then, she called her first witness, Jeffrey Loudhawk.

A dark-complexioned man with high cheekbones and straight black hair was sworn in. He was wearing the uniform of a Whitaker State campus security guard. After some preliminary questions, O'Shay asked Loudhawk if he had seen either of the defendants on the evening of May 22.

'I saw both of them.'

'Tell Judge Staley how you came in contact with them.'

'Yes, ma'am. I was patrolling around ten o'clock when I noticed the defendants seated in a car at the far end of the parking lot.'

'Was the lot crowded?'

'Yes, it was. Classes were just letting out and there were a lot of students milling around and a large number of cars.'

'What was it that attracted you to these two gentlemen?'

'The dome light came on suddenly and I was able to see into the car. Something about Mr. Booth looked odd. When I came closer I saw a rolled, ten-dollar bill in his right nostril.'

'Why did that attract your attention, Officer Loudhawk?'

'I've attended seminars on narcotics cases run by the Oregon State Police and I know, from my training, that addicts use rolled bills as straws to assist them in snorting cocaine.'

'What did you do after you saw Mr. Booth with the bill in his nose?'

'I radioed for assistance using my walkie talkie. Ron Turnbull, a fellow security guard, arrived and we approached the car. I went to Mr. Booth's side and Officer Turnbull went to the driver's side.'

'Then, Mr. Mammon was driving?'

'Yes, ma'am.'

'What did you observe when you reached the car?'

'Mr. Mammon was sitting behind the wheel of the car with his head against the headrest. Mr. Booth was in the same position in the passenger's seat with his eyes closed.'

'Where was the ten-dollar bill?'

'I found it on the floor of the car on Mr. Booth's side.'

'What happened next?'

'Officer Turnbull told Mr. Mammon to freeze and I did the same with Mr. Booth. They both complied. I looked across Mr. Booth and saw, in plain view, a transparent, plastic Ziploc bag filled with a white powder.'

'Where was this bag?'

'Halfway under Mr. Mammon's seat on the driver's side.'

'Did you see anything else that your training led you

to believe was associated with narcotics use?'

'Yes, ma'am. I saw a mirror in a map holder on the driver's side.'

'Why did the mirror interest you?'

'I know from my training that users of cocaine will prepare the drug on a mirror before snorting it.'

'What happened after you saw the bag of powder and the mirror?'

'I asked Mr. Booth what the powder was. He said he didn't know. I accused him of snorting cocaine and he denied it. Then, I placed both men under arrest and radioed the Whitaker police for assistance. When the police arrived, I turned over the prisoners, two bags of cocaine, the mirror and the rolled bill.'

'Nothing further.'

Peter thought the case against both men looked open and shut. Geary asked a few perfunctory questions of the witness, but his heart was not in it. Then, it was Steve Mancini's turn.

'Officer Loudhawk, how far from Mr. Mammon's car were you when you saw Mr. Booth with the bill in his nose?'

'It's hard to say.'

'Several car lengths?'

'About six.'

'And you saw no mirror when you observed Mr. Booth with the bill in his nose?'

'No, sir.'

'Out of curiosity, was a test administered to Mr. Booth to determine whether or not there was cocaine present in his blood?'

'Not that I know of.'

'No further questions.'

Booth leaned over to Mancini. He was upset.

'Is that all you're asking? Why didn't you make him

say he didn't see me with any coke? He's lying. They planted the dope and the bill. Call him back.'

'Calm down, Kevin. Let me do my job.'

'But he said he saw me snorting coke.'

There were beads of sweat on Booth's forehead and his eyes were dancing everywhere.

'Will you shut up? I've got to concentrate and I can't do it with you whining in my ear.'

Booth chewed on his lip for a moment. Then, he said, 'Okay. I'm sorry. I just don't want to go to jail for something I didn't do. I'm innocent. This is all bullshit. I didn't even have that bill in my hand.'

'Right, Kevin, I believe you,' Mancini answered sarcastically. 'Now how about letting me listen to this witness.'

Miles Baker, a chemist with the Oregon State Police, finished testifying about his qualifications. Then he explained how he determined that the substance in the two bags was cocaine. Geary did not cross-examine.

'Mr. Baker,' Mancini said, 'the evidence log lists several other items that were turned over to you, including a ten-dollar bill and a mirror. Did you test the bill and the mirror for traces of cocaine?'

'No, I did not.'

'Thank you. No further questions.'

'The state rests,' O'Shay said.

'Any witnesses for the defense?' the judge asked.

Geary shook his head.

'No witnesses, Your Honor,' Mancini said, 'but I have a motion for the court.'

'Very well, Mr. Mancini.'

Peter could not imagine what motion Mancini might make. If he was the judge, he would have both defendants breaking rocks on Devil's Island by now. Peter guessed that Mancini was putting on a show to make

Booth think he was earning his fee.

'I move for dismissal of the charges against Mr. Booth,' Mancini said. 'The state has accused Mr. Booth of possession of a controlled substance. Now, there was a controlled substance under Mr. Mammon's seat in a car registered to Mr. Mammon, but there has been no evidence connecting Mr. Booth with that controlled substance. Officer Loudhawk never said he saw Mr. Booth with cocaine and nothing was done to determine whether Mr. Booth had ingested cocaine, although this could have been accomplished with a simple blood test. I don't believe probable cause exists to bind over Mr. Booth.'

'What was he doing with the ten-dollar bill up his nose?' the judge asked with a straight face.

'That is for the state to explain, Your Honor. He could have been cleaning his nasal passages, he may enjoy the aroma of American currency. I don't know. But there is certainly no evidence that he was snorting cocaine with that bill. According to the officer, you do that from a mirror. There is no evidence that the mirror and the bill tested positive for cocaine.'

Judge Staley frowned. He was lost in thought for a moment. When he addressed Becky O'Shay, he sounded concerned.

'What do you have to say to Mr. Mancini's argument, Miss O'Shay?'

Peter gazed at the prosecutor. He was certain she would respond with a brilliant argument. Instead, all she managed was, 'Mr. Mancini is being ridiculous, Your Honor. It's obvious that Mr. Booth was snorting cocaine.'

'Why is it obvious? There is no evidence that there was cocaine on the bill or the mirror, the cocaine was under Mr. Mammon's seat, the car is registered to Mr.

Mammon and Mr. Booth denied using cocaine.'

'He had the bill up his nose,' O'Shay repeated in obvious frustration at her inability to counter Mancini's argument.

'That's not illegal conduct in this state, no matter how disgusting it may be. No, Miss O'Shay, I'm going to have to grant Mr. Mancini's motion.'

O'Shay looked as if she wanted to say something else, but she slumped onto her seat instead. Peter thought she looked adorable. He wanted to rush across the room and console her. Instead, he studied Christopher Mammon, expecting him to go insane with rage because his co-defendant was free and he was not, but Mammon sat passively as Judge Staley addressed Steve Mancini's client.

'Mr. Booth, don't think you have me fooled one bit. I know damn well you possessed and used cocaine on the evening of your arrest, but we are a country of law and one of our most fundamental rules of criminal procedure is that the state must prove its case with evidence, not conjecture. If the state can't do that I must set you free, no matter what my personal feelings might be. So, I am going to dismiss the case against you. But that doesn't mean I'm going to forget your face. You better not come before me again, young man. You've had your break. If I ever see you again, I will make certain that you go to prison for a long, long time.

'As for you, Mr. Mammon, this court finds probable cause to bind you over for prosecution in the circuit court on the charge of possession of a controlled substance. You will be released, Mr. Booth. Guard, you can take Mr. Mammon back to jail.'

*

Amos Geary took a long drag on a cigarette and trudged toward his office. The old lawyer was short of breath and he walked with effort. Peter hoped he would make the three blocks to the office without collapsing.

'What did you learn from this morning's outing, Mr. Hale?' Geary wheezed.

'Uh, well, I saw how a preliminary hearing works.'

Geary shook his head. 'You saw an aberration. Ninety-nine times out of one hundred, the judge binds over the defendant. I don't know what got into Brett this morning.'

'Steve was pretty amazing. I didn't know he was that good an attorney.'

'You know Mancini?'

'We went to law school together.'

'Hmm,' Geary said.

'What does that mean?'

'Watch yourself. Mancini's an opportunist.'

'Why do you say that?'

Geary took another drag on his coffin nail. 'Has he suggested that you invest in Mountain View?'

'Is that the condominium deal?'

Geary nodded. 'He's tried to get every lawyer in town to invest, except me. He knows I don't have a pot to piss in.'

'Steve seems to think those condos will make him rich.'

'Oh, they will. *If* Bend is awarded the Winter Olympics. That's a big if. If Bend doesn't get the Olympics, Steve just might end up in my tax bracket. I just hope he doesn't sucker Jesse Harmon into putting up some money.'

The name sounded vaguely familiar and Peter asked, 'Who is Jesse Harmon?'

'He's one of the most successful farmers in the county.

Mancini wasn't divorced more than a month when he put a move on Donna Harmon, Jesse's daughter.'

Geary drew on his cigarette and they walked on together in silence. Peter was not surprised that Geary was trashing Steve, especially after the way Mancini had shown him up in court. Geary never had a nice thing to say about anyone. Peter decided that Geary was just a sour old fart who, like his father, could not stand seeing a younger man succeed.

Peter's thoughts turned to Becky O'Shay. He wondered if she was seeing anyone. Peter had gone out with Rhonda Kates again. She was okay, but O'Shay was really interesting.

'The D.A. sure was bent out of shape when the judge swallowed Steve's argument,' Peter said.

'Rebecca doesn't like to lose.'

'How long has she been a prosecutor?'

Geary stopped in mid-stride and looked at Peter. Then, he shook his head in disgust.

'I know exactly what you're thinking. Forget it.'

'Forget what?' Peter asked innocently. Wearily, Geary shook his head again.

'That cute little thing has every young buck in three counties panting after her, but I'm going to give you some advice, which I assume you won't take. Stay away from Rebecca O'Shay.'

'What's wrong with her?'

'Did you see that Tom Cruise movie where he plays a vampire?'

'*Interview with the Vampire?*'

'That's the one.'

'Sure. Great flick.'

'Remember the little girl vampire?'

'Yes.'

'Rebecca O'Shay was the model.'

CHAPTER SIX

1

His mouth was dry and he could barely breathe. She was so beautiful. He knew if he touched her she would be soft like a rabbit. He wanted to close his eyes and stop his ears to make time move faster, to bring her to the moment where she would take off her clothes, but he was afraid he would miss that moment if he shut his eyes.

He heard a sound on the path that went past the girls' dormitory. Instantly he was down, hidden by the bushes. Two girls passed, chatting about a boy one of them was dating. They giggled. When they were gone he rose up slowly, until his eyes were level with the sill.

Where was she? He could not see her. She was gone. Please don't let her be gone, he prayed. Then the bathroom door opened and his heart stopped. Her jeans were off. She was holding them in her hand. Tossing them on the bed. Her legs were bare. He licked his lips and undid his zipper. Please, please, he prayed.

She walked to the chest of drawers and took out a shorty nightgown. Suddenly, she remembered the window. She turned and only his quick reaction saved him from discovery. He heard the blinds go down. No, he screamed silently. It wasn't fair. He had been here so long, waiting forever, worshiping her while she studied. Praying so hard to see her naked. And now this.

Suddenly, he noticed a wedge of light and adjusted his body. Praise God. There was a slit. A gap between the edge of the venetian blinds and the window ledge. He peeked into the room and was rewarded by a vision of a goddess with long blond hair.

She began unbuttoning her blouse slowly, as if she knew he was watching. Maybe she did know. Maybe this was for him. She would strip slowly, tantalizing him, then she would walk to the window, raise the blinds and ask him in.

He was hard now, working himself with his fingers as her blouse came off. Breasts, he thought. He could feel his body tensing as his excitement grew with each quickening stroke of his hand. The moment was now. She reached behind to unhook her bra. Now! He felt his body tremble. Now! His eyes shut tight, his teeth clenched in ecstasy as his back began to arch.

Then, a deep voice said, 'Well, well. What have we got here?' and fear and shame engulfed him.

2

Rhonda Kates was dying to see the romantic comedy playing at the Whitaker Cinema, so she and Peter caught the early show then ate dinner at an Italian restaurant on Elm. Rhonda lived just on the other side of the campus near the hospital. It was a beautiful June evening and they walked the mile or so to the theater and back. Rhonda had to get up early, so Peter only stayed for a while. Before he left, Peter promised to call, but he was not certain he would keep his promise. He liked Rhonda, but there was something about Becky O'Shay that fascinated him. In fact, Peter had called O'Shay earlier that day, but she was in court and he lost his nerve and called Rhonda instead.

Peter was starting to examine what there was about Becky that attracted him when he heard a commotion. A small crowd was watching two men struggle in the bushes under a window at the side of the women's dormitory. Peter pushed his way to the front of the crowd and saw Jeffrey Loudhawk, the campus security guard who had testified at the preliminary hearing, wrestling with a man who was thrashing around and wailing incoherently. The high-pitched, keening sound issuing from the captive was eerie and unsettling. Then Loudhawk jerked the man around and Peter recognized Gary Harmon.

'What's going on?' Peter asked just as Gary made it halfway to his knees. Loudhawk was a large, muscular man, but it took all his strength to bring Gary back down to the ground.

'Gary, don't fight. You'll only get hurt,' Peter said.

Gary turned his head toward Peter's voice as soon as he heard his name.

'I'm Steve Mancini's friend, Peter Hale,' Peter told Gary.

Gary stared at Peter, wide-eyed. He looked terrified.

'You know this guy?' Loudhawk gasped, grateful that Gary had stopped struggling.

'He's Gary Harmon. I met him through a friend. What did he do?'

'I caught him peeping in a girl's room.'

'Don't tell Mama,' Gary pleaded, his voice rising.

'You're Jeffrey Loudhawk, right?' Peter asked.

'How'd you know my name?'

'I work with Amos Geary. I heard you testify at that prelim the other day. The drug bust.'

'Right.'

'I don't suppose you could cut Gary any slack? He's retarded. I'm sure he didn't mean anything by what he did.'

'It's not my call. I radioed for backup before I arrested him. You'll have to work it out with the Whitaker police.'

'Could you wait to write this up until I talk to them. Gary is working at the college. If you report him, it will probably cost him his job.'

'It should,' Loudhawk answered indignantly.

'Well, yeah. Normally. But he seemed real slow when I was with him. Like a kid. I mean, listen to him now.'

All during their conversation, Gary had been weeping and moaning. Loudhawk took a hard look at his prisoner. Then, he said, 'Okay. I'll wait to see what the police say.'

'Thanks. Thanks a lot.'

Peter rushed home then drove to the police station while the police transported Gary. Peter knew he had to tell someone what had happened, but the way Gary was carrying on he knew he couldn't tell Gary's parents or his sister. It was almost twelve, so he decided not to call Steve Mancini right away. Peter figured he would wait at the station until he knew what was going to happen to Gary. If the police let him out, Peter would drive Gary home, then tell Steve what happened in the morning.

When Peter arrived at police headquarters, Gary was being interrogated. Peter told the officer at the desk that he was Gary's lawyer. A few minutes later, an officer escorted Peter to the back of the building. The door to the interrogation room was opened by Sergeant Dennis Downes, a jovial, thirty-four-year-old, who wore his hair in a crew cut. Downes, an avid outdoorsman, had moved to Oregon four years before for the hunting and fishing. He was roly-poly, which made some people believe he was soft, and he always smiled, which led some people to think he was dumb. Downes did not try to dispel either impression. As a policeman, he found it was an advantage to have people underestimate him.

The interrogation room was covered with white acoustic tile and the only furniture in it was a long wooden table and a few straight-backed chairs. A large, two-way mirror covered a section of one wall. Gary Harmon was seated at the table across from a uniformed officer. He had a Coke and a half-eaten hamburger in front of him, but he did not look hungry. Peter could not remember ever seeing anyone who looked so ashamed.

Downes dismissed the other officer. When the door closed, Downes asked, 'Just what is your interest in this, Mr. Hale?'

'I'm a friend of Steve Mancini. We went to law school together. Steve is engaged to Gary's sister. He introduced me to Donna and Gary. I just happened to be on campus when Gary was arrested and I recognized him.'

'Well, Gary here is damn lucky he has you as a friend.' Gary hung his head. 'I should throw the book at him, but I'm gonna let him go.'

'That's awfully nice of you, Sergeant.'

'Gary's folks are well respected. I don't know 'em that well, but I sure don't want to embarrass them.' Downes turned his attention to Gary. 'And you shouldn't either. You hear me?'

'Yes, sir, Sergeant Downes, I'm real sorry.' Gary's eyes watered. 'I'll never, never do that again,' he said, wagging his head back and forth for emphasis. 'I promise I'll be good.'

'Your promise doesn't mean anything to me, Gary. It's what you do that counts. Think of what this would do to your folks if they found out.'

Gary looked alarmed. 'You won't tell 'em, will you?'

'I should, but I won't. How would your mother feel if she learned you were creeping around the girls' dorm like some sex pervert?'

Gary started to cry.

'That baby stuff won't solve anything.'

Gary wiped his forearm across his eyes and sniffled. Downes turned to Peter.

'You better have a talk with this boy. If this happens again, he'll be seeing the inside of a cell.'

The front door of Gary's tiny cottage opened into a small living room. To the left was a narrow kitchen. A yellow, Formica-topped table was next to the stove and served as a dining area. A short hall led off the living room to the rear of the house. The bathroom was on the left side of the hall and the bedroom was across from it on the right. The beauty of the house was that it was small enough for Gary to take care of and it was within walking distance of the college.

Gary opened the front door and turned on the living

room lights. The room was neat. He cleaned it every day, just like it said on the 'To Do' list his mother had taped to the refrigerator door.

'You want a Coke?' Gary asked, the way his mother had taught him.

'Sure,' Peter answered as he surveyed the room. On the walls were a seascape and a farm scene Donna had picked out. There was a sofa against the wall that faced the front window, two armchairs, an end table by the sofa, a standing lamp and a television.

Peter heard the refrigerator door open. He wandered down the hall to Gary's bedroom. Pictures of Stallion players and Stallion banners and posters covered the walls. Gary smiled when he saw Peter looking at pictures of the football team.

'We're going all the way this year,' Gary said as he handed Peter the soft drink.

Peter sat on the bed. This room was also neat. Peter found the 'To Do' list taped to the closet door.

'Your mom write that up?' Peter asked, pointing to the list.

'Yeah. Mama didn't want me to forget nothing important.'

Gary suddenly thought of something.

'Are you gonna tell my mom what I done?'

Gary seemed pretty contrite. It looked as though Downes had done a good job of scaring the hell out of him. Sometimes, with a kid, that's all you needed to set him straight, and Gary acted more like a little kid than an adult.

'I should tell your folks, but I'm not going to.'

'Thank you.'

Peter took a sip of his drink. Gary did the same.

'You sure fucked up tonight. What were you doing looking in that girl's window?'

Gary hung his head and mumbled, 'I don't know.'

'How would you feel if you found some guy peeping in your sister's window?'

Gary did not answer.

'You wouldn't want that, would you?'

'No.'

'You have to think about things like that.'

'I will, honest. I ain't never gonna do that bad thing again.'

'You better not.'

They sat in silence for a moment while Peter drank his Coke.

'Do you date?'

Gary shook his head sadly. 'I can't get no girls to like me that way.'

'Hey, don't run yourself down. You're a good-looking guy.'

'I'm dumb. When the girls find out they don't want to be with me.'

Now it was Peter's turn to be embarrassed. He felt sorry for Gary.

'Any girl that doesn't want to be with you because you're not smart isn't worth being with. And you shouldn't be ashamed of your intelligence. Being smart is just luck. And being smart doesn't mean you're nice.

'Now, stop feeling sorry for yourself. You'll find the right girl some day. Meanwhile, you can't go around doing what you did tonight. Do you understand that? If Sergeant Downes wasn't such an okay guy, you'd be in jail and your picture would be all over the front page of the newspaper. The next time you get the urge to do something bad, think of how your folks and your sister would feel if everyone in Whitaker found out about it.'

Peter stood up and put his empty can on Gary's dresser.

'I'm going now. We both have work in the morning and we need our sleep. Do I have your word that this won't happen again?'

'Never. I swear.'

3

After Peter drove away, Gary carried the soda cans into the kitchen and put them in the garbage. He checked the 'To Do' list and was pleased to see he had done everything he was supposed to. Then, he locked the doors and turned out all the lights.

Gary changed into his pajamas, said his prayers and went to bed. He thought he would fall asleep right away because he was exhausted from the night's excitement, but as soon as he closed his eyes he saw the blond girl from the dorm in her bra and panties.

Gary opened his eyes quickly. He didn't want to see that girl. That was bad. But sure enough, when he closed his eyes again, there she was. To make matters worse, his penis was getting hard. Gary opened his eyes again. He was scared. He didn't want to think about dirty things, but he did want to go to sleep. How could he sleep if he saw that girl every time he closed his eyes?

The magazines. No, he did not want to do that tonight. What would happen if Mom came into his room and found him with those magazines? But he did want to sleep. What should he do?

Gary tossed and turned. He felt sick. Finally, he got out of bed and opened the closet. The magazines were way in the back on a top shelf stuck under some sports magazines where Mom would never find them. He took out his favorite and opened it to the centerfold. That girl was blond, too. Just like the girl at the dorm. Gary made believe that she was really in his room. He closed his eyes and took the magazine into bed with him. He imagined he was married to the girl in the magazine. When he touched her, she was as soft as a bunny and, best of all, she liked him to touch her and, when he did, she didn't laugh at him.

PART THREE

THE SUPERNATURAL MIND

CHAPTER SEVEN

Gary Harmon always felt important when he went to the Stallion because Steve Mancini was one of the owners. When he walked in the door, Steve's trophy case was the first thing he saw. The bartenders, the waiters and the waitresses knew Steve was his friend and they treated him well. If Steve came in when Gary was there, he would buy Gary a beer, even though his parents said he wasn't supposed to drink alcohol. Steve would wink and say it was their secret.

The table where Gary was sitting was on a raised area that overlooked the bar. Below Gary, couples danced frantically to the music of a raucous band. Tonight, Gary felt even more special than usual about being in the Stallion because Steve and Donna were getting married tomorrow and he was the best man. Arnie Block, one of the bartenders, had given him a free drink and so had several other people. In fact, Gary was drunk when he spotted Kevin Booth frantically scanning the faces at the crowded tables for

Christopher Mammon, who had ordered Kevin to meet him at the Stallion at ten-thirty.

Gary and Kevin Booth were both graduates of Eisenhower High. Gary remembered Booth as one of the few students not in the special education classes who would talk to him. Gary forgot that Booth paid attention to him because Gary was one of the few students at Eisenhower that Booth could bully.

'Hey, Kevin,' Gary yelled over the music as Booth walked by. Booth stopped at the sound of his name. 'It's me, Gary Harmon.'

Booth had no time to waste on a retard, but all the tables were taken and he had no idea how long it would be before Mammon showed up.

'How's it going?' Booth said, sitting down without asking.

'It's going great! Do you know Steve Mancini?'

'Sure. He's my lawyer.'

'He is?'

'Yeah. Why?'

'Steve is my friend. He's gonna marry my sister tomorrow.'

'Congratulations, man,' Booth said as he scanned the crowd again, then looked back toward the door just as Mammon walked in. Kevin stood up and waved. Mammon saw him and headed up the stairs.

'Hey, my man,' Mammon said, clapping Booth on the shoulder as he sat down at the table. Gary looked at Mammon with awe.

'Who's your friend?' Mammon asked Booth.

'Oh, this is Gary Harmon, a guy I knew in high school. Gary, this is Chris Mammon.'

'It's nice meeting your friends, Kevin,' Mammon said sarcastically, 'but we have business to discuss.'

'Do you know Steve Mancini?' Gary asked with a big smile.

'What?' Mammon asked, as if he could not believe that Gary had the temerity to address him.

'Steve is my friend,' Gary said proudly. 'He's marrying my sister tomorrow. I'm gonna be the best man.'

'Why the fuck should I care?' Mammon snapped.

'It's okay, Chris,' Booth said nervously, afraid Mammon would erupt into violence. Then, he whispered, 'Gary's a retard. He don't mean anything.'

Mammon thought about that for a moment. He had to get rid of Harmon and he had an idea. The body builder spotted what he was looking for at the bar.

'Your friend's getting married tomorrow?' Mammon asked, feigning interest.

'Yeah. At the church. I'm gonna wear a tuxedo.'

'Hey, that's great. But what are you doing here? Why aren't you at Steve's bachelor party?'

'What's that?' Gary asked, his brow furrowing.

'You ain't never heard of a bachelor party?' Mammon asked, nudging Booth with his elbow.

'No,' Gary answered, embarrassed that, once again, other people knew things that he did not.

'Where you been, Gary? That's the party your buddies throw for you the night before you get married. There's plenty of drinking and you tell stories and there's always a special gift for the groom-to-be,' Mammon concluded with a lewd wink.

'What kind of gift?'

Mammon leaned toward Gary and, in a confidential whisper, he said, 'Pussy.'

Gary flushed. 'Steve wouldn't go for a party like that.'

'Why not?' Mammon asked with exaggerated concern. 'He ain't queer, is he?'

'Oh no. He's a regular guy. He got me season tickets to the Stallion games.'

'Then, what's he got against pussy?'

'Steve's a lawyer,' Gary answered proudly.

Mammon and Booth cracked up. Gary laughed, too, because the others were laughing, but he did not know what was so funny. Steve was a good lawyer.

'You're not telling me that lawyers don't get laid?' Mammon went on when he stopped laughing. 'I bet he'll get laid on his honeymoon.'

Gary blushed. He did not like to think about anyone having sex with his sister.

'It's sure too bad there ain't no bachelor party,' Mammon said, shaking his huge head.

'Hey!' Mammon said, as if he'd just had a sudden thought. 'Just because Steve is a stick-in-the-mud doesn't mean you can't have your own bachelor party.'

Gary looked confused. Mammon slid his chair next to Gary's and put his arm around Gary's shoulder.

'Don't be too obvious,' Mammon whispered in Gary's ear, 'but look over my shoulder at the blonde at the end of the bar near the door.'

Gary turned slowly. A slender woman with straight, shoulder-length hair, wearing tight jeans and a Whitaker State tee shirt with a rearing stallion on it, was talking to a short brunette. Her emerald eyes sparkled when she laughed.

'Now, Gary, I'm a little jealous. That woman has been giving you the eye since I sat down.'

Gary looked at her again. 'Nah,' Gary said nervously, 'it wouldn't be me.'

'Who else, buddy? You're one good-lookin' stud.'

'She wasn't looking at me,' Gary repeated stubbornly, hoping Mammon was wrong and terrified that he was right.

'Kevin, did you notice that blonde giving Gary the eye?'

'Yeah, Gary,' Booth said enthusiastically, 'she's hot for you.'

'You a fan of the Stallions football team, Gary?'

'Yeah!'

'Well, my man, if I was a stud like you, and a woman like that was giving me the eye, I'd strike hard and fast like a Stallion linebacker.'

'What . . . what do you mean?'

'Get on down there. Check it out. Odds are you'll be inside that tight squeeze before I can finish my beer.'

Gary felt sick with excitement. He knew he could never have a girl like that, but Mammon seemed so certain.

'You got someplace to take her?' Mammon asked.

'I got my own house.'

'I bet that place rocks from morning to night, right?'

Gary did not answer. Mammon's arm tightened around his shoulder and Mammon's breath felt hot against his ear.

'You do know how to pick up girls, don't you?'

'Sure,' Gary answered, because he was too embarrassed to tell the truth.

'Then you know you have to go down there and ask her if she wants a beer. Now she'll say no at first. These bitches always play hard to get. You insist, though. Women like guys who won't take no for an answer. Be forceful.'

'I don't know. She really don't look that interested in me.'

'Are you kidding? Shit, man, she's creamin' over you.'

'That's true,' Booth chimed in, anxious to get rid of Gary so he could find out what Mammon wanted with him. 'She definitely wants it.'

'And she wants it from you,' Mammon said, lifting Gary to his feet. 'Now, you aren't a fag, are you?'

'Oh no. It's just . . .'

'It's just nothing, my man. And you know what? I'm jealous as shit, because you're gonna be sleeping with your ears between those silky thighs tonight. Go on.'

Mammon gave Gary a push toward the stairs. Gary walked down them slowly, twice looking over his shoulder at Booth and Mammon, who waved him on. He was sick with worry, but he could not disgrace himself by turning back. What would the guys think if he could not score with a girl who was giving him the eye? And if he did score with a girl that pretty, it would really be something. Maybe he would even ask her to come with him to the wedding.

There was an empty space next to the blonde at the bar. Up close, she was even better-looking. Gary stood there for a moment, but the girl did not seem to notice him. Finally, Gary worked up the courage to talk to her, but the words caught in his throat when he tried to speak. Gary swallowed. Then, in a quivering whisper, he asked the girl if she wanted a beer, but the noise in the bar was so loud that she did not hear him.

Gary felt nauseous. It had taken all his courage to make this attempt and he was too frightened to try again. He looked back at Booth and Mammon. They were doubled up with laughter. Mammon waved at him to go on. He turned back to the girl and tapped her on the shoulder, pulling his hand back as soon as he touched her. The girl stopped in mid-sentence and turned toward him.

'Can . . . can I get you a beer?' Gary managed.

The girl flashed a smile that barely disguised her annoyance. 'No thanks,' she answered quickly in a tone

that made it clear that she was used to being hit on
and didn't like it. When she turned back to her friend,
Gary looked at the table for help. His friends were
laughing again. Why would they laugh like that? He
wanted to run away, but he remembered what Chris
said about being persistent. He tapped the girl's shoulder again, a little harder. The girl turned around. She
looked angry.

'What do you want?' she asked.

'I like you and I want to buy you a beer.'

'Thank you, but I'm talking to someone, okay?'

'I can buy her a beer, too.'

'Look, I don't want you to buy me a beer. Neither
does my friend. Take no for an answer, okay?'

'I like you,' Gary repeated lamely.

The girl looked at the ceiling and rolled her eyes.
Gary cringed with embarrassment.

'Ch . . . Chris said you want me to buy you a beer,' he
stuttered.

'Who?'

'Chris. My friend,' Gary said, pointing toward the
table where Mammon and Booth were still laughing.
The girl saw them and figured out what was going on.

'Go tell your friends they were wrong and leave me
alone.'

'You . . . you don't like me?' Gary asked, hurt and
confused.

'Are you an idiot?' the woman asked incredulously.
'Didn't I just tell you . . .'

Gary's hand shot out and grabbed the girl's tee shirt.

'I ain't no idiot,' he yelled.

The girl staggered backward, startled by Gary's
sudden rage.

'Don't call me no names,' he shouted in her face.

'Let me go,' she screamed, as she tried to pull out of

Gary's grip. Gary yanked her toward him.

Arnie Block, the bartender closest to the commotion, turned when he heard the girl scream. At the end of the bar farthest from the front door, another attractive blonde in a Whitaker State tee shirt and jeans was sitting across from Dave Thorne, the other bartender. The girl was wearing a silver medallion around her neck. It had a cross embossed on it. The girl fingered the medallion while she sipped a beer. Thorne was working on a drink order when Arnie shouted to him.

'Dave, call Steve. Tell him Gary's causing trouble and to get over here.'

Dave looked down the bar, then grabbed the phone on the shelf behind him. He made the call. When he hung up, he noticed that the blonde with the medallion was watching two men who were walking toward the back door that led into the rear parking area. One of the men was big and flabby. The other looked like a professional wrestler. The girl looked very frightened, but Thorne had no more time to think about her because Gary was shaking the other girl by both shoulders.

'Say you're sorry,' Gary screamed. 'Say I ain't no idiot or I'll . . . I'll kill you.'

Arnie Block reached across the bar and grabbed Gary around the neck. Gary shrugged him off.

'Let her go, Gary,' Arnie yelled. This time, Gary realized who was talking to him and his grip relaxed.

'She said I was an idiot,' Gary pleaded with the bartender. Block found a clear space and leaped the bar.

'She shouldn't have said that, but you can't shake her. Can't you see she's scared?'

Gary looked at the girl. She was breathing hard, and

she was near tears and very frightened. Gary released
the girl and she staggered into the bar, upsetting her
drink.

'I called for Steve. He's really pissed,' Block said, as
Dave Thorne pushed through the crowd. 'You'll be
lucky if you don't get arrested.'

Gary's eyes widened as he remembered what would
happen to him if he was arrested again. He would go to
jail and it would be on the front page of the paper.
Mama would read it and it would kill her.

'Dave,' Block said, turning away from Gary, 'take
care of this lady. Make sure she's all right.'

When Block turned back, Gary was streaking for the
door. Arnie shook his head as Gary raced into the
night. He made no attempt to stop him.

Dave Thorne took the blonde and her friend to an
empty booth. Arnie brought over a glass of brandy just
as Steve Mancini walked in. He was wearing a suit, but
his shirt was open at the collar and his tie was pulled
down.

'What happened?' Mancini asked the bartender.

'Gary got a little out of hand with that girl.'

'The blonde?' Mancini asked, looking in the
direction Arnie was pointing.

'Yeah.'

'What did Gary do?'

Arnie told him.

'Jesus. Where is he?'

'I don't know. He took off as soon as I said you were
coming over.'

'That dumb fuck,' Mancini said, absentmindedly
running his fingers through his hair. 'All right, all
right. Damage control,' he muttered to himself.

'I'm gonna talk to her,' he told Block.

Mancini walked over to the booth. The blonde

looked up. Her makeup was smeared and she looked frightened.

'I'm Steve Mancini, one of the owners. Can I sit down?'

The girl nodded and Mancini slid into the booth across from the women.

'Are you all right, Miss . . . ?'

'Nix. Karen Nix. I'm just shaken up.' She shook her head. 'He just went crazy. I thought he was going to hit me.'

'But he didn't.'

'That's only because the bartender stopped him,' Nix said, anger flaring in her eyes. 'Do you know what he said? He threatened to kill me. I'm calling the cops as soon as I find out who that creep is.'

'I wish you wouldn't,' Steve said.

'Are you kidding? He's a lunatic. He might hurt someone else.'

'I don't think so. Gary says the first thing that comes into his head when he's angry. He doesn't mean what he says.'

'You know him?'

'I'm getting married tomorrow and Gary is going to be my best man. He's my fiancée's brother. Normally, he's a sweet kid, but he's retarded and . . .'

Nix's hand flew to her mouth.

'Oh, my God. That's why he got so angry.'

Mancini looked puzzled.

'I feel terrible,' Nix said. 'He wanted to buy me a drink. I thought he was hitting on me. I told him not to bother me a few times, but he persisted. Then, I called him an idiot. That's when he went crazy.'

'That explains it,' Mancini said. 'Gary is very sensitive about his intelligence.'

'I feel awful.'

'Don't. You had no way of knowing and Gary should

have known better, but he's like a little kid . . .'

'You don't have to say anything more. I'm not going to call the police. If I'd known I . . .'

Nix paused. She looked toward the table where Mammon and Booth had been sitting.

'Is something wrong?' Mancini asked.

'Gary told me that a friend told him I wanted him to buy me a beer. He pointed to a table on the landing. There were two men sitting there. They were laughing. Maybe they put Gary up to this joke. You know, taking advantage of him.'

'Are they still here?' Mancini asked.

'They're gone, but I'd know one of them anywhere. He was gigantic, like a body builder. Just huge. And he had tattoos on his arms.'

Mancini scowled. 'Did Gary mention any names?'

Nix thought for a moment. Then, she brightened.

'Chris! I'm certain that's what he called him.'

A flicker of fear shaped Mancini's features for a moment. Then it was gone. Nix reached across the table and touched his forearm.

'Mr. Mancini, you don't have to worry. It looks like Gary was the butt of a practical joke. I shouldn't have called him an idiot, anyway. And I don't want to spoil your wedding day.'

'Thanks a lot, Karen.' Mancini looked at his watch. 'Look, if it's all right, I'll leave now. I have some work at my office I'm wrapping up.'

'You go ahead.'

'You're terrific. I'm leaving word with the bartenders. Anytime you're in, the drinks are on me.'

'Oh, that's not necessary.'

Mancini held up his hand. 'Not a word. You've been very understanding. Not everyone in your position would be.'

At the other end of the Stallion, Dave Thorne was making up a drink order for a waitress. The blonde with the medallion was no longer on her stool. Thorne assumed she had left while he was up front, but he turned around to give the waitress her order and saw the blonde walking out of the front door behind Steve Mancini.

Christopher Mammon led Kevin Booth out of the Stallion while Gary Harmon was screaming at Karen Nix. The muffled music from the bar rumbled in the night air. Fear tightened Booth's gut when Mammon stopped in the darkest part of the rear parking lot.

'It's great seeing you out, Chris,' Booth said, trying to sound sincere. 'What's your lawyer think will happen with your case, now?'

'Geary's an old drunk, but he seems to know his stuff. He's not too encouraging, though.'

'That's too bad.'

Mammon shrugged. 'Shit happens.'

'So, Chris, what did you want to talk about?'

'We have a problem, Kevin.'

'What's that?'

'Rafael wants his thirty thousand dollars.'

Thirty thousand was the amount that Mammon was supposed to pay for the two kilos of cocaine the police seized when Booth and Mammon were arrested.

'That's not my problem,' Booth answered nervously. 'You made the deal with Rafael.'

'I agree with you, but Vargas sees it differently. He says you set up the deal, so you're responsible for the money.'

'That's not fair. I introduced you as a favor. You should have told him it wasn't my fault.'

'Oh, I did, Kevin. Unfortunately, Vargas says you and I both owe him the money and he doesn't care who pays.'

'You still have the money you were going to use to buy the dope. Give it to him.'

'No can do. See, I represent people. These people put up the money, but they won't pay it over unless they get cocaine for it. These people I represent are not big on charity.'

'Well, I don't have thirty thousand dollars. And I shouldn't have to come up with money your people owe. I'm gonna tell that to Rafael.'

'I wouldn't do that. He was very angry with you, Kevin. He said for me to tell you not to call him unless you had the money. He seemed very serious. Of course, you know Vargas better than I do. Maybe he was just funning.'

Booth knew Rafael Vargas well enough to know that he was only rational part of the time and that he was very violent all of the time. If Rafael said 'don't call' Booth was not going to risk it.

'There is a solution to our problem,' Mammon said.

'What?'

'My people are still interested in buying a very large shipment from Vargas and Vargas wants to deal with them. I'm too hot to be involved because of the arrest, so I thought up a plan that helps my people and helps you make it up to Rafael.'

A wave of nausea passed over Booth. Christopher Mammon was a sadist and a bully. Since Mammon arrived in Whitaker six months ago, Booth had never seen him do anything for anyone without an ulterior motive. Whatever Mammon had in mind, it could only mean trouble for Kevin Booth.

'You're going to do a favor for my people and Rafael. If everything works out, we'll both be off the hook for the thirty thousand.'

'I don't want to be involved, Chris. I was lucky to beat my case. You heard what that judge said he'd do if I was arrested again.'

The smile left Mammon's face and a wall of ice formed behind his eyes. Booth stopped talking and licked his lips.

'This is my ass, too,' Mammon said in a voice heavy with the threat of dire consequences. Booth felt like a small child in the presence of a stern and punitive father.

'I just . . .'

'Kevin,' Mammon said softly, 'don't be afraid. You can handle it.'

'I'm not the right guy, Chris. The cops are gonna be watching me.'

'You're small potatoes, Kevin. The cops lost interest in you the minute your case was dismissed. Besides, there's no risk. All you have to do is hold some product.'

'Chris, please. I don't want to go to jail,' Booth pleaded.

Mammon stared hard at Booth. Then, in a low, slow voice, he said, 'There are worse things than jail, Kevin. Besides, you don't have a choice. I've already assured Vargas that he can count on you.'

'Aw, Jesus. Call him back.'

Mammon placed a hand on Booth's shoulder near his neck and applied a little bit of pressure. Booth turned white.

'If you do as you're told, you won't go to jail and you'll be off the hook for the thirty grand.'

Mammon squeezed a little harder. Booth dropped

to his knees on the asphalt. He tried to pry Mammon's hand off his neck, but the iron fingers would not budge.

'On the other hand,' Mammon said quietly, 'if you fuck this up for me, you'll wish you were in jail.'

Booth gritted his teeth and twitched and wriggled in pain.

'Please, Chris.'

Mammon released Booth and he tumbled onto the asphalt. Mammon let him lie there for a moment. Then, he reached down and pulled Booth to his feet as easily as if he were a child.

'I'm sorry I had to do that, but I'd rather hurt you a little now than have to hurt you a lot later, because you failed to understand how serious I am. My people and I want this done and Vargas wants it done. I don't want to have to pay out any of my money to square this. Now, do I have your promise that you'll be a good boy?'

'Sure, Chris. I'll do what you say.'

Mammon smiled. 'I know you will.'

'What . . . what do I have to do?'

'Just sit tight. You'll be contacted soon. I don't think it's a good idea for us to be seen together from now on, so don't call me or try to see me.'

'Okay,' Booth assured Mammon, eternally grateful that he would be rid of Mammon.

Mammon started toward his car. Then, he stopped just as a man walked by the far end of the Stallion heading toward the side parking lot. Mammon turned toward Booth, who was only a few feet from him.

'One more thing, Kevin. Don't even think of running.'

Booth did not answer. He was shaking from fright. Mammon turned back toward the lot. A light at the far end of the building illuminated a slender blonde in a Whitaker tee shirt and jeans. The blonde paused under the light and headed toward the side lot. She called to the man Mammon had just seen. Mammon squinted. He knew that girl. He wondered what she was doing.

CHAPTER EIGHT

1

Two stone pillars at the end of High Street farthest from the courthouse marked the main entrance to Wishing Well Park. A wide path between the pillars led to the wishing well, which had been built in 1972 as a memorial to the men of Whitaker County who had given their lives in the Vietnam War. From the wishing well the park expanded into a large recreational area with a marina, baseball diamonds, a playground, a band shell and a series of hiking trails.

It was only one mile from Oscar Watts's house to the wishing well, but Oscar was a neophyte in the world of physical fitness and the two-mile round trip of alternate jogging and walking was pure agony. Oscar worked as a bookkeeper at the J. C. Penney on Broad. Though his doctor was always chiding him about his weight, Oscar was never troubled by the fact that his belt was lost in overlapping rolls of fat. He loved to eat, and he didn't really need to be physically fit to add up columns of numbers. Then, Oscar had a stroke and his doctor gave him a solemn lecture about blocked arteries, sky-high cholesterol counts and saturated fats. Now, instead of spending each morning consuming stacks of his wife's fabulous maple-syrup-and-butter-soaked hot-cakes, Oscar spent his mornings gasping in agony as he struggled along the hiking trails of Wishing Well Park.

Head down, feet dragging, mouth open and gulping for air, Oscar trudged ahead on legs of lead. When he looked up, the wheezing jogger saw the wishing well wavering like a ghostly beacon in the half light of dawn, reminding Oscar that his self-inflicted torture was half over. He was one hundred yards from the well when he spotted the object at its base. He was fifty yards away when he realized it might be human. Oscar stopped running and leaned forward, resting his hands on his knees, straining for a better look. Sweat obscured his vision. He ran his forearm across his eyes. Could that be a woman? It was hard to tell. Whatever sex it was, the person was curled around the base of the well, knees almost touching the red brick and hands and arms tucked out of sight, as if the person was sleeping. She could be sleeping, Oscar thought hopefully, as he crept toward the well.

At twenty-five yards, Oscar started to make out the dark stains that had soaked into the long blond hair and puddled at the base of the well. He wondered if he should call a cop now or take a closer look. Oscar didn't want to jump to conclusions and look like a fool. He decided to check things out. It was the last time Oscar thought about food for a long time.

2

Earl Ridgely could hear the gentle rush of the river from where he was standing. The summer air smelled of fresh-cut grass and roses. Morning dew shined his scuffed, black leather shoes. It was the type of balmy July day that made Ridgely wish he were lazing in a hammock sipping from a cold glass of sangria. Instead, he was sweating in a business suit, just inside the perimeter set up by the forensic experts from the Oregon State Crime Lab as they studied the body huddled next to the red brick wishing well.

Ridgely was a slender man with thinning straw-colored hair, tortoise shell glasses and a thick mustache. A local boy who graduated with distinction from Stanford, but was smart enough to attend an in-state law school because he wanted a career in politics. Ridgely was forty and at the tail end of his second term as Whitaker County D.A. A spot on the circuit court bench would be opening up soon. A good friend from law school was the governor's legal adviser and Earl had been assured that he would soon be taking his first step up a ladder that he hoped would end at the Oregon Supreme Court.

As he approached the body, a young policeman wearing latex gloves was delicately holding up for Sergeant Dennis Downes's inspection a thin metal chain at the end of which dangled a medallion. Downes had been selected by the Major Crime Team to be the officer in charge because the crime being investigated was within the Whitaker city limits. The team was composed of the same men who had viewed the body found several weeks ago in a gully in the wastelands at the border of Whitaker County. The method of murder and the type of victim were sufficiently similar to put every one of these seasoned professionals on edge.

'Should I bag this?' the officer asked.

'Where'd you find it?'

'In the bushes by the entrance.'

'Better do it,' Downes decided, even though the bushes were a distance from the wishing well. The officer walked away with his find.

'Morning, Dennis,' the district attorney said.

'Mornin', Earl.'

'Any idea who she is?'

'Not yet, but she's got to be from the college. Looks the age and she's wearing a Whitaker tee shirt.'

'Does she have any ID?'

'If she had a purse or wallet, we haven't found it.'

'Then, let's get her picture on TV and ask the *Clarion* to run it on the front page of the afternoon edition.'

Downes jerked his head toward the body. 'Like that?' he asked, wanting to be certain he understood Ridgely.

'Of course not. If she can't be cleaned up, have King make a sketch.'

Downes looked relieved. Ridgely didn't blame him. He had taken only one quick look at the corpse, but it was enough to leave him light-headed. People died unnatural deaths in Whitaker County, but the dead were usually the victims of auto accidents and farming mishaps. This girl's skull had been split, exposing the brain and drenching her long blond hair with blood that had soaked into her clothes and spilled onto the ground in such quantities that even the careful forensic experts were stained by it. The girl's face had been lacerated by chopping blows, creating open wounds that also bled profusely.

Ridgely spotted Dr. Guisti bending over the corpse.

Guisti straightened up when he saw the D.A. approaching.

'Was the murder weapon a hatchet?' Ridgely asked when they were far enough away from everyone else so they could not be heard.

'I can't say for certain, but I will say that there are enough similarities between this crime, the murder in the gully and the murder in Blaine for me to say they are either the work of the same person or a very good copycat.'

'Any signs of sexual activity?' Ridgely asked. The first two women had been raped before they were killed.

'I won't know until I examine her, but I'm guessing no. The other women were naked. She's got her clothes on. The first two were murdered in a location different from where they were found. I'm guessing the killer abducted the other women and held them for a while, but fouled up the abduction here and had to kill her.'

'I don't like this one bit, Harold. What you're telling me is that we've got a serial killer in Whitaker County.'

'Looks like it.'

'Well, shit. I don't have the personnel to investigate something like this.'

'You'd better figure out how to do it quick. I started doing a little reading on the subject after we found Emily Curran in that gully. One thing's for certain. Our boy has tasted blood and, according to the literature, once he's taken a liking to the killing, he's not going to stop.'

3

The Mancini-Harmon wedding reception was held in the dining room of the Whitaker Elks Club. A long table stocked with hors d'oeuvres, salads, desserts and a selection of roast beef and fried chicken stood against one wall next to the bar. A band played in front of a large dance floor on the opposite side of the hall. The guests chattered noisily at tables covered by white-and-red-checkerboard tablecloths. Peter was refreshing his drink at the bar when a finger poked him in the back.

'Hi, Peter.'

Peter turned too quickly and a splash of gin and tonic slopped over the lip of his glass, wetting his hand. He jerked his hand back reflexively and some more liquid jumped out of the glass.

'Having trouble holding your liquor?'

Peter looked down and found Becky O'Shay observing him with a bemused smile.

'Don't you know better than to sneak up on a person like that?' Peter asked, annoyed that Whitaker's prosecutorial pixie had made him look foolish.

'Just practicing what I was taught in law school,' answered Becky, her grin widening. Peter laughed, too, even though he was upset. He couldn't help himself. O'Shay was just too cute to stay mad at.

'Are you a friend of the bride, the groom or both?' Peter asked.

'Steve. How about you?'

'Steve. We went to law school together. Where do you know him from?'

'Oh, here and there,' O'Shay answered enigmatically. 'Steve tells me you worked at Hale, Greaves before moving to Whitaker.'

'Why did he tell you that?'

'I asked him,' O'Shay answered with a mischievous grin. Then, she cocked her head to one side and asked, 'You're related to Richard Hale, right?'

'He's my father.'

'I'm impressed. He must be great to work with.'

'Dad's a trip, all right.'

'Isn't Whitaker a little dull after the big city? Hale, Greaves must be such an exciting place to practice.'

'Dull is what I wanted after four years in the rat race,' Peter answered tersely, keeping to the story he told everyone.

'What else did Steve say about me?' Peter asked, secretly pleased that O'Shay was interested enough to pump Steve about him.

'I said you were a pervert and an incurable woman-izer,' Steve Mancini answered, draping an arm across Peter's shoulder. 'How are you two getting along? Had enough food, enough booze?'

Mancini looked dashing in his tux, but his eyes were bloodshot and his speech was a little slurred.

'Congratulations, Steve,' O'Shay told the groom.

'You're a lucky guy,' Peter added. 'Donna looks great.'

'I think so,' Mancini said.

'What have you got planned?' Peter asked.

'Portland, tonight and Sunday. Then, a week in Hawaii.'

'I could live with that,' Peter said.

'I need it. I've been breaking my ass on Mountain View.'

'Is that your condo deal?'

'Yeah,' Mancini said, flashing a smile that looked a little forced. 'We're almost there, but I have to stay on top of everyone to keep the momentum going. Then, I've got two cases set for trial early next month. I almost put off the honeymoon, but I couldn't disappoint Donna.'

'Forget about business, will you,' Peter said. 'Loosen up. This is your wedding.'

'You're right,' Mancini said as he took a scotch from the bartender and swallowed half of it.

'You need an associate to take some of the pressure off you. Why don't you put Donna through law school?' O'Shay joked.

'Donna? A lawyer?' Mancini answered derisively. 'Not a chance. Besides, she's going to be too busy with the little Mancinis to have much time for anything else.'

'What's this about little Mancinis?' asked Donna, who had a middle-aged couple in tow. She looked radiant in white.

'I was just telling Peter and Becky about our plans,' Mancini said, as he gave Donna a kiss. Donna blushed with pride.

'Steve, I want you to meet Bob and Audrey Rosemont,' Donna said. The Rosemonts and the newlyweds wandered off.

'They make a great couple, don't they?' Peter said.

'They sure do,' O'Shay answered without enthusiasm. Then, she added, 'I hope Donna's driving to Portland.'

'I just had an idea.'

'Oh?' O'Shay said, returning her attention to Peter.

'I've been told that you can get a great steak at the Range Rider. Want to help me find out if the rumors are true?'

'How would I do that?'

'By accompanying me to dinner tonight?'

'I don't know if that's such a good idea.'

'I can assure you that the idea is brilliant,' Peter said, flashing her his best smile.

'Look, Peter, this is a small town and we're adversaries. How would it look if a juror in one of our future cases remembered seeing us together on a date?'

'Ah, come on, Becky. I've spent most of my evenings staring at my TV since I moved to Whitaker. I'm going stir crazy.'

While O'Shay considered his proposal, Peter sucked in his cheeks, hunched down and made himself look pathetic.

O'Shay laughed. 'Oh, all right. If you're that desperate.'

Peter straightened up and grinned.

'Great,' he said. 'I'll pick you up at eight-thirty and I'll treat you like a goddess.'

'You'd better.'

Gary took two more shrimp from one of the silver platters on the massive table that held the hors d'oeuvres, then wandered down the line and put another chicken leg on his plate. Next, Gary spotted something wrapped in bacon near the cold cuts. He liked bacon with pancakes, but this bacon looked as if it was wrapped around liver. Gary did not like liver. He wondered if it would be okay to eat the bacon and throw out the liver. He wanted to do the right thing. He did not want to embarrass Donna and Steve. After all, he was the best man.

Gary remembered his part in the ceremony and smiled. When Steve drove him to the church this morning, he told Gary that he looked handsome in his tuxedo. Gary wondered if there had been a girl in the church who thought he was handsome. That would be something. Gary looked around the crowded room to see if any girl was looking at him. He did not see any, but he did hear a lady with gray hair tell another lady with gray-streaked brown hair about a body that had been found by the wishing well. Gary walked over to listen.

'Eric thinks this killing might be connected to the girl they found in the gully and the other girl who was murdered in Blaine,' the gray-haired lady said.

'Oh no.'

'Eric saw the body. He said it was awful. The killer used a hatchet. Her head was almost chopped off.'

'I remember when you could walk anywhere in town, any time of day,' the other woman said with a shake of her head. 'It's getting so I'm afraid to go out at night.'

'That girl was at the Stallion last night,' Gary said.

The two women looked at Gary. He smiled, proud to know something they did not.

'Hey, Gary, you look great,' said a big, balding man in an ill-fitting brown suit. Gary recognized Eric Polk, a Whitaker policeman, whom he had met at several Elks Club functions.

'Hon, we got to go,' Eric said. 'It's one-thirty and we're expected at the kids' at two.'

Wilma looked at her watch. 'I had no idea. I'm going to have to leave, Mabel. It's Kenny's third birthday.'

'Is that grandson of yours three already?' Mabel Dawes asked.

'Looks five, he's that big,' Eric said proudly.

'Donna looked lovely, Gary,' Wilma Polk said, as she, her husband and Mabel Dawes walked away. Gary's chest swelled with pride. His sister was beautiful. So was that girl at the Stallion who had been mean to him. Mrs. Polk said the girl's head had almost been chopped off. Gary thought of the hogs he had butchered on his family's farm. They would squeal and get all excited on the way to die. A picture of a mean girl all tied up and squealing came into his thoughts unbidden. For a moment, it was like it was really happening. Gary's mouth was dry and he started to get hard.

If the mean girl was tied up in his room, he could ask her why she was being mean to him. No, not his room. Mom would find her when she came to clean. But some place. He could put her someplace where no one could find her. Only he would know where she was. And she would have to do what he said. She would have to kiss him if he wanted and learn to love him. That was the most important. Love him like Donna loved Steve. Love him for ever and ever.

4

Marjorie Dooling's shoulders shook convulsively each time she sobbed into her boyfriend's shoulder. Tommy Berger held Marjorie and tried to comfort her. Dennis Downes waited patiently. He understood the shock Marjorie experienced when she saw Sandra Whiley's face, because he had experienced the same feeling that morning in the park.

'I'm sorry,' Marjorie apologized, trying hard to stop her tears.

'You take your time,' Downes answered compassionately. 'Do you want some water?'

Marjorie nodded and Downes poured some from a pitcher he made certain was on his desk before he brought her back from viewing the body.

Marjorie sat down. 'I'll be okay,' she managed after taking a few sips. 'It's just . . .'

She shook her head, at a loss for words.

'What made you call the police?' Downes asked, giving the girl an easy question to distract her from her grief.

'I saw the sketch on the front page of the afternoon *Clarion.* It looked so much like Sandy.'

Downes nodded. 'You two share a dorm room?'

'No. We live in a boardinghouse near the campus.'

'Did you worry when Sandy didn't come home last night?'

'We, uh, spent the night at my place,' Tommy answered.

'When I got back to the room this morning, Sandy wasn't there,' Marjorie told Downes. 'I figured she was studying or something.'

'When was the last time you saw her?'

Marjorie looked at Tommy.

'About ten-thirty,' he said. 'We all went to the Stallion.'

'Tommy and I wanted to leave. We offered to drop her off at the house because we came in Tommy's car, but she wanted to stay.' Marjorie's eyes teared again. 'If she'd only come with us . . .'

Downes waited patiently while Dooling gathered herself.

'Sergeant Downes, I was wondering . . . When they found Sandy, was she wearing a necklace?'

'Why do you ask?'

'Sandy always wore a medallion around her neck. A Crusader's Cross. It would be for her mom. I know she'll want it. Sandy's grandma gave it to her and it was her lucky piece.'

Sandy Whiley wasn't wearing anything around her neck when the first officer arrived on the scene, but it seemed to Downes that one of the officers had found something resembling the jewelry Dooling had described. He would check on it later. For now, the medallion was evidence and would have to be held until the killer was caught and convicted.

5

Business was usually slow at the Stallion at four in the afternoon, and the stunning summer weather was keeping all but the staunchest regulars outdoors. Dennis Downes spotted Arnie Block and Dave Thorne chatting behind the bar as soon as his eyes adjusted to the darkness inside the tavern. Downes was in uniform and the bartenders stopped talking when he sat down.

'Hi, Sergeant,' Block said. 'The usual?'

'Not today, Arnie. Were you and Dave on duty last night?'

'Yeah. We were both here.'

Downes took out a photo of Sandra Whiley that Marjorie Dooling had given him when he followed her back to the boardinghouse.

'Do you remember seeing this girl in here?'

Arnie studied the photo. 'She looks familiar, but I don't know if she was here last night.'

Thorne frowned. 'It could be . . . Yeah. Her hair was a little longer, but I'm sure . . .' He took the photo from Block and brought it closer.

'See that medallion around her neck? She was playing with it at the bar. It's definitely her.'

'When was she in?'

'It had to be around eleven. In fact, I'm sure of it, because I remember seeing her leave shortly after the fight broke up.'

'What fight?' Downes asked.

'Oh, it wasn't anything. Gary Harmon was yelling at a woman. Arnie calmed him down.'

'What's with the girl?' Block asked.

'We're trying to trace her movements. She was murdered sometime after she left the Stallion.'

'No shit!' Thorne said, looking more closely at the

photograph. 'Hey, she's not the girl they found by the wishing well?'

Downes nodded.

'Jesus. A couple of customers were talking about that earlier. We thought it might be the other one.'

'What other one?'

'The woman Gary was hassling. I saw the sketch in the *Clarion* and it looked a little like her.'

'What happened?'

'Do you know Gary?' Arnie asked.

Downes nodded.

'Then, you know he's a little slow, and he'd had one too many. He tried to hit on this girl. She shot him down and he didn't take it too well. He grabbed her by her tee shirt and yelled in her face.'

Arnie shook his head.

'What kind of tee shirt?' Downes asked, remembering the way Whiley was dressed.

'Uh, a Whitaker State one. The one with the rearing horse on it.'

'Was she wearing jeans?'

'I think so.'

'And you thought Gary might have killed this girl?' Downes asked.

'Not really,' Block said with a laugh to show how ridiculous the whole thing was. 'Gary just gets excited sometimes and acts like a kid. I mean, he did threaten to kill her, but no one took him seriously.'

CHAPTER NINE

1

Dennis Downes was normally an easygoing guy, but the possibility of busting the only serial killer in the history of Whitaker County had him on edge. Seated next to Downes in the passenger seat of their patrol car was Bob Patrick, whom everyone called Pat. Pat was tall and thin with wiry muscles. His face was narrow and pockmarked and his eyes were close-set, making him look scary and mean. Pat wore his hair long and greasy in an Elvis Presley, fifties' duck's-ass style that was a little intimidating because it was so weird. Everything about him screamed 'tough cop,' which was why Downes brought him along. Pat was as psyched up as his partner.

'Jesus, Dennis, I think you're definitely on to something here,' he said, as Downes drove toward Gary Harmon's house. Following them was another patrol car with two more officers.

'It's got to be him,' Downes responded confidently. 'I talked to Karen Nix at her dorm around six. She and

Whiley aren't twins, but they're the same type. Blond, long hair, slender. And they were both wearing jeans and that Whitaker tee shirt with the horse.

'The way I see it, Harmon has this fight with Nix. He stays mad like a little kid would and broods about the put-down. Then, he gets a weapon and waits outside the Stallion for her. The door opens, out walks a blonde. Only it's the wrong one. He follows her, waits for his chance . . .'

'And kills her, just like he threatened.'

'There's something else. A few weeks ago, Harmon was arrested for peeping a co-ed's room at the dorm.'

'Hot damn.'

They turned the corner and Gary's house came into view.

'We've got to be careful with this,' Downes cautioned. 'Everything by the book. Lots of "Please" and "Thank you." The bathroom, if he's got to pee. Coke, if he's thirsty.'

'Gotcha,' Patrick agreed with a knowing smile.

'With one exception.'

'And that is?'

'The kid's gonna trust me,' Downes said as he parked the car. 'I got him out of that peeping scrape and treated him right. We can play on that, but I might need some help. That's why I brought along the meanest prick on the force.'

Patrick's smile widened. He knew exactly what Downes wanted. They had played this game before.

It was seven-thirty and the living room lights were on in Gary's house. Downes could hear the mindless chatter of the TV set when he rang the bell. A moment later, Gary opened the door. He was barefoot and wearing jeans and a Whitaker football team tee shirt. The presence of four policemen on his doorstep confused and frightened him.

'Hi, Gary, remember me?' Downes asked with a cheerful smile.

Gary's brow furrowed. Then, he remembered Sergeant Downes. He was the nice policeman who helped him the night he . . . Gary's initial relief was replaced by anxiety as he recalled the humiliating circumstances of his arrest for peeping. Had the girl he spied on pressed charges? Were these men here to arrest him?

'What do you want?' Gary asked warily.

'Hey, Gary, there's nothing to worry about. I'm here because I need your help. Can I come in?'

Gary hesitated for a moment, but he remembered the good manners Mom had taught him and stepped aside. Downes led the other policemen inside.

'Nice place you got here,' Downes commented.

'Thank you. Do you want to sit down?' he asked, acting just the way his mom told him he should act when company called.

'Sure,' Downes said, lowering himself onto the sofa. 'Say, Gary, could we turn the TV off? It's a little loud.'

Gary turned off the set and sat opposite the burly police officer. Gary noticed that none of the other policemen sat down. One stayed by the front door, one stood near the entrance to the hall and the officer with the greasy hair made Gary uncomfortable by moving out of Gary's line of vision and standing behind his armchair.

'Have you heard about the girl who was murdered in Wishing Well Park?' Downes asked.

Gary nodded. Downes took a snapshot of Sandra Whiley out of his breast pocket and handed it to Gary. Whiley was standing on a lawn in front of the business school dressed in shorts and a tank top, acting silly. She was leaning slightly forward because the camera had caught her while she was laughing.

'She sure was pretty, don't you think?' Downes asked.

Gary nodded noncommittally, even though he did think the girl was pretty. After his problem at the Stallion and his arrest at the dorm, Gary was afraid of expressing too much interest in girls.

'We're talking to anyone who might have seen this woman last night. Did you see her?'

'I don't think so.'

'Take another look. You were at the Stallion yesterday evening, weren't you?'

Gary's heart rate increased. They were here about that girl. The one he yelled at.

'Hey, Gary, relax. You look uptight,' Downes said.

'No I ain't,' Gary answered defensively.

'Well, that's good, then, because there's no reason for you to be worried. This is just a routine inquiry. Now, you were at the Stallion last night, weren't you?'

'Yeah.'

'Why don't you tell me what you did there.'

Gary felt sick. He did not know what to say. Downes waited patiently.

'I don't remember too much what happened. I was drinking a lot.'

'Did you try to pick up a girl at the bar?' Downes prodded.

'I . . . I might have.'

Downes lifted his head a fraction of an inch and made eye contact with Bob Patrick.

'Look, Harmon,' Patrick barked, 'we know you attacked a girl at the bar, so can the shit.'

Gary's head swiveled around. Patrick loomed over him. He looked as if he might hit Gary.

'Calm down, Officer Patrick,' Downes said firmly. 'Mr. Harmon invited us into his home. He's not a suspect and that remark was uncalled for.'

Patrick stared hard at Gary, but said nothing more.

'Sorry about that, Gary, but we did talk to the bartender and some other witnesses and they told us about the argument you had with a girl. Were they telling the truth?'

Gary hung his head. He wished Steve or Donna were there to protect him, but they were on their honeymoon.

'Well, Gary?'

'I got a little mad. I shouldn't of.'

'What made you mad?'

'I don't know,' Gary mumbled.

'You wouldn't be rude to a young lady without a reason. Am I right?'

Gary looked down at the floor. He didn't know what to say. Downes let him sit like that for a while, then he said, 'I have a suggestion to make. Why don't we continue our conversation at the station. Is that all right with you?'

Gary's head snapped up. He looked panicky.

'You ain't gonna arrest me?'

Downes laughed a deep, friendly laugh.

'Arrest you? What gave you that idea? I want your help, that's all. We'll drive you home as soon as we're through. You do want to help me, don't you, Gary?'

Gary hunched forward a little and wrung his hands in his lap. He didn't like the police station. He was scared to go there.

Downes leaned close to Gary. 'Remember how I helped you out? Remember how I fixed everything for you?'

Gary nodded.

'Do you trust me, Gary? Do you think I'm your friend?'

Gary hesitated.

'I didn't tell your mom about what happened at the college with that girl, did I?'

'No,' Gary answered grudgingly.

'Then, will you be my friend and help me solve this terrible case?'

Gary squirmed in his chair. Then, reluctantly, he nodded his head.

'Terrific! Why don't you get dressed and we can go.'

Gary went to his bedroom and Downes and the mean policeman followed him. Patrick stood by the door, but Downes went inside the room. The first thing he saw were the Stallion football posters and memorabilia.

'You really are a Stallion fan,' Downes said while Gary put on his sneakers.

'Yeah,' Gary said, brightening. 'We're going all the way.'

'I sure hope so. I never miss a game.'

'Steve bought me season tickets.'

'He's a nice guy. Even when he defends his clients in court, he treats us cops with respect. He's a good citizen, just like you.'

Gary felt proud that Sergeant Downes thought he was like Steve. He didn't feel so scared now that he understood that he was just being a good citizen and helping the police solve a murder.

'Say, there's one more thing,' Downes said as soon as Gary stood up to go. 'Would you mind letting these fellas take a look around your place? I'd appreciate that.'

'Look around?'

'Yeah. As part of the official investigation. That

wouldn't be a problem for you, would it? They'd do it while we were downtown and put everything back real neat.'

'Why would they have to look around?'

'We always look around when we're investigating a case, Gary. Good citizens never object. You don't have anything to hide, do you?'

Gary's thoughts turned immediately to the magazines with the pictures of the naked women, but they were hidden so well he was certain no one could find them.

'Well, Gary?'

'I guess it's okay.'

'That's great,' Downes told him, beaming with good fellowship as he fished a piece of paper out of his pocket and handed it and a pen to Gary.

'Why don't you read this and put your John Hancock at the bottom where I've put the X?'

'What is it?'

'A consent to search form. It's just routine.'

Gary looked at the form. He could read, but it took a lot of effort and this paper had a lot of hard words on it. After a minute of struggling, he got tired and signed. Behind Gary, Bob Patrick smiled. Downes saw him, but kept his composure. Everything was going according to plan.

Gary recognized the room right away. It was the same windowless interrogation room where he was questioned the night he was arrested for peeping.

'Can I get you something to drink?' Sergeant Downes asked as soon as Gary was seated. Gary was thirsty, but he shook his head. He did not want to be left alone with the mean policeman, who was lounging in a chair by the door, staring at him.

'Okay, then,' Downes said, taking a seat across from Gary. 'I don't want to keep you long, so why don't we get down to it. What happened between you and that girl at the Stallion?'

Gary shrugged his shoulders and stared at the table-top.

'I guess I got mad.'

'That's no big thing. If I didn't get mad at you for what you did at the dorm, do you think I'm gonna get bent out of shape because you got mad at some girl? She probably didn't treat you right is what I'm guessing.'

'I was trying to get a date with that girl and she said no. That's why I was mad.'

Downes shook his head in disbelief and chuckled.

'Is that all? Hell, the way you've been acting, I thought you had some deep, dark secret. So, what happened?'

'Chris said she wanted to go out with me.'

'Chris?'

'He's a friend of Kevin Booth. Kevin and Chris was sitting with me.'

'So this Chris said this girl was giving you the eye?'

Gary nodded. 'Only I don't think she really was. I think Chris was playing a joke on me.'

'Why's that?'

'She really didn't seem to like me.'

'What made you think she didn't like you?'

'She wouldn't let me buy her a drink and she told me to go away. Then, she . . . she . . .'

'Go on.'

'She said I was stupid,' Gary blurted out. His cheeks turned scarlet.

'Well, shit, Gary, that girl had no cause to do that, did she, Pat?'

Gary looked at the other policeman to catch his response, but there was none. Bob Patrick continued to stare with his hard, cold eyes.

Downes leaned across the table. 'Gary,' he asked in a low, sympathetic tone, 'what did you do when you got mad at Karen Nix?'

'I . . . I guess I grabbed her.'

'What's all this "guess" shit?' Patrick snapped angrily. 'Either you did or you didn't.'

Patrick's loud voice startled Gary and he looked to Downes for help.

'Relax, Pat,' Downes said.

'I'm getting sick and tired of this little prick, Dennis. He's jerking us around.'

'Officer Patrick, my title is Sergeant, and I'm conducting this interview.'

Downes stared hard at Patrick. Patrick tried to meet his stare, then backed down. Gary was elated. Downes turned back to Gary.

'I know this is hard for you, but we need your help to catch the killer. So, tell me what you said to Karen Nix when you grabbed her.'

Gary hung his head. He felt nauseous.

'I . . . I guess I said something like I would kill her.'

'Then, Arnie Block came over, didn't he?' Downes asked.

Gary nodded. Downes looked relaxed, but he wasn't, because they were about to get down to the real nitty-gritty.

'What did you do after you left the bar?' he asked in a casual tone.

'I don't remember so good. I think I just walked around.'

'Did you go any special place?'

'I went to see Steve.'

'Steve Mancini?'

Gary nodded.

'Did you see him?'

'No. I went by his house, but he wasn't there.'

Downes leaned forward expectantly. 'What did you do then?'

'I went to the Ponderosa.'

Downes's pulse rate jumped. The Ponderosa was a working-man's bar near the Riverview Motel. It was a few blocks from where they were sitting. So was Sandra Whiley's boardinghouse. If Whiley was walking back to her place along High Street and Gary was walking toward the Ponderosa from Steve Mancini's house, they could have met.

'How did you get to the Ponderosa, Gary?'

'I walked down High.'

'So you went by the park?'

'Yeah.'

'What side of the street did you walk on?'

'Uhm, the other side. Not where the park is.'

Downes leaned forward. 'This is real important, Gary. The murder could have happened right when you passed by the park, so you could be an eyewitness.' Gary looked surprised. 'I want you to think real hard. Did you see anything going on in the park when you passed by?'

Gary's brow furrowed as he struggled to concentrate. Then, Gary's face broke into a wide grin.

'I did see something, Sergeant Downes. I did.'

'What did you see, Gary?'

'I seen a guy and this girl. They were hugging.'

'Where did you see this?'

'By the big park entrance, near where you go down

to the wishing well, only closer to the street.'

'What did the man look like?'

'I'm not sure. It was dark.'

'How tall was the man?'

'I don't know. He was leaning on her.'

'Leaning?'

'Yeah. You know. Hugging her. Leaning down.'

'Gary, this is important. Think real hard. Could the girl have been Sandy? Could the man be the murderer?'

Gary was quiet for a moment. Downes edged forward on his seat. When Gary raised his head, he looked apologetic.

'They was just hugging, Sergeant Downes. I'm sorry, but they was just hugging.'

An hour later, Downes and Patrick stepped into the hall, leaving Gary alone in the interrogation room.

'What do you think?' Downes asked.

'I don't know. What about you?'

Downes shook his head. 'He seems too dumb to lie, but I don't believe in coincidence. He's admitted to being at the park right around the time the murder probably was committed, he threatened to kill a girl who looks a lot like Whiley.'

'I think we need to get a D.A. in on this before we go any further,' Patrick said.

Downes frowned. Earl Ridgely had instructed Downes to call him if there was a break in the case, but Ridgely was too close to the Harmons. He'd been invited to Donna's wedding and Jesse Harmon had made a sizable contribution to Earl's campaign. Ridgely might insist on getting Gary a lawyer and that would be that.

Becky O'Shay would never suggest getting Harmon

a lawyer, but she would try to take the credit if Harmon confessed. Still, she wouldn't interfere with the interrogation and that was the main thing.

'I'm gonna find Becky O'Shay. That will give you some time to soften up Gary.'

'How do you want me to work it?' Patrick asked.

Downes thought for a moment. Then, he got an idea.

'This probably wouldn't work on most people, but Gary is dumber than a post. Why don't you try the black light?'

After Downes explained what he had in mind, Patrick frowned.

'I don't know, Dennis. That doesn't sound right to me.'

'What's the problem?'

'It's trickery. It could taint the whole confession, if we get one.'

'No it won't. Not if you don't put words in his mouth. Let me tell you how I'd do it.'

2

Peter Hale was certain that the bathroom in his rental home had been built for midgets. There was so little space between the tiny tub and the sink that he could only dry himself by standing sideways and the shower head was so low that Peter had to stoop to catch the water that drizzled out. It sure was a far cry from the walk-in shower in his condo and its four jet-stream nozzles. Still, Peter was in a good mood. He was going out tonight with an attractive, sexy woman and he was certain he was going to have a great time.

Peter wiped away some of the vapor that misted the

mirror and combed his hair. He was singing a few bars of 'Life in the Fast Lane,' one of his favorite Eagles tunes, when the phone rang. Peter wrapped a towel around his waist and rushed into the bedroom.

'Peter?'

'Hi, Becky. I was just getting ready to come over.'

'That's why I'm calling. There's an emergency and I have to go to the police station.'

'Do you want me to pick you up there?'

'I'm afraid that won't work. This could take all night. I'm going to have to ask for a rain check.'

Peter was crushed.

'You've got one,' he said jauntily, masking his disappointment. 'I know about emergencies. We had them all the time at Hale, Greaves.'

'Thanks for taking this so well. Let's talk later in the week.'

Becky hung up and a wave of despondency swept over Peter. He flopped onto the bed. He had been really pumped up for this date. He tried to look on the bright side. Having a date cancel at the last minute wasn't the end of the world. He thought of the many times he had been the canceler. Besides, he told himself, there was a gourmet lasagna microwave dinner in the freezer and a Chuck Norris movie on the tube, sustenance for both the body and the mind. He had everything he needed for an exciting evening right at home.

Peter's attempt to kid himself out of his depression failed miserably and only made him more melancholy. He couldn't stay home tonight after getting his hopes up for an evening that would vaguely resemble the good times he used to have. Peter thought about going to the restaurant by himself, but his appetite had disappeared. He contemplated calling Rhonda or picking up a college girl at the Stallion, but his heart wasn't in it. Then, he thought about calling his father.

Peter had been in Whitaker more than a month. Surely that was a long enough exile. Maybe Richard just wanted to scare him. Maybe he wasn't really written out of the will. He would call his father and explain how working for seventeen thousand a year and living in this dump had taught him about the value of money. He would recount a tale or two about the poor unfortunates he was representing. Surely Richard would see that he was a new man with a sense of responsibility. Certainly he would say that all was forgiven and welcome Peter home with open arms.

Peter dialed his father's home number. Richard picked up the phone on the third ring.

'Richard Hale,' a strong, confident voice announced.

Peter wanted to say something, but he couldn't speak.

'Hello?' his father said with a tinge of annoyance.

All Peter's energy drained away, leaving him helpless. The receiver at Richard Hale's end dropped angrily onto its cradle.

'Dad, it's Peter,' Richard Hale's son whispered into the dead line.

3

Gary looked up anxiously when the door to the interrogation room opened. He had been left alone for almost half an hour and he was getting scared. His anxiety increased when Bob Patrick entered the room.

'Hi, Gary,' Patrick said pleasantly, 'I brought you a drink.'

Before entering the room, Patrick had dried a can of

Coke and dusted it with detection powder. Although invisible to the naked eye, the powder would look orange under the ultraviolet light beamed from the tan flashlight Patrick carried. Gary did not want to take the Coke from Patrick, but he was very thirsty. He eyed the officer warily. The fact that Patrick was being nice to him made Gary suspicious.

'Where's Sergeant Downes?'

'He had something to do. He'll be back soon.'

Gary took the Coke with his right hand and drank it greedily. Patrick sat down next to Gary and placed the tan flashlight where Gary could see it. Then, Patrick took several crime scene photographs of Sandra Whiley and laid them next to the flashlight. Gary took one quick look at the photos and turned his eyes away.

'What's the matter, Gary?'

'I don't like them p . . . pictures.'

'Is it the blood that bothers you?'

'Y . . . yes.'

'Most of the killers I've interviewed couldn't look at their victim's blood,' Patrick lied. There had been only two homicides in Whitaker County since he had been on the force and he had never interviewed any of the prisoners. 'I don't know what it is, but the blood of their victim scared them. Maybe they thought I could see that blood on them even when they had taken great pains to wash it off. What do you think about that, Gary?'

'I don't know,' Gary answered, still averting his eyes from the photos.

Patrick gathered up the pictures and put them away. Gary relaxed visibly. Patrick tapped the black light.

'Know what this is?'

Gary shook his head.

'It's a blood machine, a light that can pick up the

smallest drop of blood on a killer's hands. Most murderers think that you can wash off the blood of a victim, but you can't. Oh, you can scrub and scrub, but the blood of a murdered person works its way into the skin and no amount of cleaning can make it completely disappear.'

Patrick paused to let Gary absorb what he had just said.

'Now you say you didn't kill that girl. Well, I'm open-minded.' Patrick picked up the tan flashlight and pointed it at Gary. 'Why don't you stick out your hands and we can settle this right now.'

Gary wrapped both hands around the Coke can and drew it into his chest.

'What's the matter, Gary? You aren't worried about what the blood machine might show, are you?'

'N . . . no.'

'Then open your hands and hold them palm up.'

Gary put the can down. He opened his hands and stared at them. There was nothing on them. Very slowly, Gary extended his hands toward Patrick. Patrick pressed the button on the flashlight and directed the ultraviolet beam at Gary's palms. Large iridescent orange splotches appeared on both hands. Gary stared at the orange splotches in horror.

CHAPTER TEN

Dennis Downes and Becky O'Shay conferenced in the small room on the other side of the two-way mirror. Through the glass, Becky could see Gary Harmon. The suspect huddled on his chair, casting frequent frightened looks at Bob Patrick.

'I called Don Bosco from County Mental Health and he's going through his records to see if he has anything on Gary,' Downes said.

'Good idea,' Becky agreed. 'I definitely think you're on to something. Take the magazines.' Becky pointed at the pile of sex books the police had found in Gary's house. 'We can assume Harmon saved these particular issues for a reason and I've noticed something they have in common. The centerfolds are all blondes like our victim and Karen Nix.'

'Good going, Becky. I didn't spot that.'

'Were the victim in the gully and the victim in Blaine blond?'

'One was and the girl he peeped on at the college was blond.'

'All right!' Becky exclaimed.

'What about the absence of blood on his clothing and in the house?' Downes asked.

'I don't think we should spin our wheels worrying about that. Let the criminalists run their tests. If they don't come up with anything, we can worry about it then. Harmon may have done something as simple as getting rid of his bloody clothes.'

'You're right. If he confesses, we'll find out what happened to the blood.'

Downes stood up. 'It's about time I started questioning Gary again. Do you think I should Mirandize him?'

'You haven't done that yet?'

'I didn't want to spook him. Besides, he's not in custody. I made it clear that he's free to leave whenever he wants to.'

'Technically, you may be right, Dennis, but I'd do it now. Harmon's been here for several hours. Some judges would consider him to be in custody.'

'Okay. I'm gonna start taping the conversation. You'll be able to hear everything we say in here once I switch on the intercom.'

'Good. You know, it might not be a bad idea to have Don Bosco sit in here with me. The observations of a trained psychologist could be useful at trial.'

Downes left to get a tape recorder. Becky was really excited. She rarely got a chance to be in on an investigation from the beginning and this was no ordinary investigation. Her date with Peter Hale was forgotten. Dating Richard Hale's son might have been useful, but Peter wasn't going anywhere. She might not need him to get a job, anyway. O'Shay's plans did not include a long stay in Whitaker. She would gain experience here, then try to land a job with the Multnomah County District Attorney's Office in Portland or the more prestigious United States Attorney's Office. After a few years, she planned to parlay that experience into a job in a big firm where she could make some real money. If she could claim credit for breaking a case involving a serial killer she might not have long to wait before she was on her way.

'What happened with the black light?' Downes asked Patrick. They were in the hall outside the interrogation room.

'Gary freaked. He started moaning and wringing his hands as soon as I turned on the light.'

'Did he admit to anything?'

'No, but he's pretty scared. If he's going to crack, it'll be now.'

Gary stood up when Dennis Downes preceded Bob Patrick into the room.

'Can I go home now? I don't want to stay here,' he pleaded, casting a worried glance at Bob Patrick.

'I have just a few more questions I want to ask you.'

'Can I go then?'

'Oh, sure. And don't think I don't appreciate all you're doing to help the police. I wouldn't keep you here if I didn't think you could help the people of this city solve this terrible case.'

Downes held up the tape recorder. While Gary looked at it, Downes flashed a quick look at Bob Patrick.

'To make sure I get what you say down right,'

Downes said, 'I'd like to use a tape recorder. My memory ain't what it used to be and this gadget saves me from having to write everything down. Do you mind if I tape record our conversation?'

'No.'

'Great. Before we get started, I'm going to read you your *Miranda* rights.'

'What are you doing that for?' Patrick asked angrily. 'This punk's just gonna hide behind a lawyer's skirts like every other guilty asshole.'

Downes jumped to his feet.

'I've had enough out of you, Officer Patrick. Gary has nothing to hide. If he does want a lawyer that's his right. Now, I expect you to apologize to Mr. Harmon.'

'You've got to be kidding?'

'Apologize, then get out.'

Gary watched Bob Patrick flush with anger, then he heard him mumble an apology and storm out, slamming the door behind him. He felt so relieved that he sagged on his chair.

'Good riddance,' Downes said.

'I don't like him.'

Downes leaned forward and told Gary, in a confidential tone, 'I don't either. The guy has no respect for a good citizen like you. Hell, you'd never hide behind a lawyer, would you?'

'No,' Gary answered, shaking his head vigorously.

They smiled at each other. Downes turned on the tape recorder.

'Well, Gary, to business. First, though, I'm going to give you those *Miranda* warnings we talked about.'

Downes proceeded to tell Gary that he had a right to remain silent and could have a lawyer present during questioning. Gary said he understood his rights, but wanted to talk to Downes, anyway.

'I want to help catch the guy who killed that girl,' Gary said.

'That's great.'

Downes had Gary talk about the incident at the Stallion again, so it would be on the tape. Then he drew his chair a little closer.

'Gary, I want to go back to something you told me that I think is really important. Remember you said you were on the way to the Ponderosa after you left Steve's house when you saw a man and woman at the entrance to Wishing Well Park?'

Gary nodded.

'I want you to think about that couple again.'

Gary thought real hard. Then, he shook his head.

'I just remember they was hugging, Sergeant Downes.'

'Can you remember what they were wearing?'

'No.'

'Hair color?'

'Uh uh.'

Downes seemed frustrated for a moment. Then, he thought of something.

'Gary, you think you can't remember anything else, but I'm going to tell you a few things I learned in police work. Have you ever heard of the subconscious mind?'

'I think so,' Gary answered hesitantly, not wanting to admit that he had no idea what Downes was talking about.

'Right now you're hearing me and seeing me with the conscious mind. That's what you use when you're awake. But you aren't watching those two at the park now, are you?'

'No.'

'How could you tell me about them?'

Gary thought for a moment. Then, his face lit up.

'I remembered.'

'Absolutely right. But where was that memory stored all this time?'

Gary thought some more. 'I don't know,' he said, a little dejected that he was not able to answer Sergeant Downes's question.

'Hey, don't feel bad. The answer is tricky. See, you have a subconscious mind that stores stuff when you aren't thinking about it. Not too many people know that. The trick in police work is to help a witness unlock his subconscious mind so he can remember things he thinks he's forgotten.'

'How can I do that?' Gary asked eagerly.

'By getting relaxed and concentrating. The more you relax, the easier it becomes to unlock the sub-conscious. I want you to close your eyes and get real loose and we'll see what we can do together to catch Sandy's killer, because, from what I know, I think there's a good chance you saw Sandy and her killer when you walked by Wishing Well Park.'

Gary did as he was told. The two men sat in silence for a few minutes, until Gary opened his eyes.

'It's no use. All I see is them two hugging.'

'Hmm,' Downes said thoughtfully. 'You know, Gary, if those two weren't Sandy and her killer, they probably were hugging, but what if it was Sandy and the murderer?'

'You mean they wouldn't be hugging?'

'I didn't say that. I don't want to put words in your mouth. What I'm saying is that the mind can play tricks. For instance, you wanted to hug Karen Nix, didn't you?'

Gary squirmed in his seat and blushed.

'Come on, Gary,' Downes said with a hearty laugh. 'Karen Nix is pretty. Any red-blooded American man would want to hug her. Don't tell me it didn't enter your mind.'

Gary hesitated.

'Come on now. We've got to be honest with each other here. You did want to hug her, didn't you?'

Gary hung his head and mumbled, 'Yeah.'

'All right. So, when you saw this boy and girl together, you put them in a romantic situation. But there are other things that look like hugging. What they were really doing could be registered in your subconscious mind.'

'What could they be doing if they weren't hugging?'

'You tell me.'

Gary puzzled out the problem. It took a while, then he brightened.

'They coulda been wrestling.'

'Hey, why didn't I think of that? You're one step ahead of me already, Gary. This is great! Do you see what I mean about the subconscious mind? Your conscious mind saw two people hugging, but they might also have been doing something else. Your subconscious mind will know the truth. What I want you to do is relax, close your eyes and picture that night.'

'I'll try,' Gary said, closing his eyes and leaning his head back.

'Okay. Now, maybe this will help. Think about what you were wearing. Can you do that?'

Gary nodded.

'What do you see?'

'Uh, I think it was jeans and a short-sleeve shirt.'

'Jeans like you've got on now?'

'Yeah. I got four pairs of jeans and it was another one.'

'Where is that pair now, Gary?'

'In the closet.'

Downes tried not to show his excitement. 'Have you done anything to those jeans since you wore them?'

'Oh, yeah. I have to wash them when they're dirty. It's on the list my mom made up. Every Saturday is wash day and I washed everything in the hamper right when I got up, because I was going to the wedding.'

Downes's heart sank. Whiley had been murdered Friday night or early Saturday morning. If there was blood on Gary's jeans and shirt, it was gone now. Out loud, Downes said, 'Okay, you're doing great. Keep your eyes closed and feel how warm it is. Picture yourself in your jeans and short-sleeve shirt. You're walking by the park. Can you see the park?'

'Yeah.'

'Is it warm, Gary?'

'Yeah.'

'Hey, that's great. You're cookin'. So, go on. What do you see?'

'I see them stone fences.'

'Good. Now slow up a little. What do you see? Relax and let it come.'

There was silence in the room. Downes leaned forward expectantly. He could see Gary's features contort with effort. Then, Gary's eyes opened.

'It's no good. I didn't see anything new.'

'Not a thing?' Downes said, making no effort to hide his disappointment. Gary felt terrible. Sergeant Downes had so much faith in him and he was letting him down.

'Can I try again?' Gary asked. He closed his eyes and tried to relax. There were the two stone pillars and the path between them. And on the path were the boy and the girl. He was holding her, leaning down, which meant he was taller. And she was . . . what? Leaning into him? No. Gary slowed time in his mind, trying hard to see, because he wanted to help Sergeant Downes.

'She's leaning back, pushing him away.'

'You saw that?' Downes asked excitedly.

'Real clear.'

'Is it Sandy?'

'I can't say for sure.'

'You've got to try, son. You're doing so well and this is so important.'

'I am trying, but . . .'

'You know what might help? Why don't you picture a movie screen in your head and watch what's happening on it. That way, you can slow down the movie to make it easier to see.'

'That's what I done,' Gary said proudly.

'Pictured a movie screen?'

'No, slowed everything down.'

'You done that yourself?'

'Yeah.'

'Well, I'll be damned. You know, Gary, you might be a natural at this stuff.'

Gary blushed at the compliment. 'I just want to get this guy.'

'I know you do, so let's see if you can tell for sure if it's Sandy.'

'Okay,' Gary said, letting his head sag back. This time he did what Sergeant Downes had suggested and watched the action on a big movie screen take him back in time. The park appeared, flowing like water at first, then solidifying until only the edges were wavy. As he approached the park entrance the scene slowed to a crawl and the two people started to appear. Who were they? He was taller than she, but his face and body were in shadow. Gary was opposite them now. He willed the picture to grind to a halt and strained to see if the woman's features were the same as . . . as those in the photograph of Sandra Whiley at the college that Sergeant Downes had shown him.

'I can see them. She's kind of turning and he grabs her.'

'By her shoulders, her shirt?'

'By the shirt. She's making this real fast turn when he grabs her and she whips around and I think they're probably hanging on to each other, kinda . . . you know.'

'Go on, Gary. This is great. Can you see her face?'

'Sorta, but it's like . . . I don't know. You probably wouldn't know me if I was on a dark street.'

'But you were directly across from her.'

'Yeah, when he pulled her back and grabbed her.'

'Was it her, Gary? Was it Sandy? Slow the picture. Make it lighter on the screen. You can do it, Gary. You can add some light. What do you say?'

'I'm . . . I think . . .'

'Go ahead. Say it.'

'I'm sure it's her. The one that got killed. And . . . and that's the murderer, too, because he jerked her back. They weren't hugging.'

'They weren't?'

'No, no. 'Cause he was grabbing her and she was pulling away and he . . .'

'What? Jerked her back?'

'Yeah. Like that. A jerk, so she spinned around. And that's when I seen her.'

'Did you see anything shiny, Gary? It would probably have been right then. In that split second.'

'Shiny?'

'We know there was a weapon.'

'Boy, I don't . . .'

'You don't see a weapon? We haven't found the weapon, yet. We don't know what he used to kill Sandy.'

'Oh.'

'So, look at his right hand. Most people are right-handed. It would probably be there.'

Gary concentrated real hard, running the picture forward and backward while Downes waited quietly. He could see Sandy. She looked scared.

'What have you got, Gary?'

Gary's eyes opened. 'Nothing more,' he answered groggily. He was getting tired.

'But you know it's the killer and Sandy?'

Gary nodded. 'I could see she was scared.'

'Really? You didn't say that before. That's good. See, we're making progress. How are you holding up?'

'I'm hungry.'

'Do you want a Coke and a burger?'

'A burger would be good.'

'Let's take a break. Then, we'll try again.'

An hour and a half later, Dennis Downes was frustrated and Gary Harmon looked exhausted. Gary's eyes were bloodshot and his hair was in disarray from the times he had run his fingers through it. The remains of a greasy hamburger, an empty can of Coke and several paper containers for coffee littered the table-top. They had been over and over Gary's walk by the entrance to Wishing Well Park and Gary still would not give any more details. Downes knew he had reached a dead end with his current approach. He was thinking of giving up when an idea occurred to him.

'Straight across from me,' Gary mumbled sleepily. 'I know he's taller than she is, but I still can't see enough. I'm sorry, Sergeant.'

'It's okay, Gary. Don't apologize. You've given us our first clues and you've also given me an idea. A way to break through to the truth. Would you be willing to try one more thing before you go home?'

'I'm awful tired, but if you think I can help, I'll try.'

'Terrific, Gary. Now, let me tell you my idea. If this doesn't work, we'll call it a night. Have you seen people on TV who can predict the future or read minds?'

Gary nodded.

'Those people are called psychics and some of them help the police. If there's a murder, you give them an object that belonged to the murdered person and they can project their supernatural mind into the mind of the killer through this object and find a missing body or see who did the killing through the dead victim's eyes. Based on what I've seen you do, I suspect you have a very developed supernatural mind. I want you to use it to help me out.'

'Gee, Sergeant, I've never done anything like that,' Gary said. He was beat. All he wanted to do was sleep. He didn't even think he had a supernatural mind.

'I'm not surprised you haven't used your supernatural mind,' Downes said. 'You didn't even know you had these powers of the subconscious mind, until tonight.'

Downes stood and stretched. 'We're gonna need something of Sandy's for this. You sit here while I get it. Do you want another burger or some coffee?'

'That would be good.'

Downes left the interrogation room and went next door. Becky O'Shay looked as if she was ready to fall asleep. Sitting next to her was Don Bosco, a short, squat man dressed in tan chinos and a short-sleeve shirt. Bosco had monstrously hairy forearms and bushy eyebrows. There was even an extra-thick growth of black hair on the psychologist's ears.

'What was that all about?' Bosco asked when Downes entered the room.

'Just an idea I want to try,' Downes said.

After he explained his plan, Downes asked, 'What do you think, Becky?'

'I think he's covering up. You've got him admitting he saw the murder. We need to have him slip up on a detail that will prove he committed the murder. I say, go for it.'

'Do you see any problems, Don?' Downes asked.

Bosco looked troubled. 'I think it could get risky. Harmon is reacting like someone who's mentally handicapped . . .'

'He's not that dumb.'

'I don't know,' Bosco answered hesitantly. 'And, even if he's of normal intelligence, he's awfully tired. He's going to be susceptible to suggestion. You have to be very careful not to lead him. Even telling him that he will be able to see things with his psychic powers is suggestion.'

'Okay. I'll be extra careful. Don't worry.'

Gary held the picture of Sandra Whiley in one hand and her Crusader's Cross in the other. He was leery of holding the dead girl's jewelry, but Downes assured him the object would heighten the psychic forces.

'Okay, Gary, close your eyes and relax like you did before.'

Downes waited in silence as Gary tilted his head back. After a moment, his head sagged sideways until his cheek almost touched his shoulder. Gary's head was swimming. Fatigue loosened his grip on the Crusader's Cross and the chain slipped out of his hand and dangled just off the floor.

'Can you feel the cross in your hand?' Downes asked.

'Uh huh.'

'Good. Gary, I'm going to teach you a trick you can do with that cross because of your special powers. It's a trick us ordinary folks can't do and it's called "projection transfer." That's Sandy's cross. She was wearing it when she was killed. I want you to project your supernatural mind into that cross and tell me what Sandy saw and what the killer saw. Let yourself go.'

Gary let his mind run loose but the picture on the screen was scrambled.

'Do you see Sandy?' Downes asked.

'I'm starting to see them more along. You know, after I walked by,' Gary said in a voice so heavy with fatigue that his words were slurred. 'She . . . she's . . . He's holding her.'

'All right,' Downes said, suddenly excited. 'This is what we want.'

'He's hanging onto her.'

'Like she's trying to get away?'

'Yeah. It seems like she slapped him.'

'Sandy fought back?'

'Uh huh. And then . . .'

'Yes, Gary. Concentrate. Use your powers.'

'His right hand. It's like it was going down.'

'Dropping or . . . ?'

'Like he was hitting her.'

'This is what we want. This is it, Gary. Now, we

know he grabbed her and pulled her back and she
whipped around. That's what you saw as you passed by.
Then she hit him and he hits her with his right hand.
Now I want you to look for one more thing. At this
point, the unknown man is hitting her. It had to be
with something. Something in his right hand. What is
he using? It's very important. I want you to look at his
right hand through Sandy's eyes and tell me what you
see.'

Gary concentrated as hard as he could. What would
it be? Then he remembered what the two women said
at the wedding about the girl's face being chopped up.
What was it they said the killer used?

'I'm trying, but I can't picture it.'

'If anyone can, you can, Gary. You have a power that
no one else has. You are the man with the power.'

Gary opened his eyes. 'It's almost there, but . . .'

Downes thought about the location of the head
wounds. He stood up.

'Picture it, Gary,' he said, unconsciously moving his
right hand up and down. 'Tell me what's in his hand.'

Gary closed his eyes and recalled the autopsy photograph that Bob Patrick had shown him, just before he
used the black light. Then, he remembered what the
lady at the wedding had said.

'It's shiny,' he said suddenly.

'Huh?'

'It's metal shiny.'

'Like a . . . like what? Shiny like a knife blade?'

'Yeah, shiny.'

'You've got knives, Gary. Is it like a knife you own?'

'Not a knife.'

'Not a knife?'

'He chopped her up. Chopped her with a . . . a
hatchet.'

Downes heart leaped. 'What kind of hatchet?'

'I can't see the blade, but it seems like a hatchet.'

There was a drawer in the long interrogation table. In it were pens, paper and a ruler. Downes took the picture of Sandy from Gary's right hand and replaced it with the ruler.

'Take hold of this ruler.'

Gary did as he was told.

'Gary, you are unbelievable. I've never seen anyone with your powers. Now, to me, this is a ruler, but with your supernatural mind, you can use "projection transfer" to transfer this ruler to the hatchet. Do you have it? Can you feel the shiny, silver hatchet?'

Gary nodded.

'All right. Here's where you do your thing. I'm gonna stand and so are you. I'm gonna be Sandy, so I'll squat down some, and you're gonna let that hatchet lead you to strike like the killer did, so we can see how Sandy was killed.

'Okay, stand up and keep your eyes closed. I'm right in front of you. Only now I'm Sandy. Are you ready?'

Gary nodded.

'Let it flow, Gary. First hit. Where was it?'

Gary brought his arm up sluggishly. 'Top of the head,' he said, as his arm slowly descended.

'This is great. Then what?'

Gary saw it all. His arm swung sideways.

'Another to the right side,' he said. 'And another.'

Blood was spraying from Sandy's face as the blade sliced into it. Gary's arm rose and fell. Her face was breaking up as she fell back, flying away like shards from a fractured mirror. Gary stopped.

'What's the matter?' Downes asked.

'I don't like her face like this.'

'What do you mean?'

'The blood.'

'You can see her face chopped up?'

'Yes.'

'Where is the killer, Gary?'

'Over her.'

'Can you see his face?'

'No.'

'Try hard, Gary.'

'I can't see it.'

'Okay, guy. You're doing fantastic. Hang in there. I've never met anyone with powers like yours. So, let's use those powers. Let them flow through Sandy's medallion. Let God help you see that hatchet. Can you see it?'

'Yes.'

'Okay. The killer took the hatchet away. Where is it now?'

'He . . . he threw it away.'

'Where, Gary?'

'He threw it 'cause of the blood. He didn't want to see all that blood.'

'But where did he throw it? Help us find it. Project yourself into that hatchet.'

Gary's head wobbled. He wet his lips.

'He's running to a dark place because he's scared.'

'Someplace dark? But where?'

'Just dark. I don't know.'

'Come on, Gary. Don't let me down now. Use your special powers.'

'I'm trying, Sergeant, but he's too far from Sandy to see him.'

'You mean he's out of the park?'

'Yeah. She can't see him.'

'Where is Sandy?'

'By the well.'

'How did she get there?'

'She . . . she ran.'

'Okay.'

'Then, after he chopped her, she was by the well.'

'You saw that?'

'Yeah.'

'Is there much blood on the killer?'

'Yes.'

'Did the killer clean off that blood?'

'I can't see. He's too far away.'

'Okay. One last try at something. Why did the killer murder Sandy? Do you know why he did it?'

Gary thought about the girl at the dorm and the girl at the Stallion and how he wanted them to love him. Maybe the killer asked Sandy to be his girl and she said no, like the girl at the bar.

'He wanted Sandy to be nice to him, but she said no.'

'To be nice?'

'To love him, but she wouldn't love him and he got mad.'

'Like you got mad at Karen Nix?'

'Yeah.'

Downes should have been exhausted, but he was so elated he did not feel the fatigue.

'Did I help you?' Gary asked.

'Oh, yeah. You've been a big help.'

'Can I go home now?'

'Not just yet.'

'Why?'

'Gary, I'm gonna be honest with you. We have a problem here.'

'What problem?'

'The problem of how you know so much about Sandy's murder.'

'I seen it with my powers.'

'Well, that's probably it, but that wouldn't explain one thing. Bob Patrick told me what he saw on your hands.'

Gary's eyes widened.

'What did you see, Gary?'

'B . . . blood.'

'Why do you think you saw the blood?'

'I don't know.'

'Blood doesn't just appear on someone's hands. Where did it come from?'

Gary understood what Downes was suggesting and he started to squirm on his chair.

'Oh no, Sergeant. I couldn't of done that.'

'Do you know what you just said, Gary? You said "couldn't." You didn't say "I did not kill that girl." Why didn't you say, flat out, that you did not kill Sandy?'

'I . . . I don't know.'

'You were drunk that night, weren't you?'

'Yeah.'

'And you told me that you don't remember everything clearly because you had too much to drink.'

Gary nodded.

'Think about it. Why did you say "couldn't" instead of "didn't"?'

Gary looked at Downes with pleading eyes and asked, 'Do . . . do you think I killed that girl?'

'I don't know, Gary. I wasn't there. Only Sandy and her killer were there. But you'd know in your heart, if you did it. Even if you couldn't remember with your conscious mind, because you were so drunk, your subconscious mind would know.'

'I . . . I don't remember killing anyone, Sergeant. Honest. If . . . if I did, I don't remember.'

Gary licked his lips. Could he have killed Sandy and

forgotten? Could he have done the things he saw on the movie screen?

'Well, Gary?'

'I ... I couldn't have done that,' Gary said, desperately. 'No, no, I couldn't. Could I?'

'I don't know, Gary. Why don't we talk about that?'

PART FOUR

THE CHANCE
OF A LIFETIME

CHAPTER ELEVEN

1

Peter was so depressed that he did not fall asleep until two-thirty in the morning, giving him a grand total of two hours sack time before he was wrenched out of bed by the ringing of the phone.

'Hello,' he rasped as he squinted at the clock.

'Pete, it's Steve Mancini.'

'Steve? Aren't you on your honeymoon?'

'I was. Donna and I are on our way back to Whitaker. Gary's been arrested.'

'He didn't get arrested for peeping again?' asked Peter. He had told Steve about Gary's arrest and Steve had saved Gary's job. He had also decided to keep the information about the arrest from Donna and Gary's parents.

'Gary is charged with murder, Pete. It's that girl at the wishing well.'

'Holy shit!'

'I won't be back in Whitaker until eleven or so. He needs a lawyer, right away. The cops will make mincemeat out of him if they get Gary alone.'

'Steve, I'm very sympathetic. I mean, Gary seems like a nice guy, and I was glad to help him out, but I'm not your man. I've been handling criminal cases for . . . what? Two months? The only case I tried by myself was a suspended license charge, and I lost it.'

'I'm not asking you to take the case. I just want you to make certain that Gary doesn't do anything stupid before I talk to him.'

'Why don't you call Amos or someone else with more experience?'

'No offense, but I doubt Geary is sober at this hour and the attorneys who practice criminal law in Whitaker make Bozo the Clown look like Perry Mason. You're the only one I can trust to do this the right way.'

Peter had met some of the other lawyers who practiced in the Whitaker criminal courts. Mancini was right. They weren't all that swift. And Steve only wanted Peter to baby-sit with his brother-in-law until he got back to town. It was the least he could do for one of the few people in Whitaker he could call a friend.

'What do you want me to tell Gary?' Peter asked.

'You'll do it?'

'Yeah, yeah. Come on. Brief me.'

'I owe you big.'

'And don't forget it. So, what should I do at the jail?'

Peter stood when Gary stumbled into the room where Peter's abortive interview with Christopher Mammon had taken place. In the weak rays of dawn, Harmon's face seemed drained of color. There were dark circles under his eyes and his uncombed hair was mussed from his brief sleep.

'I'm Peter Hale, Gary. I helped you out when you were arrested at the college. Do you remember me?'

Gary nodded.

'Why don't you sit down.'

Peter indicated the metal folding chair on the other side of the wooden table. Gary shuffled forward. A sour odor assailed Peter as soon as Gary drew close. It was a unique combination of fear, sweat and disinfectant that Peter had come to associate with the incarcerated. He pushed himself back from the table to widen the distance between himself and the prisoner.

'Are they treating you all right?' Peter asked.

Gary nodded. 'When can I go home?'

'I don't know, Gary. I think you'll have to stay for a while.'

'I don't like it here.'

'Yeah, well, no one likes jail.'

'Can't you get me out?'

'I'm not going to be your lawyer, Gary. Steve Mancini asked me to help out until he comes back. He's driving here from Portland, right now. He should be in Whitaker by noon and I'm sure he'll come see you.'

'Sergeant Downes said I was helping to catch the killer. He said I was a good detective. Why won't he let me go?'

'Maybe the sergeant can't let you out. You're charged with a pretty serious crime. I think you'll need a judge's permission.'

'Will Steve ask the judge to help me?'

'You bet,' Peter answered. Steve had told Peter that bail was not automatic in a murder case. If the state opposed release, there would have to be a hearing.

Gary looked so pathetic that Peter did not have the heart to tell him that he might not be able to get out of jail.

'I don't like jail. I'm all locked in. And I don't like the people here. They scare me. They call me names and say things about that girl. They say I'm going to die in the electric chair. They say my brain will boil and melt.'

'Gary, there is no electric chair in Oregon. Those men are teasing you. Ignore them.'

'I can't. They say it all the time. Please get me out. You got me out when I was arrested before.'

'That was different. I just happened to be walking through the campus when you were caught. I really didn't do anything. Sergeant Downes decided not to arrest you. If you'd been charged, I wouldn't have been your lawyer.'

Gary looked so sad that Peter asked, 'Have you talked to the police?' in an effort to distract him.

'Uh-huh.'

'How long did you talk to them?'

'A long time.'

'An hour? Two hours? Can you tell me the exact time?'

'It was a really long time. I got sleepy. I ate three burgers.'

'And you were talking to the cops all that time?'

Gary nodded.

'Why do the police think you killed Sandra Whiley? Did you tell Sergeant Downes you killed her?'

'No. I just seen the girl killed.'

'You saw the murder?'

'Part with my eyes and part with my mind.'

'I'm not following you. What do you mean, you saw part of the murder with your mind?'

'I got these powers. Supernatural powers. I never knew I had 'em, but I do. Sergeant Downes showed me how to use them to see who killed Sandy. I was real tired, but I did it to help. Now I'll lose my job because I can't go to work. Mom will be so mad.'

'I'm sure someone will talk to the college about your job and your mom won't be mad. She loves you. She knows it's not your fault you can't go to work. Now, try to think about why you're locked up. What do you mean you saw Sandy killed?'

'With my powers, I can close my eyes and see what happened in the past.'

'You mean you make it up?'

'No, I really see it happen. Only a few people got my powers. Sergeant Downes said I had the best powers of anyone. Better even than those people on TV.'

'What did you tell Sergeant Downes you saw using your powers?'

'I seen Sandy being killed.'

'Did you see who killed her?'

Gary shook his head. 'It was dark. I couldn't see his face. But I seen him do it.'

'How much of the evening can you remember when you don't use your powers?'

Gary looked sheepish.

'I don't remember a lot of it too well. Everyone was buying me drinks because of the wedding.'

'I'm going to ask you a serious question and I want you to try real hard to answer it.'

Gary sat up straight and concentrated so he could give Peter the right answer.

'Is it possible that you killed that girl, but you don't remember because you were drinking?'

Gary licked his lips. He looked very frightened.

'I . . . I don't think I killed her.'

'You don't think you killed her? That's not the same as being sure.'

'I . . . I couldn't have killed that girl,' Gary said uncertainly.

'Then how do you know so much about the murder? I don't buy this superpower stuff. I want you to be honest with me. Did you do it?'

Gary swallowed. He was chewing his lip and looking around the narrow room as if trying to find a way out.

'Gary?'

Gary's head swung back slowly toward Peter. There were tears in his eyes.

'I want to go home.'

'Try to stay on track, Gary. We were talking about the murder.'

'I don't want to talk about that no more. I didn't do nothing bad. I'm a good boy. I want Mama. I want to go home.'

2

At eight o'clock Sunday morning Becky O'Shay called District Attorney Earl Ridgely at home and asked him to meet her at his office. When he arrived at nine-thirty, Becky was waiting for him. Ridgely's spacious corner office looked out on Wishing Well Park and the slow meanderings of the Camas River, but O'Shay had no interest in the scenery. She sprang to her feet as soon as her boss walked in.

'We got him,' Becky said excitedly. 'He confessed. We have motive . . .'

'Slow down, Becky. Who are you talking about?'

'The man who killed Sandra Whiley. We nailed him.'

Ridgely flushed with anger. 'Why wasn't I informed? I was supposed to be notified if there was a break in the case.'

'We weren't certain we had the right man until early this morning. Dennis Downes and I decided against waking you at 4 A.M.'

Ridgely's anger disappeared as quickly as it had come. Catching Whiley's killer was the important thing.

'Who is it?'

'Gary Harmon.'

'Not Jesse and Alice's boy?'

Becky nodded. Ridgely walked slowly to his chair and sat down. He felt sick.

'I've known Gary since he was born. I was at Donna's wedding, yesterday.'

'I know. It's terrible. But there's no doubt he did it.'

'What's your evidence?'

Becky started with the peeping incident and explained about the pornography discovered in the search of Gary's home. Then she moved to the attack on Karen Nix and Gary's threat to kill her.

'Nix and Whiley look alike. We think Nix was the intended victim and Harmon attacked Whiley by mistake. It's obvious from the peeping incident, the porno and the way he handled his rejection by Nix that Harmon is weird where women are concerned.'

'Do you know anything about Gary?' Ridgely asked.

'I watched part of the interrogation.'

'He's mildly retarded. He's like a kid.'

'And children have poor impulse control. Besides, we have what amounts to a confession. At first, Harmon claimed he didn't know anything about the murder. Then, he admitted seeing the killer fighting with Whiley at the entrance to Wishing Well Park. The more he talked, the more detail he gave.'

'Did he ever admit he killed Whiley?'

'No, but he didn't deny doing it.'

'What did he say?'

'He started by claiming he was too drunk to remember anything, but he ended up giving Dennis details about the murder that only the killer would know.'

'Such as?'

'He knew the location of the blows that killed Whiley and he said the murder weapon was a hatchet.'

'What?!'

'A pretty odd choice for a murder weapon, right? And, coincidentally, the weapon used to kill those other two women.'

Ridgely looked stunned. 'Did you question Gary about the other murders?'

'No. We wanted to concentrate on Whiley. We were afraid we'd spook him if we started asking about other crimes. But the hatchet did it for me. Dennis says we've been keeping the type of weapon used on the other women a secret as a check against false confessions.'

Ridgely swiveled his chair. Morning fog was twisting through the low brown hills across the river. Becky waited expectantly while her boss digested what she had just told him. When he swiveled back, Ridgely looked exhausted.

'Jesse and Alice love that boy. They've sacrificed so much for him.' He shook his head. 'There are times when I hate this job.'

3

Steve Mancini's office was in a square, earth brown, single-story building on the outskirts of city center, five blocks from the courthouse. On one side of the building was Pearl Street. On the opposite side, a narrow parking area formed a buffer between the building and a Mexican restaurant. In the back was more parking and a high wooden fence that separated the lot from a residential area of run-down homes. LAW OFFICES OF STEPHEN L. MANCINI was affixed to the building beside the front door in black block letters. Smaller lettering below Mancini's name listed two other sole practitioners who rented from him.

Steve's office was at the rear of the building next to the back door. It was furnished with cheap wood paneling, a large, imitation Persian rug and a battleship-size desk. A month ago, Peter would have thought the office pretentious, but serving time in Amos Geary's rat-trap offices had dulled his senses.

'Did you talk to Gary?' Mancini asked as soon as Peter was seated. Both men looked exhausted from lack of sleep.

'I saw him this morning, right after you called.'

'How's he holding up?'

'Not too well. The poor kid kept asking for you.'

'I'll see him this afternoon.'

'Uh, just how slow is Gary?'

'He's retarded, but he got through high school and he can work. Why?'

'It looks like Dennis Downes played some games with his head.'

'What do you mean?'

'Downes conned Gary into talking about the case by

convincing him he's a detective. He has Gary believing he has supernatural powers and can read minds or some such nonsense.'

Mancini looked puzzled. 'I know Dennis. He's a good guy. I can't see him taking advantage of Gary like that.'

'I don't care how nice Downes has been in the past. This supernatural mind thing sounds like a trick you'd use to take advantage of someone who's not too bright. You better check it out.'

Mancini looked uncomfortable. He picked up a pencil and tapped it on his desk.

'I've got a problem, Pete. I had a lot of time to think on the drive back. There's no way I can be lead counsel in this case. Ridgely might go for the death penalty. Think of what it would do to my marriage if I lost. Donna loves that kid. She'd never forgive me.'

'I see what you mean. You're going to have to bring in someone from Portland to handle a case like this. Maybe Michael Palmer or Ann Girard?'

Mancini shook his head. 'Whitaker juries won't take to an outsider. I've seen what happens when one of those slick big-city types rolls into town. Ridgely eats them for dinner. No, Pete, I was thinking of you.'

'Me?' Peter laughed uneasily. 'You've got to be kidding. I've lived in Whitaker for barely two months. I'm as much of an outsider as any other Portland lawyer. And I've already explained how little criminal law experience I have.'

Mancini looked Peter in the eye.

'You don't have to take this case, but you'll regret it, if you don't. I'm giving you a once in a lifetime opportunity. If you win Gary's case, you'll be the most famous lawyer in the eastern part of the state. You are going to be the "go to" guy for every farmer and ranch hand who's injured between Whitaker and the California border. I don't have to tell you how much money Ron Sissler, Dave MacAfee and Ernie Petersen make defending claims for the insurance companies. Pete, there's a lawyer on the other side of every claim they defend. That lawyer could be you.'

'That would be great, Steve. But I'd only be famous if I won. A murder case is out of my league.'

'Don't be ridiculous. It's not as complex as some of the stuff you handled at Hale, Greaves. Besides, I'll help you. I've got plenty of experience with criminal cases.'

Mancini had Peter thinking. He had second-chaired several major cases with his father and he had tried a number of smaller matters that were much tougher than any criminal case.

'Don't tell me you can't use the money?' Mancini said.

'Well, sure, but ... What kind of money are we talking about?'

'You'd have to ask for at least a hundred grand. What with expert witnesses, investigation.'

'Do the Harmons have that kind of dough?'

'Jesse Harmon is worth a lot and he doesn't spend a nickel he doesn't have to, but he'd clean out his savings for Gary.'

'What about Amos?' Peter asked, suddenly remembering his boss. 'He'd never let me defend Gary. We're up to our eyeballs in court-appointed stuff. If I was representing Gary, I wouldn't have time to do any other work.'

Mancini leaned back in his chair and held the pencil in both hands. Then, he said, 'Fuck Amos Geary.'

'What?'

'Fuck him. For Christ's sake, Pete, he's an old,

washed-up drunk. I can't believe a guy like you is saddled with that run-down sot.'

Mancini leaned forward. He pointed the pencil at Peter.

'Have you seen what passes for the bar in this burg? We're bigger than that, Pete. When Mountain View gets going I'll be a millionaire, but I'm also going to have to spend a lot of time with the project. I could use a partner right now, but there hasn't been a lawyer in the three counties I'd let near one of my files, until you came along.

'Think about it, Pete. You and me and all of those clients who'll want to be represented by the man who won the Wishing Well case. What does Amos pay you? I bet it's not one hundred thousand a year. And that's just one case.'

Peter's heart was beating fast. Amos Geary was in Cayuse County trying a robbery case. He'd be there all week. What would he say if he came back and found out that Peter was Gary's attorney? What could he say? With Peter on the case for a week, it would be a *fait accompli*. Geary would have to accept the fact that Peter was representing Gary Harmon.

'It sounds tempting,' Peter said, 'but I really should think about this.'

'Pete, I hate to pressure you, but the Harmons are here, now.'

'What?'

'They're in the conference room waiting to meet you.'

'They are?'

'I've been building you up as the only guy in Whitaker who is qualified to represent Gary. They're ready to hire you.'

'I don't know . . .'

'Jesse wants his boy represented right away. If you don't hop on this, he's going to see it as a sign that you don't think you're big enough to handle the case.

'And I need you to be Gary's lawyer. He's my brother-in-law. The poor kid needs my help. If you're lead counsel, I can work with you. We'll make a great team.'

For a nanosecond, it occurred to Peter that Gary Harmon could die if he screwed up the case, but he banished this pang of conscience from his thoughts. With Steve as his partner, Gary would have a great defense.

Peter imagined himself as the most famous attorney in eastern Oregon, rolling in money and picking and choosing from the supplicants who would beg him to take their cases. He conjured an image of his father staring, openmouthed, at a headline in *The Oregonian* that read:

PETER HALE WINS ACQUITTAL IN BIGGEST
DEATH CASE IN EASTERN OREGON HISTORY

Peter had no intention of spending his life trying traffic cases for peanuts. Steve Mancini had confidence in Peter's abilities and he was handing Peter the chance of a lifetime.

'Let's do it!' Peter said.

Mancini grinned at him. 'That was the smartest decision you ever made. Let's meet your new clients.'

Mancini led Peter down the hall to the conference room. Jesse Harmon was pacing the floor when Steve opened the door. Harmon's fifty-nine years showed in his thatch of white hair and the lines on his tanned, weather-beaten face. He was barrel-chested and broad-shouldered from years of farmwork. Donna was sitting next to Alice Harmon, a tall, raw-boned woman with more gray than brown in her hair.

'I've got good news,' Mancini said enthusiastically, as soon as the introductions were made. 'Pete's going to take the case.'

Jesse and Alice Harmon's faces showed none of Steve Mancini's excitement. They were drawn with worry.

'Steve tells us you've got lots of experience in these cases,' Jesse Harmon said, getting down to business immediately.

Before Peter could think up an answer that would satisfy Harmon and not be a lie, Mancini said, 'Pete's spent the last four years with the most prestigious firm in Portland working with its top litigator, who just happens to be his father. You might say that Pete's got high-level litigation in his genes.'

'Did that firm handle criminal cases?' Jesse asked, ignoring Steve's attempt to skirt the issue of Peter's experience.

'Jesse,' Mancini interjected, his expression turning somber, 'there is something that Peter and I know about Gary that we've kept from you, Alice and Donna. Something that bears very strongly on the suitability of Peter to represent Gary.' Donna and Alice cast worried glances at each other and Jesse's features hardened. 'A few weeks ago, Gary was arrested when he was caught peeping in a window at the girls' dormitory while a young woman was undressing.'

Alice's hand flew to her mouth and Donna said, 'Oh, my God.'

'Pete just happened to be walking across campus when this happened. He calmed down campus security, accompanied Gary to the police station and convinced the police that Gary should not be charged. Then, he came to me. I squared things with the college so Gary could keep his job.

'Jesse, not only is Pete a top-flight lawyer, but Gary trusts him. In a case like this, trust between a lawyer and his client is essential.'

Peter was concerned that Jesse Harmon would become suspicious if Steve kept speaking up for him. He decided it was time for him to say something. Peter knew almost nothing about the state's case, so he had no idea whether Gary was guilty or innocent, but he had a very good idea of what Jesse and Alice wanted to hear.

'Mr. and Mrs. Harmon,' he said with as much sincerity as he could muster, 'I know how concerned you are about Gary, so I want you to know why I am willing to undertake Gary's defense. I am convinced that the police knew about Gary's mental handicap and took advantage of it to trick him into confessing to something he never did. What the police have done to Gary is wrong and I intend to do something about it.'

Jesse Harmon's features softened and a tear trickled down Alice Harmon's cheek.

'We appreciate what you did for our boy,' Jesse said, 'and we would be grateful if you would help him out now.'

CHAPTER TWELVE

1

Peter had not expected to see Becky O'Shay sitting next to Earl Ridgely's desk when the receptionist showed him and Steve Mancini into the district attorney's office. He started to smile, but caught himself. He remembered how reluctant Becky had been to go out with him because of their adversarial position and decided she might not appreciate an outward show of affection in front of her boss.

'How are Jesse and Alice holding up?' Ridgely asked Mancini when everyone was seated.

'As well as can be expected.'

'They're awfully good people. I'm sorry they have to go through this ordeal.'

'It would be a lot easier on them if you'd agree to let Gary out on bail.'

'I can't do that.'

'Earl, you've known Gary his whole life. Do you think he murdered that girl?'

'Look, I feel terrible about the arrest. You know how

much I respect Jesse and Alice. But the evidence is very strong. We're still investigating, of course, but we have a taped confession . . .'

'He admitted killing her?'

'Not in so many words, but . . .' Ridgely paused. 'I'm sorry. I can't discuss this any further. We'll be going before a grand jury tomorrow. If an indictment is returned, I'll give you all the discovery the law allows, but I'm going to play this one by the book.'

'Earl, we've known each other how long? I don't understand the problem in letting us know what you've got on Gary.'

'The statutes say the defense isn't entitled to discovery until there's an indictment. I know that's not how this office usually does things. We've only got a handful of lawyers in the county and I know every one of them, so I usually bend the rules. But not this time. Not in this case.'

Peter put his hand on Mancini's arm.

'I respect that, Mr. Ridgely. We can wait. I'd appreciate it if you'd let us know as soon as the grand jury votes and I'd also appreciate seeing the discovery as soon as possible.'

Peter handed Ridgely his business card.

'Steve, why don't we let Mr. Ridgely get back to work?'

Mancini looked like he wanted to say something else, but he held it in. The two men shook hands with Ridgely and nodded at O'Shay. Just before he left, Peter managed to flash a smile at Becky. She was standing so Ridgely could not see her and she returned the smile. Peter's heart soared.

The door closed and Ridgely sat lost in thought. After a moment, he looked over at his deputy and said,

'There's no way I can prosecute Gary Harmon. I know the family too well.'

O'Shay had been hoping the district attorney would reach this decision. She had been very worried that he would want to prosecute Gary Harmon himself.

'You were at the wedding, weren't you?' he asked after a while.

O'Shay was ready for this. 'Yes,' she said, 'but I don't know the Harmons and I only know Steve Mancini professionally.'

Ridgely was a little put off by O'Shay's eagerness, but he understood it. Prosecuting a murder case was the ultimate challenge for a district attorney and the chance to do it in Whitaker was rare.

'I can ask the Attorney General for assistance. They provide help to small counties in major cases.'

Becky knew it was now or never. She pulled her chair up to the desk and leaned toward Ridgely.

'Earl, I can do this. You know I'm good. I'm running a ninety-five percent conviction rate.'

'This is a murder case, Becky. What's the most complex case you've tried?'

'*Peck,* and I won. Three weeks, toe to toe with a hired gun from Portland. I kicked his ass around the courtroom and you know it. Ask Judge Kuffel.'

'I don't have to. He went out of his way to tell me what a great job you did.'

'Then you know I can try *Harmon.* Give me the chance.'

Ridgely could not think of a reason to deny O'Shay the case.

'*Harmon* is yours,' he said.

'Thank you. I'll never forget this.'

'Before you prosecute Gary, I want you to be damn certain he's the right man.'

'Definitely.' O'Shay paused. She looked a little nervous when she asked, 'What about the death penalty?'

Ridgely paled. He started to say something, then he caught himself.

'I can't answer that question for the same reason I can't try the case. If you ask for the death penalty, it must be your decision.'

Becky nodded solemnly like a person beset by a moral quandary of epic proportions, but Becky O'Shay had decided she was going for the death penalty as soon as she realized that she had a chance to prosecute Gary Harmon. A lot of doors would open for a lawyer who was tough enough to successfully prosecute a death case.

2

Kevin Booth lived six miles outside of Whitaker at the end of a gravel road in a single-bedroom house that was little better than a shack. The paint on the outside of the house had been scarred by endless waves of wind-blown debris. A dismantled junker sat on blocks in the yard in front of a small, litter-filled garage. Booth's nearest neighbor was half a mile away. The view was brown flatlands and desolation, broken only by the wavering outline of another shack, a forlorn apparition abandoned long ago that served as a reminder of the inhospitable nature of the desert.

The inside of the house looked no better than the outside. Empty pizza boxes, crumpled cigarette packs and soiled skin magazines lay scattered around. In the kitchen, the rust-stained refrigerator was almost empty and dried soup congealed around the burners on the dilapidated stove.

Booth had staggered in around one and collapsed on his unmade bed. He was in such a deep sleep that the pounding on his front door did not arouse him immediately. When the din finally penetrated, he jerked awake, upsetting the lamp on his end table. It was pitch black in his room and his heart was beating so loudly that he could not distinguish between the two thumping sounds.

'One minute,' he called out, but the pounding continued.

Booth swung his legs over the side of the bed. He was wearing boxer shorts and an undershirt. His mouth felt gummy. Awakening suddenly in the dark had disoriented him. The pills he'd taken before he went to sleep did not help. Booth fumbled for the switch on the lamp and had trouble finding it because the lamp was on its side.

'Just a minute,' he yelled again.

This time the pounding stopped. Booth found the switch. The light hurt his eyes. He winced and groped around for his jeans, then pulled them on. After slipping into his sneakers, Booth staggered into the front room.

'Who is it?' he called through the door.

'Rafael Vargas,' said a voice with a faint trace of Spain.

'Oh, shit,' Booth said to himself.

'Open the fucking door,' a deeper voice commanded.

The moment Booth opened the door he regretted it, but refusing to let the two men in would have been useless. The first man through the door could have eaten it if he wanted to. He wore a suit jacket over a tight black tee shirt that stretched across corded muscles. When he moved, the jacket flapped back revealing the butt of a large handgun. The man wore his long hair tied back in a pony tail and a gold earring dangled from his left ear. A jagged scar cut across his cheek, his nose was askew and his eyes were wild. As soon as he was inside, he searched the house.

Rafael Vargas was lean, wiry and obviously Latin. His amused smile revealed even, white teeth and there was a pencil-thin mustache over his upper lip.

'Sit down, Kevin,' Vargas commanded after he took the most comfortable chair in the shabby living room. Booth sat on the couch across from his visitor.

'There's no one else here,' Vargas's bodyguard said when he was finished searching. Vargas nodded, then turned his attention back to Booth.

'Did Chris explain what we want from you?' he asked.

Booth swallowed. He was still groggy from the pills.

'When Mr. Vargas asks a question, he expects an answer,' the bodyguard said, taking a threatening step forward.

'Yeah,' Booth answered quickly. 'I'm just sleepy. It's three in the morning.'

'Then you must wake up quickly, Kevin,' Vargas said. 'There are things to do.'

'Uh, look, Mr. Vargas,' Booth said anxiously, 'I told Chris I didn't think I was right for this.'

Vargas held up his hand and Booth froze.

'Look, amigo, Chris is hot. DEA is gonna have him under surveillance. He's smart enough to know that.'

'I was arrested with Chris. They probably suspect me, too.'

Vargas shook his head. 'DEA forgot you the minute you left the courtroom.'

'Right, but . . .'

'Kevin, wheels are in motion. It's too late to stop them from turning.'

Vargas stood up. 'I've got twenty kilos of cocaine in a van parked out front. All you have to do is hold it for a few days. Do you think you can do that?'

Booth felt the way he would have if Vargas had asked him to stand at ground zero on the day they dropped the A bomb on Hiroshima.

'Twenty . . . Mr. Vargas, I really don't want to be around twenty kilos of snow.'

'There is nothing to worry about. We don't plan to leave the merchandise here for very long,' Vargas said. 'Let's go to the van.'

Booth got up quickly and Carlos and Vargas followed him outside. There was almost no moon and there was no light in the yard except for the headlights of a brown van and the light that filtered into the yard through the living room curtains. The only sound was Booth's breathing and his sneakers scraping across the dirt. Booth stumbled on his way to the van, but neither man made any effort to catch him. Vargas found a flashlight in the glove compartment while Carlos opened the back of the van revealing two large, black plastic trashbags secured with ties.

'Take them out,' Carlos commanded.

Booth grabbed the bags by their necks and pulled them out. As soon as he started for the garage, lights flooded the yard.

'Freeze! Federal agents!' shouted a man in a dark blue windbreaker. Stenciled on the back in yellow letters was DEA. Vargas dropped the flashlight and started to run, but two armed men appeared from the side of the garage. Carlos held his hands away from his body. Booth froze.

'Drop the bags,' commanded the man in the windbreaker. Booth complied instantly. One of the garbage bags broke and a fine white powder seeped out of the tear. Booth was slammed against the side of the van. Rough hands frisked him, then his arms were wrenched behind him and metal cuffs were snapped on his wrists. When he was jerked around, Booth found himself standing next to Vargas. The slender Hispanic said nothing until they were left alone for a moment while their captors conferred. As soon as the agents were far enough away, Vargas turned to Booth and whispered, 'You are a dead man.'

3

Kevin Booth looked worse than Steve Mancini had ever seen him. Not only was his acne acting up and his body odor more repulsive, but he appeared to be on the brink of a psychotic break. Sweat was pouring off Booth, he jerked around constantly and Mancini could swear that his client had not blinked once since he sat down.

'Kevin, Kevin. You've got to get ahold of yourself,' Mancini cautioned.

'Ahold? What are you talking about? I was arrested with ten kilos of cocaine in each hand and Rafael Vargas, the executioner for one of Colombia's biggest drug cartels, has personally threatened to kill me. How can I get ahold of myself? You tell me.'

'I admit you're in some serious shit here, but Vargas was probably venting his anger at you. These threats are made all the time and rarely carried out. And as far as the dope goes, you said you were forced to carry the bags. I'll explain that to the feds, we'll agree to cooperate in the prosecution of Vargas and . . .'

'No. No way will I testify against Rafael Vargas. And, besides,' Booth said in a suddenly subdued voice, 'the feds aren't interested.'

'How do you know?'

Booth ran his tongue across his lips. 'I tried. When I was arrested, I begged them to let me cooperate. They said they didn't need me. They . . . they said they were going to send me away forever and . . . and nothing I could say would help.'

'What happened exactly?' Mancini asked.

Booth told him. Mancini digested this information. He looked at the case from the feds' point of view. The DEA must have been onto Vargas all along and followed him to Booth's home. Carlos and Vargas had probably been photographed loading the cocaine into the van and the three men had been caught red-handed. The case was open and shut. No search-and-seizure problems, no statements to be suppressed. Just three amigos standing around with enough cocaine to get every man, woman, child and household pet in the state high.

Mancini shook his head solemnly. 'This is going to be tough, Kevin. I'm going to have to work overtime to save your butt.'

'You think you can win, Steve?' Booth pleaded, looking so pathetic that Mancini had to choke back a laugh.

'Didn't I take care of you the last time?'

'Yes. Yes you did,' Booth responded eagerly.

'Now, with a case this big, I'll need twenty thousand up front,' Mancini continued.

'Twenty . . . The last time you only charged me seventy-five hundred.'

'The last time we were in state court and you weren't

caught with twenty kilos of snow. Fighting the feds is expensive. They have the resources of the entire government. I'm fighting Washington, D.C., not some small-town D.A.'

'I don't have twenty thousand dollars,' Booth said desperately.

'What about your parents?'

'My father ran off when I was two. I don't even remember him. And my mother,' Booth said bitterly, 'she's dead.'

'Where did you get the dough last time?'

'Chris Mammon lent it to me.'

'Well?' Mancini said with a shrug. 'From what you've told me, you're in this scrape because of Mammon. Ask him to go your fee.'

Booth hung his head. 'I already called him. He won't talk to me.'

Mancini sighed. 'I want to help you, Kevin, but I can't work for free. Not on a case this big. You understand that, don't you?'

'You won so easy the last time. Can't you give me some credit. If you get me off I'll pay you double.'

'No can do. Sorry, but I have an iron-clad rule about fees in criminal cases.'

Mancini looked at his watch. 'Hey, I'm going to have to break this off. I'm due in court.'

'Wait a minute. You can't just walk out on me.'

'I'm afraid I have other clients, Kevin.'

'Don't do this to me, man,' Booth whined, 'you gotta help.'

'I really am due in court.'

Mancini started to rap for the guard, but Booth grabbed him by the arm.

'I'll ... I'll tell the cops about you,' Booth threatened.

Mancini did not move his arm. Instead he turned until his face was inches from Booth's.

'Oh, really?' Mancini said. 'What exactly will you tell them?'

The former quarterback's bicep felt like steel through his suit jacket and Booth knew he had made a mistake.

'You . . . you know,' Booth stuttered.

'Let go of my arm, Kevin,' Mancini said softly.

Booth's grip loosened. Mancini still did not move. Finally, Booth's eyes dropped and he released Mancini's arm. Mancini slowly lowered it.

'Never touch me again, Kevin. And never, ever threaten me. But if you feel compelled to talk, remember that two can play that game. Would you like me to visit Rafael Vargas and confirm his suspicions about you?'

Booth swallowed. Mancini smiled coldly, then made a point of turning his back on Booth. Booth sank back on his chair, shaking with terror at the thought of a life in prison, if he was fortunate enough to escape the vengeance of Rafael Vargas.

CHAPTER THIRTEEN

1

Reporters from the *Clarion,* several other eastern Oregon papers and the local TV station were waiting for Peter outside the courtroom where Gary was to be arraigned. Peter made a brief statement expressing his total belief in his client's innocence. During the statement, Peter made numerous references to the Bill of Rights, the Constitution and the American System of Justice. He loved every moment in the spotlight.

Donna, Jesse and Alice Harmon were sitting with Steve Mancini in the front row of spectator seats. Peter stopped briefly to say hello, then walked through the low wooden gate that separated the spectators from the court. There were several defendants waiting to be arraigned and Gary was last on the list. Peter expected Earl Ridgely to handle Gary's arraignment, but Becky O'Shay was handling all the arraignments today and she called the case.

A guard brought Gary into the courtroom. He was used to his status as a prisoner by now and looked more confused than afraid. Gary spotted his parents. He started toward them, but the guard grabbed Gary by the elbow and pointed him toward Peter.

The clerk presented Peter and Gary with copies of an indictment charging Gary with aggravated murder, the most serious degree of homicide in Oregon and the only charge that carried the death penalty. The judge explained the charge and his rights to Gary, then the judge asked Gary what plea he wanted to enter. Peter told him to say, 'Not guilty,' and Gary said the words in a nervous whisper that could be heard easily only by those within the bar of the court. Peter and Becky discussed scheduling with the judge for a few minutes; then the arraignment was over.

'Hold up, will you?' Peter asked Becky. She waited patiently at her counsel table while Peter told Gary he would see him later in the afternoon, after he had a chance to read the discovery. As soon as Gary was led out, Peter smiled and asked O'Shay, 'How've you been?'

'Great. Sorry about the other night.'

'Me, too. Maybe I can collect on that rain check soon?'

'The Harmon case is a real plum for you,' Becky said, skillfully avoiding Peter's question. Peter tried to look modest.

'A death penalty case is a big responsibility,' he answered solemnly. 'Where's Earl? I thought he'd want to handle Gary's arraignment personally.'

'Earl isn't prosecuting Gary.'

'He isn't? Then, who . . .'

O'Shay smiled.

'You? You're going to prosecute?'

O'Shay nodded and looked suddenly somber. 'Unfortunately, Peter, that means that we won't be able to see each other for a while, except, of course, in the courtroom.'

Peter had been looking forward to going out with Becky. He felt a little depressed. Gary's case was going to put a damper on his social life.

O'Shay touched Peter lightly on the arm. 'Come up to my office and I'll give you the discovery. And don't look so glum. We can make up for lost time when the trial is over.'

After court, to his delight, Peter was interviewed by the press again, then Jesse Harmon gave him a twenty-five-thousand-dollar installment of the retainer. The money and the rush from being the center of attention put Peter in a very good mood.

Peter was so excited about the prospect of being the lead counsel in a major case that he had not given much thought to whether Gary had killed Sandra Whiley. Gary's claim that he did not have a clear memory of the hours when the killing occurred and his evasive answers when asked point blank if he had killed Sandra Whiley had aroused Peter's suspicions, but he had little basis for forming an opinion until he read the police reports.

When he returned to his office, Peter dumped the stack of police reports and the box of tapes O'Shay had given him onto his desk and hunted up a tape recorder so he could hear Gary's interrogation. As he listened, Peter's mood changed from excitement to confusion to concern. Something was not right. Peter could see that Gary knew a lot about the murder, but what was this 'projection transfer' and 'super-natural mind' stuff? It sounded to Peter as if Sergeant

Downes had tricked Gary into making many of the statements that were incriminating. What if Gary was repeating what Downes said and not remembering it? What if Gary was innocent?

2

Several hours after the arraignment, a guard let Gary into the attorney-client interview room at the jail.

'Can I go home now?' Gary asked as soon as he saw Peter.

'No, Gary. I've explained this all to you before. You're charged with murder, so there isn't any way you can get out of jail for a while.'

Gary looked agitated. 'How will I do my job?'

'Gary, you've got to focus on what's important. Okay? We're talking about your life here. That job at the college is just a janitor's job. That job isn't important.'

'Oh no, my job is important,' Gary told Peter with great seriousness. 'Mom says every job is important and my job is very important. There are germs. They are very small. You can't see them. They make people sick. I scrub and scrub. I clean away the germs. I make the floor shine so you can see your face. I take out the garbage so the room won't smell bad. If I don't do my job people will be sick, the room will smell.'

Gary grew more agitated as he spoke. Peter was surprised by how serious Gary was about his work. He felt a little bad about putting down his job.

'Look, Gary,' Peter said gently, 'I'm sure they have someone filling in for you. Someone to clean away the germs and take out the garbage until you can come back.'

'Is someone taking my job?' Gary asked. He was pacing back and forth. 'I want my job.'

'No, no. No one is taking your job. Listen to me. Did I help you when you were arrested for looking at that girl?'

Gary nodded, but his eyes were darting back and forth with worry.

'Did Steve and I make sure you kept your job?'

Gary stopped pacing. He looked less worried.

'Gary, do you think Steve and I will let them take your job?'

'You helped me keep my job,' Gary said, relaxing a little.

'Right. Your job is important, Gary. It's very important. The college needs you to do that job. They won't let anyone take your job because you're so good at it. Okay? But you won't be able to go back at all unless you help me.'

Gary's breathing settled. He stopped pacing.

'Now, why don't you sit down and we'll take that first step toward getting you out of here so you can work.' Peter indicated one of the metal chairs on the other side of the wooden table. Gary sat down obediently. He wiped the palms of his hands on his jumpsuit and waited for Peter to continue. Peter sighed with relief then pointed to several tape cassettes and the stack of police reports he had reviewed over the past few hours.

'I've received some discovery from the district attorney and I wanted to go over it with you. I've read a summary of the statement you made to Sergeant Downes and I've listened to a few of the tapes of your interrogation. I want you to tell me again how you know so much about this murder.'

'It's my powers.'

'Your supernatural and subconscious minds?'

Gary nodded. Peter shifted uncomfortably on the metal chair as he searched for the words he wanted to say. Gary watched him hopefully. Peter felt sorry for his client. He wondered what it must be like to go through life with the mind of a very slow child. What did Gary think about? Did he think at all without a stimulus? Was Gary nothing more than a machine with malfunctioning circuits? Were the rich patterns of life mere shadows for him? Or was there more to Gary than was apparent at first? According to the police reports, Gary had flown into a rage when Karen Nix insulted his intelligence. Would a machine care what a person thought of its capabilities?

Peter had thought a lot about the fame and fortune Gary's case could bring him, but very little about Gary Harmon. At first, he was even put off by his client. Peter liked to be around intelligent, well-educated and presentable people. People on the go. People like himself before the Elliot case. Peter would never associate with someone like Gary under normal circumstances, but Peter found Gary's childlike dependence on him endearing as well as flattering. After the way he had been treated at Hale, Greaves, it was nice being appreciated.

Peter stopped musing and looked directly at Gary. Gary met his eye without wavering.

'Gary, I want you to listen carefully to what I'm going to say.' Gary leaned forward expectantly. 'You do not have any special powers.'

Peter waited for a response. Gary looked confused. When he didn't reply, Peter pushed on.

'Do you understand what Sergeant Downes did to you?'

Gary shook his head. Peter tried to think of a diplomatic way of breaking the bad news to Gary.

'I'm your friend, Gary. Do you trust me?'

'Yeah.'

'And you know if I say something that hurts your feelings, I'm saying it because I have to in order to save you?'

Gary nodded, again.

'Okay. Do you understand that you aren't as smart as some other people?'

Gary flushed, but he nodded.

'Do mean people take advantage of you sometimes? Play tricks on you or try to fool you?'

'Yeah. I don't like them mean people. They hurt my feelings.'

'Gary, Sergeant Downes played a trick on you. He took advantage of you. He said you have supernatural powers, but you don't.'

Gary's expression was blank for a moment. Then his brow furrowed.

'How did I see the murder if I don't have powers?'

'There are only two explanations I can think of, Gary. Either you murdered Sandra Whiley . . .'

'Oh no, Mr. Hale. I couldn't do that.'

'. . . or you made up what you said.'

'No. I didn't make it up. I seen it.'

'Sergeant Downes told you to imagine what you saw in your head, didn't he?'

'Yeah.'

'That's all it was, Gary. Your imagination.'

'But it seemed so real.'

'Do me a favor. Close your eyes.'

Gary obeyed Peter's request.

'Now imagine this room. Do you have it?'

Gary nodded.

'What time of year is it?'

'Summer.'

'In your mind, imagine it's winter.' Peter waited a few seconds. 'Can you see snow on the window? Is it cold?'

'Yeah.'

'Now, imagine Santa Claus is in this room with us. Do you see him? Can you see the icicles hanging from his beard? Can you see the twinkle in his eye?'

Gary smiled.

'Gary, have you ever seen Santa in this jail?'

'No.'

'But you're seeing him in the jail now.'

'That ain't . . .'

Gary stopped. His eyes opened slowly. The smile faded to a look of puzzlement.

'Do you see what Sergeant Downes did to you? Do you understand it now?'

'I . . . I know I seen something. I know I seen two people in the park when I passed by.'

'Can you swear you saw Sandra Whiley?'

Gary shook his head. He looked dejected. Peter's heart went out to him.

'This is our job, then. To find out what you really saw and what you made up. It's going to be a hard job, but we're going to work together and we're going to do it. Will you work with me, Gary? Will you help me?'

'Yes I will, Mr. Hale. I'll try real hard.'

'Good, Gary. That's a start.'

3

It was almost five o'clock when Peter left the jail. Working with Gary was exhausting. He was so open to suggestion that Peter had to watch every word, and he could never be certain if Gary really understood him or was nodding to be polite. Representing Gary Harmon was going to be very frustrating and very time consuming.

As he walked up the stairs to Geary's office, Peter checked his watch. He was going to Steve's house after dinner to discuss strategy. There were all sorts of technical defenses, like diminished capacity, they might employ with a guilty client with Gary's intelligence. After today's session with Gary. Peter was wondering if they shouldn't dispense with them and go with a straight not guilty on the grounds that Gary did not commit the crime.

The autopsy report described the carnage to Sandra Whiley in graphic detail. The person who inflicted those wounds was in a rage. Gary had been in a rage when he attacked Karen Nix, but Gary's rage was a spontaneous response to Nix's insult. The hatchet screamed premeditation. Who walks around with a hatchet? No, the killer carried the hatchet with him to use on the victim and that meant the killer planned his moves. Peter had a hard time picturing Gary Harmon planning breakfast.

'Mr. Geary wants to speak to you,' Clara said as soon as Peter opened the office door.

'He's here?' Peter asked nervously.

'Nope,' Clara answered without looking up from her typing. 'He's at the Bunkhouse Motel in Cayuse County. Said to have you call the minute you walked in.' Clara stopped typing and looked at Peter. 'Those were his exact words. "The minute he walks in the door." '

'Do you know why he wants to talk to me?'

'That's none of my business, Mr. Hale. I'm just a secretary. But he did seem a mite annoyed.'

Peter wondered if Geary knew he was on the case

already. He had hoped for more time to cement his position as Gary's attorney before having to confront his boss.

'Mr. Geary,' Peter said as soon as he was put through by the motel clerk, 'Clara said you wanted to talk to me.'

'Yes. Yes I do. I was sitting in Judge Gilroy's chambers after court and he jokingly offered me condolences on getting stuck with the Harmon case. I told him I didn't know what he was talking about, because our office doesn't handle death penalty cases. With all the work in the office, we would never be able to commit the time we would have to commit in order to do a competent job. Not to mention that no one in my office is qualified to handle a death case, which, I'm sure you know, is a case that requires a specialist.

'The judge said he could be mistaken, but Judge Kuffel had phoned him during a break in our trial and he thought Kuffel said that my young associate had appeared at the arraignment for Mr. Harmon. That isn't true, is it, Peter?'

'Well, uh, yes it is. I mean, the judge is right. But you don't have to worry. This isn't a court appointment. The Harmons are going to pay us one hundred thousand dollars and expenses.'

Peter held his breath as he waited for Geary to absorb the amount of the fee. Peter assumed that one hundred thousand dollars would allay any qualms his boss might have. There was silence on the line for a moment. When Geary spoke again, he sounded as if he was fighting to keep himself under control.

'Peter, I want you to call Jesse Harmon and tell him you made a mistake when you accepted his son's case without consulting me. Then, you march down to Judge Kuffel's office and resign as quickly as you can.

First thing in the morning is fine, but tonight would be better, if you can catch him in. You might want to call as soon as I hang up.'

'But, Mr. Geary . . .'

'No buts, Peter. You and this office are off the Harmon case as of now. Do you understand me?'

'Well, no, I don't understand. How much do we make on one of your crummy court appointments? What, a few hundred bucks? I just brought in a one-hundred-thousand-dollar fee and you're acting like I did something wrong.'

'You did do something wrong, Peter,' Geary said in a tone that had Peter picturing swelling blood vessels and tightly clenched teeth. 'First, you took this case without consulting me, your boss.

'Second, our firm has a contract to represent indigent defendants in three counties. A contract is a binding promise between two or more parties to undertake particular tasks. In order to honor my part of the contract I need to have you available to represent the indigent accused, no matter how crummy they may be. You will not be available if you are in court on one case for two to four months.

'Third, and most important, this is not some shoplifting case. If you fuck up, Gary Harmon will have lethal chemicals injected into his veins. And you will fuck up, Peter, because *you* are a fuck-up. Did you forget that your father exiled you to this intellectual Devil's Island because of your gross incompetence. Are you so shallow that you want to compound your felony by risking Gary Harmon's life for money?'

'I resent the implications that I took this case for the money,' Peter said indignantly.

'I don't give a shit what you resent,' Geary shouted. 'You either march down to the courthouse and resign the minute I hang up or clear out of your office.'

The line went dead. Peter's hand was shaking. He hung up and slumped in his chair. What was he going to do? If he didn't resign from Gary's case, his last chance to get back in his father's good graces would be gone. But if he did resign, a golden opportunity to make a name for himself on his own would disappear. A chance like this might never come his way again.

Peter had rationalized his banishment to this dust bowl as a temporary inconvenience. He always believed that his father would welcome him back after he had done his penance as a low-paid advocate of the indigent accused. What Peter pondered long and hard was his father's reaction to a call from Amos Geary telling him that Peter had lasted barely two months before he had to can him.

Before *Elliot,* Peter would never have believed his father would punish him for anything he did. When he was suspended from high school after tearing up the football field with his jeep in a drunken frenzy, Richard paid for the damage and somehow kept the suspension off his record. When there was that unfortunate problem with the sorority girl in college, Richard fumed and hollered, then paid for the abortion. And what about law school? To this day, Peter had no idea how he would have gained admission with his grades, if Richard had not stepped in. That was why it had been such a shock when his father lowered the boom after his fiasco in *Elliot* and it was the reason why he could not dismiss the possibility that Richard would cast him out forever if he failed him again.

The thought of quitting Geary's firm made Peter feel like a kid getting ready to make a high dive for the first time. He could edge back along the board to safety by dropping Gary Harmon or he could take a frightening plunge into the unknown by staying on the case. Was he willing to trade his freedom for security? Did he want to stay a child his whole life, totally dependent on his father, or did he want to become a man who could stand on his own two feet?

Then, Peter remembered Steve Mancini's advice. 'Fuck Amos Geary,' Mancini had said. Mancini was right. With one hundred thousand dollars he could say 'Fuck you' to a lot of people. And there was the partnership waiting. When Peter thought about it, the choice wasn't all that hard.

4

'What are you going to do?' Steve Mancini asked as soon as Peter finished his account of his phone conversation with Amos Geary. They were seated on the couch in Mancini's living room. Police reports and tape cassettes were stacked next to a tape recorder in front of them on the coffee table. Donna was in the kitchen brewing coffee and slicing a coffee cake.

'I know what I'd like to do, but I have one huge practical problem. If I stay on as Gary's lawyer, I've got to clear out of my office.'

'That's no problem, at all. I have an extra office at my place you can rent. You'd have a receptionist and you can pay one of my secretaries by the hour to type your stuff. My place is a hell of a lot nicer than Geary's mausoleum. What do you say?'

'Are you still serious about going into partnership?'

'You bet. Of course, we can't do it right now, because I've got to get Mountain View squared away and you've got Gary's case to try.'

'Right.'

'But I'm definitely interested.'

'That's terrific, because I think it could work.'

'Okay. So, we'll talk.'

Peter shook Steve's hand and smiled bravely, but his insides were churning with fear.

'Now that we've got that settled, let's get to work,' Steve said.

'I want you to read this report.' Peter handed a thick, stapled stack of paper to Mancini. 'It's a summary of Downes's interrogation. Then I want you to listen to sections of these tapes. The whole interrogation is about seven hours. I only had time to listen to two tapes, but the parts I'm going to play will give you some idea of what's going on.'

Donna came out of the kitchen carrying a tray shortly after Peter started playing the tapes. She gave Peter and her husband cups of coffee and a slice of cake. Then, she sat on the couch next to Steve and listened as Dennis Downes explained to Gary the marvelous powers he possessed.

'Are Gary's statements the reason he was arrested?' Donna asked Peter when the tapes were finished.

'They're a big part of it.'

'But that's so unfair. Gary thought he was being a detective. He thought he was helping Downes. Gary wouldn't understand that Downes was fooling him. No jury is going to believe that what Gary said was a confession.'

'It would if Gary knows something that only the killer could know,' Mancini said, 'and I'm betting that somewhere on these tapes is something like that.'

'Keeping Gary's statement out of evidence is definitely the key to winning the case,' Peter said. 'The question is how to do it.'

'Doesn't the fact that Downes lied to Gary mean anything?' Donna asked.

'I seem to remember reading some cases in law school that held that a confession that is elicited by deceit won't hold up,' Peter said.

'Maybe I can help find them,' Donna volunteered. 'When I was studying to be a legal secretary I took a course on how to do legal research. Mr. Willoughby lets me do research for him, every once in a while.'

'I can use all the help I can get,' Peter said.

Mancini frowned. 'When would you fit it in, honey? You're pretty busy at work.'

'I could do the research after work or on the weekend. Please, Steve. I want to do something more to help Gary than make coffee.'

'Well . . . I guess if it's okay with Pete . . .'

Donna leaned over and kissed her husband on the cheek. Then, she stood up.

'I'll let you two get back to work while I clean up. Holler if you need anything. And, Peter, let me know what you want me to do.'

Donna almost skipped out of the room. There was a big smile on her face.

'You did okay, Steve. Donna's terrific.'

'Why thanks,' Mancini answered with a self-satisfied smile. 'One thing, though. Don't count on Donna for much help. She's a good legal secretary, but legal research . . . ?' Mancini flashed Peter a patronizing smile. 'Still, if you can find a make-work project for her, she'll be happy as a clam.'

'She seems pretty sharp to me,' Peter said, surprised to hear his friend put down his wife. 'Let's see what she can do.'

'Sure,' Mancini said. He took a sip of coffee. 'Let's get back to the confession. We should make a list of possible attacks on it. I noticed that Don Bosco observed a lot of the questioning. Why don't I talk to him and see what he has to say about it.'

'Good idea.'

'I'll do it first thing in the morning.'

'I'm going to need a good investigator. Can you suggest someone?'

'There aren't many in this area. Ralph Cotton is pretty good. He does some work for the Sissler firm. And Mike Compton does some investigation.'

Mancini thought for a moment. 'You know, there's a guy I've used, Barney Pullen. He works as a mechanic at his brother's garage, but he used to be a cop. You might check to see if he's available.'

Peter jotted down the names Steve had given him. Then, he said, 'There are a few other things we have to go over. Becky included a police report about the peeping incident. Another report mentions some pornographic magazines that were found in the closet in Gary's bedroom. I think Becky is going to try and have the porno stuff and evidence of the peeping incident admitted. What can we do about that?'

'We have to file a motion to keep that out. The jurors are going to believe Gary's a pervert if they hear it.'

'I agree. Why don't I concentrate on this issue.'

'Okay.'

'There's something else,' Peter said.

Mancini noticed a change in Peter's voice. Whatever this new thing was, it had Peter worried.

'What's the problem?'

Peter handed Mancini a stack of police reports.

'I'm hoping these reports are in here by mistake. If they're not, Gary may be in big trouble.'

Mancini skimmed the first report. His features clouded.

'Did Becky mention anything about this?'

'No.'

Mancini laid the stack of reports on his desk.

'She can't think Gary was also involved in these cases.'

'She must. Why would she give me police reports about the murders of two other women if she didn't think Gary committed them?'

CHAPTER FOURTEEN

1

The prisoners in the Whitaker jail were allowed an hour a day to exercise in the yard. Gary waited for that hour like a marooned sailor longing for rescue. Inside, the jail was musty gray and the air was heavy. Outside, there was the sun, birds in flight and air sweet with reminders of the way his life used to be. This afternoon, Gary leaned against the chain-link fence and watched several prisoners pumping iron on the far side of the yard. Gary wanted to lift weights, but he was afraid to go near them. Besides, he wasn't feeling so good. The meeting with Peter Hale had left him confused. Peter said he did not have supernatural powers, but he was certain he did. If he didn't have those powers, how did he know so much about the murder? How had he seen Sandra Whiley die?

'Hey, Gary?' a familiar voice said. Gary turned around and saw Kevin Booth. Booth was sweating and he could not stand still. He had been using so many drugs that his system was having trouble adjusting to the deprivations jail imposed. Gary did not notice. All he knew was that he finally had a friend to talk to.

'Hi, Kevin! Are you arrested too?'

'Yeah. I got busted a few days ago.'

'What did you do?' Gary asked with concern.

'I fucked up, big time. Federal stuff.'

Booth's shoulders twitched a little.

'I don't like it here,' Gary confided.

'Why is that?'

'Some of the men pick on me. They say mean things.'

'You've got to learn how to deal with those motherfuckers,' Booth responded with false bravado. He wanted Gary to think he was not afraid of being in jail, but he had barely slept during the short stint he had spent when he was arrested at Whitaker State and last night had been hell. 'If anyone messes with you, you mess them up first or you won't get any respect.'

'My mom says I shouldn't fight,' Gary said nervously.

'Yeah? Well, your mom isn't in jail.'

Just as he said this, Booth noticed Rafael Vargas sitting in the bleachers near the body builders. Not far away, his bodyguard, Carlos Rivera, was completing a set of curls with weights that were the size of car tires. Every time he brought the bar to his chest, his body would swell up like a balloon. Booth felt his bowels loosen and he looked away quickly.

'So, man,' Booth said, moving so Gary's body blocked Vargas's view of him, 'I read about you. You're a fuckin' media star. Front page! Murder! That's heavy.'

'I didn't do anything to that girl,' Gary assured his friend. 'I just seen it.'

'Seen what?'

'My lawyer doesn't want me to talk about the case to anyone.'

An idea suddenly occurred to Booth. He shot a quick look at Vargas. When he turned back to Gary, he was wearing an ingratiating smile.

'Hey, Gary, this is me. We've been buddies since high school. What do you think I'm gonna do, rat you out?'

'Oh no,' Gary said, coloring with embarrassment.

'Your lawyers probably don't want you talking to someone you don't know. Now, that makes sense. But I'm your friend, right?'

'Oh, sure,' Gary agreed.

'So, what gives?'

Gary hesitated. Peter was emphatic about not talking to anyone about his case. He said that some people in jail would tell the D.A. he had confessed to them so they could get a deal on their own case. Then, they would testify against him in court and tell lies. Peter had warned him to look out for those men, but he couldn't have meant Kevin. Peter probably meant he shouldn't talk to strangers, like Mom had always warned him. Kevin Booth wasn't a stranger. He was a friend. So, Gary proceeded to tell him everything about his case.

2

It was late afternoon when Steve Mancini returned to his office. He picked up his message slips at the reception desk and glanced through them as he walked down the hall. One of the messages was from Harold Prescott. Mancini's mouth went dry and the hand holding the message shook. He closed his office door.

As he dialed Whitaker Savings and Loan, he shut his eyes and said a little prayer.

The United States Olympic ski team trained at Mount Bachelor near Bend, Oregon. Three years ago, the state of Oregon had launched a campaign to bring the Olympics to Bend. Shortly after, Mancini had joined a group of investors to form Mountain View, Inc., with the goal of building a ski lodge and condominiums near Bend. Harold Prescott had engineered a construction loan at his bank. The loan was used to start work on the lodge and the first condo units, but the weather, labor problems and escalating costs had eaten up most of the loan and slowed progress on the project. The loan was due soon. Mountain View was trying to get a long-term loan from the bank to pay off the construction loan and complete the first phase of the project. Mancini had invested heavily in the project. If it failed, he would be ruined.

'I'm afraid I have bad news, Steve,' Prescott said as soon as they were connected. 'The committee met this afternoon. It voted against authorizing the loan.'

Mancini felt as if he was going to throw up. He squeezed his eyes shut and fought the nausea.

'Steve?'

'I don't get it,' Mancini managed.

'I argued for it, but there was too much opposition.'

'What's the problem?' Mancini asked desperately. 'We've been dealing with Whitaker Savings and Loan since the project started. Nothing's changed.'

'Steve, I warned you about this potential problem two years ago. The Federal National Mortgage Association would not approve the project. Without their approval we can't sell the loan on the New York market. I tried to persuade the others to take a chance, but it was no go.'

'Fannie Mae wouldn't approve because it's a resort area and we don't have earnest money for fifty percent of the units. That will change as soon as Bend wins the bid for the Winter Olympics.'

'The problem is that there's no assurance Bend will get the games. The rumor we're hearing is that one of the European countries has the edge. The committee was unwilling to take the risk.'

'Harold, I don't know who you've been talking to. Roger Dunn told me his sources say we've got a terrific shot. Once the announcement is made, those condos will sell like hotcakes.'

'That wasn't the only problem. There aren't enough liquid assets in your group. Most of the land is only optioned. The feeling was that there wasn't enough hard equity in the project.'

The rest of the conversation went by in a dull hum. Mancini responded automatically as a sharp throbbing pain filled his head. After a few more minutes, he hung up and stared at the wall. He knew he should call the other partners, but he could not move. All he could think about was his financial ruin.

Mancini told his secretary to hold his calls. Then he took a glass and a half-filled bottle of scotch out of his bottom drawer. He poured a stiff drink, downed it and poured another. The whiskey burned and the numb feeling wore off and was replaced by rage.

It was Shari, his first wife, who had talked him into investing in Mountain View, filling him with tales of the millions they would make. Then, the bitch bailed out, leaving him to face financial destruction. She'd probably known this would happen all along. He could imagine her laughing at him when she read about the collapse of Mountain View. Mancini's stomach knotted and pain ripped through his skull. His hands squeezed

together and the whiskey glass shattered, spraying
scotch and blood onto the carpet.

3

'Donna Harmon is here to see you, Mr. Hale,' Clara
said over the intercom.

'Send her back,' Peter answered, relieved that Clara
had not buzzed him to say that Amos Geary was on the
line. Peter had spent the day in torment as he pondered
his decision to leave Amos Geary. He had come to work
late, timing his arrival to coincide with the start of
court in Cayuse County, and had been out of the office
during every conceivable time that Geary could call.
Clara had given him several messages from his boss,
each longer and more threatening, but Peter had
returned none of them.

'Hi,' Peter said when Donna stuck her head in the
door. She looked excited.

'I think I found some good cases about tricking
people into confessing,' Donna said, thrusting a manila
envelope at Peter.

'Sit down. Let me take a look.'

Peter pulled out copies of the cases and articles
Donna had photocopied for him.

'There's a great sentence in *Miranda v. Arizona*,'
Donna told him, referring to her copy of the famous
United States Supreme Court case that established the
rule that police had to warn suspects about their constitutional rights to remain silent and to have counsel
before questioning them. 'It says that even a voluntary
waiver of your rights is no good if the accused was
threatened, tricked or cajoled into giving the waiver.
And listen to this from a University of Pennsylvania

Law Review article about "Police Trickery in Inducing Confessions."

'The author says that "A form of deception that totally undermines the Fifth and Sixth Amendment protections available to an individual occurs when the police deceive a suspect about whether an interrogation is taking place." That's what Downes did. He made Gary think there was no interrogation. He made him believe he was a detective.'

'You're pretty good,' Peter said with genuine admiration after he skimmed the material. The cases were old and the *Law Review* article had been written in 1979, but they would make it easier for him to zero in on more recent cases.

'Thanks,' Donna answered, blushing from the compliment.

'When did you do this?'

'During lunch.'

'Well, I couldn't have done better in that amount of time. This will really help.'

'You think so?' Donna asked hopefully.

'Definitely.'

Donna's features clouded. 'Have you talked to Gary?' she asked.

'Not since yesterday. He's doing pretty well, under the circumstances. He seems to have accepted the jail.'

'He would. Gary never complains about anything.'

'You really love your brother, don't you?'

'I love him very much. We all do.'

'It must be hard with his being, uh . . . so slow.'

Donna smiled. 'You mean "retarded"?'

Peter flushed. 'I didn't mean . . .'

'No, that's okay. I'm used to it. People always think that a person who's "retarded" is harder to love, but that's not true. When Gary was small, he was so much fun. You know how handsome he is. Well, he was a beautiful little boy. Always running and laughing. It wasn't until he was older that we realized how dreadfully slow he was and how hard it was for him to learn. One day Mom came back from school. It had never been official before. Just something we knew, but never admitted. Mom told us what Gary's teacher had said about a special class with other "slow learners". Then, Mom said that Gary was God's child like everybody else and that was all she was interested in. If Gary needed extra help he would get it, but she was not going to treat Gary differently because of his intelligence. As far as she was concerned, Gary was a kind and moral boy and that was all that mattered.

'I never loved Mom more than I loved her when she said that. It shaped Gary's life. We never made him feel like a freak or demanded less than he could accomplish.'

Donna paused. Her features were set in stone.

'He is a good boy, Peter. A good, simple boy, just like Mom said. He's always been like that. He couldn't do what they're saying.'

Peter wanted to say something to reassure Donna, but he knew that anything he said would sound wrong. Donna took a deep breath and stood up. She was embarrassed by her sudden display of emotion.

'I . . . I'd better go. I have to shop for dinner.'

'Thanks for the cases.'

'I hope they help,' Donna said as she left the office.

Peter closed the door behind Donna and wandered back to his desk, lost in thought. Donna really trusted him, so did Gary. They believed that he would set Gary free. Was their faith misplaced? Peter remembered his phone conversation of the day before with Amos Geary.

His boss had told him bluntly that he was not competent to try an aggravated murder case. Was Steve Mancini mistaken in his belief that Peter had the tools to handle a capital murder? Was Peter fooling himself? What if a death case was too complicated for him at this stage of his career? What did he really know about trying a charge of aggravated murder? It occurred to Peter that he should talk to someone with a little experience in this area in order to get some idea of what he was getting into.

Peter looked up the phone number for the Oregon Criminal Defense Lawyers Association. The secretary at the OCDLA gave him the names of three experienced death penalty attorneys. Peter decided not to call the first two names on the list. They practiced in Portland and he was afraid they would know who he was. Sam Levine was a Eugene attorney and he was in.

'So this is your first death case,' Levine said after Peter explained why he was calling.

'First one.'

'I remember my first. I'd tried about seven, eight murder cases and I thought I was a hotshot.' Levine chuckled. 'I had no idea what I was getting myself into.'

'Why is that?' Peter asked nervously.

'No other case is like a death case. They're unique. The biggest difference is that you have to prepare for two trials from the get-go. The first trial is on guilt and innocence. If your guy is convicted of aggravated murder, there is a whole second trial on what penalty he should receive.

'With your usual case, you don't think about sentencing until your client is convicted. With a capital case, you have to assume he's going to be convicted even if you're personally convinced you're going to win, because the penalty phase starts almost immediately after a conviction in front of the same jury that found your client guilty and you won't have time to prepare for the penalty phase if you wait until the last minute.'

Peter asked question after question and felt more and more insecure with each answer. Levine explained the special jury selection procedure he should request and told Peter that there was an entire body of law peculiar to capital murder cases. After three quarters of an hour, Levine said that he had to meet a client, but he told Peter he would be glad to speak to him again.

'Thanks. I really appreciate the time you've taken.'

'You'll learn that there's a real fraternity among death penalty lawyers. I always call other attorneys for help. You've got to. When you try a driving while suspended, you can afford to fuck up. What are they going to do to your client, give him a weekend in jail? But with a death case, you have to be perfect. If you make one small mistake, the state eats your client.'

4

Donna Harmon's arms were loaded with groceries, so she backed through the front door, then pushed it shut with her foot.

'Steve, I'm home,' she shouted cheerfully, as she deposited her packages on the counter next to the sink. The house was dark. Donna turned on the kitchen light. It was late and Donna assumed Steve would be home by now. She called out his name again as she walked down the hall to the living room. When the lights went on, Donna was startled to see her husband sitting silently by the fireplace.

'Why didn't you answer me?' she asked, still smiling. But the smile faded as her husband looked up at her. Mancini's eyes were bloodshot and his clothing was rumpled. He was holding a drink and it was obvious that it wasn't his first. The hand holding the glass was bandaged.

'What happened to your hand?'

'I cut it.'

'How?' she asked, crossing to him.

'If you were concerned about me, you would have been here when I needed you.'

The anger in Steve's voice made Donna stop.

'I had no idea you were hurt, but I have something that will make you feel better. Veal and spinach pasta with a sauce I read about in *Gourmet* magazine.'

'Do you know what time it is?'

'I lost track of time. I was meeting with Peter about some research I did in Gary's case. I'm sorry if I'm late.'

'I'm sorry,' Mancini mimicked. 'Is that supposed to make everything better? I bust my ass all day for you and all I ask is that you have my dinner ready when I get home.'

Mancini stood up slowly and walked over to Donna. He was speaking in a monotone. The muscles in his neck stood out and his face was flushed. For the first time since she'd known him, Donna was frightened of her husband. Mancini stopped in front of her. She could smell the thick odor of alcohol when he spoke.

'Now, let's get one thing straight here. You are not a lawyer and I don't expect you to pretend to be one. You're a goddamned secretary and my wife. You work from eight to five, then you get your ass home. Is that clear?'

Donna was so hurt it was hard for her to speak. Tears welled up.

'I . . . I said I'm sorry. I appreciate how hard you work . . .'

Mancini stared at his wife with what looked, unbelievably to her, like contempt.

'I would like a little less appreciation,' Steve said between clenched teeth, 'and some food. Do you think you can manage that?'

'You . . . You're not being fair,' Donna stuttered. 'I was trying to help Gary. I . . . I know I'm not as smart as you, but I can do research. I . . . I can be useful.'

'What did I just say, you cunt?' Mancini shouted.

The first blow was backhand and rattled her teeth. The second was openhanded and sent her stumbling backward. Donna was in shock. She gaped at her husband, unable to accept what was happening even though she could see Steve's fist moving toward her. The blow struck her in the solar plexus, driving all the air from her. Donna sank to her knees, then crumpled onto her side, flailing for oxygen. Mancini kicked her in the ribs and watched her writhe on the floor.

Mouth open, Donna sucked in air. She could not breathe and she thought she would die. Nothing but air mattered. Her lungs filled and a sob escaped from her. As her breath returned, she was gripped by terror. Donna rolled on her side and saw her husband put on his jacket. By the time she could speak, he was gone.

Had Steve really hit her? It seemed incredible, even though she knew it was true. Donna curled up on the floor and tried to piece together what had happened from the moment she opened the front door. What had she done to deserve a beating? She was late, but that was because she was helping Gary and Peter. She was sorry she was late. She was sorry dinner wasn't ready.

Sorry, sorry, sorry. But did she deserve to be beaten because she was late with Steve's dinner? There must be something else, but what could she have done that was so awful that it had driven her husband to hit her? Donna asked that question over and over as she lay sobbing on the living room floor.

CHAPTER FIFTEEN

1

When Donna awoke, it was to the scent of roses. The pungent smell confused her, because there hadn't been any roses in her bedroom when she had finally passed out from exhaustion, alone, in the early hours of the morning. Donna sat up to find every inch of the bed, the floor and the furniture covered by roses of every color and her husband sitting in a corner of the room watching her. Memories of the night before flooded in. Donna shrank back against the headboard.

Steve was unshaven. His clothes appeared to have been slept in. There was no anger in him. Only contrition. He walked over to Donna and knelt by the side of the bed on a carpet of red and yellow roses. His head hung down.

'I have no excuse for what I did to you. All I can do is explain why it happened and pray for your forgiveness.'

The rose fragrance was overpowering in the closed room. The memory of her husband looming above her as his blows rained on her body was vivid and frightening. But Steve seemed so chastened that Donna let him try to explain his savage attack.

'I'd been drinking. I started in the afternoon and never stopped.' Mancini paused and took a deep breath before continuing. 'The bank turned down the Mountain View loan.' There were tears in Steve's eyes, but Donna was still too frightened of him to move. 'I didn't know what to do,' he sobbed, and Donna's heart began to break. 'We could be ruined. I sank everything I had into that project.'

Her husband raised his eyes to hers. He looked so sad.

'Can you ever forgive me? I was so full of anger and so afraid, but I should never have taken it out on you. Please, Donna, I don't want to lose you.'

'Where . . . where have you been?' Donna asked, as she tried to sort out her jumbled thoughts and emotions.

'I drove around for hours thinking about what I'd done. When I was too tired to drive anymore I pulled into the first motel I saw, but I couldn't sleep. I felt so bad about . . . about hurting you. God, how could I have hit you?'

Mancini's face crumpled. Kneeling by the bed, his head down, framed in the multihued bouquets of roses, Steve looked like a little boy. Donna reached out and touched him on the cheek. He took her hand and pressed his lips to the palm, then pressed it against his cheek again.

'I'm sorry about the loan,' Donna said, 'but we'll pull through. You have your practice and your brains and you have me.'

Steve looked at Donna with the rapt glow of a supplicant whose prayers have been answered. Then, he squeezed her hand and wiped away the tears that had clouded his vision.

'Thank you, Donna. I should have known you'd

stand by me. But I was so depressed. I wanted Mountain View to succeed so much.'

'I love you, Steve. I don't need Mountain View to be happy.'

'You don't understand. I want to do things for you that I can't do now. I wanted us to be important, not just in Whitaker, but everywhere. If Mountain View is successful, we'll be rich. But now . . .' Mancini shook his head slowly. 'I don't think we can make it. I'm tapped out and I can't think of any place to turn for money, now that the bank's turned us down.'

'Maybe . . .' Donna started. Mancini looked up at her. 'I could talk to my father . . .'

'Oh no, Donna, I couldn't ask you to do that.'

'How much money do you need?'

'I'd have to talk to my partners,' Mancini answered excitedly. 'If we could buy some of the property instead of having it on option, we might get Whitaker Savings to rethink the loan.'

Mancini stood up and sat next to Donna on the bed. They fell into each other's arms and Steve hugged her to his chest.

'I don't deserve you, Donna. What I did can't be excused. I must have been out of my mind.'

'Just hold me,' Donna said, not wanting to think about the horror of the past evening.

'I will. I'll hold you forever. And I swear to you that I will never, ever hurt you again.'

2

'I don't think this is important,' Eric Polk told Dennis Downes, 'but I figured, better safe than sorry, so I had Wilma come down.'

Eric was also on the Whitaker police force, but he was several years older than Downes and was not working on the Harmon case.

'How you doin', Wilma,' Downes said, smiling at Eric's wife.

'Just fine. How are Jill and Todd?'

'Damn kid of mine runs me ragged. He's only ten and he's almost as big as me.'

'I heard he's tearing up Little League,' Eric said.

'Don't get me started on Todd or I'll chew off your ear. So, what do you have for me, Wilma?'

Wilma Polk was a heavy-set woman in her mid-fifties with curly gray hair and a round, pleasant face, who was not used to being the center of attention.

'It's probably nothing. I'd even forgotten about it until Eric said something about Donna Harmon's wedding and, well, it just popped into my head.'

'Go ahead, Wilma,' her husband said.

'Mabel Dawes and I were over by the food table at Donna Harmon's wedding reception. We were talking about the murder because Eric had been at the scene that morning. Gary was nearby and he must have overheard us. He came over and started talking about the murder, too.'

'What did he say?' Downes asked.

'I've tried to remember exactly, but it's been a while, and I wasn't really interested at the time.'

'Just give me the gist, if you can't remember the exact words.'

'He didn't get to say much, because Eric came up and interrupted us.'

'We were due at Mary's at two and it was one-thirty, so we had to get moving,' Eric explained. 'It was Kenny's third birthday.'

'So, go ahead,' Downes prodded as he jotted down

some notes about the time of the conversation.

'As I remember, I was saying something about Eric being at the crime scene. I believe I had just explained about the horrible wounds when Gary walked over. He said he had seen the girl at the Stallion, the night before. I was about to ask him some more about the girl when Eric reminded me of the time.'

'How did Gary seem? Was he nervous, excited?'

'He didn't seem nervous. Maybe a little excited, but we all were. The murder is very frightening.'

'Okay,' Downes said, smiling at Wilma as he scribbled some more notes. 'Thanks for dropping by. I'll write a report about the conversation for the D.A.'

Eric Polk escorted his wife out of Downes's office. Downes looked at his watch. It was time for a coffee break. He decided to dictate his report on his interview with Wilma Polk, then see if anyone wanted to go over to Mel's Café for a piece of pie and a cup of coffee. He was finishing the dictation when the phone rang.

'Dennis, are you busy?' Becky O'Shay asked.

'I was going out for a cup of coffee. Why?'

'Put the coffee on hold. I just received a call from the jail. One of the prisoners claims Gary Harmon confessed to him. I want you to come along with me. If this pans out, I'll buy the coffee and treat you to lunch.'

3

'The last time you escaped justice by a nose, Mr. Booth,' Becky O'Shay said with a smirk, 'but your luck seems to have run out.'

Booth flushed with anger and looked at the floor,

afraid to let O'Shay see the hatred in his eyes. He could not stand being humiliated by a woman, but he was in no position to do anything about it.

'I understand you have something for us.'

'Yeah, I got something. What I want to know is what I get in return.'

'What do you want?'

Booth licked his lips. His right foot could not stop tapping and Booth could not sit still. Withdrawal, O'Shay thought immediately. She bet every nerve in Booth's body felt like a live wire. When he looked up, O'Shay read stark terror on Booth's face.

'I want witness protection. I want to go somewhere Rafael Vargas and Chris Mammon can't get me.'

'That's asking a lot. Your beef's federal. I don't know if they'll go along, even if I wanted to.'

'Hey,' Booth pleaded, 'I'm small potatoes. I'm nothing. The feds don't want me. I'm an undersize catch. But I can deliver Mammon or Vargas and I can ice Gary Harmon.'

'Tell me about Harmon.'

Booth shook his head vigorously from side to side.

'Uh uh. What do you take me for? I'm not giving up anything until I know I'm going to be protected.'

O'Shay turned to Dennis Downes. 'Can we transfer Mr. Booth to the jail in Stark?'

'We've done that before. Sheriff Tyler will keep you warm and comfy, Kevin. They got a nice security wing. Real modern.'

'I don't care where I go, as long as it's away from anyone connected with Rafael Vargas.'

'I'll check to see if any of his people are incarcerated in Stark. If there's a problem, I've got another couple ideas.'

'So, Mr. Booth?' O'Shay asked.

'What about my deal? If I talk, what do I get?'

'Let me explain something to you. If we make a deal before you testify it will affect the value of your evidence. The first thing Peter Hale will ask you on cross-examination is what reward you're getting for your testimony. If you can say that you are testifying as a service to humanity, it will make you much more believable.'

'You want me to testify for nothing?'

'I didn't say that, did I?'

'No, but . . .'

'Do you think I'll let you down if you come through for me?'

Booth licked his lips. O'Shay made him very nervous and she was so sexy it was distracting.

'How do I know you won't screw me? What if I testify and you lose anyway? I need a guarantee.'

'You need help, Mr. Booth, and the only person in the galaxy who can help you is sitting in front of you in this room. Do you want my help?'

'Yeah. That's why I'm here.'

'Good. Then we'll do things my way or not at all. If you ask for anything in return for your testimony, I'll walk out of here. If you want to be a good citizen and help me out, I'll be very receptive to any pleas for assistance you might make after Harmon's trial.'

'Man, I don't know. I don't like this.'

'You don't have to like it, Mr. Booth. You only have to accept the fact that you have no choice but to do as I say. Right now, I would appreciate hearing a summary of what you can tell me about Harmon.'

Booth didn't trust O'Shay, but he realized he had no choice.

'Gary confessed to me. He told me he done it.'

'Why would he do that?'

'I've known Gary since high school. He thinks I'm his friend. He's so fuckin' dumb, it was easy. At first, he denied doin' it, but I told him it took balls to commit murder. I built him up. Gary's such a retard, he never figured out what I was doin'. Soon, I had him bragging about how good it felt to snuff Whiley.'

'That's certainly interesting, but how do we know you're not making up this whole story? You're facing a long sentence in a federal prison, you have some very scary people mad at you. That's a lot of motivation to lie.'

Booth looked wild-eyed. He felt his only chance at safety and freedom slipping away.

'I ain't lying. This is the truth. He spilled his guts to me.'

'Maybe he did, but I only have your word for that. Unless you can give me something concrete, something that proves Harmon killed Sandra Whiley, your testimony will be useless.'

Booth put his hands to his head. He closed his eyes and shifted on his seat.

'Let me think,' he begged.

O'Shay felt disgust for Booth, but she did not let it show. If Harmon really had confessed to Booth, Booth's testimony would be very important to her case. Now that the first flush of excitement had faded, she realized that her case was not as strong as she first imagined. Although she would argue that Harmon's statements to Downes contained so much detail that he had to be the killer, Harmon had not really confessed to killing Whiley. And there was the problem of the blood, or lack of it. Police technicians had not found any of Whiley's blood on Harmon's clothes or in his house. And the murder weapon was still missing.

Suddenly, Booth's face lit up. 'I got it,' he said. 'I got something solid. Something that will prove I'm not lying.'

4

Peter watched Clara Schoen leave Amos Geary's office from the coffee shop across the street. Geary had left half an hour before. Peter gave it fifteen minutes more to be certain Clara would not return before scurrying across to the law office.

Peter felt a little bit like a thief, though he had convinced himself that there was nothing wrong with clearing out his own belongings from his own office after everyone was gone. He wasn't taking anything that wasn't his and coming in when Geary wasn't there would prevent a nasty scene. Everyone was better off this way.

Peter had brought an empty liquor carton with him. He set it on the desk and was filling it with law books and personal items when he looked up to find Amos Geary watching him from the doorway.

'He . . . hello, Mr. Geary,' Peter said with an uneasy smile.

Geary shook his head slowly.

'You are some piece of work.' Geary's voice was filled more with sadness than anger. 'How are you going to defend a man's life when you don't even have the guts to leave my office in broad daylight?'

'I . . . Uh, I was, uh, going to drop in tomorrow to, uh, thank you for . . .' Peter started, but Geary cut him off with a sound that was half laugh, half bark.

'You really don't have any pride, do you? It's beyond

me how a man like your father could sire someone as
worthless as you.'

Peter flushed, but he was too embarrassed at being
caught to reply.

'Where are you sneaking off to?' Geary asked.

'I'm not sneaking anywhere. These are my things,'
Peter said, tilting the carton to show Geary the
contents. Geary kept his eyes on Peter's face and didn't
look down. Peter was able to keep eye contact for only a
moment before he lost his nerve.

'I'm moving to Steve Mancini's offices,' he answered.
His voice quivered a little.

Geary nodded slowly. 'You and Mancini should get
along just fine.'

Peter straightened up. He realized that he had
packed all his things and there was no more need to
stay, but Geary was blocking the doorway.

'I, uh, I really do appreciate the chance you gave me.
I learned a lot these past weeks,' Peter said, hoping that
he sounded suitably grateful.

'You didn't learn a thing, Peter. You're the same
sorry son of a bitch you were when you cheated that
poor woman in Portland. Is it going to take the death of
Gary Harmon to make you see how truly pathetic you
are?'

It suddenly occurred to Peter that Geary might be
angry enough to try to talk Jesse Harmon into firing
him.

'What are you going to do?' he asked nervously.

Geary made no effort to hide his contempt.

'Don't worry. I won't interfere with your precious
case. You've been admitted to practice law in this state,
so you're entitled to try any type of case you want to,
and the Constitution gives Gary Harmon the right to
be represented by the counsel of his choice, no matter

how sorry a son of a bitch that lawyer may be. But I will leave you with a thought. Gary Harmon is a living, breathing human being. If you continue with this farce and he is executed, you will be as much a murderer as the bastard who killed that poor girl in the park.'

PART
FIVE

DEATH
CASE

CHAPTER SIXTEEN

1

There were no fancy decorations in the Whitaker County Circuit Court. The county could not afford them and the penny-conscious rural constituents did not want them. They wanted justice, fast and without frills. So, the benches for the spectators were hard, the judge's dais was unadorned and the only dashes of color were in the flags of Oregon and the United States that flanked Circuit Court Judge Harry Kuffel's high-backed chair.

Judge Kuffel was someone you could easily picture in a bow tie, vest and bowler hat tap dancing across a vaudeville stage. He was five six with a dancer's slender, but compact, build. He wore his gray hair slicked down and his mustache was neatly trimmed. Kuffel's suits were expensive and conservative, but the judge had a ready smile and tried to keep the atmosphere in his courtroom from being overly stuffy.

'The state calls Don Bosco, Your Honor,' Becky O'Shay said.

As the psychologist walked to the front of the packed courtroom to take the oath, Judge Kuffel sneaked a look at the clock. It was four-thirty. In one half hour, he would recess for the night. Kuffel looked interested, but was secretly bored. He had decided how he would rule on the defendant's motion to suppress Gary Harmon's statements to Dennis Downes hours ago.

'Will this be your last witness?'

'Yes, Your Honor.'

'Very well.'

Peter had been relieved when Steve Mancini volunteered to handle the pretrial motion. He knew very little about the law of confessions and was only too glad to let Mancini do the research, write the brief and examine the witnesses.

Peter barely listened while Bosco explained his academic and professional credentials and gave the court a brief outline of his duties as Director of Mental Health for the county. This testimony was strictly for the record, since Bosco was well known to the court.

Peter glanced at Gary. Poor kid. Peter had to admire him. He really tried. Mancini had told Gary to take notes when witnesses were testifying. They had to train Gary now, so he would know how to fake it when there was a jury in the room. Peter and Steve agreed that subjecting Gary to cross-examination would lead to disaster. Since he would probably not take the stand, it was important to create the illusion that Gary was involved in his defense.

Gary had taken the note writing to heart and scribbled constantly, even though he understood little of what he heard. Peter had glanced at Gary's notes and they were gibberish. Still, he looked great writing.

Very intense. Thank God for his good looks.

'Mr. Bosco,' O'Shay asked, 'were you summoned to the Whitaker police station on the evening of Sandra Whiley's murder?'

'I was.'

'Do you remember when you arrived?'

'Not exactly, but I'm certain it was sometime between nine and ten.'

'Where did you go when you arrived at the station?'

'Into a small room next to the room where Mr. Harmon was being questioned.'

'Could you see and hear the defendant?'

'Yes. There was a two-way mirror and an intercom that let me hear what was said.'

'Was Mr. Harmon's interrogation under way when you arrived?'

'Yes.'

'How much of it did you hear?'

'Several hours. Maybe five. The interrogation went on for some time.'

'Did Sergeant Downes make any promises in exchange for Mr. Harmon's cooperation?'

'No.'

'Did you ever hear Sergeant Downes threaten the defendant?'

'No.'

'Did it sound like Mr. Harmon was being coerced into talking to Sergeant Downes?'

Bosco hesitated before answering and looked at Steve Mancini. Peter caught the look, but Mancini did not react at all.

'No,' Bosco said.

Becky O'Shay checked her notes. Then, she smiled at the witness.

'No further questions.'

'Mr. Mancini?' Judge Kuffel asked.

'No questions.'

Bosco frowned. He tilted his head slightly, as if he was attempting to signal Mancini, but Steve was absorbed in his notes. Bosco stood slowly, as if trying to give Mancini extra time to act. Mancini saw Bosco staring at him and smiled. Bosco's brow knitted, but he walked out of the courtroom. Peter noticed the psychologist's confusion and leaned over to Steve.

'Bosco hesitated when Becky asked whether Gary seemed to be coerced. I think he wanted to say something. Why didn't you follow up?'

'I already interviewed Bosco. He can't help us,' Mancini whispered.

'Do you have any rebuttal witnesses, Mr. Mancini?' Judge Kuffel asked.

'No, sir.'

'Then, we'll recess for the day and I'll hear argument in the morning.'

Judge Kuffel left the bench quickly and the reporters surged forward. Peter walked over to them, but Becky O'Shay intercepted him.

'Drop by my office before you leave the courthouse,' she said.

Steve Mancini talked to Gary while the guards handcuffed him. Mancini patted Gary on the shoulder and said something that made Gary smile. While Peter and Becky talked to the reporters, Mancini gathered up his notes and law books.

'Becky wants to see us,' Peter told Steve when he returned to the table.

'What for?'

Peter shrugged. The two attorneys hefted their briefcases and books and headed upstairs.

'What's up?' Peter asked the deputy D.A. when they were all in her office. O'Shay handed Peter copies of a police report.

'We received this information last week, but we've been checking it out. Now that I've decided to use this witness, I'm obligated to give you his statement.'

The two defense lawyers read the police report. When Mancini finished it, he shook his head and chuckled.

'You're not serious about using Kevin as a witness, are you?'

'Dead serious,' Becky answered.

'Come on. You can't believe a thing Kevin says. You know he's just trying to weasel out of this federal drug bust.'

'I'm sure that's what you'll argue to the jury.'

'We've got a problem,' Steve Mancini told Peter as soon as they were outside the courthouse. 'I've got to get off Gary's case.'

'Why?'

'I've got a conflict of interest. I can't represent a client if another client is going to be a key witness against him.'

'What if I cross-examine Booth?'

Mancini shook his head. 'If I know something about Booth that will help Gary and I don't tell you, I'm violating my duty to Gary. But if I use confidential information I obtained from Booth to help Gary, I'm violating my duty to Booth. Even staying on as co-counsel presents the appearance of impropriety. I have no choice. I've got to get off the case.'

'Jesus, Steve. How am I supposed to try this case alone?'

'Hey, I'm sympathetic. I feel bad about talking you

into taking the case. If you don't think you can do it, you can resign.'

But Peter knew that resigning was not an option. He had cut himself off from his father and quit his job. If he tried to get a position anywhere, he would receive references from Hale, Greaves and Amos Geary that would make Saddam Hussein look like a better job candidate. Without the Harmons' retainer he would be dead broke. A victory for Gary Harmon was his only way out of the hole he'd dug for himself.

'No, I can't let Gary down,' Peter said.

Mancini clapped Peter on the back. 'That's what I wanted to hear. Besides, I have confidence in you. You're a quick study, Peter. This criminal stuff is a cinch. This might even work out better for you in the long run. When you win, you won't have to share the credit.'

2

The Ponderosa was on the opposite side of Whitaker from the Stallion. It catered to workingmen and solitary drinkers. Its juke box played country and the waitresses were older women who had lost a few rounds to life. Most of the time it was a place where a man could get totally sloshed in peace and quiet. Occasionally, it was the scene of violent barroom brawls.

Barney Pullen fit right in with the Ponderosa regulars. He had a beer gut, a bushy black beard and a don't-fuck-with-me attitude he had picked up in the Marines. He liked to fish, hunt and drink beer. NFL football was as intellectual as he got. After the Marines, Pullen worked as a cop in Eugene, Oregon, until an incident with a suspect occurred. Pullen wasn't exactly fired, but he didn't exactly quit the force, either. The whole affair was left murky and Pullen moved to Whitaker, where he worked in his brother's body shop.

One day, Pullen was assigned the job of figuring out what caused the knocking sound that Steve Mancini heard whenever his Cadillac went over fifty. In between discussions of car engines and pro football, Pullen mentioned his police background. Mancini needed an investigator with a knowledge of cars for a personal injury case and Pullen agreed to work on the case. He had done spot investigation for Mancini ever since and Peter had hired him for the Harmon case on Mancini's recommendation when the other investigators Mancini had mentioned turned out to be unavailable.

Jake Cataldo was tending bar when Pullen stepped in out of the late afternoon sun. Pullen blinked a few times and waited for his eyes to adjust to the dark.

'Hi, Jake,' Pullen said, as he hoisted himself onto a bar stool next to a couple of regulars.

Cataldo was a big man with short, curly black hair and the pale complexion of a someone who is indoors during the day.

'Hi, Barney. What can I do you for?'

Pullen ordered a beer. Cataldo turned to get it for him.

'What are you doin' with yourself lately?' the bartender asked, when he placed the glass of beer in front of Pullen.

'You been reading about the girl who was murdered in the park?'

Cataldo nodded.

'I'm still working at the garage and I'm doing a little

investigating for the guy who's trying the case.'

'No shit? You know, that Harmon kid was in here the night that girl was killed. Sat right here at the bar. I served him myself.'

'Is Harmon a regular?'

'Not really. I mean, he's stopped in once or twice.'

'Then why do you remember him?'

'He was picked up the next day for the murder. It was on the news. His picture was in the paper.'

'You don't happen to remember what time he came in, do you?'

'Actually, I do. It was around eleven fifty-five.'

'How do you remember that?'

'There was a Mariners game on and the damn thing was still going after seventeen innings. Then, Griffey hits this shot and the game's over. I glanced at my watch. It was eleven fifty-three, eleven fifty-four. Something like that, but not exactly midnight. That's when the Harmon kid sat down and asked for coffee. I didn't hear him, because I turned away to switch the channel. I told him to hang on. I remember that clear as day.'

'How'd he look?'

'A little rocky.' Cataldo shrugged. 'He was quiet. He had the coffee and something to eat. Then, he had a few drinks. When he left, he was weaving, but I thought he'd make it home okay.'

'What did he eat?'

'Some biscuits and gravy.'

'Biscuits and gravy?' Pullen repeated, while thinking that this wouldn't be his dish of choice if he'd just slaughtered a woman. 'Did you notice anything unusual about Harmon's clothes?'

The bartender considered the question for a moment, then shook his head.

'No blood?' Pullen asked.

Cataldo thought about that. 'You see how the lighting is in here. There coulda been something I didn't see. But I didn't notice blood.'

CHAPTER SEVENTEEN

1

Carmen Polinsky was a forty-six-year-old mother of two who was married to an accountant. For twenty years, she had been a housewife. Before that she worked in a bookstore. Nothing in her past had prepared her for a job interview for the position of assassin for the state of Oregon. This job interview was technically called 'voir dire' and it denoted the process by which a jury was selected in Gary Harmon's trial.

Judge Kuffel had denied the motion to suppress Gary's statements, but he had granted Peter's motion for individual voir dire because of the unusual nature of a death case. None of the other jurors were in the courtroom to witness Carmen Polinsky's distress when Becky O'Shay asked her if she had an attitude concerning the death penalty that would make it impossible for her to vote for a death sentence if Gary Harmon was convicted of aggravated murder. Whenever anyone mentioned the death penalty, Mrs. Polinsky gripped her purse so tightly that her knuckles turned white. It was obvious that she would rather be in Zaire during an Ebola outbreak than in this courtroom in Whitaker. It was equally obvious that Mrs. Polinsky would never, ever condemn anyone to death.

'To tell the truth . . .' Mrs. Polinsky started.

O'Shay leaned forward, praying that Polinsky would confess her inability to kill for the state. Normally, O'Shay would have gotten rid of her with a peremptory challenge, which can be used to excuse a juror without stating a reason, but it was near the end of the second week of jury selection and the prosecutor had used all of her peremptories. Now, she could get rid of Mrs. Polinsky only by convincing the judge that she could not be fair to the state.

Polinsky shook her head. 'I honestly don't know,' she concluded.

O'Shay went at Mrs. Polinsky from a different angle. Her job was to manipulate the woman into saying that she could never condemn someone to death. If O'Shay succeeded, it would be Peter's job to rehabilitate the woman by convincing her that she could vote to kill Gary Harmon, because that was the only way he would be able to keep her on the jury. The absurdity of the position in which he found himself was not lost on Peter.

Mrs. Polinsky vacillated again. Judge Kuffel glanced at the clock and said, 'It's almost five. I'm going to stop for the day. Mrs. Polinsky, I want you to think about Ms. O'Shay's question. When we reconvene tomorrow morning, I'll expect a decisive answer from you. A "yes" or "no" answer. Understood?'

Mrs. Polinsky sped out of the courtroom.

'I'll see you two in chambers,' the judge commanded as he left the bench. Peter gave a few words of encouragement to Gary as the guards cuffed him and led him away. While he was gathering up his paperwork, Peter noticed Becky in an animated discussion with Dennis Downes at the rear of the courtroom. Downes was nodding his head vigorously in response to something O'Shay had asked and Becky was grinning broadly.

The court reporter was not present when Peter and O'Shay walked into chambers, and Judge Kuffel was puffing on a smelly cigar in violation of a no-smoking ordinance he stubbornly chose to ignore, so Peter knew the conference was off the record.

'For Christ's sake, Peter,' the judge said, 'let that woman off the jury.'

'It's up to Becky to lay a foundation if she wants to kick her off,' Peter answered stubbornly, dropping onto an overstuffed couch that stretched along a wall covered with diplomas, certificates of appreciation from community organizations and pictures of Kuffel holding up fish of various sizes.

'Be reasonable, Peter,' O'Shay said. 'Even if she gets on, she won't last a day. She's already a wreck and she hasn't even seen the autopsy pictures.'

'You might be right,' Peter answered with a condescending smile, 'but there's still no legal basis for excusing her. Being nervous doesn't do it. Everyone on that jury is going to be nervous.'

Judge Kuffel shook his head in disgust. Hale was right to fight O'Shay on this. Gary Harmon would be better off with Polinsky on the jury and O'Shay would have to give him a legal basis for kicking her off or the reluctant housewife would become one of Gary Harmon's judges.

'I have something I wanted to mention,' O'Shay said. 'Several weeks ago, we interviewed an inmate at the jail who claimed that the defendant confessed to him.'

'Did you notify the defense?' the judge asked.

'Oh yes. Mr. Booth is awaiting trial on a serious drug charge and has a reason to try to ingratiate himself with our office, so I asked him for some corroboration for his story. We just got it.'

O'Shay handed Peter and the judge a copy of a document.

'What the hell is this?' Peter asked, as soon as he scanned it.

'It's a report from the FBI laboratory in Washington, D.C. We sent them a hatchet we found in a storm drain on the Whitaker campus. It was right where Mr. Harmon told Kevin Booth he threw it after he hacked Sandra Whiley to death. The handle was wiped clean of fingerprints, but Sandra Whiley's blood and hair are on the blade.'

When Peter found his voice, he said, 'I move to have this evidence suppressed. This is a clear violation of the discovery statutes. This should have been revealed to the defense as soon as it was discovered so we could have our own experts test the blood and hair.'

O'Shay smiled sweetly at Peter. 'I don't think we violated the discovery statutes. They only require the prosecution to reveal the existence of evidence we intend to introduce at trial. I had no intention of introducing this hatchet until I was certain it had some connection with this case and I did not become convinced until I read the FBI report. After all, Peter, Kevin Booth is a criminal. We weren't sure he was telling the truth about your client's confession. Until now, that is.'

2

'Move it, Booth,' the guard commanded as Kevin Booth lathered up for the second time. 'This ain't a resort.'

Booth thought of some choice retorts, but he didn't dare make them to the six-five, two-hundred-and-fifty-pound corrections officer who was lounging just outside the bars next to the shower. Inmates in the security block of the jail in Stark were allowed only two showers a week and these were precious moments for Booth.

A minute later, the guard cut off Booth's hot water and he screamed. The guard doubled over laughing and Booth choked back a 'motherfucker' that surely would have led to some diabolical punishment.

'I warned you to move your ass. Now, finish up. We got other guests in this hotel.'

Booth dodged in and out of the freezing water until all the soap was off. His clean clothes were in his cell at the other end of the security tank. He wrapped as much of his shivering body as he could in a towel that barely covered his private parts and huddled his shoulders as he walked past the fags, psychos and snitches who shared the security block with him.

Booth hated his new situation. At least he had human beings to talk to in Whitaker. The security block was for prisoners who could not be allowed to live in the normal jail population: escape risks, homosexuals, ultraviolent prisoners and informants. Booth hated queers, was scared to death of psychos and considered himself different from the other snitches, but he was going to have to stay in this madhouse if he expected to live long enough to trade Gary Harmon's freedom for his own.

Booth's cell was long and narrow and contained a sink, a flush toilet and two bunks, but he was the sole occupant. As soon as the guard saw that his prisoner was inside, he closed the moving bars electronically. The guard never entered the security block unless there was an emergency. He patrolled the long corridor on the other side of the bars occasionally, but when it was shower time, he stayed in his chair and used the controls to open and close the bars of each cell as each prisoner's turn to shower arrived.

'How you doin', Kevin?' a voice asked as Booth was getting into his underpants. Booth paused with one leg raised and looked through the bars. The prisoner who had spoken to him was a slender young man with pale skin and a blond crew cut. The only distinguishing mark on his body was a swastika tattoo on his right forearm. Booth noticed the tattoo at the same time he noticed the milk container concealed under the prisoner's bath towel. The young man kept his easy smile as he tossed the contents of the milk container over Booth's naked body. Lighter fluid, Booth thought as a lighted match followed the liquid through the bars and transformed him into a human torch.

3

Peter ran as fast as he could along the jogging trails in Wishing Well Park, pushing himself to exhaustion in the hope that his brain would be too busy working on his oxygen supply to concern itself with Gary Harmon. But Peter's brain would not cooperate and images of blood-encrusted hatchets dominated his thoughts.

The feds used a system for determining sentences

that allowed judges almost no discretion. If he was convicted under the Federal Sentencing Guidelines, Kevin Booth would do a lot of federal time without the possibility of parole. There was, however, a motion for reduction of sentence that the prosecutor could make if a defendant turned in someone. In cases like Booth's, this system created tremendous pressure to lie about the criminal involvement of an innocent person.

What troubled Peter was the possibility that Gary might be guilty. Gary would not state unequivocally that he did not kill Sandra Whiley. He claimed he drank so much that he did not have a clear memory for the hour or so when the murder was probably committed. Did he kill Whiley and repress the memory or was he simply lying? Peter could not believe Gary was capable of sustaining a lie for this long, but Peter had read about repressed memory. He had a hard time buying into the idea that someone could witness a murder or be sexually abused and have no memory of the event, but he knew it happened. Maybe a person with Gary's IQ was more susceptible to that kind of thing. If he had not killed Whiley, how was he able to tell Dennis Downes that the killer used a hatchet and how was he able to tell Kevin Booth where the murder weapon could be found?

There was no endorphin rush during his run and Peter reached his house depressed and exhausted. He had barely caught his breath when the phone rang.

'Mr. Hale?' a shaky voice asked.

'Gary? You sound upset. Has something happened? Why are you calling?'

'I said I had to talk to you. I said I wanted to call my lawyer.'

'That's good, Gary. You did just what I told you to

do, if you were in trouble. Are you in trouble?'

'They say I burned up Kevin. I didn't burn him. Please tell them I didn't burn him.'

'Calm down, Gary. Who says you burned someone?'

'That lady lawyer and Sergeant Downes,' Gary gulped in a voice close to tears.

'Are Sergeant Downes and Becky O'Shay with you?'

'Yeah.'

'Put Ms. O'Shay on the phone.'

There was dead air for a moment. Peter heard Gary saying something he could not make out. As soon as O'Shay took the phone, Peter said, 'What's going on? Why are you questioning Gary?'

'Kevin Booth was set on fire in his cell in the Stark jail,' O'Shay answered, her rage barely under control. 'Unfortunately for your client, there was a fuck-up. Booth's still alive.'

'You don't think Gary was involved, do you?' Peter asked incredulously. 'He's not bright enough to plan something like that.'

'We'll soon find out.'

'How will you do that?'

'Sergeant Downes and I are going to question Gary.'

'I can't let you do that. You two shouldn't be anywhere near Gary without my permission.'

'This is a totally different crime, Peter. You don't represent Gary on this.'

'The hell I don't,' Peter said, losing his patience. 'Now, listen, Becky. I want you and Downes out of there.'

'Don't tell me what to do,' Becky answered angrily.

Peter did not want to upset O'Shay. He still had hopes of going out with her. But protecting Gary was crucial.

'Damn it, Becky. I'm Gary's lawyer. I *can* tell you what to do in this case.'

'Why are you afraid to let Gary talk to us?'

'Are you nuts? You're prosecuting him. Downes arrested him. I don't want either of you within a mile of him. Now, get Gary back to his cell immediately and don't you dare ask him any questions. If I find you have, I'll move for a mistrial. You know what you're doing isn't ethical.'

'I don't think you're in any position to discuss ethics, Hale.'

'What . . . what do you mean?'

'Do you think I believed for one moment that story about quitting Hale, Greaves to get out of the rat race? I called a few friends in Portland. They knew all about the way you lied to Judge Pruitt and lost that case for that crippled woman. You're pretty famous.'

Peter felt sick. 'Look, Becky . . .' he started, but O'Shay had already hung up.

4

Donna's doorbell rang at nine-thirty. She wondered who was calling so late. She smiled when she found Peter on her doorstep, but the smile faded as soon as she saw the expression on his face. Peter usually looked as if he had just stepped out of the pages of a menswear catalog, but tonight his suit was rumpled, his tie was askew and his hair was a mess.

'What's wrong?' she asked as she stepped aside to let him in.

'Everything. Where's Steve?'

'He's staying overnight in Salem. He has a business meeting there about Mountain View, tomorrow.'

'Damn! That's right. I forgot.'

'Is this about Gary? Has something happened?'

Peter nodded. 'You know the inmate who's going to say Gary confessed?'

'Yes.'

'Another prisoner set him on fire this afternoon.'

'They can't think Gary's involved.'

'Becky and Downes tried to question Gary without me, but he remembered what I told him about demanding a call to his lawyer if any policeman tried to talk to him. I went down to the jail and they backed off. They're grasping at straws on the torching, but something else has come up. That's what I really wanted to talk to Steve about.'

'What happened?'

'They found the murder weapon and they've linked it to Gary.'

'Oh no.'

Donna's hand flew to her mouth. She looked stricken.

'Don't cry,' Peter said when he saw Donna's shoulders start to shake. She tried to control herself, but she couldn't.

'I'm sorry,' she sobbed. 'It's just too much.'

Peter didn't know what to do. He wanted to hold Donna, but he felt awkward. Donna was Steve's wife and this was Steve's house. He settled for handing her a handkerchief and stood red-faced while she dabbed at her eyes and tried to stop crying.

'It just seems like it's one thing after another.' Then she was in Peter's arms, her body trembling as she sobbed into his shoulder. He let her lean against him, but he was afraid to hold her. He could smell Donna's hair and feel her breasts pushing against him. Peter held his breath and ended by giving her a few feeble pats on the back.

'I'm sorry,' Donna managed, suddenly pulling away.

'Everything will be okay,' he replied lamely.

'I've got to get ahold of myself,' Donna answered, as she wiped at her eyes. Then she stopped and took Peter's hand.

'I want you to know I appreciate how hard you're working for Gary. He really trusts you.'

Donna squeezed Peter's hand and held it for a moment before releasing it. Her hand felt warm and her proximity evoked in him a combination of embarrassment and sexual desire. Peter felt himself flush. They both looked down. Donna stepped back.

'Tell Steve what happened,' Peter said. 'I need to see him as soon as he gets back.'

'I'll call him at his motel.'

The Mancinis only lived a short distance from Peter and he had walked over. It had cooled down since his run and the air was pleasant. It took a few blocks to shake off his sexual excitement and refocus on Gary's problem, but every so often Peter's thoughts would drift back to Donna.

CHAPTER EIGHTEEN

1

'What did he say?' Earl Ridgely asked the man in the gray-pinstripe suit.

'What did you expect, Mr. Ridgely?' Frank Ketchell answered. Ketchell, an investigator with the State Department of Justice, was tall and gray-haired with a square jaw and bright blue eyes that wowed the ladies, but his good looks had not done him a bit of good with Elmer Maddox. After spending Saturday morning talking to the man who had set Kevin Booth on fire, Ketchell had driven to Whitaker for this late afternoon meeting.

'Maddox thought the whole thing was a big joke. He kept cracking up when he described the way Booth hopped around and rolled on the floor while he was burning.'

'Jesus,' Becky O'Shay said, shaking her head with disgust.

'The only thing that upset Maddox was that the guard shoved him back in his cell before helping

Booth. They found a shiv when they searched him. I guess he was going to finish off Booth when the guard went into the cell to put out the fire.'

'How did he expect to get away with this?' O'Shay asked in disbelief.

'I don't think it occurred to him. Like he said to me when I offered him a deal, "What are you gonna do if I don't cooperate? Give me more time?" Maddox and a buddy were on a spree for over a year, running around the country knocking off banks and killing people. He's already serving three consecutive life terms in Tennessee, he's got a consecutive federal bank robbery for a job in Idaho, he's facing the death penalty for a robbery-murder in Stark and there are four other states waiting in line to get their hands on him.'

'Why did he do it, then?'

Ketchell shrugged. 'He's got a wife and family in Washington State. I hear he loves his kid. Maybe someone promised to take care of them.'

'Who?'

'I've got no idea. I know you want Gary Harmon to be involved. The feds would love to hear that it was someone in the organization that Rafael Vargas works for. But I've got to tell you that there's no evidence connecting anyone other than Maddox to this right now.'

'Someone smuggled in the lighter fluid and the matches.'

'Oh, yeah. But Maddox could have set Booth on fire for his own amusement or for some real or imagined slight.'

'How did he get the lighter fluid, matches and shiv into the security block? What kind of security do they have in Stark?' O'Shay asked.

'Human security.'

Ridgely sighed. 'I guess finding out who gave Maddox the stuff would help.'

'And we're looking into it. There are only a few guards who could have done it, and a few prisoners, but we haven't cracked anyone yet.'

'How is Booth doing?' Ridgely asked.

Ketchell consulted a small notebook before answering.

'He was flown to the burn center in Portland as soon as possible. I talked to Dr. Leonard Farber, who's treating Booth. Farber says he's in critical condition with burns over thirty-five percent of his body. Seventy-five percent of the burns are full thickness, which means he'll need skin grafts. Additionally, Booth's bedding caught on fire and he suffered minor smoke inhalation injuries.'

'Will he be able to testify?' Becky asked.

'Farber thinks he might be up to it, but not right away. Booth will be operated on about three times in the first three to four days. They use as much of his skin as they can for the grafts and pigskin for the rest. Two weeks later, they'll use more of his skin to replace the pigskin. He can't be moved back to Whitaker for at least four weeks because they're afraid of losing the grafts.'

'Damn,' O'Shay swore angrily. 'I need Booth. He's my key witness.'

'You can always ask for a continuance,' Ridgely suggested.

'I know I can, but I don't want to if there's any chance Booth can testify now. Think of the sympathy he'll evoke in his condition.'

Ridgely was taken aback by O'Shay's callousness, but she did not notice because she was lost in thought.

'Frank,' she said, 'as I understand it, Booth can't be

moved back to Whitaker because they're afraid of endangering the skin grafts.'

'Right.'

'Call Dr. Farber for me and ask him how soon Booth could testify if we held court in Portland.'

2

Peter was at the office on Sunday afternoon when he heard the front door open. He walked into the corridor and saw Steve Mancini checking his messages at the reception desk.

'Am I glad to see you,' Peter said.

For a moment, Mancini looked as if he was not happy to see Peter. Then, his face changed rapidly and he smiled.

'How's the trial going?'

'We've got our jury and Becky's putting on her first witness on Monday.'

'Donna called and told me about Booth.'

'Then you know what's going on. Can we talk?'

Mancini looked at his watch. 'I'm really pressed for time. I haven't even been home yet. I drove right here from Salem.'

'Please, Steve. I'm afraid I'm getting in over my head and I need your advice.'

Mancini clapped Peter on the back and started for his office. 'You have any coffee up?' he asked.

During the next half hour, Peter brought Mancini up to speed on the torching of Kevin Booth and the discovery of the hatchet. When he finished, Mancini said, 'There's no way Gary was involved with setting Booth on fire. He doesn't have the brains to think up a scheme like that. This sounds more like something

Rafael Vargas would do. What did Becky say about that?'

Peter flushed. 'She didn't say much. In fact, she's been really hostile since Booth was attacked.'

'Oh?'

Peter hesitated before speaking again, but he decided it was best for his friend to hear about his real reason for leaving Portland from him. It was bad enough that he had misrepresented his reason for moving to Whitaker. If Steve heard about the Elliot case from someone else, he might decide not to go through with the partnership.

'There's another reason why Becky is upset. I, uh, haven't been straight with you about why I left Portland. When we met that night at the Stallion . . . Well, I hadn't seen you for years and, uh . . . This is a little embarrassing . . .'

'Are you going to tell me about that personal injury case you tried for Hale, Greaves?'

Peter was stunned. 'You know about that?'

'No one gives up a job with Hale, Greaves to go to work for Amos Geary. I was suspicious from the start.'

'Who told you what happened?'

'Becky.'

'When did she tell you?' Peter asked, wondering how long Becky had known about his disgrace.

'I don't remember exactly, but it's been a few weeks. It was sometime after the arraignment. I figured you'd get around to telling me when you decided you wanted me to know.'

Peter suddenly realized something. 'You knew about *Elliot* and you still wanted me to go into partnership with you.'

'Everyone fucks up, Pete. I'm not going to judge you by one case. You're a sharp guy and we get along. That's what's important.'

Peter felt an immense rush of gratitude. After so much disapproval, Steve's words were life savers.

'Thanks. You don't know how much I appreciate the vote of confidence.'

'Hey, I say what I mean. Now, let's get back to Gary's case. Have you talked to Becky about a plea?'

'A plea? No.'

'You should look into it after these new developments.'

'You don't think Gary is guilty, do you?'

'I don't know what to think. I wouldn't have believed he was a Peeping Tom, either. And look at the way he jumped on that girl in the Stallion. Gary doesn't think the way we do. He's impulsive.'

'Gee, Steve, I don't know . . .'

'I'm not saying you should plead him out. I'm suggesting you explore the possibility with Becky. From what you tell me, the case isn't going all that well. You don't want to see Gary executed, do you?'

'I've got to think about this.'

'Of course. I don't expect you to decide this minute,' Mancini said as he hoisted his briefcase onto the desk.

Peter stood up. 'Thanks for talking to me. And thanks for being in my corner.'

'Get out of here,' Mancini answered with a laugh.

'Oh, one other thing. This investigator, Barney Pullen, is he any good?'

'Why do you ask?'

'He doesn't seem to be doing anything. Whenever I've been able to get him on the phone, which isn't often, he says he's investigating, but I've only received a few reports, and they weren't worth much. I'm getting worried.'

'If you're dissatisfied, why don't you fire him and hire one of the other guys I told you about?'

'They're not available. The one who works for the Sissler firm said he's been working for them exclusively since February.'

'I didn't know that.'

'Yeah. And the other one . . .'

'Mike Compton?'

'Right. He moved to Pendleton.'

'No kidding?'

'It's too late to switch investigators, anyway. It would take someone new too long to get familiar with the case. By the time he was up to speed, the trial would be over.'

'You're right. Look, why don't you let me give Barney a call.'

'That would be great.'

Peter shut Steve's door and went back to his office. He was depressed about Gary's chances, but he was not going to approach Becky about a plea just yet. If things got much worse though, he might have to consider the possibility.

CHAPTER NINETEEN

1

Each morning, the guards waited to take Gary out of the holding cell until all of the jurors were in the jury room, so they would not see him in manacles. The Harmons had purchased a conservative blue suit and a conservative gray suit for their son and he looked very handsome in them. Lawyer and client had fallen into a routine. As soon as Gary was seated, Peter would tell him how good he looked in the suit. Gary would beam and Peter would ask Gary how he was feeling. Gary would answer that he was feeling good. Finally, Peter would remind Gary about sitting up straight, listening to the witnesses and taking notes and Gary would grow very serious and turn his yellow pad to a blank page.

Becky O'Shay was presenting her case in chronological order. On the first day of testimony, she led off with Karen Nix, who told the jury about Gary's attack and his threat to kill her. Several people who were present at the Stallion that night corroborated Nix's version of the events. Marjorie Dooling testified that

Sandra Whiley had been at the Stallion on the evening of the fight. After Dooling described how Whiley was dressed, the bloodstained clothing was introduced into evidence. A photograph of the jeans and the Whitaker State tee shirt Nix was wearing was shown to the jurors so they could compare the similarities between her clothing and the victim's.

Arnie Block gave his account of the fight and told about Gary's flight from the bar. Dave Thorne established that Sandra Whiley left the Stallion around eleven-twenty, about twenty minutes after Gary ran outside.

On the second day of Gary's trial, Oscar Watts told the jury about discovering Whiley's body. Then, several police officers and forensic technicians described the crime scene investigation and the gathering of evidence.

On the morning of the trial's third day, Becky O'Shay called Harold Guisti's name. The hall door opened to admit the doctor and Peter turned toward the back of the courtroom. His attention was momentarily diverted from the witness by Christopher Mammon, who was watching the proceedings from a seat near the back wall. Peter could not imagine why the gargantuan drug dealer would be interested enough in Gary's case to spend his morning in the tightly packed and overheated courtroom. But Peter did not have much time to spend worrying about Mammon because Dr. Guisti had been sworn and was about to begin his testimony.

After establishing the doctor's credentials, O'Shay asked him, 'In your official capacity as a pathologist did you perform an autopsy on Sandra Whiley?'

Dr. Guisti turned to the jurors and answered the question as if they had asked it.

'Yes I did.'

'When was this?'

'Around 5 P.M. on the day Miss Whiley was murdered.'

'Why did you wait so long?'

'We held off until the body was identified. That was between three and four in the afternoon, if I remember correctly.'

'Where did the autopsy take place?'

'Parson's Mortuary.'

'Please describe what you found when you performed your autopsy on Sandra Whiley.'

'I found several bruises on the left side of the jaw and above the left cheekbone. More important, there were eight cutting or chopping types of wounds on the body. Seven of them were located on the head. The eighth was located on the top of the left hand and was consistent with a defensive wound.'

'What is a defensive wound?'

'That is a wound inflicted when the victim interposes her hand defensively between the weapon wielded by the killer and the object of the murderer's attack.'

'Please describe the head wounds.'

'Five produced skull fractures. Of these five, three were severe enough to produce injuries to the underlying brain. There was another wound which was in the region of the right eye that also produced extensive fracturing of the bones between the eyes and a considerable amount of bleeding with the blood present in the air passages as well as swallowed blood in the stomach. The remaining wounds produced a variable amount of soft-tissue injury or injury to the skin or muscles that did not fracture bone or involve the brain.'

'Do you have an opinion, Dr. Guisti, after looking at these injuries and conducting your investigation, as to the type of instrument that might have been used to inflict these wounds?'

'I do.'

'What is that opinion?'

'Either an ax or a hatchet would cause the type of wounds inflicted on the deceased.'

Becky O'Shay bent down and reached into a large cardboard box containing many items, most of which were enclosed in plastic evidence bags. She rummaged around in the box until she found what she wanted. O'Shay carried the item to the witness.

'Dr. Guisti, I hand you what has been marked as State's Exhibit 23 and I ask you if the wounds on the victim could have been inflicted with this exhibit?'

Dr. Guisti opened the plastic bag. It contained a small hatchet. He turned it around a few times, all for show since he had examined the hatchet on several occasions.

'The blows could have been inflicted by this weapon.'

'Thank you,' O'Shay said, taking the hatchet from the doctor and slowly returning it to the plastic bag while standing directly in front of the jury. She placed the hatchet on the rail of the jury box and turned back to the witness. Several jurors had trouble moving their eyes away from the weapon.

'Dr. Guisti, do you have an opinion as to the cause of death of Sandra Whiley?'

'Yes. I think the eventual cause of death was hemorrhaging caused by the wounds I have described.'

'In other words, Sandra Whiley bled to death through the hatchet wounds inflicted by her killer?'

'That is correct.'

'Dr. Guisti, do you have an opinion as to the direction in which the deadly hatchet blows were struck?'

'Yes, but only as to the blow to the top of the skull. I believe that blow was struck in an up to down direction because of the way the wound slants. As to the others, I cannot say.'

'Do you have an opinion as to whether the blow to the top of the skull was the first blow struck to the head?'

'In my opinion it was.'

O'Shay checked her notes then turned the witness over to Peter.

'Dr. Guisti, what side of the head were the wounds on?'

'As I said, one was to the top of the head. It's difficult to say right or left side because the wound is midway. One blow was to the right eye. The rest were delivered to the left side of the victim's head.'

'Thank you, Doctor. I have no further questions.'

2

The red paint on the gas tanks in front of Art's Garage was barely holding its own against the ravages of rust and wind and the old wooden garage was not doing much better. The elements had eaten away at an advertisement for Coca-Cola that covered one outer wall and the once blue garage now looked a weathered gray. Barney Pullen was bent under the hood of an old Buick when Peter entered the garage during the lunch recess. Peter called out twice before he got Pullen's attention. When Pullen turned around, he looked annoyed, then his features morphed into a brown-nosing smile when he remembered that Peter was the one who paid him for investigating the Harmon case.

'Afternoon, Mr. Hale,' Pullen said, wiping his hands on a greasy rag.

'Good afternoon, Barney. I've had trouble reaching you, so I thought I'd drop by the garage to see how the investigation's been going.'

Barney shook his head ruefully. 'It's real slow. I've been talking to lots of people, but nobody seems to know anything helpful.'

'Who have you talked to?'

'Uh, well, I don't have my notes right here. Family, of course. I do have a lot of good information for you for the penalty phase from the mother, the father and Steve's wife. Lots of good stuff.'

Peter recalled receiving several poorly typed reports rife with misspellings that were accompanied by a bill claiming hours way out of proportion to the information Pullen had collected.

'I have the family interviews, but that's all. You have been doing more than just talking to family?'

'Uh, let's see, there's the bartender at the Ponderosa. You have his statement, right?'

'No, I don't. What about Kevin Booth? Have you found out anything I can use there?'

'Not yet. His father split a long time ago and the mother died last year. She was an alcoholic. Got drunk and fell down the stairs.'

'Did you talk to Booth's neighbors, run a rap sheet?'

'Rap sheet's the first thing I thought of. That arrest for drugs he beat is the only thing I could find. There aren't any neighbors. Booth lives way the hell out of town.'

'What about school records, his mother's neighbors?'

'I'll get right on it.'

'You mean you haven't done that already? We talked about this two weeks ago.'

'Yeah. And I'm sorry. I really did mean to get on it, but Art's kept me hoppin' at the shop here.'

'Barney, you have to get moving on this. If you don't come up with something on Booth soon, we'll be facing a penalty phase for sure.'

'I am investigating, Mr. Hale. As soon as I'm done with this car, I'm gonna get right on it.'

'Look, Barney, you're going to have to give this case priority until it's over. Tell your brother you can't work at the shop until it's done.'

'Okay,' Pullen answered agreeably.

Peter was going to say something else, but there wasn't anything more to say. He was just going to have to hope that Pullen would come through for him.

3

Trying a death penalty case was incredibly exhausting. While Peter was in court, he was so focused that he did not know where the day went. Most of the time, he was coasting on pure adrenaline because no person could concentrate on every word that was said for hours at a time without it. As soon as the case ended for the day, he felt instantly like someone who had gone for days without sleep.

After a fast dinner, Peter went to his new office in Steve Mancini's building and completed his preparations for the next day of trial. It was a little after eight-thirty when Peter opened the front door of his house. The phone was ringing. He raced to it in the dark, stumbling over an ottoman and almost knocking over a floor lamp.

'Mr. Hale?' an unfamiliar voice asked.

'Yes.'

'I've been calling all night. I'm glad I caught you.'

'Who is this?'

'Don Bosco. I'm the Director of Mental Health for the county. I was a witness at the pretrial hearing.'

'Right. I remember you. You were present when Gary was questioned by Dennis Downes. What's up?'

'I know I shouldn't be disturbing you at home, but I've been wondering since that pretrial hearing why no one from the defense asked me any questions on cross and why you haven't gotten in touch with me about my trial testimony.'

'Do you know something that might help Gary?'

'Didn't Steve Mancini tell you about our conversation?'

'All Steve said was that he didn't think you could help us.'

'You're kidding. Do you mean to say he didn't tell you that I believe Gary Harmon was inadvertently hypnotized by Dennis Downes during the interrogation?'

Peter blinked. 'No. He never told me anything about hypnotism.'

'That really surprises me. I told Miss O'Shay that she shouldn't be using Harmon's statements to convict him, but she won't listen to me.'

'I want to make sure I'm understanding you. You're saying that you told the D.A. there was something wrong with Gary's interrogation?'

'Yes.'

'And you also told Steve Mancini about this?'

'I told him over a month ago. I thought you'd be interested.'

Peter was dazed. Gary's statements were the basis

for the state's case. Without them . . .

'Can we get together tonight? This is very important and Steve never mentioned a thing to me about what you're saying.'

'Okay. There's an all-night restaurant near the turn-off to the interstate. The Jolly Roger. Can you be there in half an hour?'

'No problem.'

'Boy, I can't understand why Mr. Mancini didn't say anything to you,' Bosco said right before he hung up.

'Neither can I,' Peter said to the dead phone. He had been standing during the phone conversation, but he sank into an easy chair as soon as he hung up. Peter didn't know what to think. He remembered the look Bosco had given Mancini during his testimony at the motion to suppress. Peter had even commented on it to Steve. He reached for the phone to call Mancini, but he stopped in mid-dial. It would be better if he waited until he heard what Bosco had to say.

'How did you get involved in this case?' Peter asked as soon as he and Don Bosco were seated in a booth in the rear of the Jolly Roger with two cups of coffee.

'Dennis Downes called me at home around eight-thirty, nine. He wanted me to check my records to see if we had anything on Harmon. You know, a history of mental health problems. Something like that.'

'Did you find anything?'

'No.'

'What did you do after that?'

'I went over to the station house to tell him. He'd already said that the inquiry concerned the girl who was killed in the park, so I thought it was important enough to tell him in person and see if there was any other way I could help out.

'When I arrived, Becky O'Shay asked me to watch the interrogation with her through a two-way mirror. She brought me up to date and showed me pictures of the victim.' Bosco shuddered. 'Pretty gruesome.'

'Yeah, I've seen them. But why did Becky want you to observe the questioning?'

'She wanted my take on Harmon.'

'Were you there when Downes gave Gary his *Miranda* warnings?'

'No. That must have been earlier. I got the impression that Dennis had been going at Harmon for a while by the time I started watching.'

'Was there anything unusual about the way Gary was responding to Downes?'

'I didn't like the way Dennis conducted the interview. Not one bit. I even told him to be careful, but he didn't pay any attention to my suggestions.'

'What was the problem?'

Bosco took a sip of coffee and thought carefully about what he was about to say.

'The first thing I noticed was all the leading. You know, asking a question that suggests the answer. I mean, Dennis was feeding him everything. And Harmon would go along with every suggestion. I think he really trusted Dennis and wanted to please him. So, Dennis would ask him a question and Harmon would parrot back the answer Downes had fed him.'

'And you warned Downes about this?'

'During the breaks. Harmon was exhausted by the end and the more tired you are, the more open you are to suggestion. I told that to Dennis, but he and Becky didn't seem to care. They were too excited about cracking the case. In my opinion, most of what

Harmon said is worthless. Especially the last third or so of the interview.'

'Why is that?'

'Well, this is only my opinion, but I think Downes induced a trance state and anything Harmon said then, well . . .'

Bosco shrugged.

'Wait a minute,' Peter said, 'what's a "trance state"? Do you mean he was in a trance? Like hypnotized?'

'He could have been. I think he was.'

'How could that happen? I listened to the tape of the interrogation and I didn't hear Downes saying anything about putting Gary in a trance.'

'He wouldn't have to do it intentionally. Dennis could have hypnotized Harmon without either of them knowing.'

'Explain that to me.'

'Okay. "Hypnosis" and "trance" are words that make people think about magicians or Svengali, but hypnotizing a person isn't all that mysterious. All you're really doing when you induce a trance is getting a person relaxed and focused enough to block out exterior noises and influences, so they can go into a quiet, inner space. We all do that when we drop off to sleep at night or when we're so engrossed in a book that we don't hear someone ask us a question, even though they're right next to us.

'If someone is tired and under a lot of stress, like Harmon was that night, they will tend to focus their attention narrowly. Dennis helped Harmon along when he told him to shut his eyes and imagine he was watching events on a movie screen. That's a fairly common technique that hypnotists use when they're trying to intentionally induce a trance.'

'What would be the consequences of Gary being in a trance?'

'The big problem is reliability. If he was in a trance, it would be difficult, if not impossible, to tell what Harmon was really remembering and what he was repeating as a result of Downes's suggestions, or just plain making up. See, a person in a trance is not only wide open to suggestion, they also fantasize in order to please the questioner or to fill in gaps in their memory, in order to give the interrogator a complete picture.'

'I'm not certain I understand what you mean about the fantasizing.'

'Okay. Let me give you an example. A month ago, you got up at seven in the morning, you dressed in a blue suit, a white shirt and a red tie. Then, you ate a breakfast of cornflakes. I hypnotize you and ask you to tell me what you did that morning. You remember everything except the color of your tie and what you ate. I tell you to really concentrate, but you still can't remember. So, I help you a little. 'Peter,' I say, 'you usually eat Raisin Bran, don't you? Did you eat Raisin Bran that morning?' Now, a person in a trance is likely to say he ate Raisin Bran in order to please the questioner. He knows the questioner wants some answer and seems to be happy with that answer being Raisin Bran, so the person in the trance accommodates those wishes.

'Now, the questioner asks you to think about the tie without making a specific suggestion about color. Again, you know an answer is expected, so your subconscious imagines a green tie and fills in the blank with that color. By the time you're through, you'll believe the tie was green, so you will appear to be telling the truth on the witness stand and you will pass a polygraph test.'

'And you didn't warn Sergeant Downes or Becky about this?'

Bosco looked embarrassed. 'I mentioned it to both of them, but I really didn't catch on to what was happening until I'd been there awhile. By then, the questioning was pretty far along. And, remember, I was only there as an observer. I mean, I wasn't supposed to take part in the interrogation. I guess I should have been more forceful, but most of the harm had already been done by then and I didn't think it was my place to interfere because the case was so important. I didn't do anything wrong, did I?'

4

Peter drove directly to Steve Mancini's house from the Jolly Roger. At first, Bosco's information elated him. Then he realized how much Steve had cost them by failing to use the information at the pretrial hearing. By the time Peter rang Steve Mancini's doorbell at a little before eleven, he was in an emotional quandary. Mancini was his best friend in Whitaker and he was holding out the possibility of a lucrative partnership that would help Peter climb out of the hole he had dug for himself. But Steve might have ruined Gary Harmon's best chance to win his freedom by concealing information from Peter that explained away Gary Harmon's so-called confession, the basis for all of the charges against Gary.

As soon as Steve opened the door, Peter asked, 'Why didn't you tell me about Don Bosco?'

Mancini looked confused. Donna walked out of the living room. She was wearing a bathrobe over a night-gown. Mancini glanced at his wife, then back to Peter. When he answered, he sounded nervous.

'We're getting ready to go to bed, Pete. Can't this wait until tomorrow?'

'You know it can't. If Gary was in some kind of trance when he was questioned by Downes, the interrogation was no good. We could have gotten the whole thing thrown out before the trial. There wouldn't have been a trial. Without Gary's statements, the state doesn't have a case. Don't tell me you didn't know that?'

'What's this about, Peter?' Donna asked, confused by his intensity and her husband's obvious discomfort.

'Tell her, Steve.'

'Tell her what? I still don't know what you're talking about.'

'I just came from the Jolly Roger where Don Bosco, the county's Director of Mental Health, a man with expertise in hypnosis, told me how he explained to you that he believed Gary was in a trance state during most of the interrogation. He called me at home because he was surprised that you never brought that out during the hearing on the motion to suppress. He was also surprised that you never told me about your conversation with him. Quite frankly, Steve, so am I.'

'I didn't tell you about the conversation because I didn't buy into what Bosco said. You heard the tape. Downes didn't say anything about trying to hypnotize Gary.'

Peter looked astonished. 'What Downes did or did not say is irrelevant. We have a witness who would have testified that Gary was hypnotized during the most important part of his interrogation. Didn't you know that there is a statute that forbids the use of hypnotized testimony unless the most stringent precautions are taken? There are cases from around the country that exclude the testimony of hypnotized witnesses. Bosco knew all about them and he's not even a lawyer.'

Mancini looked surprised. 'I didn't know about the statute. You have to believe me. I've never had anything like this come up in one of my cases.'

'Did you know about this and keep it from Peter?' Donna asked her husband.

Mancini turned on Donna. 'I can handle this, thank you. Bring us some coffee. Come on, Pete. Let's discuss this calmly.'

'It's hard to be calm when I'm busting my ass day and night only to find out that you fucked up on the single most important issue in the case.'

'Peter . . .' Donna started, but her husband barked, 'The coffee, please.'

When Steve turned back to Peter he looked concerned, but calm.

'I can see why you're upset. I'm upset too. Especially if you think I may have screwed up Gary's case. Come on. Let's sit down and talk this out.'

The anger drained out of Peter in the face of Mancini's calm demeanor. He walked into the living room and sat down on the couch.

'I just don't understand this, Steve. Can you explain it to me? Even Bosco saw the problem. He called me tonight because he could not figure out why you didn't ask him about the trance state at the hearing. I can't believe you didn't see the significance of what Bosco told you.'

'It's the truth. I didn't know about the statute. I thought the issues were whether Downes gave Gary his *Miranda* rights and whether he coerced him into talking.'

'Can't you reopen the hearing?' Donna asked as she lowered a serving tray onto the coffee table.

'I'll try, but Becky has a very legitimate ground for objecting.'

'What's that?' Donna asked.

'Steve was Gary's lawyer. He knew all about this evidence at the time of the suppression hearing.'

'But I didn't understand the significance of what Bosco told me,' Mancini protested.

'That doesn't matter. You should have known it was important. That's the point, I wish there was some way to sugarcoat this, but there isn't.'

'Isn't there anything you can do?' Donna asked.

'There might be,' Peter said cautiously. 'I read a little about confessions for this case before Steve said he would handle the motion to suppress. A defendant can always argue to a jury that they should not accept a defendant's statements because they are involuntary. The problem is that there's no appeal from a jury's decision like there is from a pretrial decision by a judge, because appellate courts won't review the factual finding of a jury.'

'If Gary was hypnotized, he wouldn't be responsible for what he told Downes!' Mancini said. 'That's great thinking, Pete.'

'Yeah, but I've got to convince the jury that Gary was hypnotized. That may mean hiring experts and that's expensive.' Peter looked at Donna. 'Can your folks afford it?'

'Don't worry about the money, Peter,' Donna said. 'If my folks can't do it, Steve and I will pay.'

Peter did not see Mancini's sudden anger, but Donna did. She was shocked by its intensity and she remembered what happened the last time he was angry with her.

'I think you've come up with a potential solution,' Mancini said quickly, 'and I also think we should all get some rest. Don't forget, you have to be in court tomorrow.'

Peter suddenly realized how much today's court session and this evening's events had taken out of him.

'You're right,' he said as he stood up. 'Sorry I came down on you so hard.'

'I understand completely. I deserve it if I screwed up as badly as it seems.'

As soon as the door closed, Mancini returned to the living room. Donna was bent over the coffee table gathering up the coffee cups and the creamer.

'What was that about our paying for Gary's experts?' Mancini demanded angrily.

Donna straightened up with the tray in her hands.

'If Gary needs our help . . .'

'Gary made his own mess. We cannot afford to bail him out. Didn't you understand a thing I said about Mountain View? I'll bet you haven't even talked to your father about helping with it.'

'I haven't had the chance,' Donna answered, feeling guilty about letting down her husband.

'That's great. You can't take the time to help your own husband and you expect me to spend my money on some Portland shrink.'

'The experts can't be that expensive.'

'They could be dirt cheap, Donna. I've got to work like a slave at my practice just to keep our heads above water. What are we going to pay them with?'

'Gary is my brother.'

'That's right, Donna. He's your brother. Not mine.'

Steve's cold and cruel reply shocked Donna. She had always believed that her husband liked Gary.

'We wouldn't need the money for experts if you hadn't made a mistake,' Donna said angrily.

The open-hand slap spun Donna's head to the right and the tray went flying. Donna watched the cups and spraying cream sail away in slow motion as Steve grabbed the lapels of her robe and used them to fling her to the ground.

'You cunt!' Steve screamed as she hit the floor.

Donna tried to crawl away, but the pain from two strong kicks to her ribs stopped her. Another kick landed on her leg and she straightened in pain. Then, as swiftly as it started, the assault stopped. When she dared to look up, Mancini was pacing back and forth. Donna started to crawl across the floor toward the hall. Steve saw her and dropped next to her on the floor. Donna curled into a ball with her hands protecting her head.

'No, baby, no. You don't have to be afraid. I'm sorry. Please. I'm sorry.'

Donna looked up and Mancini saw the blood. The blow to Donna's face had split her lip.

'Oh, God! What have I done?'

Mancini jumped up and sprinted to the bathroom. He ran cold water over a towel. When he returned to the living room, the front door was open. Donna was gone. Mancini threw the towel on the floor and raced out of the house. The car was parked in front. He looked right and left. Where was she? He couldn't call out. He could not let anyone know what had happened. Mancini ran down the street and stopped on the corner. Where had she gone? He had to find her. Without the car, she couldn't get far. He ran inside and grabbed the car keys. He would find her. He had to find her.

*

Donna waited for the car to drive away before pulling herself to her feet by hanging on to the bushes behind which she had been hiding. A sharp pain in her ribs doubled her over. She gritted her teeth and eased into a standing position. Tears and blood mixed on her face. She loved Steve, but how could he beat her if he really loved her?

Donna wanted to change into her clothes, but she was afraid to go back to the house. Her parents' house was too far to walk. Besides, they were worrying so much about Gary that she could not let them know that her marriage was failing.

Then she thought of Peter. He lived nearby. She could keep to backyards and Steve would not see her from his car. Donna checked the street for any sign of her husband, then she crossed the road and hobbled behind a house. She wanted to run, but the pain in her ribs was so intense that she had to walk hunched over.

A dog barked and Donna's stomach tightened. She kept moving, gasping for air when a sudden bolt of pain knifed through her. Donna waited for the pain to pass before going on. The next street was Elm and cars drove by frequently. Donna waited for a break and crossed the street as quickly as she could manage, paying in pain for speed. 'Just a few more blocks,' she repeated over and over until, moments later, she was ringing Peter's door bell.

Headlights turned onto Peter's street just as his porch light came on. When Peter opened his door, Donna was crouched down, looking over her shoulder with terrified eyes.

'Please, let me in,' Donna begged.

Peter took one look at her tearstained and bleeding face and he had her through the door.

'What happened to you?' he asked. Then Donna was

sobbing in his arms and Peter was too startled to say anything. Peter led her to the living room. She clung to him. As he lowered her to the couch, she spasmed and gripped her side.

'Are you hurt?' he asked stupidly.

'He hit me, Peter. He hit me.'

'Who hit you? Is Steve all right?' Peter asked, confused by Donna's sudden, dramatic appearance and thinking that the couple had been attacked.

Donna shook her head. 'You don't understand. It was Steve. Steve hit me.'

'Steve?' Peter repeated inanely. Donna dissolved into tears and pressed herself against Peter's chest.

'Has . . . has he done this before?' Peter asked.

Donna managed a nod. She got her crying under control and wiped an arm across her eyes.

'How long has this been going on?'

Donna did not answer right away and Peter touched her shoulder.

'I want to help. You and Steve are my friends.'

Donna looked at the rug.

'I know this is hard for you, but you have to talk about it. If Steve is doing this . . . You can't let him keep hurting you, Donna.'

'It's been a nightmare, Peter.' She started to cry again. 'I never know what will set him off. He's so kind to me, so loving. Then, all of a sudden . . . I can't take it anymore.'

Donna was too exhausted to go on. Peter stared at her. Her hair was in disarray and her robe was open. She was wearing a short nightgown because of the heat. Peter could not help noticing her slim, tanned legs and the swell of her breasts as she breathed deeply. Peter raised his eyes to Donna's face, embarrassed.

'How badly are you hurt?' he asked.

'He kicked me in the ribs. He . . . It was a hard kick. It really hurts if I move quickly.'

'I'll drive you to a hospital.'

'No! No hospital. They'd have to report Steve.'

Peter thought for a moment. Then he got an idea.

'I have a friend. A nurse. Rhonda Kates. She works at the hospital. Let me call her. I'll explain what happened. Maybe she can check you out to make sure you don't have any internal injuries. If there's a problem, we'll make up a story and I'll drive you to the nearest hospital outside of Whitaker.'

Peter made the call and Rhonda told him to bring Donna to her place immediately. She even said that Donna could spend the night with her. While Peter talked on the phone, Donna tried to find a comfortable position on the couch and closed her eyes. She was so ashamed that her marriage was a failure and she felt she must be partly to blame, but she could not figure out what she had done wrong. She wanted to talk to someone but the Harmons were not a family that discussed their domestic troubles.

'Let's get going,' Peter said, as soon as he hung up.

'Thank you, Peter. You're a good friend.'

CHAPTER TWENTY

1

'Mr. Hale,' Judge Kuffel said, addressing Peter formally because they were in court and on the record, 'your former co-counsel, Mr. Mancini, conducted the hearing on the motion to suppress Mr. Harmon's statements. You've conceded that he was fully aware at the time of the hearing of the evidence you argue is grounds for reopening. Now, there is no question that Mr. Bosco's evidence favors the defense, but Mr. Mancini made a decision not to use it. I have no idea why he made that choice, but it doesn't really matter. Since he was aware of the evidence at the time of the hearing, I have to deny your motion to reopen the motion to suppress.'

If Peter was the judge, he would have ruled exactly the way Judge Kuffel ruled, but his failure to win his hastily fashioned motion still depressed him. Peter closed his eyes briefly while he tried to regain his composure. This was a mistake. Suddenly he was half asleep and it took all his willpower to raise his eyelids and return to full consciousness.

It had been two-thirty in the morning when Peter had returned home after leaving Donna with Rhonda Kates. He was totally exhausted, but Don Bosco's revelation and Donna's dramatic appearance filled his head with so many disturbing thoughts that he had as much of a chance of dozing off in the privacy of his room as he had of sleeping at a rock concert. Peter had moved through the morning in court in a sleep-deprived fog.

'I've given a lot of thought to the matter of testimony about the peeping incident, the pornographic magazines found in Mr. Harmon's bedroom and evidence concerning the other two murders,' Judge Kuffel continued.

'I will permit the state to introduce evidence concerning the peeping incident on the Whitaker campus and the pornographic magazines. This evidence may make Mr. Harmon look bad to the jury, but it is relevant to the state's theory that Mr. Harmon had a sexual obsession with women with physical characteristics very similar to the victim.'

Peter sat forward to hear the judge's ruling on the other murders. He had battled very hard to keep any reference to them out of the trial.

'Miss O'Shay, you have made a very persuasive argument that the murder of Sandra Whiley is part of a series of murders, but I am not going to permit you to put that theory to the jury. A few factors led me to this decision.

'First, there is no evidence connecting Mr. Harmon to the other killings. Second, there are substantial differences between the murder of Miss Whiley and the other murders. The other women were sexually assaulted and blood tests revealed the presence of cocaine in their systems, whereas Miss Whiley's blood did not reveal the presence of cocaine and the autopsy found no evidence of sexual assault . . .'

'Your Honor,' Becky interrupted, 'Wishing Well Park is a public place. We believe Mr. Harmon was frightened away by other individuals in the park before he could have sex with Miss Whiley.'

'Your theory may be correct, but I have to make my ruling based on the evidence.'

'There's the hatchet,' O'Shay argued. 'The weapon is a trademark of this killer. It is very unusual.'

'Not in a farming community, Ms. O'Shay. Without something more I have no choice but to bar you from mentioning the other murders. Introduction of that evidence would lead to speculation by the jury and deprive Mr. Harmon of a fair trial.'

The judge's ruling snapped Peter out of his funk. He was concerned about the introduction of evidence about the peeping incident and the magazines, but he had been scared to death that Judge Kuffel would admit evidence about the other murders. If the judge had let O'Shay argue that Gary was a serial killer, there was no way Peter could have won an acquittal.

'Do you have an update on Kevin Booth's condition?' the judge asked. Peter leaned forward. If Booth was too ill to testify, Peter's day would be complete.

'I spoke with Mr. Booth's surgeon this morning,' O'Shay said as she consulted her notes. 'Dr. Farber says that Mr. Booth cannot be transported to Whitaker without endangering the success of the skin grafts. However, Mr. Booth is metabolically more stable. His fever is down, he's gaining weight and he requires less pain medication, which makes him more coherent.

'According to the doctor, Mr. Booth will be able to testify in his hospital room in Portland by Monday. Dr.

Farber is willing to postpone further skin grafts so the trial will not be delayed. It's my intention to examine Mr. Booth in Portland, if the court is agreeable.'

'I object, Your Honor,' Peter said.

'What are your grounds, Mr. Hale?'

'Booth's testimony is crucial to the state's case. If the jury sees him in a hospital room it's going to generate a lot of sympathy. Booth has been burned to a crisp. I'm going to look like an ogre if I go after him.

'And how am I going to cross-examine effectively? What happens to Mr. Harmon's right of confrontation if Dr. Farber says that I shouldn't excite Booth? And he's on pain medication. He'll be sedated. That means the jury won't be seeing the way he would normally react to questions.'

'Your concerns are valid, Mr. Hale, but it seems to me that they are theoretical. It may be that you will be able to carry on a vigorous cross of the witness without any medical problems occurring. We'll deal with confrontation problems if the doctor tries to restrict you. Of course, we could have a mistrial or Mr. Booth's testimony may be struck, if you are foreclosed from examining Booth because of medical problems, but that's a risk the state runs.

'As to the prejudice caused by Booth's appearance and the location where he will be examined, I plan on instructing the jurors that they may not let any sympathy caused by Booth's appearance affect their decision. I'll draft a jury instruction to that effect and I'll give it to you to review tonight. Let me know if you want any changes by tomorrow morning, before court.

'With that in mind, I'll have a bus meet us here at seven o'clock on Monday morning. Ms. O'Shay, please notify the hospital that I plan on taking testimony at two in the afternoon.

'If there's nothing further, we'll take a short recess. Then I'll have the clerk bring in the jury.'

Judge Kuffel left the bench and the guards took Gary to the holding cell so he could use the restroom. Steve Mancini walked to Peter's side as soon as Gary was out of earshot. There were dark circles under his eyes and Peter noticed nicks on his face where he had cut himself shaving. It was obvious that Mancini had not slept last night either.

'I really fucked up, didn't I?'

'What's done is done,' Peter answered resignedly. 'I'll just have to call Bosco as a witness and hope that the jury buys his theory.'

'I wonder what else will go wrong.'

'What do you mean?'

Mancini hesitated. Then, he said, 'Donna left me.'

'What!' Peter responded, hoping that he looked suitably surprised.

'We had a fight after you went home because I didn't tell you about Bosco.'

'Jeez, I'm sorry. I shouldn't have barged in like that. I feel awful.'

'It's not your fault. I don't even know why I'm burdening you with this. I guess I just needed someone to talk to.'

'How serious is this?'

'Pretty serious. I feel really bad. I love her so much.' Mancini's voice caught and Peter was afraid he was going to cry. If he did, Peter didn't know if he could keep lying.

'Hey, it'll work out. It's just a newlywed spat. She loves you, too. She'll come back.'

'I hope so, Pete. I can't stand being away from her. If you run into Donna, tell her I love her, will you? Ask her to call me. I'm sure everything would be all right if we could just talk.'

'You bet,' Peter said, but he did not mean it. He felt terrible about deceiving his friend, but he remembered Donna's pain and terror too vividly to help Mancini find his wife.

'I shouldn't have bothered you in the middle of trial.'

'It's no trouble,' Peter answered guiltily. 'Maybe we should go out for dinner tonight . . .'

'No. This was selfish of me. You've got to prepare your case. Gary's life is at stake. I'm just feeling sorry for myself. I'll be okay.'

2

During the rest of the morning session, witnesses told the jury about the peeping incident and the pornographic magazines. Becky O'Shay started the afternoon session of court by calling Sergeant Dennis Downes to the stand. Just before he started to testify, Christopher Mammon entered the courtroom. This was the second time Mammon had been a spectator at Gary's trial and Peter remained puzzled by his interest.

Downes testified calmly and professionally about the history of his investigation and the evidence that led him to Gary Harmon. He emphasized the courtesy shown to the defendant and explained how Gary had agreed to come to the station house. When his narrative reached the point where the taping began, Becky introduced the tapes of Gary's interrogation into evidence and supplied everyone with a transcript of the five-hour interrogation. Then, Becky played a two-hour, edited version of the interrogation to the jury. The day's session of court ended with a recitation by Downes of his part in finding the hatchet in a storm drain near the Whitaker State College campus.

After court, Peter went directly to his office to finish the work on his cross-examination of Sergeant Downes. He hoped Steve Mancini would not be working late, because he felt a little guilty about helping Donna hide from her husband. Fortunately, Mancini was not in the building

Peter tried to work on the case, but he kept thinking about his encounter at the courthouse with Steve. Mancini seemed so sad. Maybe Donna had exaggerated when she described her beating. Mancini had definitely hit her, but based on how contrite he seemed, it was hard to believe that Steve had really meant to hurt her.

Peter was also troubled by his part in the Mancinis' marital problems. He should never have barged into their house the way he did, throwing accusations at his friend in front of Donna. He had made it sound as if Steve was intentionally sabotaging Gary's case. The more Peter thought about it, the more he decided that he owed it to Steve to tell Donna how sorry he seemed in court.

As soon as he wrapped up his work, Peter drove across town. Rhonda Kates lived near the hospital in a garden apartment on the other side of the Whitaker campus from city center. Peter rang the doorbell and noticed the curtain that covered the kitchen window move. Donna looked apprehensive when she opened the door. She had been afraid to go back to her house for her own clothes, so she was wearing shorts and a green tank top that belonged to Rhonda.

'I thought I'd drop by to see how you're doing.'

Donna's apprehensive look turned into a smile of

relief and she ushered him in.

'You all alone?' Peter asked.

'Rhonda has an evening shift at the hospital.'

'How are your ribs?'

'Nothing's broken. I'm still sore, but it could have been worse.'

They sat down in the living room.

'I was too upset to thank you last night,' Donna said.

'Oh, hey . . .'

'No. Some men wouldn't have wanted to get involved. Especially with the wife of a friend.' She paused. 'You haven't said anything to Steve, have you? About where I am.'

'No. He doesn't know I helped you. I was afraid if I said anything, he'd want to know where you are. That would have put me in the middle. I like both of you and I . . . Well, I really find it hard to believe that Steve hit you like that.'

'I know what you mean,' Donna answered bitterly.

'Actually, Steve did talk to me today at the courthouse. He's a mess. I think he's really sorry for what he did.'

'Sorry isn't good enough. I am not going to be Steve's punching bag. If you love someone . . .'

Donna left the thought unfinished. They sat quietly for a moment. Then, Donna asked, 'Are you hungry? I'm fixing some dinner for myself.'

'I'm starved.'

Peter followed Donna into a kitchen separated from the living room by an L-shaped, waist-high counter. Tomatoes, lettuce, an avocado and pods of fresh green peas were spread out near a large salad bowl on a counter next to the sink.

'I was going to make myself a steak and salad. I've got another steak. Is that okay?'

'Great.'

'Do you want a drink?'

'Does Rhonda have the fixings for a gin and tonic?'

'Let me check,' she answered as she looked in a cabinet over the stove. 'You're on,' she said, handing a bottle to Peter. 'I saw the tonic in the refrigerator. Why don't you fix me one, too.'

Peter found the ice and fixed the drinks. When he set down Donna's glass on the counter, she asked, 'How did the trial go today?'

Peter told Donna about Judge Kuffel's decision to keep out evidence of the other murders. Then he recounted the testimony concerning the sex magazines and the peeping incident and Gary's reaction to it. The heat in the apartment caused sweat to bead on Donna's body. While Peter talked, she picked up the cold glass of gin and touched it to her forehead. With her hair in casual disarray, she looked attractive even with her split lip and bruises. The cruel reminders of Steve's beating made Peter want to protect her from any further harm. When he realized that he was staring, Peter averted his eyes, hoping that Donna had not noticed.

'Poor kid,' Peter finished. 'Here he is facing a death sentence and all he can think about is your mom knowing he's been reading *Playboy*.'

'How do you think the jury reacted to the books and the peeping?'

'Tough to say. A couple of them looked upset about the peeping. I don't know what they thought about the magazines. I did see a couple of kindly looks when Gary started bawling.'

'Give Gary my love, will you. Tell him . . . tell him I have to go out of town for a few days so he won't wonder why I'm not in court.'

'I will.'

Donna paused. She looked worried.

'If I ask you a question, will you give me an honest answer?'

'Of course,' Peter said.

'Is Gary going to be convicted?'

Peter's first thought was to assure Donna that he would win Gary's case, but he found that he could not lie to her.

'I don't know, Donna. I wish I could assure you that he'll be okay, but I just don't know.'

CHAPTER TWENTY-ONE

Peter began his cross-examination of Dennis Downes by asking, 'How well do you know the Harmon family, Sergeant?'

'Not all that well. I know them to say hello to, but we don't socialize.'

'Have you met Gary Harmon in a social setting?'

'No.'

'Are you aware that Gary is mildly retarded?'

'I never heard that.'

'But you knew he was slow?'

'Well, I knew he wasn't a scholar.'

'That's obviously true,' Peter said, 'because you would have had some trouble convincing a scholar that he had supernatural powers, wouldn't you?'

Downes shrugged uneasily and Peter did not press him for a verbal answer.

'In fact, you had a pretty easy time convincing Gary that he had psychic powers, didn't you?'

'I guess.'

'That's because he trusted you, didn't he, Sergeant?'

'I suppose he did.'

'There's no doubt in your mind about that, is there? After all, when he was arrested for peeping at that girl at the college, you fixed it so he wasn't charged.'

'I did.'

'You must not have felt Gary was very dangerous, or you wouldn't have let him go, would you?'

Downes suddenly saw where Peter had led him. He hesitated before answering 'No' and Peter noted with satisfaction that several of the jurors took notes when they saw Downes hesitate.

'Let's discuss Gary's supernatural powers, Sergeant. Until you came up with that idea, didn't Gary insist that he knew nothing about the murder of Sandra Whiley?'

'No, that's not true. He said he saw her and the killer by the park entrance.'

'That's not really accurate, is it?' Peter asked as he walked across the courtroom and handed the witness a two-volume transcript of the interrogation. Sticking out of several pages were yellow Post-its with numbers on them. Peter carried his own copy of the transcript with similarly marked Post-its.

'Let me direct your attention to the page marked by the Post- it labeled number one. Have you got that?'

Downes nodded.

'What Gary told you initially was that he had seen a man and a woman hugging in the park, did he not?'

'Yes, but later . . .'

'I'm not concerned with "later," Sergeant. I'm concerned with what Gary told you at first. And that was simply that he had seen a man and a woman hugging.'

'I guess he did.'

'He had no idea who they were?'

Downes scanned the page, then agreed.

'He did not say the man was killing the woman?'

'No.'

'Not until you started this business about the subconscious mind.'

Downes did not answer.

'In fact, it took you a long time to convince Gary that he had seen Sandra Whiley in the park.'

'I didn't convince him of anything.'

'Oh, didn't you? Look at number five. What is Mr. Harmon's response when you tell him "There's a good chance that you saw Sandy and her killer when you walked by Wishing Well Park"?'

Downes scanned the page until he found the question and answer.

'He said, "All I see is them two hugging," ' Downes answered reluctantly.

'And at nine, when you tell him to relax and let it come, doesn't Mr. Harmon tell you, "It's no good, I didn't see anything new"?'

'Yes.'

'And at ten, what does Mr. Harmon tell you when you ask, "Is it Sandy?"?'

'He says, "I can't say for sure." '

'That's right. Now, you had Mr. Harmon believing he was some kind of detective, didn't you?'

'What do you mean?'

'Look again at ten. I'm quoting. "You know, Gary, you might be a natural at this stuff." And Gary says, "I just want to get this guy." He thinks he's helping the police, doesn't he?'

'Or fooling the police.'

'He figured that out with an IQ of 65?'

'Objection,' O'Shay said. 'Sergeant Downes has no

way of knowing what was going on in the defendant's head during this interview.'

'Sustained,' Judge Kuffel said.

'Very well, Your Honor,' Peter answered. 'Sergeant Downes, isn't it true that you told Mr. Harmon to guess at what happened in the park?'

'They were pretty good guesses.'

'Oh, really? Like the guesses about where the blows fell on Miss Whiley's head?'

'That was accurate.'

'It was?'

'Yes, sir. He described right where the wounds were.'

'Let's look at twenty-two. Read that to the jury, if you please, starting at line thirteen.'

'I said, "Let it flow, Gary. First hit. Where was it?" and he said, "Top of the head," which is where the first hit was.'

'Go on.'

'I said, "This is great. Then what?" and he started swinging his arm and said, "Another to the right side. And another." '

'Stop there, Sergeant. You are aware, are you not, that Dr. Guisti testified that the killer struck his blows to the left side of Miss Whiley's head?'

'Yes, but . . .'

'Yes or no?'

'Yes.'

Peter did not let the jury see how elated he felt. If he could convince the jurors that Downes had taken advantage of Gary's low intelligence to trick him, he would destroy a major part of the state's case.

'When you questioned Mr. Harmon, did he appear sleepy to you?'

'We were both tired by the end.'

'How long did the interrogation last?'

'About seven hours from the time we got him to the station house.'

'So, there are two hours of interrogation that are not on the tape?'

'Yes.'

'It was during that part of the interrogation that you had Officer Robert Patrick play a little trick on Mr. Harmon, wasn't it?'

'I don't understand the question.'

'What is a black light, Sergeant?'

Downes colored. 'A, uh, black light is like a flashlight, but it shoots out an ultraviolet light beam.'

'Did you have Officer Patrick dust a Coke can with an invisible powder that shows up orange under ultraviolet light?'

'Yes.'

'After Gary handled the can, did Officer Patrick, on your orders, shine the black light on Gary's hands?'

'Yes,' Downes answered uncomfortably.

'Did Officer Patrick then tell this young man, who has an IQ of 65, that the orange splotches on his hands were the blood of Sandra Whiley?'

'Yes.'

'That was a lie, wasn't it?'

Downes looked as if he was going to say something else at first, but ended by simply agreeing.

'Where did you learn your "projection transfer" technique, Sergeant?'

'Nowhere,' Downes answered proudly. 'I made it up.'

'Made it up?' Peter responded incredulously.

'Yes, sir.'

'Are you aware that the technique you used on Mr. Harmon is identical to the technique used by hypnotists to induce a trance?'

'Objection,' O'Shay said. 'That question assumes facts that are not in evidence.'

'We intend to offer such evidence, Your Honor,' Peter told the judge.

'Very well. With that assurance, I will order the witness to answer.'

'I don't know what technique a hypnotist would use, Mr. Hale.'

'Whether you knew or not, isn't it true that you led Mr. Harmon to give those answers that you wanted to hear?'

'No, sir. That's not true.'

'Look at marker seventeen. Don't you suggest that the man and woman Mr. Harmon said he saw hugging in the park might be doing something other than hugging, despite the fact that Mr. Harmon told you several times that was the activity in which they were involved?'

'I suggested that they would not have been hugging if the couple was Whiley and her killer.'

'Thus planting that suggestion in a mind susceptible to suggestion both because of Mr. Harmon's fatigue and IQ.'

'Objection,' O'Shay said. 'Mr. Hale is making a speech.'

'Sustained. Save the oratory for closing, Mr. Hale.'

'Sergeant Downes, did you not lead Mr. Harmon to say that the man he saw in the park was holding a weapon after Mr. Harmon repeatedly told you that he had not seen a weapon in the man's hand?'

'Gary brought up the hatchet.'

'Look at marker twenty-nine. Read the top few lines on that page, please.'

'I ask, "Did you see anything shiny, Gary? It would probably have been right then. In that split second."

and he says, "Shiny?" and I say . . .'

'Stop there. You were the first person to mention the word "shiny," weren't you?'

'Yes,' Downes said, after a moment's hesitation.

'And it is you who mentioned that the weapon would probably be in the killer's right hand?'

Downes read the page, stopping to reread one sentence.

'I . . . I may have mentioned that first.'

'You put those words in Mr. Harmon's mouth.'

'No, sir. I just asked the questions and he supplied the answers.'

'Only some of them were your answers, weren't they?'

'Nothing further, Your Honor,' Peter said before O'Shay could object.

'I only have a few questions on redirect, Sergeant.' The deputy district attorney sounded undisturbed by Peter's cross. 'Mr. Hale pointed out that the defendant described the hatchet wounds the killer inflicted as being on the right side of Miss Whiley's face, whereas the wounds were actually on the left side.'

'Yes.'

'When Mr. Harmon was describing these wounds verbally, was he also demonstrating the strikes?'

'Yes, ma'am. I gave him a ruler to hold and I told him to pretend this was the weapon. Then I stood in front of him and dipped down a little, so I would be more like Miss Whiley's height. Then I asked him to act out the blows.'

'Were the defendant's physical actions consistent with what he said?'

'No, ma'am, they were not. See, while he was talking I stood opposite him. Now Mr. Harmon had that ruler in his right hand and he was saying the blows were landing on my right side, but really, with me facing him, it was on his right, but the left side of my face. See what I mean.'

'I'm certain the jurors understand,' O'Shay said. Peter also understood with sickening clarity that he had lost one of his major points.

'Mr. Hale asked you if you had Officer Patrick shine a black light on the defendant's hands after a powder had been transferred to Mr. Harmon's hands from a Coke can,' O'Shay said.

'Yes.'

'This powder then showed up orange on Mr. Harmon's hands under the ultraviolet light, is that correct?'

'Yes.'

'What did Mr. Harmon do when Officer Patrick told him that the orange glow was Sandra Whiley's blood?'

'He stared at his hands and began wringing them in an effort to scrape off the blood.'

'Now, Mr. Hale asked you if you led the defendant to say that the man in the park had a weapon.'

'Yes.'

'Did you ever suggest that the weapon used by the person who murdered Sandra Whiley was a hatchet?'

'No, ma'am. When I was talking to Gary we didn't know what was used to kill her, other than it was a sharp-bladed instrument.'

'Who is the first person to say that the murder weapon was a hatchet?'

'Gary. The defendant.'

'And, lo and behold, the murder weapon did turn out to be a hatchet, didn't it, Sergeant?'

'Yes, ma'am. Much to my surprise, it certainly did.'

CHAPTER TWENTY-TWO

1

Dr. Leonard Farber, Kevin Booth's treating physician, had thinning brown hair, clear blue eyes and an easy smile. His cheerful disposition seemed odd when you considered that he spent his days with people who were often in horrible pain. While he walked with Becky O'Shay, Farber explained that his patient had recovered enough to be moved out of isolation in the burn ward to a regular hospital room. O'Shay showed no emotion when the doctor described Booth's injuries and the process of grafting human skin and pigskin onto areas that had been horribly burned, but listening to a scientific explanation of the effect of ignited lighter fluid on human skin was not the same as seeing a person who had been set on fire.

Dr. Farber had arranged for Booth to be temporarily placed in a hospital room that was big enough for the judge, the court reporter, the attorneys and the jury. A policeman stationed outside Booth's door looked up as the doctor and the D.A. approached.

'We're set for two, right?' Farber asked.

'You should probably be here a little before two. Say, one forty-five. Just in case the judge or Harmon's attorney has any questions.'

'See you then,' Farber said and he headed back to his office.

The police guard opened the door to Booth's room as soon as he checked Becky's ID. Booth was sitting up in a hospital bed that had been elevated so he could watch television. The set was showing a game show. As soon as the door opened, Booth turned off the set.

O'Shay kept her poise when Booth turned his head toward her. His face was covered with silver sulfadiazine, a white, greasy cream. The right side of the face looked normal, but O'Shay could see bright red circles and blobs of healing outer skin through the cream that covered the left side. In addition, Booth had an eighth-of-an-inch tube in his right nostril through which supplemental nutrition was administered. O'Shay also noticed that Booth's left eyebrow was gone.

Booth was wearing a short-sleeved hospital gown. The gown bulged in numerous places where bandages covered the grafts. On the back of Booth's left arm and hand were square patches of pinkish-purplish skin. A clear yellow serum oozed out of numerous perforations in the skin. O'Shay felt light-headed, even though Booth did not look as bad as she had imagined.

'How are you feeling, Mr. Booth?' O'Shay asked as she sat next to the bed on a gray metal chair.

'Bad,' Booth managed. His speech had a harsh, rasping quality that startled O'Shay. The word was said so softly that she had to strain to hear it. Dr. Farber had explained that Booth had suffered a minor inhalation injury when he breathed in smoke from the bedding that burned in his cell. Booth's pain medication had also been withheld so he would be clearheaded for his testimony.

'You'll feel better when you're through testifying and I let the U.S. Attorney know how much I appreciate your help.'

O'Shay could see that Booth was frightened.

'Don't worry, Kevin. This won't take long. The doctor will be here. The judge will let you take breaks, if you need to. You'll do fine.'

'We don't start for a while. I'm here because I want to tell you the questions I'm going to ask you, so you won't be surprised by them. Okay?'

Booth nodded and O'Shay rewarded him with a smile. For the next half hour, O'Shay went through her direct examination with Booth. For the most part, O'Shay let Booth answer without comment, but every once in a while, she would advise Booth to phrase an answer differently so it would have a greater impact on the jurors. By the end of the half hour, Booth seemed to be flagging, so O'Shay decided to wind up their meeting.

'That was great, Kevin. I wanted to go over one more thing, then I'll let you get some rest. Do you think you can hang in there for a few minutes more?'

Booth nodded slowly. His eyelids fluttered with fatigue.

'Jurors are impressed by details. Little things that lend authenticity to what a witness says. There are a lot of good details in your account of Harmon's confession, but there's one thing I realize we've never talked about. Something Gary Harmon may have told you that only the killer would know.'

'What . . . thing?'

'You told me that Harmon said that Sandra Whiley

wore a good luck piece around her neck. A small, silver medallion on a chain. Did Harmon ever mention anything else about this necklace to you?'

'What . . . would he . . . have said?'

'The necklace was found in some bushes near the entrance to the park. By those stone pillars. We think that the killer tore it off of her neck while they were struggling. Did Harmon ever mention anything about that?'

'I . . . I'm not sure.'

'Try and remember. I don't want you to testify about anything Harmon didn't tell you. I don't want you to make up anything. But it would be important, if Harmon did say it. Why don't you think about it while you rest.'

Booth nodded. O'Shay stood up.

'I'll come by before everyone else arrives and you can tell me if you remember anything about the necklace or anything else of importance.'

2

Peter Hale and Becky O'Shay sat on either side of Judge Kuffel on the left side of Kevin Booth's bed. Behind them, against the wall, sat the jurors. Dr. Farber and the court reporter sat on the right side of the bed. Gary Harmon sat behind Peter. Two guards stood against the wall. Another policeman was stationed outside the room in the hospital corridor.

Peter had his back to the jurors, but he had stolen a glance at them when he was setting up his notes on the bridge table the hospital provided. They seemed uneasy so close to a person who had been horribly burned. Peter appreciated how the jurors felt. He remembered his temporary feeling of disorientation when he saw his father in intensive care for the first time. Hospitals were unpleasant places and patients were graphic reminders of human frailty.

'Mr. Booth, are you feeling well enough to talk to the jury?' Becky O'Shay asked with unctuous concern.

Booth nodded. It had been agreed that he could respond with a nod or shake of the head to questions that could be answered yes or no.

'Good. If you want to rest for a while, please let me know and I'll ask the judge for a recess. Dr. Farber will also be here during the questioning. Do you understand that you can talk to him at any time, if you need to?'

Again, Booth nodded.

'Okay. Now, even though you are recuperating from your terrible burns in this hospital in Portland, you are technically a prisoner awaiting trial in jail on various charges relating to narcotics, are you not?'

Booth nodded.

'After your arrest, were you placed in the Whitaker County Jail?'

Booth nodded.

'Was Gary Harmon in the same jail?'

Booth's head turned slowly until he was staring directly at Gary. Then he turned back toward the prosecutor. Though it took only seconds, the action seemed to take forever.

'Yes,' Booth rasped. Several jurors seemed disturbed by the way Booth's voice sounded.

'How long have you known Mr. Harmon?'

'High . . . school.'

'Can you estimate the number of years?'

'Six . . . seven years.'

'Were you friends in high school?'

Booth nodded.

'So, Mr. Harmon would trust you.'

'Objection,' Peter said. 'Leading.'

'That is a leading question, Mr. Hale. Now, I am going to permit more leading than I normally would because of Mr. Booth's condition, but I think this is too important an area to permit it. Why don't you rephrase the question, Ms. O'Shay.'

'Very well, Your Honor. Mr. Booth, describe your relationship with Mr. Harmon.'

'Gary . . . was my . . . friend.'

The effort to get out this halting sentence seemed to exhaust Booth. He closed his eyes and rested while O'Shay asked the next question.

'Did Mr. Harmon appear to have other friends when he was in jail in Whitaker?'

'No,' Booth answered, his eyes still shut. 'Seemed lonely. Gary . . . stayed by self.'

'Did you talk to Mr. Harmon in jail?'

Booth nodded.

'In the course of these conversations did he ever discuss his case?'

Booth nodded.

'Tell the jury how that happened.'

Booth took a deep breath. His eyes opened and he slowly turned his head toward the jurors.

'First time I saw Gary in yard, he seemed . . . glad to see me. Excited. We just talked. When I asked about murder . . . he said he didn't . . . didn't kill girl . . .'

Booth paused and sipped from a straw in a plastic water bottle. The jury waited. Booth turned back to them.

'I was . . . a friend. He could trust me. He was nervous. Scared. Later, he told me the truth. He said . . . he killed her.'

'Did he just come out and confess?'

'No. It wasn't . . . first time. First time we talked, he said he didn't. Next day . . . he was upset. I told him he didn't have to be afraid. If . . . he wanted to get something . . . off chest . . .' Booth took a deep breath. 'Gary was scared . . . He needed to tell . . . someone.'

'What did he need to talk about?'

'Mistake. Girl at bar insulted Gary. He was confused. He attacked wrong girl. Then . . . too late.'

'So, the defendant thought Sandra Whiley was another girl who had insulted him in a bar and he told you he killed her by mistake.'

Booth nodded.

'Tell the jury the defendant's description of the murder.'

Booth drank some more water and gathered himself. His testimony was obviously exhausting him. Booth was generating so much sympathy that Gary would be dead and buried by the end of the hospital session if something dramatic did not happen.

'Gary tried to get date with . . . girl at Stallion. She said no. Gary . . . kept after her. She called him stupid . . . Made him angry. Gary grabbed her. Yelled at her.

'Gary said he . . . ran away. Still mad. Ran to his . . . house. Got hatchet. Went back to Stallion.'

'Did the defendant say that anything happened on his way back to the Stallion?'

'He saw girl. Thought she was . . . girl from bar.'

'The one who insulted him?'

Booth nodded.

'Where did he see her?'

'Near entrance to . . . park.'

'Was this the main entrance to Wishing Well Park that leads to the Wishing Well Memorial?'

Booth nodded again.

'What did the defendant say he did after spotting this woman?'

'He threatened her. She backed into the park.' Booth paused and took a sip of water. 'Gary grabbed her. They struggled. She had . . . necklace. Gary . . . grabbed her . . . by the necklace. It came off. She broke away.' Booth paused again. 'Ran to the well.'

'Who ran to the well?'

'The girl.'

'Then what happened?'

'Gary threw away . . . the necklace. Ran after her. Caught her.'

'Did he say what he did after catching her?'

Booth nodded. He stared at the jury.

'He killed her.'

'Did he say how many times he struck her or where?'

Booth shook his head. 'He was . . . upset. Crying. Gary just said he . . . hit her. More than once.'

'What happened after the defendant hit Miss Whiley with the hatchet?'

'She was . . . dead. He stood over her. That's when he saw he killed the wrong one.'

'What did the defendant do then?'

Booth sipped some water before continuing his testimony.

'He was scared. Ran away.'

'What did the defendant do with the hatchet?'

'Put it in storm drain . . . near college.'

'And after that?'

'Gary went to the Ponderosa.'

'That's a bar?'

Booth nodded.

'Did the defendant ever express remorse for killing Sandra Whiley?'

'He was sorry.'

'Sorry?'

Booth looked at the jury and waited a beat before saying, 'Sorry he killed the wrong girl.'

'Was anyone else present during these conversations between Mr. Harmon and yourself?' Peter Hale asked, when court resumed after a twenty-minute recess.

Booth shook his head.

'So, the jury has only your word that Mr. Harmon made this confession.'

Booth did not answer.

'You stand to benefit greatly from your testimony, don't you?'

'I don't . . . understand.'

'Well, let's start with the drug charges you're facing. You were arrested holding two garbage bags containing a total of twenty kilos of cocaine, weren't you?'

'I . . . didn't . . .'

'Your Honor, will you instruct Mr. Booth to answer the question, please?'

'Yes, Mr. Booth. You must answer yes or no, if you can.'

Booth ran his tongue across his lips, then nodded.

'And you had just been given the twenty kilos by Rafael Vargas, an enforcer for a Colombian drug cartel?'

Again, Booth nodded.

'Agents of the federal Drug Enforcement Administration made the arrest, did they not?'

Booth nodded.

'Which means you're facing charges in federal court?'

Booth nodded again.

'Has your lawyer told you that under the Federal Sentencing Guidelines you will most likely be sentenced to more than ten years in prison if you are convicted for possession of that much cocaine?'

'I . . . don't have . . . a lawyer.'

'I see. But you know the possible sentence?'

'Yes.'

'Did Ms. O'Shay tell you about that sentence?'

The question caught Booth off guard and he could not help looking at the prosecutor.

'Don't . . . remember.'

'That's interesting. You would think you would remember the person who told you that you were going to spend ten years in prison.'

Peter paused and Booth said nothing.

'You're not worried about spending any time in prison, are you, Mr. Booth?'

'What do . . . you mean?'

'Why don't you tell the jury about the deal you're going to receive for testifying?'

'No deal.'

'Are you telling this jury that you're not going to receive any benefit from the prosecutor or the federal government for testifying against Gary Harmon?'

'No deal.'

'Are you going to trial to contest the narcotics charge?'

'Don't know.'

'If you plead guilty or go to trial and are found guilty, do you think Ms. O'Shay will put in a good word for you with the judge at sentencing?'

'I hope so.'

'You know so, don't you, Mr. Booth, because you and Ms. O'Shay have a deal worked out already.'

'Asked and answered, Your Honor,' Becky said quickly. 'Mr. Booth has already explained that he is testifying without any promise of assistance from my office or the federal prosecutor.'

Peter could not believe this. There was obviously a deal. O'Shay and Booth had to be lying.

'Do you want this jury to believe that you are testifying out of the goodness of your heart?'

'Didn't want to,' Booth managed. 'Gary is my friend. But . . .' Booth shook his head slowly. 'That girl. To kill her like that. What if Gary was free . . . and killed again?' Booth paused. 'Couldn't have that . . . on conscience.'

'Did it bother your conscience when you lied to Mr Harmon at the Stallion by telling him that Karen Nix wanted to go out on a date with him?'

'Not me. Chris Mammon told Gary . . . about girl.'

'But you went along with it?'

Booth nodded.

'You've known Mr. Harmon since high school?'

Booth nodded again.

'Then you know he's mentally handicapped?'

Booth hesitated before nodding.

'And knowing this, you went along with Mammon's cruel joke?'

Booth ran a tongue over his lips. 'Didn't want to. Felt bad.'

'Oh? Does that mean that the witnesses who said you were laughing hysterically at Gary's discomfort were mistaken?'

Booth did not answer.

'You enjoyed tricking and teasing Mr. Harmon, didn't you?'

'No,' Booth rasped, but he did not sound convincing.

'And you had no difficulty lying to Gary to gain your ends at the Stallion, just like you have no trouble lying to this jury about what Gary said to you to save yourself from a federal prison sentence?'

'Objection,' O'Shay shouted.
'Sustained,' Judge Kuffel said.
'Then I have no further questions, Your Honor.'

3

Peter replayed Kevin Booth's testimony over and over during the five-hour ride from Portland to Whitaker and he always came to the same conclusion. Booth sounded as if he was telling the truth and Peter's cross-examination had not given the jury any reason to disbelieve him. His cross-examination of Booth had been as disheartening as his cross-examination of Dennis Downes. Neither witness had been broken because Peter was not sure how to cross-examine effectively. He'd had few chances to examine witnesses and his inexperience in court was killing him.

Peter considered going to the office and working on the case, but he was too depressed and tired. Then, he thought about going home, but he did not want to be alone. Finally, he decided to visit Donna and he felt better immediately. He had really enjoyed being with Donna the other night. It had been one of the few times since the trial started that he had been able to relax. Donna was attractive, but Peter tried not to think of her in that way because she was Steve's wife. He tried to think of her as a friend. Someone he could talk to. Someone he just enjoyed being around.

Peter hoped he would find Donna alone, but Rhonda Kates opened the door when he knocked. Rhonda had also proved to be a good friend. She had been great about helping Donna. When he saw her, Peter smiled warmly.

'Hi, Rhonda. Is Donna here?'

'She's freshening up.'

Peter noticed that Rhonda looked as though she was getting ready to go out.

'What's up?'

'Donna's moving back to her folks' house. I was going to drive her.'

'I'll do it. I have some stuff I have to go over with her about the trial.'

'Okay. How is the trial going?'

Peter stopped smiling. 'Not good,' he said.

The bathroom door opened and Donna walked out. She looked surprised to see Peter. Then, the look of surprise changed to a welcoming smile.

'Rhonda tells me you're going to your folks.'

Donna sobered. 'I'm sick of hiding. I didn't do anything wrong. Steve did. My brother is on trial for his life and Steve is not going to keep me from being in court to support him.'

'Are you going to tell your folks what happened?' Peter asked.

'Yes. I've decided that I have no reason to feel ashamed.'

'Good for you. If you want me to, I'll take you to the farm. I can fill you in on the case while we're driving.'

Donna hugged Rhonda and thanked her for putting her up.

'What happened at the hospital?' Donna asked as soon as they were on the road. Peter recounted Booth's testimony.

'Do you think the jurors believed him?'

'I don't know. What scares me is that he seemed to be telling the truth. And he was so pathetic.' Peter shook his head. 'The poor bastard could hardly talk.'

'Didn't your investigator find anything you could use against Booth?'

'Pullen has been a disaster.'

'I thought he was supposed to be good.'

'That's what Steve said, but I haven't seen any evidence of it. I can never find the guy. His reports are useless. The few times I have gotten in touch with him, he's been working at his brother's body shop instead of working on the case.'

'Why don't you fire him and hire someone new?'

'It's too late. We're in the middle of the trial.'

The road to the Harmon farm followed the river. It was a pretty stretch lined with elm and maple trees. Donna had lapsed into silence so Peter rolled down the driver's window and enjoyed the rich summer air until she said, 'I have an idea. I've lived in Whitaker my whole life. I know a lot of people here. Why don't you let me help with the investigation?'

'What?'

'I know I can do it. If . . . if we do go to a penalty phase, I can line up a million witnesses with good things to say about Gary. It would take another investigator weeks to make up a list of people I could remember in an afternoon.'

'You've never done any investigation, Donna. You wouldn't know how to go about it. You need a police background or training.'

'Barney Pullen has a police background. How much good has he done for Gary?'

'It wouldn't work.'

'Maybe not, but I can't do worse than Pullen, from what you've said, and I might do a hell of a lot better. At least you'd know I wasn't going to quit on you.'

Peter dropped Donna off at the Harmons' and headed back to town. During the drive, he thought over Donna's offer to act as his investigator. She meant well, but she had no experience and he needed someone who knew what he was doing. One thing she said had made sense, though. If Gary was convicted, the penalty phase would start after a short break. In the penalty phase, the defense told the defendant's life story to humanize him. Donna would not only know what people would be of use at trial, but those people would trust her and talk to her.

The phone was ringing when Peter walked in the door of his house. He answered on the third ring.

'Is this Peter Hale, the lawyer who's defending that guy who's supposed to have killed the girl in the park?'

'Right. Who's this?'

'Zack Howell. I'm a student. I go to Whitaker.'

'What's up, Zack?'

'I, uh, read the ad. The one you put in the *Clarion* asking anyone who was near Wishing Well Park when Sandy Whiley was murdered to call you.'

'Yes?'

'Well, uh, I didn't want to call, at first. But the guy is charged with murder. So, I talked it over with Jessie, my girlfriend, and she said we had to call.'

'You were near the park on the evening of the murder?'

'Yeah, we were.'

CHAPTER TWENTY-THREE

After talking to Zack Howell, Peter called Barney Pullen's house. A woman answered and told him that Pullen wasn't in. Peter left a message for the investigator, telling him to bring his reports to the courthouse at eight o'clock the next morning.

Peter was in front of the courthouse at eight sharp. At eight-twenty, Pullen showed up, looking annoyed.

'You're late,' Peter said.

'Sorry,' Pullen mumbled, but it was obvious that he didn't mean it.

'Where are your reports?'

'I haven't found a lot of useful stuff yet, Mr. Hale,' Pullen said, handing Peter a thin stack of paper, 'but I think I'm close to some good information.'

Peter thumbed through the reports quickly, because there was so little to read. He was stunned at first, then furious. When he looked up at Pullen, the investigator would not meet his eye.

'I can't believe this is everything you've done.'

Pullen shrugged.

'Have you walked off the distances between the Stallion, the Ponderosa and Gary's house, like I asked? I don't see a report on it in here.'

'I haven't had a chance to get to it, yet.'

'I asked you to do that weeks ago.'

'Yeah, I know. I was going to do that on the weekend, but something came up.'

'What was that, Barney?'

Pullen looked very uncomfortable. 'I promised my brother I'd take his kid fishing. I thought I'd have plenty of time to walk off the distances when we got back to town, but my car broke down. By the time I fixed it and got the kid back to his folks, I was beat. I should be able to get to it today.'

'Barney, this isn't working out.'

'What do you mean?'

'I mean that I'm getting someone else to take over the investigation. I just don't think you're doing a professional job and there's too much at stake.'

'What are you talking about? I've been busting my ass on this case.'

'We've got a difference of opinion on that. Send me a bill for your time. I've got to get to court.'

A reporter from the *Clarion* spotted Donna and her parents in the corridor outside Judge Kuffel's court-room. Before they could get inside, the reporter cornered Jesse and asked him for a comment. While her father talked to the reporter, Donna took a step back, hoping she would be left alone.

'Hi, Donna.'

She turned. Steve was standing next to her. Her breath caught and fear froze her.

'I have an appearance in Judge Staley's court. I

was heading there when I saw you.'

'I don't want to talk to you, Steve. Please go away.'

'You have every right to be angry. I just wanted to find out how you're doing.'

'I'm doing fine, now that you can't hit me.'

Mancini looked down. He seemed contrite.

'You don't deserve what I did. I'm . . . I don't know what I am. But I know that I love you and I want our marriage to work. I'm willing to go to counseling, if you think that's what I need.'

'I don't trust you, Steve, and this isn't the time.'

'I understand. I don't expect you to come back to me right away, but I want you to know that I still love you very much and I feel sick about what I've done to our marriage. I just want to know if we have a chance.'

'I don't know if we do,' Donna answered firmly.

Jesse Harmon turned away from the reporter and saw Steve. He flushed with anger and took a step forward. Donna put a hand on his arm.

'It's all right, Dad.'

Jesse glowered at Mancini, but held his tongue.

'Now isn't a good time,' Donna told Steve.

'Will you at least agree to talk this over?'

'I have to think.'

'Let's go, Donna,' Jesse said and Donna followed her parents into the courtroom.

Peter and Gary were already at their counsel table. Gary noticed Donna and grinned. He had been upset when she was not in court. Peter walked over to the bar of the court and motioned toward Donna.

'I thought over your idea about investigating for me. There are a few things I'd like you to do.'

'Oh, Peter,' Donna said excitedly.

'Look, I don't have any time now, but Becky told Judge Kuffel that she only has one short witness before she rests her case. Kuffel will send the jurors home when she rests, then hear motions. I think I'll be done by noon. Why don't I drive out to the farm after lunch. I'll make copies of all the investigative reports. You can read them over and we can talk about it tonight.'

'That would be great.'

The bailiff called the court to order and Donna and Peter took their seats just as Becky O'Shay recalled Dennis Downes to the stand.

'I have one more matter I want to discuss with you, Sergeant Downes,' O'Shay said, after the judge reminded the policeman that he was still under oath. O'Shay handed Downes a plastic evidence bag.

'Do you recognize the item of evidence marked State's Exhibit 76 that is contained in this plastic bag?'

'Yes.'

'What is it?'

'It's a Crusader's Cross on a chain.'

'A necklace?'

'Yes, ma'am.'

'Who owned this necklace?'

'We established that this medallion was Sandra Whiley's good luck charm. She was last seen wearing it by one of the bartenders at the Stallion shortly before she left the bar around eleven-twenty.'

'Was she still wearing the necklace when her body was discovered?'

'No. There was a bruise on Miss Whiley's neck that was consistent with a narrow object like the chain on the necklace being torn off forcefully.'

'Where was the necklace found?'

'In a bush near the entrance to Wishing Well Park.'

'Was the necklace damaged in any way when it was found?'

'The clasp had been broken in a manner consistent

with the necklace having been jerked off of the victim while she was wearing it.'

'How many people knew that Miss Whiley was not wearing the necklace when she was found?'

'Not many. It would only be the police at the scene, the medical examiner. Not all of the officers saw the body or learned about the discovery of the necklace.'

'So very few people would know that the necklace had been ripped from Miss Whiley's neck when she was killed as opposed to being removed from her neck by the police when her body was discovered at the well?'

'Yes, ma'am.'

'What conclusion would you draw as an experienced law enforcement officer, if you learned that Gary Harmon told someone that Sandra Whiley's killer had ripped a necklace from her just before he murdered her?'

Peter objected to the question and Judge Kuffel sustained his objection, but Downes's answer did not matter. The jury had heard Kevin Booth's account of Gary's confession and they were going to wonder how Gary could possibly have known that Sandra Whiley's Crusader's Cross had been ripped from her neck just before she was killed. Peter was wondering about that too when Becky O'Shay told the judge that the state was resting its case.

CHAPTER TWENTY-FOUR

1

The defense case was short and that worried Peter. He wondered if the jury would hold it against Gary that he was able to muster so few witnesses to speak on his behalf after so much testimony from the prosecution.

During the morning session of court Peter called several of the policemen who searched Gary's house to establish that no blood had been found on Gary's clothes. He also called the bartender from the Ponderosa, who testified that he saw Gary around midnight on the evening of the murder and did not notice any blood on his clothes. Then, he called Elmore Brock, whose shaggy brown hair, smooth skin and blue blazer made him look like a student in a parochial school. Gary's face lit up when he saw Brock and he waved at the witness. Brock looked unsure about smiling back, but he did when Gary started to look upset.

'That's Mr. Brock,' Gary told Peter excitedly.

'How are you employed, Mr. Brock?' Peter asked after getting Gary to quiet down.

'I'm the school psychologist at Eisenhower High School here in Whitaker.'

'Can you tell the jury your educational and professional background?'

Brock hunched over a little. He looked uncomfortable talking to the jury.

'I graduated from Portland State University with a B.A. in Psychology. Then, I obtained a master's degree from the University of Oregon in Special Education. After I received my master's, I spent one year in Portland at the Allen Center, a treatment facility with programs for preschool through adolescence. When the school psychologist position at Eisenhower High opened up six years ago, I applied for it and I've been there since then.'

'Mr. Brock, did you work with mentally handicapped children at the Allen Center?'

'Yes I did.'

'Does Eisenhower High have classes for the mentally handicapped?'

'It does.'

'What is the definition of "mentally handicapped"?'

'Uh, I'd say it means that a person has diminished capacity to take in and organize new information and diminished ability to use the information. The negative effects of this condition can be seen in all aspects of the handicapped person's life and it affects his educational, social and vocational functions.'

'Did you know Gary Harmon when he was a student at Eisenhower?'

'Yes, I did,' Brock said, turning toward Gary and smiling at him warmly. Gary smiled back.

'Was he classified as mentally handicapped?'

'Yes.'

'What is Gary's IQ?'

'Somewhere between 65 and 70.'

'What is the IQ of an average, normal person?'

'One hundred.'

'Would a person with an average IQ do well in college?'

'No. Most college students have IQ's in the range of 120.'

'Mr. Brock, what is the difference between Gary and someone with an average IQ?'

'Well, if you looked at a photograph, it wouldn't show any difference, but if you talked to Gary you would notice several things after a while. Gary's speech is going to be slower and less distinct. His vocabulary will be significantly smaller. His coordination and fine motor skills will also be more awkward and less developed.

'Gary also functions in the here and now. He doesn't have the ability to make plans that extend very far into the future and the plans he does make are going to be vague and may be unrealistic.'

Peter shot a quick look at Gary, but he showed no reaction during this clinical discussion of his intelligence level.

'What classes did Gary take in school?'

'They were special education classes designed to give Gary living skills and vocational skills. He also received some very basic education in mathematics, English and other subjects that normal children study.'

'Did Gary have an individualized education plan?'

'Yes. He trained to be a janitor and he worked at the college with the janitorial staff while in high school.'

'Was his work as a janitor satisfactory?'

'Definitely,' Brock answered enthusiastically. Gary sat up straight and smiled proudly. 'Gary works very hard at any task you give him. It took him a while to catch on, but Gary never stops trying to learn a skill.'

'Did Gary do any work for you?'

'Yes. He was always asking me if he could help me around the office. I usually told him no, because most of the work was too complicated for him, but I did have him Xerox items on occasion and he was great at stuffing envelopes.'

'I did good work for Mr. Brock,' Gary said.

'May I have a moment, Your Honor?' Peter asked.

Judge Kuffel nodded. Peter turned toward his client and put a hand on his shoulder.

'Gary, we talked about this,' Peter said quietly. 'You can't talk while a witness is testifying. Okay? You write down anything you think is important and we'll talk about it. But don't talk now.'

'I'm sorry,' Gary said.

'Mr. Brock, do you have Gary's school records?' Peter continued.

'Yes,' Brock said, holding up a manila folder.

'Was Gary a discipline problem at Eisenhower?'

'No, sir. In fact, there are very few negative comments in Gary's folder.'

'Do children with Gary's handicap tend to fight?'

'No. To the contrary. Mentally handicapped children tend to shy away from fights, even if they are big and strong like Gary, unless they come from a dysfunctional family and have developed antisocial traits.'

'Why is that?'

'They feel inadequate compared to so-called normal people. They get frightened easily and believe they need permission to do things.'

'Was Gary a mean or aggressive young man while at Eisenhower?'

'Definitely not. He was usually docile and very

sensitive to other people's feelings. Let me give you an example. Gary loves football. I remember one game where a teammate was injured. Mentally handicapped kids have feelings like everyone else, but they have a harder time controlling them. They sort of wear their heart on their sleeves. I remember Gary being in tears while the coaches attended to this kid.'

'As an expert in mental retardation and as someone who knows Gary personally, were you surprised to learn that Gary was charged with this murder?'

'Yes I was. Nothing I know about Gary would have prepared me for this. The amount of violence involved . . . Just the idea of Gary inflicting that kind of pain on another person is inconsistent with Gary's personality and the way someone of his intelligence would function.'

'No further questions.'

Becky O'Shay glanced through the copy of Gary's school records she had received weeks ago with Peter's discovery material. When she was done, she smiled warmly at Elmore Brock. Brock's shoulders hunched a little more, but he flashed back a brief, nervous smile.

'It's Mr. Brock, not Dr. Brock?' O'Shay asked sweetly.

'Yes.'

'So, *Mr.* Brock, you don't have a Ph.D.?'

'No.'

'Am I correct that your master's is not in psychology?'

'Yes.'

'In fact, you are not a licensed psychologist, are you?'

'No.'

'A licensed psychologist has to complete a one-year residency where he performs two thousand hours of therapy assessment in the area of his specialization while under the supervision of a licensed psychologist, doesn't he?'

'Yes.'

'You didn't do that, did you?'

Brock flushed.

'No,' he said.

'And a licensed psychologist has to take national written exams and an oral examination given to him by the Oregon State Board of Psychologist Examiners, doesn't he?'

'Yes.'

'But you didn't do that, did you?'

'No,' he answered tersely.

'Now, you've explained that the defendant is not as bright as normal folks, is that correct?'

'Yes.'

'Could you tell the jurors what Gary's high school average was?'

'That doesn't mean . . .'

'Your Honor . . . ?' O'Shay asked the judge.

'Yes, Mr. Brock. Please answer the question. If there is something Mr. Hale wants you to explain, he'll get a chance after Ms. O'Shay is done asking her questions.'

Brock ducked his head a little and said, 'Sorry.'

'That's okay, Mr. Brock,' the prosecutor said pleasantly. 'This is all new to you. Do you want the question read back?'

'No, I remember it. Gary had a 3.20 grade average.

'A 4.00 is straight A's, isn't it?'

'Yes.'

'And a 3.50 is honor roll?'

'Yes.'

'Now, I believe you said that someone like Mr. Harmon would have poor coordination?'

'Yes.'

'Didn't the defendant earn a varsity letter in football his senior year?'

Brock started to say something, then choked it back.

'Yes,' he answered tersely.

'You talked about things that the defendant can't do. I'd like to ask you about some things he can do. For instance, can Gary Harmon lie?'

'Well, yes. Gary could learn how to lie.'

'If he murdered a young girl would he be frightened?'

'Yes.'

'Would fear motivate a person with even an IQ of 65 to 70 to lie?'

'Yes.'

'Now, you told a touching story about the defendant weeping when he saw a teammate injured during a football game.'

'Yes.'

'Then, I believe you testified that Mr. Harmon wept because mentally handicapped people have the same emotions as normal people but they have a harder time controlling their feelings.'

'Yes.'

'Anger is an emotion, isn't it?'

Brock saw the trap into which he had fallen, but he had no choice but to respond affirmatively.

'Mr. Brock, if someone with an IQ of 65 to 70 was drinking and very frightened because he had just butchered a young girl with a hatchet while in an uncontrollable rage, might he not block out the memory of what he had done?'

'That's . . . that's possible.'

'Mentally handicapped people are capable of persevering at tasks, are they not?'

'Yes, they can be very single-minded.'

'So, if Mr. Harmon committed a particularly bloody and violent murder, fear might spur him to lie and he would be capable of sticking to that lie?'

'Yes.'

'What effect would being drunk have on this scenario?'

'Alcohol might make it more likely that Gary would not remember killing someone, if he did kill anyone,' Brock answered reluctantly.

'I didn't kill that girl,' Gary said.

'Your Honor,' O'Shay said, staring at the defendant.

'Mr. Harmon, you may not speak out in court,' Judge Kuffel admonished Gary. 'Do you understand me?'

Gary nodded. He looked upset. Peter whispered something in his ear and Gary looked down at the tabletop.

'You said that planning is more difficult for someone with Mr. Harmon's IQ, did you not?' O'Shay continued.

'Yes.'

'But he could plan a killing, couldn't he?'

'What type of killing are you talking about?'

'Let's say he was told that a woman at a bar wanted to go out with him by someone who was playing a practical joke. When Mr. Harmon asks the woman if she wants a beer, she not only rejects him, but insults his intelligence, a subject about which he is very sensitive. Let's say further that Mr. Harmon physically assaults this woman. My question, Doctor . . . Pardon me. *Mr.* Brock, is whether Mr. Harmon is intelligent enough to make a plan that involves going to his house to obtain a weapon, returning to the area of the bar, following a woman from the bar, killing her and getting rid of the murder weapon?'

'He . . . he could carry out that plan.'

O'Shay smiled. 'Thank you. I have no further questions.'

'Mr. Brock, you aren't a Ph.D., but you are a specialist in dealing with the mentally handicapped, are you not?' Peter asked the witness.

'Yes. That's where my training lies.'

'What does Gary Harmon's 3.20 grade point average mean?'

'Not much. His grades are only relative to his ability to perform the tasks he's given. Gary does not have an A in Advanced Physics. He has an A in life skills, which means he knows how to make his bed, tie his shoes and things of that sort. The grades are given to make the students feel good about themselves, not to reflect real academic merit.'

'Ms. O'Shay pointed out that Gary was on the varsity football team at Eisenhower. Tell the jury about that.'

Gary looked up at the mention of his favorite sport.

'Gary loves football. He went out for the team in ninth grade. The coach let him work out with the other boys, but he did not have the ability to really play. Learning all but the simplest plays would be beyond him. So, the coach let him suit up. Every once in a while, if the team was really behind or really ahead, Gary would go in for a play or two. He would be told to block a specific person.

'His senior year, the coach put Gary on varsity, but he was only in five or so plays all year. They gave him a varsity letter because he tried so hard, not because he did the things the other kids did to earn the letter.'

'I have one final series of questions, Mr. Brock. How easy would it be to fool Gary into believing that he had supernatural powers that would enable him to project himself into the mind of a dead woman and see how she was killed?'

'It would be very easy. Gary wants very much to please people. He would do or say anything for approval.'

'Would he invent a story to make a person in authority happy?'

'Most definitely. Gary has a very limited imagination, but he would pick up cues if the person talking to him suggested what he wanted to hear.'

'What effect would there be on Gary if the person questioning him was a policeman?'

'That would have a big effect. Someone with Gary's IQ will follow people in authority without question. If a policeman made suggestions to someone like Gary, there would be no way of telling if the mentally handicapped person was remembering something or making it up to please the policeman.'

2

After lunch, Peter called Don Bosco, who voiced his opinion that Dennis Downes had unwittingly placed Gary Harmon in a trance state during the interrogation, thus making any statement he made unreliable for evidentiary purposes. Bosco told the jury that Sergeant Downes's 'projection transfer' technique would invite someone of Gary's limited intelligence to fantasize in order to please his interrogator. He pointed out many sections of the transcript where leading and suggestive questions had elicited answers from Gary that echoed suggestions made by Downes.

'Mr. Bosco,' Becky O'Shay said, when it was her turn to cross-examine, 'if I understand you correctly, you are concerned that the defendant's statements may be unreliable because he may have parroted back suggestions made by Sergeant Downes instead of relating incidents in which he was actually involved.'

'That's right.'

'You weren't at Wishing Well Park when the murder was committed, were you?' O'Shay asked with a kind smile.

'No.'

'So you don't know whether Gary Harmon committed this murder and was telling Sergeant Downes about an incident he remembers or whether he was not present during the murder and is making up a story?'

'That's true.'

'Would one way of telling whether the defendant was making up what he told the officer be to see if he knew things about Sandra Whiley's murder that were not common knowledge and were not suggested to him by Sergeant Downes?'

'Yes.'

'Thank you. No further questions.'

Peter had saved his final witness for late in the day, so his testimony would be the last thing the jurors heard. He wanted the jurors to think about that testimony all night.

'Mr. Harmon calls Zachary Howell,' Peter said.

A slender young man with curly brown hair entered the courtroom and walked to the witness stand.

'Mr. Howell,' Peter asked, 'are you a freshman at Whitaker State College?'

'Yes, sir.'

'What are you studying?'

'Uh, I haven't settled on a major, yet. I'm thinking, maybe, biology.'

'Do you have a girlfriend, Mr. Howell?'

'Yes.'

'What's her name?'

'Jessie Freeman.'

'How did you come to be a witness in this case?'

'There was an ad in the school paper. It asked anyone with any information about the murder to call you.'

'Was the ad more specific?'

'You wanted to talk to anyone who'd been around Wishing Well Park from eleven P.M. to two-thirty A.M. on the evening that Sandra Whiley was killed.'

'Do you remember what you were doing on the evening that Sandra Whiley was murdered?'

'I was on a date with Jessie. We went to a late movie. Afterward, we went to Wishing Well Park and, uh, we were in the park for a while.'

Peter did not press Howell for more detailed testimony. He could tell from the amused looks of some of the jurors that they were well aware of what a young couple would be doing in the park on a romantic summer evening.

'When did you start to leave the park?'

'A little before eleven-thirty.'

'How can you be certain of the time?'

'We were going white water rafting the next day and we had to get up early, so I looked at my watch to see what time it was.'

'What path did you take to get out of Wishing Well Park?'

'We walked along the river until we reached the wishing well. Then we walked up the path and left through the main entrance.'

'Did you see a dead body next to the well when you passed by?'

'No, sir.'

'Would you have noticed a body?'

'Yes, sir. Jessie made a wish at the well and threw in

a penny. We were standing there looking down.'

'Do you know what Jessie wished for?'

'Yes, sir,' Howell smiled.

'Tell the jury how you figured out Jessie's wish?'

'When we reached the place where the stone pillars are, Jessie kissed me.'

'And did you kiss her back?'

'Yes, sir.'

'What happened then?'

'Jessie was holding onto my hand and she swung away from me and said, "See, wishes do come true." '

'She swung away,' Peter repeated.

'Yes.'

'Why do you remember all this so well, Mr. Howell?'

'The girl who was murdered, Sandy, she was in one of my classes. Everyone was talking about it the next day when we got back from rafting. I realized that we must have been right where the murder took place, right before it happened. That really scared me.'

'Mr. Howell, how long did it take between the time you decided to leave the park at a little before eleven-thirty and the time you actually left the park?'

'Not long. We were pretty near the well. Then, we stopped so Jessie could make her wish. That wasn't much time. I'd say no more than five minutes.'

'So, it was around eleven thirty-five when you were at the entrance to the park?'

'Yes.'

'How was Jessie dressed?'

'Jeans and a tee shirt.'

'Mr. Howell, are you taller or shorter than Jessie?'

'Taller. She's only about five four, five five.'

'One last question. What is the color of Jessie Freeman's hair and does she wear it short or long?'

'Jessie's hair is blond. She has long blond hair.'

3

'Are you telling me that you didn't know a thing about this witness?' Becky O'Shay shouted at Dennis Downes.

'Calm down, Becky.'

'Don't you realize that our whole case depends on the theory that Harmon made up his story about seeing two people kissing at the entrance to Wishing Well Park? Didn't you hear me tell the jury during opening statement that there were never two people kissing at the park entrance, that the two people at the entrance were Sandra Whiley and the murderer, Gary Harmon? Now, we've got two cute teenagers smooching at the pillars at eleven thirty-five. He is taller than she is, just as Harmon said. She swings away from him, just as Harmon said. And the girl has blond hair and was wearing jeans and a tee shirt, just like Sandra Whiley. Finally, we have Harmon eating biscuits and gravy at the Ponderosa without a drop of blood on him at midnight. The case is falling apart.'

Downes shrugged his shoulders. 'I don't know what to tell you. No one knew about Howell until he called Hale. It's just a bad break.'

O'Shay clenched her fists in frustration. Then she sank onto her chair and sagged.

'I'm sorry I yelled, Dennis. I'm just tired. You go and interview Howell for me. See if you can get me something I can use on cross. Call me at home if you come up with anything.'

Downes left and O'Shay stared at the stacks of police reports that covered her desk. Each one dealt with some aspect of the Harmon case. She had read through them countless times, but she vowed to go through them again in hopes of finding anything that would help her deal with Zack Howell's testimony.

Becky missed it her first time through because the clues were scattered around. A report here, a fragment of remembered conversation there. In fact, O'Shay did not put it all together until she caught sight of that afternoon's edition of the *Clarion* lying unread on top of her filing cabinet.

Becky sat up, openmouthed. Then she rummaged through the police reports until she found the one she wanted. A surge of energy coursed through her as she reread it. When she was done she placed several calls. The people with whom she spoke confirmed her conclusion. Zack Howell and Jessie Freeman may have been kissing at the entrance to Wishing Well Park and Gary Harmon may have been sitting in the Ponderosa at midnight eating biscuits and gravy, but Harmon had also murdered Sandra Whiley and Becky could prove it.

CHAPTER TWENTY-FIVE

1

The next day, Peter rested the defense case as soon as court convened, and Becky O'Shay called Dennis Downes as her first rebuttal witness.

'Sergeant Downes, you are aware that Dr. Guisti places Sandra Whiley's time of death sometime between eleven-thirty P.M. and two-thirty A.M.?'

'Yes, ma'am.'

'And the body was discovered early on Saturday morning?'

'Yes.'

'Did the authorities know Miss Whiley's identity immediately?'

'No. We couldn't find a wallet or purse, so it took a while to identify Miss Whiley.'

'When was the identification made?'

'After four that afternoon.'

'How did you discover the identity of the victim?'

'Marjorie Dooling, Miss Whiley's roommate, saw a sketch of the victim in the afternoon edition of the

Clarion and came down to the station house.'

'No further questions.'

'Any cross, Mr. Hale?' Judge Kuffel asked.

Peter had no idea why Becky had asked Downes about the time of the identification so he shook his head.

'The state calls Martin Renzler.'

Martin Renzler raised his hand and took the oath. He was tall and slender with wavy gray hair. Wire-rimmed glasses made him look studious. Renzler adjusted his suit jacket when he took the stand.

'How are you employed, Mr. Renzler?'

'I'm the managing editor of the *Whitaker Clarion*.'

'Is the *Clarion* the only daily paper in Whitaker County?'

'Yes.'

'On the morning of the day that Sandra Whiley's body was found did you receive a request from Sergeant Dennis Downes of the Whitaker police?'

'Yes.'

'What was the request?'

'He told me that the body of an unidentified female had been found in Wishing Well Park. Sergeant Downes asked if the paper would publish an artist's sketch of the woman because the police could not establish her identity.'

'Did the *Clarion* publish the sketch?'

'We ran the sketch on the front page.'

'When does the paper hit the streets?'

'I checked our records. The earliest the edition would have been out in the community is two-thirty P.M.'

'Nothing further,' O'Shay said.

Something Peter had read in a police report began to nag him. It had been a short report. Something about . . . about . . .

'The state calls Harry Diets.'

As Peter thumbed through the huge stack of reports, an overweight, thirtyish man in a business suit walked quickly up the aisle and was sworn. O'Shay established that he was the manager of KLPN, the local television station. Diets had also been contacted by Dennis Downes.

'Mr. Diets, did you broadcast the police sketch of the murdered girl?'

'We did. In fact, we made it part of a special bulletin and slipped it in at three P.M., because our next regular newscast is at five.'

Peter found the report he was looking for just as O'Shay called her next witness. As Wilma Polk walked to the witness stand, Peter read her statement to the police. By the time she had sworn to tell the whole truth and nothing but the truth, the reason she, Diets, Renzler and Downes had been called to testify dawned on Peter. As she testified to her recollections of the Harmon-Mancini wedding reception, Peter felt a sick, swirling feeling in the pit of his stomach.

'Did you learn about anything unusual that had occurred in Whitaker on the morning of the wedding?' the prosecutor asked.

'My husband, Eric, is a policeman. He was called out early. When he came back, he told me that a young woman had been murdered in Wishing Well Park.'

'Did you discuss the murder with Mabel Dawes, a friend of yours, at the wedding reception?'

'Yes, I did.'

'Please tell the jury what happened while you were talking to your friend.'

'We were at the food table. Gary Harmon walked over. He had a plate of food. I remember that, because it was piled very high and I was afraid some of the food might fall off.

'Gary seemed very interested in the murder. I remember Mabel saying that she would hate to be the person who had to break the news to the parents.'

'Did the defendant say anything to you at that point?'

'Yes. Yes he did.'

'What did he say?'

'He told us that the girl had been at the Stallion the night of the murder.'

Peter paled as he anticipated Becky O'Shay's next question and the answer he knew Wilma Polk would give.

'Do you remember when this converation with Gary Harmon took place?'

'Oh yes,' Wilma Polk answered with a vigorous nod. 'We were due at my daughter's house at two. My grandson, Kenny, was having a birthday party. He's three.'

'And the time?' O'Shay prodded.

'It was one-thirty. Eric said we had to hurry because the birthday was at two and it was already one-thirty.'

'One-thirty,' O'Shay repeated. 'And you're certain of that?'

'Oh yes, because I looked at my watch. Eric said it was one-thirty and that was exactly what my watch said.'

2

Donna had stayed up until after midnight going through the investigative reports again, after Peter left the Harmon farm. The first job Peter gave her was to use a stopwatch while tracing the possible paths Gary could have followed on the evening of the murder so

Peter could set up a time chart of Gary's movements. While she was making a list of all the routes she would have to walk, she noticed that she would be near the house where Sandra Whiley had lived with Marjorie Dooling.

The boardinghouse was a yellow, two-story Victorian with white trim. The lawn was neatly tended, but the front porch needed painting. A middle-aged woman answered the doorbell.

'Good afternoon,' Donna said nervously. 'Is Marjorie Dooling in?'

'I believe so,' the woman answered pleasantly. 'Who should I tell her is calling?'

Donna hesitated before identifying herself. She wondered if Dooling would recognize her last name and refuse to see her. After a moment's reflection, she decided that it was best to be honest.

Donna looked around the entry hall while the landlady went upstairs. After a minute, Donna heard the landlady knock on a door on the second floor and call out 'Marge.' A few minutes later, the landlady descended the stairs followed by a girl wearing a Grateful Dead concert tee shirt and cut-off jeans. Her brown hair was cut short. Donna recognized her because she had seen Marjorie Dooling testify.

'Ms. Dooling, I'm a private investigator working for Peter Hale.'

Dooling looked surprised. 'You're an investigator?'

'Just for this case,' Donna explained nervously. 'Most of the time, I'm a legal secretary.'

Suddenly, Dooling's brow furrowed. 'Isn't Hale the lawyer representing the . . . the man who killed . . . ?'

'We don't think he killed anyone.'

'I've already talked to the cops. They know your client killed Sandy. They told me he confessed.'

'The police can make mistakes. They're making a big one in this case.'

'Right.'

'Look, all I'd like to do is ask you a few questions about your friend. If it wasn't important, I wouldn't take up your time.'

Dooling worried her lower lip for a minute. Then she said, 'All right, but can you make it quick? I'm studying for a test.'

'I promise I won't be too long.'

'Come on up to my room.'

Dooling's apartment consisted of a large living room, a bathroom and two bedrooms. The living room walls were decorated with framed posters. Dooling sat on an old couch. In front of her was a low coffee table covered with textbooks and an open looseleaf notebook. Across from the couch was a TV and a CD player. Two old armchairs made up the rest of the furniture in the living room. Donna took one of the armchairs and opened her notebook. She noticed that the door to one of the bedrooms was closed.

'Was that Sandra Whiley's room?'

'Yeah,' Dooling answered quietly.

'Do you miss her?' she asked.

Dooling gave the question a lot of thought.

'We weren't super close, but she was nice. I guess I do miss her.'

'Can you tell me a little about her?'

'She was quiet. She was a good listener, too. I could talk to her, if I had a problem.'

'Did she date?'

'A little.'

'Do you think she might have been killed by someone she dated?'

'The police asked me the same question. I only met

a few of the guys she dated. None of them seemed like the type who would . . . You know.'

'How did you two meet?'

'Both of us were working our way through school by waitressing at Clark's. We got friendly and decided it would be cheaper for both of us to share my place.'

'Marjorie, can you think of anything unusual that happened around the time Sandy was killed?'

Dooling looked a little nervous. Then, she sighed.

'I guess it can't hurt now, and I already told the D.A. Sandy used drugs. A few months before she was killed, I started worrying that she was getting in too deep, but she wouldn't listen to me.'

'What drugs are we talking about?'

'Cocaine.'

'What did you mean when you said she was getting in too deep?'

'She didn't always use coke. Not when I met her. I mean, she may have experimented with it, but mostly it was grass. I started getting worried when the coke became a regular thing. I think she was seeing someone who turned her on to it. She was staying in her room a lot and skipping classes. She said everything was okay, but I didn't believe her.'

'Was this around the time of her death?'

'Actually, right around the murder I began thinking maybe she was trying to quit. She was acting different. She seemed scared of something, too. She was locking the door and not going out at night as much.'

'Did Sandy have family? Someone she might have talked to if something was bothering her?'

'I don't think she was close with her folks. They're divorced and she didn't see them much.'

'What about at school? Did she have friends other than you?'

'There was a girl in some of her classes. Annie something.'

'Do you have a phone number or address for this Annie?'

'No.'

'You mentioned that Sandy seemed scared. Was it of anyone in particular?'

Dooling hesitated. 'There was a guy.'

'Do you have a name?'

'No. But I know he scared her.'

'Can you describe him?'

'I only saw him once from the upstairs window. He came to pick her up and he stayed in his car.'

Donna asked her some more questions about Whiley's interests, her courses and her personal life. When Donna noticed that Dooling was glancing at the clock and her schoolwork, she stood up.

'Thanks for talking to me. I'm sorry I bothered you, but this has been helpful.' Donna handed Dooling the business card of the lawyer for whom she worked with her name handwritten on it. 'If you remember anything else, please give me a call.'

Donna waited until she was outside before taking a deep breath. She was nervous, but she decided that her first interview as an investigator had not gone too badly. She just didn't know if anything Dooling said would be of use to Peter.

3

The guard closed the door to the interview room and Gary sat down across from Peter. There was a dull smile on Gary's face. He started playing with the end of his tie. Peter shook his head. His client was totally oblivious to the havoc that had been wreaked on their case by the state's witnesses, but Wilma Polk's testimony had put Peter into a state of shock.

'I want you to listen up, Gary.'

'Okay.'

'I have a very important question for you and I want you to think before you answer it. Can you do that for me?'

'Sure.'

Gary sat up straight and stopped smiling.

'Sandy was murdered between eleven-thirty on Friday night and two-thirty on Saturday morning. You got that?'

'Uh huh,' Gary answered with a nod.

'Good. When Sandy's body was found early Saturday, she didn't have any identification on her. No one knew her name. So, the police asked the newspaper and the TV to show her picture and ask for help in finding out who she was. Are you following me?'

'Yeah, Pete. They didn't know Sandy's name.'

'Right. Good. Okay. Now the newspaper came out around two-thirty in the afternoon and the TV showed Sandy's picture at three. Sandy's roommate told the police Sandy's name around four. Two-thirty in the afternoon is the earliest anyone could have known who Sandy was because that's when the paper came out with her picture. Do you see that?'

'They coulda seen the picture,' Gary said with a smile.

'Right. But there was no picture before two-thirty.'

'No one coulda seen it before two-thirty.'

'Right. Now listen up. Here's my question, Gary. Mrs. Polk says that at one-thirty, at the wedding reception, you told her the dead girl was at the Stallion on Friday evening. Do you remember her saying that?'

'Who's Mrs. Polk?' Gary asked.

'The last witness. That lady with the gray hair.'

Gary looked down at the table. He was embarrassed.

'I didn't listen to her too good. I was hungry.'

Peter calmed himself with a deep breath. He did not want to get upset. He did not want to yell at Gary.

'That's okay. I was hungry too. Do you remember Mrs. Polk from the wedding?'

Gary's brow furrowed as he tried to remember Mrs. Polk. Finally, he shook his head.

'I don't remember that lady.'

'Do you remember telling anyone that the girl was at the Stallion.'

'No.'

'Well, you did. That's what Mrs. Polk said. So, how could you do that? If no one else knew who was killed at one-thirty, how did you know the girl had been at the Stallion?'

'I don't know.'

'Well, think.'

Gary started to look worried. He shifted in his seat.

'Maybe it was my powers. Maybe I seen it with my mind,' Gary said, anxious to please Peter.

'We've been over this already, Gary. You do not have powers. No one has those powers. Sergeant Downes fooled you.'

Gary thought hard for a moment. Then he looked confused. Finally he turned to Peter and asked, 'If I don't have those powers, how did I do it, Pete? How did I know who that girl was?'

4

'Shit! Shit! Shit!' Peter screamed as soon as he was safely locked in his car with the music cranked up. The session with Gary had driven him insane. Tomorrow, he would have to give his closing argument. What was he going to say? How was he going to explain all of the facts that Gary knew about this case that only the murderer could possibly know?

Peter wanted to believe that Gary was innocent, but he was starting to wonder. Gary was capable of physical violence. He had attacked Karen Nix. Elmore Brock had testified that Gary was intelligent enough to plan the murder of Sandra Whiley.

Gary seemed so gentle, so childlike, but he had been drinking on the night of the murder.

How could Gary fool him for this long if he was guilty? Brock said Gary could lie and stick to a lie. Mentally handicapped individuals could persevere at a task. If Gary was frightened of exposure could he maintain a lie for this long? What if he did not need to lie? That was the most frightening possibility. What if Gary murdered Sandra Whiley and did not even know it? What if the combination of alcohol and fear had erased the horrible deed from Gary's memory?

The Harmons lived in a white, two-story colonial farmhouse. There was a large front lawn bounded by a white board fence. Donna came onto the front porch as soon as she heard Peter's car chewing up the gravel on the circular driveway. She was dying to tell him all of the things she had done on her first day as his investigator. Her smile disappeared as soon as she saw Peter's face.

'What's wrong?'

'That's what I have to talk to you about.'

Donna ushered Peter into the large front room. Jesse and Alice were at a church function, so they were alone. As soon as they were seated, Peter related the testimony that established that Gary knew the victim had been at the Stallion before anyone else knew her identity. Donna looked more and more troubled as Peter spoke.

'Where was Gary before he went to the Stallion Friday night?'

'With us. Mom cooked a meal for Steve and the family. Steve had to leave early to work on his cases so he could go on our honeymoon. He gave Gary a lift into town.'

'Did Steve tell you where he dropped off Gary?'

'I think it was at home. Gary must have walked to the Stallion on his own. It's not that far from his house.'

'Gary says he went to Steve's house from the bar. When he didn't find him home, he walked to the Ponderosa. Gary ate there, but he also did some more drinking. The bartender at the Ponderosa says he was pretty tipsy when he left around two A.M. Gary doesn't remember going to bed, but he does remember getting up early and doing his wash. When did you see him next?'

'When he and Steve arrived at the church. Steve picked up Gary and drove him over. I asked him to do it in case Gary was having any trouble with his tuxedo.'

'Was Gary home when Steve arrived?'

'Steve said he was.'

Peter thought for a minute. Then, he asked, 'Did Gary say anything to you at the church or the reception that relates to the murder?'

'Gary did say there were police cars at the park. You pass it on the way to the church. I remember that he was excited. But I had the impression that he just saw them as they drove by.'

'You know Gary better than anyone. Could he have killed that girl?'

'I'll never believe Gary could be so cruel.'

Peter shook his head. He looked exhausted and thoroughly dejected.

'I'm afraid that he's going to be convicted. He knew Whiley was at the Stallion before anyone else knew who she was. He told Booth about the necklace. He knew the killer used a hatchet and where it was hidden. How can you explain all that?'

'I can't,' Donna answered softly. 'I just know Gary.'

'I don't think he killed Whiley, either, but I don't think I can save him, Donna. I . . . I probably shouldn't have taken the case in the first place. Maybe with another lawyer . . .'

Donna put a hand on Peter's shoulder. 'You're doing a great job. You can't blame yourself because the state's witnesses are saying things that hurt Gary.'

Peter felt awful. Donna had so much faith in him, but she wasn't a lawyer who would know how poor a job he was really doing. He could no longer hide the truth from himself.

'I can blame myself. I had no business taking on this case. Amos Geary was right. He said I would screw it up and I have. I'm no criminal lawyer. I'm no lawyer at all.'

'That's not true. You've worked harder than anyone. You've done a wonderful job.'

Donna was so trusting. Peter felt sick.

'There's something I have to tell you. It's about why I came to Whitaker. I . . . I didn't choose to leave Hale, Greaves. I was fired. I was helping out in a big personal injury case my father was trying. Right before we went to court, he had a heart attack. Dad told me to ask for a mistrial, but I wanted to show him and everyone at the firm that I was a great trial attorney, so I lied to the judge and said that Dad wanted me to finish the trial.

'The case was so easy that a first-year law student could have won it. It took a real genius to screw it up, but I did and . . . and this poor woman . . .' Peter shook his head. 'You should have seen her, Donna. She had nothing. She was dirt poor with five kids to raise by herself and then she became this cripple. Then, the worst thing happened. She got me for her attorney and I destroyed any hope she and her kids had in one afternoon. And now I'm doing the same thing to Gary.'

'You're being too hard on yourself.'

Peter looked directly at Donna.

'When I took your brother's case, I didn't even think about him. All I was thinking about was how famous I'd be if I won. I didn't care enough about him to think of what might happen if I screwed up his case the way I did Mrs. Elliot's.'

'You care for him now, though, don't you?' Donna asked quietly.

'I do. I admire Gary. He's a much better person than I am. I don't think he would ever intentionally hurt anyone. He thinks about the feelings of other people. When he has to do a job, he tries to do his very best. He's not like me at all and I wish I could be a little more like him.'

Donna reached up and touched Peter's cheek.

'I don't know what kind of person you were in Portland. I just know you now. I can see how much you care for Gary.' Donna paused and looked down. 'I know what you did for me.'

Peter wanted to take Donna in his arms, but he couldn't take advantage of her when she was so vulnerable. Donna must have realized how close they were to doing something they would regret, because she pulled her hand back. For a moment, they sat on the couch in an awkward silence, then, Donna said, 'I . . . I paced off those distances for you this afternoon.'

'Great,' Peter answered in a shaky voice, relieved that the danger was over. 'What did you find out?'

'I started at the Stallion and walked to Gary's house. It's a little over three quarters of a mile and it took me about twelve minutes. Then, I went back to the bar and continued to the park entrance. It's one-quarter mile from the Stallion to the entrance, so it took me sixteen minutes to walk from the house to the park.'

'That means Gary got home at about eleven-twelve if he left the Stallion at eleven and walked straight home.'

'If he was walking my speed,' Donna corrected. 'He could have run or walked faster.'

'Okay, but he's still got to take some time trying to find a weapon.'

Peter worked the numbers in his head.

'Damn. It could still work out. If he leaves his house around eleven-twelve, follows Whiley and gets to the park around eleven thirty-six . . . If Howell and his girl friend left the park around eleven thirty-five and Whiley passed by a little after . . .'

'I've been thinking about that, Peter. If it's only a quarter mile from the Stallion to the main park entrance, and it takes about fifteen minutes for the average person to walk one mile, it would only take about three minutes to walk a quarter of a mile. If Whiley left the bar around eleven-twenty, she should have reached the entrance to the park before those kids.'

'You're right! That would put her there around eleven twenty-five. But Howell said that Jessie made a wish at the well around eleven-thirty and the body wasn't there. Where was Whiley between eleven-twenty, when she left the Stallion, and eleven thirty-five, when

Howell and Freeman left the park?'

'Did you ask Howell and his girlfriend if they saw anyone when they were in the park?'

'Yeah. They don't remember spotting anyone, but they were probably too wrapped up in each other to notice anything. Tell me about the rest of your results.'

'Gary could have made it to the Ponderosa from the park in fifteen to twenty minutes, so he could have killed Whiley around eleven thirty-seven and made it to the bar by eleven fifty-five.'

'Did you go from the park to the storm drain where the hatchet was found and back to the Ponderosa?'

'Yes. The storm drain is near the campus. We're talking a little under two miles. Even if Gary ran it in a seven-minute mile, there's no way he could kill Whiley after eleven thirty-five, ditch the hatchet and make it to the Ponderosa by midnight.'

'So he'd have to hide the hatchet somewhere before going to the Ponderosa, then pick it up later. That sounds a little complicated for someone of Gary's intelligence, but I'll have to ask Elmore Brock about that.'

Peter stood up. He looked depressed.

'I've got to go back to the office to work on my closing argument. You keep working on character witnesses for the penalty phase. I hope we don't need them, but I'm afraid we will.'

CHAPTER TWENTY-SIX

1

They came for Gary just as the sun was setting. His heart fluttered like the wings of a trapped bird. In the back of the police car, the city fading in the gathering darkness, Gary prayed, 'Please, God, please, God,' over and over. He promised God he would be good. He promised he would never make Mom and Dad ashamed or mad again. Please, God.

The reporters were waiting on the courthouse steps, cigarettes dangling, cameras resting on the concrete slabs, engaged in loose conversation or lost to the stillness of sundown, until someone spotted the police car. All at once, they were up, jerked into action like marionettes. When the car doors opened, the mob pressed in, jabbing at him with microphones and screaming questions at him. Gary cringed in a corner of the backseat. The sheriff's deputies cleared a path as Gary struggled out of the car, the task more difficult because he was handcuffed. He looked for a friendly face and saw Peter pushing through the crowd.

'What did they say?' Gary asked, as Peter helped him up the steps.

'I don't know. They have to read the verdict in court. The jurors are waiting in the jury room.'

'Are Mom and Dad here?' Gary asked as they took the elevator up to the courtroom, surrounded by sheriff's deputies.

'Yes. I called them, first thing. Donna is with them.'

The guards escorted Peter and Gary to the defense table. As they took off Gary's handcuffs, a stir in the back of the courtroom signaled Becky O'Shay's entrance. She looked grim and intentionally avoided eye contact with Peter and his client. The bailiff scurried into the judge's chamber to tell him that all of the parties were in the courtroom. Moments later, the bailiff emerged from chambers and entered the jury room. When the door to the jury room opened, the undercurrent of noise in the courtroom stopped. There was a rustle of clothing and a tap of heels as the jurors worked their way to their seats in the jury box. Peter searched their faces for a clue to the verdict, but the jurors would not look at him or O'Shay. Beside Peter, Gary twisted anxiously in his seat.

As soon as the jurors were settled, the bailiff pressed a button at the side of his desk to signal the judge. Everyone stood when Judge Kuffel entered the courtroom. When he was seated, the judge turned toward the jury box.

'Ladies and gentlemen, have you reached a verdict?'

Ernest Clayfield, a farmer, stood slowly. He held a folded sheet of paper in his hand.

'We have,' Clayfield answered grimly.

'Please hand your verdict to the bailiff,' the judge commanded.

Clayfield held out his hand and the bailiff took the verdict form from him and gave it to the judge. Kuffel unfolded it and read it once. Then he looked at Gary.

'Will the defendant please stand,' he said in a subdued voice. Gary jumped up, but Peter felt dizzy from tension and his legs were weak. It took an effort to get to his feet.

'Omitting the caption,' Judge Kuffel said, 'the verdict reads as follows: "We the jury, being duly impaneled and sworn, find the defendant GUILTY as charged." '

There was complete silence for a moment, then Peter heard Alice Harmon moan as Donna softly cried out, 'No.' He was looking down at the courtroom floor and did not see the wide smile of satisfaction on Becky O'Shay's face. A babble of voices filled the air.

Judge Kuffel gaveled for silence, then asked, 'Do you want the jury polled, Mr. Hale?'

'Yes,' Peter managed. He touched Gary's shoulder and slumped down in his seat as the judge asked each juror if he or she agreed with the verdict.

'What happened?' Gary asked.

'They found you guilty, Gary,' Peter said. 'They think you killed that girl.'

Gary looked stunned. He rose slowly to his feet and stared at the judge. The guards started forward.

'I didn't do it,' Gary said.

The judge stopped polling the jury and said, 'Please sit down, Mr. Harmon.'

'I didn't hurt that girl,' Gary cried out, his voice breaking.

'Mr. Harmon,' the judge repeated as the guards drew closer.

'I'm a good boy,' Gary wailed. 'I want to go home.'

Peter stood and placed a hand on Gary's shoulder.

Behind him he could hear Donna's sobs.

'I wanna go home. I want my momma. I don't like that jail. I wanna go home.'

Peter wrapped his arms around Gary and held him. Gary's body shook as he took gigantic breaths and wailed like a confused and frightened child.

2

Gary had been transferred to the security block in the Whitaker jail as soon as the guilty verdict was received. It consisted of a row of fifteen narrow cells. Each cell was wide enough for a bunk and a bunk's width of floor space. At the back of the cell was a toilet. Outside the row of cells was an area where the inmates could take their only exercise by walking back and forth along the bars. A color television was affixed to the bars high up, in the middle. The guards controlled the programs and the viewing hours. Gary hated his narrow cell. It was like a coffin.

Entry to the security block was made through a sally port. Gary heard the grating sound of the sally port door sliding open and strained through the bars of his cell to see the visitor. When Peter was safely inside the sally port, the outer door slid shut and the guard opened the inner door electronically. The other inmates were locked down while Peter visited. They stared as he walked by. Life on the block was so dull that any change in routine was as great a diversion as a Broadway show.

Gary's cell door was operated from the same master control that opened the sally port gates. When Peter was in front of the cell, the guard opened it and Peter stepped inside. He had planned on a cheery greeting but Gary looked so sad that all he could manage was, 'Hi, Gary' in a voice so subdued that he wasn't certain he had even said the words aloud.

'Can I go home, Peter?'

Peter ignored the question.

'Sit down, Gary. There are some things we have to discuss.'

Gary sat on the bunk and Peter joined him. There was no other place to sit in the cell, except the toilet, which had no lid.

'You're going to have to stay in this cell for a while.'

'Why? Why can't I go back to my other cell? That cell was bigger.'

'That cell was for when you weren't convicted. Now you are. The penalty phase of your trial will start next week and the sheriff is afraid you might try to escape, so he wants you here.'

'I won't try to escape, Pete. I promise. Tell the sheriff I won't try to escape.'

'I did tell him, but he has rules he has to follow if a person is convicted. You know about rules, right, Gary? If there are rules, you have to follow them.'

Gary looked glum. 'I guess if it's the rule, he has to follow that rule.'

'Right. Now I have something serious we have to talk about, so listen hard.'

'Okay, I'm listening.'

'Do you know what happens during the penalty phase of your trial?'

'No, Pete. What happens?'

'You . . . you've, uh, been convicted of aggravated murder. That's the most serious crime in Oregon. The jury is going to listen to the D.A. and your lawyer and decide which of three punishments to give you. Two of the punishments are life sentences. One life sentence lets you have a possible parole after thirty years. One life sentence doesn't have parole. That means you can't get out ever.'

'I don't like that. I want to get out.'

Peter started to explain to Gary that he could not get out of prison, but he stopped himself. It was all so futile.

'There's another punishment, Gary. You could receive a death sentence. The jury could say that you should be execu . . . killed. Do you understand?'

'I don't want that one,' Gary said. He sounded scared.

'And I don't want you to get that punishment either,' Peter said, his words catching in his throat. 'That's why we're having this talk.

'Now pay close attention, Gary. It's very important that you have a really good lawyer in the penalty phase and I don't think I should be your lawyer.'

Gary looked surprised, then even more frightened.

'Don't you want to be my lawyer? You're a good lawyer.'

'I'm not so sure about that, Gary. I haven't done very well with this case so far. I . . . I've never tried a penalty phase. If I told the judge that I'm not good enough to represent you, he'd get you a good lawyer.'

'No, no,' Gary said in a panic, 'you're my lawyer.'

'Yes, Gary, but I think you'd do better with another lawyer.'

'Oh no. You're the best lawyer,' Gary said with conviction. 'And you're my friend. My best friend. You'll save me. I know you won't let them give me those bad punishments.'

'Jesus, Gary . . .' Peter started, but he did not have the heart to go on. 'Think about it, will you. Really think about it. Because, I don't know . . . Just think about it.'

PART SIX

THE FLATLANDS

CHAPTER TWENTY-SEVEN

1

Judge Kuffel set the start of the penalty phase for a week from Monday, which gave Peter very little time to recover from the trial. On Sunday, Peter woke up a little after nine from a restless sleep haunted by unsettling dreams. He did not want to spend the day in his depressing rental house and he did not have the energy for a run, so, after a shower and breakfast, he went to the office.

Peter had no plan to save Gary. He spent the first half hour aimlessly stacking everything in his case files on his desk. He had been through the police reports, the autopsy report and witness statements several times. The only thing new were Donna's neatly typed investigative reports. Peter picked them up and went through them without enthusiasm. He found nothing of interest until he read Donna's summary of her interview with Marjorie Dooling. Something she'd written triggered a memory and Peter shuffled through the police reports until he found David Thorne's statement.

*

As Peter entered the Stallion, a man in a Pittsburgh Steeler uniform spun away from two Oakland Raider defenders and gained five yards before being brought down by another Raider. Several patrons groaned and several more cheered. The bartender turned away from the television when the Steelers called a time-out.

'Dave Thorne?'

'That's me,' the bartender answered with a smile.

'I'm Peter Hale, Gary Harmon's lawyer.'

The smile disappeared. 'Tough loss, man.' Thorne shook his head. 'I have a hard time believing Gary could do something like that.'

'I don't think he did. That's why I'm here. I wanted to ask you about something you told the police. It was in the statement you gave to Dennis Downes.'

'I remember that.'

'I was interested in what you had to say about Sandra Whiley. She was sitting at the end of the bar farthest from the door, right?'

'Yeah, near my station.'

'So you saw her for a while?'

'I wasn't paying that much attention. I was pretty busy.'

'Right, but in the report you said that there was a time when she seemed nervous or frightened.'

'I did?'

Peter gave him a copy of his statement and Thorne read it carefully. He stopped at a section of the report that Peter had highlighted in Magic Marker. Thorne read it twice, then nodded vigorously.

'I remember now. What do you want to know?'

'You said that she was watching two men who were walking toward the back door and she seemed frightened. Tell me about that.'

'It was after I called Steve Mancini. When I turned around, Whiley looked shocked or scared. I thought she was staring at two guys on the level above the dance floor, up there.'

Peter looked where Thorne was pointing.

'Did you get a good look at the men?' Peter asked.

'No. It was dark and I only glanced at them. Things were pretty frantic up front.'

'Can you describe them at all?'

Thorne thought for a second. Then he brightened.

'One guy made no impression, but the other guy was huge. I remember thinking he looked like a pro wrestler.'

Marjorie Dooling had appeared briefly as a witness in the state's case-in-chief. Peter asked her no questions, but he remembered what she looked like. It only took him a few minutes to locate her in the Whitaker State College library, where her landlady said she was studying. Dooling was hunched over a history text at a large table next to a row of book-filled stacks. The seat across from her was empty and Peter took it.

'Miss Dooling, my name is Peter Hale.' He handed her a business card. 'I represent Gary Harmon. You testified at the trial.' Dooling's features clouded. 'You were kind enough to talk to my investigator the other day, and there was one small item in her report that I wanted to clear up.'

'All right,' Dooling sighed. 'One question. But that's all. I have a test tomorrow.'

Peter showed Dooling the section of Donna's report where she had mentioned the man who came to the house to pick up Sandy.

'You said you thought Sandy was frightened of him.'

'She was real nervous all day. When he honked the

horn for her, she seemed scared to me.'

'Can you remember anything more about the man who picked her up? His hair color, his size?'

Dooling started to shake her head. Then, she stopped as something occurred to her.

'I only saw him from the second-floor window and he was in his car. But there was something. When Sandy came out of the door, his arm was resting on the car window. I only saw it for a second, because he brought it inside as soon as he saw her.'

'What about the arm?'

'He was wearing a short-sleeve tee shirt and I could see part of his biceps and his forearm. They were really big, like a weight-lifter's, and they were covered by tattoos.'

'Can you describe the tattoos?'

Dooling closed her eyes. When they opened, she said, 'I'm not certain. Like I said, I was looking from a second-floor window and I only saw his arm for a moment, but I think I saw snakes and a panther.'

Peter drove back to his office in a fog. Sandra Whiley knew, and was afraid of, Christopher Mammon. Was Mammon monitoring Gary's trial to make certain that he was not implicated by any of the evidence? Mammon had the opportunity to commit the crime. He left the Stallion around the time that Whiley left the bar. If Peter could show that a monster like Mammon had a reason to harm Whiley, Gary Harmon would cease to be the only viable suspect in her murder.

As Peter parked in front of Mancini's building, he remembered Amos Geary telling him to read Mammon's file before the preliminary hearing, but Peter had only given the documents in the file a cursory glance. Now he wished he had been more thorough. There might have been something in the file that would help Gary. Asking Geary to see the file would be useless. He doubted Geary would even talk to him. Besides, the file was confidential and Peter no longer worked for Geary. However, Steve Mancini represented Kevin Booth in the case involving the Whitaker State bust. He would also have the police reports.

All of the closed files in the office were in a large room behind the secretarial station. Peter turned on the lights. Mancini's files were arranged alphabetically, so Peter found Booth's file quickly. It was not that thick, since the case had not gotten past the preliminary hearing. There was a table with a reading lamp at the front of the file room. Peter sat down and opened the file. He took out the envelope holding the police reports and piled them on the table. He read through the reports slowly, but discovered nothing helpful until he found two reports halfway down that looked strange. They were different in form from the other reports and seemed neater. It did not take Peter long to figure out why the reports looked different. They had not been written by the Whitaker police or the campus police. They were reports written by agents of the DEA, the federal Drug Enforcement Administration.

The first report detailed the activities of an unnamed, confidential, reliable informant, or CRI, who had been busted with cocaine and had agreed to work off the case by setting up Kevin Booth. The report was a chronological history of the contacts between Booth and the CRI in Whitaker. The CRI was to purchase increasingly larger amounts of cocaine from Booth until Booth was unable to supply the CRI's demand and had to agree to put the CRI in touch with someone who could.

The second report detailed the arrest of Kevin Booth and Christopher Mammon on the Whitaker campus, but it contained information about the arrest that was new to Peter. The CRI was supposed to be bringing thirty thousand dollars to Booth for two kilos of cocaine. After the sale went through, the CRI was going to up the ante to a point that would force Booth to use his contacts to supply a very large amount of cocaine. It was hoped that this deal would be handled directly by Booth's supplier. From the report, it appeared that the arrest by campus security had been totally unexpected and neither the DEA nor the Whitaker police wanted the arrest to occur.

Peter was certain he had never seen either of the DEA reports in Geary's file. Why would Mancini have them, but not Geary? Peter reread the reports. A thought occurred to him and he felt himself grow cold. What if Sandra Whiley was not simply an innocent bystander who was murdered by mistake? What if she was working off an arrest for cocaine and had betrayed Christopher Mammon to the DEA? That would give Mammon a huge motive for murder.

Peter put the envelope with the police reports back in the file. He was about to close it when he spotted a telephone message slip that Mancini had clipped into the folder on the left side. The slip was dated the day before the preliminary hearing.

The letters ASAP underlined in red and written in capital letters caught Peter's eye.

Peter read the message carefully. It was from Becky O'Shay. She wanted Steve to call as soon as he came in – ASAP – so they could discuss a deal in the Booth case. Peter wondered what the deal had been. Maybe

that's what Steve and Becky had been discussing when
he saw them in the hall outside the courtroom before
the prelim. But the deal had obviously fallen through
because Booth had not pled guilty.

Peter replaced the file and was about to leave the file
room when another thought struck him. Becky O'Shay
must have given Steve Mancini the DEA reports. That
meant she knew about the existence of the CRI. Did
she also know the identity of the CRI? If Whiley was the
CRI and Becky knew it, but kept it a secret, Peter could
use that fact as a basis for a motion for a new trial. But
before he confronted O'Shay or filed a motion, he had
find out if Sandra Whiley was the CRI and Peter
thought he knew how he could do that.

2

'I don't know, Peter. I could get in a lot of trouble,'
Rhonda Kates said.

'I know that. I wouldn't ask if I wasn't desperate.'

'Why don't you just tell the district attorney that you
need to talk to Booth. Don't they have to let you talk to
witnesses?'

'They do. But the D.A. would insist on coming along
or she'd convince Booth to refuse to see me.'

'I thought that was illegal.'

'The reason I have to sneak into Booth's room is
because I think the D.A. has already done something
illegal. Becky will do anything to win.

'Look, all you've got to do is get the guard away from
Booth's door. I only have one question to ask him. I'll
be in and out.'

'This is a lot to ask.'

'Rhonda, Donna's brother may be innocent. If

Kevin Booth says what I think he will, I may be able to set Gary's verdict aside and give the police the real killer. If I don't get in to see Booth, Gary will most probably be on death row by the end of next week.'

Kevin Booth had been moved to a room at the Whitaker hospital two days before. A guard sat in front of his door at all times. Peter waited in an alcove a short distance from Booth's room and used his cellular phone to call the hospital. He asked for the extension at the nurses' station farthest from Booth's room. Rhonda picked up on the first ring and pretended to carry on a conversation. Then, she placed the receiver down and told the other nurse to make sure the phone was not hung up.

Peter watched as Rhonda told the guard that there was a call for him. He seemed nervous about leaving his station, but Rhonda said the call was from the station house and the caller had said it was urgent. As soon as the policeman got up, Peter slipped into Booth's room.

Booth's hospital gown covered most of his burns, but here and there Peter saw patches of shiny, bright red and purple skin surrounded by bunches of scars. Booth's face was still covered with cream.

'Hi, Mr. Booth. I'm Peter Hale, Gary Harmon's lawyer,' Peter said with what he hoped was a winning smile. 'We met in Portland.'

'What are you doing here?' Booth asked. His speech was normal now. 'I thought the case was over.'

'It is. Actually, I had a question about the Whitaker State bust. The one you beat.'

'Why do you want to know about that case?'

'Chris Mammon still has to go to trial on it.'

'Well, fuck him. I don't give a rat's ass about Mammon.'

Peter thought fast.

'This may not help Mr. Mammon. Actually, your answer could really hurt his case. But I've got to know if he's telling us the truth. If he's not, he could end up serving a long prison term.'

'What did you want to know?' Booth asked, interested in anything that would keep Christopher Mammon off his back.

'You know when you were busted at Whitaker State. Was Sandra Whiley bringing you thirty thousand dollars or three thousand? It will make a big difference at sentencing. Mammon claims that Whiley was only going to bring three thousand and that he didn't know how much cocaine was in the Ziploc bags.'

Booth snorted. 'Mammon's lying. He knew exactly how much dope was in the bags. He weighed them himself. And he knew how much dough Whiley was bringing because he told her to bring the thirty grand.'

'Sorry to hear that. Say, was Mammon aware that Whiley was working for the feds?'

'Not before we got busted. But after, I said the bitch must have turned us in. Chris was furious. He said he was gonna check it out.'

'That's what we heard,' Peter said solemnly. 'Where'd you meet Whiley?'

Booth tilted his head to the side and looked at Peter suspiciously. 'I thought you were interested in Mammon.'

'I am. He says he didn't know Whiley well. I thought, if you knew her, you could set the record straight.'

'He's lyin' to you. Personally, I think he was screwing her.'

'You do?'

'The bitch would do anything for cocaine.'

Suddenly Booth laughed.

'What's so funny?'

'If Whiley was working for the feds there's gonna be a lot of nervous people in this burg.'

'Why's that?'

'She never had much money, so she had to earn her snow. One way she did that was by making deliveries. She could name a lot of names.'

'Like who?'

' "Mr. Football" for one. It would serve the cocksucker right, the way he left me hanging as soon as I said I didn't have any money.'

'Who are you talking about?'

Before Booth could answer, the door opened and the guard walked in. When he saw Peter, he put his hand on his gun.

'Who are you and what are you doing in here?'

'I'm an attorney,' Peter said with righteous indignation. 'This man is a witness in the Harmon case. I have a constitutional right to talk to him.'

'Let's see some identification,' the guard said, taking the gun out and pointing it at Peter.

'No problem. I'm just going to get my wallet, see.'

Peter pulled the wallet out slowly and handed a business card to the officer. The policeman studied Peter for a minute.

'Yeah, you're Harmon's lawyer. I recognize you now. I don't know what you think you're doing, but sneaking in here on my watch is going to get your ass hauled down to the station.'

'You better check before you try that,' Peter said with more bravado then he felt. 'Whitaker doesn't have enough money to cover the damages I'll win if you arrest me for talking to a witness in a death penalty case.'

The guard looked a little uncertain, but he stood his ground. Several people had clustered in the doorway to see what was going on. The officer turned to one of them.

'Nurse, call the station house and ask for one of the sergeants. Tell them we have a situation here.'

3

Dennis Downes had no idea whether Peter's shenanigans were legal or illegal. Peter was an attorney and Booth was a key witness. As soon as he learned what Peter had done, he called Becky O'Shay. O'Shay had sworn long and loudly, then told Downes she would be at the station in a few minutes.

'Just what do you think you're doing, Hale?' O'Shay demanded the minute the door to the interrogation room closed behind her.

'My duty under the Constitution of the United States.'

'Your duty, my ass. That man is my witness and he's in protective custody. You are in big trouble. The worst you're looking at is a bar complaint and I've got someone checking to see if you've broken any laws.'

Peter was furious with O'Shay, but he did not let it show. Instead, he asked in a casual tone, 'Do you think what I did was as bad as hiding the fact that your victim, Miss Whiley, was the woman who was bringing the thirty thousand dollars to Christopher Mammon and Kevin Booth on the evening of their arrest?'

Peter noticed, with satisfaction, that O'Shay's

normally pale complexion was now thoroughly bleached of color.

'Do you think it's as bad as concealing from me the fact that Miss Whiley was working with the cops, a fact that Mammon suspected and that drove him into a murderous rage, thus making him a very viable suspect in Miss Whiley's murder?'

'What ... what are you talking about?' O'Shay stuttered.

'I'm talking about a serious violation of your duty as a prosecutor to turn over to the defense *all* exculpatory evidence in your possession. I think the fact that you knew a homicidal maniac like Christopher Mammon had it in for the deceased and failed to mention that little tidbit to me constitutes a gross violation of your duties as a prosecutor, an officer of the court and a human being.'

'Mammon didn't kill Whiley, your client did,' O'Shay said.

'That's for a jury to decide, not you.'

'In case you've forgotten, hotshot, a jury did decide.'

'They didn't have all the facts.'

'This bullshit about Mammon is just that, bullshit,' O'Shay shot back, seemingly over her initial shock. 'I gave you all the information you were entitled to.'

'We'll see about that. I think it's time to go to Judge Kuffel.'

For a brief second, O'Shay looked panicky. Then, she sat down across from Peter and, in a reasonable tone, said, 'Listen, Peter, I shouldn't have gotten so angry. I know the pressure you've been under. And there's Harmon's family. This has been tough on everyone. But I can tell you that you're barking up the wrong tree.'

'I've seen the DEA reports you sent to Steve Mancini.'

'What are you talking about?'

'The reports that mention the CR1 who was involved with the drug deal at Whitaker State where Mammon and Booth were arrested.'

'I didn't send any DEA reports to Steve Mancini.'

'Someone did. They were in with your discovery material.'

'Let me see them.'

'I don't have them. They're in Steve's file.'

'I think you're confused, Peter. If Whiley was working with the government, I would have been told.'

O'Shay stood up and headed for the door.

'Where are you going?'

'Home. It's Sunday.'

'Are you going to tell Downes to let me go?'

'As soon as I'm certain that you haven't broken any laws.'

'And when will that be?'

'When the deputy I've got working on the project lets me know.'

'That's fine by me, Becky. You're just increasing the damages I'm going to receive when I sue the Whitaker police, the Whitaker District Attorney's Office and you, personally.'

The door to the interrogation room slammed shut and Peter swore.

4

The police held Peter for two more hours, then they let him go. While he was in custody, it occurred to Peter that he should make a copy of the DEA reports to show to the judge when he filed his motion for a new trial. Peter's car was still at the hospital, so he hiked there and picked it up. He arrived at the office a little after eight. All the lights were out. Peter went directly to the file room and took out the envelope with the police reports. He shuffled through them twice before realizing that someone had removed the DEA reports from the file.

Peter's first reaction was anger at Becky O'Shay. She had to be behind the theft. She was the only person to whom he had mentioned the reports. He felt so stupid for doing that, but he never would have believed she would go this far to hold on to her victory. She must have kept him in custody long enough to send someone to the office to retrieve the reports from the file.

Unfortunately for O'Shay, there was someone else who knew about the reports. Peter walked to his office and dialed Steve Mancini. It was going to look very bad for O'Shay when Steve confirmed the existence of the two documents in front of Judge Kuffel. There would definitely be enough circumstantial evidence to support an inquiry by the Oregon State Bar into O'Shay's behavior.

'Steve, this is Peter,' he said as soon as Mancini picked up.

'How are you doing?' Mancini asked. 'You didn't look so good after the verdict.'

'I didn't feel so good, either, but something has happened that's gotten me excited. I found out that Sandra Whiley was involved with the drug deal that went sour at Whitaker State. The one where Chris Mammon and Kevin Booth were arrested.'

'What!'

'Yeah. I think Whiley was working with the police and Mammon found out. It gives him a terrific motive to kill her.'

'That's incredible. How did you work that out?'

'I hope you're not mad, but after I learned about the relationship between Mammon and Whiley I looked in your file on Kevin Booth. I couldn't ask Amos Geary to let me see Mammon's file and I remembered that you'd have the same discovery. I should have called you first, but I was so excited I just did it.'

'That's okay. You shouldn't have looked at the file. It's confidential. But Gary's life is at stake.'

'Thanks, Steve. Anyway, I found two reports in your file from the DEA,' Peter went on. Then, he told Steve about his interview with Booth at the hospital, his detention by the police and his discovery that the reports had been removed from the file.

'Becky must have had someone break in here and remove them while I was at the police station,' Peter concluded, 'but she made one mistake. She forgot that you've seen the reports. You can confirm their existence. Once the judge realizes that I saw the reports around noon, I told her about them around four and they were gone by eight, he's going to reach the same conclusion I have and O'Shay's ass will be grass. Kuffel is going to have to give Gary a new trial, once he determines that Becky failed to turn over key evidence that points to another suspect.'

'These reports,' Mancini asked hesitantly, 'what did they look like?'

'They were typed up. Each one was a couple of pages long. They were written by DEA agents.'

'Pete, I honestly don't remember seeing any reports from the DEA in the discovery I received from Becky.'

'Well, they were in there.'

'I'm sure they were. I mean, you just read the reports a few hours ago. All I'm saying is that I haven't looked at that file in a while and I just don't recall those reports.'

'How can that be?'

'Booth's case wasn't that big a deal. I think I read through the reports once, real fast. He told me his version. All the stuff I needed to win at the prelim was in the report that the campus security guy filed. I'm sorry. I'll spend some serious time thinking about it, but right now I don't remember any DEA reports.'

Peter hung up in a daze. He had been counting on Steve to support him. If Mancini could not remember the reports, he had nothing. Then, Peter recalled the last thing Kevin Booth said before the guard burst into Booth's hospital room. Something about Whiley making cocaine deliveries to pay for her drugs. Booth had said that several people in Whitaker would have to worry if Whiley was working for the police and she named names. The only person he'd had time to mention before the guard came in was 'Mr. Football,' who had dropped Booth when he found out Booth did not have any money.

Peter walked to the front door of the law office and inspected it. He did the same with every other door that led into the building. None of them showed signs of forced entry. The person who took the DEA reports had a key to Steve Mancini's law office. Peter did not want to believe it. Could Steve have taken the reports? Peter raced back to the file room and opened the Booth file again. The phone message about the deal offer from O'Shay was also missing. Peter felt sick. Why was Mancini helping Becky O'Shay, and what were they covering up?

Suddenly, Peter recalled Steve's failure to tell him about his interview with Don Bosco. It was Steve who suggested that Peter convince Gary to plead guilty. Mancini had given him the names of three investi-gators, but the only one who was available was the incompetent Barney Pullen. Peter had assumed that Steve Mancini was his ally from the moment he'd become Gary Harmon's lawyer, but now it appeared that Mancini had a hidden agenda of his own and Peter suspected that it included saddling Gary with the lawyer least qualified to handle his case.

5

Peter parked his car at the edge of the dirt drive that led to the garage and surveyed Amos Geary's house. Like its owner, it was broken down and aging. Weeds had overgrown a front yard that had not seen a mower in recent times, the paint was peeling and faded. Only God knew the original color.

There was a light on behind a worn curtain in the front room. Peter hesitated before getting out of the car. He could drive away, but to what destination?

One of the steps leading to the porch was cracked and Peter stumbled over it. He caught himself by breaking his fall with his hands. This was not an auspicious sign. Peter thought about turning back, but the door opened. When Peter looked up, he found Amos Geary, dressed in a bathrobe and striped pajamas, looking down at him with contempt.

'Jesus, Hale, you are pathetic. Can't you even walk up a flight of stairs without making a mess of it?'

'Good evening, Mr. Geary,' Peter stuttered as he stood up awkwardly. His hands stung where they had smacked into the wooden porch.

'What are you doing on my property?' Geary demanded.

'I'm in trouble.'

'I'm not interested.'

Geary turned to go inside.

'Wait!' Peter shouted. 'It's not me. It's Gary. Gary Harmon is in trouble.'

Geary paused. He turned back. There was a chill in the evening air. A gust of wind went right through Peter and he shuddered.

'What do you want from me?'

'You're the only person I can turn to.'

'What happened to your good buddy Steve?'

'There's something going on and Steve may be part of it.'

'Going on?'

'A, uh, cover-up.'

Peter said the word hesitantly, knowing that it would make him appear paranoid.

'Something like the Kennedy assassination?' Geary asked with a snort. 'Something involving the CIA, perhaps? Go home, Hale. You sound ridiculous.'

'Please, Mr. Geary. I know I let you down . . .'

'You didn't let me down. I expected you to fuck up. In fact, Peter, you've confirmed my faith in my ability to judge the merits of my fellow man.'

Geary almost had the door shut. Peter was desperate.

'Goddamn it,' he shouted, 'this isn't about you or me. It's about Gary. That poor bastard is in jail for a murder he didn't commit.'

Geary held on to the screen door and looked at Peter over his shoulder.

'Whose fault is that, Hale?'

'Mine! Are you happy? There, I said it. It's my fault. I'm everything you said I was. I'm a self-centered, shallow asshole and I'm asking for your help because I know I don't have what it takes to save Gary.'

'My advice to you is to return the retainer you took

under false pretenses to the Harmons, confess your misrepresentations and tell them to hire a real lawyer to represent their son.'

'It's not that simple. Please, hear me out. There's more to this than the murder in the park. I think Steve Mancini and Becky O'Shay have been working together to cover up something. I don't know what it is, but it's tied into the arrest of Christopher Mammon and Kevin Booth at Whitaker State.'

Peter thought that Geary's eyes suddenly looked clearer and that the old lawyer was standing a little taller. Geary pushed the screen door open.

'Come inside. It's too cold to talk on the porch.'

'Thank you,' Peter answered.

The inside of Geary's house was in as much disorder as the exterior. The living room couch Geary indicated was covered in a flower pattern that had nothing to do with anything else in the room. It was worn and the springs sagged when Peter sat on it.

'You want a drink?' Geary asked.

'Actually, yes.'

Geary shuffled out of the room and returned with a fifth of Johnnie Walker and two moderately clean glasses. He poured a liberal amount of scotch in each glass and handed one of them to Peter.

'Talk,' he said after taking a sip.

Peter started at the beginning. He told Geary how Steve Mancini had manipulated him into taking Gary's case and he explained his suspicions about the ways Mancini had sabotaged it. Finally, he told Geary about the day's incidents, ending with his discovery that the reports and the phone message slip were missing and his suspicion that they had been removed by Steve Mancini.

'That's quite a story,' Geary said when Peter was

finished. 'Some people might think that you're inventing excuses to explain why you lost Gary Harmon's trial.'

'I can see how someone might think that,' Peter answered, his eyes locked on Geary's.

'The way I understand it, with the DEA reports missing and Mancini and O'Shay denying their existence, you have no evidence at all to support your highly unbelievable story of a government cover-up.'

'That's true.'

'Then why do you think I can help you?'

This was the hard part. Peter took a deep breath.

'When I learned the reports were missing and Steve was most probably the one who'd removed them, I decided that the only thing left was to go to the source. I called the DEA office in Portland. There was only one agent on duty because it's a weekend, but eventually I was put through to Guy Price, the agent in charge. I told him everything and I told him how important it was to get copies of the reports so I could go to Judge Kuffel and ask him to reopen the case. I was certain Price would help me. He isn't some ambitious, small-town D.A. like Becky. He's a federal agent.'

Peter paused. He was exhausted and remembering one of the most depressing moments in his day didn't make him feel any better.

'He didn't help, did he?' Geary said.

Peter shook his head. 'He told me that he couldn't confirm or deny any ongoing investigation.'

'Is that all he said?'

'No,' Peter answered with a tired smile. 'He wished me good luck.'

Geary laughed. 'That sounds like your government in action, son. If nothing else, you're certainly learning a lot about the real world here in Whitaker.'

'Yeah,' Peter answered ruefully.

'You still haven't told me how you think I can help you.'

'I almost gave up after my call to Price. Then I remembered that there was one person I knew who had enough clout to make someone like Price talk.'

'I hope you don't mean me?' Geary asked incredulously.

'No, Mr. Geary. I . . . I came here tonight to ask you to please call my father and ask him to talk to me.'

CHAPTER TWENTY-EIGHT

Peter had not slept well and the five-hour drive from Whitaker should have exhausted him, but he was floating by the time he saw the skyline of downtown Portland and the high green hills that formed its backdrop. He was home and he was welcome once again in his father's house.

The night before, Amos Geary had talked to Richard Hale on the phone in his den for almost half an hour while Peter waited nervously in the living room. When Geary finally told Peter that his father wanted to talk to him, he had hesitated. Now that his opportunity for reconciliation had arrived, he was afraid.

When Peter entered the den, the receiver lay on its side on the edge of an old, rolltop desk. Peter had reached toward it, then stopped just before his fingers touched the plastic. What was he going to say to Richard? He hadn't thought that far ahead. Should he tell his father that he loved him? Should he say how sorry he was for disappointing him so often? Should he ask forgiveness for falling so far below his father's expectations? In the end, all he managed was 'Dad?' in a voice choked with emotions he was not yet able to express.

'Amos gave me an outline of your problem, but I'd like you to tell me everything from the beginning,' Richard had responded. It was as if there had never been an Elliot case or the intervening months of exile. One part of Peter was relieved that he was able to avoid the emotional exchange he assumed would precede their discussion of Gary's case, but there was another part of him that longed for a tearful reconciliation in which he confessed his sins and inadequacies and Richard forgave him. Thinking about it during the drive, Peter came to the conclusion that his father was not capable of crushing his son to him in a warm and forgiving hug. Peter knew he would never see tears trickling down his father's cheeks. Richard Hale was simply not the type of man who could express his emotions. This assistance in his hour of greatest need might be all his father was able to give.

The office of the United States Attorney for Oregon was in downtown Portland, a few blocks from the offices of Hale, Greaves. It was a little after five when Peter studied his reflection in the glass at the entrance to the office building. He had worn a charcoal gray pinstripe suit, a Hermès tie and his best silk shirt for the meeting. Sunlight rebounded from the shine on his black wing tips.

When Peter entered the lobby, Richard was standing off to one side. He had put on weight since the day he sent Peter into exile, but Richard was still thinner than Peter's mental image of his father.

'How was the drive?' Richard asked.

'Long and boring.'

Richard smiled.

'Thanks for doing this for me,' Peter said.

'You're my son,' Richard answered simply. Then he turned toward the elevators.

'I don't know what to expect, Peter. There are no guarantees. Katherine probably knows nothing about what's going on in Whitaker. At best, one of the assistant U.S. attorneys is working with the DEA agent in charge of the case. Price might not even know that much about the operation or, if he does, his people may not be involved in this cover-up. That might be the work of the D.A. in Whitaker and your friend, Mancini.'

'I know that. I just want to find out if Whiley was working for the DEA and whether O'Shay knew it. And I want copies of any reports that will prove O'Shay knew about the Mammon-Whiley connection.

The elevator doors opened into a reception area. Richard announced their presence to a receptionist who sat behind a window of bullet-proof glass. Minutes later, a door opened and a tall, well-dressed woman with glasses and short black hair walked into the waiting area.

Katherine Hickox owed her appointment to the state circuit court bench to Richard Hale and others at Hale, Greaves, and it was to Richard Hale that she had turned when she decided to apply for the position of United States Attorney. Richard had quietly touted her to Oregon's United States senators and had made a phone call to a high-ranking official in the Justice Department with whom he had served on a committee of the American Bar Association. So, it was no surprise when Hickox agreed to meet with Peter's father at five-thirty and to make certain that Guy Price attended the meeting.

'Richard,' she said, offering him her hand.

Richard took it, then motioned Peter forward.

'This is my son, Peter. He's just driven in from Whitaker.'

'It's nice meeting you,' Hickox said warmly. If she knew about Peter's disgrace she hid her feelings well. 'Let's go back to my office. Guy is waiting for us there.'

Hickox led them along a series of corridors to a corner office with a panoramic view of the city. When they entered, a short, muscular man in a brown sports coat stood up. After she made the introductions, Hickox sat down behind a large oak desk and Price sat beside it.

'Why don't you tell us why you needed to meet?' Hickox suggested.

'Mr. Price,' Richard said, looking directly at the DEA agent, 'my son called you from Whitaker yesterday.'

When Richard called Hickox to set up the meeting, he had not mentioned that his son would be accompanying him. Price suddenly made the connection. He did not looked pleased.

'For your benefit, Katherine, Peter has been trying a death penalty case in Whitaker. Last week, his client was convicted of murdering a woman named Sandra Whiley. Until yesterday, there did not appear to be anyone else in Whitaker with a motive to murder the young woman. Then, Peter discovered two DEA reports in the files of a Whitaker attorney named Steve Mancini. The reports, coupled with other information, led him to conclude that Whiley had been working as an informant for the DEA in a case in Whitaker involving a very dangerous and violent drug dealer named Christopher Mammon.

'These DEA reports were mixed in with police reports that had been given to Mancini in the drug case by the district attorney who is prosecuting the death penalty case. When Peter asked her about the reports, she denied knowing anything about them. Peter returned to his office to make copies of the reports and found them missing. He called Mr. Price for assistance and was told that it was against policy to confirm or deny the existence of an ongoing investigation. I'm here to ask Mr. Price to tell Peter if Sandra Whiley was working for the DEA in a case involving Christopher Mammon so that Peter can try to avert a miscarriage of justice.'

Price looked uncomfortable. 'I told your son that I can't discuss ongoing investigations, even to confirm or deny them. I'm afraid that's still my position. I wish you'd called me before having your son drive all the way here from Whitaker for nothing.'

'I understand the official position of your office, Mr. Price. What you need to understand is the effect of following it,' Richard told the agent coldly. 'If Sandra Whiley was working for the DEA and the Whitaker district attorney intentionally concealed this fact from Peter, she is guilty of a gross violation of the discovery rules. If she conspired to have the reports destroyed to prevent Peter from proving her misconduct, she may be guilty of a crime.'

'Mr. Hale, I know you want to help your son, but I'm not going to discuss DEA business with either of you. If this D.A. is violating some law, your son should take it up with the judge who's trying the case.'

Hale stared hard enough to make Price break eye contact. Then, in a level tone, he said, 'Katherine will tell you that I am not without influence. If I find out that you're aware that Sandra Whiley was an informant for the DEA in the Whitaker case and you kept quiet about it, knowing it could cost a young man his life, I will personally make sure that you wish you were never born.'

Price's eyes widened and he leaped to his feet.

'Guy!' Hickox said, holding out her hand in his direction. Price remained standing, but he restrained himself. The U.S. Attorney turned to Richard.

'I won't have you threatening Guy in my office, Richard.'

'You're quite right,' Richard said, in a tone that let Price know he still meant to keep his promise. 'I apologize, Mr. Price. I'm sure you probably don't know what's going on in Whitaker and I'm equally certain that you'll do the right thing, if you discover that an obstruction of justice is occurring there.'

Price glared at Richard, but held his tongue.

'Thank you for meeting with Peter and me, Katherine.'

'Let me show you out,' Hickox answered stiffly.

As soon as they were out of Price's hearing, Hickox said, 'How dare you pull a stunt like that? I don't work for you and I won't let you involve me in one of your cases.'

Peter's father stopped and looked directly at Katherine Hickox.

'You don't work for me, but you are the chief law enforcement officer for the United States Government in this district. I wanted you to know that something very dirty may be going on in your baliwick. Something you don't want to be part of. Have a talk with Mr. Price after we're gone. Listen carefully to what he tells you. Price may be clean, but he can find out if someone else is dirty and he can make certain that Peter gets a copy of those reports. I've known you a long time, Katherine, and I know you'll do what is right.'

When the elevator doors closed, leaving Peter and his father alone, Peter exhaled with relief.

'Jesus, Dad, are you sure you know what you're doing? Price is a really powerful person.'

Richard turned to Peter with a wry smile.

'It's because Price is so powerful that I called him out. I'm sure no one has talked to him like that for some time. As soon as we left the room, I bet he started thinking about what type of person would have the balls to dress him down like I did. And Katherine is going to tell him as soon as he asks her, which should be right about now.'

'You might have made him so angry, he won't help out of spite.'

'I weighed that risk, but Price is a bureaucrat. He can't afford a scandal. If someone is fucking around with one of his investigations, he won't like it.'

'I hope you're right.'

'We'll know soon enough.'

'Dad, thanks. You put yourself out for me and I really appreciate it.'

'I haven't done a thing. You're the one who's going the extra mile for a client and I'm very proud of you.'

Peter's chest swelled and he felt a lump in his throat. The elevator doors opened and Peter followed his father into the lobby.

'What are your plans?' Richard asked.

Peter looked at his watch. It was after six.

'It's too late to drive back to Whitaker. I guess I'll get a room at a hotel and head back in the morning.'

'Nonsense. We'll have dinner and you'll stay with

me. You can sleep in your old room.'

'I'd like that,' Peter said. He didn't know if his father realized it, but he had just given Peter the best present he had ever received.

CHAPTER TWENTY-NINE

Peter was exhausted but happy when he pulled into his driveway the next evening. He and his father had not talked about the future, but it was obvious that they had one together. Not right away. Peter still had a lot to prove to Richard, but the wall between them had come down.

As soon as he entered his house, Peter slapped together a quick dinner, showered and put on jeans and a sweatshirt. Then, he checked the TV listings for something completely mindless. Tomorrow morning, Peter planned to plunge back into the Harmon case with a vengeance. Tonight, he would relax and get a good night's sleep.

The phone rang during the sitcom he was watching. Peter turned down the sound. The voice on the other end of the phone was soft and indistinct, as if the speaker was trying to disguise it.

'Peter Hale?'

'Yes?'

'I'm only going to say this once, so pay close attention. If you want to find out the truth about Christopher Mammon and Sandra Whiley, take the highway east. Eight point three miles from the WELCOME TO WHITAKER sign, there's a dirt road on the right. Drive down the road until you come to a barn. I'll be waiting. If you're not here by ten-thirty, I'll be gone. And come alone or I won't show.'

The flatlands was a desolate stretch of cracked brown earth that began a few miles east of the Whitaker city limits. No one lived in the flatlands. It was a place to drive through, not a place to visit in the dead of night. As soon as the glow of the city lights faded away, Peter felt he was riding through a sea of ink. There was no moon and no other source of illumination but his headlights and the stars, which hid behind a cover of thick clouds. The highway was one lane east and west. The only trace of color was the broken white line that divided it. To the left and right the only variety was provided by an occasional tumbleweed or a patch of sagebrush.

Peter set his odometer as soon as he passed the WELCOME TO WHITAKER sign. When it read eight point one, he slowed down and strained toward the side of the highway. The turnoff was more of a dirt track than a road and he almost missed it. The car started to buck as soon as it began traversing the narrow, rutted trail. Peter stared around nervously. His isolation was complete. There was not even the broken white line to break up the monotonously bleak and barren landscape that loomed up in his headlights, then disappeared as he passed by.

After a while, Peter's headlights settled on a shape in the distance. As he drew closer, he made out the burned and rotting timbers of an abandoned barn. Peter wondered why anyone would have dreamed that farming was possible in this desert, but the thought was fleeting and it was replaced by a feeling of dread when he realized that there were no other cars in sight.

Peter kept the lights on and the motor running. There was a flashlight in the glove compartment. He took it and stepped out of the car. It felt very strange to be out at night in a place where there was no artificial light. Without the headlights, Peter would be in complete darkness.

A wind ripped across the flat, dry ground and knifed through Peter. He used his free hand to zip his windbreaker tight around his neck. Then he took a few steps from his car and stared hard at the barn. No shapes emerged, no lights flickered in its dark recesses.

Peter turned slowly in a circle. He strained for any sound, but there was only the low hum of the wind. Nerves made Peter's stomach tighten. Maybe it would be for the best if no one did show. He was beginning to seriously question the wisdom of coming to this wasteland on the darkest of nights. He remembered the autopsy photographs of Sandra Whiley and the descriptions of the way the other victims had perished. It had to take time to die like that. He imagined the blade biting in, the pain, the terror.

'Have any trouble finding this place?'

Peter's heart streaked through his chest. He spun toward the voice, reflexively raising the flashlight like a weapon, but there was no one to strike. The area around him was black and empty.

Peter looked right and left as he tried to catch his

breath. Suddenly, there was a break in the dark curtain that surrounded him. A blur became a vague shape and Christopher Mammon stepped out of the darkness. Peter took a step back. Mammon watched him. Could he get into the car and lock the doors before Mammon got to him? Could he streak away and outdistance Mammon in the stygian darkness of this desert hunting ground?

'I hear you've been telling people that I killed Sandra Whiley.'

Peter tried to talk, but he couldn't.

'Not smart. Everyone else thinks Gary Harmon murdered Whiley. If I did kill her, you'd be the only one who suspected it. It would be in my best interest to lure you to an isolated spot like this and get rid of you before you could cause any trouble.'

Mammon let Peter think about that for a moment. Then he took a step forward. There was something small and black in his hand. Peter's next step brought him hard against the side of the car. Mammon raised his hand and pointed the object at Peter. 'Oh, God,' Peter thought. 'Don't let me die now. I'm not even thirty.' Then part of the object dropped down revealing something shiny.

'You can relax,' Mammon said. 'I'm not going to kill you. I'm a cop.'

It took a moment for the words to register. About the same amount of time it took for Peter's brain to recognize the object in Mammon's hand as a leather carrying case for a badge. Peter sagged against his car. If it had not been there to hold him up, he would have sunk onto the dusty, rock-strewn ground.

'Now listen up,' Mammon said. 'If you want to learn the truth, I need a guarantee that you will never, ever tell anyone about this meeting.'

'What are you talking about?'

'I'm deep cover in an operation that has been going on for two years. As soon as we finish talking, I'm leaving this continent. No one at DEA will acknowledge my existence. You can file subpoena duces tecums until you're old and gray and you won't find a trace of me in any of the files you'll be searching. So you play this by my rules or I'm gone and you'll never know what happened to Sandra Whiley.'

'I . . . I've got no choice, then.'

'That's right. And there's something else you should know. You and your father really pissed off a couple of people. I've got instructions from the top to stay as far away from you as I can.'

'Then, why are you doing this?'

Mammon took a breath. For a moment, his hard features reflected doubt.

'It's Gary. That poor bastard. If it wasn't for me, he wouldn't be in this fix. I was hoping he'd be acquitted. Then I could have forgotten him. But now . . . If he was executed, I would be to blame.'

'What do you mean?'

'Kevin Booth lived in Seattle for a while. An acquaintance of his worked for Rafael Vargas, who runs the cocaine in the Pacific Northwest for a Colombian cartel. Kevin got to know Vargas and picked up pin money acting as a mule. When he decided to move back to Whitaker last year, Vargas asked him to set up a distribution network.

'About eight or nine months ago, Sandra Whiley was busted on her way to deliver cocaine to a customer of Booth. The locals had no idea who Booth worked for. Whiley spilled everything. One of the Whitaker cops called the state police and they contacted us. OSP knew we were trying to find a way into the organization

Vargas works for. We had been running into a stone wall until we got this break.

'I've been in deep cover for two years building a background and trying to make contacts. I was transferred here to get close to Booth and force him into a position where he had to introduce me to Vargas.'

'Did Whiley know who you were?'

'No, We couldn't risk that. She thought I was working for organized crime. Her orders were to assist me so the DEA could bust me and Booth's group. The night Booth and I were arrested at Whitaker State, I was waiting for Whiley to bring me thirty thousand dollars to pay for the two kilos of coke that were found in the car. This buy was going to give me credibility when I negotiated for an amount large enough to bring Vargas into the open.

'Our arrest was bad luck and it came at a really bad time. I had to stay credible in Vargas's eyes, so it was arranged for Booth to win his preliminary hearing and for me to lose mine.'

'Wait a minute. What do you mean when you say it was arranged for Booth to win at the prelim?'

'That whole thing was a hoax. O'Shay was contacted by a higher-up in the Justice Department. He asked her to throw the prelim and she did.'

Peter was stunned. He'd never heard of anything like this.

'Who was in on the fix?'

'O'Shay, Mancini and the judge.'

'What about Earl Ridgely?'

'He was out of town for the week and O'Shay was asked to keep the whole thing from him. He's too much of a straight arrow to go along with fixing a court case. She told the judge that she had Ridgely's approval, but that was a lie. Ridgely still doesn't know why Booth won his prelim. Even Booth didn't know.

'O'Shay, Mancini and the judge worked out a scenario that would provide a legal basis for cutting Booth free. I stayed in jail to make it look like I could be trusted, then I made bail.

'The night of the murder, I was meeting Booth to convince him to take over my part in the final stage of our plan to bring down Vargas. The plan worked. We not only caught him red-handed with twenty kilos of cocaine, but we have wiretaps and other evidence that implicate him in the importation and sale of many times that amount. Vargas knows he's facing life without possibility of parole. We hoped he would cave and give us a way to get to the next level in the cartel. He broke three days ago.

Mammon paused. He looked embarrassed.

'When I arrived at the Stallion on the night of the murder, Harmon was sitting with Booth. I had to get rid of him, so I told him Karen Nix had the hots for him. I'm the one who caused his argument with Nix. If I hadn't taken advantage of him, the poor bastard wouldn't have been convicted for a crime he didn't commit.'

'How can you be so certain that Gary is innocent?'

'I know who killed Whiley.'

'Who is it?' Peter asked anxiously.

'While Gary was arguing with Nix, I went outside and talked with Booth. While we were talking I saw Whiley follow a man to his car. They argued over something, then they drove off together. The man was a customer of Booth. Someone to whom Whiley had delivered cocaine. Steve Mancini.'

'Oh, my God,' Peter said. Everything made sense now. Whiley must have threatened Steve. Mancini could not afford a scandal with Mountain View's finances hanging in the balance. When Gary was arrested, it was a godsend, and Mancini did his best to make certain that Gary would be convicted by hooking up Peter with an inept investigator, sabotaging the motion to suppress and making certain that Gary was represented by a self-centered, incompetent fool.

'You've got to testify for Gary.'

'No. Not now. Maybe not ever.

'How can you refuse? Gary may die if you don't come forward.'

'I'm leaving for South America tomorrow. If I stay and testify, my cover will be destroyed. I'm this close to being accepted by the cartel. If Mancini is going to be caught, you're the one who has to do it. I've risked my career by meeting you. I'm not going to destroy it.'

'How am I going to prove any of this?'

'I don't know, Hale, but I hope to God you can.

CHAPTER THIRTY

1

Peter had been sitting in Amos Geary's waiting room for half an hour when the office door opened. During that half hour, Clara Schoen had not spoken one word and the few times she stared in Peter's direction it had been to beam death rays at him. As soon as Geary stepped into the waiting room, Clara's head swiveled in his direction and her thin lips twitched in anticipation of the dressing down Peter was certain to receive from her boss. So, it was with astonishment that she saw Geary smile at the scoundrel whom he had so recently driven from their offices.

'Come on back,' Geary said, as he walked past Peter. Clara's mouth gaped open. Geary was almost out of sight when she remembered to remind him about his first court appearance.

'I know, Clara. Lenny Boudreau at ten-fifteen in Judge Staley's court,' Geary said without looking back. Clara's mouth gaped wider. 'Hold my calls until Peter and I are finished.'

Geary closed the door behind them and went to his filing cabinet while Peter took a chair.

'Clara thinks I can't remember my schedule without her,' Geary said as he pawed through his filing cabinet in search of the *Boudreau* file. 'I let her keep thinking that way. It makes her feel needed.'

Geary lit up as soon as he found the file. 'Did Dick save the day?' he asked as he settled in behind his desk.

'No, but there has been a break of sorts in the case.'

Geary filled the room with a dense cloud of smoke as Peter told him about the meeting at the U.S. Attorney's office, his encounter with Christopher Mammon and everything he knew about Steve Mancini.

'Mancini, huh?' Geary said thoughtfully when Peter finished. 'I wouldn't put it past him.'

'My problem is how to prove Steve killed Whiley without Mammon as a witness and how to get Gary a new trial on the grounds that O'Shay concealed exculpatory evidence. The Justice Department has put a lid on this, so there's no way I can get the DEA reports without a major lawsuit, and O'Shay won't admit what she's done. With Mammon gone, I've lost my key witness. There's also a good chance all copies of the reports have been destroyed.'

'You definitely have problems,' Geary agreed.

Peter sighed. 'I've only got a few days before the penalty phase starts. There's got to be some way to show that Whiley was the CRI.'

Peter suddenly noticed that Geary had a faraway look in his eyes and the hint of a smile on his lips. The cigarette, forgotten for the moment, dangled from his nicotine-stained fingers, the ash flaking off the tip and falling onto his carpet. Suddenly, Geary chuckled.

'Rebecca fucked up.'

'How?' Peter asked eagerly.

'Come on, think. If an old drunk like me can figure it out, a sober young stud like yourself should be able to crack this case in no time. I'll even give you a hint. There's a witness who can bury O'Shay.'

Peter went over everything he knew while Geary watched his struggle with glee. Finally, Peter gave up.

'Ah, me. The younger generation,' Geary cackled.

'Stuff it, Amos. I've lost my sense of humor.'

Geary sat up and blew a plume of smoke across the desk. Peter coughed.

'Lighten up, then listen up and I'll tell you how we're going to bust this case wide open.'

2

Earl Ridgely looked surprised when he walked into the chambers of District Court Judge Brett Staley with Becky O'Shay and saw Peter Hale and Amos Geary sitting next to the judge's desk.

'What's up, Brett?' Ridgely asked.

'Something pretty unpleasant, Earl. Why don't you and Miss O'Shay sit down and I'll let Mr. Hale explain.'

O'Shay noticed that the judge had avoided eye contact with her. She looked at Peter warily, but said nothing.

'On Sunday, I made a very unsettling discovery, Mr. Ridgely,' Peter said. 'Almost by accident, I learned that Miss O'Shay has been withholding exculpatory evidence that casts the whole Harmon case in a different light.'

'Earl, this is a crock,' O'Shay said contemptuously. 'What really happened on Sunday is that Mr. Hale snuck into Kevin Booth's room at the hospital and was arrested. I'm preparing a bar complaint. I don't know what story he's concocted, but it's his way of trying to get back at me for reporting his conduct to the ethics committee.'

'Why don't we hear what Peter has to say, Becky?' Ridgely said. O'Shay started to protest. Then, it suddenly dawned on her why they were meeting in Judge Staley's chambers instead of Judge Kuffel's and she turned pale.

'Becky has known for several months that Sandra Whiley was working as an informant for the DEA in a case involving Christopher Mammon, Kevin Booth, Rafael Vargas and a very violent Colombian drug cartel and she has intentionally concealed this information from the defense,' Peter said.

'Is this true?' Ridgely asked her.

'Earl, this is nonsense,' O'Shay answered angrily.

'I suppose I'd also be crazy to suggest that you fixed the Booth-Mammon prelim?' Peter said. 'I'm sure your boss will be interested in knowing that you told Judge Staley that he knew all about your deal with the Justice Department.'

'What deal?' Ridgely asked O'Shay.

'Miss O'Shay came to me with Steve Mancini and a Justice Department official from Washington, D.C., before the preliminary hearing for Christopher Mammon and Kevin Booth,' Judge Staley answered. 'She told me that you had approved a plan that involved my dismissal of Kevin Booth's case at the hearing so that a federal undercover operation would not be endangered.'

'I what!'

'You did assure me that your scheme had Mr. Ridgely's approval, didn't you, Miss O'Shay?' Judge Staley asked.

'Earl, there was no time to track you down,' O'Shay

said desperately. 'We shouldn't even be discussing this. We could be endangering a major undercover operation.'

'Will someone explain what's going on here?' Ridgely asked.

'The feds were monitoring a drug deal that was supposed to go down on the Whitaker State campus,' Peter explained. 'The deal was being used to help an undercover agent infiltrate a Colombian drug cartel. Then, the campus security guards screwed everything up by arresting Booth and Mammon.

'You were out of town on vacation, so Becky was contacted by the DEA. They wanted her to get Booth back on the street. The feds concocted a plan to fix Booth's prelim. Becky lied to Judge Staley and said she'd cleared everything with you.

'When Gary was arrested for Whiley's murder, Becky knew Whiley was an informant. She'd been briefed by the DEA and she even sent Steve Mancini two DEA reports about the Whitaker State case when they worked up the hoax. I found out about the reports by accident and she convinced Steve to destroy them and deny he'd ever seen them. She knew Judge Kuffel would have to throw out Gary's conviction if he learned about her cover-up.'

'I don't believe this,' Ridgely said incredulously.

'There's more and it's worse than what I've told you.'

Peter paused and looked directly at O'Shay. He was about to bluff and he hoped O'Shay could not tell how scared he was that he had guessed wrong.

'Steve Mancini has been sabotaging Gary Harmon's defense from the beginning of this case. His last act was destroying the reports, but he had done several other things to make certain Gary was convicted. What I couldn't understand was why he would want to send his brother-in-law to death row. But Becky knows the answer to that riddle, don't you?'

'I . . . I don't know what you're talking about.'

'Why would Steve destroy the DEA reports for you, Becky? Why would you trust him to do that instead of running to me with evidence that would win Gary a new trial? You knew that Steve had a reason to want Gary convicted. You knew that Steve had to obey you or risk exposure. You knew that Steve Mancini was with Sandra Whiley right before she was murdered.'

'Is this true?' Ridgely demanded.

'What does all this matter?' O'Shay implored Ridgely. 'Harmon's guilty. How did he know that the victim had been at the Stallion hours before anyone knew Whiley's identity, if he didn't kill her?'

'I talked with Gary before I set up this meeting to see if I could figure out how he knew some of the things he seemed to know. The morning that the body was found was the morning that Steve was married. He drove Gary to the church. They passed by the park and saw the police cars. Donna remembered that Gary was excited by all the activity. He probably asked Steve why there were police all over the park. I'm betting Steve slipped and said some girl who'd been at the Stallion last night had been murdered.

'I also spoke to Wilma Polk. Her husband was at the crime scene. He told Mrs. Polk that the man who killed Whiley chopped her up with a hatchet. Mrs. Polk told her friend about the killer using a hatchet when they were at the food table at the reception following the wedding. Mrs. Polk remembers Gary standing next to her and listening intently to what she said.

'And the placement of the blows. Before Bob Patrick tricked Gary with the black light, he showed him several autopsy photos of Whiley's head wounds.

'There are reasonable explanations for a lot of the evidence that incriminates Gary, but you weren't interested in the truth, were you, Becky?'

'I . . . I thought it was Gary. I still do. I didn't know that Steve was with Whiley that night until I debriefed Booth. He saw them together at the Stallion.'

'And you told Booth to keep his mouth shut,' Peter said accusingly.

'I couldn't tell you. The jury would never have convicted if it knew about Whiley being an informant and Steve being with her right before she was killed. There would have been too many other suspects. And Steve swore he didn't kill her.'

'You still don't understand what you've done, do you?' Peter asked, amazed by O'Shay's continued defiance. 'You still don't see that you've done something terribly wrong. How could you blind yourself to the possibility that Steve killed Whiley when it was right in front of you? How could you . . .'

All of a sudden Peter knew why O'Shay had shielded Steve. He remembered the way Steve and Becky acted when they were together, he recalled a cryptic remark Becky had made at the wedding reception when Peter asked her how she knew Steve.

'Did Steve swear he was innocent while you were having sex or after you were finished screwing?' Peter asked O'Shay.

Becky's eyes widened. 'What are you talking about?'

'Are you denying that you've been sleeping with Steve Mancini?'

Earl Ridgely stared at O'Shay with a growing sense of horror.

'If Earl learned that you lied to Judge Staley in order to fix the prelim and that you were secretly sleeping with a defense attorney against whom you've tried cases, he would have fired you on the spot. Did you keep quiet about Mancini because he threatened to expose you?' Peter asked.

'No, no, it wasn't like that. As soon as Kevin Booth told me he had seen Steve with Whiley at the Stallion I confronted Steve. He swore he was innocent. Then, he reminded me of . . . of something I should have remembered. Steve and I . . . Well, uh, we've been together off and on since I moved to Whitaker. And, well . . . We'd made plans to spend the evening before his wedding together.'

'What!' Peter said.

'You don't think Steve married Donna Harmon for love, do you?' O'Shay said scornfully. 'He was worried about Mountain View and he figured Jesse Harmon would come through with a sizable investment once he was married to Jesse's daughter.'

'That son of a bitch,' Peter said. Amos Geary put a restraining hand on Peter's arm.

'You were telling us how you knew Mr. Mancini was innocent, Miss O'Shay,' Geary prodded. 'Why don't you continue.'

'Steve was with me the night Whiley was killed. He showed up around midnight. He seemed upset. When I asked, he said it was because Gary had been in some trouble at the Stallion.

'Later, I confronted him about Booth seeing him with Whiley. He admitted it was true. He said Whiley was at the Stallion. When he left, she cornered him. It was in the parking lot. She was almost hysterical. She told him she had to leave town. She was scared to death of Christopher Mammon. Whiley thought he was in jail. Then she saw him in the Stallion. Whiley thought Mammon would suspect her of setting him up at Whitaker State and kill her.

'She was making a scene, so Steve told her to get in his car. They drove around for a while. She demanded money from Steve so she could run away. He tried to reason with her, but she was irrational. She said she would tell everyone Steve was using cocaine if he didn't give her money. She even threatened to crash his wedding.

'Steve told her he had some money at his office. He didn't want to be seen with her so he dropped her at the entrance to Wishing Well Park and said he'd meet her at the well as soon as he got the money.'

'When did he say he dropped off Whiley?'

'Eleven-fifty. He checked his watch because he was supposed to come to my place around midnight.'

Peter controlled his excitement. The bartender at the Ponderosa had testified that Gary came into the bar at eleven fifty-three or eleven fifty-four. If everyone's times were accurate, it would be impossible for Gary to be the killer.

'What did Steve say happened next?'

'He said he went to his office, picked up every penny he could find, which was about three thousand dollars in cash, and went right back to the park. Steve said he parked on a side street and walked over. He saw someone running away from the well when he approached. At first, he thought it was Whiley. Then, he saw her body.'

'When did you learn all this?' Earl Ridgely asked in a tone that made it clear that he was having trouble believing what he was hearing.

'Right before Booth was set on fire.'

'And . . . and you kept this to yourself? You made that poor bastard and his family go through a trial for murder when you knew he wasn't guilty?' Ridgely asked as he looked at O'Shay with disgust.

'I didn't know that. Steve denied killing Whiley and I believed him. I still think Gary committed the murder.'

'How could you?' Ridgely demanded. 'Whiley was blackmailing Mancini, he was at the park with her at the time of the killing. My God, are you an idiot?'

'No, Earl. I'm sure he didn't kill her. I remembered the suit he was wearing when he came to my house. I'd seen him in it earlier in the day. It was the same suit and the same tie. The same shoes. I confirmed that he was wearing the suit at the Stallion by checking with Karen Nix, the bartenders and some other witnesses.'

O'Shay paused and breathed deeply. She stared at the floor when she spoke.

'I . . . I undressed Steve that night. I saw his shirt, his suit. The killer would have had blood all over him and there wasn't a drop of blood on Steve Mancini.'

CHAPTER THIRTY-ONE

The Harmons sat in the front row of the courtroom. Peter had told them to come to court, but little else, because he did not want to get their hopes up. Steve Mancini sat in a row behind the Harmons on the other side of the courtroom. A deputy sheriff had served him a subpoena while he was eating breakfast. Mancini wondered why Earl Ridgely was sitting alone at the prosecution table. He was not aware that Becky O'Shay was in a jail cell charged with tampering with a witness and official misconduct.

Gary Harmon looked desperate when the guards led him into Judge Kuffel's courtroom. He was twitching from nerves and had not slept.

'Please get me out of jail, Pete,' he begged as soon as he was seated between Peter and Amos Geary, 'I'm scared there. I just want to go home.'

'Well, you might be doing just that, Gary. So, try to calm down.'

While Peter was talking to Gary, Judge Kuffel

emerged from chambers carrying the motion for a new trial that Peter had hastily prepared after the meeting in Judge Staley's chambers. He looked perplexed.

'You're joining in this motion, Mr. Ridgely?' the judge asked to make sure he understood correctly what he had just read.

'Yes, Your Honor. In light of certain matters that have come to my attention, I believe that the interests of justice require the court to set aside the guilty verdict against Mr. Harmon.'

The judge still looked puzzled. He wondered where Becky O'Shay was and why Amos Geary was sitting with Peter Hale.

'What's the basis for this motion, Mr. Hale?' Judge Kuffel asked.

'I think my first witness will clear up your confusion, Your Honor.'

'Very well, call the witness.'

'Mr. Harmon calls Kevin Booth.'

Yesterday afternoon, after the meeting in Judge Staley's chambers, Earl Ridgely, Peter Hale, Amos Geary and a detective from the Oregon State Police had interviewed Booth at the hospital. Booth was brought into court in a wheelchair and allowed to testify from it. He was wearing a hospital gown and a bathrobe.

'Mr. Booth,' Peter said, after the witness was sworn, 'you have already testified in the case of *State v. Harmon*, have you not?'

'Yes.'

'Was the testimony that you gave in Portland truthful testimony?'

'One second here, Mr. Hale,' Judge Kuffel said. 'You're asking this man if he committed perjury. If he says he lied, he's admitting to a crime.'

'That's true, Your Honor. But Mr. Booth is also testifying under a grant of immunity from prosecution for any false testimony given in Mr. Harmon's case, a promise that he will not be prosecuted for his part in the incident at Whitaker State College and a promise from state and federal authorities that he will not be prosecuted for his part in the crime that led to his arrest at his home.'

Peter did not tell the judge that the cooperation from the feds had been obtained when Earl Ridgely threatened to go public with what he knew about the rigged preliminary hearing and the undercover operation against the Colombian cartel.

'Very well. Proceed.'

'Mr. Booth, I repeat, did you testify truthfully in this case?'

'No.'

'When you said that Gary Harmon discussed his case with you at the Whitaker jail, was that true?'

'Yes.'

'Did Mr. Harmon ever tell you that he murdered Sandra Whiley?'

'No. He said he didn't do it.'

'Why did you lie about what Mr. Harmon told you?'

'I was scared I'd go to prison on my federal drug charge, so I had to make a deal. It was my only way out.'

'The prosecutor in Mr. Harmon's case is Rebecca O'Shay. Did you worry about her learning that you were lying about Mr. Harmon's guilt?'

'No. She wanted Harmon convicted.'

'Mr. Booth, did Ms. O'Shay instruct you to conceal from the defense certain information that would have cast doubt on Mr. Harmon's guilt, if made known to the jury?'

'Yeah.'

'What was one thing she didn't want you talking about?'

'Whiley was a coke head and she bought from me. She didn't have a lot of money, so sometimes she had to work off her debt. On the evening I was busted at Whitaker State with Chris Mammon, Whiley was late bringing thirty thousand dollars to the meet. When we were arrested, Mammon thought Whiley set us up. He told me he was going to kill her, if he found out it was true.'

'And you told Ms. O'Shay about the threat?'

'Yeah. She knew Mammon was at the Stallion at the same time as Whiley on the night of the murder. I thought she'd be interested, but she said Harmon did it and I wasn't to tell anyone that Mammon knew Whiley.'

'Did Ms. O'Shay tell you to keep quiet about anything else?'

Booth located Steve Mancini and his scarred lips twisted into a malicious grin.

'Yeah. I told her I saw Steve Mancini drive off with Sandra Whiley from the Stallion on the evening that Whiley was killed.'

Donna put her hand over her mouth. Jesse Harmon fixed Mancini with a look of pure hatred. Mancini looked around nervously. He started to stand, but stopped when he noticed the armed guards that Earl Ridgely had stationed inside the courtroom doors.

'What happened when you told this information to Ms. O'Shay?'

'She said I'd better forget about it or she'd see I spent the rest of my life in prison.'

'Did Mr. Mancini know Sandra Whiley before the evening of the murder?'

'Sure. Mancini bought cocaine from me. Whiley delivered it to him at his office and his house a few times. One time, she told me she had sex with Mancini for some of the blow.'

Mancini had broken out in a sweat. His eyes darted around the courtroom, desperately seeking a way out.

'No further questions, Mr. Booth.'

'Mr. Ridgely?' the judge asked.

'No questions.'

'Do you have another witness, Mr. Hale?'

Peter faced the spectator section and said, 'We call Steve Mancini, Your Honor.'

'I didn't kill her,' Mancini shouted.

Judge Kuffel pounded his gavel. Mancini froze. The judge glared at him, then said, 'You've been called as a witness, Mr. Mancini. Please come forward.'

Mancini hesitated. He looked around at the accusing eyes that stared at him from every corner of the room. Then, he walked unsteadily to the witness box. Peter looked directly at Mancini, but Steve would not look back.

'On the evening that Sandra Whiley was murdered, did you drive away from the Stallion tavern with her?' Peter asked.

'I'm . . . I want to speak to a lawyer,' Mancini said in a trembling voice.

'Mr. Hale, I'm going to have to adjourn this hearing so Mr. Mancini can consult with counsel. From what I've heard here, he may need one.'

Peter knew this would happen and he did not object. Mancini started to stand up. Ridgely signaled to two police officers, who approached Mancini.

'I have a warrant for your arrest, Mr. Mancini,' Ridgely said.

Steve froze. 'Hey, Earl, this isn't true. I didn't kill her.'

Ridgely ignored him. 'Please bring Mr. Mancini to

the jail,' he told the officers. 'See he's read his *Miranda* rights and is allowed to call an attorney.'

'Earl,' Mancini begged, but Ridgely turned his back on him and Mancini was led out of the courtroom.

'May Mr. Harmon be released into the custody of his parents, Your Honor?' Peter asked, as soon as the courtroom had quieted down.

'That would be highly unusual. He's been convicted of aggravated murder.'

Earl Ridgely stood slowly and addressed the court.

'Rebecca O'Shay is not present today because she is under arrest. Ms. O'Shay intentionally concealed crucial evidence from the defense. Evidence which casts grave doubt on Mr. Harmon's guilt.

'I haven't had time to investigate this case thoroughly in light of the new information that the court has just heard, but I know enough to feel that justice will be served best by releasing Mr. Harmon into the custody of his parents while I sort everything out.'

Judge Kuffel pursed his lips and considered the request.

'Very well,' he said. 'Mr. Harmon, I am ordering your release to the custody of your parents. There will be certain conditions you will have to follow, which I will devise after consultation with counsel. Do you follow what I'm saying?'

Gary looked scared and uncertain. He turned to Peter.

'He's sending you home, Gary,' Peter said.

Gary's mouth opened for a moment. Then it formed into a wide smile.

'I'm going home?' he asked as if he could not believe it.

Peter could not help smiling back. 'Yeah, Gary, you're going home.'

Gary's eyes shone. Then he whooped and threw his arms around Peter.

'You're a good lawyer, Pete. You're the best lawyer. You made them send me home.'

Judge Kuffel started to gavel for order. Then he thought better of it and lay the gavel down. Peter stood helpless and speechless in Gary's embrace, blushing wildly.

CHAPTER THIRTY-TWO

1

'Will you have another piece of pie, Peter?' Alice Harmon asked.

'Mrs. Harmon, if I eat one more slice of your apple pie, I'll explode.'

'I believe I can fit in another piece somewhere,' Amos Geary said.

'Gary, hand me Amos's plate, please,' Alice told her son. When Gary picked up the plate his back was to Alice Harmon and he did not see how his mother beamed.

Donna stood up and turned to Peter.

'I'm going to get some fresh air. Do you want to join me?'

'Sure.'

Donna opened the screen door and led Peter onto the front porch of her parents' house. It was mid-September, the sun was almost down and the night air was nippy. Donna and Peter both wore sweaters. They walked into the front yard. Donna wrapped her arms around herself as she strolled slowly next to the white board fence that ran along the edge of the Harmons' property.

'It's so great having Gary home,' Donna said. 'You can't believe the change in Mom and Dad.'

'It's not over yet,' Peter cautioned. 'We still have to get the charges dismissed.'

'They won't send him back,' Donna said confidently. 'They couldn't. Mr. Ridgely is too decent a man.'

They walked in silence for a while. Then, Donna said, 'It is amazing how everything conspired to make Gary look so guilty. His overhearing Wilma Polk, O'Shay telling Booth about the Crusader's Cross and Steve letting it slip that the dead woman was at the Stallion . . .'

'That's why Earl's going to go slowly before he charges anyone else. He won't want to make another mistake.'

'Who do you think killed Sandra Whiley?' Donna asked when they reached the large oak that shaded the front lawn.

'I don't know. I really haven't given it that much thought. In the movies, the defense attorney always saves his client by figuring out who the killer is. In real life, defense attorneys really don't care. I've spent this whole case trying to counter the state's evidence in order to raise a reasonable doubt. I mean, it would be great if I did prove who killed Sandra Whiley, but as long as I can convince Earl that he should set Gary free, I've done my job.'

'You must have some idea. What about Christopher Mammon? I heard that he's disappeared.'

'Mammon is definitely not the killer.'

'How can you be so certain?'

'In order to tell you, I'd have to break a promise I

made. Just trust me. I know it's not Mammon.'

Donna turned her back to Peter and bowed her head.

'If Christopher Mammon isn't guilty, then Steve probably is.'

'I guess that's true,' Peter answered thoughtfully. 'He's certainly the most likely suspect. We just learned that his first wife left him because he also beat her, so he clearly has a propensity for violence. The problem with the case against Steve is Becky O'Shay's evidence.'

Peter caught himself. Donna turned toward him and he turned red.

'I'm sorry . . .' he started, but Donna shook her head.

'Don't be. I'm glad I found out that he screwed her on the night before our wedding. It relieves me of any lingering doubts I may have had about Steve.'

They walked on in silence until Donna asked, 'Will you be moving back to Portland when you've wrapped up Gary's case?'

'No. I was really thoughtless leaving Amos short-handed, so I'm going back to work for him tomorrow. I don't think I'll stay in criminal law forever, but it is sort of exciting.'

'I'm glad you'll be around,' Donna said, looking directly into Peter's eyes. Peter hesitated for a second. Then he reached out and took her hand.

'There's another reason I'm sticking around Whitaker.'

Peter waited for Donna to pull free. When she didn't, he said, 'I don't know if this is the right time to say this. You're going through so much right now and I'm still trying to figure out who I am and what I want. There are a lot of things about me you don't know, too. Things you might not like.'

'We don't have to rush, Peter. Now that you're staying in town, we can take our time. Let's just see how things work out. Okay?'

Then Donna kissed him. It was a soft kiss, but it stunned Peter. Donna rested her head on his shoulder and they held each other in the dark. Peter had never made a commitment to a woman before. Even thinking about it was a little scary. Was he capable of being true to one person? He thought he might be able to do it. He had done some pretty amazing things since arriving in Whitaker.

2

'You look pretty satisfied with yourself,' Amos Geary said when they were on their way back to town in Peter's car.

'What do you mean?' Peter asked self-consciously. He had been reliving his kiss with Donna.

'She's not someone to play with. Donna's been through a lot. If you're not serious about her, don't start anything.'

'Jesus, Amos, give me some credit, will you,' Peter protested.

'Given your track record, I decided to be blunt.'

'Hey, the old Peter is gone.'

'We'll see.'

They drove on in silence for a while. Peter drifted back to thoughts of love, but Geary was thinking about something else. After a while, he let out a long breath.

'What?' Peter asked.

'I was thinking about that poor girl. The police have

lost so much time that I don't think they'll ever catch Whiley's killer.'

'We know it's not Mammon. I haven't ruled out Steve, but it's pretty unlikely that he killed her if O'Shay is telling the truth.'

'Which she may not be doing. Just thinking about O'Shay makes me sick.'

'Something just occurred to me. Ridgely should check on Steve's alibi for the time when those other two women were killed. With all the excitement, we forgot that the person who killed Whiley probably killed them, too.'

'Earl's no dummy. I'm sure he's already thought about seeing if he can tie Mancini into the other killings. I'll say one thing – whoever committed those murders is one sick son of a bitch. Killing someone is bad enough, but butchering a defenseless woman with a hatchet, like she was some kind of farm animal . . .'

Geary lapsed into silence at the thought of such senseless slaughter. Suddenly, Peter pulled the car over to the side of the road. Geary wasn't wearing a seat belt and he was thrown forward. Fortunately, he caught the dashboard with his hands.

'What the fuck is wrong with you?' Geary shouted.

Peter wasn't listening. He looked stunned.

'Hale, are you having some sort of yuppie fit? Talk to me.'

Peter turned slowly. He looked pale.

'The hatchet. My God, I didn't even think . . . We've got to go to the office and look up something in Mammon's file.'

'What are you talking about?'

Instead of answering, Peter hit the accelerator and Geary was thrown back into his seat.

'I'll explain on the way,' Peter said, as Geary hurriedly fastened his seat belt.

'Is this where we turn?' Peter asked.

'I'm not certain,' Geary answered.

'I thought you lived here most of your life.'

'I'm a lawyer, not a goddamn surveyor. Now, shut up and give me a minute.'

Geary studied a map of Whitaker and the surrounding area while Peter impatiently drummed his fingers on the steering wheel.

'Okay. This is the road that was listed in the police report in Mammon's file.'

Peter drove a mile up an unpaved, dirt track. There was a full moon and they soon saw the object of their search. Peter stopped in front of the dilapidated house.

'You're sure this is legal?' Peter asked.

'It's not legal. It's breaking and entering. But we aren't working for the government, so Earl can use any evidence we find at trial while we are serving our sentence for burglary.'

'Thanks for clearing that up. I feel much better now,' Peter said, as he tried the door. It wasn't locked. Peter had brought along a flashlight, but Geary flipped on a light switch and he didn't need it.

'Looks like the electricity is still paid up,' Geary commented.

'God! What's that smell?'

Both men winced as a sour and fetid odor assailed them. It was the essence of the decay that permeated the house. Flies buzzed around rotting pizza crusts and decomposing cheese that hung on the sides of oil-stained pizza boxes. Unwashed clothes lay in clumps on the couch.

'This place is a fucking sty,' Peter declared.

'Let's search it fast, so we can get out of here,' Geary said.

They split up, Peter taking the bedroom and bathroom and Geary searching the living room and kitchen. The search did not take long, since the house was so small.

'Anything?' Peter asked.

'Not a thing,' Geary answered when they both finished.

'I was so sure.'

'Your reasoning is sound. He probably killed the women somewhere else.'

'I guess,' Peter answered dejectedly.

Peter walked outside. Geary turned out the lights and shut the door. Peter was about to get in the car when he froze.

'What's that?' he asked.

Geary looked where Peter was pointing. Another house could barely be made out in the moonlight.

'It's worth a look now that we're out here.'

The two men turned on their flashlights and walked a dusty quarter mile. It was not until they reached the shack that they could tell it was deserted, but there was a padlock on the door.

'What do we do now?' Peter asked.

Geary raised his foot and kicked the door with all the force his near three hundred pounds could bring to the task. The rotting door splintered and gave. A second kick and it swung inward. An odor, different and more foul than the one they had smelled in the other house, assailed Peter when he crossed the threshold. He clamped his hand over his mouth and moved the flashlight beam around the interior of the shack.

'Holy shit!' he whispered when the beam found the bloodstained mattress pushed up against the far wall. Geary was speechless. Peter moved his beam around the floor and gagged when he realized that almost every square inch was encrusted with dried blood.

'Peter,' Amos called. Peter looked at the corner of the room that Geary's beam was illuminating. He saw piles of women s clothes, a purse and two wallets.

'What do you want to bet that one of those wallets belongs to Sandra Whiley?' Geary asked.

'If you're right, I'm not going to be the one who discovers it. Let's get out of here and call the police.'

3

Kevin Booth was asleep when Earl Ridgely entered his hospital room followed by members of the Major Crime Team. He stirred when the nurse turned on the lights, then sat up.

'What's going on?' Booth asked, rubbing his eyes as he searched for the clock. Then he saw how many people were in his room.

'I have a few questions for you, Kevin,' Ridgely said.

'It's three in the morning, for Christ's sake. Can't this wait?'

'Actually, no.' Ridgely pulled a chair next to Booth's bed. 'But I promise not to take up too much of your time. First, though, I'm going to give you your *Miranda* rights.'

Ridgely took a laminated card out of his wallet and read Booth his rights. Booth looked at Ridgely as if the D.A. was insane.

'What is this?' Booth asked when Ridgely was through.

'Can you explain why Sandra Whiley's wallet and the clothing of Emily Curran and Diane Fetter were found in a shack less than a quarter mile from your house and why the floor of the shack was covered with blood?'

'What . . . what are you talking about? What shack?'

'Kevin, at this very moment, fingerprint technicians are going over every inch of the shack and forensic experts are combing it for hair, fibers and other trace evidence.'

'Well, you won't find anything belonging to me in some fucking blood-covered shack. I don't know what you think you've got, but you ain't got shit connecting me to no murders.'

'Actually,' Ridgely said, 'we've got quite a lot. For instance, Curran and Fetter both had a lot of cocaine in their system when they died. Background checks on both women showed that they used cocaine frequently. I think you supplied both women with cocaine and lured them to your house with promises of free drugs. I think you got them high, then raped and killed them.'

'You can think all you want.'

'I also think you made one monumental error. Peter Hale explained it to me. It's so obvious that I feel really stupid for missing it.'

Ridgely waited for Booth to say something. When he didn't, Ridgely continued.

'You were terrified when you were arrested with Rafael Vargas. Not only were you facing serious federal time, but Vargas threatened to kill you, the feds refused to bargain with you and Steve Mancini wouldn't represent you. That's when you decided to trade testimony against Gary Harmon for a deal that would keep you out of prison. You gained Gary's confidence and tricked him into telling you all of the details of the murder of Sandra Whiley that he told the police. Since you killed Whiley, you were able to add some extra information that made the confession sound real, but that wasn't enough for Becky O'Shay. She knew that no jury would ever buy your story without corroboration, so she told you that you wouldn't get a deal unless you could provide proof that Gary confessed.

'You were in a panic, going through withdrawal and not really thinking straight. O'Shay was about to walk out on you and O'Shay was your last chance, so you told her something that only the killer would know. You told her where to find the hatchet you used to murder Curran, Fetter and Whiley. The hatchet you threw in the storm drain because you were afraid that Steve Mancini might have seen you running from the murder scene.

'Gary Harmon couldn't have told you where the murder weapon was hidden. It was impossible for him to have killed Whiley. He was at the Ponderosa when the murder occurred. If Gary didn't tell you it was in a storm drain near the Whitaker campus, how did you know?'

Booth stared wide-eyed at Ridgely, then scanned the stone-hard faces of the men who ringed his bed.

'I want a lawyer,' he said finally. 'I want a lawyer.'

Ridgely nodded. 'I figured that's what you'd want, Mr. Booth, and I think you're wise to ask for one, because if anyone needs a lawyer right now, you do.'

EPILOGUE

The scoreboard on top of Stallion Stadium showed that there were fifty-eight seconds remaining in the game between the Whitaker Stallions and Boise State, with Whitaker leading by a touchdown and driving for another. Peter figured that fifty-eight seconds was about as long as he could take the frozen rain that had turned the last game of the season into a mud-wrestling contest. Donna huddled against him, just as miserable as he was. Only Gary seemed oblivious to the ghastly weather conditions. He was on his feet screaming with each play, transported by the very real possibility that the undefeated Whitaker Stallions might actually go all the way.

Many things had happened in the three months since the dramatic termination of the charges against Gary Harmon. Kevin Booth had not been able to hold out for long. Connections between Booth and the three murdered women were easily established once the police started concentrating on Booth as the prime suspect. In order to escape the death penalty, Booth cut a deal that would keep him in prison for the rest of his life without the possibility of parole. Booth had shocked the prosecutors by confessing not only to murdering Sandra Whiley, Emily Curran and Diane Fetter, but to the murder of his mother, whom he had pushed down the stairs.

Booth told Earl Ridgely that he had watched from his pickup truck as Whiley and Mancini argued. Then, he followed them as they drove aimlessly through Whitaker. Whiley had haunted Booth's sexual fantasies since she began buying cocaine from him, but he had been afraid to touch a woman whom he believed belonged to Christopher Mammon. Booth suspected Whiley of betraying him as soon as he was arrested at Whitaker State and he longed to make her suffer. His humiliation at Mammon's hands had driven Booth into a rage. He was terrified of Mammon, but he thought of Whiley as prey. When Mancini dropped off Whiley at Wishing Well Park, Booth had taken his hatchet from the pickup and followed her with the idea of taking her to his shack where he could torture and rape her, but Whiley had fought Booth and had paid with her life.

As soon as Steve Mancini was certain that he would not be prosecuted for killing Whiley, he confessed his attempts to cover up his involvement with Whiley on the night of the murder. His motive in sabotaging Gary's case was simple cowardice. Mancini was terrified that a competent lawyer and a competent investigator would uncover his meeting with Whiley. He feared an arrest for her murder and he could not afford a scandal involving his use of cocaine with the Mountain View project on the verge of destruction.

'As soon as this game ends, we're heading for my place

and a gallon of hot toddies,' Peter managed to chatter.

'Two gallons, but we'll have to figure a way to get Gary out of the stadium. He's going to want to run down on the field when the game ends and shake hands with the players.'

'Oh, shit. I forgot.'

This was Gary's postgame ritual and he always went through it.

'I'll make it up to you,' Donna smiled.

'When? It's going to take us a year to thaw out.'

The whistle blew and Gary's face lit up.

'All the way, all the way,' he shrieked, as his fists pummeled the air. He grabbed Donna and dragged her to her feet, then hugged her so tight she had to tell Gary to stop.

'Pete, Pete,' Gary screamed, 'all the way, all the way.'

Then Gary was scrambling down the icy grandstand and streaking onto the field.

'It looks like the only good thing that asshole husband of yours did was to get Gary these season tickets,' Peter joked as he and Donna cautiously made their way out of the stands.

'Soon-to-be ex-husband. Judge Kuffel is hearing the divorce next week. At least Steve had the grace not to contest it.'

'He's got a lot more on his mind than the divorce. Ridgely has agreed to dismiss the criminal charges if he resigns from the bar. And Mountain View bankrupted him. I hear he's going to leave town.'

'How could he stay here? Everyone in Whitaker knows what he's done.'

'I saw Earl at the courthouse yesterday. O'Shay won't plead. She's also fighting disbarment.'

'I hope she ends up in prison for what she did to Gary.'

Donna and Peter found shelter near the concession stand where they always waited for Gary after a game. Peter bought two cups of hot coffee. They drank in silence for a few minutes, savoring the warmth provided by the steaming hot liquid. After a bit, Peter decided it was time to talk about something he had been meaning to say all day, but had not had the courage to bring up.

'Dad called last night.'

'Oh?'

'He asked me to come back to Hale, Greaves. I guess all is forgiven.'

'What did you tell him?' Donna asked cautiously.

'I said I couldn't give him an answer right away. I told him my answer depended on the answer to another question.'

'What question?'

'Well, uh, my practice is going pretty good. I've picked up a lot of business because of Gary's case. Enough so Amos and I are going to hire an associate to help him handle the indigent criminal cases so I can concentrate on personal injury and retained criminal stuff. So, that's a reason to stick around. But there would be a bigger reason if you'd marry me when your divorce is final.'

Donna blinked, then her eyes filled with tears and she threw her arms around Peter. Her half-filled cup of coffee went sailing through the air.

'Does that mean yes?' Peter asked as he broke out laughing.

Before Donna could respond, Gary burst up the concrete ramp and ran toward them. He was holding a jersey that was so covered with mud that the numbers were almost illegible.

'Look, look,' he shouted, holding up his prize. 'The coach said I could keep it. He said I'm lucky. He said the Stallions couldn't win without me.'

'That's great, Gary,' Donna managed.

'We did it, Pete. We went all the way and the coach said I helped.'

Donna and Peter broke out laughing as they watched Gary bounce up and down with joy. Donna hugged Peter, then she hugged her brother.

'Let's get you home,' Donna said to Gary, as they started toward the parking lot. She had to shout to be heard over the blaring horns and raucous shouts from the jubilant Stallion rooters who seemed oblivious to the cold and rain.

'Hey,' Peter shouted, 'what about my proposal?'

'We're going all the way,' Gary shouted at a group of boisterous students.

'My sentiments exactly,' Donna told Peter Hale.

The Undertaker's Widow

For Aunt Bea

Acknowledgments

Research is one aspect of novel writing that is always fun. I want to thank Bryan Ostrum, Dick Solomon, Mike Prahl, Joseph Ceniceros, Patricia Green, and Scott LaPine, who took the time to explain the technical information that I needed to write *The Undertaker's Widow*.

I also want to thank Vince Kohler, Steve Perry, Larry Matasar, Susan Svetkey, Norman Stamm, and Joseph, Eleonore, Jerry and Judy Margolin for reading early drafts and giving me the benefit of their wisdom.

Many thanks to Pat Mulcahy and Elisa Petrini for their unstinting editorial efforts, the crew at Jean V. Naggar's literary agency (the best agency in the known universe) for their terrific support and everyone at Doubleday and Bantam.

And, finally, just plain thanks to Daniel, Ami and Doreen.

Part One

The Undertaker's Widow

One

LEROY DENNIS began making dire predictions about the driving conditions as soon as the police dispatcher said that the scene of the shooting was a mansion on Crestview Drive. A week of torrential rains had devastated Oregon. Rivers were flooding, towns were being evacuated, power failures were the norm and mud slides were closing roads and highways around the state. The worst slides in Portland were in the hills that loomed above city center. Crestview Drive was at the top of Portland's highest hill.

Lou Anthony took the most direct route to the crime scene. A mountain of oozing earth almost stopped the homicide detectives halfway up Southwest Chandler Road. A series of flares had been spread along the pavement to warn off motorists. The unearthly rain, the devouring darkness on the edges of the headlights and the curling smoke from the flares made Anthony wonder if he had detoured into a corner of Hades.

'What have we got, Leroy?' Anthony asked as he maneuvered around the slide.

'A James Allen called in the 911,' the slender black detective answered. 'He works for the owner, Lamar Hoyt. Allen says that there are two dead. A man broke in and shot Hoyt. Then the wife shot the perp.'

'Hoyt! That's Ellen Crease's husband.'

'Isn't Crease the state senator who used to be a cop?'

Anthony nodded. 'She was good, too, and a crack shot.'

Dennis shook his head. 'This guy sure picked the wrong house to burgle.'

There were few streetlights on Crestview Drive and the road was pitch-black in spots, but Anthony and Dennis had no trouble finding the crime scene. This part of the West Hills had been carved into large estates and there were only a few homes on the narrow country lane. A high brick wall marked the boundary of the Hoyt estate. Just above the wall, the branches of a massive oak tree flailed helplessly against the elements like the tiring arms of a fading boxer. Anthony stopped in front of a wrought-iron gate. A yellow and black metal sign affixed to the seven-foot, spear-tipped bars warned that the estate was protected by an electronic security system. A black metal box with a slit for a plastic card stood even with the driver's window. Beside it was a speakerphone. Anthony was about to try it when Dennis noticed that the gate was slightly ajar. He dashed into the storm and pushed it open.

When Dennis was back in the car, Anthony drove

slowly up a winding drive toward the three-story Tudor mansion that loomed over the landscape. Most of the house was dark, but there were lights on in a downstairs room. The driveway ended at a turnaround. As soon as Anthony brought the car to a stop the ornately carved front door swung open and a frightened man in a robe and pajamas dashed into the rain. He was just under six feet tall and slender. The rain matted his uncombed, graying hair and spotted the lenses of his wire-rimmed glasses.

'They're upstairs in the master bedroom,' he said, pointing toward the second floor. 'She won't leave him. I've called for an ambulance.'

The man led the detectives into a cavernous entry hall, where an immense Persian carpet covered a good portion of the hardwood floor. Before them was a wide staircase with a polished oak banister.

Anthony brushed the rain from his thinning red hair. He was a large man with a square jaw, a broken nose and pale blue eyes. The detective's shoulders were too wide and his clothes never fit properly. Under his raincoat he wore a brown tweed sports jacket that was frayed at the elbows and wrinkled tan slacks. Anthony had started buttoning the jacket to conceal an emerging beer gut. The blue knit tie his son had bought him for his fortieth birthday was at half-mast.

'Just who are you, sir?' Anthony asked.

'James Allen, Mr. Hoyt's houseman.'

'Okay. What happened here, Mr. Allen?'

'I live over the garage. It's across from the master bedroom. There was a shot. At first, I thought it was

5

thunder. Then there were more shots. I ran next door and saw a man on the floor near the bed. There was a lot of blood. And Ms. Crease . . . she was sitting on the bed holding Mr. Hoyt. I . . . I think he's dead, but I can't say for sure. She wouldn't let me near him. She's got a gun.'

'Take us upstairs, will you, Mr. Allen?' Anthony said.

The detectives followed the houseman up the winding stairs with barely a glance at the oil paintings and tapestries that hung over the staircase. Dennis had his gun out but felt a little foolish. It sounded as if the danger was over. Allen led them to a room at the end of a dimly lit, carpeted hall. The door to the room was open.

'Please tell Senator Crease that we're with the police,' Anthony instructed Allen. The detective knew Crease well enough to call her Ellen, but he had no idea what frame of mind she was in. He wasn't taking any chances if she had a gun.

'Ms. Crease, this is James. James Allen. I have two police officers with me. They want to come into the bedroom.'

Allen started in, but Anthony put a restraining hand on his arm.

'I think it will be better if you wait downstairs for the ambulance and the other officers.'

Allen hesitated, then said, 'Very well,' and backed down the corridor.

'I'm Lou Anthony, Senator. You know me. I'm a detective with the Portland Police. My partner and I are coming into the room.'

Anthony took a deep breath and stepped through the

doorway. The bedroom lights were off, but the light
from the hall bathed the large room in a pale yellow
glow. A man sprawled on the floor roughly halfway
between the door and the west wall. The dead man's
legs were bent at the knee as if he had crumpled to the
floor. His feet were almost touching a French Provincial
armoire that stood against the south wall across from a
king-size bed. The doors of the armoire were partly open
and Anthony could see a television. The man's head was
near the foot of the bed, surrounded by a halo of blood.
Near one of his hands lay a .45-caliber handgun.

Anthony pulled his attention away from the dead
man and stared at the tableau directly in front of him.
Seated on the side of the bed farthest from the door, as
if posing for one of Caravaggio's dark oils, was Ellen
Crease. She was facing away from Anthony and the
back of her plain white nightgown was spattered with
blood. Lamar Hoyt's naked body lay sideways across the
bed. Crease's back shielded part of his upper body from
Anthony, but he could make out two entry wounds and
rivulets of blood running through the thick gray hair that
covered Hoyt's bearlike torso. Hoyt's large head rested
in his wife's lap and Crease was rocking slightly, making
little mewing sounds. Anthony noticed that her right
hand was resting on her husband's massive chest and
that her left hand held a .38 Special.

'Senator,' Anthony said gently, 'I'm going to walk
around the bed.'

Crease continued to rock and sob. The detective edged
past the armoire, then stepped over the dead man's
faded jeans and took in his navy-blue windbreaker. The

dead man's hair was wet from the rain and saturated with blood. His clothing was waterlogged.

Anthony looked away and focused on Crease. She was holding the gun, but lightly, and she was staring at her husband. What was left of Hoyt's face was covered with blood that was soaking through the white nightgown. As Anthony arrived at her side, Crease looked up. Her face was tearstained and torn by grief.

Forty-five minutes later, police cars, an ambulance and the van from the Medical Examiner's Office choked the driveway in front of the Hoyt mansion. While forensic experts worked the crime scene, Lou Anthony waited patiently for Ellen Crease in one of the deep, red leather armchairs in the library. The room was unusually clean and he sensed that neither Hoyt nor Crease entered it much. Anthony had examined some of the hand-tooled, leather-bound volumes stacked tightly in the floor-to-ceiling, cherrywood bookshelves. His brief inspection had uncovered no book with a spine that had been cracked. The detective was holding a volume of Hemingway short stories when Ellen Crease entered the library wearing jeans, an Oxford-blue shirt, and a baggy, dark green, Irish wool sweater.

State Senator Ellen Crease was thirty-five, but she had the compact, athletic body of a woman ten years younger. Crease's personality was as rugged as her physique. Her complexion was dark and her sleek black hair framed a face with features that were always on guard. There was nothing coy about Ellen Crease. She was an iron fist that never fit inside a velvet glove.

'Hello, Lou,' Crease said, holding out her hand the way she might at a political rally. Anthony hastily replaced the book and shook it.

'I'm sorry about Lamar. How are you holding up?'

Crease shrugged. Anthony marveled at her composure. He had seen Crease's grief, but there was no trace of tears now. The detective assumed Crease was repressing any feelings she had about the death of her husband. She would also be repressing her feelings about killing the intruder, but Anthony knew the guilt would soon surface to haunt Crease as it had haunted him when he had killed a man in the line of duty. A board of inquiry had cleared Anthony. He had even been decorated. Still, it had taken several years before he could put the shooting behind him. For most people, taking a human life, even in self-defense, was very difficult to live with.

'Do you feel up to answering questions?' Anthony asked.

'I want to get this over, Lou, so let's do it.'

Crease took a chair opposite Anthony and selected a slender Mouton Davidoff Cadet from a humidor on an oak end table. Anthony watched Crease light up the cigar. Her hand was remarkably steady.

'I have to give you your *Miranda* warnings, because there's been a shooting,' Anthony said apologetically.

'Consider them given.'

Anthony hesitated, uncertain whether to still read the rights. Then he thought better of it. He wanted to spare Crease as much discomfort as possible and speeding up his interview was one way to accomplish his purpose.

'Why don't you just tell me what happened?'

Crease drew in smoke from her cigar. It seemed to calm her. She closed her eyes for a moment. Anthony thought that she looked totally spent. When she spoke, Crease sounded listless.

'Lamar wanted to go to bed early, but I had to work. You know that I'm right in the middle of a primary campaign against Ben Gage for the Republican nomination to the U.S. Senate?'

Anthony nodded.

'There's a speech I'm supposed to give tomorrow night and a bill on the light rail I needed to study. Lamar wanted to make love before he went to sleep, so we did. Then I got up to change into a nightgown so I could go down to my study. I was going to go to the bathroom when there was a particularly bright flash of lightning. I walked over to the window. As I watched the storm there was another lightning flash. It illuminated the area around the pool. I thought I saw someone standing under one of the trees near the wall, but the light faded before I could focus on the spot. I wrote it off as a figment of my imagination.'

'We found a set of footprints under one of the trees. The intruder must have been watching from there.'

'Do you know who he is yet?'

'No. He wasn't carrying any ID, but it's only a matter of time before we identify him. Why don't you go on?'

For a second, Crease's self-control deserted her. She closed her eyes. Anthony waited patiently for the senator to continue.

'When I got out of the bathroom, Lamar wanted to

cuddle, so I turned off the bathroom light, put on my nightgown and got in bed with him. We talked for a little while. Not long. Then I told Lamar I had to start working. I sat up on my side of the bed . . .'

'That's the side nearest the window and away from the bedroom door and the bathroom?' Anthony asked.

'Right.'

'Okay, what happened?'

'The door crashed open and this man came in. I could see he had a gun, because there was a light on in the hall.'

Crease's façade cracked again, but she caught herself and was back in control quickly.

'I keep a Smith & Wesson .38 snubnose under my side of the bed. It's always loaded with hollow points. I ducked over the side to get it. I heard three shots and I came up firing. I saw the man go down. When I was certain he was dead, I turned toward Lamar.'

Crease's voice grew husky and her eyes grew moist. She shook her head and took an angry pull on her smoke.

'The bastard had killed Lamar, just like that. I didn't even get to say anything to him.'

Crease stopped, unable to go on.

'Are you okay?'

'Shit, no, Lou.'

Anthony felt awful. He gave her a moment to collect herself.

'Look, I'm gonna cut this short. If there's anything else I need to ask, I can get it later. Just two more things, okay?'

Crease nodded.

'When I got here I found the front gate open. With all the security your husband had, why wasn't it locked?'

'It was locked, earlier. There was a power outage. We never relocked it when the power came back.'

'Is that why the house alarm was off?'

'No. I set the alarm when I'm ready for bed. I was going to work for an hour or so, like I said.'

'This has been hard for me, Ellen. I want you to know that. You're a real star with everyone at the Police Bureau. No one blames you for this. You did the right thing.'

'I know, Lou,' Crease said, cold as ice now, 'I'm just sorry I didn't kill the fucker sooner, so Lamar would be . . .'

A crash and shouts brought Anthony to his feet. When he opened the library door, he saw two men from the Medical Examiner's Office frozen in place halfway down the stairs to the second floor. Supported between them on a stretcher was a body bag containing the corpse of Lamar Hoyt, which they were maneuvering toward a gurney that sat at the foot of the stairs. Sprawled across the gurney was a tall, muscular man dressed in jeans, a plaid, flannel shirt and a raincoat. Three police officers were trying to pin him to the gurney, which slid back and forth across the hardwood floor during the struggle. One of the officers wrenched the man's arm behind him and a second tried to apply a chokehold. The man writhed and twisted until he was facing Anthony. There was no way of missing the resemblance to Lamar Hoyt.

The officer who had the chokehold applied pressure

and the man stopped struggling. One of the officers cuffed his hands behind his back. Then the three officers dragged him off the gurney and wrenched him to his feet. Before Anthony could say anything, Ellen Crease brushed past him and strode across the entryway. As soon as the intruder saw Crease his face contorted with rage and he lunged at her, screaming, 'You did this, you bitch.'

Crease paused in front of the man, stared at him with contempt, then slapped him across the face so hard that his head snapped sideways. Anthony grabbed Crease's arm before she could strike again.

'Who is this?' the detective asked Crease.

'This sniveling piece of shit is Lamar Hoyt, Jr.'

Anthony stepped between Crease and her stepson, facing the furious man.

'Calm down,' Anthony said firmly.

'That bitch killed him. She killed my father,' Junior screamed.

The officers immobilized Junior, and Anthony grabbed the flannel shirt at the collar and jerked him upright. Anthony could smell liquor on his breath.

'Do you want to spend an evening in the drunk tank?'

'It wouldn't be the first time,' Crease snapped. Junior lunged for her again but could not break Anthony's iron grip.

'Please wait for me in the library, Senator,' Anthony commanded angrily. Crease hesitated, then strode away from the melee.

Anthony pointed toward the staircase. 'That's your

father's body, for Christ's sake. Let these men take care of him.'

Junior stared at the body bag as if seeing it for the first time.

'Take him in there,' Anthony told the officers, indicating a small sitting room just off the foyer. When the officers did as they were told, Anthony motioned them away. Junior dropped to a small sofa. Anthony sat beside him. Hoyt's son was a little over six feet tall and husky. His large head was topped by curly black hair, his eyes were brown and his nose was thick and stubby, like his father's.

'Do I have to keep these cuffs on?'

'I'm okay,' Junior mumbled.

'I have these taken off and you act up, it's a night in jail.'

Anthony motioned and the officer with the key unlocked the cuffs. Junior rubbed his wrists. He looked properly chagrined.

'What was that all about? That screaming?'

Junior's features hardened. 'Why isn't she in custody?'

'Senator Crease?'

'I know she killed him.'

'Mr. Hoyt, your father was murdered by a burglar. He broke into the bedroom and shot your father. Senator Crease shot him. Ellen Crease didn't kill your father, she tried to save him.'

'I'll never believe that. I know that bitch is behind this. She wanted him dead and she got her wish.'

Two

THE HONORABLE Richard Quinn, judge of the Multnomah County Circuit Court, was almost six foot three, but he walked slightly stooped as if he were shy about his height. Despite his size and position, the thirty-nine-year-old judge was not intimidating. He smiled easily and seemed a bit distracted at times. His blue eyes were friendly and his thick black hair tended to fall across his forehead, giving him a boyish look.

Quinn's workday usually ended between five and six, but he had stayed in his chambers until seven working on the *Gideon* case. Then his normal twenty-minute commute stretched to fifty minutes because of an accident on the Sunset Highway that had been caused by the rain. When Quinn arrived at Hereford Farms, he was famished and exhausted.

Homes in the Farms started at half a million. Quinn and Laura could easily afford the place when they moved in five years ago. Quinn was making a six-figure salary at Price, Winward, Lexington, Rice and Quinn, and Laura, an associate at the firm on the fast track to a partnership, was pulling down high five figures with the promise of more to come. Still, Quinn loved the old colonial in Portland Heights where he was living when he proposed to Laura, and he had fought the move to the suburbs.

Quinn could trace the strains in the marriage to the arguments over the house in Portland Heights. Laura felt it was too small for the parties she wanted to throw and too far from the country club she wanted to join. In the blush of new love it had been easy for Quinn to give in, but he had never felt comfortable in this house that seemed more like a display model than a real home. There was a vaulted ceiling in the dining room and living room and no walls to separate the areas. A chandelier hung high above the stone floor in the entryway. Walls of glass let light flood in everywhere during the day. A circular stairway led up to the second floor. Quinn had to admit the house was impressive, but Hereford Farms and all the houses inside its walled perimeter were sterile and Quinn doubted that he would ever feel at home in this suburban encampment.

Quinn opened his front door. He started to call out to Laura, then he remembered that she was competing in the club tennis tournament tonight. He hung up his saturated raincoat in the hall closet and fixed himself dinner in the kitchen. There were assorted salads from yesterday's meal and soup he could reheat. Meals for both of them were catch-as-catch-can and they usually ate out or grabbed prepared dinners from a local super-market because of the hours Laura kept. None of the lawyers at Price, Winward worked a normal, eight-hour day. Many of them worked so hard that they developed health problems, burned out or drank excessively. Laura was one of the firm's hardest workers, but she was in excellent health and rarely touched liquor. The work exhilarated her.

Quinn was reading in bed when he heard the front door open. He checked the clock. It was a little before ten. Quinn listened to Laura as she rustled around in the kitchen. He heard the refrigerator door swing shut. There were small impacts as a glass or plate touched down on the counter where Laura liked to snack. Later, there were muffled footfalls as Quinn's wife climbed the spiral staircase to the second floor.

Laura entered the bedroom in her warm-ups. She was thirty-three, six years younger than the judge. Her skin was pale, her hair was caramel and her eyes deep blue. Even without makeup and with her hair in disarray, Laura was attractive. She was also one of the smartest women Quinn had ever met. Her rapid rise to partner was a testament to her intelligence and to the single-minded determination she brought to everything she did. But single-minded determination could also cause problems when there were conflicts in a marriage. Laura rarely gave in on something she wanted. She had prevailed on the house and she refused to consider children while her career was on the rise. The only issue of importance on which Quinn had not yielded to Laura's wishes was his judgeship.

'How did you do?' Quinn asked as Laura pulled off her sweats and unzipped her tennis whites.

'I beat Patsy Tang two sets to love,' Laura answered matter-of-factly. 'That puts me in the quarterfinals.'

'Great. Did you have any problem driving?'

'No. They cleared that mud slide on Quail Terrace.'

Laura stepped out of her clothes and took off her bra and panties. Quinn had seen his wife naked almost every day for seven years and she still aroused him.

'When did you get home?' Laura asked.

'About eight.'

'What kept you so late?'

'Gideon. He had two supreme court justices, four circuit court judges, a mayor and several clergymen testifying on his behalf. We ran over.'

Frederick Gideon was a Lane County Circuit Court judge who sat in Eugene, Oregon, a small city one hundred miles south of Portland that was best known for being the home of the University of Oregon. Gideon was a popular, conscientious jurist who had made several bad investments. The losses had left him unable to pay for his daughters' schooling. Gideon was severely depressed when the owner of a construction company, the defendant in a multimillion-dollar lawsuit, approached him with the offer of a bribe. In a moment of weakness, Gideon accepted the money and granted the defense a directed verdict in its favor.

The attorneys for the plaintiffs had been stunned by the ruling, which had no logical basis. A private investigator working for the plaintiffs unearthed evidence of the bribe. Judge Gideon, the owner of the construction

firm and two other men were arrested. Gideon struck
a bargain with the prosecution. He resigned from the
bench, testified against the other defendants and was
allowed to plead to a single felony that carried a maximum of five years in prison. Quinn was hearing the case
because all of the Lane County judges had disqualified
themselves. He had spent the day listening to witness
after witness extol Gideon's virtues and plead for leniency. Tomorrow morning the attorneys would sum up
and he would be expected to impose a sentence.

'What are you going to do?' Laura asked.

'I'm still undecided.'

Laura bundled up her dirty clothes and sat beside
Quinn on the bed.

'Did the D.A. bring up some new evidence against
him?'

'No. Jane even let it drop that she wouldn't be upset
if I gave him probation. Still . . .'

Quinn stopped, frustrated by the conflicting emotions
that had been battling inside him ever since he had been
assigned the *Gideon* case.

'I don't understand why this case is so hard for you,'
Laura said.

'He's a judge. Different rules apply when a judge
breaks the law.'

'A judge is also a human being.'

'That's true, but he has to set his standards higher.
When you put on the robe you separate yourself from
the rest of humanity.'

'Nonsense. You don't become some kind of god as
soon as you're sworn in. Gideon was under a lot of

pressure. You might have done the same thing if you were in his place.'

'No, never,' Quinn answered firmly.

'How can you say that if you haven't been faced with Gideon's predicament?'

'Being a judge is more than just performing a job. Americans are brought up to respect the rule of law and they expect judges to administer the law fairly. When a judge takes a bribe, he undermines that faith.'

'I think you're getting a little dramatic. We're talking about one judge in Lane County, Oregon. I don't think the country is going to self-destruct because Fred Gideon took some money so he could pay his kids' college tuition.'

'So you'd go easy on Gideon?'

'I'd give him probation.'

'Why?'

'For Christ's sake, Dick,' Laura snapped, 'he's a father. Send him to jail and you're destroying a family. And for what? Some theory you learned in high school civics?'

Quinn looked amazed. 'How can you say that? You're a lawyer. Don't you respect the system you work in?'

'I work in the real world, not some ivory tower. Fred Gideon is a poor overworked and underpaid bastard who became desperate when he thought that his kids might have to drop out of college.'

'Gideon's kids could have gone to the U. of O.,' Quinn answered angrily. 'They don't have to go to Ivy League schools. You worked your way through. Lots of kids do.'

Laura's features tightened and Quinn was sorry the

moment the words were out of his mouth. Until Laura was ten, she had lived in an upper-class suburb on the North Shore of Long Island, New York. Then her father had lost his job as an engineer. After a year of unemployment he became depressed. The family dropped the country club and beach club memberships, Laura's private tennis and piano lessons stopped and her mother started saving coupons and shopping for clothes at discount stores. Laura's father was forced to take a temporary job as a salesclerk, but he refused to let his wife work. His depression deepened and Laura's parents started fighting. By the time Laura was thirteen, her father had taken up with another woman, her parents were divorced and she was living with her mother in a tiny apartment in Queens.

Laura coped with her new situation by spending all of her time doing schoolwork and playing tennis. Although she had a partial athletic scholarship, she still had to work her way through college. She viewed her father's failure to contribute to her college education as more evidence of his betrayal.

'I'm sure you'll make the right decision,' Laura told Quinn coldly. She went into the bathroom without another word. Quinn knew that he had hurt Laura and he felt bad, but his wife's lack of respect for his work depressed and upset him.

Quinn tried to read, but his book no longer held his interest. A little while later, the bathroom door opened. Laura walked over to her dresser and slipped into her nightgown. She still looked upset. Quinn did not want Laura to go to bed mad. When she was under the covers Quinn remembered that he had some good news.

'I'm going to be speaking at that judicial conference at the Bay Reef Resort on St. Jerome. The organizers confirmed late this afternoon.'

Quinn's reading light was still on and he could see little interest on Laura's face.

'I thought maybe you'd come with me. We can go a few days early and make it a vacation. The only day I'm speaking is Thursday. We'd have the rest of the week free.'

'I'm busy, Dick,' she answered coldly. 'There's the Media Corp. litigation and the Hunter Air contract.'

'The conference is the last week in February. You have plenty of time to rearrange your work. Come on, Laura. It will be good for us. We haven't had a real vacation in two years.'

Quinn waited.

'I'd really like you to come with me,' Quinn said when he could stand the silence no more. 'I can use the break, too. We'd have a great time on St. Jerome. I checked around and the island is supposed to be beautiful. Sand, sun. We'd lie out by the pool and sip banana daiquiris until we were blotto. What do you say?'

Laura began to thaw. 'I can't promise right now,' she told Quinn.

'It won't be anything but work if you're not with me.'

'I'll talk to Mort Camden.'

Quinn brightened and that made Laura smile. Quinn moved against her.

'I'll be miserable if you're not there.'

Laura touched Quinn's cheek. 'You're like such a little boy sometimes.'

Quinn slid his hand under Laura's nightgown. She tensed for a moment, then relaxed and kissed him. Quinn made the kiss last. Laura stroked his neck. They had not made love for a week and a half. Her touch was like a live wire on his nerve endings and he was instantly erect. Quinn stroked down Laura's spine until he was cupping her backside. He enjoyed the tension in her muscles. Quinn felt Laura unsnapping his pajama bottoms. His mouth was dry with excitement. He longed to play with Laura so he could draw out their pleasure. His fingers found her nipples and he began stroking them to make them hard. Before he could finish, Laura was drawing him inside her and he was trapped in the rapid pull and push of her rhythm until, moments later, he exploded and collapsed, spent but not satisfied because of the rapidity of their intercourse.

Quinn felt the bed move as Laura left it for the bathroom. He replayed the quick sexual encounter in his mind and it occurred to him that sex with Laura had been less and less satisfying in the past year. Quinn stared at the ceiling and tried to remember when making love to Laura had stopped being fun. He knew he enjoyed sex with her tremendously before they were married and he was certain that the sex was still good when they lived in the old house in Portland Heights, but somewhere along the way he started suspecting that Laura was only going through the paces and he began to feel alone and lonely when they coupled.

Quinn was still excited by Laura and she never denied him sex. On the other hand, Laura rarely initiated the act the way she had when they were dating and she seemed to work hard at finishing quickly, as if sex was another chore, like dish washing, that she wanted to complete so she could move on to more important things.

Quinn wondered what would happen if he stopped having sex with Laura for a while, but he was afraid that her lack of interest was only in his imagination and that withdrawing from her would hurt her. Quinn could never do that to Laura. He was even more afraid that she would say nothing and that theirs would become a marriage of convenience.

The toilet flushed and Quinn heard the water running in the sink. He got out of bed and walked by Laura. It would have been so nice if she had touched him as they passed just to show that she was thinking of him. Quinn closed the bathroom door. All of a sudden he felt sad and defeated. He longed desperately to recapture the early days of their relationship when her passion matched his, sex left them both exhausted and fulfilled and he would drift off to sleep with a mind unclouded by doubt.

Three

LOU ANTHONY went straight from the Hoyt estate to the Justice Center to dictate his initial report The last section recounted the incident with Lamar Hoyt, Jr., whose behavior was partially explained by the alcohol he had been drinking and partially by his intense hatred of Ellen Crease.

Lamar Hoyt, Sr., had been sixty-two when he was murdered. He was a hard-nosed businessman who had turned his father's funeral parlors into a business empire. Junior was the sole issue of Hoyt's first marriage. He had barely made it through college, where he had paid far more attention to football than academics, and had floundered around, failing at various jobs, until his father put him in charge of his mortuaries. Junior had not exactly thrived in the family business, but he had managed to keep it turning a profit. He had also earned himself a reputation as a drunk, a womanizer and a brawler, and he resented his father's refusal to let him play a bigger part in Hoyt Industries, his father's conglomerate. Anthony had learned all this from Ellen Crease, after Junior was escorted off the estate grounds and driven home by a Portland Police officer. Crease despised Junior for being a drunk and a weakling.

Anthony lived alone, so there was no one to disturb when he stumbled into the bedroom of his split-level at two-thirty in the morning. Lou's wife of twenty-two years had died of cancer three years before but he had kept the house for visits from their kids. The hostile invader had been discovered during a routine physical; the battle to save Susan's life had been furious but short. She was gone eight months later. Lou's son was a freshman in college at the time and their daughter had just been accepted at Oregon State. He was thankful that Susan had died knowing that they had turned out well. There wasn't much else that he was thankful for except the job, which kept him occupied and distracted him from his grief.

After a few hours of sleep, Anthony was back at his desk reviewing the draft of his report and waiting for the reports from the crime lab and the results of a house-to-house canvas for witnesses that he had instituted shortly after his arrival at the Hoyt estate. Anthony did not expect much from the canvas. A stolen car had been found near the wall that surrounded the estate. He assumed that it was the burglar's getaway car. The fact that it was still parked at the scene meant that the burglar had probably been working solo, but you never knew. There might have been an accomplice who left on foot, though he could not imagine that happening in the previous night's storm when a nice, dry car was available. The estates on Crestview Drive were all set so far back from the street that he doubted the neighbors would have seen an accomplice slogging from the scene, anyway. Still, stranger things had happened and some crazy neighbor might have been out jogging or walking a dog. Anthony was not holding his breath.

'Lou.'

Anthony looked up and saw an excited Leroy Dennis bearing down on him with several sheets of paper in his hand.

'How do you feel about buying me lunch?' Dennis asked.

'Why would I buy you lunch, Leroy? The last time I sprung for you, you ate so much I almost had to file for bankruptcy.'

One of life's great mysteries was how Dennis could eat and eat and still not put on a pound.

'I'm a growing boy, Lou. My body just needs more than the average man. It has something to do with my sexual prowess.'

'Give me a break,' snorted Anthony, 'or give me a reason why I should assist you in committing suicide by cholesterol overdose.'

Dennis not only ate like a machine, but he had an aversion to any kind of food that was even remotely healthy.

'This is the reason,' Dennis said, shaking the documents he held at Anthony.

'What is that?'

'Uh-uh. No food, no facts. Hell, I'm so hungry I might just eat this exceptionally fine, and difficult-to-find, evidence.'

Anthony laughed. 'You have to be the biggest asshole in the bureau, Leroy, but I was going to eat soon, anyway.'

Anthony stood up and walked over to the closet to get his raincoat. Dennis followed him.

'Now, what have you come up with?' he asked.

'The name of our perp,' Dennis answered, his tone suddenly serious. 'I ran the burglar's prints through AFIS,' Dennis explained, mentioning the Automated Fingerprint Identification System that used computers to compare unknown prints to the prints stored in the computer's data banks. 'We got a hit an hour ago.'

'Who do we have?'

'Martin Jablonski. He's got the rap sheet for the job. Armed robbery, assault, burglary. He was paroled from OSP eight months ago where he was serving time for a pretty brutal home invasion that happened six years ago. Pistol-whipped an elderly couple. I talked to his parole officer. Jablonski's supposed to be living with his wife, Conchita Jablonski, and their two kids in an apartment off Martin Luther King near Burnside. He's been unemployed or working as temporary labor since he got out of prison.'

'Let's get a D.A. to write up an application for a search warrant, then visit the little woman,' Anthony said.

Dennis grinned. 'Where do you think I've been this last hour? I'm two steps ahead of you. Sondra Barrett is working on the affidavit as we speak. She'll have it ready to take to a judge after lunch. Now, where shall we go?'

Anthony parked his car in front of an old brick apartment house a few blocks from the Burnside Bridge. The Jablonskis lived on the third floor. It was a walk-up. As they climbed the stairs, Dennis complained about the lack of an elevator and the god-awful smell in the stairwell.

The third floor was poorly lit. The outside light had to fight its way through a grime-covered window on one end of the corridor and was so weak from the effort that it ended up dull yellow. The lightbulbs that hung from the ceiling were either broken or of such low wattage that Anthony wondered why the super bothered to turn them on.

The Jablonskis' apartment did not have a bell, so Anthony bashed a meaty hand against the door and bellowed 'Mrs. Jablonski' while he strained to hear if there was any movement inside. After his third try, Anthony heard a nervous 'Who is it?' from the other side of the door.

'I'm Detective Anthony with the Portland Police, Mrs. Jablonski.'

'I don't wanna talk with you,' Conchita Jablonski answered. Her speech was thickened by a heavy Spanish accent. 'Go away.'

'What?'

'I said, I don't wanna talk to no cops. Leave me alone.'

'I'm sorry, Mrs. Jablonski, but you have no choice. I

have a search warrant. If you don't open the door, I'll have the super bring the key. It's about your husband.'

There was no sound inside the apartment. When the silence stretched to thirty seconds, Anthony turned to Dennis.

'Wait here while I round up the key.'

Dennis nodded. Anthony was about to walk to the stairs when he heard locks snap. The door opened a crack and Conchita Jablonski stared at Anthony through a gap in the door. The safety chain was still on. Anthony held up his badge so Mrs. Jablonski could see it through the narrow opening.

'This is Detective Dennis,' Anthony told her as he pointed over his shoulder. Dennis flashed her a friendly smile, but Mrs. Jablonski continued to regard the men with suspicion. 'We need to talk to you about Martin.'

'For why?'

'Can we come in, please? I really don't want to discuss your business out here in the hall where all of your neighbors can hear.'

Mrs. Jablonski hesitated. Then she closed the door for a moment and took off the safety chain. A second later, the door swung into the apartment and Dennis followed Anthony inside.

The apartment was small, with two narrow bedrooms, a small living room and a tiny kitchen area that was separated from the living room by a low counter. Both detectives were impressed by how clean Conchita Jablonski kept the apartment. Her two children huddled in the doorway of one of the bedrooms watching the detectives. They looked well cared for. A boy and a girl, both about six or seven, big-eyed and brown-skinned with soft black hair.

Conchita Jablonski was a heavyset, dark-complexioned woman with a pockmarked face. She led the detectives into the living room and seated herself in a frayed and shabby armchair. Dennis and Anthony sat across from her on a sagging couch.

'I have some bad news for you,' Anthony said. Conchita Jablonski's facial features stayed frozen, but her shoulders hunched as if she were preparing for a blow. She clasped her hands in her lap. 'Martin broke into a home last night.' Conchita's features wavered. Her hands tightened on each other. 'While he was in the house, he shot and killed someone.'

Conchita began to shake. The children saw the change in their mother and they looked frightened.

'Martin was also shot. He's dead.'

Conchita bent at the waist as if she had been punched in the stomach. She started to sob. Her shoulders shook. The children's eyes widened. They huddled together. Dennis stood up and walked over to the shaking woman. He knelt beside her chair.

'Mrs. Jablonski,' he began in a soft and sympathetic voice. Before he could say another word, Conchita Jablonski spun in her chair and slapped him across the face. Dennis was off balance. He fell onto the floor awkwardly, almost in slow motion, into a sitting position, more stunned than hurt.

'You bastards!' Conchita shrieked. 'You killed my Marty!'

Anthony raced to her chair and restrained Mrs. Jablonski.

'He was robbing a house, Mrs. Jablonski. He murdered a woman's husband. He would have killed her, too, if she hadn't shot him.'

Conchita heard only parts of what Anthony said as she strained against him. Dennis struggled to his feet and helped subdue the distraught woman. She collapsed, sobbing, her head in her hands.

'Please, Mrs. Jablonski,' Dennis implored. 'Your kids are scared. They need you.'

She fought for control, gulping air. The two children raced over to her and buried themselves in her skirt. She talked quietly to them, submerging her own grief. The detectives waited while she calmed them. Dennis brought her a glass of water, but she would not take it.

'Are you gonna be okay?' Dennis asked.

'What do you care?' the woman shot back angrily. 'You cops never cared about me or Marty before. All you wanna do is lock him up.'

Anthony saw no reason to argue with Mrs. Jablonski. He held out the search warrant. 'This is a court order that gives us the right to search your apartment. Detective Dennis will sit with you while I conduct the search.'

Mrs. Jablonski suddenly looked frightened. Anthony wondered why, but he did not ask. If there was something hidden in the tiny apartment, it would be easy to find. He decided to start in the bedroom that the adults used. He could hear Detective Dennis talking soothingly to Mrs. Jablonski as he tossed the covers off the small bed where the Jablonskis slept. He knelt down and looked under it but saw nothing.

There was men's and women's clothing in the cheap wooden chest of drawers but nothing else. When he was through with it, Anthony opened the door of the closet. Dirty men's clothes lay crumpled on the floor, but there was nothing under them. Anthony peered up at a shelf that was just above his head. He pulled over a wooden chair that swayed slightly when he climbed up on it. Toward the back of the shelf was a shoe box. Inside were stacks of currency bound by rubber bands. Many stacks. The top bills were hundreds, fifties and twenties. Anthony stepped down from the chair and carried the shoe box into the living room.

'I've read Marty's file,' Anthony told her. 'It says that you're on welfare and Marty was having trouble getting steady work. There's a lot of money in here. Where did it come from? Drugs? Was Marty selling drugs?'

'I ain't saying anything to you. You cops are all the same. I knew I shouldina let you in my house.'

'Listen, Conchita, I'm not gonna mess around with you,' Anthony said harshly. 'Your husband killed a very important man. Now, all of a sudden, you're rolling in dough. You tell me where Marty got that money or I'll arrest you as an accessory to murder. What do you think happens to your kids if you're in jail?'

Conchita Jablonski wrapped her arms around her children and looked at Anthony with a combination of fear and loathing. He felt like a first-class heel, but Anthony did not let her know it.

'It's up to you, Conchita. You want your kids in foster care, keep playing games.'

The fight went out of Mrs. Jablonski. 'I don't know

where Marty got the money,' she answered in a small voice. 'He just got it.'

'He never said from who?'

'Just that it was from some guy.'

'Did he tell you what this guy looked like?'

'No.'

'Marty didn't say what this guy wanted him to do for this money?' Dennis asked.

'When he was doin' something bad he wouldn't tell me what it was because he didn't want me or the kids involved, but I knew it was no good.' She shook her head and started to cry. 'I tol' him to give back the money, but he said it was for me and the kids. He felt real bad how we lived and how he couldn't get no job because of his record. He wanted to do something for us. And now he's dead.'

'I'm going to have to take this with me,' Anthony said. 'I'll give you a receipt.'

'You can't take that money,' she sobbed. 'I got the kids. How I gonna feed them?'

'That's blood money, Mrs. Jablonski,' Dennis told her. 'Your husband may have been paid to kill someone for that money. You seem like a good woman. You take real good care of your kids and your home. You don't want that money. You know that money will only bring you grief.'

Anthony and Dennis spent twenty more minutes with Conchita Jablonski, but it soon became clear that she did not know anything more about the money, the man who had given it to her dead husband or the reason he had been given it. While Dennis finished searching the apartment, Anthony counted the cash in the shoe box and gave Mrs. Jablonski a receipt for $9,800. The detective figured that the actual amount Jablonski had been given was $10,000. The bills were secured by rubber bands in five-hundred-dollar bundles. Anthony had discovered a solitary rubber band under three hundred dollars in loose bills.

'I don't like this,' Dennis said when they were driving back to the Justice Center.

'I don't either. I didn't see anything in Jablonski's file about drugs. From what his wife says, he didn't score the money in a burglary. Some guy gave it to him because he wanted Jablonski to do something. Why would Jablonski run out in the middle of one of the worst storms in Oregon history to burglarize an estate with the security system Hoyt's had if that wasn't the job he was paid to do?'

'Yeah, Lou, that's what I was thinking. Only, robbery might not have been the motive. What if Jablonski was paid to hit Lamar Hoyt?'

'That's one possibility, but there's another.'

Leroy Dennis carried the shoe box full of money to the evidence room while Anthony made the call. James Allen answered the phone and Anthony asked to speak to Senator Crease.

'I'm afraid she's resting, Detective. She does not wish to be disturbed.'

'I can appreciate that, Mr. Allen, but this is an urgent police matter and I have to talk to her.'

Two minutes later, Ellen Crease picked up the phone.

'I'm glad I got you,' Anthony said. 'I wasn't sure you'd be staying at your house.'

'I'm using the guest room tonight,' Crease said. She sounded exhausted. 'Tomorrow is the funeral. Then I'm going out to eastern Oregon to campaign.'

'Oh,' Anthony said, surprised that she was going back on the campaign trail so soon after her husband's murder.

Crease could hear the note of censure in Anthony's tone.

'Look, Lou, everything I see in this house reminds me of Lamar. If I don't get out of here and keep busy, I'll go crazy.'

'I understand.'

'Did you call just to see how I'm doing?'

'That and one other thing. A few hours ago, we identified Martin Jablonski as the man who broke into your house. Does that name mean anything to you?'

'No. Should it?'

'Probably not. He was a real bad guy. Multiple arrests and convictions. Home burglaries accompanied by assaults. We thought we had ourselves a simple solution to what happened at your house. Then we discovered almost ten thousand dollars in cash in a shoe box in Jablonski's closet. His wife says someone gave it to him, but he wouldn't tell her why. We think Jablonski may have been paid to break into your estate.'

'But why . . . ?' Crease started, stopping when the obvious answer occurred to her. 'Lamar? You think this Jablonski was paid to kill Lamar?'

'We have no concrete evidence that is what happened. I just found the money an hour ago. It could be completely unconnected to the break-in.'

'But you don't think so.'

'The timing bothers me. The fact that he broke in when the weather was so bad.'

'Thank you for letting me know about this, Lou. I appreciate it.'

'This wasn't just a courtesy call. If Jablonski was paid to make a hit, Lamar may not have been the intended victim.'

There was dead air for a moment. 'You're suggesting that I might have . . . that Jablonski was sent to kill me?'

'I don't know. But I'm not taking chances. There's going to be a patrol car parked outside the estate while you're in Portland. You're going to have an around-the-clock guard until we sort this out. I suggest that you arrange your own security when you're out of the city.'

'I don't believe this.'

'I could be wrong. I just don't want to take any chances.'

'Thanks, Lou. I'm not going to forget this.'

'Yeah, well, let's hope I'm way off base. In the meantime, I'd appreciate it if you could work up a list of people who might want you or Lamar out of the way bad enough to pay someone to kill you. It could be a business thing, something personal. If there's even a possibility, write it down and let me look into it. I'll be discreet.'

'I'll work on it right away.' Crease sounded nervous, distant. 'And thanks again.'

Anthony hung up the phone and leaned back in his chair. He hoped he was wrong about the money. He hoped it was for drugs or a payoff for something Jablonski had already done, but he didn't think so.

Four

[1]

IT WAS STILL RAINING when Richard Quinn left for work on the morning after Lamar Hoyt's murder. Not the monster rain of the night before, but a steady, wearying drizzle that was profoundly depressing. The main roads had been opened during the night, but there were places where two lanes narrowed to one because of half-cleared mud slides or still active road crews. Quinn parked in the county garage shortly after seven-thirty and walked through the drizzle to the Multnomah County Courthouse, an eight-story, gray concrete building that takes up an entire block between Fourth and Fifth and Main and Salmon in the heart of downtown Portland. Quinn waved to the guard at the front desk and took the elevator to the fifth floor.

The door to Quinn's chambers was halfway down the

marble corridor on the south side of the courthouse. Copies of the *Oregonian* and the *New York Times* were lying in front of it. The judge usually started his day by doing the crossword puzzle in both papers while drinking a cup of coffee, but he was too distracted by the *Gideon* case to try them this morning.

Quinn picked up the papers and opened the door to his chambers. After flipping on the lights in the reception area, Quinn started coffee in the pot that sat on the low, gray metal filing cabinet behind his secretary's desk. Then he switched on the lights in his chambers.

A large rain-streaked window looked out at the ornamental ribbons decorating the north side of Michael Graves's post-modern Portland Building. Behind Quinn's massive oak desk was a bookshelf filled with a complete set of the Oregon Supreme Court and Court of Appeals case reporters and the Oregon Revised Statutes. In front of the desk were two high-backed armchairs. A couch stood against the wall behind the chairs. Above it hung a modern oil painting that made no sense whatsoever. Given the choice, Quinn would have set the oil on fire, but Laura had bought it for him as a swearing-in present. Quinn was not about to destroy the only indication of support for his decision to ascend the bench that his wife had made since the governor's call, three years ago.

Quinn dropped the newspapers on the bookshelf and surveyed his desk. It was as he had left it the preceding evening. Every square inch was covered with paperwork pertaining to Gideon's sentencing. Quinn eyed the reports, letters and lawbooks as he hung up his jacket on the coatrack that held his judicial robes. He sat behind the desk and stared some more. He had read every piece of paper several times. He knew some of the documents by heart. What he did not know was the proper sentence to impose on Frederick Gideon.

On Quinn's wall was a framed quotation from Abraham Lincoln, which read: 'I'll do the very best I know how – the very best I can; and I mean to keep doing so until the end. If the end brings me out all right, what is said against me won't amount to anything. If the end brings me out wrong, ten angels swearing I was right would make no difference.'

The judge's father, Oregon Supreme Court Justice Patrick Quinn, had framed the quotation and it had hung in the elder Quinn's chambers in the Supreme Court Building during his years on the bench. Justice Quinn had died when Richard was fifteen. If his father had faults, Richard never learned of them. His wife, who died in the same car accident that killed her husband, adored him. No one Richard had ever met had an unkind word for Patrick Quinn. Certainly not Frank Price, senior partner in Richard's old firm, former partner and best friend of Patrick, and the man who raised Quinn after his parents died. True or not, Patrick Quinn's perfection lived in his son's memory as a model and a challenge, and the framed quote that Quinn had inherited was the creed the judge tried to live by. But doing the right thing was not always easy.

Quinn reread the quotation. He thought about Lincoln's words. At this level, all decisions were hard and the certainty of mathematics was usually unattainable. He could only do his very best, then hope that, in the end, he had chosen correctly. That knowledge did not make the knot in his gut less painful, only a bit easier to bear.

'Your Honor,' Stephen Browder said as he launched into the conclusion of his argument in favor of probation, 'Frederick Gideon is a local boy who pulled himself out of poverty and worked his way through college and law school. Much of his early legal career was devoted to helping the poor. As his fortunes improved, he expanded his involvement in civic affairs. I am not going to repeat the testimony of the friends, business associates and community leaders who have testified in Judge Gideon's behalf at this sentencing hearing, but the gist of the testimony of these highly respected citizens is that Fred Gideon is a good man, a man worthy of your compassion. He is a man who made one tragic mistake in an otherwise blameless life.'

Browder paused and Quinn studied the defendant. He knew that everything Browder said was true. Gideon was basically a good person and he was repentant. Quinn's mental image, formed during his brief contacts with Gideon at judicial conferences, was of a rotund and jovial man who was always quick with a smile and a joke. The months following his arrest had taken the heart out of the jurist. His skin was pasty and there were circles under his eyes. He had lost a lot of weight. He had also lost his pride. The eyes that Quinn remembered for their twinkle were lifeless and had not raised high enough to meet the eyes of Quinn or any witness during the sessions in court.

'No one, including Judge Gideon, is asking you to

excuse what he did,' Browder continued. 'Frederick Gideon sold his judicial opinion for money and he will regret his decision to do so every day that remains to him in this life. But, Your Honor, Judge Gideon has been severely punished for his transgression in ways far more severe than any jail sentence this Court can impose on him. He is a judge no more, having voluntarily relinquished his position soon after his arrest in order to protect the bench from further controversy.'

In the front row of the courtroom, Martha Gideon hid her face in her hands. Her shoulders shook with each sob. Gideon's daughters tried to comfort their mother while fighting back their own tears.

'In addition, my client will be disbarred and lose not only his means of earning a living but his right to practice a profession in which he has spent most of his adult life. A profession he loves.

'There is more, and it is the worst punishment. Before he brought this shame on himself, the name Frederick Gideon stood for integrity, honesty. My client was someone who was widely admired. Judge Gideon has disgraced his good name and he may never be able to reclaim his dignity.'

Browder was an imposing attorney with wavy gray hair and a dignified bearing. He paused and placed his hand on his client's shoulder. Gideon flinched, as if the touch had burned him.

'The ability to show compassion is essential in a judge,' Browder said. 'I ask you to show compassion to this man. Please look beyond this single transgression to Fred Gideon's countless good deeds. He is a decent person who made one tragic mistake. Probation is the appropriate sentence for this man.'

Browder sat down. Quinn could put off his decision no longer. He looked across his courtroom at the defendant.

'Mr. . . . ,' Quinn began. Then he corrected himself. 'Judge Gideon. Even though you are no longer on the bench, I will address you as a judge because you have served as a judge for a long time. By all accounts, with the exception of the incident that brings you to this sorry pass, you have been a good judge.'

Quinn's voice caught in his throat and he was afraid that he might not be able to go on. There was a pitcher of water and an empty glass at his elbow. Quinn filled the glass slowly to give himself time to recover. He sipped the water until he felt his composure return.

'I'm relatively new to the bench. I suspect that's why I was assigned your case. You sat in another county, our contacts have been few. Most of what I know about you I have learned during this sentencing hearing. As I said, I'm new to the bench, but I suspect that I may never have to make a more difficult decision than the one I will make today.'

In front of Quinn were notes he had made in his chambers the night before. He consulted them for a moment.

'Judge Gideon, some of the finest people in this state have spoken on your behalf and your lawyer has been eloquent in his plea for leniency, but there is a presence that speaks more eloquently than any of your lawyers or your witnesses. It is this courtroom with its high ceilings, marble floors and walls of dark wood. This courtroom reminds me of the dignity and majesty of the law and it speaks to the duties of a judge.'

Gideon's head hung down and he stared at the top of the counsel table.

'We have a code of judicial conduct in Oregon. It forbids judges to commit criminal acts or engage in fraudulent conduct. You would expect that. But it also says that judges have to act honorably not just because fraudulent and criminal acts are forbidden by law but because acting at all times in an honorable way promotes public confidence in our judges and our courts.'

Quinn paused. This was as hard as he thought it would be.

'Judge, I know how much you have suffered and will suffer every day of your life. You are a decent man who knows that you have committed a great wrong. When you sold your judicial decision for money, you did far more than simply rob a litigant of a fair hearing. You committed an act that called into question the integrity of the American system of justice. You committed an act that undermined the confidence of our citizens in the judiciary. In effect, you betrayed the people of this state. I know that you understand what you did and I can see how much you are suffering. I want to give you probation, but I would be committing a great wrong myself if I did not sentence you to prison.'

Martha Gideon moaned. The defendant was sobbing quietly. His attorney looked as if it were he who would soon be behind bars.

'If you are the person I believe you are, you will know

that I am doing the right thing today by sentencing you to the Oregon State Penitentiary for two years. If you are not able to appreciate your sentence, then I have probably been far too lenient.'

[2]

Presiding Circuit Court Judge Stanley Sax found Quinn in his chambers shortly after noon. Quinn's secretary was at lunch and his clerk was also gone. An uneaten ham and cheese sandwich and a sealed bag of potato chips lay on Quinn's desk next to an unopened can of Coke in a small space that had been created by pushing aside some of the paperwork in Judge Gideon's case. Quinn was seated in shirtsleeves in front of his untasted food.

Sax sat in a chair across from Quinn without being asked. He was a small, solemn-looking man with a paunch. Except for a fringe of curly black hair that was going gray and a few odd strands on the top of his head, Sax was bald.

'You going to eat those?' Sax asked, pointing at the bag of potato chips. Quinn shook his head and Sax leaned across the desk and grabbed the bag.

'You look down in the dumps,' Sax said as he wrestled the bag open.

'It wasn't easy sentencing a fellow judge to prison.'

'That's why they pay us the big bucks.'

Sax popped a few chips in his mouth. He chewed for

a moment. Then he said, 'There's something I want you to think about.'

Quinn waited while Sax popped some more potato chips into his mouth.

'You gonna drink all of your Coke?' he asked.

Quinn opened the tab. As he handed the can to Sax, he asked, 'Do you want my sandwich, too?'

'Thanks, but I ate already.' Sax took a swig from the can. 'Katherine Rowe is moving over to domestic relations from the homicide rotation. Craig Kittles was supposed to take her place, but it looks like he'll be getting the U.S. magistrate appointment. That leaves me a judge short.'

It took Quinn a moment to catch on. In order to develop expertise, the judges in Multnomah County were assigned to rotations where they heard particular types of cases for set periods of time. Judge Rowe was transferring to the panel that dealt only with divorces, adoptions and other family matters. Some judges heard civil or criminal cases exclusively for a year or two. There were three judges who handled only homicide cases. The rotation was for one or two years, based on the judge's preference. Homicide was the most prestigious and demanding rotation and was usually reserved for judges with years of experience.

'You want me to go into the homicide rotation?' Quinn asked incredulously.

'You catch on fast. That's what I like about you. You're also not afraid to do what's right. You need brass balls to handle a death case. Not everyone can drop the hammer. You showed me a lot today.'

'I'm flattered, but I've only been sitting as a judge for three years.'

'Don't go modest on me, Dick. I've heard Frank Price say that you were giving out legal opinions on your daddy's lap when you were three, and you don't make partner at Price, Winward without getting a little bit of experience along the way. You're smarter than any other judge in this county with the exception of yours truly. Plus, and this is a big plus for someone who's going to deal in matters of life and death, you wanted to be a judge for all the right reasons. You didn't take this job because your practice wasn't going well or for the prestige or the power. I've been watching you. You're Pat Quinn's son, all right.'

Sax paused. He ate another chip. While he chewed he looked Quinn in the eye.

'You want it, it's yours.'

'How soon do you need to know?'

'Take a day or two to think about it.' Sax stood up. 'Don't let me down. And stop feeling guilty. If it's any comfort to you, I would have given Gideon the whole five years. So would your dad.'

[3]

Francis Xavier Price, the Price in Price, Winward, Lexington, Rice and Quinn, had been a major force in Oregon legal and political circles for almost fifty years. He and Alan Winward had founded the firm in 1945, as soon as they were discharged from the army after serving with distinction in World War II. Both men jumped into the political arena at the same time they were forging their legal careers. Alan Winward became a state representative, a state senator and governor, while Frank Price maneuvered behind the scenes. By the mid-fifties, Roger Lexington, Bill Rice and Patrick Quinn were name partners. By the sixties, the firm had over one hundred attorneys and its political connections and its list of lucrative clients made Price, Winward the most powerful law firm in Oregon.

The relationship between Frank Price and Patrick Quinn had always been special. When politics began taking more and more of Alan Winward's time, the firm hired the slender, nervous young man as its first associate. Within three years, Price and Winward made Quinn a partner, partly to recognize his magnificent record of success and partly out of fear that he would leave and set up his own practice. Neither partner wanted to face his protégé in court.

When Quinn tired of the grind of a high-level law practice, Frank Price used his political connections to secure an appointment to the Oregon Supreme Court for the man who had become like a son to the Prices, who had no children of their own. When Richard's parents were killed three years into the justice's first term on the court, Frank and Anna Price had not hesitated to take in Richard and raise him.

Frank Price was a gaunt and wiry bantamweight who still went to work every day at the age of eighty. For most of his adult life, Price had lived in a large house in Dunthorpe, but he had moved to a condominium in downtown Portland soon after his wife died. Quinn visited his surrogate father after work whenever he could. He knew how much in love Frank had been with his wife and how lonely he was since Anna's death. Quinn hoped that his visits helped Frank get through his dark period.

By the time Quinn left the courthouse shortly after six, the rain had let up. When Price opened the door for Quinn, the judge could see the lights of cars streaming over the bridges that spanned the Willamette River through the wide and high windows that made up the outer wall of the apartment.

'Come on in,' Price said with a smile. 'Can I get you something to eat? Some coffee?'

'Just coffee. I'm meeting Laura for Thai food in half an hour.'

Price walked into the kitchen. He was a little stiff. Arthritis. His complexion was pale, too, but he still swam fifteen hundred meters every weekday. Price had never surrendered in court and he was not giving in to old age.

'I heard about Gideon,' Price called in from the kitchen.

'It was a tough call,' Quinn said.

'A good result, though. I've never been able to stomach lawyers and judges who break the law. They always have an excuse.'

Quinn shrugged. He still felt lousy about what he had done, even though he felt that his sentence could not be avoided.

Price returned to the living room, carrying two steaming mugs of coffee. Quinn was sitting on the couch in front of a low table. Price set one mug in front of him and took a seat in an antique wooden rocker.

'I bet you feel like shit.'

Quinn smiled wearily. Frank had always been able to read his mind.

'It'll pass. Come this time next week, you'll be feeling a whole lot better. Know why? By next week, you'll have figured out that you did the right thing.'

'I don't know—' Quinn started, but Price cut him off impatiently.

'Of course you know. Gideon is a crook and a disgrace to the bench. He knew what he was doing when he took that money and he deserves every day of the sentence you imposed on him.

'Besides, if it's any comfort, you can count on the Parole Board cutting him loose inside of six months.'

Quinn looked up.

'You don't think a man with that many friends is going to do hard time, do you?'

Quinn didn't answer.

'You're thinking of Gideon's wife and kids, right? Gideon didn't think about what would happen to them if he got caught. Why should you? He's an adult, Dick. He was a judge. The son of a bitch knew right from wrong and he chose to do wrong. Don't forget that. This was the sentence he knew he could get, but he probably convinced himself that he would skate if he was caught because he was a judge with friends in high places. Maybe the next judge who is tempted to cross the line will think twice because you hammered Gideon. Have you considered that?'

'No.'

'Well, stop feeling sorry for yourself and think about it.'

'I will.'

Quinn took a sip of coffee. Then he said, 'Stan Sax came to my chambers today. He wants me to go on the homicide rotation. What do you think?'

'It sounds interesting.'

'I'm not that experienced in criminal law.'

'You're a quick study, Dick. Stan wouldn't have asked if he didn't think you could handle the job.'

'Yeah.' Quinn smiled. 'I've already made up my mind to do it.'

'Good. Say hello to Stan for me, the next time you see him.'

'I will. Say, did I tell you that I've been asked to speak at the National Association of Litigators' annual convention on St. Jerome next month?'

'No.'

'Laura's coming with me. We'll go a few days early. It will be good for her to get away and just relax.'

'St. Jerome should be beautiful this time of year. I'm jealous.'

Quinn grinned. 'I'll be thinking of you as I lie on the beach. The paper said it was eighty-four and sunny today.'

Price laughed. 'Go ahead, rub it in, you ingrate. I hope you get hit by a hurricane.'

Five

SHORTLY AFTER NOON, one week after the Hoyt homicide, Lou Anthony returned to the Homicide Bureau and found two messages from Gary Yoshida, the lead forensic expert on the case. Anthony found the criminalist bent over a microscope in the crime lab.

'Lou,' Yoshida said with a smile. He swiveled the stool on which he was perched. Anthony leaned against the counter. Around them, other forensic experts were testing drugs, examining objects under microscopes and recording observations on reports that were often the difference between a guilty and not guilty verdict.

'You called twice,' Anthony said, and Yoshida's smile faded.

'Thanks for getting back to me so quickly.'

Anthony shrugged. 'What's up?'

'Has the Hoyt crime scene been turned back to Senator Crease?'

'Yeah. We released it two days ago.'

'Damn.'

'What's the matter?'

'I'd really like to look it over again.'

'Why?'

Yoshida walked over to his desk and picked up a stack of photographs that had been taken in Lamar Hoyt's bedroom. When he found the two that he wanted, Yoshida brought them over to Anthony.

'I was going through the evidence again when I was writing my report and I spotted this,' Yoshida said, pointing to a section of each photo that showed the armoire that held the television.

'Is that blood spatter?'

'Yeah. And it's got me concerned. I don't like to screw up, but I may have, big-time.'

'I don't get it.'

Yoshida explained the problem to Anthony. When he was finished, the detective looked upset.

'How certain about this are you?'

'I've got to see the scene in three dimensions to be sure. That's why I want to look at the bedroom again.'

'Shit.' Anthony took a deep breath. 'Okay. Look, two days isn't that long, and I don't imagine Crease is staying in the bedroom. Maybe the scene hasn't been altered yet. We could take a drive out to the estate. Can you go now?'

'You bet.'

'Then let's head out.'

'Great.'

'Not if you find what you're looking for,' Anthony answered grimly.

Days of biting cold followed the heavy rains that had disrupted the commerce of the city. Low gray clouds drifted in an iron sky and threatened more rain. The winding country roads that led to the Hoyt estate were clear of debris, but the landscape looked bedraggled and grimy.

Anthony rolled down his window so he could use the speakerphone at the front gate. A gust of cold wind rushed into the police car. After a brief wait, James Allen buzzed Anthony and Yoshida through the gate. The estate grounds had been hard hit by the weather. The colors had been leeched out of the hedges and the lawn by the pale light, and the foliage bowed down, cowed by the cold and the threat of rain. The house looked deserted and dispirited as if it were in mourning.

Anthony circled the turnaround and parked near the front door. The houseman was waiting for them. He had the door open as soon as Anthony and Yoshida were out of their car. The men hunched their shoulders and walked with speed into the entry hall.

'Good afternoon, Mr. Allen,' Anthony said. 'Is Senator Crease in?'

'No, sir. She's campaigning in eastern Oregon. I don't expect her back until Monday. Is there something I can do for you?'

'Yeah. It's actually better if we don't have to bother the senator. This is Gary Yoshida from our crime lab. We want to take another look at the bedroom.'

'I'm not sure I can let you do that. Ms. Crease left me strict orders that no one but the cleaning people were to be allowed in the bedroom.'

'Has the bedroom been cleaned up already?' Anthony asked, trying hard to hide his concern.

'No, sir. A crew is coming tomorrow morning.'

'Senator Crease probably wanted to keep reporters out of the house. She wouldn't want to interfere with our investigation.'

'I'm sure you're right, but I can't let you in the room without talking to her.'

'Why don't you phone?'

'I can try. I have the number of her hotel in Pendleton. Do you want to wait in the living room?'

'Sure.'

'Can I get you something to drink? Some coffee or tea?'

Anthony glanced at Yoshida. The forensic expert shook his head.

'No, thanks,' Anthony told the houseman.

Anthony knew where the living room was from his official visit to the estate on the evening of the murder, but he let Allen direct him to it. The vast room was dominated by a massive stone fireplace. A Persian carpet, similar to the carpet in the entry hall, lay over the hardwood floor. Yoshida tried to be nonchalant, but as soon as Allen was gone, he said, 'This room is almost as big as my house. We're in the wrong business, Lou.'

'I don't know, Gary. The owner's dead and we're still ticking.'

Anthony and Yoshida settled themselves on one of

the large sofas that flanked the fireplace, and waited for the houseman to return. A fire had not been laid in the grate and the room was chilly. Anthony was beginning to regret turning down the offer of coffee when Allen reentered the room. The policemen stood up and met him halfway.

'I'm sorry. Ms. Crease has already left the hotel and I have no idea when I'll be able to talk to her.'

'Thanks for trying, but we really do have to see the room.'

'I thought the investigation was complete.'

'For the most part, but we have a few loose ends to tie up.'

'I don't want to impede your investigation, but without Ms. Crease's permission . . . ,' Allen said hesitantly.

Anthony tired of diplomacy. He was all for civility, but he was used to getting his way, like most policemen.

'Look,' Anthony said sharply, 'this is an official police investigation into the death of your employer and Senator Crease's husband. You're telling me the bedroom is going to be cleaned tomorrow. By the time you talk to Senator Crease any evidence in that room will be destroyed. We need to get into the bedroom and we need to do it now.'

'All right,' Allen said reluctantly. 'You can go up. The room is locked. I'll get the key for you.'

'Thanks. We won't be long.'

Anthony knew the way to the bedroom and he did not want the houseman tagging along, so Anthony told

Allen that there was no need for him to accompany them. He sensed that Allen was relieved that he would not have to reenter the bedroom.

As soon as Yoshida opened the door, Anthony started to envy Allen. The room had been sealed and the windows were closed. The stench of death still hung in the stale air.

Anthony took a step into the bedroom, but Yoshida held out his arm to block him. Anthony stepped back into the corridor as Yoshida switched on the lights. The forensic expert stood in the doorway and slowly surveyed the room. He was carrying the Hoyt file in an attaché case. When he had seen what he wanted to see from the doorway, Yoshida walked over to the bed and set down the attaché on Lamar Hoyt's end table. Then he took out the crime scene photographs and the lab reports and shuffled through them. Every so often, he compared a photograph to the section of the room it portrayed. When he was through with the photographs, Yoshida began studying sections of the room. He stood at the door to the bathroom for a while, then inspected the armoire that stood opposite the foot of the bed against the south wall. After he was shot, Martin Jablonski had crumpled to the floor with his feet almost touching the side of the armoire that faced the west wall. A fine spray of blood that discolored the west-facing side of the armoire about six feet above the carpet attracted Yoshida's attention.

Occasionally, Yoshida made notes on a yellow pad. Other times he asked Anthony to hold one end of a roll of string over a particular patch of blood while he unrolled the string and straightened it at some point before squatting down and sighting back along it toward Anthony. Sometimes Yoshida employed a tape measure. Except to clarify Yoshida's instructions, Anthony kept quiet, even though he was anxious to learn Yoshida's conclusions.

Yoshida put everything back in the attaché and snapped the locks closed. Anthony looked at him expectantly. Yoshida looked very grim. He explained his conclusions to Anthony with scientific detachment while walking the detective through every step in his reasoning and showing him the physical evidence that supported his opinion. Anthony's mood grew more morose with each new detail.

When Yoshida was through, Anthony told him to wait in the living room while he went in search of James Allen. The detective found the houseman in the kitchen. A huge, tiled center island with several stove lights dominated the room. Anthony spotted two dishwashers and two ovens. Copperware hung from the ceiling. Allen was seated at a large wooden table polishing silverware. He stood up when Anthony entered.

'Are you through, sir?'

'Just about. I wanted to ask a few questions, though.'

'Please.'

'How long did you work for Mr. Hoyt?'

'A long time. Mr. Hoyt first employed me in the West Side Home of Heavenly Rest. When he purchased this estate, he asked me if I would work for him here.'

'Was Mr. Hoyt a good employer?'

'He was the best, sir,' Allen answered. He paused

and it was clear to Anthony that the houseman was struggling.

'I want to be completely honest, Detective. I don't want you thinking that I have concealed information. When I was a young man . . . well, sir, I killed a man. There is no other way to put it.'

Allen looked down, embarrassed by his confession.

'I was convicted of manslaughter and I served two years in prison. I was twenty when I was paroled. I was a high school dropout with no job skills who bore the stigma of a felony conviction. No one would hire me. I was sleeping in missions, barely able to keep myself together. I seriously considered suicide on more than one occasion. Then Mr. Hoyt hired me. He . . . well, sir, it would be quite accurate to say that he saved my life. Simply giving me a job would have been enough, but he did much more. When my mother grew ill, Mr. Hoyt paid for her care and he financed my education.'

Allen looked directly into Anthony's eyes. 'Mr. Hoyt was not merely my employer. He was my savior. His death has been very hard on me.'

'I appreciate your candor.'

'Thank you, sir.'

'If you worked for Mr. Hoyt since you were twenty, I guess you were with him through all three marriages.'

'Yes, sir.'

'I gather that the first two were pretty stormy toward the end.'

'They were.'

'How about his marriage to the senator? Did Mr. Hoyt and Senator Crease get along?'

Allen looked uncomfortable. 'I shouldn't be discussing Mr. Hoyt's private life.'

Anthony nodded. 'I appreciate that, but this is a murder investigation and it's suddenly become important that I learn a little more than I already know about the personal life of Mr. Hoyt and Ellen Crease.'

'Really, Detective Anthony, I don't feel it's proper for me to comment.'

Anthony placed his slablike forearms on the kitchen table and leaned forward slightly.

'Mr. Allen, there is no place for delicacy here. Martin Jablonski splattered your boss's brains all over his expensive bed linens. Life doesn't get more indelicate than that. What I want to know is why he did that. If you respect Mr. Hoyt as much as you seem to, you'd want to help me out here.'

Allen looked confused. 'I thought Mr. Hoyt was killed during a burglary. What possible relevance could the state of his marriage have to your investigation?'

'Let's just say that we're looking into other possibilities.'

'And you suspect Ms. Crease?'

'I'm afraid that I can't go into that.'

Allen considered the implications of Anthony's answer. Then he said, 'For most of their marriage, Mr. Hoyt and Ms. Crease got along quite well.'

'Most?'

'Yes, sir.'

'When did they stop getting along?'

'Recently.'

'What made you think there were problems?'

'They quarreled. Not all of the time, you understand. But there were arguments.'

'About what?'

'I really can't say.'

'Do you think Senator Crease was in love with her husband?'

Allen thought about the question for a moment before answering.

'Yes. When he died she took it very badly. I know that she has not made a public display of her grief, but in the privacy of this house . . . in my opinion she is still grief-stricken.'

'Was Mr. Hoyt in love with Senator Crease?'

'I believe so.'

'Believe?'

'Well, there were the arguments.'

'Was she cheating on him?'

'Not that I knew, but she wouldn't have brought men back here, would she?'

'What about Mr. Hoyt? Was he cheating on her?'

The houseman's eyes dropped briefly.

'Not that I knew,' Allen replied.

'What does that mean?'

'If you're aware of Mr. Hoyt's marital history, you know that he has always had a problem with fidelity.'

'Did you ever hear Senator Crease accuse her husband of cheating on her?'

'No.'

'Did the senator ever threaten her husband?'

'I never heard any threats,' Allen answered evasively.

'Let me put this another way. Did you ever get concerned for Mr. Hoyt because of anything Ellen Crease did?'

Allen considered the question.

'The arguments . . . some of them were very loud. I couldn't hear what was said, but the tone . . . I'm afraid that's all I can say.'

Anthony stood up. 'Thank you for talking to me. I know it wasn't easy.'

'No, sir, it wasn't.'

Anthony was grateful that Yoshida did not say much during the short ride back to the Justice Center. The detective liked Ellen Crease. He respected her. But there was no way of avoiding the implications of the blood spatter patterns in the master bedroom.

The discovery that Jablonski may have been paid to break into the Hoyt mansion had complicated the investigation by turning a simple burglary into a possible murder conspiracy. Now the discovery of the blood spatter evidence forced Anthony to add Crease to the list of people who might have paid Jablonski to murder Lamar Hoyt. If it turned out that Ellen Crease was behind her husband's murder, he would arrest her. He did not want to do that, either, but he would if his duty demanded it.

Six

CEDRIC RIKER looked around the interior of the Lumberjack Tavern with jerky head movements that betrayed his nervousness. The Multnomah County district attorney was not used to meeting people after midnight in workingmen's bars. He liked to conduct business over power breakfasts at upscale hotels or pricey dinners at trendy restaurants.

Riker was a slender man of medium height who wore wire-rimmed glasses and styled blond hair. He usually dressed elegantly, but he was wearing jeans, a flannel shirt and a navy-blue ski jacket for this clandestine meeting with Benjamin Gage's hatchet man, Ryan Clark. Riker's attempt to blend in with the customers in the Lumberjack was doomed to failure. None of the construction workers or bikers who drank there wore polished wing-tip shoes.

As soon as Riker's eyes adjusted to the dark interior,

he spotted Clark waiting for him in a booth in the bar's darkest corner. Riker slid onto the bench across from Clark until he was pressed against the wall. There was an empty glass and a pitcher of beer between the two men, but Riker ignored them.

'Ben appreciates your meeting with me.'

'He won't be so happy if some reporter sees us here,' Riker snapped. 'Let's get this over with.'

Cedric Riker was an arrogant and insecure man who liked to throw his weight around. He could not afford to antagonize Benjamin Gage, a powerful political ally and a source of campaign funds, but Clark was only an employee. Riker detested Clark with his mysterious ways and intimidating scar, and he was never civil to him. Riker's bullying tactics had no effect on Clark. He despised Riker, but he kept his contempt well hidden because Riker was useful to his boss on occasion.

'We're very worried about the impact of Lamar Hoyt's murder on Ben's campaign,' Clark said.

'You should be. Crease is playing this for all she can get. The press is making her sound like a cross between Joan of Arc and Annie Oakley.'

'Ben understands that there are new developments in the case. He'd like to know what they are.'

'What kind of developments?' Riker asked warily.

'Something to do with Jablonski and some money. Our source wasn't clear.'

Riker was angry. Someone was leaking the details of the Hoyt investigation. Still, if Gage wanted to know, Riker was not going to keep the information from him.

'Jablonski's an ex-con with a history of violence. He

just got out of the Oregon State Penitentiary eight months ago. He was serving time for a series of home burglaries in wealthy neighborhoods. In a few cases, he pistol-whipped the victims. He hurt one of them pretty badly. Killing Hoyt would be consistent with his modus operandi. But Lou Anthony's found a few things that don't look right.'

'Such as?'

Riker took a quick and nervous look around the tavern. When he was satisfied that no one was listening, he said, 'The search of Jablonski's apartment turned up ten thousand dollars in cash in a shoe box. It was hidden in the bedroom closet. Jablonski may have been paid to make a hit.'

'On Hoyt?'

'Or Crease. Then again, the money and the Hoyt break-in might be unconnected. Except . . .'

'Yes?' Clark prodded.

Riker leaned across the table and lowered his voice.

'Lou went back to the crime scene with a forensic expert. There's something wrong with the blood.'

'The blood?'

Riker explained what Anthony had told him. When he finished, Clark looked thoughtful.

'What are you planning to do?' he asked.

'I know Ben's losing votes, but I've got to move very slowly. Ben should understand that. Everyone knows that he's one of my supporters. If I go after Crease without the goods, it will hurt both of us.'

Clark nodded. Riker waited for him to say something else. Instead, Clark stood up.

'It would be better if we left separately. I'll let Ben know how helpful you've been.'

Riker watched Clark walk out of the tavern. When the door closed, Riker shuddered involuntarily. He just did not feel right around Gage's A.A. The guy was spooky. A few minutes later, Riker left the Lumberjack. Outside, the rain had let up, but the wind was blowing. Riker hunched his shoulders and walked quickly to his car.

Seven

[1]

HOYT INDUSTRIES corporate headquarters was housed in a three-story, no-frills concrete box a few minutes from the Wilsonville exit on I–5. A parking lot surrounded the building and a field surrounded the parking lot. There were minimal attempts at landscaping. Anthony parked in a spot reserved for visitors. A receptionist sat behind a wide desk in the lobby. Anthony named the person whom he wanted to see. A few minutes later, he was sitting across the desk from Stephen Appling, Hoyt's senior vice-president.

Appling was dressed in a gray, pinstriped Armani suit and a silk Hermès tie. His curly salt-and-pepper hair had been styled and he had a tan in spite of the weather. He seemed the antithesis of someone who would work for a good old boy like Lamar Hoyt. Then, again, anyone as country smart as Hoyt would see the value in hiring a shrewd businessman who would feel at home with blue-blood bankers and wealthy investors.

Anthony noticed several golf trophies on a low credenza behind Appling's desk and a framed Wharton M.B.A. next to several photographs of Appling playing golf with various celebrities.

'Is that Michael Jordan?' Anthony asked.

Appling smiled. 'Hoyt Industries hosts a celebrity golf tournament every year to raise money for charity.'

'Did you play with Jordan?'

'No. I played with Gerald Ford that time. I did get in a round with Michael at Pebble Beach, though. We were trying to recruit him for an endorsement contract. It didn't work out.'

Anthony's brow furrowed. 'What product was Jordan supposed to endorse? Not the mortuary business?'

Appling threw his head back and laughed.

'No, Detective, not the mortuaries. Actually, the funeral parlors were only a small part of Lamar's financial interests. Hoyt Industries owns a company that manufactures supplies for funeral homes nationally, a trucking company and Modern Screen Theaters.'

'That's Hoyt Industries?'

Appling nodded. 'We operate eighty percent of the movie theaters in Oregon, Washington and Idaho and we're expanding into northern California. We were talking to Michael about being a spokesman for the theaters.'

'So this is a big operation.'

Appling smiled sadly. 'Lamar liked to come across

as a hick, but he was anything but. His business expertise rivaled that of any of the M.B.A.'s he employed, yours truly included, even though he never graduated from high school. He is sorely missed around here.'

'Who's running the company now that Mr. Hoyt is dead?'

'I'm the interim president, but the Board of Directors is going to have to select a permanent president.'

'Is Senator Crease going to inherit her husband's stock?'

'You'll have to talk to Charles DePaul, Lamar's lawyer, about that.'

'If she does inherit Mr. Hoyt's shares, will that give her a controlling interest in the company?'

'Yes,' Appling responded. Anthony noticed that he was not smiling now.

'So she'll have a big say in how the company runs.'

'If she wants to, no one can stop her.'

'You don't seem happy about that.'

'I'm sure that Senator Crease will do what is best for the company.'

'But you're not certain?'

'Is this just between us, Detective?'

'Sure, if that's how you want it.'

'Ellen Crease is a . . . how shall I say this? Headstrong is a good description. She has her own opinions about how to do things. Once those opinions are formed, it is difficult to change them. Unfortunately, the senator's views on how to run this company are not based on a background in business.'

'You don't think she's competent to head up Hoyt Industries?'

'Don't get me wrong. I have the highest respect for the senator's intelligence, and I think she believes that she is capable of running Hoyt Industries. I'm not convinced, though.'

'Who would profit if the senator had been murdered along with her husband?'

'You mean with regards to the company?'

Anthony nodded.

'I guess Junior, if he inherited.'

'Could he run Hoyt Industries?'

'Off the record again?'

'Yes.'

'Junior is a fool and a spendthrift. He would bankrupt this company.'

'So you don't think Mr. Hoyt contemplated any part in running the company for his son?'

'I'm certain of it. They weren't even on good terms personally. In fact, shortly before his death, Lamar and Junior had a yelling match right here.'

'About what?'

'I don't know. Lamar wouldn't talk about it. I just caught the tail end. I was walking over to Lamar's office when his door burst open and Junior came storming out. He almost knocked me down. Junior looked furious. When I went into Lamar's office, he was just as angry.'

'Mr. Appling, can you think of anyone who would want Mr. Hoyt dead?'

'No, and I have thought about it. We have union problems with the trucking concern, of course, and

71

there are employees that we've had to let go, but that's just grasping at straws. If you're looking for serious suspects, I can't give you any.'

'Thank you for your time, Mr. Appling,' Anthony said as he stood up. He placed a card on the vice-president's desk. 'If you think of anything else, please give me a call.'

[2]

Charles DePaul's office was not as grandiose as Anthony had expected the office of a senior partner in a major law firm to be. It was sparsely furnished and functional. DePaul's desk was almost bare. There was an antique reading lamp, some correspondence neatly stacked under a glass paperweight, a picture of DePaul's wife and three daughters and a single file sitting squarely in the center of the desk. DePaul was as unimposing as his office, a short, balding, slightly overweight man who looked nothing like the image suggested by his reputation in the Oregon Bar.

'You said on the phone that you wanted to discuss the terms of Lamar's will. Can you tell me why?'

'This is confidential information, Mr. DePaul. So let me ask you first, who is your client?'

'Lamar Hoyt, Sr.'

'Not Ellen Crease?'

'No, sir.'

'Mr. DePaul, I need your promise that what is said here will not be repeated.'

'You can trust my discretion.'

'There is a possibility that the break-in at the Hoyt estate was more than a burglary. The man who broke in may have been paid to kill Mr. Hoyt, his wife or both of them. If Mr. Hoyt was the intended victim then I need to know who gains by his death . . .'

'And the beneficiary of the will is an obvious suspect,' DePaul said, completing the detective's thought.

'Exactly.'

'Aside from bequests to a few charities, Mr. Allen and some of the employees at Hoyt Industries, the major beneficiaries were Ellen Crease and Lamar's only child, Lamar, Jr. Senator Crease inherited the bulk of the estate. That would be the house, the controlling shares in Hoyt Industries and a number of other bequests.'

'And his son?'

'Lamar left Junior the mortuary business, a quarter of a million dollars in cash and a home in the mountains. Junior is an avid skier.'

Anthony remembered the incident with Lamar, Jr., at the mansion and asked, 'How did Mr. Hoyt react when the will was read?'

DePaul shook his head with disapproval. 'Junior caused quite a scene. He threatened to contest everything, then he stormed out after flinging a few choice words at Senator Crease.'

'Inheriting a quarter million dollars and a going business would make my day. What was bothering Junior?'

'The amount that he left to his son was a very small bequest when you consider that Lamar's estate is worth twenty million dollars.'

'Why didn't he leave Junior more?'

DePaul considered the question for a moment before answering. 'Junior is not an idiot, but he's lazy and irresponsible. He's been able to run the mortuaries, but Lamar had to keep a close eye on the business. I believe that Lamar wanted to give Junior an incentive to work hard. He didn't want to leave him penniless, but he was afraid that Junior would not work at all if he had too much money.'

'He obviously didn't feel that way about his wife.'

DePaul hesitated. 'Detective Anthony, I don't know if I should be telling you this, but Lamar and I go way back. If there is something amiss . . . well, I just want to make sure that you're fully informed. Shortly before his death, Lamar discussed the possibility of changing his will.'

'In what way?'

'He didn't say specifically, but I had the impression that he was going to change his bequests to his wife and son dramatically.'

'How?'

'He never came right out and said what he planned to do, but I believe that their stake in his estate would have been drastically diminished.'

'So Senator Crease and Junior benefited when Mr. Hoyt was killed before the will was changed?'

'Yes. Senator Crease in particular.'

DePaul paused. He looked troubled, as if a new thought had just occurred to him.

'Of course, if Ellen was involved in Lamar's murder, Junior would inherit her share.'

'Why is that?'
'The law forbids a person to profit from a will if they cause the death of the person who made it.'

Eight

K AREN FARGO heard the announcement of Lamar Hoyt's murder on the morning news while she was driving to work. She had pulled onto the shoulder of the highway because she could not see the traffic through her tears and she was shaking so badly that she was afraid she would lose control of her car. When she could drive, she took the first exit and returned home. She had called in sick that day and the next.

On her first day back to work, Mr. Wilhelm had called her into his office and fired her. Fargo was in a state of shock and her protests were feeble. Mr. Wilhelm had an explanation for his actions, but she barely heard them. She knew why she had been let go and who was behind the firing, though that person was so insulated by layers of middle management and executive power that she knew she would never be able to prove her suspicions.

After cleaning out her desk, Fargo drove straight home and called her parents in Michigan. She told them about being fired, though not about Lamar. Her parents were serious Baptists and would not have approved of her affair with a married man. They acted like cheerleaders, reminding her of how smart she was and what good work she did. Surely another company would hire her.

When Fargo ended her call to her parents, she was upbeat. She did not have very much money saved, but she had enough to get by until another job came along. There was always a market for a good secretary. Maybe, she thought, it was best that she not continue to work at Hoyt Industries, where every day would be a reminder of the life she had lost. Maybe being fired was a blessing in disguise.

The next day Fargo started her job search with high hopes. She had graduated at the top of her secretarial school class, she was attractive and friendly and she always received excellent efficiency ratings. Strangely, the jobs did not come. The interviewers were always enthusiastic and she left the interviews with high expectations, but her phone did not ring.

At first, she convinced herself that the companies had lost her number and she called them to see if a decision had been made. Most of the time, the person who had interviewed her would not take her call. A secretary would tell Fargo that the job had been given to someone else. On the few occasions that someone important did talk to her, they seemed embarrassed. It was only during the call that she had made two hours before to Durham

Food Products that she found out why she was being turned down for job after job. Mr. Pebbles, the man with whom she'd had such a positive interview, sounded uncomfortable when they spoke. Toward the end of their short conversation, he told her sympathetically that he would have hired her if her reference from Hoyt Industries hadn't been so negative. When Fargo asked the man what he meant, Pebbles told her that he had said too much. He wished her luck and hung up.

Fargo was too numb to think straight. Then she remembered that all of the jobs for which she had applied required references. When she figured out that someone at Hoyt Industries was blackballing her, she became frightened, then she became angry. Fargo had driven to her old company to confront Mr. Wilhelm, but the security guard would not let her into the building. On the ride home, Fargo grew scared. What if she could not find a job? How would she live? She had broken down halfway home and she was still crying when she opened the front door of her small, rented Cape Cod.

Fargo had not bothered to raise her shades that morning and her front room was thick with shadows. She turned on a floor lamp. It took her a moment to realize that a man was sitting in the armchair near the window. Fargo took a step backward. The light from the lamp did not reach all the way to the armchair and she could just make out the man's profile.

'There's no need to be afraid, Miss Fargo,' the man said quietly. 'I'm a friend, and I think you need one.'

Fargo reached behind her for the doorknob, but she made no move to open the front door.

'Who . . . who are you?' she asked anxiously.

'Someone who wants to help you. Are you upset because you've been turned down for another job?'

Fargo let go of the doorknob. 'How did you know that?'

'That's not important. What is important is that you know the identity of the person who has been stopping you from getting a job. She's the same person who made certain that you were fired from Hoyt Industries.

'Miss Fargo, there are people who are concerned about you. People who don't think that it's fair that Ellen Crease used her power to have you fired and is using her power to keep you from finding work. These people want to secure a job for you. A good job that will pay you the salary you deserve.'

'Why would these people do that for me?'

'They're the same people who believe that Ellen Crease is responsible for the murder of Lamar Hoyt. They want to see justice done.'

The man stopped talking to let Fargo absorb what he had said.

'What . . . what do you want from me?' she asked.

'There is almost enough evidence for the district attorney to indict Ellen Crease. The one thing that is missing is a powerful motive. Crease was well taken care of by Lamar Hoyt, she had her own career and everyone says that she loved Hoyt and he loved her.'

'That's not true,' Fargo interjected.

'What isn't true?'

'Lamar didn't love her. He loved me.'

'We know that, Miss Fargo, but the authorities don't.

79

If you give that information to the police, they will know Ellen Crease's motive for murder.'

'I couldn't go to the police,' Fargo said.

'Of course you could. We would protect you and we would reward you. The day after you go to the police someone will call you with a job offer. A very good job offer. Someone else will deposit a substantial sum of money into your savings account. I believe it's down to three hundred and eighteen dollars, as of this morning.'

'How . . . how did you know that?'

'We're concerned about you, Karen,' the man said with compassion. 'We were afraid that you were suffering financially, so we checked your account to see if you needed our help. It looks like we can help each other.'

The man sounded so sure of himself, so comforting. Why, then, Fargo asked herself, did she feel so frightened?

'Why don't you tell me about your relationship with Lamar, so we can decide what you can say that will help the police?'

'I don't know if I should.'

'Karen, Ellen Crease has already made Lamar Hoyt her victim. Do you want to be her victim, too? Crease did not give Lamar a chance to fight back. We are giving you that chance.'

Fargo considered what the man said while he waited patiently. Then she started talking. When she was through, the man asked her questions and she answered them truthfully. When he was satisfied with what he heard, he told her what to do.

'How do I get in touch with you?' she asked as he crossed the room.

'Don't worry about that.'

He stepped into the pool of light near the front door. Then was gone and Fargo realized that the only thing she knew about her visitor was that once upon a time something had happened to him that was violent enough to leave a jagged scar on his right cheek.

Nine

[1]

HOYT & SON'S West Side Home of Heavenly Rest was a white, three-story building that resembled a plantation home in the antebellum South. Lou Anthony knew that there were four other Homes of Heavenly Rest in Oregon, as well as two Heavenly Rests in Seattle, Washington, one in Butte, Montana, and one in Boise, Idaho. Junior's office was here on the West Side.

A crystal chandelier hung over the foyer, but the lighting was subdued. As Anthony entered through the wide front doors, a tall, solemn-looking man in a mourning coat approached him.

'Are you with the Webster party?'

'No, I'm not.' Anthony flashed his badge. 'I'm looking for Mr. Hoyt.'

The man examined the badge for a moment while Anthony listened to the soft strains of organ music that floated toward him from somewhere in the building.

'Take the hall on your right. There's a set of stairs at the end. Mr. Hoyt's office is at the top of the stairs.'

The interior of the funeral home was dark woods and dark red draperies, all under subdued lighting. There were two chapels on Anthony's left as he walked down the hall. One was empty, but a small group of mourners gathered in the other talked in hushed tones. A casket dominated the room. A heavyset woman wept in the front row. Two young men in ill-fitting black suits tried to comfort her.

Anthony found the office easily. An attractive blonde wearing too much makeup was talking on the phone when he entered. She glanced at Anthony, told the caller that she would get back to her and hung up.

'I'm here to see Mr. Hoyt,' Anthony said when he had the woman's attention.

'What does this concern?'

Anthony showed the woman his shield. The secretary disappeared behind the only other door in the office. A moment later, she emerged and held it open.

The office had the same subdued decor as the rest of the funeral home. Junior was sitting behind his desk. He did not look pleased to see Anthony.

'What's this about?' Junior asked brusquely. 'I'm pretty busy.'

Anthony sat down across from the mortician without being asked.

'I have a few questions I want to ask you. I decided to wait until after the funeral. How did it go?'

Junior's aggression disappeared.

'We gave Dad the best we had. Our Royal Deluxe.' Junior looked thoughtful. 'It was so odd seeing him laid out. I see people every day like that, but when it's your own father . . .'

Junior caught himself, embarrassed by his show of emotion. 'You said you had some questions?'

'Just a few. I'll try to make this quick. I understand that you and your father had an argument at Hoyt Industries headquarters a few days before he was killed. What was that about?'

Junior's face registered fear and surprise.

'Who told you that?'

'I'm afraid I can't reveal my sources.'

'I bet it was that turd Appling. Well, the argument was a big nothing. Just a disagreement about some changes I made at Heavenly Rest.'

'There wasn't any more to it?'

'No,' Junior answered nervously. 'Why are you interested in an argument I had with my father, anyway? I thought the police believed that this was just a burglary by that guy Jaworski.'

'Jablonski,' Anthony corrected Junior. 'Martin Jablonski. You didn't happen to know him, did you?'

'Why would I know him?'

Suddenly, Anthony's reason for asking the question dawned on Junior.

'What the fuck is going on here? You're not suggesting . . .'

'I'm not suggesting anything.'

'Well, I think you are. If you really want to find

out who's behind my father's murder, investigate Ellen Crease.'

'You made the same accusation against Senator Crease when you were at the mansion on the night your father was murdered. Why do you think your stepmother . . .'

'That cunt is not my mother . . .'

'Senator Crease, then. Why do you think that she had something to do with your father's murder?'

Junior snorted with derision. 'You're some detective Don't tell me you don't know yet.'

'Know about what?'

'Dad was going to dump her. She was on the way out. Then good-bye, sugar daddy.'

'Why do you think that your father was planning to leave Senator Crease?'

'You don't know much about my father, if you're asking that question. His wives all had a shelf life of about seven years and he began cheating on them way before he dumped them. Ask my mom.'

'So you're going on your father's history with women? You don't have any concrete evidence that your father was going to divorce Senator Crease?'

'No. I just know my father,' he answered bitterly. 'He was a user.'

'You don't seem to have liked him much.'

Junior seemed suddenly subdued. 'My father walked out on my mother and he never hid how he felt about me. No matter what I did, it was never good enough. He told me to my face what a disappointing incompetent I was, more than once.'

'He let you run this business.'

'I'll give him that. But he made it pretty clear to me that I could never expect anything more from him.'

'Like letting you run Hoyt Industries. That was something you must have wanted.'

'Are you kidding? That company is worth millions,' Junior answered with a combination of anger and wistfulness. 'The bitch will get those shares now. My only regret is that my father won't get a chance to see her run his life's work into the ground.'

[2]

Lou Anthony reached two conclusions as soon as he saw the young woman who was waiting in the reception area of the Portland Police Bureau Detective Division. The first was a no-brainer. The woman was gorgeous, with smoky emerald eyes and hair the shade of auburn that takes your breath away when the leaves change color in the fall.

Anthony's second conclusion was that the woman would rather be someplace else. Her slender hands fidgeted in her lap and she sat too straight, as if preparing for flight. Anthony walked over to her and she stood up quickly. The detective figured her for five four, but she seemed taller because she was wearing heels.

'My name is Lou Anthony. I'm the detective in charge of the Lamar Hoyt case. I understand you have something you wanted to tell me.'

The young woman looked lost. She glanced around

the reception area. Anthony guessed that she had something to say but was not sure that this was the place she should be saying it.

'Why don't you come back with me?' Anthony said, holding open the door that led to the wide-open spaces where the detectives worked on the thirteenth floor of the Justice Center. The woman walked through the door and Anthony directed her to an empty interrogation room, where they would have some privacy

'Can I get you something? Coffee?' Anthony asked. The room was small and barely held a gray metal table and four chairs.

'Coffee, please. Black,' the woman answered.

'I'll be right back,' the detective told her with a reassuring smile. When he returned with two steaming cups of coffee, she was still wearing her raincoat. Her hands were in her lap and she was twisting in her seat so she could look around the tan-painted, concrete-block room.

'Are you cold?' Anthony asked. The woman looked puzzled. 'I noticed you're still wearing your raincoat.'

Fargo looked down, as if she had not realized that she still had on the coat. She took it off and Anthony draped it over a chair. Drops fell from the coat onto the metal legs and ran down them toward the floor. When she sat, she picked up her coffee, wrapping both hands around the Styrofoam cup for warmth.

'I'm sorry,' Anthony apologized, 'but I didn't get your full name.'

The woman nervously ran her tongue across her lips before answering.

'I'm Karen. Karen Fargo.'

'Is that Miss or Mrs.?'

'I'm not married.'

'The receptionist said you wanted to speak to someone about Lamar Hoyt's murder. Like I said, it's my case, so you can tell me anything you have to say.'

Fargo hesitated and Anthony waited. Then she said, 'I read in the paper that a man broke in and shot Lamar. Is that what happened? I mean, are you certain that this man . . . that he killed Lamar?'

Anthony caught the use of Hoyt's first name but did not change his expression.

'We found the bullet that killed Mr. Hoyt and we gave it to the people at the police lab. They checked the gun we found next to the intruder. The bullet came from that gun, and the intruder's fingerprints were on the gun.'

'Oh.' Fargo looked down as if she were losing the courage that had brought her to police headquarters.

'Did you think that someone else may have shot Mr. Hoyt?' Anthony asked gently.

'I . . . Well, I thought . . .'

'Yes?'

When she answered, Anthony could see that Karen Fargo was very frightened. 'It wasn't her? His wife? You're certain?'

'Why would you think that Ms. Crease shot her husband?'

Fargo looked down again. 'I . . . I shouldn't have come here,' she said, and started to stand.

'Miss Fargo, what was your relationship to Mr. Hoyt?'

Karen Fargo burst into tears and collapsed on her chair.

'I'm so sorry,' she managed.

'Do you want some water?'

'No. I'll be okay.'

Fargo took two deep breaths. 'We loved each other. We . . .' Fargo looked down. 'We were going to be married.'

'Mr. Hoyt was already married,' Anthony said carefully.

Fargo dabbed at her tears again. 'He was going to divorce her. He told me so. Lamar was going to wait until after the campaign. Then he was going to divorce her and marry me.'

'How long did you have this relationship with Mr. Hoyt?'

'About a year. A little less. It started six months after I went to work for his company. I'm . . . I was a secretary at Hoyt Industries.'

'And you met Mr. Hoyt there?' Anthony prodded.

'At the company picnic. We just started talking. It didn't last for long. He asked me my name and how long I'd been there and if I was enjoying my job. I thought he was asking to be nice. I was sure he wouldn't even remember me. But he did. About a week later, he saw me in the cafeteria and he remembered my name. Then a week after that, he called me at my apartment and asked if he could come over. I didn't know what to say. I mean, he was the boss of the whole company. I couldn't very well say no, could I?'

She looked toward Anthony for approval and he gave it to her. She bit her lip and looked down at the tabletop.

'I was afraid. I . . . I thought . . . Well, I knew he was married and I'm not naive. But Lamar was a perfect gentleman. He was always a perfect gentleman.

'After that first time, he just started visiting. Sometimes he'd take me out to eat. Usually when his wife was busy in Salem at the legislature. He didn't come on to me. It was just to talk. He said he liked being with me and how he felt he could just be at ease when he was with me. There's so much pressure for a businessman like Lamar, you know, and he felt that his wife was so busy with her own work that she didn't have time for him.'

'So you started sleeping with him?'

Fargo looked straight at Anthony.

'He was lonely. It was sad. He had all that money and his big house, but he was lonely.'

'When did Mr. Hoyt start talking about marriage?'

'Right around when his wife said she was going to run for the U.S. Senate. That really upset Lamar, because it meant that she would be living in Washington, D.C., and he would never get to see her. He said that it would be like they weren't even married.'

'Miss Fargo, Lamar Hoyt was murdered on January seventh. Why did you wait until now to come see me?'

Karen Fargo's eyes widened with fright. Then she looked away.

'I don't know,' she answered. 'It's just been eating at me. Lamar dying like that. It didn't seem right.'

'Do you have anything concrete that would prove Ms. Crease was behind her husband's death?'

'No. Just that Lamar said he thought she might know about us.'

'He did? When did he say that?'

'A few weeks before he was killed. He said she was acting funny around him and that we had to be careful. He wanted to know if anything unusual had happened. Strange phone calls or anyone watching or following me.'

'And did any of that happen?'

'Not that I knew of.'

Anthony tried to think of something else to ask Fargo, but he couldn't. He was not surprised to discover that Hoyt had a mistress. It fit his pattern. Ellen Crease was a little older than the first two wives when she'd become wife number three, but not much older. She was now around the age of the other exes when Hoyt cut his ties with them.

'Thank you for coming in to talk to me, Miss Fargo. I can see how hard it was for you.'

Anthony thought Fargo looked relieved that he was not going to ask her any more questions. Anthony shook her hand and showed her out. Back at his desk, he swiveled his chair and looked out the wide windows. Rain again. Surprise, surprise. Some days he would give everything he owned for one sunny day.

Anthony felt sorry for Karen Fargo. He imagined that Hoyt's attentions must have seemed like something out of a fairy tale to a secretary who is suddenly transformed into the mistress of a millionaire. Was Hoyt really intending to dump Crease for Fargo or was he simply dangling the possibility of marriage in front of Fargo to keep her in his bed?

As Anthony went to get a fresh cup of coffee, he

thought about a question Fargo had asked. Was he certain that Jablonski had killed Hoyt? Definitely, as far as the physical act went, but what about the blood spatter evidence and the money? And then there was the fact that all the security systems at the estate were off when Jablonski broke in. Crease had a reasonable explanation for that, but did he believe it? Crease had definitely benefited from Hoyt's death. She had sky-rocketed in the polls, and there was the insurance and the will. These were all motives for murder. Now there was another motive for Crease to hire Jablonski.

Anthony let the thought hang in the air. He turned it around and examined it. He did not want to believe that Ellen Crease was a murderer. Anthony liked Crease. He had no doubt that Hoyt's death had really hurt her. She had shown little emotion other than anger in her press conferences, but he had seen her right after the murder and he would swear that her grief was real. That actually weighed against her. If Ellen really loved Lamar, the knowledge that he had a lover and was ready to leave her would be a powerful motive to kill. Anthony decided that it was time to have another meeting with the district attorney.

Ten

R YAN CLARK entered the pool house just as United States Senator Benjamin Gage began the final lap of his morning workout. Clark was six feet tall, darkly handsome and very fit. When he moved, he exuded a quiet confidence that warned off muggers and attracted the attention of beautiful women, who found the jagged scar on Clark's right cheek fascinating. They always asked about it and Clark had invented a story that seemed to satisfy their curiosity.

The only time Benjamin Gage had ever mentioned the scar was at the end of Clark's interview for a job at StarData, Gage's high-tech company. The conversation had taken place eight years earlier when Clark was twenty-nine and Gage was thirty-eight. Clark was wearing a beard at the time and the scar was barely visible. The formal part of the interview, which had been conducted in Gage's office at company headquarters, was over and the two men had adjourned to a smart restaurant in Northwest Portland for dinner. Their booth was in the back. Gage was a frequent customer. When he dined at the restaurant it was understood that the booth next to his would be kept vacant. Gage paid a premium for this that he could easily afford.

'Where did you get the scar?' Gage had asked. His own face was unmarked and ruggedly handsome.

Clark had hesitated before answering. That was when Gage knew that the scar had something to do with the five years on Clark's résumé that read 'Naval Intelligence – Administrative Responsibilities.' When Gage had asked Clark to describe his administrative duties during the interview at the office, Clark had been creatively evasive and Gage had let it pass. He knew he would pursue the question at dinner.

Gage had leaned back against the wine-red leather. There was no one else around. Their corner of the restaurant was suitably dark. When he spoke, Gage looked directly into Clark's eyes. A few years later, during Gage's first successful run for Congress, this ability to look people in the eye had convinced voters of Gage's sincerity. Clark was not affected at all and he was able to keep eye contact long enough to make Gage blink first, something few people could accomplish.

'Look, Ryan, you're not interviewing to be a security guard. If I wanted a rent-a-cop, I'd call Pinkerton. I wouldn't conduct my job search through the chairman of the Senate Committee on Covert Operations. I need a man who can be counted on to do odds and ends that

other people can't, or won't, do,' Gage had said, proving
that he could be as creatively evasive as Clark. 'You want
me to pay you six figures to do these odd jobs. I'm not
going to pay that kind of money or trust someone with this
type of work without knowing everything there is to know
about the man I'm hiring. So tell me about the scar.'

There had been no more hesitation. Gage liked that.
It meant Clark could make important decisions quickly.
He also liked the fact that Clark did not touch the scar
or do anything else to indicate that he even thought
about it.

'This is a knife wound I received in a Mideast country.
The man who stabbed me was lying next to two other
bodies. I thought he was dead. When I leaned down to
secure his weapon, he stabbed me.'

'Who were these men?'

'It was two men and a woman,' Clark had answered
without emotion. 'They were terrorists who directed the
suicide bombing of the American Embassy in Paris.'

'I remember the bombing, but I don't remember reading that the people behind it were caught.'

'You wouldn't have.'

'What happened to the man who stabbed you?'

'Another member of my team shot him.'

'I see. Tell me, Ryan, did this incident occur when
you were a navy SEAL?'

'No.'

'Was this one of your "administrative responsibilities"
in Naval Intelligence?'

'I'm afraid I can't answer that question, Mr. Gage.'

'Not even if refusing to answer costs you the job?'

Clark had smiled. He knew he had the job. He knew Gage was trying to play with him. Gage had held his ground for a moment. Then he had returned the smile. Clark had been doing this and that for Gage ever since.

Moments after Clark was admitted to Gage's house, a servant placed a pitcher of fresh-squeezed orange juice, a pot of steaming coffee and a plate with two croissants on a table that stood on the tiled deck of Gage's twenty-five-meter lap pool. The lap pool was four lanes wide and heated. Entering the humid air of the pool house caused beads of sweat to form on the brow and upper lip of Senator Gage's administrative assistant. Clark sat down at the table and watched Gage make his final turn. Then he lost interest and glanced out through the wall of glass on the east side of the pool house. On most days, Clark would have seen the apple orchards, lush farmlands and green foothills that stood between Gage's twelve-thousand-square-foot home of glass and cedar and the snow-covered slopes of Mount Hood. But today the landscape was gray with mist and there was little to see.

Gage boosted himself out of the pool. He was forty-six years old, but he was only slightly slower in the pool than he had been in his days as a competitive swimmer. Some of the hair that covered Gage's lanky body was starting to silver.

Gage toweled himself dry, then crossed the pool deck and sat opposite Clark.

'Have you seen the latest polls?' he asked Clark angrily.

'Crease has fifty-one percent, you've got forty-four and the rest are undecided,' Clark answered calmly.

'That's right. Before the murder, we were dead even. Crease has gotten everyone's sympathy for losing a husband, and the press has made her out to be a female version of Rambo. I am sinking fast.'

Gage took a bite of his croissant. Clark waited patiently.

'Did you listen to Crease's press conference in Bend?'

'I missed it.'

'A reporter asked Crease how her husband's murder affected her. She stared him down for a second or so. Then she told him that she would be dead, too, if the gun control lobby had its way and that Hoyt would be alive if the tough crime measures she's advocating were law. After that, she looked into the camera for a few seconds more. Then she told all those voters that she couldn't bring her husband back, but she could dedicate the rest of her life to trying to prevent similar catastrophes from happening to them and to seeing that those who break the law regret it.'

Gage smiled without humor and shook his head in wonder. 'She is one heartless bitch and she has played Hoyt's murder like a violin virtuoso.'

Clark allowed himself a rare smile.

'She may be playing a different tune by next week,' he said.

'Oh?'

'Cedric Riker called me. He wanted to make certain that you knew before the press. He's going to the grand jury this morning. It looks like Fargo tipped the scales.'

Gage grinned broadly.

'That's that, then,' the senator said with satisfaction. 'Once the indictment comes down, she's dead.'

'That's how I see it.'

'Good work, Ryan. Very good work.'

[2]

Henry Orchard knocked loudly on Ellen Crease's hotel room door because he knew she would be sound asleep after an exhausting day of campaigning. Crease's campaign manager was a slovenly, overweight dynamo who was uninterested in anything but politics. Until minutes ago, Orchard had been a happy man. His candidate had exploded in the polls, breaking away from a dead heat to take a substantial lead over Benjamin Gage.

'Who is it?' Crease snapped. She sounded wide-awake. Orchard was not surprised. Crease never seemed to tire and she needed little sleep. When she did sleep, she had a knack for waking up fully alert.

'It's Henry. Open up. Something's happened.'

Orchard heard Crease cross the room. Her door opened and he walked in. Orchard was unshaven and there were dark shadows along his fleshy jowls. The shirt he had thrown on was dotted with stains and his socks did not match. Crease was wearing a quilted bathrobe over a floor-length flannel nightgown. Only the bedside light was on in the room, but Orchard did not turn on any other lights. He spotted an armchair near the window and dropped into it.

'I just talked to a source in the Multnomah County

District Attorney's Office. Tomorrow Cedric Riker is going to ask a grand jury to indict you for murder.'

'What?'

'He's looking for two counts. Lamar and the guy who shot him.'

Crease looked stunned. 'Is this the first you've heard about this?'

'Absolutely. I knew the investigation was still open, but I haven't heard a thing suggesting that you were under suspicion.'

'What have they got? What's the evidence?'

'I don't know and neither does my informant. The first thing I asked him was what Riker's got, but only Riker and the investigating officer . . .'

'Lou Anthony?'

'Right, Anthony. They're the only ones who know for now. What do you think they have?'

'There's nothing out there, Henry,' Crease answered bitterly. 'And this really hurts. I loved that old bastard.'

Crease found a cigar in her purse and lit it. Then she paced across the room until she arrived at a writing desk. She pulled out the desk chair and sat on it, facing Orchard.

'This is unbelievable. An indictment will kill us.' Crease thought for a moment.

'It's Gage,' she said angrily. 'It has to be. He contributed heavily to Riker's campaign and they go way back. Gage and Riker cooked up this whole thing to help Gage climb back in the polls.'

'I'd like to think that,' Orchard replied cautiously, 'but

this isn't any old dirty trick. We're talking an indictment for murder. Riker would have to have some evidence to show the grand jury. And even if Riker's a prick, Lou Anthony isn't. He's an old friend of yours, isn't he?'

'I know Lou,' Crease answered thoughtfully. She blew a plume of smoke toward Orchard. 'You're right. Lou wouldn't phony up evidence.'

Crease was quiet for a moment. Orchard watched her.

'What do you suggest I do, Henry?' she asked after a while.

'The same person who warned me about the grand jury is going to call me the minute he hears that Riker has an indictment. Riker probably has your campaign schedule. I know the way he thinks. He's going to get the local sheriff to arrest you, preferably at some campaign function for maximum embarrassment. He'll work out the timing so you have to spend a night in the local jail, then he'll have you flown back to Portland in handcuffs and parade you through the airport the way the Romans used to display conquered enemy chieftains.'

Crease shook her head in disgust. 'Riker is such a creep.'

Orchard smiled. 'Of course, we won't let him do any of this. As soon as I hear that Riker's got his indictment, you'll disappear. When the sheriff arrives with his warrant, you won't be here. I've arranged for a private plane to fly us back to Portland. It's on standby. And I have Mary Garrett on retainer. She tells me that she'll set up a time to surrender you when it's convenient for us and she'll schedule an immediate bail hearing.'

'Garrett, huh.'

'We can't fuck around with this, Ellen. I've seen Garrett in court. She's a great white shark. More important, the press loves her and you need the press as much as you need a good lawyer.'

Eleven

T HE DECOR of Mary Garrett's office was ultra-modern and disorienting, as if the decorator had artistic dyslexia. Ellen Crease could not find a straight line anywhere. She did see many gleaming aluminum tubes, myriad sheets of odd-shaped glass and numerous objects whose function was not easily identifiable. The lawyer Henry Orchard had chosen for her fit into this setting quite nicely. Her wardrobe and jewelry were expensive, but the clothes and accessories did not look quite right on the birdlike, five-foot woman. It was as if Garrett were under a court-ordered punishment to wear them as a means of emphasizing her dense glasses and overbite. Had this been true, the joke would have been on the court, because Garrett knew she wasn't a beauty queen and didn't care. What she did care about was winning and that was something she did very well.

As soon as the introductions were made, Garrett asked Henry Orchard to leave the room so she and Ellen Crease would have privacy. Crease sat in a director's chair. Its arms and legs were polished metal tubing and the back and seat were black leather that sagged a little, so that the height of the chair's occupant decreased. Garrett sat behind a wide glass desk on a high-backed chair of black leather. The chair could be elevated by pushing a button so that the diminutive attorney was always taller than her clients.

'I think your politics suck,' was the first thing Garrett said to Ellen Crease when the door closed on Henry Orchard. 'In fact, I can't think of a single thing you stand for that I agree with. I thought I should put that on the table right off.'

Garrett had caught Crease completely off guard. There was a smirk on Garrett's lips and arrogance in the way she held her body. She was clearly communicating her opinion that she did not need Ellen Crease as a client but that Crease could not do without her as her attorney. If anyone else had treated her this way, Crease would have been out the door, but Garrett's combativeness endeared her to Crease. Perhaps it was the fact that her arrogance was wrapped in such a small and unattractive package. Instead of flushing with anger, Crease felt herself breaking into a wide grin.

'Then let's not talk politics,' Crease said.

Garrett grinned back at her. 'Good. I've been told that you have a thick skin. I wanted to see for myself. You're going to need it before this thing plays out.'

'What exactly do you take "this thing" to be?'

'The Prince of Darkness's dumber brother has an indictment charging you with two counts of aggravated murder. Aggravated murder, as you know from your days as a cop, carries a possible death sentence.

'Before I go any further, I'm going to explain the attorney-client relationship to you. And I want you to listen very closely to what I say, because this is not just a civics lecture.

'Anything you tell me is confidential. That means that, by law, I'm forbidden to tell anyone what you confide to me. It also gives you the freedom to tell me the most outrageous lies, but you may pay a price if you aren't completely honest. The best liar I ever represented is sitting in prison because I turned down a plea offer that would have kept him out of jail as a result of a fairy tale that he concocted. Do I make myself clear?'

'Perfectly. But I have no reason to lie to you.'

'Then why did Riker go to the grand jury?'

'Isn't it obvious? Have you seen the latest polls? Cedric Riker is one of Ben Gage's tools. Gage was a major contributor to Riker's campaign and Riker owes him his job. Indicting me is a way of paying back Gage.'

'I don't doubt that Riker is motivated by politics, but he can't go in front of a grand jury without evidence.' Crease remembered that Orchard had said the same thing. 'What does he have on you, Senator?'

'I don't know.'

Garrett formed a steeple with her fingers and thought out loud.

'We know Jablonski fired the shot that killed your husband, so the only way you would be implicated in your husband's death would be if you hired him to do it.'

'Ms. Garrett . . .'

'Call me Mary. We're going to be seeing a lot of each other.'

'Mary, then. I didn't even know Martin Jablonski existed until my husband was murdered. Cedric Riker could not have any evidence implicating me in my husband's death, because I had nothing to do with it.'

'Let's approach this problem from a different angle,' Garrett said. 'Was there something going on in your relationship with Lamar Hoyt that Riker could interpret as a motive for murder?'

Crease hesitated and Garrett concluded that her client was making a decision that would shape the direction of her representation. After a moment, Crease looked directly at her lawyer and said, 'There's the money I'm going to inherit and the Hoyt Industries stock, which will make me the majority shareholder. But if I had hired Jablonski to kill Lamar, it would have been because Lamar was cheating on me with a woman named Karen Fargo.'

'How long had you known?' Garrett asked softly.

'Since Lamar stopped having sex with me regularly.'

'Did you confront your husband?'

'Yes. I wasn't surprised. In fact, I'd been expecting this for some time. I was Lamar's third wife and each marriage followed a pattern. Lamar would marry a woman in her twenties, then tire of her when she turned thirty or so. He began cheating on his first two wives when they were about my age and I expected him to cheat on me. The difference is that I'm not a docile airhead like the first two Mrs. Hoyts. I loved Lamar and I decided to break the cycle so I could keep our marriage intact.'

'What did you do?'

'I made it crystal-clear to Lamar that I wasn't going to stand for his bullshit. He bought off his first two wives. I told Lamar that he'd be living on the street if he tried to pull this crap with me. Then I asked him point-blank if Miss Fargo could ring his bell the way I did. That got him thinking.'

'And?'

'He stopped inventing excuses to avoid getting in the sack with me.'

'So you think he broke it off with Fargo?'

'I'm not sure, but Lamar seemed like a loving husband again.'

'Do you think Riker is aware of the affair?'

'I have no way of knowing.'

Garrett made some notes on a pad. Crease waited patiently. When Garrett stopped writing, the lawyer said, 'Why don't you tell me how you met Lamar?'

'I was a policewoman in Portland and there was a burglary at one of Lamar's mortuaries. I interviewed Lamar while I was conducting my investigation. He was charming in an old-boy sort of way. Very gallant. After the official part of the meeting, we drifted into small talk. Then I left.

'The next day, Lamar left me a message at work asking me to call him. I thought it had something to do with the case, but he wanted to take me out for dinner. I turned him down. I knew he was married. He was also a witness in a police investigation.

'About six months later, we arrested the perp who'd broken into the mortuary. He was an addict looking for something to sell for a rock of crack cocaine. I dropped by Lamar's office to let him know that the case was wrapped up and ended up at dinner with him.'

Crease drifted off for a moment as if she were reliving the moment.

'Lamar was a charming bastard,' Crease said with a small smile. 'By the end of that dinner, I was hooked. See, I'd never had much. My father just took off about a year after I was born and my mom cleaned houses to put food on the table. I got through college on scholarships and waiting tables. The most money I'd ever seen was what I was pulling down as a cop. And here I was dining in elegance with a man whose pinky ring cost more than my mother made in a good year.'

'Didn't the age difference bother you?'

'It's a funny thing. I never thought about the fact that he was almost thirty years older than me. He was a big bear, and so full of life. Lamar knew all the right things to say, too, and how to make you feel important. We spent most of that dinner talking about me. He had me believing that our backgrounds were pretty similar. You know, poor boy makes good, which was pretty much bullshit, since Lamar's daddy owned two funeral parlors when he died and Lamar's mother never worked a day in her life. Still, Lamar could make you think he was a sharecropper's son who rose from poverty.

'He also gave me a taste of how things could be for

me if I continued to see him. There was the limousine, the waiters in tuxedos, his jewelry and the estate.'

Crease spaced out again and Garrett could see her thinking about that good time with a man she loved and would never see again. It made Garrett feel sad. Then Crease laughed.

'What's so funny?' Garrett asked.

'I was just remembering Lamar. You know he looked like a redneck hick with his cowboy boots and string ties, but he was smooth. When he asked to see me again, I didn't hesitate.'

'Did the subject of his marriage ever come up?'

'He was the one who raised it. I don't remember how he did it, but I left that first dinner with the impression that Lamar thought that the second Mrs. H. was as dull as a dishrag, while finding me intellectually stimulating.' Crease stared directly into Garrett's eyes. 'That part was one hundred percent accurate. Mary Lou is a dim bulb. I know why Lamar was attracted to her. I've seen pictures of her during the Miss Oregon swimsuit competition. But I'll be damned if I know what they talked about outside of bed. Lamar was very smart. Country smart. I challenged him in a way no other woman ever did.'

'What happened after the first dinner?'

'There were more dinners. They were wonderful. We talked and talked. Around the third time we met, Lamar took me back to his estate. Mary Lou was in New York on a buying spree. I suspect he sent her there to get rid of her for the weekend. I was bowled over. I'd never been inside a house like that before. That was the evening I made up my mind to marry Lamar. And it wasn't just the house or his money. I want you to understand that. I wanted those things, but I wanted Lamar more. I was fascinated by his intelligence, his energy . . .'

Crease trailed off, as if she had suddenly remembered that Lamar was dead and gone and all that energy and intelligence was now part of the void.

'Was that first evening at his estate the first time you slept together?'

'Yes.'

'I get the impression that you two were good in bed.'

'I thought so. That's why my antennae went up when Lamar started making excuses. At his age, he couldn't have sex as often as he used to, but he was pretty game whenever we made love.'

'How did Lamar feel about your career?'

Crease's smile faded. 'At first, my being a cop fascinated Lamar. I think it was a turn-on. But soon after we were married, he began complaining. Deep down, he wanted a traditional wife. Someone who looked good, had dinner waiting on the table when he got home and spread her legs whenever he was horny. He found out fast that I wasn't like that and never would be.'

'What happened when he made this discovery?'

'There were a lot of hard words at first. Then I hit him straight on. I asked him if he wanted a partner or a doormat. I told him that we could be something together, but I made it clear that I wasn't going to lose my identity in order to make him happy. For a while, it was touch-and-go.'

'But he came around?'

'He came around. And when I told him I wanted to quit the force to run for the legislature, he was my biggest supporter.' A tear formed in Crease's eye and trailed down her cheek. Crease squared her shoulders. 'He changed for me and he was always there for me. Damn, I miss him.'

Garrett studied her new client. Crease's display of emotion seemed genuine. That did not mean that Crease was not a murderer, but it made Garrett, who was a cynic at heart, reserve judgment. She looked at her watch.

'We're due in court soon, so this is enough for now. Henry told you about my fee?'

Crease nodded. 'I'll have it to you by tomorrow.'

'Good. My secretary will give you my retainer agreement.

'Now, I know you've been a cop, so you have a good idea of what is going to happen as a result of these charges, but I want to spell it out for you. Your life is about to become a living hell. There's no other way to put it and I don't believe in sugarcoating the facts for my clients.'

Garrett paused to judge how Crease was taking what she was dishing out. The senator was tense but alert.

'Bail will be the big problem. There is no mandatory bail in a murder case, but Riker is going to have to convince the judge that his case is very strong if he wants you held with no bail. If he succeeds, you'll be locked up with the type of people you used to arrest. I don't have to tell you what that will be like. The good news is that I think we've got a real shot at keeping you out of the pokey. And I mean completely out.

'That doesn't mean your life will be normal. The vultures of the press will be circling you twenty-four hours a day, and they won't have the slightest interest in your political views. You'll also find out who your real friends are.'

Garrett leaned forward. She reminded Crease of the gargoyles she'd seen perched on the Notre Dame Cathedral the first time Lamar had flown her to Paris.

'I have some advice. Most clients aren't tough enough to follow it, but I think you are. Whatever has happened has happened. No matter how much you would like to you cannot change the past, so do not dwell on the murder of your husband. That's my job. That's why you hire an attorney. So you can go on with your life and let someone else do the worrying. I'll be doing enough for the two of us.'

Garrett looked at her watch again and stood up.

'Stanley Sax, the presiding judge, is a friend of mine and he's got integrity. I talked to him this morning. He's set a special arraignment for ten-thirty. Your case will be the only one on the docket and we'll be taking up bail at the same time you're arraigned. That's unusual in a murder case, but this case is unusual because of the impact your incarceration would have on the primary. You'll plead not guilty. The press is going to be there in full force, so sing it out loud and clear. Then go back to campaigning and let me do my job.'

[2]

Richard Quinn was studying a brochure from the Bay Reef Resort on St. Jerome when his secretary told him that Stanley Sax was on the way over from presiding court. The brochure showed a white sand beach, azure waters and clear blue skies. The hotel was new and he and Laura had a room with an ocean view. There was a casino, a huge pool, a four-star restaurant, water sports, tennis and more. Lately, Laura seemed excited about their week in paradise.

Quinn set down the brochure when Sax rapped his knuckles on the doorjamb.

'Come in, Stan,' Quinn said cheerfully. 'What's up?'

Sax did not return Quinn's smile. He dropped into a chair on the other side of Quinn's desk.

'I'm here to make your day.'

'Oh?' Quinn answered cautiously.

'I know you're not scheduled to move into the homicide rotation until next month, but something has come up and I need you. Ced Riker has indicted Ellen Crease for the murder of her husband.'

'What!'

'That was my reaction, too. He went to the grand jury yesterday. Crease is represented by Mary Garrett. Garrett called me to request an expedited bail hearing and I agreed because of the impact on the campaign if Crease has to sit in jail for a week while we schedule a hearing in the normal way. I'd like you to handle the case.'

Quinn saw the brochure from St. Jerome in his peripheral

vision. He owed Stanley Sax, but Quinn was counting on the week alone with Laura as his best chance to jump-start their ailing marriage.

'I can't do it, Stan. I've agreed to speak at a seminar in two weeks on St. Jerome. Remember? Laura's coming with me.'

'That won't be a problem. I've scheduled the arraignment and the bail hearing for ten-thirty today. You take care of the hearing and I'll handle any emergencies while you're away.'

'I don't know, Stan. This is a pretty big case for me to take on for my first homicide.'

'Let me tell you something, Dick, every death penalty case is too big for any of us to handle. Only God should be deciding who should live and who should die, but we're stuck with the job.

'Now, it's true that you'll be under a spotlight in Crease's case that would not be shining on you if the defendant were some junkie lowlife. If you make a mistake, everyone in the country will know about it. But that won't make a difference to you. Want to know why?'

Quinn just stared at him.

'I know you, Dick. I know how conscientious you are and I know that you punish yourself for your mistakes much harder than anyone else can. That's why I want you on this one. You won't let yourself screw up. You'll make certain that both sides get a fair trial.'

Quinn's bailiff pressed a button under his desk in the courtroom and a light on the desk in Quinn's chambers flashed bright red to let him know that both sides in *State*

113

v. Crease were in the courtroom. Quinn slipped into his judicial robes and opened the door that led directly to the bench. As he stepped through it, the bailiff rapped the gavel, commanded everyone in the packed courtroom to rise and announced that the Honorable Richard Quinn would be presiding over the docket. Quinn noticed several members of the press in attendance and saw the lights of the TV cameras that were shooting through the glass in the courtroom doors.

'You can be seated,' Quinn said as soon as he had taken the bench. Cedric Riker remained standing, but the deputy district attorneys who accompanied him took seats on either side of the prosecutor. One deputy was a black woman and the other was an Asian male. They looked young and nervous.

Riker looked anything but nervous. He was dressed to kill and hungry for every second of publicity that this case would bring him. Quinn was willing to bet that Riker had held a news conference in the corridor. Speaking with the marble and polished wood of the courtroom as a backdrop lent authority to Riker's words and made him look good to all the voters who listened to his sound bites on the eleven o'clock news.

Seated at the other counsel table were Mary Garrett and her client. Garrett was wearing black with a pearl necklace. None of Garrett's associates were at the counsel table, though Quinn suspected that there were one or two in the audience in case of an emergency. There were no lawbooks in front of Garrett, either. Quinn had heard that Garrett had an encyclopedic knowledge of the law and was known to give accurate volume and page cites to cases in the law reports from memory. She had already delivered a concise and expertly written brief on the bail issue to Quinn's chambers. Quinn was impressed by Garrett's ability to pump out a brief of such high quality on such short notice.

Ellen Crease sat quietly beside Garrett. She was dressed in a gray business suit and a cream-colored silk blouse. Aside from a pair of small diamond earrings, she wore no jewelry. Quinn's eyes rested on the defendant for a moment. It was hard to avoid looking at her. Crease was not classically beautiful, but even dressed in a conservative business suit, she exuded an animal sexuality that attracted and held a man's attention.

'Mr. Riker and Ms. Garrett, Judge Sax has assigned *State v. Crease* to me. However, I want to make counsel aware that I will be speaking at a legal seminar in St. Jerome in two weeks. That means that I will not be in Portland for approximately one week. During that time, if there are any emergencies, Judge Sax will take care of them. Is that a problem for counsel?'

Both lawyers answered in the negative.

'Good. Now, Mr. Riker, as I understand it, we're to hold an arraignment and bail hearing this morning.'

'Well, Your Honor, we do intend to arraign the defendant on two charges of aggravated murder, but the People object to holding a bail hearing on such short notice in a case this serious.'

Garrett was on her feet before Riker had finished his sentence.

'Your Honor, Senator Crease is in the middle of a hotly contested campaign for the Republican nomination for the United States Senate. Her opponent is a political ally of Mr. Riker, who has done enough damage to her on behalf of his political cohort by bringing this spurious indictment during the campaign. Keeping the senator in jail for a week or more would cause her untold damage. She has had to cancel an entire day of campaigning already because of these absurd charges.'

'I resent the implication that this indictment was politically motivated,' Riker told Quinn self-righteously. '*I* did not charge the defendant with murder. This murder indictment was handed down by the people of this state through the agency of a duly impaneled grand jury.'

'Nonsense, Judge,' Garrett countered with a snort. 'A grand jury is a tool of the prosecutor's office. Everyone knows that. Mr. Riker would fire any of his deputies who couldn't get an indictment charging the Pope with JFK's assassination.'

The hearing was getting out of hand, so Quinn said sharply, 'Ms. Garrett and Mr. Riker, I want this sniping to stop right now. This may be a long and contentious case, but it is going to be conducted with civility by all parties. Am I understood?'

'Of course, Your Honor,' Riker assured the judge in a fawning manner intended to ingratiate him with Quinn. Garrett merely nodded.

'Good. Now, I assume you've been given a copy of Ms. Garrett's brief on the bail question, Mr. Riker.'

'Well, I was, but so soon before court that I haven't had a chance to read it.'

'Tell me why you believe holding Senator Crease in jail for a week or so during the height of this campaign would be in the interests of justice,' Quinn commanded the prosecutor.

Garrett held back a smile. Having Quinn address her client as 'Senator Crease' instead of 'the defendant' was a small but important victory.

'The defendant is charged with two counts of aggravated murder,' Riker blustered, and it was immediately obvious to Quinn that the prosecutor had not done any legal research on the issue of the proper timing for a bail hearing in a murder case. 'These charges are serious. The defendant is a flight risk and a potential danger to others.'

'The question of whether the senator is a flight risk or a danger to others is relevant to the amount of bail to be imposed, if I decide to grant bail. It is not relevant to the question of my authority to hold a bail hearing at the same time that I arraign Senator Crease. Do you have any other arguments you wish to make?'

'No, Your Honor.'

'Then I must tell you that I find the arguments in Ms. Garrett's brief persuasive and I hold that the interests of justice require me to hold Senator Crease's bail hearing this morning.

'The question of whether bail will be granted is another matter. I have no opinion on it at this moment and I will hear counsel on the question as soon as Senator Crease is arraigned.'

Quinn held the arraignment quickly. He read the charges to Crease and advised her of her rights. Then he asked her how she wanted to plead to the accusation that she had hired Martin Jablonski to murder her husband, then murdered Jablonski because he was a witness to her involvement.

Crease had been standing during the arraignment. When Quinn asked her how she wished to plead, she squared her shoulders and looked Quinn in the eye. Despite the tense atmosphere in the courtroom, Crease appeared to be confident and free of fear. When she spoke, her voice was firm and filled with resolve.

'I loved my husband very much, Your Honor. I would never hurt him. I don't know what is behind these allegations, but they are false and I am not guilty.'

For a moment, the fire in Crease's eyes trapped Quinn. Then he pulled himself away and pretended to scan some papers that lay in front of him.

'Very well,' Quinn said. 'We'll record your plea of not guilty to both charges. Now to the issue of bail. Mr. Riker, I believe that you have the burden of convincing me that there is clear and convincing evidence of Senator Crease's guilt before I can hold her without any bail. How do you wish to do that?'

'This hearing has caught me by surprise, Your Honor. I'm not prepared to proceed with witnesses at this time.'

'When could you have your witnesses here, Mr. Riker?'

Garrett was certain that Riker was not going to give her a chance to rip into his witnesses prior to trial, and she smiled when he said, 'Well, I don't know. Perhaps I could give the Court the police reports in lieu of presenting live testimony?'

'That would deprive me of the opportunity to cross-examine, Your Honor,' Garrett objected.

'I agree,' Quinn said. 'Mr. Riker, unless you want to call witnesses and subject them to examination by Ms. Garrett, I'm going to have to hold that bail is appropriate in this case and move on to the question of the proper amount of bail.'

Riker looked very uncomfortable. He shifted from one foot to another. One of the deputies tried to whisper something to him, but Riker waved him off.

'You've put me in an impossible position, Your Honor,' Riker complained.

'I'm sorry you feel that way, Mr. Riker, but you're going to have to tell me if you want to put on witnesses or argue the amount of bail.'

'Let's proceed with arguments on the amount of bail,' Riker said reluctantly. 'The defendant is a wealthy woman who can fly to any country, including those without extradition treaties with the United States. She even owns her own airplane. This makes her a flight risk. Plus, she is a former policewoman. She knows how to use a weapon. She could be a danger to our witnesses.'

Garrett stood up and addressed Quinn.

'Your Honor, until Mr. Hoyt's will is probated Ms. Crease has limited access to his wealth. She earns a salary as a state senator, but that hardly makes her rich. Furthermore, Senator Crease is in the middle of a political campaign. That, in addition to her complete innocence, is why we are fighting so hard for bail.'

'Would the senator surrender her passport as a condition of my setting bail?'

'Of course.'

Quinn reviewed the personal history that was part of Garrett's brief. He came to a decision.

'Instead of setting bail, I am going to release Senator Crease on her own recognizance . . .'

'But, Your Honor . . . ,' Riker sputtered.

'Please do not interrupt me, Mr. Riker. I will give you an opportunity to make a record when I am finished.'

Quinn dictated a series of conditions for Crease's release, then gave Riker an opportunity to vent his spleen. When the district attorney was finished ranting and raving, Quinn set a date for the state and defense to file motions and set a tentative date for hearing the pretrial motions and for the trial. When there was no further business to conduct, the bailiff rapped the gavel, everyone in the courtroom stood and Quinn returned to his chambers.

As soon as Quinn left the bench, Mary Garrett broke into a huge grin. 'So far so good, Ellen.'

'The judge seemed to be very fair.'

'That he did.'

'Will he be our trial judge?'

Garrett nodded. 'This is my first time in front of Quinn. He's a surprise choice for the homicide rotation. Before he came on the bench he was a contract law specialist in the Price, Winward firm. But I like what I've seen so far. He seems bright and he's decisive.'

'Do you think he'll work with us? He seemed to dislike Riker.'

Garrett stopped smiling. 'Don't get any ideas about Quinn being some sort of pro-defense, knee-jerk liberal because of what happened today. My book on him is that he is one hundred percent ethical and that he decides cases on the law. That means that he'll rule for Riker whether he likes him or not, if he thinks he is right. And he can be really tough. He just sent Judge Gideon to prison when everyone in the courthouse was putting money on probation.

'On the other hand, we won't have to worry about having a judge who is part of the prosecution. The bottom line is that we have the best kind of judge He's smart, he's ethical and he'll give us a fair trial. Now it's up to me to make certain that the trial ends favorably for you.'

[3]

Quinn found Laura hunched over the computer in their home office on the second floor. She was dressed in a flannel nightgown with the granny glasses she used for reading perched on her nose.

'Still working?' Quinn said.

'It's that condo deal in Maui,' Laura answered without looking away from the monitor. 'There are all sorts of problems and, of course, our client had to wait until the last possible minute to let us know.'

'Ellen Crease was indicted for Lamar Hoyt's murder. Stan Sax assigned me the case.'

Laura looked up and swiveled away from the screen.

'That'll keep you busy,' Laura said.

'Didn't you handle some litigation involving Hoyt?'

'BestCo. We sued his ass. I deposed him.'

'What was he like? I met him a few times but I never had a real conversation with him.'

Laura thought about the question. She swiveled her chair and pushed her glasses back on her nose.

'Hoyt was a real cowboy. All ready to shoot it out at high noon with us, as if the lawsuit were some kind of nineteenth-century gunfight. He impressed me as the type of guy who thinks he can conquer every situation with the force of his personality.' Laura thought for a moment, then added, 'I guess he had a sort of primal charm, but he was also a real chauvinist. He couldn't keep his eyes off my breasts.'

'Didn't he make his money in mortuaries?'

'Yeah, but that was only at the beginning. He diversified early on. Hoyt had his fingers in a lot of pies and,' Laura added with a smirk, 'up a few dresses.'

'He was cheating on Senator Crease?'

'That's the rumor.'

'I wonder if she knew.'

'If *I* knew, she probably had a clue.'

'I'm surprised she stood for it. From what I hear, that's not her style.'

'Some women will put up with a lot for twenty million dollars. She was number three. Maybe she didn't want to become the ex-number three.'

Laura paused. 'Is this going to affect our trip to St. Jerome?'

'No way. Stan is going to cover for me when we're gone. I told him I wouldn't handle the case if I had to give up the trip. I'm really looking forward to spending some uninterrupted time with you.'

'Me, too,' Laura told Quinn. He bent down and kissed her and she returned the kiss.

'That's enough smooching,' Laura said. 'If I don't get back to work, I'll be up all night.'

Quinn smiled and gave Laura a peck on the cheek. She seemed excited about the trip to St. Jerome. Maybe she realized how hard she had been working and how nice it would be to take some time off. Quinn hoped that spending time with him had something to do with Laura's good mood. When he walked downstairs to fix himself a snack, he was grinning.

Part Two

The Cove of
Lost Souls

Twelve

C AN I GET you something to drink before we take off?' the flight attendant asked.

Quinn was lost in thought, oblivious to the attendant and the passengers who were filing past his aisle seat in first class while the flight crew prepared for the plane's departure from New York for St. Jerome. When he realized that the flight attendant was speaking to him, Quinn looked up at her with a blank expression and she repeated the question with a pleasant smile.

'Scotch on the rocks, please,' Quinn answered without returning her smile. The attendant turned to the first-class passenger across the aisle and Quinn looked forlornly at the empty window seat beside him. Yesterday Laura had told him that she would not be able to go to St. Jerome.

'Honey, I have really bad news,' she had said in a midday call from her office to his chambers. 'A group of businessmen in Florida are putting together a condominium deal like the one in Maui. They heard about the job I did for Eddie Meyers. They have some of the same problems. The deal is going to be finalized this weekend and I have to fly to Miami tomorrow afternoon so we can meet on Wednesday. Then they want me with them during the negotiations through Saturday.'

There had been stunned silence on Quinn's end. The conference on St. Jerome was from Thursday to Sunday. Quinn was speaking on Thursday morning. He had planned it so that he and Laura would leave on Tuesday and have every day but Thursday to themselves. If Laura had to be in Miami from Tuesday to Saturday, there was no way she could come with him.

'Can't someone else go in your place?' he had asked, but Laura had told him that the clients insisted on her handling the matter personally and were willing to pay a large retainer to secure her services.

'Turn them down,' Quinn had snapped, unable to hide his anger and disappointment. 'There must be hundreds of lawyers in Miami who can review their damn contract.'

'I know you were looking forward to this vacation,' Laura had answered calmly. 'So was I. But this will give me a foothold in Florida. Do you know how many condo deals are made there?'

'I don't care, Laura. This vacation . . . I was hoping so much . . .'

Quinn could not finish the sentence.

'I'm sorry, Dick. I'm not in this just for myself. You

were a partner at Price. How could I explain turning down a fee like this and losing the potential business?'

Quinn wanted to remind her that she was also a partner in their marriage. Instead, he hung up after assuring Laura that he understood in a tone that let her know that he did not.

The line of boarding passengers started to thin. To distract himself, Quinn took the airline magazine from the seat pocket in front of him and found the crossword Completing the crossword before takeoff was a ritual that Quinn followed whenever he flew.

'Excuse me. I think the window seat is mine.'

When Quinn looked up he saw a woman standing in the aisle. She was about five feet four and wore a white T-shirt under a red sports jacket. Her jeans were secured at the waist by a brightly colored red and yellow fabric belt with an unusual silver buckle that resembled a seashell.

'I have 2A,' she explained, showing Quinn her ticket.

'Sorry,' Quinn said as he stumbled awkwardly to his feet. As the woman edged by him, she smiled apologetically. Quinn guessed that she was in her mid-twenties. She was not wearing makeup and she looked tired. Her straight black hair was pulled back into a ponytail. Here and there, strands had escaped to add to the picture of an exhausted traveler. The woman had a small nose, full lips and almond-shaped brown eyes that were a little bloodshot. The overall effect was vaguely oriental. Just as the woman sat down, the flight attendant brought Quinn his drink.

'Can I get you anything?' the attendant asked the

woman in the window seat. The woman looked at Quinn's drink.

'Is that a Scotch?' she asked him.

'Yes.'

'Then make mine the same.'

The attendant left to fill the order.

'I need a stiff drink,' she told Quinn while flashing a tired smile. 'I just got off a nonstop from Italy.'

'Vacation?' he asked to be polite.

'I wish,' she answered with a pleasant laugh. 'I was in Bologna checking out leather suppliers for my business.'

'What do you do?'

'I'm the president of Avalon Accessories, creators of the best custom-made belts in the known universe,' the woman answered proudly. Then her shoulders sagged dramatically. 'But sometimes I wish I had a partner. All the travel kills me. If I'm not in the shop, I'm on a plane.'

'Do you sell your belts out of your shop?'

'I don't actually have a shop. That's just a figure of speech. I make the belts in a small factory. I sell through specialty shop customers and catalog sales. But I also work with a few fashion designers. They show me their designs for the season and I make belts that are appropriate for the collection.' The woman pointed at her belt. 'This is part of Gretchen Nye's spring collection. Do you like it?'

'I noticed it when you sat down. It's very nice.'

'Nice?' the woman answered with mock indignation. 'You're supposed to say that it's a startlingly innovative combination of style and color that knocked your socks off. Nice doesn't sell Gretchen Nye originals at two thousand a pop.'

Quinn laughed. 'I did mean to say that it was startlingly innovative. It came out wrong.'

'You're forgiven.'

The flight attendant brought the woman's drink just as the plane began taxiing toward the runway. She swallowed most of it, then sat silently during takeoff. Quinn could see that her knuckles were white from tension. As soon as they were airborne, she downed the rest of her Scotch.

'No matter how many times I go through that, I still get scared,' she confided to Quinn. 'A friend of mine was killed in an air crash.'

'That's terrible.'

'Yeah. It really shook me up. I'm a mess every time I fly.'

The attendant passed by and the woman ordered a second drink. So did Quinn.

'Are you vacationing on St. Jerome?' the woman asked.

The question reminded Quinn that Laura was not with him and he lost the relaxed feeling he had been experiencing since his conversation with the woman began.

'Business, I'm afraid. Though I'm going to take advantage of the beach.'

'What kind of work do you do?'

'I'm a judge.'

The woman looked impressed. 'I've never met a judge before.'

Quinn smiled. 'Well, this is what we look like.'

She laughed. 'Where are you a judge?'

'Portland, Oregon.'

'I hear that Portland is a beautiful city. I'd like to visit someday.'

'I like it.'

Suddenly, the woman looked confused. 'You can't be a judge on St. Jerome, can you?'

'No. I can only hear cases in Oregon.'

'That's what I thought. So what kind of business do you have on the island?'

'I'm speaking at a legal seminar. I only hope I can keep my audience interested. My lecture is going to seem awfully dull compared to those white sand beaches outside the hotel.'

'I'm certain you'll hold their interest, Judge . . . Say, I don't know your name. Mine is Andrea. Andrea Chapman.'

'Richard Quinn,' he said as they shook hands. 'Dick, actually. And please don't call me Judge. That's for the courtroom.'

'Okay, Dick. Are you staying at The Palms?'

'No. I'm at the Bay Reef Resort.'

'Oh, the new one. They were just finishing it the last time I was on the island.'

'It looks beautiful in the brochures. Are you going to St. Jerome on business?'

'God, no. This trip is strictly R and R. A friend of mine owns a villa on the island. He lets me use it when I need to get away.'

'A boyfriend?'

Andrea giggled. 'Freddy is gay. Flaming. But he's a

great friend and one of my best customers. We met at a leather goods show in Milan about five years ago. He owns a catalog business and he really pushes my belts.'

'Is the villa near my hotel?'

'No. It's on the other side of St. Jerome. You should see it. The place is unbelievable. The floors are these different-colored marbles, the walls are all glass, and the view is to die for. It's right on the ocean on this cliff. When I wake up and pull the drapes it's like I'm floating in space.'

'It sounds fantastic.'

'It is.' Andrea leaned over toward Quinn and dropped her voice an octave. 'There's a story behind the villa. The way Freddy got it. Some Guatemalan drug lord owned it, but he was busted in Rhode Island of all places. He gave it to this lawyer in Boston that Freddy knows as part of his fee and Freddy bought it from the lawyer for a song. I don't think the lawyer ever saw it. He just wanted cash.'

Andrea lowered her voice even more.

'The last time I used the place, I found a stash of coke hidden behind a phony panel in the bathroom. It scared the hell out of me.'

'I can imagine. Did you turn it over to the police?'

'On St. Jerome? You're kidding? I wouldn't go within a mile of an island cop if I was being murdered. St. Jerome is great, but everyone – and I mean everyone – in the government is on the take. If I told the police about the dope, I'd either be in jail or penniless now.'

'So what did you do?'

'Flushed it as quickly as I could. Then I scrubbed down the toilet bowl to make sure there wasn't a trace of the stuff left. It was my last day on St. Jerome, thank God. If it had been my first, I would probably have been on the next flight out. As it was, I didn't sleep a wink. I kept expecting Governor Alvarez's Gestapo to kick in the door and throw me in prison.'

Quinn laughed. 'If you were so frightened, why did you come back?'

'You wouldn't ask that if you'd been on St. Jerome before. The place has got to be the most beautiful island in the world. Besides, Freddy swore to me that the place is clean now. He was just as scared as I was when I told him about the coke. Can you imagine what it would cost an American to buy his way out of a drug beef?'

Chapman paused. 'Say, are you going to be working all the time?'

'Not the first two days.'

Quinn realized where the conversation might be going and his wedding ring suddenly felt very heavy on his finger. He decided to make his marital status clear to Andrea.

'My wife was supposed to come with me, but something came up at the last minute. She's a lawyer, too, and there was a business emergency.'

'That's too bad. I bet she would have loved St. Jerome. There's a lot to do if you know your way around.'

'Such as?'

'Do you snorkel or scuba dive?'

'No. I'm a lousy swimmer.'

'You don't have to swim great to snorkel. And there are these fabulous reefs where you can see all these tropical fish. You've never seen such bright colors,' Andrea said excitedly. 'Electric blues, iridescent greens. It's wilder than a Missoni fashion show.'

'That sounds terrific. Are any of these reefs near my hotel?'

'Oh, sure. But the best one is on my side of the island, away from the hotels, where Freddy's villa is, off Cala de Almas Desoladas.'

'What was that?' asked Quinn, who spoke no Spanish.

'The Cove of Lost Souls. Freddy said it's called that because of a ship that was wrecked on the reef in 1700 something. The captain was in love with a beautiful woman. They were going to be married. On their wedding day, the bride was kidnapped by pirates. The captain chased the pirates to St. Jerome just as a terrible storm struck the island and the captain's ship and the pirate ship were wrecked. Everyone died, including the captain and his bride.

'Freddy told me that if you go to the cove at night, sometimes you can hear the souls of the captain and his bride calling to each other across the water. Isn't that sad and romantic?'

'Yes, it is.'

'There's more, though. Freddy says that there have been mysterious disappearances in the cove. Not often. Once or twice, every ten years or so. They occur when lovers come to the beach at night on the anniversary of the shipwreck. They swim out toward the reef. One

135

minute they're there, the next they're gone. The locals think that the lost souls on the reef are harvesting other souls to keep them company.'

'It's probably cramps,' Quinn said with a smile.

'See, that's the lawyer in you talking,' Andrea scolded Quinn. 'Lawyers are so unromantic.' She paused as if debating whether to say more. 'Do you want to hear something spooky?'

'Sure.'

'The last time I stayed on St. Jerome, a day before I found the coke, I went down to the cove at sunset and waited around to see if I would hear the lost souls calling. At first, I just heard what you usually hear on the beach at night, the surf and the wind. Soon after the sun went down, the temperature dropped and I got cold. I was just starting to leave when something very strange happened.'

Andrea paused. She looked distant.

'What's the matter?' Quinn asked with concern.

'I was remembering the voices. Only they weren't really voices. It was more like a moaning sound and it was so sad.'

Quinn was weaned on logic and had the overly rational mind of the contract lawyer, which has no cubbyhole where the supernatural can dwell comfortably.

'Do you think it might have been the wind?' he asked tolerantly.

'I knew you'd say that. Everyone I tell this story to says the same thing. If you'd been there, though, you'd know that it wasn't the wind. That sound . . .' Andrea shivered. 'It was inside my bones.' She shook her head. 'I just don't know how else to describe it. And the way it made me feel. At first I was really scared, but suddenly I felt so lost and alone.'

Andrea paused thoughtfully.

'What if it's true? It would be so tragic. The two lovers, so close to each other, but separated by the raging sea for eternity.'

Quinn could not think of a thing to say that wouldn't sound patronizing, so he was silent. He did not want to insult Andrea. He liked her. She was so different from Laura. Quinn thought of the way Laura would react to Andrea's ghost story and laughed.

'You don't believe me. I know. No one does.'

'I'm sorry. I wasn't laughing at you.'

'Oh, that's okay. No one takes my experience at the cove seriously. I'm used to it. Say, I just got an idea. You could hear the lost souls yourself. I could take you to the cove.'

'I don't know.'

It had been some time since he had spent a day alone with a woman other than Laura and the thought of it made him uncomfortable, especially with the way things were between them.

'Oh, come on. You'd love it. And it's not a place that the tourists get to see. They pretty much stay near the hotels. Freddy told me that the governor likes it that way. There's a lot of poverty away from The Palms and Bay Reef. Freddy said that poor people are bad for tourism, so Governor Alvarez only paved the road on one section of the island. You have to drive on a dirt road to get to the villa and the cove. It goes through these shantytowns.'

Quinn knew he was being foolish. He didn't believe for a moment in the lost lovers, but the cove and the reef with the tropical fish sounded fascinating, and he did have two days with no plans. Spending one of them in the company of an attractive woman suddenly sounded like a good idea.

'The invitation sounds tempting,' Quinn hedged.

Andrea turned slightly and put her hand on his arm.

'I insist. I'll even teach you how to snorkel. You'll love it. What do you say?'

'I . . .'

'I'm not taking no for an answer. There's no way I'm going to let you leave St. Jerome without learning how to snorkel. I can pick you up at the hotel around four, tomorrow afternoon. That will give us both time to get over our jet lag and catch up on sleep. It takes about three-quarters of an hour to get to the cove from the hotel. I'll bring a picnic basket. We can swim for a while. I have snorkeling equipment and I'll give you a lesson. Then we'll eat and wait for the sun to go down.'

Andrea grinned mischievously. 'I just got a great idea. If we hear the sound of the lost souls and you can't explain it, you have to treat me to dinner. But it's my treat if you can come up with a rational explanation. What do you say?'

Quinn made a decision. He would go and have a good time. Maybe an evening with Andrea would help him get rid of his melancholy mood. But Quinn did not want anyone connected to the conference seeing him drive off with Andrea: judges had to avoid even the appearance of impropriety.

'Why don't you give me directions to the cove and I'll meet you there? I'll rent a car.'

Andrea's smile widened. 'So, you'll come?'

'I'll come. And, if you win, we can invite the ghosts along. I'll even spring for their dinners.'

Quinn's first glimpse of St. Jerome was filtered through gauzy white clouds. A patch of sugar-white sand, a strip of crystal-clear blue water, groves of swaying emerald-leafed palms. When the plane dropped beneath the clouds and Quinn had an unobstructed view of the island, he was certain he had found paradise. After the steady diet of gray and rain he had dined on in Portland, the sight of the sun, the palm trees and the clear blue water was exhilarating.

The exhilaration ended when the hatch of the airplane opened and Quinn was engulfed by a thick soup of hot, sticky air. He had rarely experienced such all-consuming heat. It bounced off the railings of the portable, metal steps that descended to the tarmac, melted the black asphalt and stirred the tar into a sucking mixture that threatened to wrench his shoes from his feet during the walk from the plane to the one-story terminal building that shimmered before him in the undulating waves of heat. Only the breeze from the sea made the heat bearable.

The lime-green paint on the exterior walls of the terminal had been savaged by the salt-heavy sea air. On one wall hung a huge poster of a smiling, mustachioed man in a military uniform. Quinn could not read the Spanish words on the poster. A large tear almost disconnected the top of the poster from the bottom. It looked to Quinn as if the damage had been done with a knife. Lounging against the wall next to the poster were two soldiers carrying automatic weapons. Quinn could not help noticing several other soldiers who were similarly armed.

'Why all the heavy artillery?' Quinn asked.

Andrea lowered her voice.

'The soldiers are here to protect the tourists. Governor Alvarez lets drug smugglers use the island for a fee. About five years ago, he executed six dealers who tried to cheat him. They were members of a South American cartel. A few weeks later, six tourists were gunned down in an ambush in retaliation. The island's economy is dependent on tourism. The massacre had a disastrous impact.'

'You're making St. Jerome sound pretty dangerous.'

'Oh, you don't have to worry. There hasn't been any trouble since. Freddy told me that a lot of money changed hands and Alvarez worked out the problem.'

'This Alvarez sounds like a petty criminal.'

Andrea looked alarmed. She cast a quick look around to see if anyone had heard the judge's comment.

'You don't criticize Governor Alvarez here,' Andrea warned. 'Enjoy the beaches and forget politics. It's not a healthy subject for discussion on St. Jerome.'

Louvered windows let air into the terminal, but it was still hot. Quinn looked for the baggage carousel before noticing two black men in shorts and sweat-stained shirts taking luggage off a cart and stacking it near one of the interior walls. He found his bags and looked around for customs.

The dominant language on the signs inside the terminal was Spanish, the official language of the island, but there were translations in English, French, German and Japanese. Quinn heard most of these languages being spoken by the tourists who queued up in front of the customs officials. The heavyset, sleepy-eyed man who checked Quinn's passport spoke broken English. After a few perfunctory questions, he smiled at Quinn and welcomed him to St. Jerome.

'The Bay Reef Resort is supposed to provide a shuttle service between the airport and the hotel,' Quinn told Andrea.

'Don't worry about me. Freddy's driver will pick me up.'

A brand-new air-conditioned van with the Bay Reef logo was waiting at curbside.

'I'll see you at the cove at four tomorrow,' Quinn said before boarding it.

'At four.'

The air-conditioning in the van made Quinn forget about the debilitating heat. Two middle-aged couples were the only other passengers on the shuttle. From what Quinn could hear, they were Australian and they were on holiday together. Quinn turned his attention to the royal palms with their thick tan trunks and broad green leaves that shaded the highway. Beyond the palm trees, waves rushed across a white sand beach. Everywhere

141

Quinn looked he saw the sea or lush tropical vegetation. St. Jerome was every bit as beautiful as the brochure from the Bay Reef Resort had promised.

After a fifteen-minute ride, a high white stucco wall appeared on the ocean side of the highway. They drove alongside the wall for a mile. Then the van pulled up in front of a guardhouse and waited while a black man in a clean, white short-sleeved shirt and tan slacks opened a gate topped by black spikes. The bold black letters on a copper sign affixed to a column next to the gate identified the enclave as the Bay Reef Resort.

The van drove for a short distance down a wide road lined with pink bougainvillea and more palms, then stopped in front of a one-story white stucco building. To the left, Quinn could see the beginning of a line of elegant shops. To the right was a row of two-story suites. High hedges blocked Quinn's view in both directions.

Quinn got out of the van and identified his bags for a porter, who directed him through an arched portal toward the reception area. Quinn noticed that there were almost no doors in sight. The reason was soon obvious. As he stepped through the archway, the breeze that blew in from the ocean cooled him.

There was a red and yellow terrazzo floor and a dozen varieties of flowering plants in the lobby of the Bay Reef. Beyond the reception area was a wide flagstone terrace. Guests in shorts and bathing suits were eating lunch at tables covered with white cloth under the shade of sea-grape trees. The trees were strung with lights that illuminated the open-air restaurant after the sun set.

After he checked in, a porter showed Quinn to his

suite. A king-size, four-poster bed dominated the bed-room. The sight of it made Quinn sad. He had requested it after seeing pictures of the suite in the brochure for the resort. Before Laura's abrupt withdrawal from their trip, he had imagined the pleasure they would both take in making love in that bed.

Quinn tipped the bellman, put away his clothes, and switched on the air conditioner and the overhead fan. The judge was tired from his nine-hour flight, but he did not want to nap. As soon as he showered and changed into shorts and a T-shirt, Quinn wandered onto the balcony. Oleander, coconut palms and more sea grape were planted liberally along the edge of the beach, providing some shade for the bathers who lounged around, soaking up the sun. To the left, Quinn could see the thatch-roofed bar at the end of the flagstone terrace. Brown-skinned waiters and waitresses cruised back and forth between the bar and the guests with drink-laden trays. The ocean near the resort was dotted with sailboats, catamarans and splashing, laughing vacationers. Quinn checked his watch. Laura's plane would be in by now. He walked inside, lay down on the bed and called Laura at her hotel.

'Hi,' Quinn said as soon as they were connected. 'I just wanted to make sure you got in okay.'

'No problems here. How was your flight?' Laura asked.

'The flight was fine.'

'Does St. Jerome live up to your expectations?'

'Yeah, it does. It's even more beautiful than I thought it would be. The resort is unbelievable.'

'You know I want to be with you, don't you, Dick?'

Quinn wanted to tell Laura that she would have turned down her new clients or had someone else from the firm handle the business if she really wanted to be with him, but he did not want to start a fight. So he said, 'I know, honey.' Then he added, 'I really miss you,' which was true.

'I miss you, too. Maybe we can get away together soon. Just the two of us.'

Quinn wanted to remind her about the Crease trial and his other cases, which would eat up most of the year, but he didn't.

'That would be great,' he answered with as much enthusiasm as he could muster. 'I love you.'

'Love you, too,' Laura answered before she hung up.

Quinn replaced the receiver and lay back, staring at the long-bladed ceiling fan that spun slowly overhead. It dawned on him that he had not mentioned Andrea Chapman or their plans for the next day. Quinn wondered why it had slipped his mind. He felt vaguely guilty about not mentioning Andrea, but there was nothing he could do about it now.

Quinn walked onto the balcony again. He missed Laura terribly. There were so many happy couples frolicking on the beach. The sight of them made Quinn feel worse. He wished he were with Laura lying in the sun, reading a trashy novel and getting smashed on banana daiquiris. But Laura was working and he was alone.

Thirteen

THE HEAT AND LIGHT of the sun woke Laura Quinn. It was a pleasant change from the alarm clock that usually shocked her out of bed in Portland. She stretched and turned so she could see the clock on the hotel nightstand. It was eight-thirty. Laura could not remember the last weekday when she had been in bed at this hour.

Laura rolled onto her back and contemplated a lazy morning. Her client had left a message saying that she would be contacted at ten. That left her time to shower and have a leisurely breakfast. She got out of bed wearing the T-shirt and panties she'd slept in. It was hot in Miami, but Laura had switched off the air conditioner so she could enjoy the warmth after the cold and gray of the Oregon winter.

Laura found a space on the hotel carpet that was wide enough for her to do some stretching and proceeded to go through the routine she followed every morning at home. Repeating the familiar exercises made her think of Quinn, who was usually shaving and showering while she worked out. She missed her husband, and her good feelings were replaced by pangs of guilt.

Laura completed fifty crunches and twenty push-ups. The Florida heat and the exercise had covered her in a thin sheen of sweat. She stripped and went into the bathroom. Quinn had sounded so lonely during the call from St. Jerome, but it was his reaction when she told him that she could not make the trip to the island that haunted her. He had sounded betrayed and abandoned and, she admitted to herself, he had every right to feel that way.

Affection for Quinn had crept up on Laura. Bush-whacked and ambushed her. It was something she never anticipated when the two of them were teamed to work on the Remington litigation. Quinn was someone who rarely entered Laura's thoughts before the *Remington* case. He was nice-looking, but not handsome enough to moon about. He was also shy and clumsy. Laura knew that Quinn had been a varsity basketball player in college, but she still had trouble imagining him playing with grace. Of course, Quinn was very smart, even brilliant at times, but so were most of the lawyers at Price, Winward. You didn't get invited to join the firm unless you were a superstar in law school and you didn't make partner unless your talent sparkled in the real world.

Laura turned off the shower. While she toweled off, she thought about the first time she and Quinn had made love. It had been in a hotel room. They were staying at the Adolphus in Dallas while they took depositions in *Remington*. She had a small room, but Quinn was a partner, so he was staying in a suite. It was the end of a grueling fifteen-hour workday. They were in the living room of the suite under a wide skylight going over their notes of the depositions they had conducted from nine to five at the offices of Remington's attorneys. The night had been clear and Laura remembered a moment when she had leaned her head back against the couch and stared up through the skylight at a swirl of stars and a bright, white quarter moon.

Quinn had been brilliant that day. He had broken Remington's CEO and they were both excited. Laura remembered feeling like a timber wolf circling a terrified calf as she watched the CEO's expression change slowly from disdain to despair. They could both taste blood when they packed their attaché cases and left the offices of Remington's attorneys. Hours later, Quinn and Laura, exhausted by the long day and tipsy from the wine they'd drunk at dinner, were sitting next to each other on the couch when Laura said something that had struck them both as funny. What normally would have merited a good chuckle made them giddy in their weakened state. When their laughter was spent they found themselves pressed together. Laura remembered Quinn looking at her with such longing the moment before their lips touched.

The morning after their first sex, Laura had been in torment. Quinn was not a particularly good lover, but he did love her. That much Laura knew. As they lay together in the dark, Quinn had confessed the feelings that had exploded in him during the past year. He told her how he had come to care for her but had been afraid to tell her. He was a partner and she was an associate. He was concerned with appearances, worried about the difference in their ages. But he was also helplessly in love with her, he admitted, laying himself open for rejection.

Quinn's honesty impressed Laura, but intimacy terrified her. Laura's father had adored her and her mother, or so Laura had believed. Then he had left them. How could Laura trust Quinn's feelings? How could she trust her own? Laura had slept with men, but she had never let herself expose her emotions to a man. Quinn wanted that. He needed it.

Laura had told Quinn that she did not want to rush into a serious relationship. Quinn backed off. She could read the pain in his eyes. The sag in his shoulders reminded her of the defeated CEO. It upset her to think that she had hurt him.

In the week after their return from Texas, Laura thought long and hard about her feelings for Quinn. She had learned to admire and respect Quinn during the time they'd worked together, but did she love him? What was love, anyway? Her emotions were so jumbled by the life she had led that she wasn't certain that she would ever be able to answer that question. If love existed, she knew that it did not last forever. Her mother had loved her father, and her father said he loved her mother, but neither loved the other now. Laura was convinced that love could be a lie. Still, she did feel something for Quinn that she had never felt for another man. He was gentle and considerate and he respected her legal abilities. She felt safe and comfortable when she was with him. Was that the way someone in love was supposed to feel?

Laura suggested that they spend time together. Quinn agreed eagerly. He did not pressure her and he seemed to understand the difficulty she had committing herself emotionally. When Laura thought about their future, she imagined herself and Quinn working together with the same verve and success they'd had in the Remington case. Only, in her thoughts, she, too, was a partner at Price, Winward. When she agreed to marry Quinn she was still not certain that her feelings for him were love, but they were what she thought love was supposed to feel like.

Laura took the elevator to the lobby and treated herself to fresh-squeezed orange juice, cold cereal and coffee in the hotel restaurant. As she ate, she wondered what had happened between her and her husband. There had not been anything dramatic. No affair, Quinn did not drink like her father or suffer from depression. He was the same man she had married, but somewhere during the past seven years, the marriage had started to die.

Who was to blame? Laura thought that their problems started with Quinn's ascension to the bench. When Quinn told her that the governor had approached him about the appointment she had been stunned. Laura knew that Dick was Patrick Quinn's son. Everyone knew that. She knew that he was basically an intellectual who enjoyed the law because of its mental rigor and not because of the money and thrill of combat that drew her to its practice. What she could not understand was how anyone could achieve her dream of making partner at Price, Winward and abandon it for the bench. As an associate, she was making almost as much as an Oregon Supreme Court justice. When she made partner, their combined salaries would be more than $300,000 a year. How could Quinn throw away the prestige and financial security of his present position? Laura tried to understand her husband's motivation, but she could not accept what he wanted to do. Should she have tried harder to understand Quinn's feelings? The thought nagged at her. Had she lost respect for Quinn simply because his job paid less than hers? Was that fair?

Laura returned to her room. Her client had not called by ten-fifteen. She took out the letter in which the retainer check and first-class plane ticket had been enclosed. The letter had been FedExed to the firm and there was a phone number on the letterhead. Jerome Ross, the man she had spoken to on the phone, had also signed the letter. She reached for the phone, then stopped herself. Ross would call when he was ready.

Laura walked to the window and stared out at the ocean. Since Quinn's ascension to the bench, and her promotion to partner, Laura had increased her workload. Was she working hard to establish a reputation and to prove her worth to the firm, or was she hiding in her work? One thing was certain, she and Quinn were growing apart and she had to decide what she wanted to do about it. There were two choices: seal the rift or separate.

At ten-thirty, Laura dialed the number for SeaCliff

Estates. The phone rang twice. Then a recording told her that the number she had dialed was not in service. Laura redialed, assuming that she had misdialed the first time. She heard the same message again. There was a phone book in her end table. Laura could not find a listing for SeaCliff Estates or Jerome Ross, so she rang the front desk.

'This is Laura Quinn in room 517. I have a reservation for five nights. I need to call the company that made it for me and I've misplaced the phone number. Did they give it to you when the reservation was made?'

'Let me check, Mrs. Quinn.'

A moment later, the desk clerk read her the same number that was on the letterhead.

'You're certain that there aren't any other phone numbers for the company?' Laura asked.

'That's the only one.'

'Thanks.'

'Uh, Mrs. Quinn. Did you say that the reservation was for five nights?'

'Yes. I'm supposed to fly out Sunday.'

'We only have you down for two nights. Yesterday and today.'

'There must be some mistake.'

'That's what I have here.'

Laura thought for a moment. Then she asked, 'Have I received any messages?'

'Your box is clear.'

Laura hung up. She called Portland and asked for Mort Camden, another partner at Price, Winward. They talked for a few minutes, then Camden told her he would get back to her. Jerome Ross had still not contacted her when Camden called twenty minutes later.

'This is fucked, Laura. The retainer check is drawn on an account in a Miami bank that was opened a week ago, but there's only one hundred dollars in it.'

'One hundred! The damn retainer is twenty thousand.'

'I don't know what to say, but something stinks. I think you should hop on the first plane back to Portland.'

'What do you think is going on, Mort?'

'Beats me. Maybe someone is playing a joke on you.'

'It's one expensive joke. The first-class round-trip ticket and the hotel reservations cost several thousand dollars.'

'I don't know what to say.'

Laura threw her file on the floor. She was livid.

'I'm checking out. I'll see you tomorrow.'

As soon as Camden hung up, Laura angrily jabbed out the number of the airline. The phone rang. She planned to ask for a seat on the next flight from Miami to Portland, but a thought occurred to her and she hung up the phone. She had hurt Quinn when she chose a business deal over a vacation with him. It was only Wednesday morning and St. Jerome was not far from Miami.

Laura's arm dropped to her side. Quinn had given her seven good years. The hurt in his voice when she told him that she could not go to St. Jerome was proof that he still cared for her very much. If she wanted her marriage to survive, she had to act. Laura dialed the airline and asked for a seat on the next flight to St. Jerome.

Fourteen

ANDREA WAS RIGHT about the difference between the resort side of St. Jerome and the other side of the island. The Bay Reef and The Palms were palaces where the wealthy, dressed in the latest fashions, dined on lobster and caviar, played golf and sunned themselves while sipping cool drinks by the pool. Puerta del Sol, the brightly colored capital city, was filled with fashionable shops and upscale restaurants. The buildings were freshly painted sunny yellow, happy blue and festive red, and the shop owners greeted everyone with a laugh and a smile. Poverty had been banished from the immaculate streets of the capital by order of Governor Alvarez. True, the taxis were dilapidated and there were some beggars who managed to evade the ever-present police patrols, but this was local color, the source of quaint Third World stories that could be told back home for the amusement of neighbors and friends.

The far side of St. Jerome was another story. The island's only paved highway was an oval that passed through Puerta del Sol, then swung around behind the hotels on the way to the airport before curving back to the resorts. Seven miles past the capital, a dirt track branched off toward the far side of the island. This road was the only open space in a jungle of towering trees whose branches interlocked to form a dense, dark green canopy that blocked out the sun and cast thick shadows over the narrow highway. The air was filled with the sweet smell of flowering plants and the wet, fetid smell of rotting vegetation. Quinn passed only a few people during the forty-minute, cross-island trip. More than once, he nervously checked his fuel gauge, having no desire to be stranded in the dense jungle.

At the suggestion of the concierge, Quinn rented a Land Rover and soon discovered why the recommendation had been made. The road was not well maintained. Quinn felt his kidneys suffer each time the Rover hit a pothole, and the billowing dust clouds kicked up by the thick tires completely obscured the scene in the rearview mirror.

The jungle thinned, then disappeared when the road descended toward the ocean and into a civilization quite different from the one most St. Jerome tourists saw. Scattered along both sides of the road for half a mile were rusting shacks constructed from corrugated tin and a few more-substantial buildings made of concrete blocks. Some of the structures had colorful curtains strung across the doorway. None had glass windows, but some of the more solidly constructed buildings had louvered shutters. An emaciated goat was tethered to one shack and scrawny chickens wandered among many of the buildings pecking at the dusty ground.

A group of children was playing soccer with a tin can in a dirt field. They stopped when they heard the Rover and watched it drive by. An old man with nappy gray hair smiled and waved at Quinn and Quinn waved back. The old man's teeth were yellowed and decaying and there were gaping holes in his mouth where some teeth had rotted out. His T-shirt and shorts were in the same state of decay as his teeth. The clothing worn by the children who were playing soccer was also torn and tattered. All of the people he saw as he passed by the shacks were barefoot. A group of women in colorful skirts and blouses, their hair covered by multicolored scarves, walked along the road balancing tin basins filled with fruit on their heads. They also stopped to watch the Rover pass. Except for the old man with the rotting teeth, no one smiled.

Quinn drove through the village and around a curve that put it out of sight. The road straightened out. Quinn noted the location of the village on the map Andrea had drawn for him. According to her notes, four miles after the village a narrow dirt trail branched off toward the sea. Quinn looked up from the map and saw a jeep with two soldiers closing fast in his rearview mirror. The jeep pulled around Quinn to pass, then slowed when it was next to the Rover. The soldier in the passenger seat studied Quinn. His expression was hard and he cradled an automatic rifle. Quinn flashed a nervous smile at the soldier, but the soldier did not smile back.

His cold appraisal was intimidating and Quinn looked away. After what Andrea had told him, Quinn was not certain that tourists were safe on St. Jerome. The land on either side of the road was flat and sandy and totally deserted. If something happened to him here, there would be no witnesses.

The jeep drove parallel to the Rover for a few seconds more, then cut in front of it and sped up. Quinn did not relax completely until the jeep was out of sight.

The dirt trail to the cove was right where Andrea's map said it would be. The sandy track was flat for a short distance. Then the Rover climbed upward to the crest of a hill and the road ended. Quinn stopped the car and got out. He was on the edge of a high cliff. Below him was the sea, which the cliff surrounded on three sides. An overhang blocked Quinn's view of the beach except for a strip that was adjacent to the ocean. Quinn looked for Andrea's car but did not see any other vehicles. He checked his watch. It was only a few minutes after four.

Quinn grabbed a towel and locked the Rover. A moment later, he found a narrow pebble-strewn path that wound downward along the cliff side. A stiff breeze messed with his hair. He was wearing a pair of baggy, khaki Bermuda shorts over a blue boxer swimsuit and a T-shirt with a colorful map of the world on the back. His sandals had smooth soles and twice he slipped sideways on small rocks.

When he was halfway down the trail, Quinn spotted Andrea lying on a large blanket. Beside her were a towel, some clothes, a large wicker picnic basket and snorkeling equipment. During the plane trip, Andrea had looked tired and bedraggled and her clothes had concealed her figure. Today she was wearing dark glasses and a bikini that was no more than three minute patches of yellow fabric. Her trim figure impressed Quinn. Andrea's legs were smooth and faintly muscled and her waist was narrow. He could see her ribs just below the bra of the bikini, then a flat stomach. Andrea's only imperfection was a pale, half-moon-shaped scar that stood out on her hip just below the string that secured the right side of her bikini bottom. The sight of Andrea's near-naked body aroused Quinn. Before he had time to think about his feelings, Andrea sat up and waved. Quinn waved back, then walked down the trail slowly to give his erection time to subside.

'You found me,' Andrea said with a smile.

'Your directions were excellent and you're right about this place. It's beautiful.'

'Wait until you see the reef.'

Quinn lowered himself onto the blanket and eyed the snorkeling equipment nervously.

'I'm not a very good swimmer. Are you certain I can do this?'

'If you can swim at all, you can snorkel. All you really do is paddle around with your face in the water. It's a piece of cake. You'll see. I won't let you drown.'

Andrea stood up. Quinn could not help noticing the way her breasts moved under the thin fabric of her bikini top. For a second, he fantasized Andrea naked, lying next to him on the blanket in the hot sun.

'I'm going to cool off. Come on.'

Andrea reached out for Quinn and he took her hand. Her palm felt warm and smooth and she held on for a second before pulling him toward her. Quinn lurched to his feet and stumbled forward. Their bodies touched. Andrea laughed. Quinn was aroused again. The sensation was exciting but disturbing. He was certain that nothing would happen between them, but a part of him wished it would.

Quinn tossed his T-shirt and shorts on the blanket. Andrea jogged toward the water. Quinn followed, entranced by Andrea's muscular thighs and the way the movement of her buttocks made the fabric of her bikini bottom undulate. Quinn wondered what Andrea would be like in bed. She seemed so carefree and he imagined that her lovemaking would be loose and spontaneous. He remembered how quick and unsatisfying sex with Laura had become. Instantly, a wave of guilt washed over him.

Andrea ran into the surf, slowing as the water got higher and diving in when the ocean was at her waist. When she surfaced, her long black hair was wet and it gleamed in the strong sunlight.

'Come on in.'

Quinn walked into the water. From his experiences in Oregon, he expected the ocean to be freezing, but when the water touched his skin, it felt like a cool shower on a warm summer day. At first, the water was shallow and the sand was smooth. Then fields of dark green seaweed grabbed at his ankles, snarled between his toes and obscured the bottom. Without warning, the seafloor dropped abruptly and Quinn stumbled into water that reached his waist. He bucked a small wave and nearly lost his balance. When he recovered his footing, he squatted and let the waves wash over him. Quinn was still not used to the torrid heat, and the cool water felt great. He closed his eyes, stretched out flat in the water and windmilled his arms, swimming gracelessly for a short distance. When he was winded, Quinn rolled onto his back. Unlike pool water, the salt water supported Quinn and he relaxed a little.

Andrea was a polished swimmer and she swam over to him with a natural stroke.

'Feels good, doesn't it?'

'It feels great. The sun is really hot.'

Andrea rolled onto her back and closed her eyes.

'This is the most wonderful place in the world, don't you think?'

The water slipped under Andrea's bikini top and the fabric rose and fell with the motion of the sea. Andrea drifted next to Quinn and he watched as the water washed across her breasts when the fabric shifted. Andrea opened her eyes and caught Quinn staring. He blushed and she smiled. Their eyes met and Andrea rolled against Quinn. Her arms snaked around his neck. Quinn froze. He knew what was happening and he knew he should stop it, but he couldn't. He did not want to.

Andrea's lips were cold and tasted salty. Her kiss was gentle. She teased him with her lips and he responded. The kiss was long and deep. Quinn closed his eyes and savored it. When her breast brushed his chest, Quinn cupped it. Andrea let Quinn caress her breast for a moment, then broke away, laughing. Quinn was confused. Andrea's fingers brushed his cheek, a feather touch. Quinn felt desire and guilt simultaneously.

'The sun will start to go down soon,' Andrea said. 'If you want to snorkel, we better do it now.'

Quinn's mouth was dry from sexual excitement. He nodded instead of speaking, grateful for the chance to sort out what had just happened and to think about what he wanted to happen later when the sun was down and they left the water for the blanket Andrea had so carefully spread out on the sand.

Andrea swam in easily. Quinn followed her using an ungainly crawl. He was a slow swimmer and he used his time in the water to calm himself. Andrea's kiss had shaken Quinn and made him want more. He and Andrea lived on opposite coasts. They would probably never see each other again after St. Jerome. If he slept with Andrea, Laura might never know. But Quinn would know and he had no idea how that would affect his marriage.

Andrea was gathering up a set of fins, a mask and a snorkel when Quinn swam ashore. She held up the mask. 'This is the key to snorkeling,' she instructed. Quinn was still in a state of sexual confusion, but Andrea's tone gave no hint that anything had happened between them. 'Without this, you'd be blind underwater. With it, you can see clearly.'

Quinn concentrated on what Andrea was saying to distract himself.

She held up the snorkel. 'This is basically a tube with a U-bend at one end that's fitted with a mouthpiece. With the snorkel, you can breathe while you're swimming facedown on the surface of the water without raising your head.'

Andrea sat on the sand and slipped on her fins. Quinn copied her. He tried to stand up but he had trouble. When he was on his feet he took a few tentative steps and almost fell.

'God,' he laughed self-consciously, 'I feel like I'm a clown in the circus.'

'You're doing fine.' Andrea handed Quinn his mask and snorkel. 'Let's wade out a ways.'

Quinn struggled through the surf. He noticed that Andrea was holding her mask and snorkel out of the water and he did the same. When they were in waist-deep, Andrea said, 'Spit on the glass on the inside of your mask like this and rub the spittle all over it, then rinse it off. This will stop the glass from misting when you're underwater.'

Quinn did as he was told. Andrea put on the mask and slid the snorkel under the thick black rubber strap that secured the mask to her head.

'Breathe through the mouthpiece,' Andrea said, 'then bend forward and stick your face in the water. Just stand there. I want you to get used to breathing through the snorkel. I'll hold onto you so you can concentrate on what you're doing.'

Quinn bent forward hesitantly until the mask was submerged. Andrea's hands were firm and her touch aroused him again, so he tried to concentrate on her instructions. He put his face in the water and tried to breathe through the mouthpiece, immediately sucking in a mouth full of seawater. The salty taste panicked him and he stood up, spitting. Andrea showed him the correct way to breathe so he would not get water in his mouth. Quinn got it right after a few tries.

The first thing that amazed Quinn was the clarity with which he could see the underwater world beneath him. A small crab scuttled across a rock on the sandy sea bottom. Then a bright blue and indigo fish that shot into and out of his vision startled Quinn. He jerked up and spit out his mouthpiece.

'Did you see that?' he asked excitedly. 'This fish . . . it was incredible . . .'

Andrea laughed. 'You ain't seen nothing yet. Wait till we get to the reef.'

Andrea spent a little longer in the shallow area close to the beach getting Quinn used to swimming with the snorkel. The memory of the solitary blue and indigo fish spurred Quinn to learn quickly. Finally, Andrea motioned Quinn to head for the reef.

'You think I'm ready?' he asked anxiously.

'No question. Let's do it.'

Quinn was nervous about leaving the area near the beach, but he was soon swimming slowly but steadily into deep water. The most frightening thing was how far away the bottom seemed and the fact that it kept receding, but the sheer beauty of the world below kept him from turning back. He was soon looking down on chasms of coral divided by rivers of white sand on which the wave action had inscribed ripple patterns. The coral was shaped like knobs, spines, fingers and fans. Andrea pointed out several round gray boulders covered by a maze of ridges and grooves that looked remarkably like a human brain. Quinn crossed over a coral cliff from which strands of seaweed waved. Attached to the cliff were clusters of brown coral shaped like the antlers of a great stag and reddish brown spines that jutted high up in the water like the fingers of a drowning man.

Quinn noticed two small plastic bags filled with bread crumbs tied to Andrea's bikini bottom. He watched as she opened the tie that secured one of the bags and took out some bread. Andrea motioned to Quinn to look down. He could see a large section of whitish brown coral directly below him, but no sign of life. Andrea let the bread fall. The crumbs floated downward undisturbed until they were almost touching the coral. Suddenly, the sea was filled with multicolored fish. Flashes of bright yellow, garish red, electric blue and neon green swooped below him. Andrea handed Quinn the other bag. He opened it quickly, anxious to keep the sea filled with tropical fish.

Quinn shredded a piece of bread and dropped some of it into the water. A bright yellow goatfish darted out of a hole in the coral and nipped at a bread crumb, while a butterfly fish with a fat white body and broad black stripes attacked another piece.

Quinn was so absorbed by the swirl of colors that he forgot about Andrea. When he remembered, he looked along the surface for her. She wasn't there. Quinn treaded water to keep himself upright and spun in a circle. The endless ocean and limitless sky gave way to the shoreline, the beach and the high cliff walls, then the ocean and sky returned. Quinn grew anxious. Andrea had been beside him a moment ago. He started

163

to spin again when Andrea erupted from the ocean a few feet from his face. Quinn started to laugh, then Andrea screamed. Quinn froze. Something jerked Andrea underwater and Quinn dove after her without thinking. Through the glass plate in his facemask he saw Andrea clawing at the arms of a diver in scuba gear, her legs and arms flailing helplessly.

Quinn grabbed the arm that was wrapped around Andrea's throat and tried to pry it from her neck. Andrea's eyes were wide with fear behind her mask. Quinn used all his strength and the diver's arm loosened. Then Quinn's snorkel filled with salt water. Quinn gagged, panicked and bolted straight up. When he cleared the surface, Quinn spit out his mouthpiece, gulped in air and dove again. Andrea and the diver were fading away. She was no longer struggling and she looked like a rag doll in the diver's grip. Quinn took a few desperate strokes in Andrea's direction even though he knew that he could not save her. He came up for air and dropped under the water once more, but Andrea and the diver had disappeared.

Quinn surfaced and scanned the horizon. The sun was setting, the air was suddenly cold and uninviting and the stunningly beautiful ocean floor had been transformed into a frightening abyss. Andrea had been snatched away and he could be next. Terror propelled Quinn toward the beach. Each time he kicked, he expected to feel a hand clamp onto his ankle. He wanted to look down so he could see if he was in danger, but he was afraid to stop.

The shore seemed miles away and Quinn's lungs

burned. Though he swam with all his might, the beach never seemed closer. He struggled forward, but his arms felt heavy and he could barely kick his legs. He wanted to rest, but terror drove him on. Just when he thought his arms and lungs would give out, a wave carried him into shallow water and he waded ashore.

The panic-driven swim had exhausted Quinn. He threw himself onto the beach and gasped for air. When he had recovered a little of his strength, Quinn struggled to his knees and threw up. Then he collapsed on the sand and experienced a momentary rush of joy because he was alive. That feeling was rapidly replaced by fear for his own safety and guilt over his failure to save Andrea.

Quinn scanned the beach and the ocean for any sign of Andrea or the diver, but he was completely alone. He threw on his clothes and collected everything else that he had brought to the cove. The sun was starting to set. Quinn hurried up the trail. The Land Rover was the only vehicle in sight. If Andrea had not driven to the cove, Freddy's villa had to be nearby. There would be a phone he could use to call the police.

Andrea had told Quinn that the villa overlooked the ocean. He had not noticed any turnoffs between the village and the cove, so he headed away from the village. He assumed that Andrea had not walked far in the heat. After driving two miles without spotting a side road, Quinn began to wonder if Andrea had been dropped off at the cove and was counting on him to drive her back to the villa.

Another roadside collection of shacks appeared a short

distance ahead. Quinn slowed, looking for someone he could ask for directions to the villa. Halfway through the makeshift town, Quinn saw a concrete-block building slightly larger than the rest. A sign dangled from a roof that overhung a small porch. Quinn guessed that the building housed a shop. He started to slow down when he spotted a metal cooler advertising Coca-Cola at the far end of the porch. The soldiers in the jeep were sitting next to it, drinking sodas. As the Rover neared the shop, they stopped sipping their drinks and watched it.

It occurred to Quinn that he knew very little about Andrea and that the subject of drugs had come up several times since they had met. There was the drug dealer who owned the villa where she was staying and the cocaine she had found there. Andrea was also knowledgeable about Governor Alvarez's drug connections. If Andrea's murder was drug related, the authorities could be involved.

Even if Andrea's death had no connection to drugs, it might not be smart to tell the soldiers about the murder. Would they believe Quinn if he said that a diver appeared out of nowhere and spirited Andrea away? The story sounded fantastic even to Quinn, and he had witnessed the murder. It was possible that the soldiers would conclude that Quinn and Andrea were lovers who fought and that Quinn, afraid that Andrea would ruin his marriage and career, had drowned her.

Quinn made a quick decision. He would drive back to the Bay Reef Resort and explain what happened to the manager or one of the organizers of the convention. There might even be an attorney from St. Jerome at the conference with whom he could consult. Quinn made a U-turn and hoped that the soldiers did not follow him.

When Quinn arrived at the Bay Reef the sun had almost set and he was in the grip of a mind-numbing depression. Quinn dropped off the rental car with the valet and entered the lobby. Heat and fear had caused him to sweat through his T-shirt. As he walked across the terrazzo floor, he imagined that everyone was staring at him. Quinn jumped when someone touched his elbow.

'Judge Quinn?' asked a heavyset man wearing wire-rimmed glasses and a Hawaiian shirt. Quinn's vision blurred from fatigue. He could not place the man, but he faked a smile.

'Cliff Engel. We met at the ABA convention in Chicago.'

'Oh, right,' Quinn answered, vaguely remembering Engel as someone he'd had lunch with after a committee meeting.

'Been down by the beach?' Engel asked after spotting the top of Quinn's swimming trunks poking out above the waist of his shorts.

'Yes. I'm pretty wiped out,' Quinn added hastily. 'This sun takes it out of you. I thought I'd take a nap.'

'Oh, too bad. I was hoping you'd join Nancy and me for a drink and dinner. We're with the Lyles. You met Gary at the ABA. He's one of my partners.'

'Sorry,' Quinn said, forcing his smile to widen, 'but I'm all in. I'll see you tomorrow, though.'

'Sure thing. I can't wait to hear your talk. Maybe we can have that drink after you speak.'

'Sounds good.'

Engel pumped Quinn's hand and strode off toward the bar. Quinn sagged. When Engel had touched him, Quinn was certain it was a policeman making an arrest. His heart was still beating hard.

Quinn crowded into an elevator with two couples who were speaking French, and stood at the back of the car. He could not wait to get to his room. He planned to take a cold shower and clear his head, then figure out his next step.

Quinn opened the door to his room and froze. Laura was sitting in a chair, looking cool and beautiful in a T-shirt and shorts.

'What . . . what are you doing here?'

Laura laughed. 'You should see your face.'

'I . . . I thought you were in Miami all week.'

'Aren't you glad to see me?' she asked with a grin.

'Of course,' Quinn lied.

Laura stood up and started across the room toward him. Under any other circumstances, Quinn would have been overjoyed to see Laura. Two days ago he had been crushed when she refused to fly with him to this island paradise. Now, the last thing he wanted was to find Laura in his hotel room, and the thought that she might want to make love terrified him.

Laura started to put her arms around Quinn, but he stopped her.

'You're all clean and I'm sweating like a pig,' he said. 'Give me a rain check on that kiss until I've showered.'

Laura sniffed. 'You are a little ripe.'

Quinn faked a laugh and forced a smile. 'So what happened in Miami?'

Laura followed Quinn into the bathroom and told him about her experience while he got ready to shower. He only half listened as Laura told him about Miami. What, he wondered, was he going to tell his wife about his day at the beach, if she asked?

'I was pissed, as you can imagine,' Laura concluded. 'Mort told me to fly home. I was going to, but I thought about you being alone on St. Jerome. I really did feel lousy about ruining your vacation. Fortunately, there was a seat on the early morning flight.'

'Well, that's . . . that's great.'

'What have you been doing all day?'

'I, uh, I rented a car and drove around the island.'

'See anything interesting?'

'Not really. Everyone is pretty poor. Except for the capital, there's not much here. But the resort is great.'

'How's the food, because I'm starved?'

'Good. Why don't you make a reservation for us at the Plantation Room while I shower? It's a four-star restaurant.'

It was seven-thirty. Laura was able to get a reservation at eight. Quinn drew out his shower for as long as possible, using the time to decide how much he could tell Laura about the murder and Andrea. Quinn wanted to confess his infidelity and seek her counsel, but he also wanted to protect her from involvement in his nightmare, and he was terrified of her reaction to what had happened between him and Andrea.

By the time Quinn finished shaving, it was time to eat. Many of the attorneys who were enrolled in the seminar were eating in the Plantation Room and several of them recognized Quinn from American Bar Association functions. After dinner, Quinn and Laura found themselves barhopping in Puerta del Sol with Cliff Engel, Gary Lyle, their wives and two other couples. Quinn was glad to be hijacked. Laura and Cliff Engel got into a discussion about real estate transactions and Quinn was able to use the time to think about what he should do while the others became more rowdy from drink.

It was two in the morning when Quinn and Laura stumbled into their hotel room. Laura was mildly intoxicated. Quinn had hardly touched any of the drinks that had been thrust upon him. He was afraid of what he might say or do if he got drunk.

'Gary Lyle is a horse's ass,' Laura said as she collapsed on the bed fully clothed, 'but I like his friend Cliff.'

'He seemed okay,' Quinn answered as he shucked his jacket and sat down on the edge of the bed to take off his shoes.

Laura sat up and draped an arm across her husband's shoulders.

'You were quiet tonight.'

'Was I? I'm just tired, I guess.'

Laura leaned into Quinn. She slipped her hand inside his shirt and ran it slowly back and forth across his chest.

'Not too tired, I hope.'

Before Quinn could answer, Laura's lips were melting onto his. Laura pressed Quinn onto his back and finished unbuttoning his shirt. Then she slid down the straps of her dress and shrugged it off. Quinn's throat was dry. It had been so long since Laura had initiated sex.

Laura slid out of her bra and panties. Her breasts were high and firm and her skin was the color of cream. She sank to her knees between Quinn's legs and unzipped his pants. He did not move as she slid them down his legs, then did the same with his underpants. He closed his eyes and began to swim in sensation. There was a feeling of silk on skin as Laura slid against him and up the length of his body. He could smell her hair. He could taste her lips and her tongue. Then he saw Andrea's face frozen in terror as she burst from the sea.

Quinn's eyes opened. He was sweating. He held Laura tightly. Laura could not hear Andrea's scream, but she must have heard the rapid beat of his heart, because she pulled back and looked at Quinn.

'What's wrong?'

Quinn did not answer. He sat up and put his feet on the floor. His breathing was ragged. Laura's eyes widened. She was afraid that Quinn was having a heart attack.

'Are you all right?'

Quinn needed to confess, to unburden himself. But how could he talk to Laura about the things that had happened in the cove? The bed moved as she slipped to the floor in front of Quinn and took his hands in hers. She looked so concerned. Quinn saw with crystal clarity that this was the pivotal moment in their marriage. Laura was his wife, but for months he had not been certain that she loved him. If she did, they would ride out this tragedy together. If she did not, his confession could sever the slender thread that bound them together.

Laura squeezed his hand. 'Dick?'

Quinn could not keep his terror and despair inside any longer. He needed help and he prayed that Laura was the person to turn to for it.

'Something happened today,' Quinn managed. 'Something very bad. I . . . I was with a woman.'

'What?'

'She was someone I met on the plane. She sat next to me on the flight from New York. Her name was Andrea Chapman. She's dead. She was murdered.'

Laura stared at Quinn, too stunned to speak. Quinn focused on the floor as he told Laura about Andrea's invitation to spend the day at the Cove of Lost Souls. Then Quinn told Laura how Andrea died.

'One minute she was there, then she was gone. I thought she was playing a game until she screamed.' Quinn shook his head to rid himself of the image. 'I tried to save her. I dove down and grabbed the diver's arm, but I swallowed water and I had to come up for air. I was choking.' Quinn paused. He was having trouble breathing, as if he were underwater again. 'When I dove the second time, Andrea and the diver were almost out of sight. When I went under the third time, they were gone.'

'Have you told the police?'

'No. I was afraid.'

'Of what?'

'Andrea talked about drugs. She said the police are corrupt. That they work with drug dealers. The killing could be drug related. And . . .'

Quinn's voice trailed off. Laura studied him.

'Did anything happen between the two of you, Dick?'

Quinn did not answer. His head hung lower.

'Did you . . . were you . . . intimate?' Laura asked, using this bland term because it provided a barrier between her feelings and her fear.

'We didn't . . . It never got that far,' Quinn answered, his voice barely above a whisper.

'How far did it get?'

Quinn tried to answer the question, but he could not. Laura stood up and walked away from the bed.

'I don't know what happened,' Quinn told her without conviction. His eyes begged for forgiveness, but he did not see any give in Laura's rigid features.

'It was just a kiss. We . . . we only touched one time.'

Quinn wanted to tell her that nothing would have happened, that he would have remained faithful, but the lie died unspoken.

Laura paced back and forth. Quinn felt smaller and smaller as each moment passed in silence. Laura sat in a chair near the window. She was thinking like an attorney so she would not have to think like a woman.

'How certain are you that you can't be connected to the murder?' Laura asked.

'I don't know. I don't think my fingerprints are on anything, but I can't be certain. Even if they are, the St. Jerome Police won't have the technology to match them unless I become a suspect.'

'Were there any witnesses? Anyone who knows that you were with this woman?'

'I don't think so.'

Quinn told Laura about the soldiers in the jeep and the people in the village.

'But they didn't see me with Andrea. I did sit next to her on the plane. Another passenger may have heard us make plans to meet, but I doubt it.'

'How certain are you about the corruption on St. Jerome?'

'Andrea was pretty emphatic about it. I have heard other things. One of the organizers of the conference made some remarks while we were talking.'

'Given what you know about the government of St. Jerome, I think going to the authorities would be a mistake, especially now that you've waited to come forward. That looks very suspicious. If you went to the police, you wouldn't be able to tell them anything, anyway.'

'You're right. I'm not even sure of the sex of the diver.'

'If this came out, you being with this . . . this woman in the cove, the murder. If you became a suspect . . . The effect on your career would be devastating.'

'Then, you think I should say nothing?'

'It's a gamble. There's no telling when the body will be discovered. With luck, you'll be back home and no one will connect you to the crime.'

'Thank you, Laura.'

'Don't thank me,' Laura answered harshly. 'I'm doing this for me as much as for you. Do you think I want to be involved in your sordid affair or with the police?'

Laura walked over to the desk and picked up the phone.

'What are you doing?'

'I'm going to get a seat on the next flight back to Portland.'

'Don't leave me. Please. I need you.'

'You should have thought about that when you cheated on me.'

'Don't do this, Laura. I love you. We need to discuss this calmly.'

'We do, but I am not calm now. I am very, very angry, and I need some time away from you to think about what I want to do. We can talk when you get back. Right now, I can't stand the sight of you.'

Fifteen

QUINN'S PLANE landed in Portland at eight-thirty Friday evening. Laura knew his flight number and the time of arrival, but she was not waiting for him. Quinn found a taxi.

There were lights on in the house when the cab arrived at Hereford Farms. Quinn paid the driver and carried his suitcases to the front door. Laura opened it before he could ring the bell. She was wearing dark jeans and a black turtleneck. Her hair was combed, but she wore no makeup. There were circles under Laura's eyes and her complexion was paler than usual. He forced a smile, but Laura did not return it.

'We have to talk,' Laura said without any preliminaries.

Quinn left his bags in the hall and followed Laura into the living room. She sat in an armchair and Quinn took the couch.

'You don't know what you've done to me,' she said.

'Laura, I . . .'

'No. Let me say this.' She looked down. Her hands were clasped so tightly in her lap that her knuckles were white where the blood was cut off. 'I trusted you completely. You have no idea how hard that is for me. I know we've had trouble. I know I'm not the easiest person to live with. But I was certain that I could trust you.'

Laura's eyes began to tear and she swiped at the drops angrily. Quinn was shocked. Laura never cried. The sight of his wife in tears made Quinn sick. 'You don't know how difficult it was for me to fall in love with you. I swore that I would never give myself to a man the way my mother did.'

Laura shook her head, too choked with anger to go on. Quinn watched helplessly, knowing that there was nothing he could say.

'I don't want to live with you.'

'You want a divorce?' Quinn asked incredulously.

'I haven't thought that far. What I do want is to be alone for a while.'

'Can't you forgive me? Don't you see how sorry I am? I love you, Laura.'

'I don't know that. Right now, I don't want to be around you. I've made up the bed in the guest room. You can stay here until you've found somewhere else to live.'

Quinn was desperate.

'Don't do this. Don't destroy our marriage.'

Laura's head snapped up.

'Don't you dare put this off on me. No one made you go with that woman.'

Quinn could see that Laura was so angry that nothing he said would change her mind.

'I'll get an apartment for a while,' he said softly. 'Whatever you want, as long as you promise me you'll think about what we have. No matter what I've done, I still love you and I don't want our marriage to end.'

Part Three

Hell Week

Sixteen

IT WAS ALMOST THREE when Quinn signed in with the guard at the front desk of the Multnomah County Courthouse on the Sunday afternoon following his return from St. Jerome, then took the elevator to his chambers on the fifth floor. He was depressed and a little hung over, having had way too much to drink the night before. Quinn rarely drank excessively, but Laura would not take his calls and his small apartment with its ugly rented furniture had gotten him down.

Quinn hung up his raincoat and put on a pot of coffee. He was in for a solid afternoon of legal research and he hoped the caffeine would clear the cobwebs from his brain. The pretrial hearing in *State v. Crease* was set to start Monday afternoon. The defense had filed several motions. Quinn's ruling on three of them would have a significant impact on the trial. Mary Garrett was asking Quinn to suppress all of the evidence found during the search of the crime scene that had been made a week after the shootings. Ellen Crease's defense attorney was also asking Quinn to suppress certain statements as hearsay.

The State had filed only one motion of importance. Mary Garrett wanted to introduce evidence concerning Martin Jablonski's prior crimes. Cedric Riker opposed the introduction of this evidence.

Quinn organized the materials relating to each motion into a separate pile while he waited for the coffee to perk. When the coffee was ready, Quinn filled a mug and started reading the memos relating to the motion to suppress the evidence found at the crime scene. Three hours later, he was slogging through the police reports detailing Martin Jablonski's criminal history so he would have a better idea of how to handle the district attorney's motion. He finished deciphering Portland Police Officer J. Brademas's handwritten account of a six-year-old, extremely violent, home burglary and was about to start Officer K. Raptis's report of an older liquor store holdup when he heard the phone ringing in the outer office and saw one of his lines flashing.

'Hello.'

'Is this Richard Quinn?'

'Yes.'

'My name is Kyle Fletcher. I'm a detective in Missing Persons.' Quinn straightened up, suddenly alert. 'I'm looking into the disappearance of a woman named Andrea Chapman. Does that name ring a bell?'

Quinn's heart rate accelerated.

'Judge Quinn, you there?'

'Uh, yes. I was just thinking,' Quinn said to stall for time while he tried to figure out why a policeman was calling him about Andrea.

'This woman disappeared last week while she was vacationing on the Caribbean island of St. Jerome. You were there the same time she was.'

'That's right. I was speaking at a legal seminar.'

Quinn wanted to forget about St. Jerome. His failure to tell the police about Andrea's murder haunted him Detective Fletcher's call gave Quinn a chance to tell someone about the terrible thing that had happened in the cove.

'I believe Miss Chapman sat next to you on the flight from New York to the island. I got your name from the manifest.' Quinn heard a deep sigh. 'I'm stuck here calling everyone in first class. Then it's on to economy. If you could tell me what you remember about her, it would be a help.'

Quinn wanted to tell the truth, but he was afraid. So much time had passed. If he confessed to witnessing the murder now, he had no idea of the consequences.

'Okay. Now I know whom you're talking about. I didn't remember her name. The woman who sat next to me on the flight from New York to St. Jerome designed belts. She was wearing a very attractive belt that she'd designed for some collection.'

'That's her. What did you two talk about?'

'Not a lot. The type of things you discuss with a seat companion on a flight. I was reading a book for part of the time.'

'Just what you remember.'

'I believe she mentioned that she was flying back from a show for leather suppliers in Bologna, Italy. We talked about her job. That's about all I remember, except that she didn't like flying, but she had to because of her work.'

'Did she tell you her plans on St. Jerome?'

Quinn was sweating. This was his last chance to tell Fletcher what had happened, but he could not do it.

'She was going to stay at a friend's villa,' Quinn said. 'I don't remember his name.'

'That fits in with what I have so far. Did she mention someone she was going to meet or someone she knew on the island?'

Quinn felt sick and he hoped that his voice did not betray him.

'I don't remember her saying she was going to meet anyone. I got the impression that she just wanted to relax.'

'Is there anything else you can recall?'

'No. I think that's it.'

'Say, did you see her after the flight? On the island?'

Quinn froze. 'What was that?' he asked to cover his hesitation. 'You faded out there for a moment.'

'Sorry. Must be my line here. I asked if you saw Miss Chapman after you landed. Maybe at your hotel?'

'No. Not after the airport.'

'Okay. Well, thanks.'

Quinn knew that he should hang up, but he could not help asking, 'Uh, what happened? I mean, what do you think happened? She seemed like a nice person.'

'What we know for sure is that the day after she

landed she went to the beach late in the afternoon. We think she might have planned to meet someone, because she took two sets of snorkeling gear. However, the local police questioned the servants and she never said anything to them about meeting anyone.

'The St. Jerome Police tell me that there are lots of safe beaches on the island. Then you get some with real strong currents. A person could be swept out to sea. They get a tourist drowning every couple of years. There's warnings posted, but people don't listen. The locals think that's what happened.'

'And you? Is that what you think?'

'No reason to think otherwise. Except, of course, there's the extra snorkeling gear. The cops did find her blanket and stuff along with one set of equipment, not two. And the cove where they found this stuff, it's supposed to be safe. Then, again, there have been several reported disappearances in it over the years. So who knows? Anyway, thanks for your time, Judge. I'll let you get back to your work.'

Quinn hung up. His hands were sweaty and he was breathing hard. He had just lied to a police detective. If he was ever linked to Andrea . . . But he wouldn't be. If they knew that he was the person that Andrea was meeting, the detective would have questioned him further. Or would he? What if they did know and the conversation was a trap? The conversation could have been taped. He was getting a headache. Quinn stroked his temples. He should have told the detective what he knew, but anything he said would incriminate him. He could not call back, anyway, he suddenly realized. The detective had not left his phone number or the city he was calling from.

The call from the detective had drained Quinn of energy. He went into the bathroom in his chambers and took two aspirin. While he was washing them down, he saw his reflection in the mirror. He looked pale and shaken. Since his return from the island, the murder had taken on a dreamlike quality. Andrea still haunted his dreams, but her features were blurring and there were times when Quinn did not think about St. Jerome at all. The detective's call had made Quinn relive the horror in the cove and the cowardly way that he had dealt with it.

Seventeen

[1]

THE ATTORNEYS were raring to go when Quinn took the bench Monday afternoon to hear the motions in *State v. Crease*. Cedric Riker looked bright-eyed and dressed for success. He was always most excited when the gallery was full and the press was in attendance. Mary Garrett looked intense. She was wearing a gray pinstriped suit that was all business.

It was Ellen Crease whom Quinn studied most intently. Her black dress reflected a somber mood, but she seemed unafraid. Crease did not slump in her seat or look down as Frederick Gideon had. From the moment Quinn took the bench she sat square-shouldered and straight-backed, coolly confident and self-assured.

Quinn let his eyes rest on Crease for a moment too long. She sensed the judge's interest and turned her head toward him. Quinn colored and looked down at a pleading on the dais. He recovered his composure just as Lamar Hoyt, Jr., entered the courtroom. Quinn saw Junior smirk at Crease, who flushed with anger, held his stare long enough to let him know that she was not intimidated, then turned her attention to the proceedings. Just before she did, Quinn noticed Ryan Clark sitting in the back of the courtroom. Quinn had met Benjamin Gage's administrative assistant at a Republican fund-raiser. Quinn was not surprised to see Clark, given Gage's interest in the outcome of Crease's case.

'Good morning, Counsel, Senator,' Quinn said. 'For the record, this is the time set to discuss the motions filed by the parties in this case. Am I correct that only the motion to suppress the evidence found in Senator Crease's bedroom will require me to hear witnesses and that I'll be deciding Ms. Garrett's hearsay objections to the testimony of Karen Fargo and Conchita Jablonski after reading the briefs and affidavits you have submitted?'

'That's correct, Your Honor,' Mary Garrett said. Riker nodded his agreement.

'Why don't you state your positions? Then we'll hear the witnesses in the motion to suppress.'

Riker sat down and pulled a legal pad in front of him.

'We are asking the Court to suppress all of the evidence obtained as a result of the warrantless search of my client's bedroom by Detective Anthony and Gary Yoshida of the crime lab after the crime scene was released back to my client,' Garrett told Quinn.

'I want to be clear on this,' Quinn interrupted. 'As I

understand it, you have no objection to the introduction of any evidence found in the bedroom on the evening of the murder?'

'That's correct,' Garrett responded. 'The police were legally on the premises at that time. The bedroom was a crime scene, there were two dead bodies present. The situation changed when the bedroom was released back to Senator Crease. After that point, it became incumbent on the authorities to obtain a warrant to search the bedroom.'

'I'm with you. Now, why don't you think the search was legal?'

'The obvious reason is that the search was conducted without a warrant when the police had adequate time to obtain one. Our second point is that James Allen, the houseman, was coerced into opening the locked bedroom for the police. Finally, even if he was not coerced, Mr. Allen had no authority to let the police into his employer's locked bedroom.'

'Thank you, Ms. Garrett,' Quinn said as he made some notes. 'Mr. Riker?'

Riker stood slowly, then paused for effect before shaking his head.

'Your Honor, this whole motion is a ridiculous waste of time. There is a well-recognized exception to the warrant requirement that permits the police to search without a warrant if emergency conditions make an immediate warrantless search necessary to prevent the destruction of evidence. If Detective Anthony and Officer Yoshida had waited to search the bedroom, the most important evidence in this case would have been destroyed.

'Even if exigent circumstances did not exist, the entry into the bedroom was perfectly legal. The defendant was in eastern Oregon campaigning. In her absence, Mr. Allen was in charge of the house. He had authority to let people into the bedroom and he let Detective Anthony and Officer Yoshida into the bedroom willingly. The courts have long recognized that third parties may give binding consent to officials to search the premises of a defendant and seize evidence found inside the premises. This is an exception to the requirement that the police obtain a warrant before searching and to the requirement that the person searching have probable cause to believe there is evidence of a crime in the place searched.'

'As I understand it,' Quinn said, 'it's the position of the defense that the person who gave consent did not have the actual authority to give it.'

'We disagree with that assertion, but it would make no difference if the defense was correct, Your Honor. Even if Mr. Allen did not have actual authority to let the officers into the bedroom, he appeared to have that authority. As the Court knows, if a police officer has a reasonable belief that a person has authority to consent to a search, a warrantless search will be legal, even if it turns out that the officer was mistaken.'

'Okay. Why don't you call your first witness, Ms. Garrett?'

'Senator Crease calls James Allen, Your Honor.'

James Allen took the oath and sat in the witness box. He looked uneasy.

'Mr. Allen, how are you employed?'

'I work . . . worked for Mr. Lamar Hoyt as his house-man until his death. I am now employed in that same capacity for your client, Ms. Crease.'

'Do you remember the time, several days after Mr. Hoyt was murdered, when Detective Anthony and an Officer Yoshida came to the estate and told you that they wanted to reenter the master bedroom?'

'Yes, ma'am.'

'Did either gentleman show you a search warrant?'

'No.'

'What reason did they give you for wishing to look at the room?'

'Detective Anthony told me that there were loose ends in the investigation that needed to be tied up and that they had to look at the bedroom again to do that. He was never very specific.'

'Where was Senator Crease on that day?'

'She was campaigning in eastern Oregon.'

'What did you tell Detective Anthony when he asked to look in the bedroom?'

'I told him that Ms. Crease had given me strict orders to let no one into the bedroom except the cleaning people, who were coming the next day.'

'What happened when you told Detective Anthony that you had strict orders not to let anyone but the cleaners into the bedroom?'

'He said that Ms. Crease couldn't have meant to keep out the police. He said she probably just wanted to keep reporters out.'

'What happened next?'

'I told the detective that he was probably right, but I

didn't feel that I could let him in without speaking to Ms. Crease, so I tried to get in touch with her at her hotel in Pendleton. Unfortunately, she was not in.'

'What happened after you told the detective that you couldn't reach Senator Crease?'

Allen looked nervous. He licked his lips. 'Uh, well, at that point, Detective Anthony became quite agitated. He reminded me that he was investigating Mr. Hoyt's murder and said that any evidence in the room would be destroyed by the cleaners if I waited to talk to Ms. Crease before letting them into the room.'

'You said that Detective Anthony grew agitated when you refused to let him into the bedroom. Please describe his demeanor.'

'His tone grew sharp and he leaned very close to me. He was quite insistent.'

'What did you do after his demeanor changed?'

'I . . . I didn't want to impede the investigation, so I gave Detective Anthony the key to the bedroom.'

'Thank you, Mr. Allen. Your witness, Counselor.'

Riker stood up and walked over to James Allen.

'Good morning, Mr. Allen,' he said in a tone that lacked sincerity. Allen nodded.

'It's in your best interest to say things that help the defendant, isn't it?'

'Pardon me, sir?' Allen asked, clearly offended by the question.

'The defendant pays your salary. You're dependent on her for your living, for the roof over your head?'

'I have testified to the truth, Mr. Riker,' Allen answered with great dignity.

'Certainly. But what I've said is true, is it not?'

Allen started to say something, then thought better of it and ended by answering, 'Yes,' tersely.

Riker opened a thick folder and reviewed some papers. He selected one of them and looked up at the witness.

'Mr. Allen, have you ever been convicted of a crime?'

Allen paled and answered, 'Yes,' in a shaky voice.

'What crime was that?'

'Man . . . manslaughter.'

'You stabbed a man to death in a bar fight, did you not?'

Allen looked like he was going to be sick.

'Please instruct Mr. Allen to answer, Your Honor,' Riker asked the Court.

'Please answer the question,' Quinn instructed the witness.

'That is true,' Allen answered.

'Did you know about this?' Garrett whispered to Crease.

'Yes, but I forgot. It's ancient history. James is gay. When he was eighteen, two men attacked him. They were gay bashing. James had a knife and he fought them off. Lamar said that it would have been self-defense, but James ran the men down after they quit the fight and killed one of them. He gave James a break when he got out of prison and hired him. He hasn't been in trouble since.'

'You're the housekeeper at the Hoyt estate, right?' Riker asked Allen.

'Yes.'

'When Mr. Hoyt and the defendant were away, you were in charge of the house, weren't you?'

'Yes.'

'That's why you had the keys to all the rooms, including the bedroom?'

'Yes.'

'And you could go into any room in the house to clean or to get something, right?'

'Yes.'

'In fact, it was part of your duties to let people, like the cleaners, into various rooms in the house, including the bedroom, when Mr. Hoyt and the defendant were away?'

'Yes.'

'Mr. Allen, did you like Mr. Hoyt?'

'Yes, sir.'

'You'd worked for him for more than twenty years?'

'Yes.'

'And you wanted his killer brought to justice?'

'Yes.'

'How did you feel when Detective Anthony told you that keeping him and Officer Yoshida out of the bedroom might lead to the destruction of evidence that could prove who killed Mr. Hoyt?'

'I . . . Well, I didn't want to be responsible for something like that.'

'So you wanted the officers to enter that bedroom, didn't you?'

'I . . . I guess . . . Yes. I wanted to help.'

'Thank you, Mr. Allen,' Riker said before turning away from the witness and returning to his seat. Quinn noted Riker's satisfied smile and the brief look of concern on Garrett's face.

'If I might, Your Honor,' Garrett said.

'Certainly.'

'Mr. Allen, your instructions from Senator Crease were quite explicit, were they not? Didn't she tell you to keep the bedroom locked and let no one but the cleaners into it?'

'Those were my instructions.'

'She did not tell you to make an exception for the police, did she?'

'No.'

'You made it clear to the officers what your instructions were?'

'Yes.'

'And when you refused Detective Anthony admission, that is when he became agitated, sharp with you and demanding?'

'Yes.'

'Did his tone have anything to do with your decision to give him the bedroom key?'

'Well, he was a policeman and he seemed very upset with me. I didn't feel that I could refuse him.'

'Nothing further.'

Riker was already on his feet. 'Mr. Allen, did the defendant give you specific instructions to keep the police out of the bedroom?'

'No.'

'So you never discussed with the defendant what you should do if a policeman came to the house and needed access to the bedroom so he could try to secure evidence that would help find Lamar Hoyt's murderer?'

'No.'

'Before you gave Detective Anthony the key, did you try to figure out what the defendant would have told you if you had been successful in talking to her in Pendleton?'

'I . . . Yes, I did.'

'Was it your impression that the defendant wanted her husband's killer found?'

'Most assuredly.'

'So you concluded that she would never want to impede the investigation, didn't you? That she would have gladly allowed the police access to that bedroom if it would help find her husband's killer?'

Allen looked down and answered, 'Yes,' in a tone so low that Quinn had trouble hearing him.

'And that was why you gave Detective Anthony the key, wasn't it? Not because he grew sharp with you, but because you realized that his agitation stemmed from his desire to solve the murder of your employer of twenty years? Isn't that so?'

'I . . . I guess . . . Yes, that had a lot to do with it.'

'Thank you, Mr. Allen,' Riker said with a self-satisfied smile.

Quinn asked Mary Garrett if she had any other questions for the witness. Garrett thought about trying to rehabilitate Allen, but she realized that the damage had already been done. She dismissed the witness. Allen took a seat in the back of the courtroom. He looked very upset.

'How bad were we hurt?' Crease asked in a whisper.

'Riker did a good job. We can argue that Allen was bullied into consenting to the search, but Riker can argue that he was only doing what he thought was best and that he had concluded that you would have consented, too.'

'Would it do any good to call me as a witness?' Crease asked. 'I definitely told Jim to keep the bedroom locked, except to let in the cleaners.'

'Riker would ask you if you intended to keep out police officials who were trying to solve the murder of your husband,' Garrett answered. 'We both know how you would answer that question.'

'Any more witnesses, Ms. Garrett?' Quinn asked.

'No, Your Honor.'

'Then let's hear from your people, Mr. Riker.'

'The State calls Lou Anthony, Your Honor.'

The bailiff went into the hall and returned with the detective. The bailiff gave Anthony the oath, then motioned him toward the witness box. Quinn thought that the detective seemed very uncomfortable and the judge noticed that the witness avoided looking at Ellen Crease.

'Detective Anthony, are you the detective in charge of the investigation into the death of Lamar Hoyt?' Riker asked after establishing Anthony's background in police work.

'Yes, sir.'

'Were you at the crime scene on the evening of January seventh?'

'Yes, sir.'

'Did you interview the defendant and speak to the medical examiner, forensic experts and other investigators?'

'Yes, sir.'

'What conclusion did you come to about the defendant's responsibility for the death of her husband and Martin Jablonski on the evening of the shooting?'

'On the evening of January seventh, I concluded that a burglar, who we later learned was an ex-convict named Martin Jablonski, had broken into the home of Mr. Hoyt and the defendant to commit a burglary and had shot Mr. Hoyt during its commission. I also concluded that the defendant shot and killed Mr. Jablonski to protect herself.'

'Did you believe that Mr. Jablonski was working alone?'

'At that time, yes.'

'Did you later suspect that Mr. Jablonski had been hired to break into the Hoyt estate and shoot Mr. Hoyt?'

'Yes.'

'What caused you to form that opinion?'

'During a search of Mr. Jablonski's apartment, I found ten thousand dollars that his wife said Jablonski received shortly before the break-in.'

'Subsequent to learning about the ten thousand dollars, did you become aware of evidence that called into question the defendant's version of the shooting?'

'Yes, sir. Gary Yoshida, a forensic expert in our crime lab, told me that blood spatter evidence at the crime scene contradicted the defendant's version of the way the shooting occurred.'

'When did Officer Yoshida tell you about the blood spatter evidence?'

'On January 14, a week after the shooting.'

'Did Officer Yoshida tell you he needed to visit the crime scene to confirm his suspicions about the blood spatter evidence?'

'Yes. He said that he had to see the scene in three dimensions. His initial conclusions were drawn from examinations of photographs and he felt that wasn't good enough.'

'When Officer Yoshida informed you that he needed to see the bedroom again to confirm his suspicions about the blood spatter, did you drive to the estate immediately?'

'Yes.'

'Why did you go so quickly?'

'It had been a while since the murder and we had just turned the scene back to the defendant. We were both worried that the scene had been altered. I felt time was of the essence.'

'What happened at the estate?'

'Mr. Allen, the housekeeper, let us in. He told us that the bedroom was going to be cleaned the next day. I asked for his consent to enter the bedroom with Officer Yoshida so we could find any evidence that might exist before the cleaners destroyed it. He gave his consent and we conducted our investigation.'

'Why didn't you get a search warrant for the bedroom?'

'There wasn't any reason to do that. We are taught about the law of search and seizure at the Police Academy and we get updates from time to time. It has always been my understanding that a warrant is not necessary if someone with the authority to give it consents to a search of the premises.'

'Did you believe that Mr. Allen had the authority to consent to your entry into the bedroom?'

'Yes, sir. He was the housekeeper. He had the key. The defendant was away campaigning. He was the only one home.'

'No further questions. Thank you, Detective.'

'What's your take on Anthony? Is he an honest cop?' Garrett asked Crease in a whisper.

Crease thought about the question before answering. Then she leaned close to her attorney.

'Lou's a straight arrow. He won't lie.'

Garrett looked at the witness.

'As I understand your testimony, Detective, you and Officer Yoshida went to the Hoyt estate, James Allen met you, you told him you wanted to enter the bedroom, he said that was great and he took you upstairs and let you in. Do I have that right?'

'No, ma'am. That is not what happened.'

Garrett looked astonished. 'Oh! What part do I have wrong?'

'When I first asked Mr. Allen if Officer Yoshida and I could go into the bedroom, he wasn't sure that he could let us in.'

'In fact, he specifically told you, did he not, that the room was locked and that Senator Crease had instructed him to unlock the room only for the cleaners?'

'Yes, ma'am.'

'Did you take "no" for an answer?'

'No, because the defendant had no reason to believe we would need to take a second look at the room when she left for eastern Oregon. I assumed that she wouldn't want to block a police investigation.'

'Well, Detective, weren't you also assuming at this time that Senator Crease may have hired Martin Jablonski to kill her husband?'

'That was a theory.'

'If that was true, she would have every reason to impede a police investigation, wouldn't she?'

Anthony hesitated before answering, 'I guess so.'

'And every reason to want to forbid you access to the crime scene.'

Anthony did not know what to say.

'I'll assume your lack of response constitutes agreement, Detective,' Garrett said.

'Objection,' said Riker, who was obviously upset by the course of Garrett's examination. 'Detective Anthony did not just agree. Ms. Garrett is putting words in his mouth.'

'Sustained,' Quinn said. 'Detective, we need a yes or no for the record.'

Anthony looked helpless. Finally, he answered, 'I guess she would have a reason to deny us access to the room if she was the killer.'

Garrett's lips twitched. It was bad form to grin in court when you scored points, so she had to suppress a big smile.

'It is true, is it not, that Mr. Allen tried to reach Senator Crease by phone to see if she would agree to let you in the room, but he was unable to talk to her?'

'Yes.'

'He then reiterated to you that his instructions were to keep everyone but the cleaners out of the room?'

'Yes.'

'That upset you, didn't it?'

'I wasn't upset.'

'You didn't become agitated and raise your voice?'

'I . . . I was concerned about the cleaners and I was certain that . . . I mean, well, it seemed to me that Senator Crease would have let us in if she was asked. That she wouldn't have objected to the police going in.'

'Even though you just said that she had every reason to keep out the police if she was a murderer?'

'I . . . Honestly, that didn't go through my mind, about her refusing.'

'You just wanted to get into the room?'

'Yes.'

'So you applied pressure to Mr. Allen.'

'No.'

'You didn't lean into him?'

'I may have.'

'You didn't sound annoyed?'

'I . . . That may be so. I was concerned.'

'You made Mr. Allen change his mind, did you not?'

'He changed his mind. I couldn't force him. I didn't. It was his decision.'

'You're telling Judge Quinn that you didn't use your authority as a policeman and your size to intimidate Mr. Allen?'

'No. It wasn't that way.'

Garrett hesitated for a moment. Then she said, 'No further questions, Your Honor.'

Quinn studied the detective. He sounded a little desperate, but he also sounded like an honest cop. The judge did not doubt that Anthony had applied some pressure to Allen to convince him to change his mind, but it made a difference if the detective simply used his powers of persuasion as opposed to coercing the housekeeper to open the bedroom door. However, the line between persuasion and coercion could be very thin when the person who wants a result is a police officer.

'Our next witness will take a while, Your Honor,' Cedric Riker said. 'This might be a good time to break.'

'Who is the witness?'

'Officer Yoshida. He'll be explaining the basis for probable cause and talking about the exigent circumstances.'

'All right. Let's break for the day. I'll see everyone at nine in the morning.'

[2]

Quinn did not want to go back to his barren apartment, so he stayed in his chambers to work on cases that he had not been able to get to because of *State v. Crease.* The corridors of the courthouse were deserted when Quinn turned out the lights in his chambers and locked the door shortly before seven. The courthouse floors were marble and the ceilings were high. The slightest noise was magnified. At night, the silence in the darkened halls was eerie. Quinn walked down the corridor. The elevators were around the corner. When he was almost at the end of the hall, Quinn paused. He thought he heard a footfall. He stopped to listen, but the hall was silent. Maybe a security guard was walking rounds on the floor below. Sound carried in odd ways in an empty building at night.

Quinn turned the corner. There was a bank of two elevators on either side of the wide marble stairs. Just as the judge pressed the Down button to summon one a scraping sound made Quinn's breath catch in his chest. He stepped away from the elevators and peered down the deserted hallway in both directions. Quinn jumped, then sagged, startled by the bell that signaled the arrival of the elevator.

Quinn took the car to the lobby. The empty courthouse had spooked him and the dark, deserted streets looked threatening. The rain had stopped, but a stiff wind forced Quinn to turn up the collar of his raincoat. He hurried along the three blocks between the courthouse and the garage where the county rented parking spaces for the judges.

During the ride home, Quinn tried to think about the evidence he had heard, but he found himself thinking about Laura and how lonely he would be all evening. Quinn decided to call Laura as soon as he got home. Maybe she was ready to talk about their future.

Quinn opened his door and turned on the light. He shut and locked the door. A man in a black ski mask, turtleneck and jeans stepped out of the judge's bedroom and pointed a gun at Quinn.

'Stay calm,' the man said. 'I'm not here to hurt you or rob you, but I will hurt you if you don't do as you're told. If you're smart, I'll be gone in a few minutes and you'll be just fine. Do you understand me?'

'Yes,' Quinn answered, trying to keep his tone neutral so the gunman would not hear how frightened he was.

The intruder gestured toward a chair that stood in front of a low coffee table.

'Sit down.'

Quinn did as he was told.

'How did Andrea Chapman die?' the man asked.

'I told the police that I don't know anything about that.'

The man reached behind his back and pulled a manila envelope out of his waistband. He tossed it onto the coffee table.

'Open it,' he commanded.

Quinn raised the flap.

'Now, take out the photographs.'

Quinn removed three 8 ½ by 11 black-and-white photographs. All three shots showed Quinn and Andrea Chapman in the Cove of Lost Souls. Quinn's stomach rolled. The man pulled back the hammer of the gun and pointed the barrel at Quinn's head. Quinn blanched.

'I repeat, how did Andrea Chapman die?'

'She was murdered,' Quinn stammered.

'Yes, but how was she murdered?'

'Drowning. She was drowned.'

There was a slit for the mouth in the ski mask and Quinn saw the man's lips curl into a cruel grin.

'I hear that drowning is a peaceful way to die once you give in to it. Andrea didn't have it that easy.'

The man paused as if recalling a fond memory. When he spoke again, it was in the tone that confidants use with one another.

'Andrea's skin was smooth and her body was very firm. You would have enjoyed playing with her. I did. Oh, she cried and begged at first, but I soon put an end to that. Do you want to know how?'

This time the man's smile was wide and self-satisfied. Quinn's stomach clenched and bile rose in his throat. The man chuckled.

'Don't go in much for rough foreplay, do you? It's one of my favorite things. After a while Andrea was willing to do anything I asked, even to the point of inventing her own little sex games, to avoid the pain.'

The man paused. He eyed Quinn curiously, holding the judge's gaze the way a hypnotist traps his subject. The smile faded suddenly.

'Unfortunately, I had business to attend to, so I was forced to rape Andrea brutally, several times. Then I selected a very sharp hunting knife and engaged in some creative dismemberment.'

Quinn gagged and fought with all his might to keep from throwing up.

'Don't worry, Judge. You won't have to see any pictures. In fact, if you do as you're told, neither you nor anyone else will ever view my handiwork. But if you disobey me there will be terrible consequences for you.

'Tell me, Judge, what do you think would happen if the St. Jerome Police received an anonymous call telling them where to find the body of Andrea Chapman? What do you think would happen if the St. Jerome Police received copies of these photographs? Did you know that there is an extradition treaty between the United States and St. Jerome? Did you know that hanging is the punishment for murder on St. Jerome?'

Quinn had trouble breathing. He felt as if his body had turned to water.

'What do you want from me?' Quinn managed.

'One thing. If you do that one thing, you'll be safe. If you don't, Andrea Chapman's body will be found, the police will get these pictures and you will rot in a rat-infested prison on St. Jerome until the day you are hanged by the neck in the prison courtyard. Now, ask me what the one thing is.'

Quinn hesitated.

'Come on. You can do it. Ask me how you can save your life.'

'What do you want me to do?'

'Everything in your power to see that Ellen Crease is convicted of the murder of her husband. Once the jury returns a verdict of guilty, Andrea Chapman's body will disappear forever and all copies of the photographs you are holding will be destroyed.'

'I . . . I can't rig the trial. She could be sentenced to death.'

'So could you. Do you have an alibi for the day Andrea

died? Can you explain where you went in your rented car?' The man walked over to Quinn and held out his hand. 'Please hand me the photographs, Judge.'

Quinn's hand shook as he picked up the pictures. The man took them and walked to the front door.

'You know what you have to do to save your life. Keep your mouth shut, do it, and you'll survive.'

The door closed and the man was gone. Quinn concentrated on fighting the nausea, but it was no good. He raced into the bathroom and threw up several times. Then he collapsed on the bathroom floor. Quinn remembered Andrea's smile, her laugh. An image of her running toward the sea came to him unbidden. Then, superimposed on that vision was an image of her body beaten and mutilated. Quinn squeezed his eyes shut and willed the vision away. He leaned against the bathroom wall and breathed deeply.

After a while Quinn struggled to his feet, cupped his hands and gulped cold water from the tap, then splashed it on his face. He had almost regained his composure when he remembered the call from the detective. Quinn had told him that he had not seen Andrea after he left the airport. The photographs would destroy him.

Quinn went into his kitchen and poured a glass of Scotch, which he drank quickly. The Scotch burned away some of his fear. Quinn took the liquor bottle into the living room, refilled his glass and collapsed on the couch. He reviewed everything that had happened to him since Andrea sat next to him on the plane trip to St. Jerome.

The first thought that occurred to Quinn was chilling. Until this evening, Quinn believed that Andrea Chapman's murder was not connected to him in any way. Now Quinn knew that Andrea Chapman had been killed to set him up. It was the only way to explain what happened to Laura in Miami. The people who wanted Crease convicted had learned about Quinn's trip to St. Jerome. They had lured Laura to Miami with a fat retainer check so they could make certain that the first-class seat next to Quinn would be vacant. He had been played for a fool from the beginning.

[3]

Frank Price eyed Quinn as he let him into the apartment. The judge's tie was loose, his suit coat was rumpled and there were stains on his wrinkled white shirt. His complexion was pasty and there were dark shadows under his eyes.

'For someone who's just been on vacation in a tropical paradise, you don't look so hot.'

'Too much work,' Quinn mumbled without conviction. Price gave him a harder look.

'How are things with you and Laura?' Price asked as he led Quinn into the living room.

'Fine. Everything is fine,' Quinn said.

Only after he answered did it occur to Quinn that Price had asked about the health of his relationship with Laura and not the usual small-talk question about the state of his wife's health. Quinn wondered if Laura had talked to Frank at work. Price was watching him closely.

'We're separated,' Quinn confessed.

Suddenly, Price looked every bit of his eighty years. 'I'm sorry to hear that,' he said.

Quinn heard a slight tremor in Price's voice. Quinn knew that the old man loved him and hoped he would have a good marriage. He could see how much his separation from Laura hurt Frank.

'I'm living in an apartment. It's just temporary.'

'Do you want to talk about it?'

Quinn shook his head. 'We'll work it out. I still love her. I think she loves me.'

'If you need my help I'm always here for you.'

'I know that.'

'I put up some coffee, but you look like you can use something stronger.'

Quinn wanted a glass of Scotch, then thought better of it.

'Coffee will be fine.'

Price carried two mugs of steaming coffee into the living room.

'I came for some information and I need it in confidence,' he told Price.

'Oh?'

Quinn wrapped his large hands around the mug for warmth.

'I'm hearing the pretrial motions in Ellen Crease's case. Do you know her?'

'We've met at political functions and I know people who know her. We're not friends.'

'What about her husband, Lamar Hoyt?'

'He was a major contributor to the Republican Party. I've had dinner with him.'

'Frank, can you think of anyone with a grudge against Ellen Crease? I'm talking about something very serious. Something that would motivate a person to want to hurt Crease very badly.'

Price was clearly uncomfortable.

'This is highly irregular, Dick. This extra-judicial inquiry into the background of a defendant whose case you're hearing. Do you mind telling me what prompted this visit?'

'I . . . I can't explain why I'm here. You're going to have to take it on faith that the information I'm asking for is crucial to a decision I have to make.'

'If you're in some kind of trouble . . . ,' Price started.

'Frank, I know I can trust you. I just can't confide in you.'

'Does this have anything to do with Laura?'

'No,' Quinn lied.

Price hesitated for a moment, but he could see how desperate Quinn looked.

'Ellen Crease has always been confrontational and she's made several political enemies, even in her own party. We never minded her ambition when she was running aggressive campaigns against Democratic opponents, though I, and others, did find her methods objectionable on occasion, but I can tell you that she has not endeared herself to the party by challenging an incumbent Republican senator.'

'How did she get away with going after Gage?'

211

'Crease doesn't feel that she's accountable to anyone. She has a very committed following on the far right and her husband's money.'

'Is there anyone you can think of who would be so upset with Crease that he would try to have her killed?'

'Why do you need to know that?'

'What if the man who broke into the Hoyt mansion came to kill Ellen Crease and not Lamar Hoyt? Crease would be innocent.'

'Dick, do you realize what you're doing? You're a judge, for Christ's sake. You have to remain impartial. You have no business playing detective like this. In fact, you're violating your oath by taking sides in this case.'

'I know that, and I can't explain why I'm asking you these questions. Please, Frank, I need your help.'

'What have you gotten yourself into?'

Quinn looked away. Price was very troubled. For a moment, Quinn worried that he was going to end the meeting. Then Price said, 'There are two people I can think of who would have the motive and personality to do what you're suggesting. Lamar Hoyt, Jr., was a constant source of concern to Lamar since he was a child. He is irresponsible and he has a history of violence. I know of two assault charges that Lamar was able to settle out of court by paying off the complaining witnesses. Junior has been quite vocal about his hatred of his stepmother. I assume you've heard about the will contest?'

Quinn nodded.

'Then, there's Benjamin Gage. Have you heard the rumors about his connection to Otto Keeler's death?'

'I never paid that much attention to them.'

'I have no idea if there's any truth to them, but they won't go away. Gage made his fortune in the computer industry with a company called StarData. Otto Keeler and Gage started the company. For a while, StarData looked like it might take off, but it experienced a serious funding problem. Just when things looked darkest, the StarData building burned down. Otto Keeler was killed in the blaze. Gage assumed total control over the company and he used the millions the company received from Keeler's key man insurance and the fire insurance to help StarData turn the corner financially. The origin of the fire was unquestionably arson and there was no reason anyone uncovered for Keeler sleeping in the building on the evening of the blaze. There was never any evidence connecting Gage to the fire, but the police took a very hard look at him for a long time.'

'Other than Gage and Lamar, Jr., I can't think of anyone else who would have a reason to try to do what you're suggesting.'

Quinn stood. He looked drained and distant. Price gripped Quinn's shoulders.

'Let me help you, Dick.'

Quinn smiled sadly. Then he embraced Price.

'I love you, Frank. But I've got to do this on my own.'

Quinn let Price go and headed for the door.

'If you change your mind . . . ,' Price said.

'I know,' Quinn answered.

Eighteen

'OFFICER YOSHIDA, how are you employed?' Cedric Riker asked.

'I'm a criminalist with the Oregon State Police Forensic Laboratory in Portland.'

'Please give Judge Quinn your academic background.'

Yoshida turned toward Quinn. He had testified in his court on a few occasions and was perfectly relaxed on the witness stand.

'I graduated from Portland State University with a B.S. in chemistry in 1989 and returned to PSU for courses in genetic biology and forensic DNA analysis. From 1989 to 1990, I worked as an analytical chemist. Then, in 1990, I became an Oregon State Police officer assigned to the crime lab.'

'Over the years, have you had training in crime scene investigation and, more specifically, in the analysis of bloodstain patterns?'

'Yes, sir. I attended the Oregon State Medical Examiners' death investigation class in 1990, a blood pattern analysis training program at the Police Academy in 1991, an advanced crime scene training program in 1992, and I completed a basic, intermediate and advanced serology training program in 1992. Over the years, I have read numerous articles in the area and attended many seminars where these subjects were discussed.'

'As part of your duties, do you go to crime scenes and collect evidence?'

'Yes.'

'How many crime scenes have you investigated?'

Yoshida laughed. 'Gosh, I don't know. I never kept a count. It's a lot, though. I investigate several homicides each year. Then, there are other scenes.'

'Okay. Now, were you one of the criminalists who went to the Hoyt estate on the evening that Lamar Hoyt and Martin Jablonski were shot to death?'

'I was.'

'Please describe the scene for Judge Quinn.'

Yoshida left the witness box and walked over to a large diagram of the murder scene that he had prepared. The diagram was resting on an easel.

'The crime scene we are interested in is the master bedroom on the second floor of Mr. Hoyt's mansion. To get to that room, you climb a set of stairs to the second floor, then go down a long corridor in a westerly direction.'

Yoshida picked up a wooden pointer and placed its tip on a section of the drawing that represented the door to the hall.

'The master bedroom itself is a rectangle. The door between the bedroom and the hall is in the east wall at the southeast corner of the bedroom.'

Yoshida moved his pointer to the bathroom doorway.

'The northern wall in the hall is also the south wall of the bathroom. When you enter the bedroom, you can see the bathroom door if you look to your right.'

Yoshida moved the pointer again.

'If you are standing in the doorway and you look directly across the room, you'll see the west wall. A good portion of that wall is a large window with a view of the pool and part of the yard. Halfway between the west and east walls is a king-size bed. The headboard touches the north wall. Directly across from the foot of the bed is an armoire approximately seven feet high. It contains a television and its back touches the south wall. My information from the first officers on the scene and an interview with the houseman, James Allen, is that the lights in the room were off when the crime occurred and that the television was also off.'

'When you entered the crime scene, what did you see?'

Yoshida pointed to a stick figure that had been positioned between the small box that represented the armoire and the slightly larger box that represented the king-size bed.

'The first thing I saw was the body of Martin Jablonski. He was facedown with his feet almost touching the armoire and his head facing the bed. There was a pool of blood under his body approximately ten feet from the foot of the bed and one foot from the west-facing side of the armoire. There was also a .45-caliber handgun lying on the floor near Mr. Jablonski's right hand.'

'Did you determine how Mr. Jablonski was killed?'

'Yes, sir. The defendant told the investigating officers that she shot Mr. Jablonski twice with a Smith & Wesson .38 snubnose loaded with hollow point bullets. When Mr. Jablonski was autopsied, the medical examiner recovered two bullets that had lodged in the body. One was recovered from Mr. Jablonski's head and the other from his torso. They were the type of bullet that the defendant described. Ballistics tests confirmed that the defendant's gun, which was recovered at the scene, fired the two shots.'

'Why didn't the bullets exit the body?' Riker asked.

'Hollow point bullets are designed to stay inside the body so they can bounce around and cause more damage.'

'Did you see another body in the room?'

'Yes, sir. The body of Lamar Hoyt was sprawled on his back on the bed. I was told that he had been shot while in the bed, but that the defendant had been found holding him with his head in her lap. From blood spatter patterns on the headboard and bed, I concluded that Mr. Hoyt was probably sitting up on the east side of the bed when he was shot. Then he fell sideways onto the west side of the bed. The defendant pulled him even further sideways when she sat down and cradled his head.'

'Did ballistics tests identify the .45-caliber handgun found next to Mr. Jablonski as the weapon that was used to kill Lamar Hoyt?'

'Yes.'

'Now, Officer Yoshida, did the defendant explain what happened on the evening of the shooting?'

'Yes, sir. To Detective Anthony.'

'Please tell the Court how the shooting scenario was explained to you.'

'As I understood the defendant's version, she and Mr. Hoyt had engaged in sexual intercourse. The defendant has the side of the bed closest to the window. She stated that after they finished, she got up from the bed, went to the window in the west wall, then crossed in front of the bed and entered the bathroom, turned on the bathroom light and washed up.

'After finishing in the bathroom, she put on her night-gown, turned off the bathroom light and crossed back in front of the bed. She got back in the bed on her side and talked with Mr. Hoyt for a while. As they were talking, the door opened and Mr. Jablonski entered the room. The defendant said she saw that Mr. Jablonski was armed, so she ducked over her side of the bed and secured the .38 that she keeps under it. She heard three shots and came up firing. Mr. Jablonski fell and she turned her attention to her husband, whom she determined to be dead.'

'Officer Yoshida, when you looked at the crime scene on the evening of the shootings, did you see anything that called the defendant's version of the shootings into question?'

Yoshida looked embarrassed.

'The evidence was there. I just didn't pick up on it.'

'What did you conclude on the evening of the crime?'

'That the defendant was telling the truth.'

Yoshida's embarrassment deepened. He looked up at Quinn and tried to explain his failure to correctly interpret the crime scene's story.

'Everyone thought we were dealing with a burglary that went wrong. I mean, Jablonski was dead, there was no question his gun fired the shots that killed Mr. Hoyt. I guess I just assumed there was nothing to look for.'

'Did something happen after the first crime scene investigation that caused you to question your first impression?' Riker asked.

'Yes, sir. I took a second look at the evidence while I was writing my report.'

'When you reexamined the evidence, did you discover something you'd missed the first time around?'

'I did.'

'What was that, Officer Yoshida?'

'I spotted a blood spatter pattern in two of the crime scene photographs that had not made an impression on me when I was at the scene. It made me question the defendant's story of how the shooting of Martin Jablonski occurred.'

'Did you tell Detective Anthony that you had to visit the scene again?'

'Yes. I needed to see everything again in three dimensions to confirm my suspicions.'

'Did you feel time was of the essence?'

'I did. It was already a week since the shooting and I was afraid that the blood pattern would be destroyed or contaminated.'

'Can you explain to the judge what you can tell from blood spatter analysis that is relevant to this case?'

'Certainly,' Yoshida told Riker before addressing the judge. 'If I asked you to tell me what shape a drop of blood takes when it falls straight down, you would probably tell me that it would look like a teardrop, but that is a popular misconception. Actually, falling drops of blood are shaped like a sphere. The type of surface the drop strikes and the angle at which it hits affect the pattern the drop makes when it strikes a surface.

'If a drop of blood falls straight down at a ninety-degree angle it should leave a pattern that looks like a circle. As the degree of the angle changes so that the drop is hitting the surface at an angle that is moving from the vertical to the horizontal, the pattern will become more and more elongated. There is an equation that will give you the angle of impact using measurements of the length and width of the bloodstain. This helps a forensic scientist determine if the victim was standing or sitting when his blood was spattered onto a surface. You can also tell the direction in which the blood was cast by examining the shape of the blood drop after it strikes a surface.'

Yoshida placed blowups of two crime scene photographs on the easel. The first had been taken from the west side of the room shooting back toward the hall. It showed Martin Jablonski's body in front of the armoire. The second photograph was a close-up of the west-facing side of the armoire. Quinn could see a discoloration on the side of the armoire approximately six feet from the floor in the first photograph. In the close-up, the discoloration could clearly be seen as a fine spray of blood.

'When a person is struck with sufficient force to cause blood to spatter, the blood may spatter at low, medium or high velocity,' Yoshida instructed Quinn. 'If I punched you in the nose, the spatter would likely be low-velocity and would not carry very far. If the force is stronger, say because I use an object like a club or a brick, the blow may result in a medium-velocity pattern. Gunshots create high-velocity spatter patterns with an extremely high percentage of very fine blood specks. The result is a mistlike dispersion similar to an aerosol spray. Because of their low mass, these particles seldom travel a horizontal distance of over three or four feet.'

Yoshida put the tip of the pointer on the spatter pattern in the first blowup.

'The first bullet that hit Mr. Jablonski struck him in the right temple. From the high-velocity spatter pattern on the side of the armoire, I conclude that Jablonski was struck by that bullet when he was standing with the right side of his head approximately one foot from the side of the armoire facing directly forward toward the bed. When the bullet struck Mr. Jablonski in the temple area on the right side of his head, his blood sprayed onto the west-facing side of the armoire. He had to be close to the armoire for the blood to spray onto it.

'Now, here is the problem,' Yoshida continued. 'I've lined up the angles. For the bullet to enter Mr. Jablonski's right temple at an angle that would leave the spray pattern on the west-facing side of the armoire, the shot had to come from the bathroom, not the west side of the bed.'

Movement in the corridor outside the courtroom caught Quinn's eye. He turned pale and his breath caught in his chest. The woman who had passed by the door reminded him of Andrea Chapman.

Cedric Riker picked up a brown paper bag and turned to Yoshida. Quinn tried to calm down so he could pay attention to the testimony. The woman could not have been Andrea, Quinn told himself. Andrea Chapman was dead. The woman he saw simply resembled Andrea. She had passed by quickly, the distance between the bench and the corridor was considerable. The glass in the door must have distorted the woman's image. Quinn wrenched his attention back to the testimony.

'Officer Yoshida, I am handing you State's exhibit 113. What is that?'

Yoshida pulled a white nightgown out of the bag. The front was saturated with dried blood, but the back was only covered with a fine spray.

'This is the defendant's nightgown. Lab tests have determined that the blood on the front and back is her husband's.'

'According to the defendant, where was the nightgown when Lamar Hoyt was shot by Mr. Jablonski?'

'She said that she was wearing it.'

'Is the physical evidence consistent with the defendant's claim that she was wearing the nightgown when her husband was shot?'

'No.' Yoshida held up the nightgown and displayed the backside to Quinn. 'This is also high-velocity spatter.

If the defendant was wearing the nightgown when Mr. Hoyt was shot, the spray would have covered the front of the nightgown. It is my conclusion that this nightgown was not on the defendant when Mr. Hoyt was shot. I believe it was lying on the bed with the backside up.'

'What conclusions did you draw concerning the way in which the shooting occurred from your analysis of the blood spatter evidence?'

'It is my conclusion that the defendant was not wearing the nightgown when the shooting occurred. I believe that she left the nightgown front-down on the bed after having intercourse. Then she went to the bathroom. She was in the bathroom when Mr. Jablonski was in front of the bed and to the left of the armoire. Mr. Jablonski fired the three shots that struck and killed Mr. Hoyt. Then the defendant fired her first shot into Mr. Jablonski's temple from the area near the bathroom door. This shot caused high-velocity blood spatter to spray onto the side of the armoire. As soon as he was shot, Mr. Jablonski turned toward the bathroom and was shot front to back. The second bullet left no blood spatter because Mr. Jablonski was wearing heavy clothing and the bullet stayed in the body. Mr. Jablonski then crumpled to the floor with his head toward the bed and his feet almost touching the armoire.'

'I have no further questions of Officer Yoshida,' Riker said.

Mary Garrett began her cross-examination, but Quinn had trouble paying attention to it. Yoshida's testimony stunned him. Quinn had reached a tentative conclusion about how he would deal with the blackmailer's demand that he assure the conviction of Ellen Crease, but that decision had been based in part on a belief that Ellen Crease was an innocent person who was being framed by her enemies. Yoshida's testimony changed everything. He had to know if there was a flaw in Yoshida's interpretation of the blood spatter evidence.

'We have no further witnesses,' Riker said when the examination of Yoshida was concluded. Quinn glanced at the clock. It was almost noon.

'Let's break for the day and I'll hear the legal arguments tomorrow. We'll reconvene at two. I have some matters I need to attend to in the morning.'

Quinn turned to his court reporter.

'Miss Chan, please see me in chambers.'

Quinn left the bench. He took off his robes as soon as he was through the door to his chambers. An idea had occurred to him as Garrett was questioning Yoshida. He buzzed Fran Stuart just as Margaret Chan walked in.

'Fran,' Quinn said over the intercom as he motioned for Chan to sit down, 'get me the file in *State v. Schwartz*, please.'

Quinn released the intercom button and addressed the court reporter.

'Can you get me a transcript of Gary Yoshida's testimony today?'

'Sure. I should be able to finish it before five.'

'Please drop it by when you're done.'

Chan left just as Fran Stuart put the *Schwartz* file on his desk. Quinn thanked her and she returned to the outer office. Court-appointed counsel had represented the defendant in *Schwartz*. Quinn remembered signing an order authorizing payment of indigent defense funds for a court-appointed defense witness who was an expert in blood spatter. Quinn had been impressed by the testimony. The man's name, address and phone number were on the form on which the request for payment was made. Quinn jotted down the information and picked up the phone.

'Paul Baylor?' Quinn asked when the phone was answered.

'Yes.'

'This is Judge Richard Quinn of the Multnomah County Circuit Court. You testified before me in *State v. Schwartz.*'

'Oh, yes, Your Honor. What can I do for you?'

'I'd like to consult with you privately. The matter is confidential. Would you have time to meet with me tomorrow morning?'

'Do you want me to come to the courthouse?'

'No. I thought I could come to your office.'

'Sure.'

'Is eight A.M. too early?'

'No, that's fine. Uh, what is this about?'

'I'm looking for an opinion on an issue involving blood spatter evidence. I'll be bringing some pictures and a transcript.'

'Fine. See you tomorrow.'

'One more thing. Please don't mention this conversation or our meeting to anyone.'

Quinn hung up and buzzed his secretary.

'Fran, please bring all of the evidence in the *Crease* hearing into my chambers. I want to study it.'

A few minutes later, Fran Stuart placed a large

cardboard box on the floor next to Quinn's desk.

'I'm going to get my lunch, Judge. Can I get you anything?'

'I brought my lunch. Thanks, Fran.'

'I'll lock the front door to give you some privacy. I won't be long.'

Fran Stuart closed the door to Quinn's chambers. A moment later, Quinn heard the door between the corridor and the reception area close. There was a small refrigerator in Quinn's private bathroom. Quinn took out a can of Coke and a brown bag with a ham and cheese sandwich and a bag of potato chips. He had made the sandwich that morning, but he had no appetite now. Still, he forced himself to take a bite. He knew it would be a mistake to skip lunch. He needed all his energy to cope with the crisis he was facing.

While Quinn ate he mulled over Yoshida's testimony. Loud and repeated knocking on the outer door interrupted Quinn's chain of thought. He did not want company, but the knocking was insistent. Quinn went into the reception room. There was a peephole in the door to the hall. Quinn looked through it. The blood drained from his face and he felt dizzy. The woman in the corridor was the woman who had passed by the courtroom door. Quinn stared harder through the peephole. The glass distorted the woman's image but there was no getting around her resemblance to Andrea Chapman. Quinn opened the door.

The woman was Andrea and she was not. Andrea had long black hair. The woman in the hall was blonde and her hair was cut short to frame her face. She also wore glasses. Beneath her raincoat, her clothing was conservative and cheap: a drab, colorless dress, no jewelry and very little makeup.

'Are you Judge Quinn? Richard Quinn?'

'Yes. Can I help you?'

'My . . . my name is Claire Reston. I need to talk to you. It's very important.'

Quinn saw none of Andrea's breezy self-confidence in the woman. They were almost the same height, but Claire Reston slouched and her shoulders were hunched and folded in as if she were trying to hide behind them. She also had trouble looking Quinn in the eye.

'Why don't you come into my chambers?' suggested Quinn, who was anxious that no one see him with the woman.

Reston took one of the chairs across the desk from Quinn. She folded her hands in her lap.

'I . . . I know about you and Andrea,' Reston said without conviction.

'Who?'

Reston looked up. The lenses in her glasses were thick and made her eyes look large. Quinn felt terrible about lying to the woman, but he had no choice.

'Andrea Chapman is my sister. The . . . the day before she disappeared, she told me about you.'

'Okay. Now I understand. Look, Miss Reston, a police detective called me about your sister's disappearance. I'll tell you what I told him. I sat next to her on the flight to St. Jerome, but I didn't see her after we landed.'

Reston looked down. She seemed on the verge of tears.

'That's not true.' Reston's voice quivered as if the

227

effort to disagree with Quinn was monumental. 'She told me your name. She was upset. She didn't want to do it. I want you to know that.'

'Do what, Miss Reston? I don't understand.'

'They wanted her to seduce you. They were going to blackmail you.'

'Who was going to blackmail me? What are you talking about?'

'She didn't tell me anything else. Just that she had been hired to seduce a judge. She told me your name. She was very nervous, very tense.'

'Miss Reston, I assure you that I did not see your sister after we left the plane. If she was hired to do something to me, maybe she changed her mind. I only talked to her during the flight. She was friendly, but she made no attempt to seduce me. I'm married.'

Reston looked confused.

'Have you told the police that I had something to do with your sister's disappearance?'

'No. I . . . Andrea and I . . . we're not close. I don't even see her that much. In fact, the call from St. Jerome surprised me. I didn't even know that she had disappeared until the detective called to ask about her. I . . . Well, I didn't know anything but your name and that you were a judge, so I didn't tell the detective what Andrea said.' Reston looked down at her lap. She seemed embarrassed by her lack of courage. 'Then I read about Senator Crease's trial and the story gave the name of the judge . . .'

Reston trailed off. She looked very unsure of herself and Quinn believed his bluff would work.

'Miss Reston, I am sorry that your sister has disappeared. She seemed very nice. But I really can't help you. I talked to her a little on the plane. That's all. I probably mentioned where I was staying, but she never called my hotel. If she did, she didn't leave a message.'

Reston sat up a little straighter. She studied Quinn.

'I . . . I don't believe you. I think you do know something about Andrea's disappearance.'

Quinn heard the hall door open and close. Reston looked over her shoulder toward the sound. She stood up quickly and opened the door between Quinn's chambers and the reception area. Quinn saw Fran Stuart over Reston's shoulder.

'I'm staying at the Heathman Hotel in room 325. You . . . you have to be honest with me. If you know something . . .' Reston was on the verge of tears. 'I'll give you until tomorrow.'

Reston saw Stuart. She ran out of courage and bolted past the secretary.

'Who was that?' Stuart asked.

Quinn shook his head. 'Forget about her. She's confused. It wasn't anything important.'

Stuart started to say something, then thought better of it. Quinn closed the door to his chambers.

Nineteen

[1]

THE OFFICES of Oregon Forensic Investigations were located in an industrial park a few blocks from the Columbia River. Quinn had to wind through narrow streets flanked by warehouses to find the entrance to the parking lot. After parking in a space reserved for visitors, Quinn walked up a concrete ramp, then followed a walkway that led past several businesses. A door with the company name opened into a small anteroom. There were two chairs on either side of an end table that held a lamp and several copies of *Scientific American* and *Time*. In one wall of the reception area was a door and a sliding glass window. Quinn looked through the window and saw a receptionist's desk with a telephone and a second door in the back wall. The door to the receptionist's area was locked. A sign above a button on the wall instructed Quinn to ring for assistance. He pressed the button and heard a muted buzzing somewhere in the building. Moments later, the doors opened and Paul Baylor greeted Quinn.

Baylor was a slender, bookish African American with a B.S. in forensic science and criminal justice from Michigan State who had worked in the Oregon State Crime Lab for ten years before opening his own forensic consulting firm with another OSP forensic expert. Quinn had been impressed by the slow, thoughtful manner with which Baylor handled the prosecutor's questions when he testified in his courtroom. He did not appear to be taking sides and had answered truthfully, even when the answers were not favorable to the defense. Baylor was wearing a brown tweed sports jacket, a white shirt, a forest-green tie and tan slacks. After shaking hands with Quinn, Baylor brought him into a cramped office outfitted with inexpensive furniture.

'How can I help you, Judge?' Baylor asked when they were seated. Quinn was carrying a box containing the transcript of Gary Yoshida's testimony, several police reports, a sketch of Yoshida's diagram of the crime scene, a complete set of the crime scene photographs, including the two that showed the blood spatter pattern on the side of the armoire, and a brown paper bag with Ellen Crease's nightgown inside. He set the box on top of Baylor's desk.

'You may have read that I'm hearing motions in *State v. Crease.*'

Baylor nodded.

'Do you know Gary Yoshida?'

231

'Sure. We worked together for several years when I was with OSP.'

'What's your impression of him?'

Baylor looked uncomfortable about being asked to comment on another professional, but he answered the question.

'Gary does good work and he's very honest.'

'Is he an expert on blood spatter?'

'He's knowledgeable about it.'

'How exact a science is blood spatter analysis?'

Baylor thought about the question before answering.

'Blood spatter analysis is very helpful in determining what happened at a crime scene, but it's not like finger-print examination. There is a certain amount of subjectivity involved. A fingerprint is not open to interpretation, if you have enough points of comparison. That's not true with blood spatter. You can't just look at an individual blood spot and draw indisputable conclusions. You have to look at the spot in the context of the whole scene. Bloodstains just tell you in general what happened.'

'So two honest experts can look at the same scene and draw different conclusions as to what happened?'

'Sure, in certain instances.'

'I would like you to look at the evidence I've brought and read Officer Yoshida's testimony. Then I would like you to tell me if there is any analysis of the evidence that would support Ellen Crease's version of how the shoot-out in her bedroom occurred.'

Baylor's brow furrowed. He looked concerned.

'Are you questioning Gary's honesty?' he asked.

'No, no. I just want to know if there is a reasonable

explanation of the evidence that is different from his conclusions. There isn't any question in my mind that Officer Yoshida gave an honest opinion in court. I want to know if he could be wrong.'

'I assume Gary had the advantage of visiting the crime scene?'

Quinn nodded. 'He was out there twice.'

'Can I visit it?'

'No. Besides, my information is that it has been cleaned.'

'That's going to put me at a disadvantage.'

'I realize that. Just do your best. And let me know if working on the problem without visiting the scene has a critical impact on your conclusions.'

'Okay. When do you want me to get back to you?'

'Actually, I thought I'd wait. Is this something you can do right away?'

Baylor looked surprised. 'I can get to it now. It might take a while.'

'Is there someplace nearby I can eat breakfast?' Quinn asked. He did not have much of an appetite, but a restaurant would give him a place to pass the time while Baylor worked.

'Yeah. Sue's Cafe is pretty good. It's two blocks down just when you turn out of the lot on the right.'

'Okay. I'll be back in an hour.'

'I'll see what I can do by then. Uh, one other thing. Should I submit a court-appointed witness voucher for my work?'

'No. I'll be paying for this personally.'

*   *   *

When Quinn returned to Oregon Forensic Investigations, he found Paul Baylor in shirtsleeves with his collar open and his tie at half-mast.

'You find Sue's okay?' Baylor asked as he led Quinn through a door into a large work area. The walls were unpainted concrete blocks and there was fluorescent lighting hanging from the ceiling. The laboratory equipment that sat on several wooden tables looked new and Quinn figured that this was where Baylor and his partner had sunk their capital.

'It was a good suggestion.' Quinn noticed the papers and photographs that covered one of the worktables. 'Are you through?'

'Yeah. It didn't take as long as I thought it might.'

'Were you able to draw any conclusions?' Quinn asked anxiously.

'Yes.'

'And?'

'Okay. First thing, I can't disagree with Gary's findings.'

'You mean the evidence contradicts Ellen Crease's version of the shootings?'

'I didn't say that. Look, as I said before, blood spatter analysis is not an exact science. People can draw different conclusions from the same evidence in some situations. Gary's conclusions are valid. However, Gary's analysis of the significance of the blood spatter patterns on the nightgown and the side of the armoire is not the only analysis one can make.'

Crease's nightgown was lying facedown on top of butcher paper on a long table. Baylor led the judge over to it.

'The spatter pattern on the back of the nightgown was the easiest to deal with.' Baylor pointed at the dried blood that had sprayed over the back of the white fabric. 'In the transcript, it says that the lab concluded that the blood on the front of the nightgown and the spray on the back are Lamar Hoyt's blood, so I'm accepting that as a fact. No question that's high-velocity spatter. So far so good.

'Now, as I understand it, Crease said that she was in bed with the nightgown on, talking to her husband, when Jablonski entered the bedroom and shot him.'

'That's how I heard it.'

'Okay. Now, Gary concludes that she was lying about wearing the nightgown because the spray pattern from the high-velocity spatter is across the back of the nightgown. His conclusion is that she's in the bathroom lying in wait for Jablonski and the nightgown is flat on the bed, front side down. That's one explanation for the pattern being on the back, but there is another that's consistent with Crease's story.'

Baylor grabbed two wooden chairs and set them side by side. Then he motioned to Quinn.

'Stand over by that filing cabinet and face me.' Baylor sat in the chair that faced Quinn's left side. 'You're Jablonski and I'm Crease. The filing cabinet is the armoire. I'm sitting on my side of the bed. I've got my nightgown on. The other chair is the side of the bed closest to the bathroom. That's Lamar Hoyt's side.

'Jablonski comes into the bedroom. He moves to the middle of the bed and to the left of the armoire and raises the gun to shoot Hoyt.'

Baylor bent over the side of the chair to his right.

'I'm going for the gun that is under the bed. See how my back is suddenly facing my husband? The fabric is stretched out. If you shoot while I'm bent like this and Hoyt is hit at a certain angle, the spray will cover my back, not my front. Then, when I straighten up, the fabric will rumple a little, making it look like the nightgown was tossed on its front on the bed.'

Baylor straightened up.

'So Crease could have been telling the truth about wearing the nightgown,' Quinn said slowly, more to himself than to Baylor. 'If she was, she would have had to bend over the west-facing side of the bed for the spatter pattern on the nightgown to look like that. She couldn't have been in the bathroom.'

'Yes. But Gary's explanation could also be correct.'

'What about the blood on the armoire?'

'That gets trickier, but there is a way that the spray could have gotten on the armoire with Crease shooting from her side of the bed.

'Let's keep Jablonski on his feet on the west side of the armoire, exactly where Gary placed him. He shoots Hoyt as Crease goes for her gun. Crease's movements distract Jablonski. He turns his head toward the window but does not turn his body. Now Jablonski's right temple is facing Crease's side of the bed. Go on, turn your head.'

Quinn did as he was told.

'Now, the next part gets tricky.' Baylor raised his hand and pretended to fire a gun. 'Bam. Crease's first shot enters the right temple, high-velocity spatter sprays from the wound, but the spray would go forward, in front of Jablonski's body and onto the floor, and it would not travel far, since the amount of spray is small and high-velocity spray is atomized. When Jablonski collapses after the body shot, he would fall on top of the high-velocity spray and obliterate it.'

'If the high-velocity spray from the head shot landed on the floor, what caused the blood spatter pattern on the side of the armoire?'

'Aspirated blood from Jablonski's lungs. A shot to the body frequently causes people to cough up blood. If Jablonski turned his head toward the armoire after he was shot in the body, he could have coughed blood on the armoire before collapsing onto the high-velocity spatter from the head wound. Aspirated blood can resemble high-velocity spray.'

A thought occurred to Quinn. 'Is there a difference between blood that is sprayed from a head wound and aspirated blood from the lungs?'

'You mean, could we test the blood on the armoire to see if it is aspirated blood?'

'Exactly.'

'Not anymore. If the blood on the armoire was tested shortly after the crime, it's possible that amylase, an enzyme from saliva, could have been detected. Amylase could have been caught up in the blood when Jablonski coughed. But amylase breaks down and becomes undetectable in a week or two, depending on the temperature and humidity in a room. Additionally, amylase is not always found in aspirated blood, or it may go undetected because it's below the detection limit of the test that's used. Even if Gary had tested the blood on the armoire as soon as he caught on to its possible significance, I doubt that it would have told him anything.'

'So there's no way to tell if the blood on the side of the armoire is aspirated blood or high-velocity spatter.'

'Correct.'

'And there's no way to say for certain where Ellen Crease was when she shot Martin Jablonski.'

'Also correct.'

Quinn's shoulders sagged. He was hoping that Baylor would debunk Yoshida's analysis. All he had done was confuse the situation.

[2]

Quinn's head was pounding by the time he arrived at his chambers. If Baylor had told him that the blood spatter evidence proved that Ellen Crease was a liar, Quinn would have let the trial run its course. But Baylor could not say that the shooting of Martin Jablonski had not occurred exactly as Crease described it.

Quinn gave the exhibits to Fran Stuart and instructed her to hold all of his calls. He reviewed the memos on the law of search and seizure and the rules of evidence filed by the parties. From what he could determine, the blood spatter evidence was the key to the State's case. If Quinn granted all of Garrett's motions, the only evidence left in the case would be Jablonski's history as a burglar who resorted to violence and the indisputable fact that

Jablonski had broken into the Hoyt mansion and shot Lamar Hoyt. If this was the way that the evidence stood when the State rested, any judge would have to grant a motion for judgment of acquittal to the defense.

Quinn rested his head in his hands. He had slept little the night before and he was exhausted and not thinking clearly. He needed to rest, he wanted time to think out his course of action, but court was scheduled to convene in five minutes.

When Quinn looked up, he saw Lincoln's framed quote on his wall. Lincoln's counsel to do one's best while trying to do what was right had helped him reach his decision to impose a prison sentence on Frederick Gideon when everyone expected him to grant the judge probation. Doing the right thing was the centerpiece of Quinn's personal philosophy. It was something you did regardless of the consequences. Sometimes doing the right thing required courage. Quinn had not been courageous on St. Jerome. He did not report Andrea's murder to the authorities for selfish reasons. While his cowardice protected him, it helped Andrea's killer get away with murder. Now he wanted Quinn to help him destroy another life. Quinn decided that he was not going to do that. This afternoon he would act with the courage he had not shown on St. Jerome.

'Before I rule on these motions, I want to thank counsel on both sides for their excellent briefs and oral argument. They have been of great assistance to me in framing and resolving some difficult issues.'

Quinn paused. Cedric Riker leaned back, looking as

if he did not have a care in the world. He was so self-centered that he could not conceive of losing a motion. When he did lose, he always found someone else to blame. Mary Garrett shifted nervously on her chair. She was self-confident, but she had none of Riker's egomania to blind her to the fact that the questions were close. Ellen Crease watched Quinn with cool detachment.

'I'll start with the most complex question. Did the search of the defendant's bedroom violate the Oregon and United States Constitutions? The burden is on the State to prove that the search was legal because the search was conducted without a warrant. Warrantless searches are presumed to be illegal, unless the State can show the existence of an exception to the warrant requirements of the Oregon and United States Constitutions.

'Mr. Riker has argued that exigent circumstances excused Detective Anthony and Officer Yoshida from obtaining a warrant. I do not find this argument convincing. Officer Yoshida gave no scientific opinion as to why waiting a few hours while a warrant was obtained would make it any more likely that the blood spatter would be degraded or destroyed. After all, it had been over a week since the crime scene was created. True, the cleaners would have destroyed the evidence, but they were not scheduled to appear until the next day. Additionally, Detective Anthony and Officer Yoshida did not know that the cleaners were coming until after the decision was made to go to the estate without a warrant.'

Garrett leaned forward, hanging on Quinn's every word.

'The State argues that James Allen gave a valid consent to the police to enter the bedroom. I find that Mr. Allen did not have real authority to do that. He and the police were both aware that Senator Crease had specifically instructed Allen to keep everyone except the cleaning crew out of the bedroom.

'However, I do find that James Allen did have apparent authority to open the locked bedroom for the police. He was the housekeeper. He had the keys to the room. Detective Anthony could reasonably assume that the person left in charge of the house by Senator Crease could let him and Officer Yoshida into the bedroom if he wished to let them in and there was a valid reason to do so.'

Garrett's shoulders sagged and Riker smiled.

'Despite my finding that James Allen had the apparent authority to consent to a search of Senator Crease's bedroom, I must still suppress the evidence obtained during the search.'

Riker shot up in his chair. He looked stunned. Garrett looked like she could not believe what she was hearing.

'I find that Detective Anthony intentionally coerced Mr. Allen into opening the bedroom after he had been told unequivocally by Mr. Allen that he was under instructions from his employer to keep everyone but the cleaning crew out of the bedroom. I hold that Detective Anthony was not credible when he testified that he did not intentionally coerce Mr. Allen into giving consent.'

Riker was on his feet. 'Your Honor,' he started, but Quinn cut him off.

'The time for argument is over, Mr. Riker. Please sit down.'

Riker collapsed onto his chair.

'As to the other motions, I have read the briefs submitted by the parties and I have examined the affidavits submitted by the State detailing what Conchita Jablonski and Karen Fargo would testify to if called as witnesses. I will not allow Conchita Jablonski to testify to anything her husband told her concerning how he came by the money that was found in the Jablonski apartment. That is pure hearsay.

'Similarly, I am excluding any statements that Lamar Hoyt may have made to Karen Fargo about the state of his marriage and his desire to leave his wife for her on the grounds that they, too, are hearsay.'

Riker could only gape at the judge. His case against Ellen Crease was being destroyed beyond repair.

'Finally, I will allow the defense to introduce evidence concerning Mr. Jablonski's criminal background to support its position that he was acting as a burglar on the evening of the shooting.

'I'll prepare the order,' Quinn said as he stood. 'Mr. Riker, you have thirty days to decide if you want to appeal my order to the court of appeals. Court is adjourned.'

As soon as Quinn left the bench, Cedric Riker streaked out of the courtroom with his assistants in tow and Ryan Clark headed down the hall to the pay phones to let Benjamin Gage in on the bad news. James Allen stayed

seated. He watched Mary Garrett and Ellen Crease discuss the outcome of the case at their table. Allen looked
grim and undecided. After a moment's more thought he
mixed with the spectators and left the room.

'What does this mean?' Ellen Crease asked her lawyer.

'It means we won everything,' Garrett told her as
the enormity of Quinn's ruling dawned on her. 'He
suppressed everything Riker can use to convict you.
He left him with nothing.'

Garrett hoisted her attaché case and they headed out
of the courtroom.

'You sound surprised.'

'To tell the truth, I am. I had some hope of winning
the motion to keep out the hearsay, but the blood spatter
motion was a real long shot.'

'Does this mean that the case is over? That I'm free?'

'Technically, the charges still exist. But Riker's choice
is to appeal or dismiss and . . .'

Garrett stopped. Bearing down on them was Lamar
Hoyt, Jr.

'This isn't over, bitch!' he screamed in Crease's face.
'I'm contesting the will and I'm gonna sue you civilly
for wrongful death.'

'Get away from my client,' Garrett commanded.

'Shut up, you . . .'

Suddenly, Junior was up on his toes with his left arm
cranked behind his back in a hammerlock. Applying
the pressure was a tall man with a swimmer's wide
shoulders and narrow waist. Long black hair swept
across his forehead. His blue eyes looked sleepy and
his thick black mustache was shaggy. The man did not

look angry and he sounded unexcited when he said, 'Come on, Junior. Let's calm down here.'

'Ah, ah,' Junior managed as the man pressed his arm toward his shoulder blade and beyond.

'I don't want to hurt you,' the man said, 'but I can't have you threatening the senator and Ms. Garrett.'

'Let go! Ah!' Junior gasped. His face was cramped with pain and Garrett thought he was going to cry.

'If I let go, will you behave?'

'Yes!'

'Okay,' the man said as he released some of the pressure on Junior's arm. 'Now, I'm taking you at your word and I'm going to let you go. When I do, I want you to head out of here as fast as your fat legs will carry you. If you're lying to me, I'll break both your arms. We on the same wavelength?'

'Yeah! Yeah! Let me go.'

The man released Junior and took a step back. Junior grabbed his shoulder and bent forward.

'On your way. Let's not dawdle,' the man said.

Junior glared, but kept his mouth shut and headed for the elevators.

'Thank you, Jack,' Ellen Crease said calmly. She had not blinked during the encounter with Junior.

'My pleasure,' the man said, flashing her a boyish smile.

Mary Garrett had noticed the man sitting in the back of the courtroom throughout the hearing. She had assumed that he was a policeman.

'Mary, this is Jack Brademas,' Crease said. 'He's the head of security at Hoyt Industries. Jack's been protecting

ne since I learned about the money that was paid to
Martin Jablonski.'

'Pleased to meet you, Mr. Brademas.'

'Jack, please. Especially after that coup you just pulled
off in court. Was Judge Quinn's ruling as good for the
senator as it seemed?'

'Better,' Garrett answered. 'For all intents and purposes, this case is over.'

[3]

Ced, this is Lou Anthony. I just got back to my desk
and there was a note to call you. What happened at the
hearing?'

'Quinn fucked us, Lou.'

'How?'

'He suppressed everything. The blood spatter evidence, Fargo's statements about what Hoyt told her.
Everything.'

'All the evidence?' Anthony repeated as if he could
not believe his ears.

'Everything he could suppress, he threw out.'

'Jesus. Where does that leave us?'

'In outer fucking space without a ship. Quinn gutted
our case.'

'Can't you appeal?'

'Sure, but it would be useless. The court of appeals
can reverse a judge who misinterprets the law, but
Quinn based his decision to suppress the blood spatter

evidence on his personal evaluation of your credibility. The court can't review that.'

'What do you mean, my credibility?'

'He said you were a liar, Lou. That's as plain as I can say it.'

'He what?'

'He said you lied under oath when you testified that you did not intentionally pressure James Allen to let you into the bedroom.'

'But I didn't. I mean, I persuaded the guy, but I never leaned on him. We just talked.'

'That may be what really happened, but Quinn put it on the record that you are a liar. The court of appeals cannot reverse a decision that rests on a judge's evaluation of the credibility of a witness, unless there is no evidence in the record to support the finding.'

'I wouldn't lie under oath. You know that.'

'I know it, Lou, but everyone who reads Quinn's opinion is going to think otherwise.'

[4]

While she was driving home, Karen Fargo caught the end of a news story about Ellen Crease's case, but she did not hear enough to let her figure out what had happened. Fargo turned on the television as soon as she walked into her house. The case was the lead story. A reporter was talking about Richard Quinn's dramatic decision while the screen showed a triumphant Ellen Crease waving to supporters from the courthouse steps.

'I want to thank all of the people who had faith in me during these dark days,' Crease told the reporters who were massed around her. 'I loved my husband. Losing him to senseless violence was a great blow, but being accused unjustly of murdering someone you love is the cruelest blow. I thank God for Judge Richard Quinn's courage.'

'Will you continue to campaign, Senator?' a reporter shouted.

Crease stared directly into the camera. Her mouth was set in a grim line. When she spoke, there was no doubting her determination.

'I have never stopped campaigning. The Republican Party should not be represented by a man who is soft on crime, for gun control and sympathetic to the liberal forces in our society that would pervert the values that have made America the greatest country on earth. I represent the true values of our party, and the voters will validate that statement in the May primary.'

The screen was suddenly filled with a picture of Benjamin Gage dressed in a tuxedo with his beautiful wife on his arm entering the Benson Hotel to attend a fund-raiser.

'Senator,' asked a reporter from Channel 6, 'what is your reaction to Judge Quinn's ruling in Ellen Crease's case?'

Gage halted. He looked serious and thoughtful.

'Ken, it would be inappropriate for me to comment on Ellen Crease's criminal case. However, I do feel that it would be ironic if Ms. Crease was to have her case dismissed on one of the technicalities that she so frequently derides in her speeches. It would also be unfortunate for the voters if the public was deprived of a clear resolution of the murder charges against Ms. Crease because of the suppression of the evidence that the State believes will prove its allegations.'

'So you do not feel that justice is being done in Senator Crease's case?'

'Now, Ken,' Gage answered with a patient smile, 'you know better than to put words in my mouth. I will leave the business of solving Lamar Hoyt's murder to the police. My job is to represent the people of Oregon in the United States Senate.'

Gage turned from the reporter and entered the hotel. The reporter made a closing comment, but Karen Fargo did not hear him. She was concentrating on the man who followed Senator Gage into the Benson. He was tall, good-looking, dressed in a tuxedo, and he had a jagged scar on his right cheek. Fargo only had a moment to study him, but he definitely looked like the man who had offered her money and a job if she would tell the police about her involvement with Lamar Hoyt. Did the man work for Senator Gage? She wondered if the film footage showing the man with the scar would be aired again at eleven. She decided to watch the late news so she could be certain about what she had seen.

The phone rang. Fargo switched off the set and picked up the receiver.

'Ms. Fargo?'

'Yes?'

'This is Detective Anthony.'

'Yes?' Fargo answered tentatively.

'I wanted to tell you what happened in court.'

'I . . . It was on the news. That the judge suppressed the evidence. What does that mean?'

'It means that Mr. Riker cannot use the evidence we found in the second search of the crime scene to convict Ellen Crease. Mr. Riker will appeal the judge's ruling, but that could take a while. Maybe years.'

'So I won't have to go to court?'

'It's possible you might, but not in the near future.'

Fargo sagged with relief. She would never forget Lamar, but she was terrified of having to appear in court.

'Thank you for calling,' Fargo said.

'I wanted to be certain that you understood what happened,' Anthony answered kindly. 'Feel free to call me anytime if you have questions.'

Fargo thought about the man with the scar. Should she tell Detective Anthony about him?

'Detective,' she started. Then it occurred to her that she might lose her job and the money if she said anything. And it might involve her further in a matter that she wanted to put behind her.

'Yes?'

'Nothing. Just thank you.'

[5]

Quinn told Fran Stuart to hold all of his calls. Then he asked her to stay late so that she could type up the drafts and final version of the Findings of Fact, Conclusions of Law and Order in the *Crease* case. Quinn shut his door and collapsed in the chair behind his desk. He felt sick to his stomach from what he had done and sick with fear of the consequences.

Quinn gathered the materials that he would need to write the order. It took him an hour to write and polish a draft. Quinn gave it to his secretary. Fran typed it quickly and Quinn sent her to dinner while he worked on the final draft. It was already after six and night had fallen.

Fran returned around seven and typed the final draft. Quinn read it through.

'This is fine, Fran. You can go home now. I'll sign it and leave it on your desk. File the original with the clerk's office and send a copy to Cedric Riker and Mary Garrett. And thanks for staying late.'

Fran closed the door. Quinn rubbed his eyes. Then he read through his order a final time, checking the facts, rereading sections of cases he had cited and statutes he had quoted. When Quinn was convinced that he had constructed the document in a way that would make reversal in an appellate court impossible, he signed the order.

Quinn closed his eyes and rested his head against the back of his chair. He had put off thinking about the future until he had made his ruling out of fear that he would be too afraid to act. He could put off thinking about his career no longer. Quinn's life was the law, but he had violated his oath by ruling for Crease. If he had ruled honestly, he would have held that Allen's consent was not coerced. By ruling as he had, he had betrayed the trust that had been put in him by the people of his state.

Quinn looked around his chambers at the bound volumes that contained the law. His father had written some of the opinions in those books. As a boy, he revered them and dreamed of following his father's example and career. Now Quinn saw that the cases in the reports were nothing. You could write the most beautiful words, but they were meaningless without the will and the desire to follow them. Quinn had betrayed his trust. He had turned the words to dust.

Twenty

T HE NEXT MORNING Quinn overslept. By the time
he arrived at the courthouse Fran Stuart had filed
the order in *Crease* and sent copies to the parties. Quinn
told Stuart that he did not want to be disturbed. He shut
the door to his chambers and began work on a draft of
the letter of resignation that he planned to submit to
Stanley Sax. Writing the letter was more difficult than he
imagined. It was almost like writing a suicide note. There
were many false starts and a lot of time spent staring
into space. When Fran buzzed him at eleven forty-five,
she startled Quinn out of one of his reveries.

'What is it, Fran?'

'There are two Portland Police detectives to see you.
I told them that you didn't want to be disturbed, but
they insist on speaking to you.'

'What do they want?'

'They wouldn't say.'

'Okay. Send them in. I'll talk to them.'

The door to Quinn's chambers opened and a slender black man Quinn did not recognize followed Lou Anthony into the room. Anthony looked like a man who was controlling his anger. Quinn colored as it dawned on him how much the detective must dislike him.

'Good morning, Judge,' Anthony said with strained civility. 'This is my partner, Leroy Dennis.'

Quinn nodded at Dennis and asked, 'What brings you here?'

'Police business. I'd like you to come with us.'

'Come where?'

'There's been a murder and I want you to accompany Detective Dennis and me to the crime scene.'

'If you need to have a search warrant authorized, I can do the work here.'

'If I needed a search warrant, you'd be the last judge I'd contact,' Anthony snapped. Dennis put his hand on his partner's arm and Anthony looked down, embarrassed by his outburst.

'There are some things that we need to talk over with you and we can't do it here,' Dennis said.

'This is getting a little too mysterious, Detectives.'

'Sorry, but this is all we can tell you before we get to the scene,' Dennis said. 'Everything will become clear to you there.'

The Heathman Hotel was only a few blocks from the courthouse. The detectives were silent during the short walk and Quinn's imagination ran wild. When they arrived at the hotel the judge noticed several police cars parked near the entrance. Dennis and Anthony led Quinn through the lobby to the reception desk, where an officer and a harried-looking man in his forties were examining hotel records.

'Mr. Abrams,' Anthony interrupted. The man who was talking to the officer looked up. 'Did you see this man in here yesterday evening?'

Abrams studied Quinn for a few moments, then shook his head.

'It's impossible to say. We were extremely busy. The lobby was very crowded.'

Suddenly, Quinn guessed why the detectives had brought him to the hotel. Claire Reston, Andrea Chapman's sister, was staying at the Heathman. Anthony had said that there had been a murder. Was Reston the victim? If she was, why did the police think that Quinn would know anything about her death?

'What's going on here?' Quinn demanded.

'You'll see in a moment,' Dennis answered as the detectives led Quinn to the elevators. Once inside the car, Anthony pressed the button for the third floor. Reston had told Quinn that she was staying in room 325. Now Quinn was certain that he was being taken to view Reston's dead body. He remembered that Fran Stuart was standing inches away when Reston had told him her hotel and room number.

The door to 325 was open. A large Portland Police officer was guarding the entrance. The room was a corner suite. Criminalists from the Oregon State Crime

Lab were moving around inside the sitting room, photographing, dusting and measuring. Everything in the room looked orderly, except for a room service tray with a half-eaten dinner on it that sat on a coffee table across from the television.

Anthony led Quinn through the crowd to the door to the bedroom. The door was partially closed, but Quinn could see the edge of the bed and a bare foot. He knew he did not want to go into the room, but he had no choice.

'Do you recognize this woman, Judge?' Anthony asked as he thrust the door open. The bedroom looked and smelled like a slaughterhouse. Objects had been knocked onto the floor from a dresser, a chair had been overturned and the bed had been stripped of its blankets, which lay in a bundle on the bloodstained carpet. The blood on the carpet was nothing compared to the quantity of blood that saturated the bare undersheet upon which Claire Reston lay spread-eagled. Her hands had been bound to the headboard and her feet were secured to the foot of the bed. Blood had spattered on the wall behind her. She was naked. A crude gag had been stuffed inside her mouth.

Quinn's knees buckled and he leaned against the wall.

'Are you okay, Judge?' Dennis asked when he noticed Quinn's ashen pallor.

Quinn wanted to turn away from the bed, but he was mesmerized by the tableau of wanton violence.

'This is the first time . . . I've seen pictures, but . . .'

'Maybe we better go next door,' Dennis said. 'Get you outta here. You want some water?'

'Please.'

Quinn began to turn from the bed. Then he froze. The hair on Reston's head was blond, but her pubic hair was black like Andrea Chapman's. Quinn moved slightly so he could see Reston's right hip. What he saw caused his stomach to roll.

'Hey,' Dennis said, gripping Quinn's elbow. 'Come on, now. Take some breaths.'

Quinn turned from the bed. He gulped in air. Dennis led him from the room, but Quinn did not even notice that he was moving. He was trying to absorb what he had just seen. Not the corpse or the gaping wounds that covered it or the blood or the stench, but the pale, half-moon-shaped scar that Quinn had seen on the dead woman's hip: a scar identical to that which he had seen on Andrea Chapman's hip on the beach in the Cove of Lost Souls. Claire Reston did not just look like Andrea Chapman. She was Andrea Chapman. Chapman had not been murdered on St. Jerome.

Dennis led Quinn out of 325 and into the suite next door. The police had commandeered it as a temporary headquarters. Anthony followed them. A detective was on the phone in the sitting room and two police officers were drinking coffee on the couch. Dennis brought Quinn into the bedroom and Anthony shut the door. The judge sank onto the bed and held his head in his hands.

'Must be quite a shock,' Dennis said sympathetically as he walked into the bathroom to get Quinn a glass of water. 'Seeing that poor young woman like that. 'Specially if it's your first time. I got light-headed my first time, too. Couldn't eat all day.'

Quinn's senses were overloaded by the horror he had witnessed in the bedroom next door and by the discovery that no one had been murdered on St. Jerome.

'Here,' Dennis said, handing the glass to Quinn. Quinn took it gratefully and sipped a little. Dennis pulled up a chair next to the bed. 'How long you known her, Judge?'

Dennis had slipped the question in so smoothly that Quinn almost answered it. Should he admit he knew the dead woman? Should he admit to knowing her as Claire Reston or Andrea Chapman? If he admitted to knowing that the dead woman was Andrea, how could he explain that the scar was the tip-off without revealing that he had seen Andrea in a bikini? Once he admitted that, he would have to confess to seeing her after the flight to St. Jerome. Quinn made a decision.

'I . . . I just met her. I was asked to speak at a legal seminar on St. Jerome in the Caribbean in late February. My wife was supposed to accompany me, but she had to cancel at the last minute because of a business emergency. My wife's seat on the plane was taken by a woman named Andrea Chapman.'

Quinn paused and drank some more water.

'A few days ago, I received a call from a police detective who was looking into Ms. Chapman's disappearance . . .'

'Where did he call from and what was his name?' Anthony interrupted.

'I think his last name was Fletcher. He mentioned his first name, but I can't remember it. If he told me where he was calling from, I forgot. I don't think he did, though.'

'So this Chapman woman disappeared?' Dennis said.

'From St. Jerome. I didn't know anything about that.'

'You didn't see Chapman after the flight?' Anthony asked.

'Well, in the airport, but not after that.'

'You were saying that you just met the deceased?' Dennis prodded.

'Yes. She came to my chambers during the lunch break in the hearing on the pretrial motions in Ellen Crease's case. She said her name was Claire Reston and that Andrea Chapman was her sister. She wanted to know if I had any information about her sister's disappearance.'

'Why would she think you knew anything about that?' Anthony asked.

Quinn froze. He had not thought about that.

'I, uh, I assumed that she'd gotten my name from the detective who called me. He got my name from the airline manifest. She never told me how she got my name, but the detective must have told her that I sat next to her sister.'

'So that's when you talked to the sister? On the plane and in the airport?' Anthony asked.

Quinn felt panicky. Why did Anthony repeat his question? Could he prove that Quinn had seen Andrea the next day?

'Yes.'

'Not after the flight?'

'No. Not after.'

'Judge Quinn, I am going to give you the *Miranda*

rights now,' Anthony said. Quinn's pulse rate jumped. Anthony would only do that if Quinn was a suspect in Claire Reston's murder.

'You have the right to remain silent . . .'

'Why is this necessary?' Quinn asked.

'I'll answer that when I'm done,' Anthony answered curtly. Quinn sat silently while Anthony finished reading him his rights, trying to guess what the police knew.

'Judge, I'm going to ask you again. Did you see Andrea Chapman after the flight to St. Jerome?'

Quinn suddenly noticed the manila envelope that Anthony was holding. The detective had shielded it from Quinn's view while Dennis was talking to him. Anthony withdrew from the envelope a photograph of Quinn and Andrea talking on the blanket in the cove. The photograph had been taken with a telephoto lens. If they blew it up further, Quinn was certain that the scar on Chapman's hip would become visible and the police would figure out that Reston and Chapman were the same person, if they did not know that already.

'We found these photographs in the dead woman's suitcase, Judge Quinn. Would you care to explain them?'

Quinn was having trouble breathing.

'Can I get you some more water, Judge?' Dennis asked solicitously. 'You okay?'

Quinn sucked in air. He was on the verge of breaking down.

'Did you fuck Chapman on St. Jerome?' Anthony asked angrily. 'Did her sister trail you to Portland and threaten to tell your wife?' They didn't know that Reston and Chapman were the same person, Quinn realized. 'Did you slash her to ribbons to shut her up?'

'No. It wasn't like that. I didn't have sex with Andrea.'

'You want us to believe that you were all alone with this woman and you didn't try to fuck her?'

Quinn did not know what to say.

'It is a strange coincidence that this Chapman woman disappears right after you meet her, then her sister talks with you and she's dead the next day,' Dennis said.

'You have to believe me,' Quinn pleaded. 'I met Andrea on the plane. She was very nice. We talked during the flight. She told me that there was a cove on the far side of the island with a beautiful reef. It's the cove in the picture. We spent the afternoon there. That's all.'

'Why didn't you tell us that before?' Dennis asked.

'I was afraid that someone would think I was involved in her disappearance,' Quinn answered lamely.

'Did you ever see these pictures before?' Dennis asked.

'No.'

'That's funny, because you haven't asked us where we got them or who took them. You didn't even seem surprised to see them.'

When Quinn did not respond, Dennis asked, 'Judge, can you tell us where you were last night between six and eight?'

'Six and eight?' Quinn repeated inanely.

'Yes, sir.'

'I was at the courthouse, in my chambers. I . . . I was working on the order in the *Crease* case.'

'Can anyone vouch for you?'

'My secretary, Fran Stuart. She was there.'

'The whole time?'

'No. She typed up a first draft for me, then went to dinner sometime between six and seven. Then she came back and typed the final. I think she left around seven-thirty.'

'So there was an hour and a half between six and eight when you were alone?'

Quinn nodded.

'No cleaning people came in, no one called?'

Quinn shook his head. He felt completely helpless.

'You see our problem here, Judge?' Dennis asked. 'The Heathman is only a short walk from the courthouse. I'd bet five minutes max. And there was a lot going on in the hotel between six and eight, which is the time when the medical examiner estimates that Claire Reston was murdered. It would have been easy for you to walk from the courthouse to the hotel, slip up to the third floor unnoticed and . . .' Dennis shrugged. 'Can you help us out here?'

Quinn looked back and forth between the two policemen. Both men watched him with blank expressions.

'You can't think . . . My, God, I could never do something like . . . like what was done to that poor woman.'

'Nice people sometimes do terrible things under stress, Judge,' Dennis said sympathetically. 'She showed you the photos, you see your marriage and career going down

261

the toilet. We see a lot of this kind of thing. If you did it, let us know so we can help you.'

'That . . . that woman wasn't just killed. That was methodical. That was torture.'

'Maybe you got a taste on St. Jerome,' Anthony said harshly. 'The thrill of having Chapman helpless, begging. It can be a turn-on for some people. Was it a turn-on for you?'

Quinn stared at Anthony in disbelief. Then he looked at Dennis. They had been playing with him and he was too distracted to see it. They really believed that he could tie up and torture a defenseless woman.

'Gentlemen, I've tried to be cooperative, but it is now clear to me . . . I don't want to continue this conversation, except to say that I did not hurt Claire Reston. I want to go now. I won't talk to you anymore without a lawyer.'

'Why don't you sit and think a minute while I discuss this with Detective Anthony?' Dennis said as he motioned Anthony into the outer room.

Quinn let his head fall into his hands. He wanted to tell the detectives the truth, but he would be providing them with a massive motive for murder if he revealed that the dead woman had been used to blackmail him. Dennis and Anthony would believe that Quinn, enraged by her betrayal, had murdered Reston. The conclusion was logical, even if it was false.

The door opened and Dennis and Anthony reentered the bedroom.

'We're going to let you go, Judge,' Dennis told Quinn. 'Neither one of us thinks you've told the truth, but we don't want to rush this investigation. I advise you to think very seriously about your duties as a citizen. If you have information that would help us solve the death of the poor girl in the other room, you have to tell us. You're not just some nobody on the street. You're a judge. From what they say, that means something to you. Think about how you should be acting here.'

[2]

Fran Stuart stood up as soon as Quinn walked into the reception area. She looked very upset.

'I waited for you to come back. I didn't know where to reach you.'

'Calm down, Fran. What's wrong?'

'It's Mr. Price. He's had a heart attack. Richard Kahn called you ten minutes after you left with the detectives.'

'Is he . . . ?'

'No. Mr. Kahn said they were talking about a case in Mr. Price's office when he complained about chest pains. He's at St. Vincent's Hospital. They're in surgery right now.'

Quinn was nursing a cup of coffee in the hospital cafeteria when a tall, middle-aged woman wearing a black skirt and a gray sweater approached his table.

'Judge Quinn?'

'Yes.'

'I'm Dr. Loerts. I operated on Mr. Price.'

'Sit down, please. Can I get you some coffee?'

'No, thanks,' the surgeon answered with a weary smile. She looked tired. Her red hair was pulled back in a ponytail and she rubbed her eyelids as soon as she slid onto the chair across from the judge.

'Mr. Price is going to be fine. We performed a triple bypass. That sounds scary, but we do a ton of them and it's routine for my team.'

'What happened?'

'Three of Mr. Price's arteries were clogged and that was keeping an adequate supply of blood from reaching his heart. We took one vein from his leg and another from his chest and attached them to the arteries at a spot in front of and behind the area that was blocked. In other words, we literally bypassed the area. Everything is working just fine now. In fact, he's probably in better shape because there isn't anything blocking the flow of blood to his heart.'

'Can I see him?'

'Not right now. He's in the recovery room and he'll probably be there for another hour or two. He'll go to the coronary care unit when he's ready. You can see him there but he's going to be heavily medicated. He probably won't even remember your visit. When he's well enough, he'll go up to the sixth floor for the rest of his stay. That floor is reserved for people with heart problems. I expect him to be out of the hospital by next week.'

'I'd still like to see him today, even if he doesn't know. When can I do that?'

The doctor looked at her watch. 'We'll transfer him

to coronary care in an hour or so. You can only stay for a short time, but I'd guess that you'll be able to see him around six.'

'You're certain my . . . my father is okay?'

Dr. Loerts pushed herself to her feet. 'Your dad is going to be fine, so don't worry.'

[3]

Quinn could not return to the gloomy solitude of his rented apartment. The only other place he could think to go was his chambers, where he planned to finish writing his letter of resignation and put his cases in order for the judges who would inherit them. Quinn drove the route to the courthouse in a mental fog. Dr. Loerts had assured Quinn that Frank would be okay, but Frank was eighty years old and Quinn knew that the years they had together were growing short.

Quinn's eyes watered and he felt a painful lump in his throat as he recalled asking Dr. Loerts if his 'father' was okay. It was the first time that he had ever referred to Frank Price as his father, even though the quiet, taciturn man had slowly insinuated himself into Quinn's consciousness in that way.

Quinn remembered the day that he moved into the Price home. It had been the day of his parents' funeral. He'd been putting his clothes away, still dressed in his black suit and too stunned to change, when Price came into his new bedroom. Quinn could picture him standing in the middle of the room, his arms dangling at his side, looking ill at ease. Quinn had been holding a stack of white crew-neck undershirts in his hand.

'I know you're about all in, so I'll make this short,' Frank had said. 'Anna and I don't have children. We didn't plan it that way. It's just the way it worked out. Your father is as close as we came. He was a great lawyer and one of the best men I ever met. When he married your mother, we were overjoyed and we came to love her as much as we loved Pat. Anna and I can't take the place of your parents. We'd never try. But we're here for you whenever you need us.'

Quinn warmed quickly to Anna, but it took him years to feel comfortable with Frank Price. Now, when he was close to losing him, the full import of what the feisty old man had done for him flooded in and it made him realize what it would mean to lose Laura, too. Love was a precious commodity, which people possessed rarely in this life. When you found it, you could not let it slip away. Quinn loved Laura and he was going to fight for her. He vowed to call her as soon as he arrived at the courthouse. He would tell her how much he loved her and he would beg her to take him back.

The Multnomah County Courthouse had been constructed in 1914 when there were few cars and parking was easy, so it did not have a garage. Judges with seniority were assigned spaces across the park across from the courthouse in the basement of the Justice Center, but Quinn's parking space was in a garage three blocks away where the county rented space. Quinn stopped at the entrance and put a plastic card in a slot. A metal bar rose and Quinn drove in. His space was in a corner far from the entrance on the lowest floor. The ceiling above the space was low where the ramp from the floor above sloped down and the corner was always in shadow.

There were no other cars around when Quinn parked his Volvo, which was not surprising since it was after nine at night. He knew a security guard patrolled the garage but he did not see him and assumed that he was making his rounds on another level.

Quinn's attaché case was in the backseat of the car. He opened the front door and stepped out, closing it behind him. He opened the back door on the driver's side and bent down to retrieve the attaché. When he straightened up, he saw movement in the side view mirror. Quinn turned and raised the case reflexively. Whatever the attacker had in his hand bounced off its side, but the blow was hard enough to drive Quinn backward into the side of the car.

Quinn lowered the attaché enough to see a tall man wearing jeans, gloves, a dark blue windbreaker and a ski mask. There was a sap in his right hand. Quinn was certain that he was the same man who had broken into his apartment. Quinn was taller and heavier than his assailant but he had never been good with his fists. He had won his only fight in high school because of his size, not his skill. Quinn circled warily, holding the attaché in front of him like a shield. The attacker edged closer. Quinn yelled for help. As the scream echoed off the concrete, the attacker feinted with the hand that held the sap. Quinn raised the attaché and the man kicked him in his shin. Quinn gasped. His right leg gave way and Quinn dropped his arms while still holding onto the attaché. The attacker smashed the sap into the left side of Quinn's head. Quinn's hands flew to his face and he dropped the case. The man hit Quinn in the solar plexus to silence him. Quinn fell against the car, hitting his head hard on the edge of the roof. He started to slump to the floor, but his attacker propped him up.

Quinn was almost unconscious. He heard the driver's door open and felt his attacker push him into the front seat. He wanted to sit up, but his body would not obey him. His vision blurred. Quinn thought he saw his attacker take a handgun out of the windbreaker and place it on the hood of the car. Quinn tried to struggle up, but rough hands grabbed both of his legs. He heard his assailant swear. The man was trying to stuff Quinn's legs into the car.

Quinn suddenly remembered his car keys. The Volvo could be opened or locked from a distance using a small keypad that was attached to the key. The lock button on the automatic door opener doubled as a panic alarm. Quinn groped in his pants pocket until he felt the plastic keypad. Just as his assailant finished pushing one of his legs into the car, Quinn held the lock button down for a count of three. The locks on all four doors clicked down. The attacker stopped, surprised by the sharp sound. The car alarm blared. Adrenaline coursed through Quinn. He kicked out with both feet. They struck solidly and drove the man back. Quinn launched himself out of the car and landed a wild right to the side of his attacker's head. The punch had no force and the man rolled with it, then connected solidly with

Quinn's ribs. Quinn grunted and the man struck him in the throat.

'Hey! What's going on here?' a security guard yelled from the far end of the garage. Quinn's attacker glanced toward the guard, doubled up Quinn with a front kick and ran toward the exit. Quinn slumped over the hood of the Volvo just as the guard ran past him. The guard was overweight and out of shape. He chased the attacker for a short distance, then turned back to Quinn. The judge looked down and saw the handgun. He pocketed it just as the guard asked, 'Are you okay?'

Quinn slumped against the car. His throat hurt and he had trouble talking for a moment, so he just nodded.

'You're lucky I came down here on my rounds.'

The guard took Quinn's elbow and helped him to straighten up. He picked up Quinn's attaché.

'Is this what he was after?' the guard asked.

'That's just a file in one of my cases,' Quinn croaked.

The guard realized the area of the garage he was in.

'Are you a judge?'

Quinn nodded.

'You don't think this was some guy you sentenced?'

'No. He was probably after my wallet.'

Quinn sat in the car until he caught his breath. He touched the side of his head where he had been sapped, and winced. The back of his head also hurt where it had smacked against the roof of the car, but the skin was not broken. His ribs, shin and head hurt and felt a little sick from being kicked and punched in the body.

'Do you want to go to the hospital?' the guard asked.

'No.'

Adrenaline had made the attack seem surreal. Now it was wearing off and Quinn began to shake, as it dawned on him that he could have been killed.

'I'd really like to go to my chambers in the courthouse.'

'You're certain?'

'Positive.'

He was afraid to return to his apartment, which his assailant had penetrated with ease.

'I'll walk you over to make sure nothing else happens.'

'Thanks. And thank you for saving me.'

As the guard and Quinn walked to the courthouse, Quinn asked, 'Do you have to report this?'

'Definitely.'

'It's just that I can't identify the man who attacked me. He was wearing a mask. And he didn't get anything. I don't want to waste police time when there's nothing I can say that will help them.'

'This is pretty serious. This guy may have attacked someone else. Besides, it's the rules.'

'Will the police have to talk to me right away? I'm pretty tired. I'd rather give my statement tomorrow.'

'I'll see what I can do.'

The security guard rode up with Quinn to his floor. Quinn unlocked the door to his office. He heard the guard report the attack on Fran's phone while he washed his face in the bathroom.

The guard rapped on the doorjamb and Quinn stepped out of the bathroom.

'You're okay for tonight. They're gonna send over a patrolman in the afternoon.'

The guard left. As soon as the door closed, Quinn took a step forward and the gun slapped against his side. Quinn took it out. When the policeman interviewed him about the attack tomorrow, he would give it to him. As he looked at the weapon a thought occurred to Quinn. He went through the sequence of the attack. The man had used a sap, so he wanted Quinn unconscious. When the assailant believed that Quinn was unconscious, he put the gun on the hood of the car and tried to stuff Quinn's legs into the car. Why do that? Why not just use the gun?

An answer occurred to Quinn. He felt ill. The police had the photographs of Quinn and Andrea in the Cove of Lost Souls. They suspected him of killing the woman at the Heathman. His assailant was planning on making it look like Quinn had committed suicide in his car. The gun would be placed in Quinn's hand. When the body was discovered it would look like Quinn had killed himself rather than face disgrace. An investigation might have cleared Quinn. Suicide would end the case.

Quinn let the gun rest in his hand and he flashed back to the fight in the garage. He'd been beaten, but he had fought back and it had felt good. For the first time since this insanity had started, he had not been a punching bag. He wondered what he would have done if he'd had the gun when he was attacked. He knew nothing about guns, but he believed that he would have fired it. The thought unsettled Quinn. He had experienced many emotions since Andrea Chapman was murdered, but

271

anger was not one of them. Anger was not an emotion that Quinn felt often. He rarely had a reason to be angry, but he was angry now. Someone was playing with his life and he was going to find out who it was.

Quinn suddenly realized that there was someone else who was in danger, someone who had a motive as strong as Quinn's to discover the people behind the plot to fix the *Crease* case and the resources to fight back. Quinn went to his desk. He opened Ellen Crease's file and found the form that she had filled out so that she could be released on her own recognizance. Then he dialed her unlisted phone number.

[4]

Two armed and uniformed guards were waiting for Quinn just inside the front gate of the Hoyt estate in a patrol vehicle with the markings of a private security company. As soon as Quinn stopped his car, the passenger door of the patrol car opened and a man with the build of an offensive lineman walked to the gate.

'Please step out of the car, sir, and show me some identification,' he commanded. Quinn noticed that he kept one hand on the butt of a holstered revolver. The guard in the car also watched Quinn's every move.

A gray mist covered Portland and the air was cold and clammy. Quinn shivered and hunched his shoulders. He slid his driver's license through the bars of the front gate. As soon as the guard was satisfied that the judge was the person he claimed to be, he told Quinn to return to his car. Quinn waited while the guard radioed the house, glad to be in a warm place again. Moments later, Quinn heard a low hum. The gate opened wide and the guard told him how to reach the house. Quinn drove through the gate. In the night sky was a dim quarter-moon. Quinn's headlights only made the barest incursion into the thick fog that obscured most of the grounds. Twice he saw an armed guard on patrol.

A handsome man in a gray business suit was waiting for Quinn when he parked in front of the mansion.

'Come in, Judge,' the man said, extending a hand. 'I'm Jack Brademas, head of security at Hoyt Industries. The senator wanted me to sit in on this meeting.'

Quinn shook hands and Brademas led him into the library, where Lou Anthony had talked to Ellen Crease on the evening of the murder. Crease stood up when the men entered. She was wearing jeans and a white shirt under a baggy sweater. A cigar smoldered in an ashtray at her elbow.

'You look cold, Judge,' Crease said. 'Would you like tea, coffee, or something stronger?'

Quinn noticed a coffee urn and a teapot sitting on a cherrywood sideboard next to several fine-china cups and saucers.

'Coffee, please.'

'Would you, Jack?'

Quinn sat down across from Crease in a high-backed chair and Brademas handed him a cup. The senator waited patiently while Quinn took a sip. Quinn's exhaustion was apparent, as was the discolored swelling on the side of the judge's face.

'When you called me, you sounded so upset that I agreed to meet with you,' Crease said. 'Now that I've had some time to think, I'm wondering if this meeting doesn't violate some code of ethics. I am the defendant in a case you're hearing.'

'Matters have gone way beyond that, Senator. There are events happening on the periphery of your criminal case of which you have been completely unaware. Both our lives are in danger.'

'Please explain that.'

'Senator, you have some very powerful enemies. People who will stop at nothing, including murder, to harm you. They have already effectively destroyed my career as a judge. Tonight they tried to kill me.'

'What?'

'Monday evening, a man in a ski mask broke into my apartment. He had photographs of a young woman and me that have the potential of destroying my career and my marriage. The man threatened to make the pictures public if I didn't fix your case so that you would be convicted of murdering your husband and Martin Jablonski.'

'But you ruled for me. You destroyed the State's case.'

'Yes. I did the only thing I could think of to protect you,' Quinn said softly. 'Because of what I did, a woman was murdered and an attempt was made on my life.'

'Judge, this is getting a bit confusing,' Jack Brademas interrupted sympathetically. 'If we're going to help, we have to know everything that's happened to you. Why don't you start at the beginning?'

Quinn recounted the trip to St. Jerome, the ruse that was used to trick Laura into flying to Miami, the visit from Claire Reston, his discovery of the second explanation for the blood spatter evidence found on the armoire, Reston's murder, and the recent attempt on his life.

'I think that Martin Jablonski was paid to murder you, Senator,' Quinn concluded. 'When he failed and you were arrested for your husband's murder, I was set up. Now that I've double-crossed the blackmailers, they're trying to frame me for Reston's murder and kill me. But I'm not the main focus of these people. You are. And that means that you're also in danger.'

'Judge, I can't begin to thank you for the sacrifices you've made for me. I owe you everything. Quite possibly my life.'

Quinn looked down, embarrassed. Crease thought silently for a moment. Then she blew an angry plume of smoke into the air and said, 'Benjamin Gage has to be behind this. He and Junior are the only people I can think of who hate me enough to want me dead, and Junior is too stupid to dream up a scheme this complex.'

Brademas nodded. 'I drew the same conclusion.'

He turned to Quinn.

'Benjamin Gage's administrative assistant is a man named Ryan Clark. He's an ex-navy SEAL. As soon as you told us that a man in scuba gear snatched the Chapman woman I thought of Clark. Pulling off a fake abduction underwater would be a piece of cake for someone with Clark's skills.'

'How did he do it?' Quinn asked. 'I never saw Andrea surface for air.'

'She wouldn't have to. There's an emergency breathing apparatus attached to all air tanks. She could have used the one on Clark's tank while they were underwater.'

'What do you think we should do next, Judge?' Crease asked.

'I think that the key to discovering the person behind this plot is learning the true identity of Andrea Chapman or Claire Reston or whatever her real name is. If we find out who she is, we might be able to find a link between her and the people who are after us.'

'Jack can trace her, Judge,' Crease said. 'He was a Portland Police officer before he came to work for my husband's company. We knew each other on the force. He still has contacts in the bureau.

'Jack, can you get copies of the investigative reports of the murder at the Heathman? We need to know the identity of the murdered woman and where she lived. Then we can try to find out how she got mixed up in this.'

'I'll have the information by tomorrow afternoon,' Brademas assured his boss.

'Good. Why don't you also think about the information that Judge Quinn has given us and see if you can come up with any other avenues of investigation?'

Brademas left and Crease turned to Quinn. 'It looks like we're both in more trouble than we ever wanted to be.' Crease sighed heavily. 'If the latest polls hold, my political career will be over. The only way I can save it is by proving that I was framed. Otherwise, people will always believe that I hired Jablonski and beat the rap on a technicality.'

'It might help if I went public and told everyone about the blackmail attempt.'

'It would only help if we can prove that we were both set up and who is behind this conspiracy. Otherwise, anything you say will sound like an attempt to exonerate yourself in the Reston murder. Besides, going public would destroy your career and I couldn't let you do that for me.'

'My career is over, anyway. I'm stepping down from the bench tomorrow. When I was attacked, I was going back to the courthouse to write my letter of resignation.'

'Don't do that. You're a good judge. If you resign from the bench, you're letting the bastards who set us up win. It took guts to rule for me. It was the right thing to do. Let Jack and me work on this. And don't give up hope. That's what you'd be doing if you resign.'

Twenty-one

[1]

W HEN QUINN walked into Stanley Sax's chambers, the presiding judge took a hard look at the yellowish purple bruise that spread across the left side of Quinn's face.

'Are you okay?'

'Physically, I'm fine. Emotionally . . . that's something else.'

'I can imagine. You're the talk of the courthouse. First that ruling in *Crease*, then this attack in the garage.'

'I want to take some time off, Stan.'

'That makes sense. How long do you want?'

'I cleared my desk when I thought that the *Crease* trial would take most of the month. I can take a few days off without disrupting the work of the court. I'll write memos in all of my cases so that any judge you assign will be able to get up to speed easily.'

'All right. Being attacked like that has to be frightening. Go home and rest. Call me next week and let me know how you feel. Maybe you and Laura should head for the coast. Lily and I used to rent a little bungalow in Cannon Beach and watch the storms with hot buttered rums and a good fire.' Sax smiled. 'A little romance is a great remedy for the blues.'

Sax's reminder of his empty marriage hurt, but Quinn faked a smile and said, 'Thanks for the advice and for being so understanding.'

Sax waved off Quinn. The judge left Sax's chambers and headed for his own. Fran Stuart examined Quinn's face. Before she could ask, Quinn said, 'This looks pretty bad, but I'm fine.'

Fran handed Quinn a stack of messages. As Quinn thumbed quickly through the stack to see if there was one from Crease or Brademas, his secretary said, 'Most of these are from friends asking if you're okay or from reporters who want to interview you. There was also a call from an Officer Ramirez. He wanted to set up an appointment for this afternoon so he can get a statement about the attack.'

Quinn looked at his watch. It was a little after three. He could probably fit in Ramirez around four-thirty. Quinn started toward his office.

'And your wife called several times.' Quinn's heart jumped. 'She wanted you to call her as soon as you got in.'

Quinn had been too exhausted physically and emotionally to call Laura after his visit to Ellen Crease. Her calls made Quinn anxious. Was she calling to reconcile or to ask for a divorce?

'Oh,' Fran said, 'there was one unusual call. It came in ten minutes ago. A woman named Denise Ritter. She said it was urgent. She wanted to talk to you about that woman who was murdered at the Heathman Hotel. She said that she's the woman's sister.'

'Her sister?'

'Yes. She sounded very upset.'

'Thank you, Fran.'

Quinn thumbed through his messages until he found the slip with Ritter's phone number. It had a Seattle area code. The phone rang twice, then a woman answered.

'Is this Denise Ritter?' Quinn asked.

'Yes?'

'This is Judge Richard Quinn.'

Quinn could hear breathing on the other end of the phone.

'Ms. Ritter?'

'I'm sorry. Maybe I shouldn't have called.'

'Is this about the woman who was murdered?'

'Yes. Marie is . . . was my sister.'

Quinn heard the woman's breath catch. Then he heard a sob.

'Are you all right?'

'I'm sorry. I . . . I flew down this morning on the shuttle to identify Marie's body.'

'That must have been awful.'

'The detectives were very kind, but . . .'

Ritter's voice trailed off and Quinn heard her blowing her nose. She apologized again.

'Ms. Ritter, why did you call me?'

'The detectives showed me a picture of you and Marie on a beach.'

'You told them that the woman in the pictures was Marie?'

'Yes.'

'Did they seemed surprised?'

'Now that you mention it, they did.'

'What did they ask you when you said that?'

'They wanted to know if Marie had ever mentioned you, but they wouldn't tell me why they were asking.'

Ritter hesitated. Then she said, 'Judge, Marie and I weren't close. Especially these past few years. I was hoping you could tell me what went wrong. How this happened.'

'Ms. Ritter, I would like to talk with you about Marie, too. If I took the shuttle to Seattle, would you meet with me tonight?'

[2]

The shuttle touched down a little after six P.M. Twenty minutes later, the cab Quinn hired at Sea-Tac Airport rounded a curve on the freeway and the judge saw the massive, glass and concrete structures that dominated Seattle's city center. Seattle had its share of interesting architecture: the Space Needle towered over everything, and the Pike Place Market, a collection of ramshackle stalls, shops and restaurants seemingly held together by glue, tottered on a hillside overlooking Elliott Bay. However,

Seattle's buildings were nowhere near as spectacular as its geography. The 'Emerald City' sat on a narrow strip of land between Puget Sound and eighteen-mile-long Lake Washington. Massive Mount Rainier dominated the landscape east of the city, and to the west were the jagged peaks of the Olympic Mountains.

Shortly after reaching the city, the cab turned off the interstate and traveled downhill toward the Pioneer Square Historic District, an area of late-Victorian and early-twentieth-century buildings that had been built up after the Great Fire of 1889. Day and night, the district swarmed with crowds attracted to its galleries, restaurants, antique shops and theaters. Denise Ritter had agreed to meet Quinn in an espresso bar at First and James near the original Pioneer Square. Quinn spotted the totem pole in the square before he located the café, a dark and narrow space squeezed between a gallery featuring Native American art and an occult bookstore. Toward the back of the espresso bar, a woman wearing a peasant dress nervously scanned the door.

Denise Ritter bore little resemblance to her sister. She was five nine and stoop-shouldered. Her hair was black like Marie's, but it was frizzy and collected behind her in a barrette, and her blue eyes hid behind thick, tortoiseshell glasses. Behind the thick lenses, Ritter's eyes were red from crying. When she noticed Quinn walking toward her, Ritter seemed to pull into herself. It took Quinn a moment to realize that Marie had modeled her Claire Reston persona on her real sister.

'I'm Richard Quinn,' the judge said when he reached Ritter's table. Ritter held out her hand self-consciously and Quinn took it. The skin felt cold and she looked exhausted.

'Are you all right?' Quinn asked as he sat down.

'No,' Ritter answered frankly. 'Seeing Marie like that was really hard for me.'

She could not go on and Quinn was relieved when a skinny waiter in jeans and a T-shirt walked up to the table. Quinn asked for coffee. Ritter was nursing a latte.

'I appreciate your willingness to meet with me, under the circumstances,' Quinn told Ritter.

'I'm doing this as much for me as for you. Marie was my sister. What I don't understand is your interest.'

'What did the police tell you about me?'

'That you knew Marie.'

'Did they say that I was a suspect in Marie's death?'

The question startled Ritter. She shook her head while examining Quinn more closely.

'And Marie never mentioned me to you, or talked about a judge that she knew?'

Ritter looked down at the tabletop. 'I rarely talked to Marie about her business.'

'What exactly did you understand Marie's business to be?'

Ritter sighed sadly. 'Marie was a call girl, Judge. A prostitute.'

Quinn should have been shocked, but he wasn't. If you wanted to hire a woman to seduce a man, seeking the services of a professional made sense.

'Did Marie work in Seattle?'

'Yes.'

'Did she ever work in Portland?'

'I don't know. She never told me she did, but I disapproved of Marie's . . . lifestyle and she knew it, so it was rare for her to discuss her profession with me.'

'I want you to know that before today I did not know that Marie was a prostitute,' Quinn said firmly. 'She told me that she designed belts. I thought she worked in the fashion industry. Did she ever do anything like that?'

'Marie! Not that I knew of.'

'Would you mind talking about your sister?'

Ritter brushed at her eyes. Her lower lip trembled.

'Marie was two years younger than me. She was always rebellious. I was a good student. Marie was at least as intelligent as I am, but she barely passed. She was into drugs, boys. My parents tried everything. Eventually, they gave up. When she was eighteen, Marie was arrested for prostitution and my parents kicked her out of the house. She wasn't really living at home then, anyway. After that, they wouldn't have anything to do with her.'

'Do your parents know that Marie is dead?'

'No. I haven't told them. I don't know what to say. They wrote Marie off years ago.'

'How close were you to your sister?'

'That's hard to answer. We saw very little of each other when I was at college and graduate school. After I moved back to Seattle to take a teaching job we started meeting a little more, but there wasn't any plan to it. Sometimes she would just drop by or she'd call on the spur of the moment and we'd go out for dinner. A lot of the times when she called I thought it was because she was lonely, but, if I asked her, she would always pretend to be upbeat and tell me how great her life was.'

Ritter paused and took a sip of her latte. When she looked up, there were tears in her eyes.

'There were other times when she would show up out of the blue, strung out or just needing a place to stay. I knew she wanted help when she came to me like that. I even got her to go into a rehab program once. The last few times I saw her I think she was clean, but I'm so naive I don't think I could really tell if she was using.'

Quinn handed Ritter his handkerchief.

'I'm sorry,' she apologized. 'I guess we really weren't that close. We were so different. But she was my sister and she was so lost. The last time we were together I tried to talk her into getting a straight job. She just laughed. She said she was doing great and was going to do better. She looked like she was, too. She was wearing expensive clothes and jewelry I hadn't seen before.'

'Where was she getting her money? I know you said that she was a call girl. Was that her only job? Did she have a pimp?'

'No, not a pimp. From what I could figure out, she worked for an escort service. But it was a front for a call girl operation.'

Denise paused. She suddenly looked very thoughtful.

'That last time I saw Marie, the time I told you about, when she was dressed in the expensive clothes, that was in mid-February. She was very up, very excited, and that was strange, because I knew she didn't enjoy earning her money the way she did. She'd told me that much.'

Quinn had been in St. Jerome in late February. He was sure that Marie Ritter's sudden, mid-February good fortune was connected to the blackmail plot.

'Did Marie tell you why she was excited or how she got the money for the clothes?'

'Not specifically. She did talk about making a lot of money and I had the impression that the money she was going to make wasn't connected to the escort service. That it was something that she had going on the side. But I can't be certain of that.'

'Did your sister have any friends I might talk to?'

'Marie mentioned someone named Christy a few times and another woman named Robin, but all I know about them is their first names.'

'Did your sister ever talk about her customers?'

'I didn't encourage Marie to talk about what she did. It was very distasteful to me, that kind of life.' Ritter shuddered. 'I can't even imagine it.

'When she did speak about the men she'd been with, it was usually with contempt, but she never mentioned their names and I didn't ask. She thought most of them were pathetic. There were a few she said were okay, but generally she would laugh about them. As I said, I didn't enjoy discussing what she did, except to try to get her to stop.'

'Denise, did your sister ever mention any customers from Portland?'

'Not that I can recall.' Ritter paused. 'She did tell me that there was a man she had seen more than once who lived in Oregon. He had some kind of business in Seattle. It was something odd.'

'Can you remember what it was?'

Ritter brightened. 'She said he was an undertaker. Marie thought that was funny.'

Quinn felt a surge of excitement. 'Denise, this is important. Did she describe this man? Can you remember anything she said about him?'

Ritter frowned, then shook her head.

'All I remember was his business.'

'She never said how old he was?'

'She said he didn't dress or act like she thought an undertaker would. I think he was a flashy dresser and he liked to dance all night, so I assumed that he was young, but she never told me his age.'

'Do you have any idea how I can get in touch with Marie's escort service?'

'No. I don't even know where Marie was living these past few months.'

Ritter paused. Then she looked directly at Quinn.

'I've been trying to build up the courage to ask you something since you walked in, Judge.'

'Go ahead and ask your question.'

'What was your connection with my sister?'

'I met her on a plane when I flew to the Caribbean to speak at a legal conference. We spent the next day on the beach you saw in the picture. I think Marie was hired to make friends with me, then seduce me. When the police searched the hotel room where Marie was murdered, they found those pictures in her suitcase and they brought me to the hotel room. They thought that I might have killed her, but I didn't. I could never hurt someone the way your sister was hurt.'

Ritter digested this information. Then she took a deep breath and looked directly at Quinn.

'The detectives . . . They only pulled back the sheet enough to show me Marie's face and I was too upset to ask. Was she . . . ? Did she feel much pain?'

Quinn flashed back to the room. For a brief moment, he saw Marie Ritter's savaged body.

'I'm afraid she did,' the judge answered gently.

Ritter's eyes watered. She bit her lip.

'Please tell me what happened.'

'Marie, you don't want to know that. That isn't going to do you any good.'

'Please,' Ritter pleaded.

Quinn sighed and described what he had seen in the hotel room as delicately as was possible. When he was through, Ritter spaced out for a moment.

'I knew this would happen if she stayed in that life. I tried to talk to her, but she wouldn't listen to me.'

'You can only do so much. Don't make the mistake of thinking that this was your fault or that there was some way that you could have saved her. Some people don't want to be saved. Promise me that you're not going to take this burden on your shoulders.'

Ritter sighed. 'No, I won't make that mistake.'

'Good. That's good. The killer took your sister. Don't you let him take you, too.'

[3]

Quinn was barely conscious of the fifty-minute flight back to Portland. All he could think about was the information that Denise Ritter had given to him. Mary Garrett had filed a pretrial discovery motion claiming that she had not received all of the police reports in the possession of the prosecution. To resolve the issue, Quinn had been forced to review the reports. He had read Detective Anthony's interview with Charles DePaul. If Junior knew that his father was going to change his will, he would have a clear motive for hiring Jablonski to kill his father and Ellen Crease. If Junior knew that Crease could not benefit from the will if she was convicted of her husband's murder, Junior would have a motive to blackmail Quinn. Quinn suddenly remembered the argument between Junior and his father at Hoyt Industries that Anthony had learned about during his interview with Stephen Appling. Were they arguing about the will?

How could he find out the cause of the argument? Only Junior and his father were present. An idea occurred to Quinn. Karen Fargo had to be the woman who was going to be the new beneficiary of Hoyt's will. She was his mistress when the argument occurred. Men talked to their mistresses about the things that bothered them.

Quinn's first impulse was to tell Ellen Crease about his discovery in Seattle. Jack Brademas could talk to Fargo. He was a professional investigator, a former policeman. But that wouldn't work. Fargo would never talk to anyone connected to Ellen Crease. He would have to do it.

* * *

A light rain was falling when Quinn's flight landed at nine-thirty. He found Fargo's address in the phone book and drove straight from the Portland Airport to her yellow and white Cape Cod. The judge parked out front shortly after ten o'clock. There were lights on in the front room. Quinn dashed across the street and huddled under the overhang that shaded the front door. He rang the bell. The sound from a television show stopped and a curtain moved. Moments later, the front door opened as wide as the safety chain would permit.

'Ms. Fargo?'

'Yes?' she responded warily.

'I'm Richard Quinn. I'm a judge. I heard the case against Ellen Crease.'

Fargo recognized Quinn from the television broadcasts about the case.

'What do you want from me?'

Quinn smiled to put Fargo at ease. 'It would be great if I could get inside. I forgot my umbrella.'

Water was running down Quinn's face and beading on his raincoat. Fargo opened the door and let Quinn inside. He ran a hand through his hair to rid it of some of the rain.

'I apologize for coming so late and not calling first. I wouldn't disturb you if this wasn't important.'

Fargo walked into the living room and gestured toward the couch. Quinn took off his coat so he would not dampen her furniture. Fargo sat forward on her chair watching Quinn.

'You know that I ruled against the State in the pretrial hearings?'

Fargo nodded.

'Some new information has come to me that I didn't have when I made the ruling. I'm afraid I can't tell you what it is. I hope you understand.'

'Certainly.'

'I've learned that Lamar Hoyt and his son had an argument shortly before Mr. Hoyt was murdered. It's suddenly become important to find out the substance of the argument, but no one knows what they talked about. I was wondering if Mr. Hoyt mentioned it to you.'

'Yes. He did. I . . . I never told anyone about it because I didn't think that it was important.'

'That's okay, Ms. Fargo. You wouldn't have understood why I need to know about the argument. Can you tell me what Mr. Hoyt said?'

'I don't remember the date.'

'That's okay.'

'I do remember Lamar visiting in the early evening. He was very angry about Junior.'

'Why?'

'He thought he was skimming money from the mortuary business. Profits were down and he was furious. He was having Junior investigated and the investigator had found out that Junior was living way beyond his means. The argument occurred when Lamar confronted Junior with the things that the investigator found.'

'Did Mr. Hoyt mention anything specific that the investigator had found?'

Fargo colored. 'Most of it had to do with women.'

'Dates?'

Fargo shook her head. 'There was some of that, but

Lamar said that Junior was also paying expensive prostitutes. Lamar also thought that Junior was using cocaine. It was very sordid and Lamar was furious.'

[4]

Laura's calls had been on Quinn's mind all day, but he had been either too busy to call her or too afraid. If she wanted a divorce, he did not want to learn about it when he was tired and run-down. But what if she wanted him back? As soon as he returned to his apartment, Quinn poured himself a stiff drink and phoned Laura.

'Dick!' Laura responded with obvious relief when she heard his voice. 'Where are you? I've been trying to reach you all day.'

'I'm at my apartment, but I was in Seattle earlier today.'

'What were you doing there?'

'It would take too long to explain. Fran told me that you called several times. What did you want to talk to me about?'

'I need to see you.' Laura's voice wavered. 'Can you come home?'

'Now?'

'Yes. Please.'

Quinn had rarely heard uncertainty in Laura's voice and this was the first time he had ever heard her plead. If she was anything, Laura was a model of self-confidence, always certain that she was right, always the one who made the demands, never the supplicant.

'I'll come over right away.'

'Thank you, Dick.'

Quinn hung up the phone and stood quietly for a moment. He had wanted to say something more, to tell Laura that he still loved her, but he couldn't, because he was afraid of what she would say.

Laura looked tense when she opened the front door for Quinn. She was dressed casually in a blue warm up suit, but she had put on makeup and her hair was combed carefully. He hoped that was a good sign.

'Take off your coat. Let's sit down.' Laura pointed toward the living room. 'I even made you a drink.'

Quinn saw a glass of Scotch resting on an end table next to the couch. He shucked his coat and followed Laura. She sat opposite him with a coffee table between them.

'I've been rehearsing this, so let me just talk, okay? When I married you we seemed to have the same goals. Then you left the firm to become a judge. It was hard for me to accept that. I felt betrayed. It wasn't just the money. It was the life I'd planned for the two of us. I couldn't understand how you could walk away from your partnership, something that I coveted so much. I think we started drifting apart after you made that choice. I'm not saying it was your fault. But it's true. Something changed in the marriage. Or maybe I changed. It doesn't matter.

'I really was sorry when the Miami client hired me, but I honestly believed that I owed it to the firm to take him on. Then the job turned out to be a hoax. I was furious.

All I wanted to do was to fly back to Portland. I started to phone the airline when I remembered how sad you had been when I told you I couldn't go with you to St. Jerome. I remembered your voice on the phone. You sounded so . . .'

Laura shook her head. 'I stopped with my hand in the air. It was . . . I don't know . . . like a light going on, like I was suddenly hearing something clearly that had only been a murmur. I realized how much pain you were in and that I was the cause of that pain. I asked myself what I wanted to happen to our marriage and I didn't know the answer to that question. That's why I flew to St. Jerome. I hoped that I could figure out how I really felt about us by being there with you, away from Portland and the law office and my work. I knew that there was something terribly wrong with our marriage and I wanted to try and cure it. But everything fell apart after I arrived.'

Laura stopped to collect herself. She was a person who kept her feelings to herself and Quinn could see how painful it was for her to reveal her emotions.

'I was in Los Angeles on business on Wednesday and Thursday. Today, two detectives visited me at the office. They told me about the woman who was murdered at the Heathman. They wanted to know about the woman who disappeared on St. Jerome. They showed me pictures of the two of you on the beach.

'I didn't understand where they were going, at first. The black detective, Dennis, is very smooth. When it became clear that they thought you might have killed the woman at the hotel, I had to make a decision. I asked myself if I truly believed that you could murder someone the way they said that poor woman was killed. I had to decide what type of person I married and I decided that you could never do that.'

'Laura, some other things have happened to me this past week that you don't know about. They explain why the woman at the hotel was murdered. I love you very much. The one thing I want more than anything in the world is for us to be together again. But I don't want to hide anything from you.'

Laura waited for Quinn to continue. The look of wariness on her face frightened Quinn. By the time he finished explaining about the blackmail attempt by the man in the ski mask, Claire Reston's visit to his chambers and the way he had decided the *Crease* case, her expression was unreadable.

'After I suppressed the evidence, I prepared for the worst, but I never dreamed that the blackmailers would murder someone to frame me. I've been sick about it. The way that woman died . . .'

'Why didn't the blackmailers just carry out their threat and send the photographs to the authorities on St. Jerome?'

'They couldn't, Laura. Andrea Chapman did not die on St. Jerome.'

'What?'

'It was a hoax. The woman who posed as Andrea Chapman on St. Jerome and the woman who pretended to be Claire Reston were the same person, Marie Ritter, a Seattle call girl. Ritter has a distinctive scar on her hip. I saw it in the cove and I saw it on Reston's body in the hotel room. By killing Ritter, the blackmailer got rid of a witness at the same time that he set me up for her murder. Last night he tried to wrap everything up by killing me.'

Laura's eyes widened. 'Fran told me that someone attacked you in the parking garage. I thought that was a robbery attempt.'

'The man who attacked me is the same man who broke into my apartment.'

'God, Dick. Do you have any idea who's behind this plot?'

'Benjamin Gage has an aide who is an ex-SEAL. He'd have had no trouble faking the underwater murder on St. Jerome. But I talked to Marie Ritter's sister in Seattle. She told me that Marie had a customer who lives in Oregon. Denise didn't know his name, but she had the impression that he's young and he's an undertaker.'

'Lamar Hoyt's son.'

'Yes. And I've also learned that Junior and his father quarreled shortly before Hoyt's death because Senior believed that his son was skimming money from the mortuary business.'

'Then you think Junior is behind everything?'

'That's where the evidence seems to be pointing, but Lamar, Jr., and Ryan Clark are both the same size as the blackmailer and the man who attacked me in the garage.'

'Have you given this information to the police?'

'No. I just learned the information about Lamar, Jr., tonight and I really can't prove that Junior knew

Ritter. Marie never told Denise the name of her client. If Junior denies knowing Ritter, we can't prove he's lying.'

'And Hoyt's statements to Fargo are hearsay.'

Quinn closed his eyes and let his head fall back.

'I don't know what I'm going to do, Laura.'

'One thing you are not going to do is give up,' Laura said forcefully. 'We are going to get through this.'

Quinn opened his eyes and he looked at his wife hopefully.

'Does that mean that you want me back?'

Laura reached out and took Quinn's hand.

'I put up a good front, Dick, but I'm always scared. I've been scared since my parents divorced. Scared for years and years. Scared that I'll lose everything if I don't work harder than everybody. That I'll end up like my father.'

'I have a hard time picturing you failing at anything, Laura.'

'Our marriage almost failed, but I'm not going to let it. I do want you back. I want us to try to . . . to be together like we were when . . . when we first . . .'

Quinn took Laura in his arms before she could finish. Her body shuddered and so did his. Quinn stroked Laura's hair and kissed the top of her head. She raised her face and Quinn kissed her lips. The kiss was tentative at first, then they were sprawled on the carpet and Laura was opening Quinn's belt. Quinn broke away only for the brief time that it took them to struggle out of their clothes. Then they became a tangle of bodies, soft and hard, the kisses so eager that they both wondered if there would be anything left of them when they were through.

After their first frenzied bout of lovemaking, Quinn and Laura gathered their clothes and went upstairs to the bedroom. The second time they made love it was less frantic and Quinn took his time renewing his acquaintance with a body that had become foreign to him. When they were sated, Quinn collapsed beside Laura. Her hand found his and she said, 'I love you.'

'I never thought I'd hear you say that again.'

'Well, I have. I want our marriage to work, Dick. I want it more than I want anything else. No matter what happens from now on, I'm standing with you.'

[5]

Benjamin Gage listened to the recording of Richard Quinn's meeting with Ellen Crease and Jack Brademas for a second time. When the minicassette stopped spinning, Ryan Clark turned off the tape recorder. Gage looked grim.

'Can we use this?' Gage asked.

'No. The recording was obtained illegally. We'd also be forcing Quinn to go public.'

'And he'd have to admit that he fixed Crease's case. She'd be discredited.'

'Maybe not. Quinn would say that the blackmailer wanted him to make sure that Crease was found guilty. Now that there is an alternative explanation for the blood spatter evidence, a lot of voters will conclude that she's been framed. I don't think we can afford to gamble. Not with you leading in all of the polls.'

'You're right.' Gage picked up the minicassette. 'Have there been more of these?'

'One other. The information wasn't useful, but the intelligence on this cassette is certainly interesting.'

'Our man seems to be on top of things. Make sure he's taken care of. I want him working hard for us.'

Twenty-two

[1]

WHEN LOU ANTHONY arrived at work Saturday morning there was a message from Denise Ritter asking him to call. Ritter sounded nervous when the detective identified himself.

'Something happened yesterday. I wasn't going to call, at first. I . . . I don't want to get anyone in trouble. But I thought about Marie. That this might help find the person who killed her.'

'Finding your sister's killer is very important to me, Ms. Ritter. If you have information that might help, please tell me.'

'When you and Detective Dennis interviewed me you asked if Marie ever mentioned Richard Quinn. She didn't. She never said that she knew any judge.'

Denise Ritter hesitated. Anthony waited patiently for her to continue.

'I hope I didn't do anything wrong, but I couldn't stop thinking about that question, so I called Judge Quinn. He flew to Seattle yesterday evening.'

'Quinn flew up to see you?'

'Yes.'

'What did you two talk about?'

'Marie mostly. He told me how they met on St. Jerome . . .'

'He knew that the woman in the photograph I showed you was your sister? The woman who was murdered at the Heathman?'

'He seemed to know. Why?'

'Nothing. It's not that important. Go on.'

'I did tell Judge Quinn one thing that I didn't tell you. That's why I'm calling. I thought about it all night. Judge Quinn seemed to think it was important, so I decided that you should know, too.'

'What is it that you think I should know?'

'The judge asked me if Marie had any clients from Portland. I told him that Marie didn't tell me the name of any of the men she had been with, but she did tell me that one of them lived in Oregon. The only reason I remembered what Marie said was because he had an odd job. She said he was an undertaker.'

Anthony and Ritter talked for a few more moments. The detective was thanking her when Leroy Dennis strolled over to Anthony's desk. Anthony waved him into a seat, finished with Ritter and hung up.

'The person on the phone was Denise Ritter. She called to tell me that Judge Quinn flew up to Seattle yesterday and pumped her about her sister's background.'

'No kidding?'

'No kidding. She also told me that Quinn knew that Andrea Chapman and Claire Reston were the same person. But that's not the most important thing Denise told me. It seems that one of her sister's customers was an undertaker from Oregon.'

'Whoa.'

'Yeah, whoa.'

'What are you thinking, Lou?'

'What if Junior learned that his father was going to marry Karen Fargo and alter his will in her favor? Steve Appling said that the two Lamars had a pretty bad argument shortly before the murder. Maybe that's when Junior discovered Senior's plan.'

'So you think Junior may have hired Jablonski to kill his father?'

'And Crease. With both of them dead, he would inherit everything. But Jablonski screwed up and got himself killed, so Junior's plan failed. Then Crease was arrested and Junior had a second chance. If Crease was convicted of hiring Jablonski to kill her husband she couldn't benefit from the will. I think Junior used Ritter to blackmail Judge Quinn.'

'Damn, you may be right.'

'It would certainly explain the way Quinn is acting. Those photographs scream blackmail, Leroy.'

'And Denise Ritter has just supplied the link between Junior and her sister,' Dennis answered thoughtfully. Then he frowned. 'But there are problems with your scenario, Lou.'

'Such as?'

'Jablonski for one. He was in prison for a long time. When he was out, he wasn't running in Junior's circle. How did they meet?'

'I don't know, but I'm gonna nail Junior's ass as soon as I find out.'

'And another thing,' Dennis continued. 'Until you learned about this possible connection between Marie Ritter and Hoyt, you thought Crease killed her husband.'

'She still could be good for it,' Anthony answered grudgingly. 'That blood spatter evidence bothers the hell out of me.'

'Exactly. And don't forget Judge Quinn. If Ritter was blackmailing him, he'd have a powerful motive to kill her.'

Anthony sighed. 'I have to admit that I've been really pissed at Quinn since he accused me of lying, but I have a hard time seeing him as Ritter's killer.'

'Quinn has been acting like a man with something to hide.'

'No doubt about that. The judge flat out lied about knowing Ritter and he continued to lie after being confronted with the pictures, but I still don't make Quinn for the Ritter killing. Any man can commit murder under the right circumstances. Ritter threatens to ruin Quinn, go to his wife, go to the press. Quinn hits her in a rage. One moment of passion, one dead woman. But that isn't what we have here. Marie Ritter was raped and systematically tortured. My gut tells me that Quinn couldn't kill her like that.'

'So you think that the judge is concealing information

about the murder because he's being blackmailed?'

'That's the only way I can explain the way the judge has been acting. Quinn definitely saw those pictures before we showed them to him at the Heathman. He almost peed his pants when he saw them, but he didn't ask a single question about where they came from or how we got them. And why else would he be playing detective in Seattle? I think he's trying to figure out who killed Ritter himself.'

Dennis thought about what Anthony had just said. His brow furrowed. Then Dennis shot up in his seat.

'Hot damn. If someone did use those pictures to blackmail Quinn it might be our lucky break.'

'I don't follow you.'

'If Junior was the blackmailer he would have ordered Quinn to fix the case so that Crease would be convicted.'

Anthony frowned. 'Quinn rigged the case *for* Crease.'

'Right.'

'That puts us back to square one again with Crease as the main suspect.'

'Not necessarily. I've been checking on Quinn. Everybody says that the man's a saint, and I mean everybody. Real high principles. Look at the way he sent that Eugene judge to jail. Everyone was betting that he'd give him probation. It's possible that the blackmailer ordered Quinn to make certain that Crease was convicted and Quinn just couldn't do it.'

'So where does that leave us?'

'I think the key to identifying the blackmailer is finding out what Quinn was told to do, not what he really did. And to do that, we've got to ask the judge.'

[2]

On Saturday morning, Quinn and Laura slept until nine-thirty. They decided to visit Frank Price at the hospital. After that Quinn would go to the courthouse. He had put his decision to resign on hold, but he still had to prepare the memos on his cases so he could take time off.

Quinn was washing the breakfast dishes when the doorbell rang. Laura looked up from the paper when her husband walked to the door. Quinn peered through the peephole. Lou Anthony and Leroy Dennis were standing on the welcome mat.

'Good morning, Judge,' Dennis said. 'May we come in?'

'What's this about?' Quinn asked warily.

Dennis glanced at Laura. He looked uncomfortable.

'Maybe we should talk in private, Judge.'

'I have nothing to hide from my wife.'

Dennis hesitated. 'Some of the questions we're going to ask . . . The subjects are delicate.'

'I repeat. I have nothing to hide from my wife.'

Quinn led the detectives into the living room.

'What do you want to know?' he asked when they were all seated.

'Denise Ritter called me this morning and told me about your trip to Seattle,' Anthony said. 'What were you doing up there?'

'She called me. She said that she wanted to talk to me about her sister.'

'So you hop a jet and fly to Seattle?'

Quinn did not respond.

'Why didn't you tell me that Andrea Chapman and Claire Reston were the same person when we were at the crime scene?'

'I only suspected that the two women were the same when I saw the dead woman at the hotel. I wasn't certain. I was pretty upset.'

'I remember,' Dennis said, 'and I can't believe that you want the person who tortured Marie Ritter to death to get away with it.'

'I don't.'

'That's not the way you're acting,' Dennis said.

'We think that you have information that will help us identify Marie Ritter's killer,' Anthony told Quinn.

'We're counting on your decency, Judge,' Dennis said. 'We're counting on you coming through for us.'

'What is this information that you believe I have?'

'I'm gonna put my cards on the table,' Anthony told Quinn. 'We have evidence that points to a suspect other than Senator Crease. You know who I'm talking about. Denise Ritter told you that her sister had a customer from Oregon who was an undertaker. If Lamar Hoyt, Jr., is the customer, he becomes suspect number one.

'Now we come to you, Judge. I've been on the losing side of motions before. Hell, everyone screws up. But no judge has ever accused me of intentionally lying under oath. When I calmed down I asked myself why you did what you did. It was a mystery, until we found those pictures of you and Ritter. Then everything fell into place.'

'Lou and I are certain that you were blackmailed to fix Ellen Crease's case,' Dennis said, feeling vindicated by the swift shift of emotions on Quinn's face. 'What we need to know is whether the blackmailer wanted you to acquit Crease or convict her. We figure that Junior would have asked you to make certain that Crease was convicted. If Senator Crease was blackmailing you, she would want you to fix the case so that she couldn't be convicted.'

'So there it is, Judge,' Anthony told Quinn. 'If you tell us that the blackmailer wanted you to convict Ellen Crease, we'll concentrate on Lamar Hoyt, Jr. If you tell us that you were ordered to acquit Crease, we'll go to the D.A. with that.'

'And you'll ask Cedric Riker to move to set aside Dick's order on the grounds that it was obtained by fraud,' Laura told Anthony.

'Yes, ma'am,' he answered without hesitation. 'We'd have to.'

'That would expose my husband to disbarment, criminal charges and disgrace.'

'There is no way around that.'

'Of course,' Dennis said quickly, 'we could work out something with the criminal charges.'

'Like the Eugene Police did with Frederick Gideon?' Laura said.

Dennis blinked.

'Detectives,' Laura said, 'my husband won't answer any more of your questions without consulting an attorney.'

Dennis and Anthony sagged.

'Laura,' Quinn started.

'Listen to me on this, Dick.'

Quinn wanted to talk to the detectives, but he realized that Laura was right.

'I appreciate the way you've handled this case and the consideration you've shown me,' Quinn told the detectives. 'I'm not ruling out our talking further. But you know how serious a decision this is for me.'

'I know that, Judge,' Dennis agreed.

'Just give me some time to think.'

'Cedric Riker also suspects that you fixed Crease's hearing and he wants your blood. If Riker had his way, we'd be questioning you at the station with a rubber hose and klieg lights shining in your eyes. I'd rather trust your good instincts and have you cooperate because you know it's the right thing to do, but we can't wait very long for you to decide.'

'You see our position?' Dennis asked. 'We have a very dangerous person running free. That person has murdered Marie Ritter and was responsible for the death of Lamar Hoyt. He also attacked you. Remember, Judge, you're the key witness here and the killer knows that. He tried to kill you once. You can bet he'll try again.'

Quinn thought about that. If he were attacked at home, Laura would be in danger.

'Before you go,' Quinn said, 'there is something else I learned that might help you. Lamar Hoyt suspected that Junior was skimming from the mortuary business. That's why they argued at Hoyt Industries headquarters.'

'How do you know that?'

'Karen Fargo told me last night.'

Anthony colored. 'Damn it, Judge, you are not one of the Hardy Boys. Stay the hell out of this investigation. You hear me?'

Laura showed the detectives to the door. Then she returned to the living room, where she found Quinn looking totally lost.

'What should I do?' he asked as soon as Laura sat beside him.

'If you admit to the police that you fixed Ellen Crease's case you can bank on being forced to resign from the bench and you face the additional threats of being disbarred and prosecuted criminally.'

'Maybe I don't deserve to stay on the bench. I covered up what I thought was a murder. I fixed a case.'

'You had good reasons for not going to the authorities on St. Jerome and you decided the motion to suppress the way you did to protect Ellen Crease.'

'I could have told the police about the blackmail threat, withdrawn from the case and let another judge take over.'

'Yes. You probably should have, but you didn't. We have to deal with what really happened. I guess the problem is that anything you do puts you in jeopardy. The ideal solution would be for the police to arrest the killer without your assistance.'

'Without my help they might never be able to do that.'

*   *   *

[3]

Anthony dropped off Leroy Dennis at the police station, then drove to Karen Fargo's house. He got along well with the witness and he had explained to Dennis that Fargo might be more comfortable speaking to him alone.

'I just came from talking to Judge Quinn,' Anthony said when they were seated at a table in Fargo's tiny kitchen. 'He said he talked to you last night, and you told him why Lamar and his son quarreled.'

'It was okay to talk to him, wasn't it?' Fargo asked anxiously. 'He's a judge.'

'Oh, sure. No, you did the right thing. I just wanted to find out if there's anything else you remembered that you think is important.'

Fargo hesitated. Anthony thought that she seemed agitated.

'Is something wrong?' he asked.

'No, I . . .' Fargo could not meet Anthony's eye.

'Karen, if you know something that will help in this investigation, you've got to tell me. There have been three deaths already.'

'I never lied. Everything I said to you and the grand jury was true, but . . .'

'Yes?'

Fargo looked desperate.

'Is it illegal if I was paid to come to see you? Would I be breaking the law?'

'Someone paid you to come forward?'

Fargo told Anthony about the visit from the man with the scar.

'How much were you paid?' Anthony asked when Fargo was through.

'Five thousand dollars.'

'Did this man who visited you say who he was or who he was working for?'

'No, but I saw him again.'

'Where?'

'On the evening news.'

'Did the newscaster say his name?' Anthony asked excitedly.

'No. He was just someone in a news story, but . . .'

'Yes?'

'It was right after Judge Quinn suppressed the evidence. That's what the story was about. And this man, the one who came here, he looked like he was with Senator Gage.'

[4]

The courthouse was deserted when Quinn arrived. He went directly to his chambers and put on a pot of coffee. While the coffee perked, Quinn went into his office and surveyed the paperwork that was strewn across the top of his desk. Most of it was from the motions in the *Crease* case. Quinn went back into the anteroom and looked through the filing cabinet behind Fran Stuart's desk. By the time he had pulled the files in the other cases that had to be dealt with, the coffee was ready.

Quinn poured himself a mug and shut the door to his office. After tuning his radio to a classical music station,

311

the judge began organizing the documents on his desk into piles so he could return them to the file in *State v. Crease* with some sense of order. Quinn put a rubber band around the police reports that he had examined when he was deciding Cedric Riker's motion to exclude evidence of Martin Jablonski's criminal record. He was about to put them in the accordion file where he kept all of the documents pertaining to the motion when he noticed something that was written on the top report. Quinn slipped the report out from under the rubber band and examined it. It was the arresting officer's account of a six-year-old home burglary committed by Jablonski. His conviction for this crime had sent him to the penitentiary until his release last year. As Quinn reread the report his heartbeat accelerated. He tried to calm down so he could figure out what his discovery meant. When he was certain of his reasoning, Quinn phoned Ellen Crease.

'Crease residence,' James Allen said.

'Mr. Allen, this is Judge Quinn. Is Senator Crease in?'

'Yes, sir.'

Allen put Quinn on hold. When the phone came back to life, Ellen Crease was on the other end. Quinn told her about Junior's connection to Marie Ritter and what he had learned from Karen Fargo. Then Quinn explained his discovery of the police report and the conclusions he had drawn from it.

'My God,' Crease said when Quinn was finished. 'This is so hard to believe.'

'But it makes sense.'

'Yes, it does.'

Crease sounded like she was in shock.

'What do you think we should do?' Quinn asked.

Crease thought for a moment.

'The courthouse is only a block from the Justice Center. Wait for me in your chambers. I'm coming down. We'll go to the police together.'

While Quinn waited for Crease, he organized his files. The busywork helped him take his mind off the terrible events of the past few days. Periodically, Quinn checked the time. He thought it would take Crease about half an hour to drive downtown. Quinn had placed the call to Crease a little after three and it was already three-thirty. Quinn expected the phone to ring at any moment.

At three-fifty, Quinn heard the door between the anteroom and the corridor open. Quinn walked to the door to his chambers. He reached for the doorknob, then stopped himself. A peephole had been installed for security purposes. Through it, Quinn saw the man who had attacked him in the garage quietly closing the door to the corridor. His face was still concealed behind a ski mask and he was carrying a large hunting knife.

Quinn locked his door just as the man reached for the knob. Quinn saw the knob turn slowly. He backed against the desk. There was a second door in his chambers that opened onto the bench. Quinn realized that he could escape through it into the courtroom, then he could get out through the courtroom door.

Quinn started to leave when he remembered the gun that had been left on the hood of his car. It was in his desk drawer. He had meant to turn it over to the police, but he never had the chance. Quinn raced around the desk and got the gun. He had never fired one and had only a vague idea, picked up from television and the movies, of how to shoot it, but he felt better holding the weapon.

Quinn opened the door behind the bench as quietly as possible and slipped into the courtroom. He closed the door silently and crept down the stairs from the bench to the bar of the court, praying that the person in his anteroom would not think of his escape route.

Rain clouds had darkened the sky and very little light came through the courtroom windows. The weak light that illuminated the courthouse corridor seeped into the courtroom. The empty benches were cloaked in shadow. Quinn hurried to the door. It was locked, but he had the key. As he stepped into the corridor, the door to his chambers opened and he and his attacker were suddenly face to face.

Both men paused for a second. Then the man in the mask took a step toward Quinn. Quinn pointed his weapon down the corridor and fired. In the narrow confines of the marble hallway the gunshot roared like a cannon. Quinn's aim was terrible. The bullet ricocheted crazily as it bounced off the walls. The man ducked back into Quinn's chambers.

The courthouse was a square. The fifth floor consisted of four corridors built around an open center. At the front of the courthouse were the elevators and broad steps that led down to the front door. Quinn wanted to run down those stairs, but that would mean passing the door to his chambers, so he headed to the hall in the rear of the courthouse. There, two enclosed staircases at either end of the hall went down to the back corridor on the first floor. If he could make it to the first floor, Quinn could run into a tiny alcove where he would find the elevator that went up to the courthouse jail. If he got that far, he could call for help through an intercom on the wall of the alcove. Armed corrections deputies would be moments away.

Quinn took off. As he rounded the corner, he heard pounding footsteps racing after him. Quinn flung open the door to the near stairwell and leaped down the steps. He slipped on the third-floor landing and slid down half a flight before checking himself. In the second it took Quinn to regain his feet, he strained to hear his pursuer and thought he heard the sound of feet descending.

Quinn hit the bottom stair. The corridor in the back of the courthouse was dimly lit. He held his gun in front of him. His stomach was cramped and his breathing grew ragged. His senses were intensified. All he had to do was make it to the end of the hall.

Quinn sprinted for the alcove. The moment he reached it the door to the other stairwell flew open and the man in the ski mask ran into the hall. Quinn had been certain that he had heard footsteps in the stairwell he had just descended. Could there be two people hunting him? Before he could consider the question, the masked man sprang. Quinn backpedaled into the alcove and raised his gun, which was halfway up when the knife struck it. The impact jarred the gun and the knife loose and sent Quinn stumbling backward. He tripped on his own feet and fell heavily to the floor. His head smacked against the wall. Quinn's eyes wouldn't focus. He shook his head. When his vision returned, Quinn saw that the masked man was holding the gun.

Time slowed to a crawl and a feeling of overwhelming calm flooded through Quinn as he accepted his death. He saw the attacker sight down the barrel of the gun. His eyes locked on Quinn's. Then there was an explosion. The assailant's knees buckled, the gun fell and the front of the ski mask dampened with blood. There was a second shot. Quinn tried to push his way through the wall. The attacker collapsed at Quinn's feet and Ellen Crease stepped into the alcove holding a smoking .38-caliber revolver.

The jail elevator opened and two men stepped into the alcove. They were dressed in the light green shirt and dark green pants worn by the Multnomah County Corrections deputies. The first person out was Sergeant Art Bradford, a huge man with a marine crew cut who had been in Quinn's court guarding prisoners on many occasions. Clyde Fellers, the second deputy, was a black man with massive arms, a thick neck and a gut who had played football for Portland State. Bradford and Fellers stared at the dead man. Then they stared at Quinn, who was slumped on a bench outside the alcove.

'The judge is okay. He's just shaken up,' Ellen Crease said.

Quinn looked up. He was pale and spoke softly.

'The dead man attacked me in the parking garage two days ago. He just broke into my chambers and chased me downstairs. Senator Crease shot him.'

'I was supposed to meet Judge Quinn in his chambers,' Crease explained. 'I took the elevator up to the fifth floor. Someone raced around the far corner of the hall just as I came into the corridor where the judge's courtroom is located. No one was in the judge's chambers, so I ran down the back stairs looking for him.'

Crease stopped her narrative. She looked as bad as Quinn.

'I had to shoot. He was aiming at the judge.'

'Someone should call Portland Homicide,' Quinn said. 'Ask them to send Detectives Lou Anthony and Leroy Dennis over here. This is connected to one of their cases. And make sure that Anthony and Dennis are told that I know who murdered Lamar Hoyt.'

'You can turn him over now,' Dr. Marilyn Kinsey, the assistant medical examiner, said to Sergeant Bradford. Quinn, Detectives Anthony and Dennis, Ellen Crease and the other people in the group surrounding the dead man waited expectantly as Bradford rolled the corpse onto its back. Kinsey knelt down and slowly peeled back the ski mask.

'Looks like you were right,' Anthony told Quinn.

The judge looked down on the lifeless face of Jack Brademas.

'Let's go up to your courtroom so you can show us that report,' Dennis suggested.

Anthony, Dennis, Crease and Quinn went up to the fifth floor. Quinn preceded everyone into his courtroom and switched on the lights. While the others sat at the counsel table that Garrett and Crease had used during the hearing, Quinn went into his chambers through the door behind the bench and retrieved the document that had cleared up the case for him.

'Why don't you tell us how you figured out that Jack Brademas was involved, Judge?' Dennis said as soon as Quinn laid the police report of Martin Jablonski's home burglary on the table. The report was the one he had just finished reading last Sunday when the police detective called to see if Quinn could provide information about the disappearance of Andrea Chapman. It was only while Quinn waited for the police to arrive at the courthouse that the judge realized that the man on the line could not have been a police detective. The incident on St. Jerome had been staged. Andrea Chapman never existed and Marie Ritter did not disappear on St. Jerome. The call from the phony detective was part of the plan to unnerve him so that he would be easy prey for the blackmailer. The caller had probably been Jack Brademas.

'This is the police report of the arrest that sent Martin Jablonski to prison this last time,' Quinn said. 'This was the crime for which he was serving time until he was paroled last year. It was a brutal home invasion. A nighttime burglary accompanied by a violent assault on the homeowners. Take a look at the report.'

Anthony and Dennis studied the handwritten report. They looked confused.

'I don't see . . . ,' Anthony started. Then he looked as if he had been shot. He pointed at the bottom of the report where the arresting officer had signed his name.

'J. Brademas,' Dennis said out loud.

'Exactly,' Quinn said. 'Brademas knew Jablonski. He arrested him. I think he hired Jablonski to break into the Hoyt mansion and kill Lamar Hoyt and Senator Crease. If Jablonski was caught later, the crime would fit his M.O., but Brademas was probably going to murder Jablonski after Jablonski committed the double murder at the estate.'

'I've been sick ever since Judge Quinn told me about the report,' Crease said. 'Jack was my friend. I helped him get his job and Lamar treated him very well. Why did he do it?'

'I think I can answer that, Senator,' Lou Anthony said. 'Your husband suspected Junior of embezzling from the mortuary business. He had Jack Brademas investigate. My guess is that Brademas went to Junior and made a proposal. He would arrange to have you and your husband murdered for a cut of the estate. The plan must have looked great on paper. Junior had no ties to Jablonski and Jablonski was known for this type of violent crime. But neither Brademas nor Junior counted on you killing Jablonski.'

'Our problem now will be proving that Junior was Brademas's partner.'

Dennis stood up. 'You people have been through

enough for one night. Wait here and I'll see if there's any reason to keep you further.'

Dennis left and Crease slumped in her seat. She looked exhausted.

'I still can't believe that Jack was behind all this. I've known him for years.'

'If Junior confesses, maybe you can salvage your election campaign,' Quinn said in an attempt to cheer up Crease.

'Winning the primary seems less and less important to me, Dick. I've lost Lamar. Now I find out I've been betrayed by someone I really trusted. Besides, I'm so far down in the polls . . .'

Crease smiled sadly and shook her head. The court-room door opened and Dennis returned.

'You can go,' the detective said, 'but you'll have to run the gauntlet. Someone notified the press.'

Quinn walked toward the courtroom door. Crease started to follow him, but Anthony stopped her and said, 'Wait a minute, Ellen. I know I put you through hell by arresting you.'

'I don't hold it against you. You thought you were doing the right thing.'

'I did, but I might have cost you the campaign, so I figure I owe you one. I need your promise that you won't reveal where you got this information.'

Crease gave it.

'Karen Fargo was paid five thousand dollars to tell her story to me.'

'Who did it?'

Anthony repeated Fargo's description. As soon as he

mentioned the scar, Crease said, 'That's Ryan Clark, Benjamin Gage's A.A., and he doesn't spit without Gage's say-so. If he bribed Fargo, Gage is behind it.'

Part Four

Political Necessity

Twenty-three

[1]

HENRY ORCHARD popped the videotape into the VCR and pressed the Play button on the remote. Ellen Crease drew in smoke from her Cuban Cohiba Panatela. The anchor on the evening news suddenly appeared on the forty-eight-inch television screen in her home entertainment center.

'This is the Saturday night news report on Channel 6, but it's representative of the stories that the other local channels carried as the lead story last night,' Crease's campaign manager told the senator. 'The networks used local feeds.'

Crease watched herself leave the courthouse protected by a phalanx of policemen. She saw herself ignore the outstretched microphones and the reporters' entreaties. Then Judge Quinn came down the courthouse steps. He stopped at the bottom and turned to the reporters.

'This is good,' Orchard said as he turned up the volume.

'The police have asked me to refrain from making a statement or answering questions, and I am going to follow their instructions with one exception. Senator Ellen Crease saved my life tonight and I want to acknowledge her heroism and my debt to her.'

'How did she save your life?' several reporters asked simultaneously, as others asked what had happened in the courthouse, but Quinn refused to say anything more. The next shots were of Quinn's and Crease's cars driving from the scene while a voice-over informed the viewers that Senator Benjamin Gage had refused to comment on the incident at the courthouse.

'Now, here's where they hurt us,' Orchard said.

'Although Senator Gage refused to comment on the shooting, United States Congresswoman Renata Camp, a strong supporter of Senator Gage, did have this to say.'

The screen showed a stern-looking woman of fifty with short gray hair. When she spoke into the camera, she looked very concerned.

'I want to preface this statement by saying that I know very little of the facts surrounding tonight's shooting incident. I do know that the man who attempted to murder Circuit Court Judge Richard Quinn at the Multnomah County Courthouse was a longtime friend and associate of Senator Ellen Crease and the current head of security at her husband's company. I hope that the authorities will look more deeply into the facts surrounding the murder of Lamar Hoyt.'

'The information we have,' a reporter told Congress-woman Camp, 'is that Senator Crease saved Judge Quinn's life by shooting Jack Brademas. You seem to be suggesting that there was something more sinister going on here.'

'I'm not saying that at all. I do find it interesting that the senator hid behind a legal technicality in order to escape a trial of the facts of her murder charge, after spending her political career decrying the so-called legal loopholes that murderers, rapists and child molesters use to escape punishment. Then we have her good friend and associate trying to murder the judge in her case. I think these kinds of facts deserve investigation.'

Orchard stopped the tape and switched off the set.

'You don't need to see the rest, unless you want to.'

Crease waved her cigar at her political adviser.

'It's more of the same,' Orchard continued. 'What hurts is the innuendo and the accusation that you're hiding behind legal technicalities to keep the voters from learning the truth about Lamar's murder.'

Orchard leaned toward Crease. 'There's just over a month to the primary and you are way back in the polls. You've got three choices. You quit, you sit and take it or you fight back. If you choose column A or column B, you might as well concede the election and go on vacation.'

Crease blew a stream of smoke toward the ceiling. Then she looked at Orchard.

'You know the first thing I'm gonna do when I'm elected to the United States Senate, Henry? I'm going to get the embargo of Cuba lifted so I can smoke these cigars in public.'

Orchard grinned broadly. 'That's my girl! Now, I've got some ideas about how we can use Judge Quinn's statement.'

'Hold on to them until tomorrow, Henry. I'm meeting with Mary Garrett tonight. I might have something that will bring us back, but I've got to talk to her before I tell you about it.'

'What's Garrett have to do with your campaign?'

'I can't tell you. But it will be worth the wait. If I decide to go public with what I know, I've got to make sure that I don't burn myself. So hold on until tomorrow. Then we'll see.'

[2]

The Multnomah County District Attorney's Office was deserted on Sunday afternoon, so Leroy Dennis and Lou Anthony were the only people who witnessed Cedric Riker's tirade.

'Can you tell me what the fuck is going on here?' Riker swore when the detectives finished their account of the Saturday shoot-out at the courthouse.

'It's confusing, Ced,' Leroy Dennis told the D.A.

'Confusing?' Riker raged. 'What do you find confusing? It looks like simple math to me. By my count that bitch has now killed two people. We usually send serial killers to death row. What are you two geniuses proposing? That I give her a marksmanship medal?'

'Just listen to Leroy, Ced,' Anthony told the D.A. in his most conciliatory tone.

'I'm all ears.'

'Before Saturday, it looked like Senator Crease paid Jablonski to kill her husband. Then the evidence started pointing to Lamar, Jr. Now there's a possibility that Senator Gage is involved.'

'Gage! What are you talking about? Are you accusing Benjamin Gage of murder?'

'We're not accusing anyone right now.'

'Well, that's a relief. Ben happens to be a close personal friend of mine and one of my staunchest supporters. Not to mention the fact that he is a United States senator.'

'I'm just saying that there is a lot of circumstantial evidence pointing at people other than Ellen Crease. We may have acted too hastily when we arrested her.'

'Lou, I went to the grand jury on Crease on your say-so. Are you telling me that we indicted an innocent woman?'

Anthony flushed. 'We might have.'

'Where does Senator Gage come in?' Riker asked.

'Karen Fargo was paid to come forward. The day after she came in to see me five thousand dollars was deposited in her bank account and she was offered a job at a business owned by one of Gage's supporters. This morning I took Fargo to a TV studio to view a videotape that showed Ryan Clark, Gage's administrative assistant. She identified him as the person who bribed her.'

'Shit!' Riker swore as he paced back and forth in front of the detectives.

'There's a lot of circumstantial evidence linking

Brademas to Junior,' Leroy Dennis said, 'but Brademas could have sold out Crease to Gage. We think we have enough to bring in Gage for questioning.'

Riker spun around and glared at Dennis.

'You are not going to drag a United States senator down to the station house.'

'Where do you suggest that we question him?' Anthony asked calmly.

'Damn,' Riker muttered. He paced to the window and back. 'I'll call Gage. We'll talk to him someplace where the press won't see us.' Riker pointed a finger at Anthony. 'I don't want one word of this getting out. Meanwhile, you concentrate on Lamar Hoyt.'

Anthony did not say anything. He knew Riker owed Gage. Everyone knew that. But he didn't owe Gage a thing and he would follow the investigation where it led him.

[3]

Mary Garrett closed her office door behind Ellen Crease and studied the senator as she crossed the room. After what her client had been through, she expected some sign of wear, but Crease looked confident, poised and full of fight. Crease had asked for this emergency meeting, so Garrett waited for her client to explain what she wanted.

'Mary, I need your advice,' Crease said without preliminaries.

'That's what you pay me for.'

Crease told her lawyer what had happened at the courthouse. When she finished, she hesitated and suddenly looked troubled.

'This is the difficult part, Mary, because it may mean betraying the trust of someone who came to me for help. But we're also dealing with political realities here and the current reality is that I don't stand a chance in hell of winning the primary if something dramatic doesn't happen quickly.'

'If the police pin your husband's murder on Jack Brademas and Junior, that will be pretty dramatic.'

'We don't know if that will happen. Gage is already using his stalking horses to suggest that I may still be guilty and that Brademas could have been my accomplice. If Junior doesn't confess, the killing will remain officially unsolved.'

'What about going public with the fact that Gage bribed Fargo to come forward?'

'I've thought about that. Gage can admit he paid Fargo, then claim credit for bringing a witness forward. Some people will think what he did was sleazy, but they're not going to vote for me if my name hasn't been cleared.'

Crease looked very uncomfortable. 'Before I tell you anything more, I need your promise that nothing I say will leave this room unless I consent to it.'

'Of course. That's all covered by attorney-client confidentiality.'

'Would attorney-client confidentiality cover information I gave you about the criminal actions of another person?'

'Yes. It covers anything you tell me with a few exceptions that don't apply here.'

'Would the privilege apply even if the person who committed the criminal acts was a judge and he committed them while acting in his capacity as a judge?'

Garrett frowned.

'What's this all about, Ellen?'

Garrett had never seen her client look so uncertain.

'I feel awful about this, but my political future and my reputation are at stake.'

Crease told Garrett what Richard Quinn had confided to her on the night that he was attacked in the garage. As Crease related the details of the blackmail plot, Garrett looked incredulous. When she explained Paul Baylor's alternative explanation of the blood spatter evidence, Garrett took careful notes. When Crease told Garrett that Quinn had confessed that he fixed the motion to suppress, the lawyer looked stunned.

'This is very bad. I've never heard of anything like it.'

'It happened. Brademas hired Jablonski to kill me and Lamar, then he used this call girl that Junior knew to coerce the judge into assuring my conviction.'

'And you think that Junior was Brademas's partner?'

'Junior is the most likely person to have been in this with Jack, but there is another possibility. Benjamin Gage could have learned about the Ritter woman while trying to find dirt to use against me in the campaign. That must be the way he found out about Fargo.'

'Do you have any proof of that?'

'No, but the blackmail plot required money and a

high level of planning. Jack could have worked it out, but Junior never could have. Whatever else I think about Gage and Clark, there is no denying that they are extremely intelligent.'

'You still haven't told me what you want from me, Ellen?'

'Advice. If I hold a press conference and go public with the fact that I was the victim of a conspiracy, I might turn the voters around. But Judge Quinn trusted me. He saved my life by ruling as he did. I don't want to hurt him. And there's the legal problem. I need to know what would happen to Quinn's order if Riker learns that the judge fixed my case. Would I be back facing a murder charge?'

'I'm pretty certain that the order would be null and void if Quinn admits he lied about his legal conclusions, but Riker would have real problems continuing his prosecution. Even if the blood spatter evidence was ruled admissible by a new judge, we now have a reasonable explanation for it, and that's the only concrete evidence the State has to contradict your version of what happened on the night of your husband's murder.

'Then, there's all this new evidence about Jack Brademas and Junior, and Gage bribing Fargo to come forward. The fact that someone tried to blackmail Quinn into assuring your conviction also makes it look like someone else was behind your husband's murder.'

'What will happen to Judge Quinn if I go public with the information that he fixed my case?'

Garrett sighed. 'He'll be ruined. Even if he fixed the case with the best of intentions he'll be removed from the bench. He could be disbarred. He could even face criminal charges.'

'So Judge Quinn will be destroyed if I go public.'

'I'm afraid that's what it comes down to.'

'And if I don't go public, my reputation and my political career are over.'

Twenty-four

H ENRY ORCHARD and Ellen Crease sat in the back booth of a dimly lit downtown restaurant and discussed the campaign.

'I don't know what to do, Henry.'

'It's a no-brainer, Ellen. You've got to hold the press conference and blow this blackmail scheme wide open. It's the only way you can give yourself a real chance to become a United States senator.'

'I'd be climbing into national politics over the judge's body. It'd kill him, bury him so deep he might never crawl out.'

'What if Gage is behind Lamar's murder? If you do nothing, Gage will win. You could be sending a murderer to the United States Senate. There's more at stake here than the career of one person. Quinn will still

335

be alive. You've got money and influence. You can help him after you're elected.'

Crease leaned her head against the back of the booth and shut her eyes.

'I wish this would all go away, Henry. I wish Lamar was still alive and I never decided to challenge that son of a bitch Gage.'

'Yeah, well, those are wishes that won't come true, Ellen. And you're going to have to decide what you're going to do now. The days are slipping away. The primary is in May. If we're going to repair the damage caused by your murder indictment, we have to act. I agree with Garrett. Riker would be a fool to pursue his case once you reveal what you know. It's true that there are going to be casualties and Quinn will be one of them, but we're talking about your life here and about bringing your husband's murderer to justice.

'Look, why don't you talk this over with Quinn? Maybe he'll join you at the press conference and tell everyone how you saved his life and how this masked guy tried to force him into convicting you. If Quinn will help, it could be the break we need.'

Crease sighed. 'How soon can you set up the press conference?'

'I'll have you on the air Thursday night, prime time. We might even get national coverage.'

'Then, God help me, let's do it. And God help Richard Quinn.'

[2]

Quinn threw two more logs into the stone fireplace in the living room of Frank Price's beach house.

'You warm enough?' Quinn asked Laura.

'Uhm.'

Laura was bundled up in a wool sweater and jeans. A glass of wine sat on a low table at her elbow. Quinn settled on the floor beside Laura and they both stared through the huge picture window at the rain that pounded the beach and the boiling whitecaps that rolled over the beleaguered sand. The fire crackled and Quinn felt the heat on his face. He had good memories of this rustic cabin where he had spent many of his summers growing up. He was sorry that he would have to drive back to Portland tomorrow.

'What are you thinking about?' Quinn asked. 'If it's business, you're in big trouble.'

Laura laughed. 'Believe it or not, I haven't thought about my practice since we crossed the coast range. The mountains must block the brain waves from Price, Winward.'

Quinn put his arm around Laura's shoulder. He, too, had felt a lessening of tension as the landscape changed from urban sprawl to farmland and forest during their Sunday morning drive to the coast. By the time he and Laura were finishing bowls of thick, steaming clam chowder at a ramshackle restaurant of weathered wood on the Newport waterfront, he was a different person. An hour after lunch, Quinn and Laura were making love to the sound of rain pattering on the shake roof of the beach house and the murders were a universe away.

When they awoke Monday morning, a storm was brewing in the Pacific, but the rain held off until three. Quinn and Laura had walked the beach, driven into town for lunch, then spent the afternoon reading in front of the fire.

'If it's not business, then what caused that glazed look in your eyes?'

Laura looked a little guilty.

'You won't be mad at me?' she asked sheepishly.

Quinn squeezed her shoulder and kissed the top of her head.

'Speak. I know you. You'll brood all night if you don't get whatever is bothering you off your chest.'

'Why do you think Brademas told Lamar, Sr., that Junior was embezzling the money?'

Quinn groaned.

'You said you wouldn't be mad.'

Quinn sighed. 'Brademas was Hoyt's head of security. He was supposed to tell him.'

'I know, but wouldn't it have made more sense for Brademas to keep Hoyt in the dark? If Brademas hired Jablonski to kill Hoyt and Senator Crease so he would get a share of the estate when Junior inherited, wasn't Brademas risking a lot by going to Senior? What if Hoyt called in the police immediately after finding out about Junior? What if he changed his will the same day?'

'I see what you mean. Maybe Brademas didn't think of the plan until after he spoke to Hoyt.'

'That would explain it,' Laura said in a tone that let Quinn know she was not really convinced. 'And there's something else. That visit from Marie Ritter when she was pretending to be Claire Reston.'

'What about it?'

'What was the point? What possible purpose was served by having Ritter pretend to be her sister?'

Quinn shrugged. 'I guess Brademas and Junior wanted to shake me up so I'd go along with their blackmail scheme.'

'But you were already a mess. They'd threatened to frame you for murder. You thought you'd be disbarred, disgraced and incarcerated in a rat-infested prison on St. Jerome. Ritter's visit was really overkill.'

'Wait a minute. Ritter told me where she was staying just when Fran Stuart walked in. Brademas and Junior were creating a witness. After Ritter was murdered, Fran could testify that Ritter was upset when she left my chambers and that I knew her hotel room number.'

'That makes sense, but what if you saw through Ritter's makeup and figured out that Claire Reston and Andrea Chapman were the same person? You'd know Ritter wasn't murdered on St. Jerome. Brademas and Junior would have lost their leverage. Why put Marie Ritter in the same room with you when everything was going so well? Why take the risk?'

'They probably figured that I'd be so shaken up that I wouldn't be able to figure out that Reston and Chapman were the same person. And they were right. If I hadn't seen the scar on Ritter's hip I would still believe that Claire and Andrea were different women. They took a risk, but given my state, it wasn't all that big a risk.'

Laura snuggled close to Quinn. 'You're probably right.'

Quinn kissed Laura. 'Even if I'm not right, I don't care. I want to forget about Ellen Crease, Lamar Hoyt, *fils* and *père*, and Jack Brademas.'

Laura kissed Quinn. 'I've been a bad wife. I promise not to mention the case or anything even remotely connected to law for the rest of our stay.'

'Good. Because even a single slip of the tongue will be severely punished.'

'Oh? What might you do?'

'Hmm. Ravishing comes to mind.'

Laura fluttered her eyelids. 'You mean that I'll be ravished if I say anything connected with law?'

'You betcha.'

Laura smiled seductively and whispered, 'Habeas corpus.'

[3]

Lamar Hoyt, Jr., lived on the eighth floor of a brick and glass condominium near the Vista Bridge. Anthony flashed his badge at the security guard and told him not to announce the arrival of the detectives and the four uniformed officers who accompanied them. When they arrived at Junior's apartment, the officers stationed themselves on either side of the door and Dennis rang the bell. He had to press the button five times before an angry voice, thick with sleep, asked, 'Who is it?'

Anthony held his badge in front of the peephole and said, 'Open up, police.'

The door swung open, revealing a huge living room decorated with low-slung, modern furniture of polished metal, glass and smooth woods. Anthony saw the lights of Portland through a floor-to-ceiling window that stretched across the outer wall of the apartment. The other walls were decorated with framed posters or paintings with a skiing theme. The top of a glass coffee table was covered with empty beer bottles, a half-filled bottle of red wine and an open pizza delivery box containing only the half-eaten remains of a slice of pepperoni and cheese.

'Real class, Junior,' Anthony said.

'Ah, shit,' Junior replied when he recognized the detective.

Junior was wearing a dark blue silk bathrobe belted loosely at the waist. The robe hung open a little, exposing Junior's hairy legs and torso and a pair of bright red bikini underpants.

'May we step inside, Mr. Hoyt?' Dennis asked.

'No, you may not.'

'I'm afraid we have to insist,' Dennis responded patiently.

'I'm calling my lawyer.'

'Maybe you'd better do that,' Anthony said. 'Tell him to meet you downtown.'

'Down . . . It's the middle of the night. I'm not going anywhere unless you've got a warrant.'

Dennis smiled and handed Hoyt his copy of a search warrant.

'What's this about?' Junior asked nervously.

'Why don't we talk inside?'

Junior backed away from the door. Dennis noticed a dining area in front of the picture window that was relatively clean. He motioned Junior toward it. Anthony took a seat at the head of a large dining table and Dennis sat beside him. Two policemen stationed themselves near Junior and he eyed them anxiously.

'We have a new lead in your father's death and we need your help, Mr. Hoyt,' Dennis said.

'What kind of new lead?'

Anthony took an autopsy photograph of Marie Ritter out of a manila envelope and handed it to Junior.

'Jesus!' Junior said, dropping the picture the moment he saw what it was.

'That's a curious reaction for someone who works in a funeral parlor,' Dennis told Junior.

'You didn't happen to know this woman, did you?' Anthony asked.

Junior forced himself to look at the picture. He looked confused at first, then his expression changed. When he looked up, Junior's eyes shifted nervously between the detectives.

'You are two sick fucks, you know that?'

'Not as sick as the person who did this,' Anthony answered, pointing at Marie Ritter's mutilated body. 'This is a call girl named Marie Ritter. She was murdered a few nights ago at the Heathman. I understand that you were one of her customers.'

Junior twitched. He cast another anxious glance at the autopsy photo.

'Look, I'll be honest with you. I, uh, I knew this woman, but not down here. I knew her in Seattle. And not as Marie Ritter. She called herself Crystal. All these whores have whore names.' Junior forced a smile, but Anthony and Dennis did not respond. 'But I didn't know that she was dead.' Junior fidgeted nervously. 'This isn't my normal thing, you understand. A friend of mine turned me on to her. Said she was, uh, exotic. I usually don't pay for sex, if you know what I mean.'

'I'm sure you get lots of pussy, Junior,' Anthony said. 'But we're more interested in the last time you saw Marie Ritter than we are in your love life. When was that?'

'Uh. Let's see. It would be sometime in January. Late January.'

'So soon after your father's death?' Dennis asked.

'So much for a period of mourning,' Anthony added.

'Hey, I don't have to take this shit,' Junior said, half standing and glaring at Anthony. 'Especially from the person who blew the investigation of my father's killer.'

Anthony paled and he started to stand, but Dennis put a restraining hand on his partner's arm.

'Why don't you relax, Mr. Hoyt?' Dennis said. 'I'm sure it just seemed odd to my partner that you would be cavorting with a high-priced call girl so soon after your father passed away.'

'Yeah, well, it happened,' Junior answered sullenly. He settled back onto his chair. 'I was in Seattle on business and I called her.'

'Directly?'

'No. She works for an escort service. I arranged it through them.'

'I bet Crystal didn't come cheap, Junior. No pun intended,' Anthony said.

'You think you're funny?'

'Where do you get all the money for these expensive toys, Mr. Hoyt?' Dennis asked.

Junior barked out a harsh laugh. 'You are two pathetic civil servants. For a guy like me, a couple of hundred a night is nothing. I'm making a bundle from the mortuaries.'

'You must be spending a bundle, too,' Dennis said casually. He didn't sound the least offended by Junior's outburst. 'Wine, women and song, heh, heh. You know, the credit check I ran on you has you maxed out on just about every credit card there is and your bank balance . . .' Dennis shook his head sadly and Junior turned pale.

'Do you remember where you were on Wednesday evening?'

'Wednesday?' Junior asked nervously. 'Why do you need to know that?'

'That's when Ms. Ritter – Crystal – was killed.'

'Hey, I didn't have anything to do with that.'

'Of course,' Dennis said soothingly, 'but it would help if we could eliminate you as a suspect. See, so far, you're the only person connected with this case who knew Ms. Ritter.'

'I . . . I'm pretty sure . . . Yeah, Wednesday, I was by myself. I stayed home alone.'

'No one called you or dropped in to visit?' Dennis asked.

'No.'

'That's too bad. You're certain you were home and not at the Heathman with Miss Ritter?'

'Absolutely.'

Dennis smiled. 'Well, we'll know soon enough. The lab reports are expected back soon.' Dennis shook his head sadly. 'You know, it just isn't fair anymore. A good crook used to be able to beat the rap by just wearing gloves so he didn't leave fingerprints. But now with this DNA if you spit or leave a teensy-weensy head hair or an itsy-bitsy drop of semen, you're doomed.'

'You won't find any of my prints or DNA on that woman.'

'Mr. Hoyt,' Anthony asked, 'do you think you can remember a little more about that argument you had with your father? The one at Hoyt Industries headquarters. You were pretty vague about what made you and your father so upset.'

'I've had enough of this. First, you drop a picture of a dead woman on my table, then you suggest I killed her, now you're asking about some argument I already told you about . . .'

'Let me help you out here. You know Jack Brademas, the head of security for Hoyt Industries, don't you? Probably heard all about his getting killed on the TV.'

Junior did not answer. He looked desperate.

'We know that Brademas told your father that you were skimming money from the mortuaries. That's what you and your father argued about.'

'That's bullshit, pure bullshit, and I'm not talking to you two anymore without a lawyer.'

'That's your choice,' Dennis said, 'but it might be smart to cooperate with us now. That way we can tell the D.A. to give you a break.'

'What D.A.? Are you gonna charge me with some crime?'

'Why, have you done something you're worried about?'

'No, I haven't,' Junior said, but he looked confused and scared. 'Now, why don't you two get out of here?'

'We're going to leave, but you'll be coming with us while these officers search your apartment.

'Take him into the bedroom and let him dress,' Anthony told two of the officers. Two men surrounded Junior. He hesitated and Anthony said, 'We can take you downtown dressed in those skivvies and put you in the drunk tank, if you'd like.'

Junior wrenched his elbow free and strode angrily out of the room.

Twenty-five

[1]

LOU ANTHONY and Leroy Dennis met Cedric Riker at Benjamin Gage's house at three o'clock, Tuesday afternoon. Benjamin Gage ushered Anthony and Dennis into his den, where Riker was waiting drink in hand. It looked like their arrival had interrupted a chat between old friends.

'I know that you gentlemen are busy, so why don't you tell me how I can help you?'

'Do you know a woman named Karen Fargo, Senator?' Anthony asked quickly to keep Riker from conducting the questioning.

'No. I don't believe I've ever met her.'

'But you know who she is,' Dennis said.

Dennis smiled disarmingly, but Ryan Clark had briefed his boss on both detectives and he knew that he was not dealing with fools.

'Of course. I've followed Senator Crease's case very closely.'

'Have you ever paid her any money, Senator?' Dennis asked.

'Now, wait a minute,' Riker interjected, 'we're not here to . . .'

Gage held up his hand and Riker's sentence squealed to a halt.

'I have great respect for the law, Ced. I want to be completely candid with these men.'

Gage turned to Dennis. 'I hope I didn't do anything wrong in urging Miss Fargo to go to the police with what she knew, but I felt that her evidence would be of use in finding Lamar Hoyt's killer. Was it illegal to find Miss Fargo a job after Ellen Crease had her fired? Was I wrong to help her with her rent and food until she could get back on her feet?'

'No one is accusing you of doing anything illegal, Senator,' Riker assured Gage.

'I appreciate that, because, after the fact, I wondered if I'd been out of bounds.'

'Mr. Clark, he's your assistant?' Anthony asked.

'Administrative assistant. A true patriot. He was a navy SEAL. Decorated extensively.'

'Do you happen to know his whereabouts on last Wednesday?'

'I'm afraid you'll have to ask him about that. I'm sure he'll answer all your questions.'

'Do you know where we can reach him?'

'Certainly.'

Gage told them a phone number.

'Senator, did you or Mr. Clark know Marie Ritter or Martin Jablonski?'

Gage smiled patiently. 'I can only speak for myself. I recognize Mr. Jablonski's name, of course, and I can assure you that we never met. I'm unfamiliar with the other person you mentioned. I can't speak for Mr. Clark. You'll have to ask him.'

Riker stood up. 'Thank you for taking the time to talk to us.'

'Anytime, Ced. I'm a strong supporter of the police.'

Gage walked the detectives and the district attorney to the front door. When they were on their way, the senator returned to his study and phoned Ryan Clark.

'How did it go?' Clark asked.

'Piece of cake.'

[2]

The message light on the answering machine was blinking furiously when Quinn and Laura returned home from the beach late Tuesday afternoon.

'Probably reporters,' Quinn said as he carried the last of the bags in from the car.

'Or my office,' Laura answered as she hit the Play button.

They were right about the first four messages, but the fifth was from Ellen Crease.

'Judge, I've tried calling you every place I could think of, but no one knows where you are. It's urgent that we speak as soon as possible. Please call me immediately.'

'I wonder what that's about,' Laura said.

'I'd better call. She sounded upset.'

Quinn dialed the number Crease had left. James Allen answered the phone. Quinn gave his name and Ellen Crease picked up a moment later.

'I just got your message. Laura and I have been hiding out at the coast since early Sunday. What's up?'

'We need to talk.'

Crease sounded very tense.

'About what?'

'It's not something that we should discuss over the phone. Can you come to my house?'

'Now?'

'Right away.'

'Can't this wait until tomorrow? We just walked in the door and I'm bushed.'

'It has to be now. Please. This concerns both of our futures. I wouldn't ask if it wasn't important.'

Quinn hesitated. Then he gave in.

'Use the back entrance to the estate. That way, no one will see you. I'll leave the gate open. It's a little tricky to get to. You have to take some back roads.'

'Give me the directions.'

Quinn grabbed a pencil and wrote down Crease's instructions on a pad, then read them back.

'What was that about?' Laura asked when Quinn hung up.

'I have no idea.'

'Can't it wait until tomorrow?'

'She sounded very uptight, so she must think that it's important we meet. She even wants me to come by a back way so I won't be seen.'

'Call her back and tell her you'll talk to her tomorrow.'

'She saved my life, Laura.'

Laura sighed. 'You're right. Do you want me to come with you?'

Quinn squeezed Laura's hand. 'There's no reason why both of us should run out. I won't be gone long.'

Quinn left and Laura carried their bags upstairs to the bedroom. She was unpacking them when something Crease had said on the answering machine flitted in and out of her consciousness. Laura paused and tried to recapture the thought. She frowned, then shook her head. It was gone. She was tempted to replay Crease's message but that would mean going downstairs. She felt sticky from the ride. She decided to shower first. It was probably nothing, anyway.

Quinn took the back roads to the Hoyt estate and ended at a small gated entrance surrounded by woods. The gate was open, just as Crease said it would be. It was almost a mile to the house on a narrow unpaved road.

Ellen Crease was waiting for Quinn at the rear door.

'I've given James Allen the night off and I've dismissed the security guards so we can have privacy,' Crease said as she led Quinn into a sunroom in the rear of the mansion. The room was painted white and floored with terra-cotta tiles. Wide-leaf plants filled the corners of the room. Three of the walls were floor-to-ceiling windows divided into small panes through which the pale evening light entered.

Crease gestured Quinn onto one of four wicker chairs
that surrounded a glass-top table. Outside the room was
a garden. None of the flowers were in bloom and there
were no buds on the limbs of the trees. The foliage
looked cold and exposed. Just beyond the garden were
heavy woods that stretched to the boundary of the
estate. Crease got to the point immediately.

'I need your help, Dick. Believe me, I've thought
long and hard before asking you for it, but I have no
choice.'

'I'll help any way I can,' Quinn assured her.

'Don't say that so quickly. Wait until you hear what
I want from you.'

Crease sighed. She seemed sad.

'I've only known you for a short time, but you've
impressed me with your integrity and character. That's
what makes my request so difficult. I am going to lose
my bid to win the primary unless I go public about the
conspiracy against me. I trust the voters. If they know
that I was framed for Lamar's murder, I believe they
will swing over to me.'

Crease's features hardened. She captured Quinn with
her eyes. He could feel her power.

'Dick, the voters have to be told that you were threatened with blackmail if you did not fix my case. Benjamin
Gage is taking the position that I've been hiding behind
a legal technicality to keep the public from finding out
the truth about Lamar's murder. You can tell everyone
that you ruled as you did to protect me from a plan
to frame me. I know it's a lot to ask. I tried to reach
you yesterday, so you would have time to think about

what I'm asking you to do. When I couldn't find you I had to go forward. I've planned a news conference for Thursday night. I'm going public with everything.'

'You can't do that.'

Crease looked sad. She shook her head wearily. 'You have no idea how difficult this decision was for me, Dick, but I'm convinced that I must go ahead with the news conference.'

'Do you appreciate what could happen to me if it gets out that I fixed your case?'

'Yes. I consulted Mary Garrett before I made this decision. She told me that you will probably have to resign from the bench and that you might face criminal charges.'

'There is no "might." Cedric Riker is a political crony of Benjamin Gage. If my confession costs Gage the election he'll definitely come after me.'

'I've got money and influence, Dick. I won't desert you if things start to go bad.'

Quinn shook his head as if he could not believe what he was hearing.

'I know I'm asking a lot. If you go public at my press conference, I am prepared to back you with every penny I've got. You'll have the best lawyers, and I'll work behind the scenes for you. Gage isn't the only person with political influence.'

Quinn leaned back and closed his eyes. He had been prepared to resign from the bench on the evening that Brademas attacked him in the garage. Crease had convinced him to reconsider that decision. Now she wanted him to make a public confession.

'I have to talk this over with Laura. If I'm disbarred or go to prison, it will affect her, too.'

'Of course. But I'm going to go ahead with the news conference whether you help me or not. If you confess publicly, it may help you later.'

Quinn was about to respond when the rear doorbell rang.

'Stay here,' Crease said. 'I'll see who that is.'

A moment later, Quinn heard raised voices in the hall. One of them was Laura's. Quinn walked into the hall. Laura saw him and walked down the hall with Crease close behind her.

'What does she want from you?' Laura demanded.

'Your husband was just about to drive home and tell you,' Crease answered calmly. 'Why don't we discuss this in the sunroom, instead of standing in the hall?'

Quinn and Laura followed the senator into the sunroom. When they were seated, Quinn said, 'Ellen wants me to go public about the blackmail plot. She thinks it will help her win the election if the voters learn that someone tried to coerce me into fixing her case so that she would be convicted.'

Laura turned on Crease. 'You want my husband to risk prison so you can win an election?'

'The decision to go public has already been made. The only question is whether Dick helps me. I'm sorry, Laura.'

'I don't think you are. There's something very wrong here, something that I don't understand. I listened to the message that you left on our answering machine. You said that you tried to find Dick, but no one knew where he was.'

'Yes?' Crease answered with obvious confusion.

'You couldn't find us because Dick and I didn't tell anyone that we were going to the coast.'

Now Quinn looked confused, too.

'What are you getting at?' Quinn asked.

'How did Jack Brademas know that my husband was working at the courthouse on Saturday?' Laura asked Crease. 'It was a weekend afternoon. No one would expect him to be there. The only person besides me that he told was you, Senator, when he phoned to tell you about the police report.'

'Jack must have followed your husband,' Crease said.

'That's possible, but it wouldn't explain why he was so desperate to kill Dick. Only one thing could have caused that urgency. Knowing that Dick had discovered his link to Jablonski and was going to tell the police. And you are the only person who knew about Dick's discovery.'

'You think I sent Jack to kill your husband?' Crease asked incredulously.

'There were a few things that never added up. If Brademas was working with Junior so he could get a cut of the estate, it made no sense for him to tell your husband about the embezzlement scheme and run the risk that Lamar would go to the police or disinherit Junior. I think Jack Brademas was your accomplice all along, Senator.'

'You've got it all wrong, Laura,' Crease said without rancor.

'I don't think so. Jablonski was your sacrificial lamb. You hid in the bathroom while he murdered your husband. Then you ambushed him and became a grieving

355

widow and a law-and-order avenger overnight. It was a terrific little coup that helped you to skyrocket in the polls and become a multimillionaire. Everything was going great until Gary Yoshida stumbled across the blood spatter pattern on the armoire and Gage bribed Fargo to go to the police. When you were indicted for Lamar Hoyt's murder, you lost everything you had gained. Now your priority was to escape death row. That's when you dreamed up your blackmail scheme. You knew that Dick was going to St. Jerome because he announced it at your bail hearing. I bet Brademas found out about Marie Ritter while he was investigating Junior. You used her to ensnare Dick, then you killed her when she had served her purpose.'

'There's a problem with your theory, Laura,' Crease said calmly. 'If Jack and I were working together, why would we tell your husband that he would be ruined unless he did everything he could to see that I was sent to prison?' Crease flashed Laura a condescending smile. 'That doesn't sound like a very good plan to me.'

'That was the cleverest part of the plan, Senator, and it hinged on an excellent reading of the character of my husband. I could never understand why the blackmailers sent Marie Ritter to see Dick during the hearing. They were running an incredible risk that he would figure out that Claire Reston and Andrea Chapman were the same person. If that happened, the blackmail plan would be useless because Dick would know that Andrea Chapman was not murdered on St. Jerome. The blackmailers' leverage would be lost.

'On top of that, Reston let Dick know that she could

go public with the fact that he was with Chapman in the cove. It was a ridiculous thing to do if the black-mailers wanted their plot to succeed, but it was a very clever thing to do if the blackmailers wanted their plan to fail.'

For the first time since Laura arrived, Crease looked uncertain.

'You sent Reston to see Dick because you wanted him to do exactly the opposite of what Brademas ordered. You knew that my husband would never give in to blackmail if you told him to fix the case so that you would be acquitted. He would have gone to the police even if it meant his career. You used reverse psychology to get Dick to do what you wanted. You knew how decent Dick is. You gambled that he would sacrifice his career to save you.'

'This is absolute nonsense,' Crease said.

'Look at the evidence. Paul Baylor didn't say that Gary Yoshida's interpretation of the blood spatter evidence was wrong, he only gave a theoretical alternative to Yoshida's explanation. If Yoshida was right, you lied all along. You also profited the most when your husband died. You and Brademas go way back. Who does it make more sense for him to work with? And you were the only one who knew about the report that implicated Brademas, the only one who could tell him where to find Dick.'

'She saved my life, Laura,' Quinn said.

'No, Dick, she didn't save your life when she killed Brademas. She took care of a witness who could hang her. Brademas became a liability as soon as you found his name on that report.'

'But why didn't she wait until Brademas killed me? With both of us dead there would be no way to prove that her case was rigged and she would be free of the murder charges.'

'With you dead, there would be no one who could tell the voters about the conspiracy to frame her. She needed you alive to save her campaign. It all fits, Dick. She's been playing you since you were assigned to her case.'

Quinn stood up. He should have been furious, but he was too stunned to be angry.

'Where are you going?'

'To the police.'

'Don't do that, Dick,' Crease implored desperately.

'Don't be ridiculous.'

'I'll make you a deal.'

'There's nothing you can offer me.'

'But there is. I can offer you your career. In order to implicate me, you'll have to confess to fixing my case. No one can prove what you did if you don't go to the police. Keep quiet and you'll stay on the bench, you won't be disbarred, you won't have to worry about criminal charges and the disgrace.'

Quinn suddenly saw Crease's real face. An image of Marie Ritter spread-eagled on the hotel bed flashed in his mind and he remembered the terror he felt in the garage and as he lay waiting for death on the cold marble floor of the courthouse.

'Not a chance. If I have to go to jail, I will, but you're not walking away from this.'

Quinn turned his back to the senator.

'God damn it, Quinn, you'll ruin us both,' Crease shouted.

Quinn and Laura kept walking. There was an end table at Crease's elbow. She opened a drawer and pulled out a gun.

'Stop,' she yelled. When Quinn did not look back, Crease squeezed the trigger. Quinn's right leg flew out from under him and he fell to the floor. Laura screamed. Quinn stared at Crease, dazed. Blood was spreading along his pants leg near his knee. Crease took a pair of handcuffs from the drawer and tossed them to Laura. She made no move to catch them and they fell at her feet. Crease cocked the gun and pointed it at Laura.

'Pick them up and cuff him,' she ordered.

'I'm not . . . ,' Laura started, but Crease smashed her across the cheek with the revolver, driving her to her knees. Quinn threw himself at Crease, but she stepped out of reach and he collapsed sideways, grimacing with pain. Crease pointed the gun at Quinn's head and spoke to Laura.

'Do as you're told or I'll kill him.'

Laura looked at Crease wide-eyed. Crease cocked the revolver and Laura retrieved the cuffs.

'Get your hands behind you,' Crease told Quinn. Laura snapped on the cuffs.

'Was it the money? Did you kill your husband for his money?' Quinn asked to stall for time.

Crease shook her head wearily.

'I didn't care about Lamar's money. I cared about Lamar and I killed the bastard because he was going to leave me.'

Crease's voice caught and her eyes watered.

'I loved him. He's the only man I ever loved. I gave Lamar everything and he threw my love in my face.' A tear ran down Crease's cheek. 'Fargo wasn't the first tramp he'd played around with, but she was the one he was going to substitute for me. It was history repeating itself. As soon as one of his wives started to age, Lamar would trade her in. I tried to talk him out of it. I did everything I could. I really loved that son of a bitch, but I told him I'd see him dead before I'd let him make me into one of his discards. He didn't believe me.'

'What if you were wrong about me? What if I did fix the case so that you were convicted?'

'I thought of that possibility. If I saw that you were trying to help the prosecutor convict me I would have released the photographs to the media and moved for a mistrial claiming that you had been blackmailed into fixing the case. But I never had to do that, because I had you doped out one hundred percent.'

Quinn felt like a complete fool.

'What we didn't count on was that police report with Jack's name on it,' Crease said. 'If it weren't for that . . .' She shook her head.

'Did Brademas help you for the money?'

'Of course. And he was in love with me. He had been since we were on the force together. We were even lovers before I married Lamar. Jack had been shaking down drug dealers. Internal Affairs was after him, but they didn't have the evidence to make a case stick. He resigned to avoid a further inquiry. I got him his job in security at Hoyt Industries for old time's sake.

'When Lamar started cheating on me I became Jack's lover again, out of spite. But he never meant anything to me. When I decided to kill Lamar, persuading Jack to help me was easy. Then he started to get out of control. He was just supposed to kill Ritter, not torture her. I was furious when I heard what he'd done. I wanted to frame you for Ritter's murder, but you would never have killed her like that. Then you told me about the police report and I knew Jack was a liability I could not afford.

'When we got to the courthouse, I told Jack that I would follow him as backup. He thought that he was supposed to kill you and take the report. But I would never have let him kill you. Laura is right. You were worth more to me alive so you could tell everyone how I saved your life.'

'Why did Brademas go after me in the parking garage?'

'We wanted to make sure that the order suppressing evidence would stand. I couldn't risk having it set aside if you told someone that you had fixed my case. Then you came to me for help. I decided that you would be of more use to me alive, because you would be my proof of the plot to frame me for Lamar's murder.'

Crease suddenly looked very tired.

'We've talked long enough,' she said. 'Are both of your cars in back of the house?'

Quinn and Laura nodded.

'Get him up and help him outside,' Crease told Laura.

'Don't do this,' Quinn begged. 'I'll make the broadcast.'

Crease shook her head. 'It's too late for that. I'd never be able to trust you.'

'For God's sake,' Quinn started.

'Move,' Crease ordered, 'and no more talking.'

Quinn hobbled forward into the hallway. Crease followed at a safe distance.

'I love you,' Quinn whispered to Laura.

'What did I say about talking?' Crease asked angrily.

A second later, a gunshot exploded in the hall.

Twenty-six

A YOUNG COP was waiting at the front door of the Hoyt mansion when Anthony and Dennis drove up. Two marked cars were parked along the other side of the turnaround. The officer told them where everyone was and Anthony and Dennis walked along the front of the mansion until they found a slate path that led toward the pool. The path continued along the side of the house. Eventually, they rounded a corner and saw an ambulance and two parked cars. Richard Quinn was lying on a stretcher. A medic was working on his leg. A second medic was working on a nasty gash on Laura Quinn's cheek. Through the open back door, Anthony saw a forensic expert circling a third person who was lying facedown in the hall. He was carrying a camera. Every so often he would stop and take a photograph. Another cop was videotaping the scene.

Anthony walked inside and knelt next to the body of

Ellen Crease. He spotted the entry wound in the back of her head. He had no desire to see the mess the bullet had made when it exited. It was enough to know that Crease was dead.

Anthony walked outside just as Quinn gasped in pain. The medic apologized and Quinn gritted his teeth. He looked spent, but Anthony needed to find out what had happened. He squatted down beside the judge.

'Feel up to talking?'

'I can manage a little.'

'We're gonna have to take him to the hospital,' the medic said. 'Make it quick.'

'She was in it with Brademas,' Quinn said. 'She hired Jablonski to make the hit on Lamar because he was going to leave her for Karen Fargo.'

Anthony remembered his interview with Crease in the library on the evening of her husband's murder. He had been impressed by the dignity with which she had conducted herself despite her grief. Maybe the grief had not been an act.

'Crease was going to go on television Thursday night and tell everyone that I had been blackmailed to fix her case. She wanted me to speak at her press conference. Laura figured out what happened. She came here and confronted Crease. We were going to the police. Crease shot me and hit Laura. She was going to kill us.'

'Gotta go,' the medic said as he signaled his partner.

'You take care,' the detective said as the medics started maneuvering the stretcher toward the ambulance. 'I'll talk to you at the hospital.'

Anthony walked over to Leroy Dennis, who was finishing up with Laura. She joined Quinn in the back of the ambulance. When the ambulance drove away, Anthony said, 'Let's talk to the man of the hour.'

The detectives found James Allen in the sunroom.

'Mr. Allen?' Anthony said.

Allen looked up, but he seemed to have trouble focusing and he looked unstable.

'Do you remember me, sir?'

Allen made an almost imperceptible nod. Anthony sat across from him.

'I had to do it,' he said, his voice slightly louder than a whisper.

'I know, Mr. Allen,' Dennis said. 'She was going to kill them.'

'How did you happen to come back to the house? I understand from the officer who talked to you that this was your night off.'

'I didn't feel well, so I came home. I wanted to make myself some tea to calm my stomach before going to my quarters. I was going toward the kitchen when I heard them. Judge Quinn said he was going to the police. Then there was a gunshot.'

Allen paused and shook his head in disbelief.

'I froze for a moment. Then I went into the den where the gun collection is kept. She was raising the gun to fire again when I reentered the hall. I . . . I didn't feel that I had a choice.'

Allen began to sob. Anthony watched helplessly. Dennis went into the hall and returned with a doctor. Then the detectives left.

'Let's take a walk,' Anthony said. 'I want to talk to you about something.'

'Such as?'

'This blackmail business,' Anthony told Dennis as they headed back toward the pool where the other policemen would not overhear them.

'We don't have any proof that Quinn fixed Crease's case. With Crease and Brademas dead, it doesn't look like we'll get any unless the judge confesses.'

Anthony stood on the edge of the empty pool. Debris had settled on the bottom. Leaves mostly. Anthony figured the pool man would have cleaned it eventually, but he wondered what would happen now with everybody dead.

'Quinn's a good judge,' Anthony said.

'If he fixed a case, he violated the law.'

'I know that, but I'm wondering about the value of pursuing our investigation now that Crease is dead.'

'Value? That's a funny word to use, Lou. We don't get paid to deal in values. That's for philosophers. We're lawmen. The senators and representatives write the laws, the governors sign them, we enforce them. Cops aren't supposed to think about whether the laws are good or bad.'

Anthony walked away from the pool and into the garden. He could see the setting sun through the denuded tree limbs.

'Do you believe in second chances, Leroy?'

'That's what bleeding-heart defense lawyers are always whining for. Isn't that what you've told me?'

Anthony smiled. 'You got me there. Well, I'm just

one part of this team. You've got a vote, too, but I think that we should put this case to rest and leave Richard Quinn alone.'

Dennis thought about Anthony's proposal for a moment. Then he shrugged.

'I'll go along with you for now. But I won't do it for nothing.'

'What do you want, Leroy?'

'A Captain Neon burger and a pint of Terminator stout.'

Epilogue

'ARE YOU all right?' Laura asked when Quinn stopped.

'I'm a little winded. Just let me rest for a moment.'

Quinn was home from the hospital and trying to get some exercise by walking along the streets in Hereford Farms, but he did not have much stamina. Quinn leaned on his cane for a moment while Laura waited patiently. It was not hard to do. Balmy spring weather had suddenly appeared. Flowers were starting to show up, the temperature was perfect and the sky was children's-book blue.

'Okay,' Quinn said. Laura took his arm and they started down Peacock Road toward the swimming pool and the tennis courts.

'Stanley Sax stopped me in the courthouse hallway,'

Laura told Quinn, introducing a subject they had avoided. 'He wants to know when you'll be ready to go back to work.'

Quinn looked straight ahead.

'What did you say?' he asked.

'I said it's up to your doctors. Is that what I should have said?'

'Be honest with me, Laura. Do you think I deserve to be sitting as a judge?'

Laura stopped walking. She faced Quinn.

'I love the fact that you're so principled, Dick, but I wish you would recognize your humanity a little more often. You're going to make wrong choices. Don't punish yourself when you do because that's ego; that's crediting yourself with infallibility.

'You asked me if I think you should go back to the bench. I think you should do what makes you happy, and that's being a judge. I wouldn't tell you to go back if I didn't think it was right. The people of this state need good judges. If you leave the bench, you'll be letting them down so you can punish yourself.'

Quinn and Laura walked in silence for a while. Finally, Quinn said, 'I want to go back, I just . . .'

'You just acted like a human being.'

Quinn looked anguished. 'You really think it's the right thing to do?'

'Yes, Dick.'

'Then the next time you see Stan tell him I'm anxious to get back to work.'

* * *

[2]

'Un autre, s'il vous plaît,' James Allen said.

'Immédiatement, monsieur.'

The waiter took Allen's empty cup and saucer and carried it inside the café. Allen smiled. He was especially pleased because the waiter was conversing in French. Allen had noticed that many of the waiters switched to English the moment an American tried to converse in French if the American's accent or grammar was not perfect.

While Allen waited for the waiter to return with his cappuccino, he looked across the waters of Lake Geneva to the French Alps. The mountaintops were dusted with snow even though the weather in Lausanne was balmy. Every year, James Allen took his vacation on the Continent. This was his second time in Switzerland and he was enjoying it very much. It was especially nice because the $50,000 he had received from Benjamin Gage and the money in Lamar Hoyt's bequest permitted him to travel in luxury for the first time.

As per his agreement with Ryan Clark, Allen had told the police nothing about the arrangement with Senator Gage that Allen had initiated soon after the hearing on the motion to suppress. It was the blood spatter evidence that had convinced Allen that Ellen Crease had been behind the murder of his employer. Allen had never liked the woman. She was too insensitive to Mr. Hoyt's needs, too domineering. If she had won election to the United States Senate, Mr. Hoyt would have been left alone for most of the year. He knew how much that would have upset Mr. Hoyt because he had overheard several arguments in which this matter was the main subject.

Just when Allen decided that Crease was guilty, Judge Quinn had destroyed the case against her. It was then that Allen decided to give campaign intelligence to Benjamin Gage in the hopes that his information would lead to Crease's defeat. When Ryan Clark supplied him with the bugging equipment, Allen secretly hoped that Crease would confess the murder on tape, but that had never happened. Still, it was the phone conversation between Crease and Judge Quinn that Allen had overheard that eventually put the houseman in a position to avenge his employer's murder. Allen had rigged the sunroom with a listening device and had acted as soon as Crease threatened to kill Laura and the judge.

Life had been hectic following the shooting. There were the police interrogations and the interviews with the press. Appearing distraught through it all drained him, but Allen knew enough about the authorities to understand that they would not have reacted favorably if he expressed the joy he felt when he ended the life of the woman who had taken Lamar Hoyt from him.

A ferry cruised by on the lake heading toward Montreux. Tomorrow Allen was planning to travel by ferry a little farther to Château Chillon, the fortress where Lord Byron had set his famous poem. He was looking forward to the slow ride during which he planned to reread 'The Prisoner of Chillon.'

'*Monsieur*,' the waiter said with a warm smile as he placed the cappuccino in front of Allen. Allen thanked him in fluent French perfected during years of night school study and trips to France and Switzerland.

A cloud slipped in front of the sun. For a moment, the air cooled. Allen sipped his drink. The hot liquid cut the chill. He checked the time. In four hours he would be dining in one of Europe's finest restaurants. He picked up the book he was reading and took another sip of his cappuccino.